Infinite Possibilities

BOOKS BY ROBERT A. HEINLEIN

Novels

Beyond This Horizon (1948)
Sixth Column (1949)
The Puppet Masters (1951)
Double Star (1956)
The Door Into Summer (1957)
Methuselah's Children (1958)
Starship Troopers (1959)
Stranger in a Strange Land (1961)
Glory Road (1963)
Orphans of the Sky (1963)
Farnham's Freehold (1964)
The Moon Is a Harsh Mistress (1966)
I Will Fear No Evil (1970)
Time Enough for Love (1973)
The Number of the Beast (1980)
Friday (1982)
Job: A Comedy of Justice (1984)
The Cat Who Walks Through Walls (1985)
To Sail Beyond the Sunset (1987)

Juvenile Novels

Rocket Ship Galileo (1947)
Space Cadet (1948)
Red Planet (1949)
Farmer in the Sky (1950)
Between Planets (1951)
The Rolling Stones (1952)
Starman Jones (1953)
The Star Beast (1954)
Tunnel in the Sky (1955)
Time for the Stars (1956)
Citizen of the Galaxy (1957)
Have Space Suit—Will Travel (1958)
Podkayne of Mars (1963)

Short Fiction & Miscellaneous

The Man Who Sold the Moon (1950)
Waldo and Magic, Inc. (1950)
The Green Hills of Earth (1951)
Revolt in 2100 (1953)
Assignment in Eternity (1953)
The Menace From Earth (1959)
The Unpleasant Profession of Jonathan Hoag (1959)
The Worlds of Robert A. Heinlein (1966)
The Past Through Tomorrow (1967)
Expanded Universe (1980)
Grumbles from the Grave (1989)
Requiem: New Collected Works (1992)
Tramp Royale (1992)
The Fantasies of Robert A. Heinlein (1999)

Infinite Possibilities

Tunnel in the Sky
Time for the Stars
Citizen of the Galaxy

ROBERT A. HEINLEIN

50 YEARS SFBC
SCIENCE FICTION

First SFBC Science Fiction Printing: April 2002

Published by arrangement with the author and
Simon & Schuster Children's Publishing
1230 Avenue of the Americas
New York, NY 10020

Visit The SFBC online at http://www.sfbc.com

ISBN 0-7394-3385-7

PRINTED IN THE UNITED STATES OF AMERICA

Contents

TUNNEL IN THE SKY

For Jeannie and Bibs

Contents

1

The Marching Hordes

THE BULLETIN BOARD OUTSIDE LECTURE HALL 1712-A OF PATRICK Henry High School showed a flashing red light. Rod Walker pushed his way into a knot of students and tried to see what the special notice had to say. He received an elbow in the stomach, accompanied by: "Hey! Quit shoving!"

"Sorry. Take it easy, Jimmy." Rod locked the elbow in a bone breaker but put no pressure on, craned his neck to look over Jimmy Throxton's head. "What's on the board?"

"No class today."

"Why not?"

A voice near the board answered him. "Because tomorrow it's 'Hail, Caesar, we who are about to die—' "

"So?" Rod felt his stomach tighten as it always did before an examination. Someone moved aside and he managed to read the notice:

PATRICK HENRY HIGH SCHOOL
Department of Social Studies

SPECIAL NOTICE to all students Course 410 (elective senior seminar) *Advanced Survival*, instr. Dr. Matson, 1712-A MWF

1. There will be no class Friday the 14th.
2. *Twenty-Four Hour Notice* is hereby given of final examination in Solo Survival. Students will present themselves for physical check at 0900 Saturday in the dispensary of Templeton Gate and will start passing through the gate at 1000, using three-minute intervals by lot.
3. *TEST CONDITIONS:*

(a) ANY planet, ANY climate, ANY terrain;
(b) NO rules, ALL weapons, ANY equipment;
(c) TEAMING IS PERMITTED but teams will not be allowed to pass through the gate in company;
(d) TEST DURATION is not less than forty-eight hours, not more than ten days.

4. Dr. Matson will be available for advice and consultation until 1700 Friday.
5. Test may be postponed only on recommendation of examining physician, but any student may withdraw from the course without administrative penalty up until 1000 Saturday.
6. Good luck and long life to you all!

(s) **B. P. Matson, Sc.D.**

Approved:

J. R. ROERICH, *for the Board*

Rod Walker reread the notice slowly, while trying to quiet the quiver in his nerves. He checked off the test conditions—why, those were not "conditions" but a total lack of conditions, no limits of any sort! They could dump you through the gate and the next instant you might be facing a polar bear at forty below—or wrestling an octopus deep in warm salt water.

Or, he added, faced up to some three-headed horror on a planet you had never heard of.

He heard a soprano voice complaining, " 'Twenty-four hour notice!' Why, it's less than twenty hours now. That's not fair."

Another girl answered, "What's the difference? I wish we were starting this minute. I won't get a wink of sleep tonight."

"If we are supposed to have twenty-four hours to get ready, then we ought to have them. Fair is fair."

Another student, a tall, husky Zulu girl, chuckled softly. "Go on in. Tell the Deacon that."

Rod backed out of the press, taking Jimmy Throxton with him. He felt that he knew what "Deacon" Matson would say . . . something about the irrelevancy of fairness to survival. He chewed over the bait in paragraph five; nobody would say boo if he dropped the course. After all, "Advanced Survival" was properly a college course; he would graduate without it.

But he knew down deep that if he lost his nerve now, he would never take the course later.

Jimmy said nervously, "What d'you think of it, Rod?"

"All right, I guess. But I'd like to know whether or not to wear my long-handled underwear. Do you suppose the Deacon would give us a hint?"

"Him? Not him! He thinks a broken leg is the height of humor. That man would eat his own grandmother—without salt."

"Oh, come now! He'd use salt. Say, Jim? You saw what it said about teaming."

"Yeah . . . what about it?" Jimmy's eyes shifted away.

Rod felt a moment's irritation. He was making a suggestion as delicate as a proposal of marriage, an offer to put his own life in the same basket with Jimmy's. The greatest risk in a solo test was that a fellow just had to sleep sometime . . . but a team could split it up and stand watch over each other.

Jimmy must know that Rod was better than he was, with any weapon or bare hands; the proposition was to his advantage. Yet here he was hesitating as if he thought Rod might handicap him. "What's the matter, Jim?" Rod said bleakly. "Figure you're safer going it alone?"

"Uh, no, not exactly."

"You mean you'd rather not team with *me?*"

"No, no, I didn't mean that!"

"Then what did you mean?"

"I meant—Look, Rod, I surely do thank you. I won't forget it. But that notice said something else, too."

"What?"

"I said we could dump this durned course and still graduate. And I just happened to remember that I don't need it for the retail clothing business."

"Huh? I thought you had ambitions to become a wide-angled lawyer?"

"So exotic jurisprudence loses its brightest jewel . . . so what do I care? It will make my old man very happy to learn that I've decided to stick with the family business."

"You mean you're scared."

"Well, that's one way of putting it. Aren't you?"

Rod took a deep breath. "Yes. I'm scared."

"Good! Now let's both give a classic demonstration of how to survive and stay alive by marching down to the Registrar's office and bravely signing our names to withdrawal slips."

"Uh, no. You go ahead."

"You mean you're sticking?"

"I guess so."

"Look, Rod, have you looked over the statistics on last year's classes?"

"No. And I don't want to. So long." Rod turned sharply and headed for the classroom door, leaving Jimmy to stare after him with a troubled look.

The lecture room was occupied by a dozen or so of the seminar's students. Doctor Matson, the "Deacon," was squatting tailor-fashion on one corner of his desk and holding forth informally. He was a small man and spare, with a leathery face, a patch over one eye, and most of three fingers missing from his left hand. On his chest were miniature ribbons, marking service in three famous first expeditions; one carried a tiny diamond cluster that showed him to be the last living member of that group.

Rod slipped into the second row. The Deacon's eye flicked at him as he went on talking. "I don't understand the complaints," he said jovially. "The test conditions say 'all weapons' so you can protect yourself any way you like . . . from a slingshot to a cobalt bomb. I think final examination should be bare hands, not so much as a nail file. But the Board of Education doesn't agree, so we do it this sissy way instead." He shrugged and grinned.

"Uh, Doctor, I take it then that the Board knows that we are going to run into dangerous animals?"

"Eh? You surely will! The most dangerous animal known."

"Doctor, if you mean that literally—"

"Oh, I do, I do!"

"Then I take it that we are either being sent to Mithra and will have to watch out for snow apes, or we are going to stay on Terra and be dumped where we can expect leopards. Am I right?"

The Deacon shook his head despairingly. "My boy, you had better cancel and take this course over. Those dumb brutes aren't dangerous."

"But Jasper says, in *Predators and Prey,* that the two trickiest, most dangerous—"

"Jasper's maiden aunt! I'm talking about the *real* King of the Beasts, the only animal that is always dangerous, even when not hungry. The two-legged brute. Take a look around you!"

The instructor leaned forward. "I've said this nineteen dozen times but you still don't believe it. Man is the one animal that can't be tamed. He goes along for years as peaceful as a cow, when it suits him. Then when it suits him not to be, he makes a leopard look like a tabby cat. Which goes double for the female of the species. Take another look around you. All friends. We've been on group-survival field tests together; we can depend on each other. So? Read about the Donner Party, or the First Venus Expedition. Anyhow, the test area will have several other classes in it, all strangers to you." Doctor Matson fixed his eye on Rod. "I hate to see some of you take this test, I really do. Some of you are city dwellers by nature; I'm afraid I have not managed to get it through your heads that there are no policemen where you are going. Nor will I be around to give you a hand if you make some silly mistake."

His eye moved on; Rod wondered if the Deacon meant him. Sometimes he felt that the Deacon took delight in rawhiding him. But Rod knew that it was serious; the course was required for all the Outlands professions for the good reason that the Outlands were places where you were smart—or you were dead. Rod had chosen to take this course before entering college because he hoped that it would help him to get a scholarship—but that did not mean that he thought it was just a formality.

He looked around, wondering who would be willing to team with him now that Jimmy had dropped out. There was a couple in front of him, Bob Baxter and Carmen Garcia. He checked them off, as they undoubtedly would team together; they planned to become medical missionaries and intended to marry as soon as they could.

How about Johann Braun? He would make a real partner, all right—strong, fast on his feet, and smart. But Rod did not trust him, nor did he think that Braun would want him. He began to see that he might have made a mistake in not cultivating other friends in the class besides Jimmy.

That big Zulu girl, Caroline something-unpronounceable. Strong as an ox and absolutely fearless. But it would not do to team with a girl; girls were likely to mistake a cold business deal for a romantic gambit. His eyes moved on until at last he was forced to conclude that there was no one there to whom he wished to suggest partnership.

"Prof, how about a hint? Should we take suntan oil? Or chilblain lotion?"

Matson grinned and drawled, "Son, I'll tell you every bit that I know. This test area was picked by a teacher in Europe . . . and I picked one for his class. But I don't know what it is any more than you do. Send me a post card."

"But—" The boy who had spoken stopped. Then he suddenly stood up. "Prof, this isn't a fair test. I'm checking out."

"What's unfair about it? Not that we meant to make it fair."

"Well, you could dump us any place—"

"That's right."

"—the back side of the Moon, in vacuum up to our chins. Or onto a chlorine planet. Or the middle of an ocean. I don't know whether to take a space suit, or a canoe. So the deuce with it. Real life isn't like that."

"It isn't, eh?" Matson said softly. "That's what Jonah said when the whale swallowed him." He added, "But I will give you some hints. We mean this test to be passed by anyone bright enough to deserve it. So we won't let you walk into a poisonous atmosphere, or a vacuum, without a mask. If you are dumped into water, land won't be too far to swim. And so on. While I don't know where you are going, I did see the list of test areas for this year's classes. A smart man can survive in any of them. You ought to realize, son, that the Board of Education would have nothing to gain by killing off all its candidates for the key professions."

The student sat down again as suddenly as he had stood up. The instructor said, "Change your mind again?"

"Uh, yes, sir. If it's a fair test, I'll take it."

Matson shook his head. "You've already flunked it. You're excused. Don't bother the Registrar; I'll notify him."

The boy started to protest; Matson inclined his head toward the door. "Out!" There was an embarrassed silence while he left the room, then Matson said briskly, "This is a class in applied philosophy and I am sole judge of who is ready and who is not. Anybody who thinks of the world in terms of what it 'ought' to be, rather than what it is, isn't ready for final examination. You've got to relax and roll with the punch . . . not get yourself all worn out with adrenalin exhaustion at the slings and arrows of outrageous fortune. Any more questions?"

There were a few more but it became evident that Matson either truthfully did not know the nature of the test area, or was guarding the knowledge; his answers gained them nothing. He refused to advise as to weapons, saying simply that the school armorer would be at the gate ready to issue all usual weapons, while any unusual ones were up to the individual. "Remember, though, your best weapon is between your ears and under your scalp—provided it's loaded."

The group started to drift away; Rod got up to leave. Matson caught his eye and said, "Walker, are you planning to take the test?"

"Why, yes, of course, sir."

"Come here a moment." He led him into his office, closed the door and sat down. He looked up at Rod, fiddled with a paperweight on his desk and said slowly, "Rod, you're a good boy . . . but sometimes that isn't enough."

Rod said nothing.

"Tell me," Matson continued, "why you want to take this test?"

"Sir?"

" 'Sir' yourself," Matson answered grumpily. "Answer my question."

Rod stared, knowing that he had gone over this with Matson before he was accepted for the course. But he explained again his ambition to study for an Outlands profession. "So I have to qualify in survival. I couldn't even get a degree in colonial administration without it, much less any of the planetography or planetology specialties."

"Want to be an explorer, huh?"

"Yes, sir."

"Like me."

"Yes, sir. Like you."

"Hmm . . . would you believe me if I told you that it was the worst mistake I ever made?"

"Huh? No, sir!"

"I didn't think you would. Son, the cutest trick of all is how to know *then* what you know *now.* No way to, of course. But I'm telling you straight: I think you've been born into the wrong age."

"Sir?"

"I think you are a romantic. Now this is a very romantic age, so there is no room in it for romantics; it calls for practical men. A hundred years ago you would have made a banker or lawyer or professor and you could have worked out your romanticism by reading fanciful tales and dreaming about what you might have been if you hadn't had the misfortune to be born into a humdrum period. But this happens to be a period when adventure and romance are a part of daily existence. Naturally it takes very practical people to cope with it."

Rod was beginning to get annoyed. "What's the matter with *me?"*

"Nothing. I like you. I don't want to see you get hurt. But you are 'way too emotional, too sentimental to be a real survivor type."

Matson pushed a hand toward him. "Now keep your shirt on. I know you can make fire by rubbing a couple of dry words together. I'm well aware that you won merit badges in practically everything. I'm sure you can devise a water filter with your bare hands and know which side of the tree the moss grows on. But I'm not sure that you can beware of the Truce of the Bear."

" 'The Truce of the Bear?' "

"Never mind. Son, I think you ought to cancel this course. If you must, you can repeat it in college."

Rod looked stubborn. Matson sighed. "I could drop you. Perhaps I should."

"But *why,* sir?"

"That's the point. I couldn't give a reason. On the record, you're as promising a student as I have ever had." He stood up and put out his hand. "Good luck. And remember—when it gets down to fundamentals, do what you have to do and shed no tears."

Rod should have gone straight home. His family lived in an out-county of Greater New York City, located on the Grand Canyon plateau through Hoboken Gate. But his commuting route required him to change at Emigrants' Gap and he found himself unable to resist stopping to rubberneck.

When he stepped out of the tube from school he should have turned right, taken the rotary lift to the level above, and stepped through to Arizona Strip. But he was thinking about supplies, equipment, and weapons for tomorrow's examination; his steps automatically bore left, he got on the slideway leading to the great hall of the planetary gates.

He told himself that he would watch for only ten minutes; he would not be late for dinner. He picked his way through the crowd and entered the great hall—not onto the emigration floor itself, but onto the spectator's balcony facing the gates. This was the new gate house he was in, the one opened for traffic in '68; the original Emigrants' Gap, now used for Terran traffic and trade with Luna, stood on the Jersey Flats a few kilometers east alongside the pile that powered it.

The balcony faced the six gates. It could seat eighty-six hundred people but was half filled and crowded only in the center. It was here, of course, that Rod wished to sit so that he might see through all six gates. He wormed his way down the middle aisle, squatted by the railing, then spotted someone leaving a front row seat. Rod grabbed it, earning a dirty look from a man who had started for it from the other aisle.

Rod fed coins into the arm of the seat; it opened out, he sat down and looked around. He was opposite the replica Statue of Liberty, twin to the one that had stood for a century where now was Bedloe Crater. Her torch reached to the distant ceiling; on both her right and her left three great gates let emigrants into the outer worlds.

Rod did not glance at the statue; he looked at the gates. It was late afternoon and heavily overcast at east coast North America, but gate one was open to some planetary spot having glaring noonday sun; Rod could catch glimpses through it of men dressed in shorts and sun hats and nothing else. Gate number two had a pressure lock rigged over it; it carried a big skull & cross-bones sign and the symbol for chlorine. A red light burned over it. While he watched, the red light flickered out and a blue light replaced it; the door slowly opened and a traveling capsule for a chlorine-breather crawled out. Waiting to meet it were eight humans in diplomatic full dress. One carried a gold baton.

Rod considered spending another half pluton to find out who the important visitor was, but his attention was diverted to gate five. An auxiliary gate had been set up on the floor, facing gate five and almost under the balcony. Two high steel fences joined the two gates, forming with them an alley as wide as the gates and as long as the space between, about fifteen meters by seventy-five. This pen was packed with humanity moving from the temporary gate toward and through gate five—and onto some planet light-years away. They poured out of nowhere, for the floor back of the auxiliary gate was bare, hurried like cattle between the two fences, spilled through gate five and were gone. A squad of brawny Mongol policemen, each armed with a staff as tall as himself, was spread out along each fence. They were using their staves to hurry the emigrants and they were not being gentle. Almost underneath Rod one of them prodded an old coolie so hard that he stumbled and fell. The man had been carrying his belongings, his equipment for a new world, in two bundles supported from a pole balanced on his right shoulder.

The old coolie fell to his skinny knees, tried to get up, fell flat. Rod thought sure he would be trampled, but somehow he was on his feet again—minus his baggage. He tried to hold his place in the torrent and recover his possessions, but the guard prodded him again and he was forced to move on barehanded. Rod lost sight of him before he had moved five meters.

There were local police outside the fence but they did not interfere. This narrow stretch between the two gates was, for the time, extraterritorial; the local police had no jurisdiction. But one of them did seem annoyed at the brutality shown the old man; he put his face to the steel mesh and called out something in lingua terra. The Mongol cop answered savagely in the same simple language, telling the North American what he could do about it, then went back to shoving and shouting and prodding still more briskly.

The crowd streaming through the pen were Asiatics—Japanese, Indonesians, Siamese, some East Indians, a few Eurasians, but predominantly South Chinese. To Rod they all looked much alike—tiny women with babies on hip or back, or often one on back and one in arms, endless runny-nosed and shaven-headed children, fathers with household goods in enormous back packs or pushed ahead on barrows. There were a few dispirited ponies dragging two-wheeled carts much too big for them but most of the torrent had only that which they could carry.

Rod had heard an old story which asserted that if all the Chinese on Terra were marched four abreast past a given point the column would never pass that point, as more Chinese would be born fast enough to replace those who had marched past. Rod had taken his slide rule and applied arithmetic to check it—to find, of course, that the story was nonsense; even if one ignored deaths, while counting all births, the last Chinese would pass the reviewing stand in less than four years. Nevertheless, while watching this mob being herded like brutes into a slaughterhouse, Rod felt that the old canard was true even though its mathematics was faulty. There seemed to be no end to them.

He decided to risk that half pluton to find out what was going on. He slid the coin into a slot in the chair's speaker; the voice of the commentator reached his ears: "—the visiting minister. The prince royal was met by officials of the Terran Corporation including the Director General himself and now is being escorted to the locks of the Ratoonian enclave. After the television reception tonight staff level conversations will start. A spokesman close to the Director General has pointed out that, in view of the impossibility of conflict of interest between oxygen types such as ourselves and the Ratoonians, any outcome of the conference must be to our advantage, the question being to what extent.

"If you will turn your attention again to gate five, we will repeat what we said earlier: gate five is on forty-eight hour loan to the Australasian Republic. The temporary gate you see erected below is hyperfolded to a point in central Australia in the Arunta Desert, where this emigration has been mounting in a great encampment for the past several weeks. His Serene Majesty Chairman Fung Chee Mu of the Australasian Republic has informed the Corporation that his government intends to move in excess of two million people in forty-eight hours, a truly impressive figure, more than forty thousand each hour. The target figure for this year for all planetary emigration gates taken together—Emigrants' Gap, Peter the Great, and Witwatersrand Gates—is only seventy million emigrants or an average of eight thousand per hour. This movement proposes a rate five times as great using only *one* gate!"

The commentator continued: "Yet when we watch the speed, efficiency and the, uh—*forthrightness* with which they are carrying out this evolution it seems likely that they will achieve their goal. Our own figures show them to be slightly ahead of quota for the first nine hours. During those same nine hours there have been one hundred seven births and eighty-two deaths among the emigrants, the high death rate, of course, being incident to the temporary hazards of the emigration.

"The planet of destination, GO-8703-IV, to be called henceforth 'Heavenly Mountains' according to Chairman Fung, is classed as a bounty planet and no attempt had been made to colonize it. The Corporation has been assured that the colonists are volunteers." It seemed to Rod that the announcer's tone was ironical. "This is understandable when one considers the phenomenal population pressure of the Australasian Republic. A brief historical rundown may be in order. After the removal of the remnants of the former Australian population to New Zealand, pursuant to the Peiping Peace Treaty, the first amazing effort of the new government was the creation of the great inland sea of—"

Rod muted the speaker and looked back at the floor below. He did not care to hear school-book figures on how the Australian Desert had been made to blossom like the rose . . . and nevertheless had been converted into a slum with more people in it than all of North America. Something new was happening at gate four—

Gate four had been occupied by a moving cargo belt when he had come in; now the belt had crawled away and lost itself in the bowels of the terminal and an emigration party was lining up to go through.

This was no poverty-stricken band of refugees chivvied along by police; here each family had its own wagon . . . long, sweeping, boat-tight Conestogas drawn by three-pair teams and housed in sturdy glass canvas . . . square and businesslike Studebakers with steel bodies, high mudcutter wheels, and pulled by one or two-pair teams. The draft animals were Morgans and lordly Clydesdales and jug-headed Missouri mules with strong shoulders and shrewd, suspicious eyes. Dogs trotted between wheels, wagons were piled high with household goods and implements and children, poultry protested the indignities of fate in cages tied on behind, and a little Shetland pony, riderless but carrying his saddle and just a bit too tall to run underneath with the dogs, stayed close to the tailgate of one family's rig.

Rod wondered at the absence of cattle and stepped up the speaker again. But the announcer was still droning about the fertility of Australasians; he muted it again and watched. Wagons had moved onto the floor and taken up tight echelon position close to the gate, ready to move, with the tail of the train somewhere out of sight below. The gate was not yet ready and drivers were getting down and gathering at the Salvation Army booth under the skirts of the Goddess of Liberty, for a cup of coffee and some banter. It occurred to Rod that there probably was no coffee where they were going and might not be for years, since Terra never exported food—on the contrary, food and fissionable metals were almost the only permissible imports; until an Outland colony produced a surplus of one or the other it could expect precious little help from Terra.

It was extremely expensive in terms of uranium to keep an interstellar gate open and the people in this wagon train could expect to be out of commercial touch with Earth until such a time as they had developed surpluses valuable enough in trade to warrant reopening the gate at regular intervals. Until that time they were on their own and must make do with what they could take with them . . . which made horses more practical than helicopters, picks and shovels more useful than bulldozers. Machinery gets out of order and requires a complex technology to keep it going—but good old "hayburners" keep right on breeding, cropping grass, and pulling loads.

Deacon Matson had told the survival class that the real hardhips of primitive Outlands were not the lack of plumbing, heating, power, light, nor weather conditioning, but the shortage of simple things like coffee and tobacco.

Rod did not smoke and coffee he could take or let alone; he could not imagine getting fretful over its absence. He scrunched down in his seat, trying to see through the gate to guess the cause of the holdup. He could not see well, as the arching canvas of a prairie schooner blocked his view, but it did seem that the gate operator had a phase error; it looked as if the sky was where the ground ought to be. The extradimensional distortions necessary to match places on two planets many light-years apart were not simply a matter of expenditure of enormous quantities of energy; they were precision problems fussy beyond belief, involving high mathematics and high art—the math was done by machine but the gate operator always had to adjust the last couple of decimal places by prayer and intuition.

In addition to the dozen-odd proper motions of each of the planets involved, motions which could usually be added and canceled out, there was also the rotation of each planet. The problem was to make the last hyperfold so that the two planets were internally tangent at the points selected as gates, with their axes parallel and their rotations in the *same* direction. Theoretically it was possible to match two points in contrarotation, twisting the insubstantial fabric of space-time in exact step with "real" motions; practically such a solution was not only terribly wasteful of energy but almost unworkable—the ground surface beyond the gate tended to skid away like a slidewalk and tilt at odd angles.

Rod did not have the mathematics to appreciate the difficulties. Being only about to finish high school his training had gone no farther than tensor calculus, statistical mechanics, simple transfinities, generalized geometries of six dimensions, and, on the practical side, analysis for electronics, primary cybernetics and robotics, and basic design of analog computers; he had had no advanced mathematics as yet. He was not aware of his ignorance and simply concluded that the gate operator must be thumb-fingered. He looked back at the emigrant party.

The drivers were still gathered at the booth, drinking coffee and munching doughnuts. Most of the men were growing beards; Rod concluded from the beavers that the party had been training for several months. The captain of the party sported a little goatee, mustaches, and rather long hair, but it seemed to Rod that he could not be many years older than Rod himself. He was a professional, of course, required to hold a degree in Outlands arts—hunting, scouting, jackleg mechanics, gunsmithing, farming, first aid, group psychology, survival group tactics, law, and a dozen other things the race has found indispensable when stripped for action.

This captain's mount was a Palomino mare, lovely as a sunrise, and the captain was dressed as a California don of an earlier century—possibly as a compliment to his horse. A warning light flashed at the gate's annunciator panel and he swung into saddle, still eating a doughnut, and cantered down the wagons for a final inspection, riding toward Rod. His back was straight, his seat deep and easy, his bearing confident. Carried low on a fancy belt he wore two razor guns, each in a silver-chased holster that matched the ornate silver of his bridle and saddle.

Rod held his breath until the captain passed out of sight under the balcony, then sighed and considered studying to be like him, rather than for one of the more intellectual Outlands professions. He did not know just what he did want to be . . . except that he meant to get off Earth as soon as he possibly could and get out there where things were going on!

Which reminded him that the first hurdle was tomorrow; in a few days he would either be eligible to matriculate for whatever it was he decided on, or he would be—but no use worrying about *that.* He remembered uneasily that it was getting late and he had not even decided on equipment, nor picked his weapons. This party captain carried razor guns; should he carry one? No, this party would fight as a unit, if it had to fight. Its leader carried that type of weapon to enforce his authority—not for solo survival. Well, what should he take?

A siren sounded and the drivers returned to their wagons. The captain came back at a brisk trot. "Reins up!" he called out. "Reeeeeeiiiins UP!" He took station by the gate, facing the head of the train; the mare stood quivering and tending to dance.

The Salvation Army lassie came out from behind her counter carrying a baby girl. She called to the party captain but her voice did not carry to the balcony.

The captain's voice did carry. "Number four! Doyle! Come get your child!" A red-headed man with a spade beard climbed down from the fourth wagon and sheepishly reclaimed the youngster to a chorus of cheers and cat calls. He passed the baby up to his wife, who upped its skirt and commenced paddling its bottom. Doyle climbed to his seat and took his reins.

"Call off!" the captain sang out.

"One."

"Tuh!"

"Three!"

"Fo*ah!*"

"Five!"

The count passed under the balcony, passed down the chute out of hearing. In a few moments it came back, running down this time, ending with a shouted *"ONE!"* The captain held up his right arm and watched the lights of the order panel.

A light turned green. He brought his arm down smartly with a shout of "Roll 'em! *Ho!"* The Palomino took off like a race horse, cut under the nose of the nigh lead horse of the first team, and shot through the gate.

Whips cracked. Rod could hear shouts of "Git, Molly! Git, Ned!" and "No, no, you jugheads!" The train begin to roll. By the time the last one on the floor was through the gate and the much larger number which had been in the chute below had begun to show it was rolling at a gallop, with the drivers bracing their feet wide and their wives riding the brakes. Rod tried to count them, made it possibly sixty-three wagons as the last one rumbled through the gate . . . and was gone, already half a galaxy away.

He sighed and sat back with a warm feeling sharpened with undefined sorrow. Then he stepped up the speaker volume: "—onto New Canaan, the premium planet described by the great Langford as 'The rose without thorns.' These colonists have paid a premium of sixteen thousand four hundred per person—not counting exempt or co-opted members—for the privilege of seeking their fortunes and protecting their posterity by moving to New Canaan. The machines predict that the premium will increase for another twenty-eight years; therefore, if you are considering giving your children the priceless boon of citizenship on New Canaan, the time to act is now. For a beautiful projection reel showing this planet send one pluton to 'Information, Box One, Emigrants' Gap, New Jersey County, Greater New York.' For a complete descriptive listing of all planets now open plus a special list of those to be opened in the near future add another half pluton. Those seeing this broadcast in person may obtain these at the information booth in the foyer outside the great hall."

Rod did not listen. He had long since sent for every free item and most of the non-free ones issued by the Commission for Emigration and Trade. Just now he was wondering why the gate to New Canaan had not relaxed.

He found out at once. Stock barricades rose up out of the floor, forming a fenced passage from gate four to the chute under him. Then a herd of cattle filled the gate and came flooding toward him, bawling and snorting. They were prime Hereford steers, destined to become tender steaks and delicious roasts for a rich but slightly hungry Earth. After them and among them rode New Canaan cowpunchers armed with long goads with which they urged the beasts to greater speed—the undesirability of running weight off the animals was offset by the extreme cost of keeping the gate open, a cost which had to be charged against the cattle.

Rod discovered that the speaker had shut itself off; the half hour he had paid for was finished. He sat up with sudden guilt, realizing that he would have to hurry or he would be late for supper. He rushed out, stepping on feet and mumbling apologies, and caught the slideway to Hoboken Gate.

This gate, being merely for Terra-surface commuting, was permanently dilated and required no operator, since the two points brought into coincidence were joined by a rigid frame, the solid Earth. Rod showed his commuter's ticket to the electronic monitor and stepped through to Arizona, in company with a crowd of neighbors.

"The (almost) solid Earth—" The gate robot took into account tidal distortions but could not anticipate minor seismic variables. As Rod stepped through he felt his feet quiver as if to a small earthquake, then the *terra* was again *firma.* But he was still in an airlock at sea-level pressure. The radiation from massed bodies triggered the mechanism, the lock closed and air pressure dropped. Rod yawned heavily to adjust to the pressure of Grand Canyon plateau, North Rim, less than three quarters that of New Jersey. But despite the fact that he made the change twice a day he found himself rubbing his right ear to get rid of an earache.

The lock opened, he stepped out. Having come two thousand miles in a split second he now had ten minutes by slide tube and a fifteen minute walk to get home. He decided to dogtrot and be on time after all. He might have made it if there had not been several thousand other people trying to use the same facilities.

2

The Fifth Way

ROCKET SHIPS DID NOT CONQUER SPACE; THEY MERELY CHALLENGED it. A rocket leaving Earth at seven miles per second is terribly slow for the vast reaches beyond. Only the Moon is reasonably near—four days, more or less. Mars is thirty-seven weeks away, Saturn a dreary six years, Pluto an impossible half century, by the elliptical orbits possible to rockets.

Ortega's torch ships brought the Solar System within reach. Based on mass conversion, Einstein's deathless $e = Mc^2$, they could boost for the entire trip at any acceleration the pilot could stand. At an easy one gravity the inner planets were only hours from Earth, far Pluto only eighteen days. It was a change like that from horseback to jet plane.

The shortcoming of this brave new toy was that there was not much anywhere to go. The Solar System, from a human standpoint, is made up of remarkably unattractive real estate—save for lovely Terra herself, lush and green and beautiful. The steel-limbed Jovians enjoy gravity 2.5 times ours and their poisonous air at inhuman pressure keeps them in health. Martians prosper in near vacuum, the rock lizards of Luna do not breathe at all. But these planets are not for men.

Men prosper on an oxygen planet close enough to a G-type star for the weather to cycle around the freezing point of water . . . that is to say, on Earth.

When you are already there why go anywhere? The reason was babies, too many babies. Malthus pointed it out long ago; food increases by aritmetical progression, people increase by geometrical progression. By World War I half the world lived on the edge of starvation; by World War II Earth's population was increasing by 55,000 people *every day;* before World War III, as early as 1954, the increase had jumped to

100,000 mouths and stomachs per day, 35,000,000 additional people each year . . . and the population of Terra had climbed well beyond that which its farm lands could support.

The hydrogen, germ, and nerve gas horrors that followed were not truly political. The true meaning was more that of beggars fighting over a crust of bread.

The author of *Gulliver's Travels* sardonically proposed that Irish babies be fattened for English tables; other students urged less drastic ways of curbing population—none of which made the slightest difference. Life, *all* life, has the twin drives to survive and to reproduce. Intelligence is an aimless byproduct except as it serves these basic drives.

But intelligence *can* be made to serve the mindless demands of life. Our Galaxy contains in excess of one hundred thousand Earth-type planets, each as warm and motherly to men as sweet Terra. Ortega's torch ships could reach the stars. Mankind could colonize, even as the hungry millions of Europe had crossed the Atlantic and raised more babies in the New World.

Some did . . . hundreds of thousands. But the entire race, working as a team, cannot build and launch a hundred ships a day, each fit for a thousand colonists, and keep it up day after day, year after year, time without end. Even with the hands and the will (which the race never had) there is not that much steel, aluminum, and uranium in Earth's crust. There is not one hundredth of the necessary amount.

But intelligence can find solutions where there are none. Psychologists once locked an ape in a room, for which they had arranged only four ways of escaping. Then they spied on him to see which of the four he would find.

The ape escaped a fifth way.

Dr. Jesse Evelyn Ramsbotham had not been trying to solve the baby problem; he had been trying to build a time machine. He had two reasons: first, because time machines are an impossibility; second, because his hands would sweat and he would stammer whenever in the presence of a nubile female. He was not aware that the first reason was compensation for the second, in fact he was not aware of the second reason—it was a subject his conscious mind avoided.

It is useless to speculate as to the course of history had Jesse Evelyn Ramsbotham's parents had the good sense to name their son Bill instead of loading him with two girlish names. He might have become an All-American halfback and ended up selling bonds and adding his quota of babies to a sum already disastrous. Instead he became a mathematical physicist.

Progress in physics is achieved by denying the obvious and accepting the impossible. Any nineteenth century physicist could have given unassailable reasons why atom bombs were impossible if his reason were not affronted at the question; any twentieth century physicist could explain why time travel was incompatible with the real world of space-time. But Ramsbotham began fiddling with the three greatest Einsteinian equations, the two relativity equations for distance and duration and the mass-conversion equation; each contained the velocity of light. "Velocity" is first derivative, the differential of distance with respect to time; he converted those equations into differential equations, then played games with them. He would feed the results to the Rakitiac computer, remote successor to Univac, Eniac and Maniac. While he was doing these things his hands never sweated nor did he stammer, except when he was forced to deal with the young lady who was chief programmer for the giant computer.

His first model produced a time-stasis or low-entropy field no bigger than a football—but a lighted cigarette placed inside with full power setting was still burning a week later. Ramsbotham picked up the cigarette, resumed smoking and thought about it.

Next he tried a day-old chick, with colleagues to witness. Three months later the chick was unaged and no hungrier than chicks usually are. He reversed the phase relation and cut in power for the shortest time he could manage with his bread-boarded hook-up.

In less than a second the newly-hatched chick was long dead, starved and decayed.

He was aware that he had simply changed the slope of a curve, but he was convinced that he was on the track of true time travel. He never did find it, although once he thought that he had—he repeated by request his demonstration with a chick for some of his colleagues; that night two of them picked the lock on his lab, let the little thing out and replaced it with an egg. Ramsbotham might have been permanently convinced that he had found time travel and then spent the rest of his life in a blind alley had they not cracked the egg and showed him that it was hard-boiled.

But he did not give up. He made a larger model and tried to arrange a dilation, or anomaly (he did not call it a "Gate") which would let him get in and out of the field himself.

When he threw on power, the space between the curving magnetodes of his rig no longer showed the wall beyond, but a steaming jungle. He jumped to the conclusion that this must be a forest of the

Carboniferous Period. It had often occurred to him that the difference between space and time might simply be human prejudice, but this was not one of the times; he believed what he wanted to believe.

He hurriedly got a pistol and with much bravery and no sense crawled between the magnetodes.

Ten minutes later he was arrested for waving firearms around in Rio de Janeiro's civic botanical gardens. A lack of the Portuguese language increased both his difficulties and the length of time he spent in a tropical pokey, but three days later through the help of the North American consul he was on his way home. He thought and filled notebooks with equations and question marks on the whole trip.

The short cut to the stars had been found.

Ramsbotham's discoveries eliminated the basic cause of war and solved the problem of what to do with all those dimpled babies. A hundred thousand planets were no farther away than the other side of the street. Virgin continents, raw wilderness, fecund jungles, killing deserts, frozen tundras, and implacable mountains lay just beyond the city gates, and the human race was again going out where the street lights do not shine, out where there was no friendly cop on the corner nor indeed a corner, out where there were no well-hung, tender steaks, no boneless hams, no packaged, processed foods suitable for delicate minds and pampered bodies. The biped omnivore again had need of his biting, tearing, animal teeth, for the race was spilling out (as it had so often before) to kill or be killed, eat or be eaten.

But the human race's one great talent is survival. The race, as always, adjusted to conditions, and the most urbanized, mechanized, and civilized, most upholstered and luxurious culture in all history trained its best children, its potential leaders, in primitive pioneer survival—man naked against nature.

Rod Walker knew about Dr. J. E. Ramsbotham, just as he knew about Einstein, Newton, and Columbus, but he thought about Ramsbotham no oftener than he thought about Columbus. These were figures in books, each larger than life and stuffed with straw, not real. He used the Ramsbotham Gate between Jersey and the Arizona Strip without thinking of its inventor the same way his ancestors used elevators without thinking of the name "Otis." If he thought about the miracle at all, it was a half-formed irritation that the Arizona side of Hoboken Gate was so far from his parents' home. It was known as Kaibab Gate on this side and was seven miles north of the Walker residence.

At the time the house had been built the location was at the extreme limit of tube delivery and other city utilities. Being an old house, its living room was above ground, with only bedrooms, pantry, and bombproof buried. The living room had formerly stuck nakedly above ground, an ellipsoid monocoque shell, but, as Greater New York spread, the neighborhood had been zoned for underground apartments and construction above ground which would interfere with semblance of virgin forest had been forbidden.

The Walkers had gone along to the extent of covering the living room with soil and planting it with casual native foliage, but they had refused to cover up their view window. It was the chief charm of the house, as it looked out at the great canyon. The community corporation had tried to coerce them into covering it up and had offered to replace it with a simulacrum window such as the underground apartments used, with a relayed view of the canyon. But Rod's father was a stubborn man and maintained that with weather, women, and wine there was nothing "just as good." His window was still intact.

Rod found the family sitting in front of the window, watching a storm work its way up the canyon—his mother, his father, and, to his great surprise, his sister. Helen was ten years older than he and an assault captain in the Amazons; she was seldom home.

The warmth of his greeting was not influenced by his realization that her arrival would probably cause his own lateness to pass with little comment. "Sis! Hey, this is *swell*—I thought you were on Thule."

"I was . . . until a few hours ago." Rod tried to shake hands; his sister gathered him in a bear hug and bussed him on the mouth, squeezing him against the raised ornaments of her chrome corselet. She was still in uniform, a fact that caused him to think that she had just arrived—on her rare visits home she usually went slopping around in an old bathrobe and go-ahead slippers, her hair caught up in a knot. Now she was still in dress armor and kilt and had dumped her side arms, gauntlets, and plumed helmet on the floor.

She looked him over proudly. "My, but you've grown! You're almost as tall as I am."

"I'm taller."

"Want to bet? No, don't try to wiggle away from me; I'll twist your arm. Slip off your shoes and stand back to back."

"Sit down, children," their father said mildly. "Rod, why were you late?"

"Uh . . ." He had worked out a diversion involving telling about the examination coming up, but he did not use it as his sister intervened.

"Don't heckle him, Pater. Ask for excuses and you'll get them. I learned that when I was a sublieutenant."

"Quiet, daughter. I can raise him without your help."

Rod was surprised by his father's edgy answer, was more surprised by Helen's answer: "So? Really?" Her tone was odd.

Rod saw his mother raise a hand, seem about to speak, then close her mouth. She looked upset. His sister and father looked at each other; neither spoke. Rod looked from one to the other, said slowly, "Say, what's all this?"

His father glanced at him. "Nothing. We'll say no more about it. Dinner is waiting. Coming, dear?" He turned to his wife, handed her up from her chair, offered her his arm.

"Just a minute," Rod said insistently. "I was late because I was hanging around the Gap."

"Very well. You know better, but I said we would say no more about it." He turned toward the lift.

"But I wanted to tell you something else, Dad. I won't be home for the next week or so."

"Very well—*eh?* What did you say?"

"I'll be away for a while, sir. Maybe ten days or a bit longer."

His father looked perplexed, then shook his head. "Whatever your plans are, you will have to change them. I can't let you go away at this time."

"But, Dad—"

"I'm sorry, but that is definite."

"But, Dad, I *have* to!"

"No."

Rod looked frustrated. His sister said suddenly, "Pater, wouldn't it be well to find out why he wants to be away?"

"Now, daughter—"

"Dad, I'm taking my solo survival, starting tomorrow morning!"

Mrs. Walker gasped, then began to weep. Her husband said, "There, there, my dear!" then turned to his son and said harshly, "You've upset your mother."

"But, Dad, I . . ." Rod shut up, thinking bitterly that no one seemed to give a hoot about *his* end of it. After all, *he* was the one who was going to have to sink or swim. A lot they knew or—

"You see, Pater," his sister was saying. "He does have to be away. He has no choice, because—"

"I see nothing of the sort! Rod, I meant to speak about this earlier, but I had not realized that your test would take place so soon. When I signed permission for you to take that course, I had, I must admit, a mental reservation. I felt that the experience would be valuable later . . . when and if you took the course in college. But I never intended to let you come up against the final test while still in high school. You are too young."

Rod was shocked speechless. But his sister again spoke for him. "Fiddlesticks!"

"Eh? Now, daughter, please remember that—"

"Repeat fiddlesticks! Any girl in my company has been up against things as rough and many of them are not much older than Buddy. What are you trying to do, Pater? Break his nerve?"

"You have no reason to . . . I think we had best discuss this later."

"I think that is a good idea." Captain Walker took her brother's arm and they followed their parents down to the refectory. Dinner was on the table, still warm in its delivery containers; they took their places, standing, and Mr. Walker solemnly lighted the Peace Lamp. The family was evangelical Monist by inheritance, each of Rod's grandfathers having been converted in the second great wave of proselyting that swept out of Persia in the last decade of the previous century, and Rod's father took seriously his duties as family priest.

As the ritual proceeded Rod made his responses automatically, his mind on this new problem. His sister chimed in heartily but his mother's answers could hardly be heard.

Nevertheless the warm symbolism had its effect; Rod felt himself calming down. By the time his father intoned the last "—one Principle, one family, one flesh!" he felt like eating. He sat down and took the cover off his plate.

A yeast cutlet, molded to look like a chop and stripped with real bacon, a big baked potato, and a grilled green lobia garnished with baby's buttons . . . Rod's mouth watered as he reached for the catsup.

He noticed that Mother was not eating much, which surprised him. Dad was not eating much either but Dad often just picked at his food . . . he became aware with sudden warm pity that Dad was thinner and greyer than ever. How old was Dad?

His attention was diverted by a story his sister was telling: "—and so the Commandant told me I would have to clamp down. And I said to her, 'Ma'am, girls will be girls. If I have to bust a petty officer everytime one of them does something like that, pretty soon I won't have anything but privates. And Sergeant Dvorak is the best gunner I have.' "

"Just a second," her father interrupted. "I thought you said 'Kelly,' not 'Dvorak.' "

"I did and she did. Pretending to misunderstand which sergeant she meant was my secret weapon—for I had Dvorak cold for the same offense, and Tiny Dvorak (she's bigger than I am) is the Squadron's white hope for the annual corps-wide competition for best trooper. Of course, losing her stripes would put her, and us, out of the running.

"So I straightened out the 'mix up' in my best wide-eyed, thick-headed manner, let the old gal sit for a moment trying not to bite her nails, then told her that I had both women confined to barracks until that gang of college boys was through installing the new 'scope, and sang her a song about how the quality of mercy is not strained, it droppeth as the gentle rain from heaven, and made myself responsible for seeing to it that she was not again embarrassed by scandalous—her word, not mine—scandalous incidents . . . especially when she was showing quadrant commanders around.

"So she grumpily allowed as how the company commander was responsible for her company and she would hold me to it and now would I get out and let her work on the quarterly training report in peace? So I threw her my best parade ground salute and got out so fast I left a hole in the air."

"I wonder," Mr. Walker said judicially, "if you should oppose your commanding officer in such matters? After all, she is older and presumably wiser than you are."

Helen made a little pile of the last of her baby's buttons, scooped them up and swallowed them. "Fiddlesticks squared and cubed. Pardon me, Pater, but if you had any military service you would know better. I am as tough as blazes to my girls myself . . . and it just makes them boast about how they've got the worst fire-eater in twenty planets. But if they're in trouble higher up, I've got to take care of my kids. There always comes a day when there is something sticky up ahead and I have to stand up and walk toward it. And it will be all right because I'll have Kelly on my right flank and Dvorak on my left and each of them trying to take care of Maw Walker all by her ownself. I know what I'm doing. 'Walker's Werewolves' are a team."

Mrs. Walker shivered. "Gracious, darling, I wish you had never taken up a calling so . . . well, so *dangerous.*"

Helen shrugged. "The death rate is the same for us as for anybody . . . one person, one death, sooner or later. What would you want, Mum? With eighteen million more women than men on this continent did you want me to sit and knit until my knight comes riding? Out where I operate, there are more men than women; I'll wing one yet, old and ugly as I am."

Rod asked curiously, "Sis, would you really give up your commission to get married?"

"Would I! I won't even count his arms and legs. If he is still warm and can nod his head, he's had it. My target is six babies and a farm."

Rod looked her over. "I'd say your chances are good. You're quite pretty even if your ankles are thick."

"Thanks, pardner. Thank you too much. What's for dessert, Mum?"

"I didn't look. Will you open it, dear?"

Dessert turned out to be iced mangorines, which pleased Rod. His sister went on talking. "The Service isn't a bad shake, on active duty. It's garrison duty that wears. My kids get fat and sloppy and restless and start fighting with each other from sheer boredom. For my choice, barracks casualties are more to be dreaded than combat. I'm hoping that our squadron will be tagged to take part in the pacification of Byer's Planet."

Mr. Walker looked at his wife, then at his daughter. "You have upset your mother again, my dear. Quite a bit of this talk has hardly been appropriate under the Light of Peace."

"I was asked questions, I answered."

"Well, perhaps so."

Helen glanced up. "Isn't it time to turn it out, anyway? We all seem to have finished eating."

"Why, if you like. Though it is hardly reverent to hurry."

"The Principle knows we haven't all eternity." She turned to Rod. "How about making yourself scarce, mate? I want to make palaver with the folks."

"Gee, Sis, you act as if I was—"

"Get lost, Buddy. I'll see you later."

Rod left, feeling affronted. He saw Helen blow out the pax lamp as he did so.

He was still making lists when his sister came to his room. "Hi, kid."

"Oh. Hello, Sis."

"What are you doing? Figuring what to take on your solo?"

"Sort of."

"Mind if I get comfortable?" She brushed articles from his bed and sprawled on it. "We'll go into that later."

Rod thought it over. "Does that mean Dad won't object?"

"Yes. I pounded his head until he saw the light. But, as I said, we'll go into that later. I've got something to tell you, youngster."

"Such as?"

"The first thing is this. Our parents are not as stupid as you probably think they are. Fact is, they are pretty bright."

"I never said they were stupid!" Rod answered, uncomfortably aware of what his thoughts had been.

"No. But I heard what went on before dinner and so did you. Dad was throwing his weight around and not listening. But, Buddy, it has probably never occurred to you that it is hard work to be a parent, maybe the hardest job of all—particularly when you have no talent for it, which Dad hasn't. He knows it and works hard at it and is conscientious. Mostly he does mighty well. Sometimes he slips, like tonight. But, what you did not know is this: Dad is going to die."

"*What?*" Rod looked stricken. "I didn't know he was ill!"

"You weren't meant to know. Now climb down off the ceiling; there is a way out. Dad is terribly ill, and he would die in a few weeks at the most—unless something drastic is done. But something is going to be. So relax."

She explained the situation bluntly: Mr. Walker was suffering from a degenerative disease under which he was slowly starving to death. His condition was incurable by current medical art; he might linger on, growing weaker each day, for weeks or months—but he would certainly die soon.

Rod leaned his head on his hands and chastised himself. Dad dying . . . and he hadn't *even noticed.* They had kept it from him, like a baby, and he had been too stupid to see it.

His sister touched his shoulder. "Cut it out. If there is anything stupider than flogging yourself over something you can't help, I've yet to meet it. Anyhow, we are doing something about it."

"What? I thought you said nothing could be done?"

"Shut up and let your mind coast. The folks are going to make a Ramsbotham jump, five hundred to one, twenty years for two weeks. They've already signed a contract with Entropy, Incorporated. Dad has resigned from General Synthetics and is closing up his affairs; they'll kiss the world good-by this coming Wednesday—which is why he was being stern about your plans to be away at that time. You're the apple of his eye—Heaven knows why."

Rod tried to sort out too many new ideas at once. A time jump . . . of course! It would let Dad stay alive another twenty years. But— "Say, Sis, this doesn't get them anything! Sure, it's twenty years but it will be just two weeks to them . . . and Dad will be as sick as ever. I know what I'm talking about; they did the same thing for Hank Robbin's great grandfather and he died anyhow, right after they took him out of the stasis. Hank told me."

Captain Walker shrugged. "Probably a hopeless case to start with. But Dad's specialist, Dr. Hensley, says that he is morally certain that Dad's case is not hopeless . . . twenty years from now. I don't know anything about metabolic medicine, but Hensley says that they are on the verge and that twenty years from now they ought to be able to patch Dad up as easily they can graft on a new leg today."

"You really think so?"

"How should I know? In things like this you hire the best expert you can, then follow his advice. The point is, if we don't do it, Dad is finished. So we do it."

"Yeah. Sure, sure, we've got to."

She eyed him closely and added, "All right. Now do you want to talk with them about it?"

"Huh?" He was startled by the shift. "Why? Are they waiting for me?"

"No. I persuaded them that it was best to keep it from you until it happened. Then I came straight in and told you. Now you can do as you please—pretend you don't know, or go have Mum cry over you, and listen to a lot of last-minute, man-to-man advice from Dad that you will never take. About midnight, with your nerves frazzled, you can get back to your preparations for your survival test. Play it your own way—but I've rigged it so you can avoid that, if you want to. Easier on everybody. Myself, I like a cat's way of saying good-by."

Rod's mind was in a turmoil. Not to say good-by seemed unnatural, ungrateful, untrue to family sentiment—but the prospect of saying good-by seemed almost unbearably embarrassing. "What's that about a cat?"

"When a cat greets you, he makes a big operation of it, bumping, stropping your legs, buzzing like mischief. But when he leaves, he just walks off and never looks back. Cats are smart."

"Well . . ."

"I suggest," she added, "that you remember that they are doing this for their convenience, not yours."

"But Dad has to—"

"Surely, Dad must, if he is to get well." She considered pointing out that the enormous expense of the time jump would leave Rod practically penniless; she decided that this was better left undiscussed. "But Mum does not have to."

"But she has to go with Dad!"

"So? Use arithmetic. She prefers leaving you alone for twenty years in order to be with Dad for two weeks. Or turn it around: she prefers having you orphaned to having herself widowed for the same length of time."

"I don't think that's quite fair to Mum," Rod answered slowly.

"I wasn't criticizing. She's making the right decision. Nevertheless, they both have a strong feeling of guilt about you and—"

"About *me?*"

"About you. I don't figure into it. If you insist on saying good-by, their guilt will come out as self-justification and self-righteousness and they will find ways to take it out on you and everybody will have a bad time. I don't want that. You are all my family."

"Uh, maybe you know best."

"I didn't get straight A's in emotional logic and military leadership for nothing. Man is not a rational animal; he is a rationalizing animal. Now let's see what you plan to take with you."

She looked over his lists and equipment, then whistled softly. "Whew! Rod, I never saw so much plunder. You won't be able to move. Who are you? Tweedledum preparing for battle, or the White Knight?"

"Well, I was going to thin it down," he answered uncomfortably.

"I should think so!"

"Uh, Sis, what sort of gun should I carry?"

"Huh? Why the deuce do you want a gun?"

"Why, for what I might run into, of course. Wild animals and things. Deacon Matson practically said that we could expect dangerous animals."

"I doubt if he advised you to carry a gun. From his reputation, Dr. Matson is a practical man. See here, infant, on this tour you are the rabbit, trying to escape the fox. You aren't the fox."

"What do you mean?"

"Your only purpose is to stay alive. Not to be brave, not to fight, not to dominate the wilds—but just stay breathing. One time in a hundred a gun might save your life; the other ninety-nine it will just tempt you into folly. Oh, no doubt Matson would take one, and I would, too. But we are salted; we know when not to use one. But consider this. That test area is going to be crawling with trigger-happy young squirts. If one shoots you, it won't matter that you have a gun, too—because you will be dead. But if you carry a gun, it makes you feel cocky; you won't take proper cover. If you don't have one, then you'll *know* that you are the rabbit. You'll be careful."

"Did you take a gun on your solo test?"

"I did. And I lost it the first day. Which saved my life."

"How?"

"Because when I was caught without one I ran away from a Bessmer's griffin instead of trying to shoot it. You savvy Bessmer's griffin?"

"Uh, Spica V?"

"Spica IV. I don't know how much outer zoology they are teaching you kids these days—from the ignoramuses we get for recruits I've reached the conclusion that this new-fangled 'functional education' has abolished studying in favor of developing their cute little personalities.

Why, I had one girl who wanted to—never mind; the thing about the griffin is that it does not really have vital organs. Its nervous system is decentralized, even its assimilation system. To kill it quickly you would have to grind it into hamburger. Shooting merely tickles it. But I did not know that; if I had had my gun I would have found out the hard way. As it was, it treed me for three days, which did my figure good and gave me time to think over the philosophy, ethics, and pragmatics of self-preservation."

Rod did not argue, but he still had a conviction that a gun was a handy thing to have around. It made him feel good, taller, stronger and more confident, to have one slapping against his thigh. He didn't have to use it—not unless he just had to. And he knew enough to take cover; nobody in the class could do a silent sneak the way he could. While Sis was a good soldier, still she didn't know everything and—

But Sis was still talking. "I know how good a gun feels. It makes you bright-eyed and bushy-tailed, three meters tall and covered with hair. You're ready for anything and kind of hoping you'll find it. Which is exactly what is dangerous about it—because you aren't anything of the sort. You are a feeble, hairless embryo, remarkably easy to kill. You could carry an assault gun with two thousand meters precision range and isotope charges that will blow up a hill, but you still would not have eyes in the back of your head like a janus bird, nor be able to see in the dark like the Thetis pygmies. Death can cuddle up behind you while you are drawing a bead on something in front."

"But, Sis, your own company carries guns."

"Guns, radar, bombs, black scopes, gas, warpers, and some things which we light-heartedly hope are secret. What of it? You aren't going to storm a city. Buddy, sometimes I send a girl out on an infiltration patrol, object: information—go out, find out, come back alive. How do you suppose I equip her?"

"Uh—"

"Never mind. In the first place I don't pick an eager young recruit; I send some unkillable old-timer. She peels down to her underwear, darkens her skin if it is not dark, and goes out bare-handed and bare-footed, without so much as a fly swatter. I have yet to lose a scout that way. Helpless and unprotected you do grow eyes in the back of your head, and your nerve ends reach out and feel everything around you. I learned that when I was a brash young j.o., from a salty trooper old enough to be my mother."

Impressed, Rod said slowly, "Deacon Matson told us he would make us take this test bare-handed, if he could."

"Dr. Matson is a man of sense."

"Well, what would *you* take?"

"Test conditions again?"

Rod stated them. Captain Walker frowned. "Mmm . . . not much to go on. Two to ten days probably means about five. The climate won't be hopelessly extreme. I suppose you own a Baby Bunting?"

"No, but I've got a combat parka suit. I thought I would carry it, then if the test area turned out not to be cold, I'd leave it at the gate. I'd hate to lose it; it weighs only half a kilo and cost quite a bit."

"Don't worry about that. There is no point in being the best dressed ghost in Limbo. Okay, besides your parka I would make it four kilos of rations, five of water, two kilos of sundries like pills and matches, all in a vest pack . . . and a knife."

"That isn't much for five days, much less ten."

"It is all you can carry and still be light on your feet. Let's see your knife, dear."

Rod had several knives, but one was "his" knife, a lovely all-purpose one with a 21-cm. molysteel blade and a fine balance. He handed it to his sister, who cradled it lightly. "Nice!" she said, and glanced around the room.

"Over there by the outflow."

"I see." She whipped it past her ear, let fly, and the blade sank into the target, sung and quivered. She reached down and drew another from her boot top. "This is a good one, too." She threw and it bit into the target a blade's width from the first.

She retrieved both knives, stood balancing them, one on each hand. She flipped her own so that the grip was toward Rod. "This is my pet, 'Lady Macbeth.' I carried her on my own solo, Buddy. I want you to carry her on yours."

"You want to trade knives? All right." Rod felt a sharp twinge at parting with "Colonel Bowie" and a feeling of dismay that some other knife might let him down. But it was not an offer that he could refuse, not from Sis.

"My very dear! I wouldn't deprive you of your own knife, not on your solo. I want you to carry both, Buddy. You won't starve nor die of thirst, but a spare knife may be worth its weight in thorium."

"Gee, Sis! But I shouldn't take your knife, either—you said you were expecting active duty. I can carry a spare of my own."

"I won't need it. My girls haven't let me use a knife in years. I want you to have Lady Macbeth on your test." She removed the scabbard from her boot top, sheathed the blade, and handed it to him. "Wear it in good health, brother."

3

Through the Tunnel

Rod arrived at Templeton Gate the next morning feeling not his best. He had intended to get a good night's sleep in preparation for his ordeal, but his sister's arrival in conjunction with overwhelming changes in his family had defeated his intention. As with most children Rod had taken his family and home for granted; he had not thought about them much, nor placed a conscious value on them, any more than a fish treasures water. They simply were.

Now suddenly they were not.

Helen and he had talked late. She had begun to have strong misgivings about her decision to let him know of the change on the eve of his test. She had weighed it, decided that it was the "right" thing to do, then had learned the ages-old sour truth that right and wrong can sometimes be determined only through hindsight. It had not been fair, she later concluded, to load anything else on his mind just before his test. But it had not seemed fair, either, to let him leave without knowing . . . to return to an empty house.

The decision was necessarily hers; she had been his guardian since earlier that same day. The papers had been signed and sealed; the court had given approval. Now she found with a sigh that being a "parent" was not unalloyed pleasure; it was more like the soul-searching that had gone into her first duty as member of a court martial.

When she saw that her "baby" was not quieting, she had insisted that he go to bed anyhow, then had given him a long back rub, combining it with hypnotic instructions to sleep, then had gone quietly away when he seemed asleep.

But Rod had not been asleep; he had simply wanted to be alone. His mind raced like an engine with no load for the best part of an hour, niggling uselessly at the matter of his father's illness, wondering what it was going to be like to greet them again after twenty years—why, he would be almost as old as Mum!—switching over to useless mental preparations for unknown test conditions.

At last he realized that he had to sleep—forced himself to run through mental relaxing exercises, emptying his mind and hypnotizing himself. It took longer than ever before but finally he entered a great, golden, warm cloud and was asleep.

His bed mechanism had to call him twice. He woke bleary-eyed and was still so after a needle shower. He looked in a mirror, decided that shaving did not matter where he was going and anyhow he was late—then decided to shave after all . . . being painfully shy about his sparse young growth.

Mum was not up, but she hardly ever got up as early as that. Dad rarely ate breakfast these days . . . Rod recalled why with a twinge. But he had expected Sis to show up. Glumly he opened his tray and discovered that Mum had forgotten to dial an order, something that had not happened twice in his memory. He placed his order and waited for service—another ten minutes lost.

Helen showed up as he was leaving, dressing surprisingly in a dress. "Good morning."

"Hi, Sis. Say, you'll have to order your own tucker. Mother didn't and I didn't know what you wanted."

"Oh, I had breakfast hours ago. I was waiting to see you off."

"Oh. Well, so long. I've got to run, I'm late."

"I won't hold you up." She came over and embraced him. "Take it easy, mate. That's the important thing. More people have died from worry than ever bled to death. And if you do have to strike, strike low."

"Uh, I'll remember."

"See that you do. I'm going to get my leave extended today so that I'll be here when you come back." She kissed him. "Now run."

Dr. Matson was sitting at a desk outside the dispensary at Templeton Gate, checking names on his roll. He looked up as Rod arrived. "Why, hello, Walker. I thought maybe you had decided to be smart."

"I'm sorry I'm late, sir. Things happened."

"Don't fret about it. Knew a man once who didn't get shot at sunrise because he overslept the appointment."

"Really? Who was he?"

"Young fellow I used to know. Myself."

"Hunh? You really did, sir? You mean you were—"

"Not a word of truth in it. Good stories are rarely true. Get on in there and take your physical, before you get the docs irritated."

They thumped him and x-rayed him and made a wavy pattern from his brain and did all the indignities that examining physicians do. The senior examiner listened to his heart and felt his moist hand. "Scared, son?"

"Of course I am!" Rod blurted.

"Of course you are. If you weren't, I wouldn't pass you. What's that bandage on your leg?"

"Uh—" The bandage concealed Helen's knife "Lady Macbeth." Rod sheepishly admitted the fact.

"Take it off."

"Sir?"

"I've known candidates to pull dodges like that to cover up a disqualification. So let's have a look."

Rod started removing it; the physician let him continue until he was sure that it was a cache for a weapon and not a wound dressing. "Get your clothes on. Report to your instructor."

Rod put on his vest pack of rations and sundries, fastened his canteen under it. It was a belt canteen of flexible synthetic divided into half-litre pockets. The weight was taken by shoulder straps and a tube ran up the left suspender, ending in a nipple near his mouth so that he might drink without taking it off. He planned, if possible, to stretch his meager supply through the whole test, avoiding the hazards of contaminated water and the greater hazards of the water hole—assuming that fresh water could be found at all.

He wrapped twenty meters of line, light, strong, and thin, around his waist. Shorts, overshirt, trousers, and boot moccasins completed his costume; he belted "Colonel Bowie" on outside. Dressed, he looked fleshier than he was; only his knife showed. He carried his parka suit over his left arm. It was an efficient garment, hooded, with built-in boots and gloves, and with pressure seams to let him use bare hands when necessary, but it was much too warm to wear until he needed it. Rod had learned early in the game that Eskimos don't dare to sweat.

Dr. Matson was outside the dispensary door. "The late Mr. Walker," he commented, then glanced at the bulkiness of Rod's torso. "Body armor, son?"

"No, sir. Just a vest pack."

"How much penalty you carrying?"

"Eleven kilograms. Mostly water and rations."

"Mmm . . . well, it will get heavier before it gets lighter. No Handy-Dandy Young Pioneer's Kit? No collapsible patent wigwam?"

Rod blushed. "No, sir."

"You can leave that snow suit. I'll mail it to your home."

"Uh, thank you, sir." Rod passed it over, adding, "I wasn't sure I'd need it, but I brought it along, just in case."

"You did need it."

"Sir?"

"I've already flunked five for showing up without their snuggies . . . and four for showing up *with* vacuum suits. Both ways for being stupid. They ought to know that the Board would not dump them into vacuum or chlorine or such without specifying space suits in the test notice. We're looking for graduates, not casualties. On the other hand, cold weather is within the limits of useful test conditions."

Rod glanced at the suit he had passed over. "You're sure I won't need it, sir?"

"Quite. Except that you would have flunked if you hadn't fetched it. Now bear a hand and draw whatever pig shooter you favor; the armorer is anxious to close up shop. What gun have you picked?"

Rod gulped. "Uh, I was thinking about not taking one, Deacon—I mean 'Doctor.' "

"You can call me 'Deacon' to my face—ten days from now. But this notion of yours interests me. How did you reach that conclusion?"

"Uh, why, you see, sir . . . well, my sister suggested it."

"So? I must meet your sister. What's her name?"

"Assault Captain Helen Walker," Rod said proudly, "Corps of Amazons."

Matson wrote it down. "Get on in there. They are ready for the drawing."

Rod hesitated. "Sir," he said with sudden misgiving, "if I did carry a gun, what sort would you advise?"

Matson looked disgusted. "I spend a year trying to spoon-feed you kids with stuff I learned the hard way. Comes examination and you ask me to slip you the answers. I can no more answer that than I would have been justified yesterday in telling you to bring a snow suit."

"Sorry, sir."

"No reason why you shouldn't ask; it's just that I won't answer. Let's change the subject. This sister of yours . . . she must be quite a girl."

"Oh, she is, sir."

"Mmm . . . maybe if I had met a girl like that I wouldn't be a cranky old bachelor now. Get in there and draw your number. Number one goes through in six minutes."

"Yes, Doctor." His way led him past the school armorer, who had set up a booth outside the door. The old chap was wiping off a noiseless Summerfield. Rod caught his eye. "Howdy, Guns."

"Hi, Jack. Kind of late, aren't you? What'll it be?"

Rod's eye ran over the rows of beautiful weapons. Maybe just a little needle gun with poisoned pellets . . . He wouldn't have to *use* it . . .

Then he realized that Dr. Matson had answered his question, with a very broad hint. "Uh, I'm already heeled, Guns. Thanks."

"Okay. Well, good luck, and hurry back."

"Thanks a lot." He went into the gate room.

The seminar had numbered more than fifty students; there were about twenty waiting to take the examination. He started to look around, was stopped by a gate attendant who called out, "Over here! Draw your number."

The lots were capsules in a bowl. Rod reached in, drew one out, and broke it open. "Number seven."

"Lucky seven! Congratulations. Your name, please."

Rod gave his name and turned away, looking for a seat, since it appeared that he had twenty minutes or so to wait. He walked back, staring with interest at what his schoolmates deemed appropriate for survival, any and all conditions.

Johann Braun was seated with empty seats on each side of him. The reason for the empty seats crouched at his feet—a big, lean, heavily-muscled boxer dog with unfriendly eyes. Slung over Braun's shoulder was a General Electric Thunderbolt, a shoulder model with telescopic sights and cone-of-fire control; its power pack Braun wore as a back pack. At his belt were binoculars, knife, first aid kit, and three pouches.

Rod stopped and admired the gun, wondering how much the lovely thing cost. The dog raised his head and growled.

Braun put a hand on the dog's head. "Keep your distance," he warned. "Thor is a one-man dog."

Rod gave back a pace. "Yo, you are certainly equipped."

The big blond youth gave a satisfied smile. "Thor and I are going to live off the country."

"You don't need him, with that cannon."

"Oh, yes, I do. Thor's my burglar alarm. With him at my side I can sleep sound. You'd be surprised at the things he can do. Thor's smarter than most people."

"Shouldn't wonder."

"The Deacon gave me some guff that the two of us made a team and should go through separately. I explained to him that Thor would tear the joint apart if they tried to separate us." Braun caressed the dog's ears. "I'd rather team with Thor than with a platoon of Combat Pioneers."

"Say, Yo, how about letting me try that stinger? After we come out, I mean."

"I don't mind. It really is a honey. You can pick off a sparrow in the air easily as you can drop a moose at a thousand meters. Say, you're making Thor nervous. See you later."

Rod took the hint, moved on and sat down. He looked around, having in mind that he might still arrange a survival team. Near the shuttered arch of the gateway there was a priest with a boy kneeling in front of him, with four others waiting.

The boy who had been receiving the blessing stood up—and Rod stood up hastily. "Hey! *Jimmy!*"

Jimmy Throxton looked around, caught his eye and grinned, hurried over. "Rod!" he said, "I thought you had ducked out on me. Look, you haven't teamed?"

"No."

"Still want to?"

"Huh? Sure."

"Swell! I can declare the team as I go through as long as you don't have number two. You don't, do you?"

"No."

"Good! Because I'm—"

"NUMBER ONE!" the gate attendant called out. " 'Throxton, James.' "

Jimmy Throxton looked startled. "Oh, gee!" He hitched at his gun belt and turned quickly away, then called over his shoulder, "See you on the other side!" He trotted toward the gate, now unshuttered.

Rod called out, "Hey, Jimmy! How are we going to find—" But it was too late. Well, if Jimmy had sense enough to drive nails, he would keep an eye on the exit.

"Number two! Mshiyeni, Caroline." Across the room the big Zulu girl who had occurred to Rod as a possible team mate got up and headed for the gate. She was dressed simply in shirt and shorts, with her feet and legs and hands bare. She did not appear to be armed but she was carrying an overnight bag.

Someone called out, "Hey, Carol! What you got in the trunk?"

She threw him a grin. "Rocks."

"Ham sandwiches, I'll bet. Save me one."

"I'll save you a rock, sweetheart."

Too soon the attendant called out, "Number seven—Walker, Roderick L."

Rod went quickly to the gate. The attendant shoved a paper into his hand, then shook hands. "Good luck, kid. Keep your eyes open." He gave Rod a slap on the back that urged him through the opening, dilated to man size.

Rod found himself on the other side and, to his surprise, still indoors. But that shock was not as great as immediate unsteadiness and nausea; the gravity acceleration was much less than earth-normal.

He fought to keep from throwing up and tried to figure things out. Where was he? On Luna? On one of Jupiter's moons? Or somewhere 'way out there?

The Moon, most likely—Luna. Many of the longer jumps were relayed through Luna because of the danger of mixing with a primary, particularly with binaries. But surely they weren't going to leave him here; Matson had promised them no airless test areas.

On the floor lay an open valise; he recognized it absent-mindedly as the one Caroline had been carrying. At last he remembered to look at the paper he had been handed.

It read:

SOLO SURVIVAL TEST—Recall Instructions

1. You must pass through the door ahead in the three minutes allowed you before another candidate is started through. An overlapping delay will disqualify you.
2. Recall will be by standard visual and sound signals. You are warned that the area remains hazardous even after recall is sounded.
3. The exit gate will not be the entrance gate. Exit may be as much as twenty kilometers in the direction of sunrise.
4. There is no truce zone outside the gate. Test starts at once. Watch out for stobor. Good luck!

—**B. P. M.**

Rod was still gulping at low gravity and staring at the paper when a door opened at the far end of the long, narrow room he was in. A man shouted, "Hurry up! You'll lose your place."

Rod tried to hurry, staggered and then recovered too much and almost fell. He had experienced low gravity on field trips and his family had once vacationed on Luna, but he was not used to it; with difficulty he managed to skate toward the far door.

Beyond the door was another gate room. The attendant glanced at the timer over the gate and said, "Twenty seconds. Give me that instruction sheet."

Rod hung onto it. "I'll use the twenty seconds."—*as much as twenty kilometers in the direction of sunrise.* A nominal eastward direction—call it "east." But what the deuce was, or were, "stobor"?

"Time! Through you go." The attendant snatched the paper, shutters rolled back, and Rod was shoved through a dilated gate.

He fell to his hands and knees; the gravity beyond was something close to earth-normal and the change had caught him unprepared. But he stayed down, held perfectly still and made no sound while he quickly looked around him. He was in a wide clearing covered with high grass and containing scattered trees and bushes; beyond was dense forest.

He twisted his neck in a hasty survey. Earth-type planet, near normal acceleration, probably a G-type sun in the sky . . . heavy vegetation, no fauna in sight—but that didn't mean anything; there might be hundreds within hearing. Even a stobor, whatever that was.

The gate was behind him, tall dark-green shutters which were in reality a long way off. They stood unsupported in the tall grass, an anomalism unrelated to the primitive scene. Rod considered wriggling around behind the gate, knowing that the tangency was one-sided and that he would be able to see through the locus from the other side, see anyone who came out without himself being seen.

Which reminded him that he himself could be seen from that exceptional point; he decided to move.

Where was Jimmy? Jimmy ought to be behind the gate, watching for him to come out . . . or watching from some other spy point. The only certain method of rendezvous was for Jimmy to have waited for Rod's appearance; Rod had no way to find him now.

Rod looked around more slowly and tried to spot anything that might give a hint as to Jimmy's whereabouts. Nothing . . . but when his scanning came back to the gate, the gate was no longer there.

Rod felt the cold ripple of adrenalin shock trickle down his back and out his finger tips. He forced himself to quiet down and told himself that it was better this way. He had a theory to account for the disappearance of the gate; they were, he decided, refocusing it between each pair of students, scattering them possibly kilometers apart.

No, that could not be true—"twenty kilometers toward sunrise" had to relate to a small area.

Or did it? He reminded himself that the orientation given in the sheet handed him might not be that which appeared in some other student's instruction sheet. He relaxed to the fact that he did not really know anything . . . he did not know where he was, nor where Jimmy was, nor any other member of the class, he did not know what he might find here, save that it was a place where a man might stay alive if he were smart—and lucky.

Just now his business was to stay alive, for a period that he might as well figure as ten Earth days. He wiped Jimmy Throxton out of his mind, wiped out everything but the necessity of remaining unceasingly alert to all of his surroundings. He noted wind direction as shown by grass plumes and started crawling cautiously down wind.

The decision to go down wind had been difficult. To go up wind had been his first thought, that being the natural direction for a stalk. But his sister's advice had already paid off; he felt naked and helpless without a gun and it had reminded him that he was not the hunter. His scent would carry in any case; if he went down wind he stood a chance of seeing what might be stalking him, while his unguarded rear would be comparatively safe.

Something ahead in the grass!

He froze and watched. It had been the tiniest movement; he waited. There it was again, moving slowly from right to left across his front. It looked like a dark spike with a tuft of hair on the tip, a tail possibly, carried aloft.

He never saw what manner of creature owned the tail, if it was a tail. It stopped suddenly at a point Rod judged to be directly down wind, then moved off rapidly and he lost sight of it. He waited a few minutes, then resumed crawling.

It was extremely hot work and sweat poured down him and soaked his overshirt and trousers. He began to want a drink very badly but reminded himself that five litres of water would not last long if he started drinking the first hour of the test. The sky was overcast with high cirrus haze, but the primary or "sun"—he decided to call it the Sun—seemed to burn through fiercely. It was low in the sky behind him; he wondered what it would be like overhead? Kill a man, maybe. Oh, well, it would be cooler in that forest ahead, or at least not be the same chance of sunstroke.

There was lower ground ahead of him and hawklike birds were circling above the spot, round and round. He held still and watched. Brothers, he said softly, if you are behaving like vultures back home, there is something dead ahead of me and you are waiting to make sure it stays dead before you drop in for lunch. If so, I had better swing wide, for it is bound to attract other things . . . some of which I might not want to meet.

He started easing to the right, quartering the light breeze. It took him onto higher ground and close to a rock outcropping. Rod decided to spy out what was in the lower place below, making use of cover to let him reach an overhanging rock.

It looked mightily like a man on the ground and a child near him. Rod reached, fumbled in his vest pack, got out a tiny 8-power monocular, took a better look. The man was Johann Braun, the "child" was his boxer dog. There was no doubt but that they were dead, for Braun was lying like a tossed rag doll, with his head twisted around and one leg bent under. His throat and the side of his head were a dark red stain.

While Rod watched, a doglike creature trotted out, sniffed at the boxer, and began tearing at it . . . then the first of the buzzard creatures landed to join the feast. Rod took the glass from his eye, feeling queasy. Old Yo had not lasted long—jumped by a "stobor" maybe—and his smart dog had not saved him. Too bad! But it did prove that there were carnivores around and it behooved him to be careful if he did not want to have jackals and vultures arguing over the leavings!

He remembered something and put the glass back to his eye. Yo's proud Thunderbolt gun was nowhere in sight and the corpse was not wearing the power pack that energized it. Rod gave a low whistle in his mind and thought. The only animal who would bother to steal a gun ran around on two legs. Rod reminded himself that a Thunderbolt could kill at almost any line-of-sight range—and now somebody had it who obviously took advantage of the absence of law and order in a survival test area.

Well, the only thing to do was not to be in line of sight. He backed off the rock and slid into the bushes.

The forest had appeared to be two kilometers away, or less, when he had started. He was close to it when he became uncomfortably aware that sunset was almost upon him. He became less cautious, more hurried, as he planned to spend the night in a tree. This called for light to climb by, since he relished a night on the ground inside the forest still less than he liked the idea of crouching helpless in the grass.

It had not taken all day to crawl this far. Although it had been morning when he had left Templeton Gate the time of day there had nothing to do with the time of day here. He had been shoved through into late afternoon; it was dusk when he reached the tall trees.

So dusky that he decided that he must accept a calculated risk for what he must do. He stopped at the edge of the forest, still in the high grass, and dug into his pack for his climbers. His sister had caused him to leave behind most of the gadgets, gimmicks, and special-purpose devices that he had considered bringing; she had not argued at these. They were climbing spikes of a style basically old, but refined, made small and light—the pair weighed less than a tenth of a kilogram—and made foldable and compact, from a titanium alloy, hard and strong.

He unfolded them, snapped them under his arches and around his shins, and locked them in place. Then he eyed the tree he had picked, a tall giant deep enough in the mass to allow the possibility of crossing to another tree if the odds made a back-door departure safer and having a trunk which, in spite of its height, he felt sure he could get his arms around.

Having picked his route, he straightened up and at a fast dogtrot headed for the nearest tree. He went past it, cut left for another tree, passed it and cut right toward the tree he wanted. He was about fifteen meters from it when something charged him.

He closed the gap with instantaneous apportation which would have done credit to a Ramsbotham hyperfold. He reached the first branch, ten meters above ground, in what amounted to levitation. From there on he climbed more conventionally, digging the spurs into the tree's smooth bark and setting his feet more comfortably on branches when they began to be close enough together to form a ladder.

About twenty meters above ground he stopped and looked down. The branches interfered and it was darker under the trees than it had been out in the open; nevertheless he could see, prowling around the tree, the denizen that had favored him with attention.

Rod tried to get a better view, but the light was failing rapidly. But it looked like . . . well, if he had not been certain that he was on some uncolonized planet 'way out behind and beyond, he would have said that it was a *lion.*

Except that it looked eight times as big as any lion ought to look.

He hoped that, whatever it was, it could not climb trees. Oh, quit fretting, Rod!—if it had been able to climb you would have been lunch meat five minutes ago. Get busy and rig a place to sleep before it gets pitch dark. He moved up the tree, keeping an eye out for the spot he needed.

He found it presently, just as he was beginning to think that he would have to go farther down. He needed two stout branches far enough apart and near enough the same level to let him stretch a hammock. Having found such, he worked quickly to beat the failing light. From a pocket of his vest pack he took out his hammock, a web strong as spider silk and almost as thin and light. Using the line around his waist he stretched it, made sure his lashings would hold and then started to get into it.

A double-jointed acrobat with prehensile toes might have found it easy; a slack-wire artist would simply have walked into it and sat down. But Rod found that he needed sky hooks. He almost fell out of the tree.

The hammock was a practical piece of equipment and Rod had slept in it before. His sister had approved it, remarking that it was a better model than the field hammock they gave her girls. "Just don't sit up in your sleep."

"I won't," Rod had assured her. "Anyway, I always fasten the chest belt."

But he had never slung it in this fashion. There was nothing to stand on under the hammock, no tree limb above it close enough to let him chin himself into it. After several awkward and breath-catching attempts he began to wonder whether he should perch like a bird the rest of the night, or drape himself in the notch of a limb. He did not consider spending the night on the ground—not with that *thing* prowling around.

There was another limb higher up almost directly over the hammock. Maybe if he tossed the end of his line over it and used it to steady himself . . .

He tried it. But it was almost pitch dark now; the only reason he did not lose his line was that one end was bent to the hammock. At last he gave up and made one more attempt to crawl into the hammock by main force and extreme care. Bracing both hands wide on each side of the head rope he scooted his feet out slowly and cautiously. Presently he had his legs inside the hammock, then his buttocks. From there on it was a matter of keeping his center of gravity low and making no sudden moves while he insinuated his body farther down into the cocoon.

At last he could feel himself fully and firmly supported. He took a deep breath, sighed, and let himself relax. It was the first time he had felt either safe or comfortable since passing through the gate.

After a few minutes of delicious rest Rod located the nipple of his canteen and allowed himself two swallows of water, after which he prepared supper. This consisted in digging out a quarter-kilo brick of field ration, eleven hundred calories of yeast protein, fat, starch, and glucose, plus trace requirements. The label on it, invisible in the dark, certified that it was "tasty, tempting and pleasing in texture," whereas chewing an old shoe would have attracted a gourmet quite as much.

But real hunger gave Rod the best of sauces. He did not let any crumb escape and ended by licking the wrapper. He thought about opening another one, quelled the longing, allowed himself one more mouthful of water, then pulled the insect hood of the hammock down over his face and fastened it under the chest belt. He was immune to most insect-carried Terran diseases and was comfortably aware that humans were not subject to most Outlands diseases, but he did not want the night fliers to use his face as a drinking fountain, nor even as a parade ground.

He was too hot even in his light clothing. He considered shucking down to his shorts; this planet, or this part of this planet, seemed quite tropical. But it was awkward; tonight he must stay as he was, even if it meant wasting a day's ration of water in sweat. He wondered what planet this was, then tried to peer through the roof of the forest to see if he could recognize stars. But either the trees were impenetrable or the sky was overcast; he could see nothing. He attempted to draw everything out of his mind and sleep.

Ten minutes later he was wider awake than ever. Busy with his hammock, busy with his dinner, he had not paid attention to distant sounds; now he became aware of all the voices of the night. Insects buzzed and sang and strummed, foliage rustled and whispered, something coughed below him. The cough was answered by insane laughter that ran raggedly up, then down, and died in asthmatic choking.

Rod hoped that it was a bird.

He found himself straining to hear every sound, near and far, holding his breath. He told himself angrily to stop it; he was safe from at least nine-tenths of potential enemies. Even a snake, if this place ran to such, would be unlikely to crawl out to the hammock, still less likely to attack—if he held still. Snakes, button-brained as they were, showed little interest in anything too big to swallow. The chances of anything big enough to hurt him—and interested in hurting him—being in this treetop were slim. So forget those funny noises, pal, and go to sleep. After all, they're no more important than traffic noises in a city.

He reminded himself of the Deacon's lecture on alarm and could not see sky; he floated in a leafy cloud. He traced it to the body's coming too urgently to battle stations, remaining too long at full alert. Or, as his sister had put it, more people worry themselves to death than bleed to death. He set himself conscientiously to running through the mental routines intended to produce sleep.

He almost made it. The sound that pulled him out of warm drowsiness came from far away; involuntarily he roused himself to hear it. It sounded almost human . . . no, it *was* human—the terrible sound of a grown man crying with heartbreak, the deep, retching, bass sobs that tear the chest.

Rod wondered what he ought to do. It was none of his business and everyone there was on his own—but it went against the grain to hear such agony from a fellow human and ignore it. Should he climb down and feel his way through the dark to wherever the poor wretch was?

Stumbling into tree roots, he reminded himself, and falling into holes and maybe walking straight into the jaws of something hungry and big.

Well, should he? Did he have any right *not* to?

It was solved for him by the sobs being answered by more sobs, this time closer and much louder. This new voice did not sound human, much as it was like the first, and it scared him almost out of his hammock. The chest strap saved him.

The second voice was joined by a third, farther away. In a few moments the peace of the night had changed to sobbing, howling ululation of mass fear and agony and defeat unbearable. Rod knew now that this was nothing human, nor anything he had ever heard, or heard of, before. He suddenly had a deep conviction that these were the stobor he had been warned to avoid.

But what were they? How was he to avoid them? The one closest seemed to be higher up than he was and no farther than the next tree . . . good grief, it might even be *this* tree!

When you meet a stobor in the dark what do you do? Spit in its face? Or ask it to waltz?

One thing was certain: anything that made that much noise in the jungle was not afraid of anything; therefore it behooved him to be afraid of it. But, there being nothing he could do, Rod lay quiet, his fear evidenced only by tense muscles, gooseflesh, and cold sweat. The hellish concert continued with the "stobor" closest to him sounding almost in his pocket. It seemed to have moved closer.

With just a bit more prodding Rod would have been ready to sprout wings and fly. Only at home on the North American continent of Terra had he ever spent a night alone in the wilderness. There the hazards were known and minor . . . a few predictable bears, an occasional lazy rattlesnake, dangers easily avoided.

But how could he guard against the utterly unknown? That stobor—he decided that he might as well call it that—that stobor might be moving toward him now, sizing him up with night eyes, deciding whether to drag him home, or eat him where it killed him.

Should he move? And maybe move right into the fangs of the stobor? Or should he wait, helpless, for the stobor to pounce? It was possible that the stobor could not attack him in the tree. But it was equally possible that stobor were completely arboreal and his one chance lay in climbing down quickly and spending the night on the ground.

What was a stobor? How did it fight? Where and when was it dangerous? The Deacon evidently expected the class to know what to do about them. Maybe they had studied the stobor those days he was out of school right after New Year's? Or maybe he had just plain forgotten . . . and would pay for it with his skin. Rod was good at Outlands zoology—but there was just too much to learn it all. Why, the zoology of Terra alone used to give oldstyle zoologists more than they could handle; how could they expect him to soak up all there was to learn about dozens of planets?

It wasn't *fair!*

When Rod heard himself think that ancient and useless protest he had a sudden vision of the Deacon's kindly, cynical smile. He heard his dry drawl: Fair? You expected this to be *fair,* son? This is not a game. I tried to tell you that you were a city boy, too soft and stupid for this. You would not listen.

He felt a gust of anger at his instructor; it drove fear out of his mind. Jimmy was right; the Deacon would eat his own grandmother! A cold, heartless fish!

All right, what would the Deacon do?

Again he heard his teacher's voice inside his head, an answer Matson had once given to a question put by another classmate: "There wasn't anything I could do, so I took a nap."

Rod squirmed around, rested his hand on "Colonel Bowie" and tried to take a nap. The unholy chorus made it almost impossible, but he did decide that the stobor in his tree—or was it the next tree?—did not seem to be coming closer. Not that it could come much closer without breathing on his neck, but at least it did not seem disposed to attack.

After a long time he fell into restless sleep, sleep that was no improvement, for he dreamed that he had a ring of sobbing, ululating stobor around him, staring at him, waiting for him to move. But he was trussed up tight and could not move.

The worst of it was that every time he turned his head to see what a stobor looked like it would fade back into the dark, giving him just a hint of red eyes, long teeth.

He woke with an icy shock, tried to sit up, found himself restrained by his chest strap, forced himself to lie back. What was it? What had happened?

In his suddenly-awakened state it took time to realize what had happened: the noise had stopped. He could not hear the cry of a single stobor, near or far. Rod found it more disturbing than their clamor, since a noisy stobor advertised its location whereas a silent one could be anywhere—why, the nearest one could now be sitting on the branch behind his head. He twisted his head around, pulled the insect netting off his face to see better. But it was too dark; stobor might be queued up three abreast for all he could tell.

Nevertheless the silence was a great relief. Rod felt himself relax as he listened to the other night sounds, noises that seemed almost friendly after that devils' choir. He decided that it must be almost morning and that we would do well to stay awake.

Presently he was asleep.

He awoke with the certainty that someone was looking at him. When he realized where he was and that it was still dark, he decided that it was a dream. He stirred, looked around, and tried to go back to sleep.

Something *was* looking at him!

His eyes, made sensitive by darkness, saw the thing as a vague shape on the branch at his foot. Black on black, he could not make out its outline—but two faintly luminous eyes stared unwinkingly back into his.

"—nothing I could do, so I took a nap." Rod did not take a nap. For a time measured in eons he and the thing in the tree locked eyes. Rod tightened his grip on his knife and held still, tried to quell the noise of his pounding heart, tried to figure out how he could fight back from a hammock. The beast did not move, made no sound; it simply stared and seemed prepared to do it all night.

When the ordeal had gone on so long that Rod felt a mounting impulse to shout and get it over, the creature moved with light scratching sounds toward the trunk and was gone. Rod could feel the branch shift; he judged that the beast must weigh as much as he did.

Again he resolved to stay awake. Wasn't it getting less dark? He tried to tell himself so, but he still could not see his own fingers. He decided to count to ten thousand and bring on the dawn.

Something large went down the tree very fast, followed at once by another, and still a third. They did not stop at Rod's bedroom but went straight down the trunk. Rod put his knife back and uttered, "Noisy neighbors! You'd think this was Emigrants' Gap." He waited but the frantic procession never came back.

He was awakened by sunlight in his face. It made him sneeze; he tried to sit up, was caught by his safety belt, became wide awake and regretted it. His nose was stopped up, his eyes burned, his mouth tasted like a ditch, his teeth were slimy, and his back ached. When he moved to ease it he found that his legs ached, too—and his arms—and his head. His neck refused to turn to the right.

Nevertheless he felt happy that the long night was gone. His surroundings were no longer terrifying, but almost idyllic. So high up that he could not see the ground he was still well below the roof of the jungle and could not see sky; he floated in a leafy cloud. The morning ray that brushed his face was alone, so thoroughly did trees shut out the sky.

This reminded him that he had to mark the direction of sunrise. Hmmm . . . not too simple. Would he be able to see the sun from the floor of the jungle? Maybe he should climb down quickly, get out in the open, and mark the direction while the sun was still low. But he noticed that the shaft which had wakened him was framed by a limb notch of another forest giant about fifteen meters away. Very well, that tree was "east" of his tree; he could line them up again when he reached the ground.

Getting out of his hammock was almost as hard as getting in; sore muscles resented the effort. At last he was balanced precariously on one limb. He crawled to the trunk, pulled himself painfully erect and, steadied by the trunk, took half-hearted setting-up exercises to work the knots out. Everything loosened up but his neck, which still had a crick like a toothache.

He ate and drank sitting on the limb with his back to the trunk. He kept no special lookout, rationalizing that night feeders would be bedded down and day feeders would hardly be prowling the tree tops—not big ones, anyway; they would be on the ground, stalking herbivores. The truth was that his green hide-away looked too peaceful to be dangerous.

He continued to sit after he finished eating, considered drinking more of his precious water, even considered crawling back into his hammock. Despite the longest night he had ever had he was bone tired and the day was already hot and sleepy and humid; why not stretch out? His only purpose was to survive; how better than by sleeping and thereby saving food and water?

He might have done so had he known what time it was. His watch told him that it was five minutes before twelve, but he could not make up his mind whether that was noon on Sunday or midnight coming into Monday. He was sure that this planet spun much more slowly than did Mother Earth; the night before had been at least as long as a full Earth day.

Therefore the test had been going on at least twenty-six hours and possibly thirty-eight—and recall could be any time after forty-eight hours. Why, it might be today, before sunset, and here he was in fine shape, still alive, still with food and water he could trust.

He felt good about it. What did a stobor have that a man did not have more of and better? Aside from a loud voice, he added.

But the exit gate might be as much as twenty kilometers "east" of where he had come in; therefore it behooved him to reach quickly a point ten kilometers east of where he had come in; he would lay money that that would land him within a kilometer or two of the exit. Move along, hole up, and wait—why, he might sleep at home tonight, after a hot bath!

He started unlashing his hammock while reminding himself that he must keep track of hours between sunrise and sunset today in order to estimate the length of the local day. Then he thought no more about it as he had trouble folding the hammock. It had to be packed carefully to fit into a pocket of his vest pack. The filmy stuff should have been spread on a table, but where he was the largest, flattest area was the palm of his hand.

But he got it done, lumpy but packed, and started down. He paused on the lowest branch, looked around. The oversized and hungry thing that had chased him up the tree did not seem to be around, but the undergrowth was too dense for him to be sure. He made a note that he must, all day long and every day, keep a climbable tree in mind not too far away; a few seconds woolgathering might use up his luck.

Okay, now for orientation— Let's see, there was the tree he had used to mark "east." Or was it? Could it be that one over there? He realized that he did not know and swore at himself for not checking it by compass. The truth was that he had forgotten that he was carrying a compass. He got it out now, but it told him nothing, since east by compass bore no necessary relation to direction of sunrise on this planet. The rays of the primary did not penetrate where he was; the forest was bathed by a dim religious light unmarked by shadows.

Well, the clearing could not be far away. He would just have to check. He descended by climbing spurs, dropped to spongy ground, and headed the way it should be. He counted his paces while keeping an eye peeled for hostiles.

One hundred paces later he turned back, retracing his own spoor. He found "his" tree; this time he examined it. There was where he had come down; he could see his prints. Which side had he gone up? There should be spur marks.

He found them . . . and was amazed at his own feat; they started high as his head. "I must have hit that trunk like a cat!" But it showed the direction from which he had come; five minutes later he was at the edge of the open country he had crossed the day before.

The sun made shadows here, which straightened him out and he checked by compass. By luck, east was "east" and he need only follow his compass. It took him back into the forest.

He traveled standing up. The belly sneak which he had used the day before was not needed here; he depended on moving noiselessly, using cover, and keeping an eye out behind as well as in front. He zigzagged in order to stay close to trees neither too big nor too small but corrected his course frequently by compass.

One part of his mind counted paces. At fifteen hundred broken-country steps to a kilometer Rod figured that fifteen thousand should bring him to his best-guess location for the exit gate, where he planned to set up housekeeping until recall.

But, even with part of his mind counting paces and watching a compass and a much larger part watching for carnivores, snakes, and other hazards, Rod still could enjoy the day and place. He was over his jitters of the night before, feeling good and rather cocky. Even though he tried to be fully alert, the place did not feel dangerous now—stobor or no stobor.

It was, he decided, jungle of semi-rainforest type, not dense enough to require chopping one's way. It was interlaced with game paths but he avoided these on the assumption that carnivores might lie waiting for lunch to come down the path—Rod had no wish to volunteer.

The place seemed thick with game, mostly of antelope type in many sizes and shapes. They were hard to spot; they faded into the bush with natural camouflage, but the glimpses he got convinced him that they were plentiful. He avoided them as he was not hunting and was aware that even a vegetarian could be dangerous with hooves and horns in self or herd defense.

The world above was inhabited, too, with birds and climbers. He spotted families of what looked like monkeys and speculated that this world would probably have developed its own race of humanoids. He wondered again what planet it was? Terrestrial to several decimal places it certainly seemed to be—except for the inconveniently long day—and probably one just opened, or it would be swarming with colonists. It would be a premium planet certainly; that clearing he had come through yesterday would make good farm land once it was burned off. Maybe he would come back some day and help clean out the stobor.

In the meantime he watched where he put his hands and feet, never walked under a low branch without checking it, and tried to make his eyes and ears as efficient as a rabbit's. He understood now what his sister had meant about how being unarmed makes a person careful, and realized also how little chance he would have to use a gun if he let himself be surprised.

It was this hyperacuteness that made him decide that he was being stalked.

At first it was just uneasiness, then it became a conviction. Several times he waited by a tree, stood frozen and listened; twice he did a sneak through bushes and doubled back on his tracks. But whatever it was seemed as good as he was at silent movement and taking cover and (he had to admit) a notch better.

He thought about taking to the trees and outwaiting it. But his wish to reach his objective outweighed his caution; he convinced himself that he would be safer if he pushed on. He continued to pay special attention to his rear, but after a while he decided that he was no longer being followed.

When he had covered, by his estimate, four kilometers, he began to smell water. He came to a ravine which sliced across his route. Game tracks led him to think it might lead down to a watering place, just the sort of danger area he wished to avoid, so Rod crossed quickly and went down the shoulder of the ravine instead. It led to a bank overlooking water; he could hear the stream before he reached it.

He took to the bushes and moved on his belly to a point where he could peer out from cover. He was about ten meters higher than the water. The ground dropped off on his right as well as in front; there the ravine joined the stream and an eddy pool formed the watering place he had expected. No animals were in sight but there was plenty of sign; a mud flat was chewed with hoof marks.

But he had no intention of drinking where it was easy; it would be too easy to die there. What troubled him was that he must cross the stream to reach the probable recall area. It was a small river or wide brook, not too wide to swim, probably not too deep to wade if he picked his spot. But he would not do either one unless forced—and not then without testing the water by chucking a lure into it . . . a freshly killed animal. The streams near his home were safe, but a tropical stream must be assumed to have local versions of alligator, piranha, or even worse.

The stream was too wide to cross through the tree tops. He lay still and considered the problem, then decided that he would work his way upstream and hope that it would narrow, or split into two smaller streams which he could tackle one at a time.

It was the last thing he thought about for some time.

When Rod regained consciousness it was quickly; a jackal-like creature was sniffing at him. Rod lashed out with one hand and reached for his knife with the other. The dog brute backed away, snarling, then disappeared in the leaves.

His knife was gone! The realization brought him groggily alert; he sat up. It made his head swim and hurt. He felt it and his fingers came away bloody. Further gingerly investigation showed a big and very tender swelling on the back of his skull, hair matted with blood, and failed to tell him whether or not his skull was fractured. He gave no thanks that he had been left alive; he was sure that the blow had been intended to kill.

But not only his knife was gone. He was naked, save for his shorts. Gone were his precious water, his vest pack with rations and a dozen other invaluable articles—his antibiotics, his salt, his compass, his climbers, his matches, his hammock . . . everything.

His first feeling of sick dismay was replaced by anger. Losing food and gear was no more than to be expected, since he had been such a fool as to forget his rear while he looked at the stream—but taking the watch his father had given him, that was stealing; he would make somebody pay for that!

His anger made him feel better. It was not until then that he noticed that the bandage on his left shin was undisturbed.

He felt it. Sure enough! Whoever it was who had hijacked him had not considered a bandage worth stealing; Rod unwrapped it and cradled Lady Macbeth in his hand.

Somebody was going to be sorry.

4

Savage

Rod Walker was crouching on a tree limb. He had not moved for two hours, he might not move for as long a time. In a clearing near him a small herd of yearling bachelor buck were cropping grass; if one came close enough Rod intended to dine on buck. He was very hungry.

He was thirsty, too, not having drunk that day. Besides that, he was slightly feverish. Three long, imperfectly healed scratches on his left arm accounted for the fever, but Rod paid fever and scratches no attention—he was alive; he planned to stay alive.

A buck moved closer to him; Rod became quiveringly alert. But the little buck tossed his head, looked at the branch, and moved away. He did not appear to see Rod; perhaps his mother had taught him to be careful of overhanging branches—or perhaps a hundred thousand generations of harsh survival had printed it in his genes.

Rod swore under his breath and lay still. One of them was bound to make a mistake eventually; then he would eat. It had been days since he had thought about anything but food . . . food and how to keep his skin intact, how to drink without laying himself open to ambush, how to sleep without waking up in a fellow-denizen's belly.

The healing wounds on his arm marked how expensive his tuition had been. He had let himself get too far from a tree once too often, had not even had time to draw his knife. Instead he had made an impossible leap and had chinned himself with the wounded arm. The thing that had clawed him he believed to be the same sort as the creature that had treed him the day of his arrival; furthermore he believed it to be a lion. He had a theory about that, but had not yet been able to act on it.

He was gaunt almost to emaciation and had lost track of time. He realized that the time limit of the survival test had probably—almost certainly—passed, but he did not know how long he had lain in the crotch of a tree, waiting for his arm to heal, nor exactly how long it had been since he had come down, forced by thirst and hunger. He supposed that the recall signal had probably been given during one of his unconscious periods, but he did not worry nor even think about it. He was no longer interested in survival tests; he was interested in survival.

Despite his weakened condition his chances were better now than when he had arrived. He was becoming sophisticated, no longer afraid of things he had been afraid of, most acutely wary of others which had seemed harmless. The creatures with the ungodly voices which he had dubbed "stobor" no longer fretted him; he had seen one, had disturbed it by accident in daylight and it had given voice. It was not as big as his hand, and reminded him of a horned lizard except that it had the habits of a tree toad. Its one talent was its voice; it could blow up a bladder at its neck to three times its own size, then give out with that amazing, frightening sob.

But that was all it could do.

Rod had guessed that it was a love call, then had filed the matter. He still called them "stobor."

He had learned about a forest vine much like a morning glory, but its leaves carried a sting worse than that of a nettle, toxic and producing numbness. Another vine had large grape-like fruits, deliciously tempting and pleasant to the palate; Rod had learned the hard way that they were a powerful purgative.

He knew, from his own narrow brushes and from kills left half-eaten on the ground, that there were carnivores around even though he had never had a good look at one. So far as he knew there were no carnivorous tree-climbers large enough to tackle a man, but he could not be certain; he slept with one eye open.

The behavior of this herd caused him to suspect that there must be carnivores that hunted as he was now hunting, even though he had had the good fortune not to tangle with one. The little buck had wandered all over the clearing, passed close by lesser trees, yet no one of them had grazed under the tree Rod was in.

Steady, boy . . . here comes one. Rod felt the grip of "Lady Macbeth," got ready to drop onto the graceful little creature as it passed under. But five meters away it hesitated, seemed to realize that it was straying from its mates, and started to turn.

Rod let fly.

He could hear the meaty *tunk!* as blade bit into muscle; he could see the hilt firm against the shoulder of the buck. He dropped to the ground, hit running and moved in to finish the kill.

The buck whipped its head up, turned and fled. Rod dived, did not touch it. When he rolled to his feet the clearing was empty. His mind was filled with bitter thoughts; he had promised himself never to throw his knife when there was any possibility of not being able to recover it, but he did not let regrets slow him; he got to work on the tracking problem.

Rod had been taught the first law of hunting sportsmanship, that a wounded animal must always be tracked down and finished, not left to suffer and die slowly. But there was no trace of "sportsmanship" in his present conduct; he undertook to track the buck because he intended to eat it, and—much more urgently—because he had to recover that knife in order to stay alive.

The buck had not bled at once and its tracks were mixed up with hundreds of other tracks. Rod returned three times to the clearing and started over before he picked up the first blood spoor. After that it was easier but he was far behind now and the stampeded buck moved much faster than he could track. His quarry stayed with the herd until it stopped in a new pasture a half kilometer away. Rod stopped still in cover and looked them over. His quarry did not seem to be among them.

But blood sign led in among them; he followed it and they stampeded again. He had trouble picking it up; when he did he found that it led into brush instead of following the herd. This made it easier and harder—easier because he no longer had to sort one spoor from many, harder because pushing through the brush was hard in itself and much more dangerous, since he must never forget that he himself was hunted as well as hunter, and lastly because the signs were so much harder to spot there. But it cheered him up, knowing that only a weakened animal would leave the herd and try to hide. He expected to find it down before long.

But the beast did not drop; it seemed to have a will to live as strong as his own. He followed it endlessly and was beginning to wonder what he would do if it grew dark before the buck gave up. He *had* to have that knife.

He suddenly saw that there were two spoors.

Something had stepped beside a fresh, split-hooved track of the little antelope; something had stepped on a drop of blood. Quivering, his subconscious "bush radar" at full power, Rod moved silently forward. He found new marks again . . . a man!

The print of a shod human foot—and so wild had he become that it gave him no feeling of relief; it made him more wary than ever.

Twenty minutes later he found them, the human and the buck. The buck was down, having died or perhaps been finished off by the second stalker. The human, whom Rod judged to be a boy somewhat younger and smaller than himself, was kneeling over it, slicing its belly open. Rod faded back into the bush. From there he watched and thought. The other hunter seemed much preoccupied with the kill . . . and that tree hung over the place where the butchering was going on—

A few minutes later Rod was again on a branch, without a knife but with a long thorn held in his teeth. He looked down, saw that his rival was almost under him, and transferred the thorn to his right hand. Then he waited.

The hunter below him laid the knife aside and bent to turn the carcass. Rod dropped.

He felt body armor which had been concealed by his victim's shirt. Instantly he transferred his attention to the bare neck, pushing the thorn firmly against vertebrae. "Hold still or you've had it!"

The body under him suddenly quit struggling.

"That's better," Rod said approvingly. "Cry pax?"

No answer. Rod jabbed the thorn again. "I'm not playing games," he said harshly. "I'm giving you one chance to stay alive. Cry pax and mean it, and we'll both eat. Give me any trouble and you'll never eat again. It doesn't make the least difference."

There was a moment's hesitation, then a muffled voice said, "Pax."

Keeping the thorn pressed against his prisoner's neck, Rod reached out for the knife which had been used to gut the buck. It was, he saw, his own Lady Macbeth. He sheathed it, felt around under the body he rested on, found another where he expected it, pulled it and kept it in his hand. He chucked away the thorn and stood up. "You can get up."

The youngster got up and faced him sullenly. "Give me my knife."

"Later . . . if you are a good boy."

"I said 'Pax.' "

"So you did. Turn around, I want to make sure you don't have a gun on you."

"I left—I've nothing but my knife. Give it to me."

"Left it where?"

The kid did not answer. Rod said, "Okay, turn around," and threatened with the borrowed knife. He was obeyed. Rod quickly patted all the likely hiding places, confirmed that the youngster was wearing armor under clothes and over the entire torso. Rod himself was dressed only in tan, scratches, torn and filthy shorts, and a few scars. "Don't you find that junk pretty hot in this weather?" he asked cheerfully. "Okay, you can turn around. Keep your distance."

The youngster turned around, still with a very sour expression. "What's your name, bud?"

"Uh, Jack."

"Jack what? Mine's Rod Walker."

"Jack Daudet."

"What school, Jack?"

"Ponce de Leon Institute."

"Mine's Patrick Henry High School."

"*Matson's* class?"

"The Deacon himself."

"I've heard of him." Jack seemed impressed.

"Who hasn't? Look, let's quit jawing; we'll have the whole county around our ears. Let's eat. You keep watch that way; I'll keep watch behind you."

"Then give me my knife. I need it to eat."

"Not so fast. I'll cut you off a hunk or two. Special Waldorf service."

Rod continued the incision Jack had started, carried it on up and laid the hide back from the right shoulder, hacked off a couple of large chunks of lean. He tossed one to Jack, hunkered down and gnawed his own piece while keeping sharp lookout. "You keeping your eyes peeled?" he asked.

"Sure."

Rod tore off a rubbery mouthful of warm meat. "Jack, how did they let a runt like you take the test? You aren't old enough."

"I'll bet I'm as old as you are!"

"I doubt it."

"Well . . . I'm qualified."

"You don't look it."

"I'm *here,* I'm alive."

Rod grinned. "You've made your point. I'll shut up." Once his portion was resting comfortably inside, Rod got up, split the skull and dug out the brains. "Want a handful?"

"Sure."

Rod passed over a fair division of the dessert. Jack accepted it, hesitated, then blurted out, "Want some salt?"

"*Salt!* You've got *salt?*"

Jack appeared to regret the indiscretion. "Some. Go easy on it."

Rod held out his handful. "Put some on. Whatever you can spare."

Jack produced a pocket shaker from between shirt and armor, sprinkled a little on Rod's portion, then shrugged and made it liberal. "Didn't you bring salt along?"

"Me?" Rod answered, tearing his eyes from the mouth-watering sight. "Oh, sure! But—Well, I had an accident." He decided that there was no use admitting that he had been caught off guard.

Jack put the shaker firmly out of sight. They munched quietly, each watching half their surroundings. After a while Rod said softly, "Jackal behind you, Jack."

"Nothing else?"

"No. But it's time we whacked up the meat and got out of here; we're attracting attention. How much can you use?"

"Uh, a haunch and a chunk of liver. I can't carry any more."

"And you can't eat more before it spoils, anyway." Rod started butchering the hind quarters. He cut a slice of hide from the belly, used it to sling his share around his neck. "Well, so long, kid. Here's your knife. Thanks for the salt."

"Oh, that's all right."

"Tasted mighty good. Well, keep your eyes open."

"Same to you. Good luck."

Rod stood still. Then he said almost reluctantly, "Uh, Jack, you wouldn't want to team up, would you?" He regretted it as soon as he said it, remembering how easily he had surprised the kid.

Jack chewed a lip. "Well . . . I don't know."

Rod felt affronted. "What's the matter? Afraid of me?" Didn't the kid see that Rod was doing him a favor?

"Oh, no! You're all right, I guess."

Rod had an unpleasant suspicion. "You think I'm trying to get a share of your salt, don't you?"

"Huh? Not at all. Look, I'll divvy some salt with you."

"I wouldn't touch it! I just thought—" Rod stopped. He had been thinking that they had both missed recall; it looked like a long pull.

"I didn't mean to make you mad, Rod. You're right. We ought to team."

"Don't put yourself out! I can get along."

"I'll bet you can. But let's team up. Is it a deal?"

"Well . . . Shake."

Once the contract was made Rod assumed leadership. There was no discussion; he simply did so and Jack let it stand. "You lead off," Rod ordered, "and I'll cover our rear."

"Okay. Where are we heading?"

"That high ground downstream. There are good trees there, better for all night than around here. I want us to have time to settle in before dark—so a quick sneak and no talking."

Jack hesitated. “Okay. Are you dead set on spending the night in a tree?”

Rod curled his lip. “Want to spend it on the ground? How did you stay alive this long?”

“I spent a couple of nights in trees,” Jack answered mildly. “But I’ve got a better place now, maybe.”

“Huh? What sort?”

“A sort of a cave.”

Rod thought about it. Caves could be death traps. But the prospect of being able to stretch out swayed him. “Won’t hurt to look, if it’s not too far.”

“It’s not far.”

5

The Nova

Jack's hideaway was in a bluff overlooking the stream by which Rod had been robbed. At this point the bluffs walled a pocket valley and the stream meandered between low banks cut in an alluvial field between the bluffs. The cave was formed by an overhang of limestone which roofed a room water-carved from shale in one bluff. The wall below it was too sheer to climb; the overhanging limestone protected it above and the stream curved in sharply almost to the foot of the bluff. The only way to reach it was to descend the bluff farther upstream to the field edging the creek, then make a climbing traverse of the shale bank where it was somewhat less steep just upstream of the cave.

They slanted cautiously up the shale, squeezed under an overhang at the top, and stepped out on a hard slaty floor. The room was open on one side and fairly long and deep, but it squeezed in to a waist-high crawl space; only at the edge was there room to stand up. Jack grabbed some gravel, threw it into the dark hole, waited with knife ready. "Nobody home, I guess." They dropped to hands and knees, crawled inside. "How do you like it?"

"It's swell . . . provided we stand watches. Something could come up the way we did. You've been lucky."

"Maybe," Jack felt around in the gloom, dragged out dry branches of thorn bush, blocked the pathway, jamming them under the overhang. "That's my alarm."

"It wouldn't stop anything that got a whiff of you and really wanted to come in."

"No. But I would wake up and let it have some rocks in the face. I keep a stack over there. I've got a couple of scare-flares, too."

"I thought—Didn't you say you had a gun?"

"I didn't say, but I do. But I don't believe in shooting when you can't see."

"It looks all right. In fact it looks good. I guess I did myself a favor when I teamed with you." Rod looked around. "You've had a *fire!*"

"I've risked it a couple of times, in daylight. I get so tired of raw meat."

Rod sighed deeply. "I know. Say, do you suppose?"

"It's almost dark. I've never lighted one when it could show. How about roast liver for breakfast, instead? With salt?"

Rod's mouth watered. "You're right, Jack. I do want to get a drink before it is too dark, though. How about coming along and we cover each other?"

"No need. There's a skin back there. Help yourself."

Rod congratulated himself on having teamed with a perfect housekeeper. The skin was of a small animal, not identifiable when distended with water. Jack had scraped the hide but it was uncured and decidedly unsavory. Rod was not aware that the water tasted bad; he drank deeply, wiped his mouth with his hand and felt at peace.

They did not sleep at once, but sat in the dark and compared notes. Jack's class had come through one day earlier, but with the same instructions. Jack agreed that recall was long overdue.

"I suppose I missed it while I was off my head," Rod commented. "I don't know how long I was foggy . . . I guess I didn't miss dying by much."

"That's not it, Rod."

"Why not?"

"I've been okay and keeping track of the time. There never was any recall."

"You're sure?"

"How could I miss? The siren can be heard for twenty kilometers, they use a smoke flare by day and a searchlight at night, and the law says they have to keep it up at least a week unless everybody returns . . . which certainly did not happen this time."

"Maybe we are out of range. Matter of fact—well, I don't know about you, but I'm lost. I admit it."

"I'm not. I'm about four kilometers from where they let my class through; I could show you the spot. Rod, let's face it; something has gone wrong. There is no way of telling how long we are going to be here." Jack added quietly, "That's why I thought it was a good idea to team."

Rod chewed it over, decided it was time to haul out his theory. "Me, too."

"Yes. Solo is actually safer, for a few days. But if we are stuck here indefinitely, then—"

"Not what I meant, Jack."

"Huh?"

"Do you know what planet this is?"

"No. I've thought about it, of course. It has to be one of the new list and it is compatible with—"

"I *know* what one it is."

"Huh? Which one?"

"It's Earth. Terra herself."

There was a long silence. At last Jack said, "Rod, are you all right? Are you still feverish?"

"I'm fine, now that I've got a full belly and a big drink of water. Look, Jack, I know it sounds silly, but you just listen and I'll add it up. We're on Earth and I think I know about where, too. I don't think they meant to sound recall; they meant us to figure out where we are . . . and walk out. It's a twist Deacon Matson would love."

"But—"

"Keep quiet, can't you? Yapping like a girl. Terrestrial planet, right?"

"Yes, but—"

"Stow it and let me talk. G-type star. Planetary rotation same as Earth."

"But it's not!"

"I made the same mistake. The first night I thought was a week long. But the truth was I was scared out of my skin and that made it seem endless. Now I know better. The rotation matches."

"No, it doesn't. My watch shows it to be about twenty-six hours."

"You had better have your watch fixed when we get back. You banged it against a tree or something."

"But—Oh, go ahead. Keep talking; it's your tape."

"You'll see. Flora compatible. Fauna compatible. I know how they did it and why and where they put us. It's an economy measure."

"A what?"

"Economy. Too many people complaining about school taxes being too high. Of course, keeping an interstellar gate open is expensive and uranium doesn't grow on trees. I see their point. But Deacon Matson says it is false economy. He says, sure, it's expensive—but that the only thing more expensive than a properly trained explorer or pioneer leader is an improperly trained dead one.

"He told us after class one day," Rod went on, "that the penny-pinchers wanted to run the practices and tests in selected areas on Earth, but the Deacon claims that the essence of survival in the Outlands is the skill to cope with the unknown. He said that if tests were held on Earth, the candidates would just study up on terrestrial environments. He said any Boy Scout could learn the six basic Earth environments and how to beat them out of books . . . but that it was criminal to call that survival training and then dump a man in an un-Earthly environment on his first professional assignment. He said that it was as ridiculous as just teaching a kid to play chess and then send him him out to fight a duel."

"He's right," Jack answered. "Commander Benboe talks the same way."

"Sure he's right. He swore that if they went ahead with this policy this would be the last year he would teach. But they pulled a gimmick on him."

"How?"

"It's a good one. What the Deacon forgot is that any environment is as unknown as any other if you don't have the slightest idea where you are. So they rigged it so that we could not know. First they shot us to Luna; the Moon gates are always open and that doesn't cost anything extra. Of course that made us think we were in for a long jump. Besides, it confused us; we wouldn't know we were being dumped back into the gravity field we had left—for that was what they did next; they shoved us back on Earth. Where? Africa, I'd say. I think they used the Luna Link to jump us to Witwatersrand Gate outside Johannesburg and there they were all set with a matched-in temporary link to drop us into the bush. Tshaka Memorial Park or some other primitive preserve, on a guess. Everything matches. A wide variety of antelope-type game, carnivores to feed on them—I've seen a couple of lions and—"

"You *have?"*

"Well, they will do for lions until I get a chance to skin one. But they threw in other dodges to confuse us, too. The sky would give the show away, particularly if we got a look at Luna. So they've hung an overcast over us. You can bet there are cloud generators not far away. Then they threw us one more curve. Were you warned against 'stobor'?"

"Yes."

"See any?"

"Well, I'm not sure what stobor are."

"Neither am I. Nor any of us, I'll bet. 'Stobor' is the bogeyman, chucked in to keep our pretty little heads busy. There aren't any 'stobor' on Terra so naturally we must be somewhere else. Even a suspicious character like me would be misled by that. In fact, I was. I even picked out something I didn't recognize and called it that, just as they meant me to do."

"You make it sound logical, Rod."

"Because it *is* logical. Once you realize that this is Earth—" He patted the floor of the cave. "—but that they have been trying to keep us from knowing it, everything falls into place. Now here is what we do. I was going to tackle it alone, as soon as I could—I haven't been able to move around much on account of this bad arm—but I decided to take you along, before you got hurt. Here's my plan. I think this is Africa, but it might be South America, or anywhere in the tropics. It does not matter, because we simply follow this creek downstream, keeping our eyes open because there really are hazards; you can get just as dead here as in the Outlands. It may take a week, or a month, but one day we'll come to a bridge. We'll follow the road it serves until somebody happens along. Once in town we'll check in with the authorities and get them to flip us home . . . and we get our solo test certificates. Simple."

"You make it sound too simple," Jack said slowly.

"Oh, we'll have our troubles. But we can do it, now that we know what to do. I didn't want to bring this up before, but do you have salt enough to cure a few kilos of meat? If we did not have to hunt every day, we could travel faster. Or maybe you brought some Kwik-Kure?"

"I did, but—"

"Good!"

"Wait a minute, Rod. That won't do."

"Huh? We're a team, aren't we?"

"Take it easy. Look, Rod, everything you said is logical, but—"

"No 'buts' about it."

"It's logical . . . but it's *all wrong!*"

"Huh? Now, listen, Jack—"

"*You* listen. You've done all the talking so far."

"But—Well, all right, say your say."

"You said that the sky would give it away, so they threw an overcast over the area."

"Yes. That's what they must have done, nights at least. They wouldn't risk natural weather; it might give the show away."

"What I'm trying to tell you is that it *did* give the show away. It hasn't been overcast every night, though maybe you were in deep forest and missed the few times it has been clear. But I've seen the night sky, Rod. I've seen stars."

"So? Well?"

"They aren't *our* stars, Rod. I'm sorry."

Rod chewed his lip. "You probably don't know southern constellations very well?" he suggested.

"I knew the Southern Cross before I could read. These aren't our stars, Rod; I know. There is a pentagon of bright stars above where the sun sets; there is nothing like that to be seen from Earth. And besides, anybody would recognize Luna, if it was there."

Rod tried to remember what phase the Moon should be in. He gave up, as he had only a vague notion of elapsed time. "Maybe the Moon was down?"

"Not a chance. I didn't see our Moon, Rod, but I saw *moons* . . . two of them, little ones and moving fast, like the moons of Mars."

"You don't mean this is *Mars?"* Rod said scornfully.

"Think I'm crazy? Anyhow, the stars from Mars are exactly like the stars from Earth. Rod, what are we jawing about? It was beginning to clear when the sun went down; let's crawl out and have a look. Maybe you'll believe your eyes."

Rod shut up and followed Jack. From inside nothing was visible but dark trees across the stream, but from the edge of the shelf part of the sky could be seen. Rod looked up and blinked.

"Mind the edge," Jack warned softly.

Rod did not answer. Framed by the ledge above him and by tree tops across the stream was a pattern of six stars, a lopsided pentagon with a star in its center. The six stars were as bright and unmistakable as the seven stars of Earth's Big Dipper . . . nor did it take a degree in astrography to know that this constellation had never been seen from Terra.

Rod stared while the hard convictions he had formed fell in ruins. He felt lost and alone. The tree across the way seemed frightening. He turned to Jack, his cocky sophistication gone. "You've convinced me," he said dully. "What do we do now?"

Jack did not answer.

"Well?" Rod insisted. "No good standing here."

"Rod," Jack answered, "that star in the middle of the Pentagon—it wasn't there before."

"Huh? You probably don't remember."

"No, no, I'm sure! Rod, you know what? We're seeing a *nova."*

Rod was unable to arouse the pure joy of scientific discovery; his mind was muddled with reorganizing his personal universe. A mere stellar explosion meant nothing. "Probably one of your moonlets."

"Not a chance. The moons are big enough to show disks. It's a nova; it has to be. What amazing luck to see one!"

"I don't see anything lucky about it," Rod answered moodily. "It doesn't mean anything to us. It's probably a hundred light-years away, maybe more."

"Yes, but doesn't it thrill you?"

"No." He stooped down and went inside. Jack took another look, then followed.

There was silence, moody on Rod's part. At last Jack said, "Think I'll turn in."

"I just can't see," Rod answered irrelevantly, "how I could be so wrong. It was a logical certainty."

"Forget it," Jack advised. "My analytics instructor says that all logic is mere tautology. She says it is impossible to learn anything through logic that you did not already know."

"Then what use is logic?" Rod demanded.

"Ask me an easy one. Look, partner, I'm dead for sleep; I want to turn in."

"All right. But, Jack, if this isn't Africa—and I've got to admit it isn't—what do we do? They've gone off and *left* us."

"Do? We do what we've been doing. Eat, sleep, stay alive. This is a listed planet; if we just keep breathing, someday somebody will show up. It might be just a power breakdown; they may pick us tomorrow."

"In that case, then—"

"In that case, let's shut up and go to sleep."

6

"I Think He Is Dead"

ROD WAS AWAKENED BY HEAVENLY ODORS. HE ROLLED OVER, BLINKED at light streaming under the overhang, managed by great effort to put himself back into the matrix of the day before. Jack, he saw, was squatting by a tiny fire on the edge of the shelf; the wonderful fragrance came from toasting liver.

Rod got to his knees, discovering that he was slightly stiff from having fought dream stobor in his sleep. These nightmare stobor were bug-eyed monsters fit for a planet suddenly strange and threatening. Nevertheless he had had a fine night's sleep and his spirits could not be daunted in the presence of the tantalizing aroma drifting in.

Jack looked up. "I thought you were going to sleep all day. Brush your teeth, comb your hair, take a quick shower, and get on out here. Breakfast is ready." Jack looked him over again. "Better shave, too."

Rod grinned and ran his hand over his chin. "You're jealous of my manly beard, youngster. Wait a year or two and you'll find out what a nuisance it is. Shaving, the common cold, and taxes . . . my old man says those are the three eternal problems the race is never going to lick." Rod felt a twinge at the thought of his parents, a stirring of conscience that he had not thought of them in he could not remember how long. "Can I help, pal?"

"Sit down and grab the salt. This piece is for you."

"Let's split it."

"Eat and don't argue. I'll fix me some." Rod accepted the charred and smoky chunk, tossed it in his hands and blew on it. He looked around for salt. Jack was slicing a second piece; Rod's eyes passed over the operation—then whipped back.

The knife Jack was using was "Colonel Bowie."

The realization was accompanied by action; Rod's hand darted out and caught Jack's wrist in an anger-hard grip. "You stole my knife!"

Jack did not move. "Rod . . . have you gone crazy?"

"You slugged me and stole my knife."

Jack made no attempt to fight, nor even to struggle. "You aren't awake yet, Rod. Your knife is on your belt. This is another knife . . . mine."

Rod did not bother to look down. "The one I'm wearing is Lady Macbeth. I mean the knife you're using, Colonel Bowie—*my* knife."

"Let go my wrist."

"Drop it!"

"Rod . . . you can probably make me drop this knife. You're bigger and you've got the jump on me. But yesterday you teamed with me. You're busting that team right now. If you don't let go right away, the team is broken. Then you'll have to kill me . . . because if you don't, I'll trail you. I'll keep on trailing you until I find you asleep. Then you've had it."

They faced each other across the little fire, eyes locked. Rod breathed hard and tried to think. The evidence was against Jack. But had this little runt tracked him, slugged him, stolen everything he had? It looked like it.

Yet it did not *feel* like it. He told himself that he could handle the kid if his story did not ring true. He let go Jack's wrist. "All right," he said angrily, "tell me how you got my knife."

Jack went on slicing liver. "It's not much of a story . . . and I don't know that it is *your* knife. But it was not mine to start with—you've seen mine. I use this one as a kitchen knife. Its balance is wrong."

"Colonel Bowie! Balanced wrong? That's the best throwing knife you ever saw!"

"Do you want to hear this? I ran across this hombre in the bush, just as the jackals were getting to him. I don't know what got him—stobor, maybe; he was pretty well clawed and half eaten. He wasn't one of my class, for his face wasn't marked and I could tell. He was carrying a Thunderbolt and—"

"Wait a minute. A Thunderbolt gun?"

"I said so, didn't I? I guess he tried to use it and had no luck. Anyhow, I took what I could use—this knife and a couple of other things; I'll show you. I left the Thunderbolt; the power pack was exhausted and it was junk."

"Jack, look at me. You're not lying?"

Jack shrugged. "I can take you to the spot. There might not be anything left of him, but the Thunderbolt ought to be there."

Rod stuck out his hand. "I'm sorry. I jumped to conclusions."

Jack looked at his hand, did not shake it. "I don't think you are much of a teammate. We had better call it quits." The knife flipped over, landed at Rod's toes. "Take your toadsticker and be on your way."

Rod did not pick up the knife. "Don't get sore, Jack. I made an honest mistake."

"It was a mistake, all right. You didn't trust me and I'm not likely to trust you again. You can't build a team on that." Jack hesitated. "Finish your breakfast and shove off. It's better than way."

"Jack, I truly am sorry. I apologize. But it was a mistake anybody could make—you haven't heard my side of the story."

"You didn't wait to hear *my* story!"

"So I was wrong, I *said* I was wrong." Rod hurriedly told how he had been stripped of his survival gear. "—so naturally, when I saw Colonel Bowie, I assumed that you must have jumped me. That's logical, isn't it?" Jack did not answer; Rod persisted: "Well? Isn't it?"

Jack said slowly, "You used 'logic' again. What you call 'logic.' Rod, you use the stuff the way some people use dope. Why don't you use your head, instead?"

Rod flushed and kept still. Jack went on, "If I had swiped your knife, would I have let you see it? For that matter, would I have teamed with you?"

"No, I guess not. Jack, I jumped at a conclusion and lost my temper."

"Commander Benboe says," Jack answered bleakly, "that losing your temper and jumping at conclusions is a one-way ticket to the cemetery."

Rod looked sheepish. "Deacon Matson talks the same way."

"Maybe they're right. So let's not do it again, huh? Every dog gets one bite, but only one."

Rod looked up, saw Jack's dirty paw stuck out at him. "You mean we're partners again?"

"Shake. I think we had better be; we don't have much choice." They solemnly shook hands. Then Rod picked up Colonel Bowie, looked at it longingly, and handed it hilt first to Jack.

"I guess it's yours, after all."

"Huh? Oh, no. I'm glad you've got it back."

"No," Rod insisted. "You came by it fair and square."

"Don't be silly, Rod. I've got 'Bluebeard'; that's the knife for me."

"It's yours. I've got Lady Macbeth."

Jack frowned. "We're partners, right?"

"Huh? Sure."

"So we share everything. Bluebeard belongs just as much to you as to me. And Colonel Bowie belongs to both of us. But you are used to it, so it's best for the team for you to wear it. Does that appeal to your lopsided sense of logic?"

"Well . . ."

"So shut up and eat your breakfast. Shall I toast you another slice? That one is cold."

Rod picked up the scorched chunk of liver, brushed dirt and ashes from it. "This is all right."

"Throw it in the stream and have a hot piece. Liver won't keep anyhow."

Comfortably stuffed, and warmed by companionship, Rod stretched out on the shelf after breakfast and stared at the sky. Jack put out the fire and tossed the remnants of their meal downstream. Something broke water and snapped at the liver even as it struck. Jack turned to Rod. "Well, what do we do today?"

"Mmm . . . what we've got on hand ought to be fit to eat tomorrow morning. We don't need to make a kill today."

"I hunt every second day, usually, since I found this place. Second-day meat is better than first, but by the third . . . phewy!"

"Sure. Well, what do you want to do?"

"Well, let's see. First I'd like to buy a tall, thick chocolate malted milk—or maybe a fruit salad. Both. I'd eat those—"

"Stop it, you're breaking my heart!"

"Then I'd have a hot bath and get all dressed up and flip out to Hollywood and see a couple of good shows. That superspectacle that Dirk Manleigh is starring in and then a good adventure show. After that I'd have another malted milk . . . strawberry, this time, and then—"

"Shut up!"

"You asked me what I wanted to do."

"Yes, but I expected you to stick to possibilities."

"Then why didn't you say so? Is that 'logical'? I thought you always used logic?"

"Say, lay off, will you? I apologized."

"Yeah, you apologized," Jack admitted darkly. "But I've got some mad I haven't used up yet."

"Well! Are you the sort of pal who keeps raking up the past?"

"Only when you least expect it. Seriously, Rod, I think we ought to hunt today."

"But you agreed we didn't need to. It's wrong, and dangerous besides, to make a kill you don't need."

"I think we ought to hunt people."

Rod pulled his ear. "Say that again."

"We ought to spend the day hunting people."

"Huh? Well, anything for fun I always say. What do we do when we find them? Scalp them, or just shout 'Beaver!'?"

"Scalping is more definite. Rod, how long will we be here?"

"Huh? All we know is that something has gone seriously cockeyed with the recall schedule. You say we've been here three weeks. I would say it was longer but you have kept a notch calendar and I haven't. Therefore . . ." He stopped.

"Therefore what?"

"Therefore nothing. They might have had some technical trouble, which they may clear up and recall us this morning. Deacon Matson and his fun-loving colleagues might have thought it was cute to double the period and not mention it. The Dalai Lama might have bombed the whiskers off the rest of the world and the Gates may be radioactive ruins. Or maybe the three-headed serpent men of the Lesser Magellanic Cloud have landed and have the situation well in hand—for them. When you haven't data, guessing is illogical. We might be here forever."

Jack nodded. "That's my point."

"Which point? We know we may be marooned; that's obvious."

"Rod, a two-man team is just right for a few weeks. But suppose this runs into months? Suppose one of us breaks a leg? Or even if we don't, how long is that thornbush alarm going to work? We ought to wall off that path and make this spot accessible only by rope ladder, with somebody here all the time to let the ladder down. We ought to locate a salt lick and think about curing hides and things like that—that water skin I made is getting high already. For a long pull we ought to have at least four people."

Rod scratched his gaunt ribs thoughtfully. "I know. I thought about it last night, after you jerked the rug out from under my optimistic theory. But I was waiting for you to bring it up."

"Why?"

"This is your cave. You've got all the fancy equipment, a gun and pills and other stuff I haven't seen. You've got salt. All I've got is a knife—two knives now, thanks to you. I'd look sweet suggesting that you share four ways."

"We're a team, Rod."

"Mmm . . . yes. And we both figure the team would be strengthened with a couple of recruits. Well, how many people are there out there?" He gestured at the wall of green across the creek.

"My class put through seventeen boys and eleven girls. Commander Benboe told us there would be four classes in the same test area."

"That's more than the Deacon bothered to tell us. However, my class put through about twenty."

Jack looked thoughtful. "Around a hundred people, probably."

"Not counting casualties."

"Not counting casualties. Maybe two-thirds boys, one-third girls. Plenty of choice, if we can find them."

"No girls on this team, Jack."

"What have you got against girls?"

"Me? Nothing at all. Girls are swell on picnics, they are just right on long winter evenings. I'm one of the most enthusiastic supporters of the female race. But for a hitch like this, they are pure poison."

Jack did not say anything. Rod went on, "Use your head, brother. You get some pretty little darling on this team and we'll have more grief inside than stobor, or such, can give us from outside. Quarrels and petty jealousies and maybe a couple of boys knifing each other. It will be tough enough without that trouble."

"Well," Jack answered thoughtfully, "suppose the first one we locate is a girl? What are you going to do? Tip your hat and say, 'It's a fine day, ma'am. Now drop dead and don't bother me.'?"

Rod drew a pentagon in the ashes, put a star in the middle, then rubbed it out. "I don't know," he said slowly. "Let's hope we get our team working before we meet any. And let's hope they set up their own teams."

"I think we ought to have a policy."

"I'm clean out of policies. You would just accuse me of trying to be logical. Got any ideas about how to find anybody?"

"Maybe. Somebody has been hunting upstream from here."

"So? Know who it is?"

"I've seen him only at a distance. Nobody from my class. Half a head shorter than you are, light hair, pink skin—and a bad sunburn. Sound familiar?"

"Could be anybody," Rod answered, thinking fretfully that the description did sound familiar. "Shall we see if we can pick up some sign of him?"

"I can put him in your lap. But I'm not sure we want him."

"Why not? If he's lasted this long, he must be competent."

"Frankly, I don't see how he has. He's noisy when he moves and he has been living in one tree for the past week."

"Not necessarily bad technique."

"It is when you drop your bones and leavings out of the tree. It was jackals sniffing around that tipped me off to where he was living."

"Hmm . . . well, if we don't like him, we don't have to invite him."

"True."

Before they set out Jack dug around in the gloomy cave and produced a climbing line. "Rod, could this be yours?"

Rod looked it over. "It's just like the one I had. Why?"

"I got it the way I got Colonel Bowie, off the casualty. If it is not yours, at least it is a replacement." Jack got another, wrapped it around and over body armor. Rod suspected that Jack had slept in the armor, but he said nothing. If Jack considered such marginal protection more important than agility, that was Jack's business—each to his own methods, as the Deacon would say.

The tree stood in a semi-clearing but Jack brought Rod to it through bushes which came close to the trunk and made the final approach as a belly sneak. Jack pulled Rod's head over and whispered in his ear, "If we lie still for three or four hours, I'm betting that he will either come down or go up."

"Okay. You watch our rear."

For an hour nothing happened. Rod tried to ignore tiny flies that seemed to be all bite. Silently he shifted position to ward off stiffness and once had to kill a sneeze. At last he said, "Pssst!"

"Yeah, Rod?"

"Where those two big branches meet the trunk, could that be his nest?"

"Maybe."

"You see a hand sticking out?"

"Where? Uh, I think I see what you see. It might just be leaves."

"I think it's a hand and I think he is dead; it hasn't moved since we got here."

"Asleep?"

"Person asleep ordinarily doesn't hold still that long. I'm going up. Cover me. If that hand moves, yell."

"You ought not to risk it, Rod."

"You keep your eyes peeled." He crept forward.

The owner of the hand was Jimmy Throxton, as Rod had suspected since hearing the description. Jimmy was not dead, but he was unconscious and Rod could not rouse him.

Jim lay in an aerie half natural, half artificial; Rod could see that Jim had cut small branches and improved the triple crotch formed by two limbs and trunk. He lay cradled in this eagle's nest, one hand trailing out.

Getting him down was awkward; he weighed as much as Rod did. Rod put a sling under Jim's armpits and took a turn around a branch, checking the line by friction to lower him—but the hard part was getting Jim out of his musty bed without dropping him.

Halfway down the burden fouled and Jack had to climb and free it. But with much sweat all three reached the ground and Jim was still breathing.

Rod had to carry him. Jack offered to take turns but the disparity in sizes was obvious; Rod said angrily for Jack to cover them, front, rear, all sides; Rod would be helpless if they had the luck to be surprised by one of the pseudo-lions.

The worst part was the climbing traverse over loose shale up to the cave. Rod was fagged from carrying the limp and heavy load more than a kilometer over rough ground; he had to rest before he could tackle it. When he did, Jack said anxiously, "Don't drop him in the drink! It won't be worthwhile fishing him out—I know."

"So do I. Don't give silly advice."

"Sorry."

Rod started up, as much worried for his own hide as for Jim's. He did not know what it was that lived in that stream; he did know that it was hungry. There was a bad time when he reached the spot where the jutting limestone made it necessary to stoop to reach the shelf. He got down as low as possible, attempted it, felt the burden on his back catch on the rock, started to slip.

Jack's hand steadied him and shoved him from behind. Then they were sprawled safe on the shelf and Rod gasped and tried to stop the trembling of his abused muscles.

They bedded Jimmy down and Jack took his pulse. "Fast and thready. I don't think he's going to make it."

"What medicines do you have?"

"Two of the neosulfas and verdomycin. But I don't know what to give him."

"Give him all three and pray."

"He might be allergic to one of them."

"He'll be more allergic to dying. I'll bet he's running six degrees of fever. Come on."

Rod supported Jim's shoulders, pinched his ear lobe, brought him partly out of coma. Between them they managed to get the capsules into Jim's mouth, got him to drink and wash them down. After that there was nothing they could do but let him rest.

They took turns watching him through the night. About dawn his fever broke, he roused and asked for water. Rod held him while Jack handled the waterskin. Jim drank deeply, then went back to sleep.

They never left him alone. Jack did the nursing and Rod hunted each day, trying to find items young and tender and suited to an invalid's palate. By the second day Jim, although weak and helpless, was able to talk without drifting off to sleep in the middle. Rod returned in the afternoon with the carcass of a small animal which seemed to be a clumsy cross between a cat and a rabbit. He encountered Jack heading down to fill the water skin. "Hi."

"Hi. I see you had luck. Say, Rod, go easy when you skin it. We need a new water bag. Is it cut much?"

"Not at all. I knocked it over with a rock."

"Good!"

"How's the patient?"

"Healthier by the minute. I'll be up shortly."

"Want me to cover you while you fill the skin?"

"I'll be careful. Go up to Jim."

Rod went up, laid his kill on the shelf, crawled inside. "Feeling better?"

"Swell. I'll wrestle you two falls out of three."

"Next week. Jack taking good care of you?"

"You bet. Say, Rod, I don't know how to thank you two. If it hadn't been for—"

"Then don't try. You don't owe me anything, ever. And Jack's my partner, so it's right with Jack."

"Jack is swell."

"Jack is a good boy. They don't come better. He and I really hit it off."

Jim looked surprised, opened his mouth, closed it suddenly. "What's the matter?" Rod asked. "Something bite you? Or are you feeling bad again?"

"What," Jim said slowly, "did you say about Jack?"

"Huh? I said they don't come any better. He and I team up like bacon and eggs. A number-one kid, that boy."

Jimmy Throxton looked at him. "Rod . . . were you born that stupid? Or did you have to study?"

"Huh?"

"Jack is a *girl.*"

7

"I Should Have Baked a Cake"

There followed a long silence. "Well," said Jim, "close your mouth before something flies in."

"Jimmy, you're still out of your head."

"I may be out of my head, but not so I can't tell a girl from a boy. When that day comes, I won't be sick; I'll be dead."

"But . . ."

Jim shrugged. "Ask her."

A shadow fell across the opening; Rod turned and saw Jack scrambling up to the shelf. "Fresh water, Jimmy!"

"Thanks, kid." Jim added to Rod, "Go on, dopy!"

Jack looked from one to the other. "Why the tableau? What are you staring for, Rod?"

"Jack," he said slowly, "what is your name?"

"Huh? Jack Daudet. I told you that."

"No, no! What's your full name, your legal name?"

Jack looked from Rod to Jimmy's grinning face and back again. "My full name is . . . Jacqueline Marie Daudet—if it's any business of yours. Want to make something of it?"

Rod took a deep breath. "Jacqueline," he said carefully, "I didn't know. I—"

"You weren't supposed to."

"I—Look, if I've said anything to offend you, I surely didn't mean to."

"You haven't said anything to offend me, you big stupid dear. Except about your knife."

"I didn't mean that."

"You mean about girls being poison? Well, did it ever occur to you that maybe boys are pure poison, too? Under these circumstances? No, of course it didn't. But I don't mind your knowing now . . . now that there are three of us."

"But, Jacqueline—"

"Call me 'Jack,' please." She twisted her shoulders uncomfortably. "Now that you know, I won't have to wear this beetle case any longer. Turn your backs, both of you."

"Uh . . ." Rod turned his back. Jimmy rolled over, eyes to the wall.

In a few moments Jacqueline said, "Okay." Rod turned around. In shirt and trousers, without torso armor, her shoulders seemed narrower and she herself was slender now and pleasantly curved. She was scratching her ribs. "I haven't been able to scratch properly since I met you, Rod Walker," she said accusingly. "Sometimes I almost died."

"I didn't make you wear it."

"Suppose I hadn't? Would you have teamed with me?"

"Uh . . . well, it's like this. I . . ." He stopped.

"You see?" She suddenly looked worried. "We're still partners?"

"Huh? Oh, sure, sure!"

"Then shake on it again. This time we shake with Jimmy, too. Right, Jim?"

"You bet, Jack."

They made a three-cornered handshake. Jack pressed her left hand over the combined fists and said solemnly, "All for one!"

Rod drew Colonel Bowie with his left hand, laid the flat of the blade on the stacked hands. "And one for all!"

"Plus sales tax," Jimmy added. "Do we get it notarized?"

Jacqueline's eyes were swimming with tears. "Jimmy Throxton," she said fiercely, "someday I am going to make you take life seriously!"

"I take life seriously," he objected. "I just don't want life to take me seriously. When you're on borrowed time, you can't afford not to laugh."

"We're all on borrowed time," Rod answered him. "Shut up, Jimmy. You talk too much."

"Look who's preaching! The Decibel Kid himself."

"Well . . . you ought not to make fun of Jacqueline. She's done a lot for you."

"She has indeed!"

"Then—"

" 'Then' nothing!" Jacqueline said sharply. "My name is 'Jack,' Rod. Forget 'Jacqueline.' If either of you starts treating me with gallantry we'll have all those troubles you warned me about. 'Pure poison' was the expression you used, as I recall."

"But you can't reasonably expect—"

"Are you going to be 'logical' again? Let's be practical instead. Help me skin this beast and make a new water bag."

The following day Jimmy took over housekeeping and Jack and Rod started hunting together. Jim wanted to come along; he ran into a double veto. There was little advantage in hunting as a threesome whereas Jack and Rod paired off so well that a hunt was never hours of waiting, but merely a matter of finding game. Jack would drive and Rod would kill; they would pick their quarry from the fringe of a herd, Jack would sneak around and panic the animals, usually driving one into Rod's arms.

They still hunted with the knife, even though Jack's gun was a good choice for primitive survival, being an air gun that threw poisoned darts. Since the darts could be recovered and re-envenomed, it was a gun which would last almost indefinitely; she had chosen it for this reason over cartridge or energy guns.

Rod had admired it but decided against hunting with it. "The air pressure might bleed off and let you down."

"It never has. And you can pump it up again awfully fast."

"Mmm . . . yes. But if we use it, someday the last dart will be lost no matter how careful we are . . . and that might be the day we would need it bad. We may be here a long time, what do you say we save it?"

"You're the boss, Rod."

"No, I'm not. We all have equal say."

"Yes, you are. Jimmy and I agreed on that. Somebody has to boss."

Hunting took an hour or so every second day; they spent most of daylight hours searching for another team mate, quartering the area and doing it systematically. Once they drove scavengers from a kill which seemed to have been butchered by knife; they followed a spoor from that and determined that it was a human spoor, but were forced by darkness to return to the cave. They tried to pick it up the next day, but it had rained hard in the night; they never found it.

Another time they found ashes of a fire, but Rod judged them to be at least two weeks old.

After a week of fruitless searching they returned one late afternoon. Jimmy looked up from the fire he had started. "How goes the census?"

"Don't ask," Rod answered, throwing himself down wearily. "What's for dinner?"

"Raw buck, roast buck, and burned buck. I tried baking some of it in wet clay. It didn't work out too well, but I've got some awfully good baked clay for dessert."

"Thanks. If that is the word."

"Jim," Jack said, "we ought to try to bake pots with that clay."

"I did. Big crack in my first effort. But I'll get the hang of it. Look, children," he went on, "has it ever occurred to your bright little minds that you might be going about this the wrong way?"

"What's wrong with it?" Rod demanded.

"Nothing . . . if it is exercise you are after. You are hurrying and scurrying over the countryside, getting in a sweat and nowhere else. Maybe it would be better to sit back and let them come to you."

"How?"

"Send up a smoke signal."

"We've discussed that. We don't want just anybody and we don't want to advertise where we live. We want people who will strengthen the team."

"That is what the engineers call a self-defeating criterion. The superior woodsman you want is just the laddy you will never find by hunting for him. *He* may find *you,* as you go tramping noisily through the brush, kicking rocks and stepping on twigs and scaring the birds. He may shadow you to see what you are up to. But *you* won't find *him.*"

"Rod, there is something to that," Jack said.

"We found *you* easily enough," Rod said to Jim. "Maybe you aren't the high type we need."

"I wasn't myself at the time," Jimmy answered blandly. "Wait till I get my strength back and my true nature will show. Ugh-Ugh, the ape man, that's me. Half Neanderthal and half sleek black leopard." He beat his chest and coughed.

"Are those the proportions? The Neanderthal strain seems dominant."

"Don't be disrespectful. Remember, you are my debtor."

"I think you read the backs of those cards. They are getting to be like waffles." When rescued, Jimmy had had on him a pack of playing cards, and had later explained that they were survival equipment.

"In the first place," he had said, "if I got lost I could sit down and play solitaire. Pretty soon somebody would come along and—"

"Tell you to play the black ten on the red jack. We've heard that one."

"Quiet, Rod. In the second place, Jack, I expected to team with old Stoneface here. I can always beat him at cribbage but he doesn't believe it. I figured that during the test I could win all his next year's allowance. Survival tactics."

Whatever his reasoning, Jimmy had had the cards. The three played a family game each evening at a million plutons a point. Jacqueline stayed more or less even but Rod owed Jimmy several hundred millions. They continued the discussion that evening over their game. Rod was still wary of advertising their hideout.

"We might burn a smoke signal somewhere, though," he said thoughtfully. "Then keep watch from a safe spot. Cut 'em, Jim."

"Consider the relative risks—a five, just what I needed! If you put the fire far enough away to keep this place secret, then it means a trek back and forth at least twice a day. With all that running around you'll use up your luck; one day you won't come back. It's not that I'm fond of you, but it would bust up the game."

"Whose crib?"

"Jack's. But if we burn it close by and in sight, then we sit up here safe and snug. I'll have my back to the wall facing the path, with Jack's *phht* gun in my lap. If an unfriendly face sticks up—*blooie!* Long pig for dinner. But if we like them, we cut them into the game."

"Your count."

"Fifteen-six, fifteen-twelve, a pair, six for jacks and the right jack. That's going to cost you another million, my friend."

"One of those jacks is a queen," Rod said darkly.

"Sure enough? You know, it's getting too dark to play. Want to concede?"

They adopted Jim's scheme. It gave more time for cribbage and ran Rod's debt up into billions. The signal fire was kept burning on the shelf at the downstream end, the prevailing wind being such that smoke usually did not blow back into the cave—when the wind did shift it was unbearable; they were forced to flee, eyes streaming.

This happened three times in four days. Their advertising had roused no customers and they were all getting tired of dragging up dead wood for fuel and green branches for smoke. The third time they fled from smoke Jimmy said, "Rod, I give up. You win. This is not the way to do it."

"No!"

"Huh? Have a heart, chum. I can't live on smoke—no vitamins. Let's run up a flag instead. I'll contribute my shirt."

Rod thought about it. "We'll do that."

"Hey, wait a minute. I was speaking rhetorically. I'm the delicate type. I sunburn easily."

"You can take it easy and work up a tan. We'll use your shirt as a signal flag. But we'll keep the fire going, too. Not up on the shelf, but down there—on that mud flat, maybe."

"And have the smoke blow right back into our summer cottage."

"Well, farther downstream. We'll make a bigger fire and a column of smoke that can be seen a long way. The flag we will put up right over the cave."

"Thereby inviting eviction proceedings from large, hairy individuals with no feeling for property rights."

"We took that chance when we decided to use a smoke signal. Let's get busy."

Rod picked a tall tree on the bluff above. He climbed to where the trunk had thinned down so much that it would hardly take his weight, then spent a tedious hour topping it with his knife. He tied the sleeves of Jim's shirt to it, then worked down, cutting foliage away as he went. Presently the branches became too large to handle with his knife, but the stripped main stem stuck up for several meters; the shirt could be seen for a long distance up and down stream. The shirt caught the wind and billowed; Rod eyed it, tired but satisfied—it was unquestionably a signal flag.

Jimmy and Jacqueline had built a new smudge farther downstream, carrying fire from the shelf for the purpose. Jacqueline still had a few matches and Jim had a pocket torch almost fully charged but the realization that they were marooned caused them to be miserly. Rod went down and joined them. The smoke was enormously greater now that they were not limited in space, and fuel was easier to fetch.

Rod looked them over. Jacqueline's face, sweaty and none too clean to start with, was now black with smoke, while Jimmy's pink skin showed the soot even more. "A couple of pyromaniacs."

"You ordered smoke," Jimmy told him. "I plan to make the burning of Rome look like a bonfire. Fetch me a violin and a toga."

"Violins weren't invented then. Nero played a lyre."

"Let's not be small. We're getting a nice mushroom cloud effect, don't you think?"

"Come on, Rod," Jacqueline urged, wiping her face without improving it. "It's fun!" She dipped a green branch in the stream, threw it on the pyre. A thick cloud of smoke and steam concealed her. "More dry wood, Jimmy."

"Coming!"

Rod joined in, soon was as dirty and scorched as the other two and having more fun than he had had since the test started. When the sun dropped below the tree tops they at last quit trying to make the fire bigger and better and smokier and reluctantly headed up to their cave. Only then did Rod realize that he had forgotten to remain alert.

Oh well, he assured himself, dangerous animals would avoid a fire.

While they ate they could see the dying fire still sending up smoke.

After dinner Jimmy got out his cards, tried to riffle the limp mass. "Anyone interested in a friendly game? The customary small stakes."

"I'm too tired," Rod answered. "Just chalk up my usual losses."

"That's not a sporting attitude. Why, you won a game just last week. How about you, Jack?"

Jacqueline started to answer; Rod suddenly motioned for silence. "Sssh! I heard something."

The other two froze and silently got out their knives. Rod put Colonel Bowie in his teeth and crawled out to the edge. The pathway was clear and the thorn barricade was undisturbed. He leaned out and looked around, trying to locate the sound.

"Ahoy below!" a voice called out, not loudly. Rod felt himself tense. He glanced back, saw Jimmy moving diagonally over to cover the pathway. Jacqueline had her dart gun and was hurriedly pumping it up.

Rod answered, "Who's there?"

There was a short silence. Then the voice answered, "Bob Baxter and Carmen Garcia. Who are you?"

Rod sighed with relief. "Rod Walker, Jimmy Throxton. And one other, not our class . . . Jack Daudet."

Baxter seemed to think this over. "Uh, can we join you? For tonight, at least?"

"Sure!"

"How can we get down there? Carmen can't climb very well; she's got a bad foot."

"You're right above us?"

"I think so. I can't see you."

"Stay there. I'll come up." Rod turned, grinned at the others. "Company for dinner! Get a fire going, Jim."

Jimmy clucked mournfully. "And hardly a thing in the house. I should have baked a cake."

By the time they returned Jimmy had roast meat waiting. Carmen's semi-crippled condition had delayed them. It was just a sprained ankle but it caused her to crawl up the traverse on her hands, and progress to that point had been slow and painful.

When she realized that the stranger in the party was another woman she burst into tears. Jackie glared at the males, for no cause that Rod could see, then led her into the remote corner of the cave where she herself slept. There they whispered while Bob Baxter compared notes with Rod and Jim.

Bob and Carmen had had no unusual trouble until Carmen had hurt her ankle two days earlier . . . except for the obvious fact that something had gone wrong and they were stranded. "I lost my grip," he admitted, "when I realized that they weren't picking us up. But Carmen snapped me out of it. Carmen is a very practical kid."

"Girls are always the practical ones," Jimmy agreed. "Now take me—I'm the poetical type."

"Blank verse, I'd say," Rod suggested.

"Jealousy ill becomes you, Rod. Bob, old bean, can I interest you in another slice? Rare, or well carbonized?"

"Either way. We haven't had much to eat the last couple of days. Boy, does this taste good!"

"My own sauce," Jimmy said modestly. "I raise my own herbs, you know. First you melt a lump of butter slowly in a pan, then you—"

"Shut up, Jimmy. Bob, do you and Carmen want to team with us? As I see it, we can't count on ever getting back. Therefore we ought to make plans for the future."

"I think you are right."

"Rod is always right," Jimmy agreed. " 'Plans for the future—' Hmm, yes . . . Bob, do you and Carmen play cribbage?"

"No."

"Never mind. I'll teach you."

8

"Fish, or Cut Bait"

THE DECISION TO KEEP ON BURNING THE SMOKE SIGNAL AND THEREBY to call in as many recruits as possible was never voted on; it formed itself. The next morning Rod intended to bring the matter up but Jimmy and Bob rebuilt the smoke fire from its embers while down to fetch fresh water. Rod let the accomplished fact stand; two girls drifted in separately that day.

Nor was there any formal contract to team nor any selection of a team captain; Rod continued to direct operations and Bob Baxter accepted the arrangement. Rod did not think about it as he was too busy. The problems of food, shelter, and safety for their growing population left him no time to worry about it.

The arrival of Bob and Carmen cleaned out the larder; it was necessary to hunt the next day. Bob Baxter offered to go, but Rod decided to take Jackie as usual. "You rest today. Don't let Carmen put her weight on that bad ankle and don't let Jimmy go down alone to tend the fire. He thinks he is well again but he is not."

"I see that."

Jack and Rod went out, made their kill quickly. But Rod failed to kill clean and when Jacqueline moved in to help finish the thrashing, wounded buck she was kicked in the ribs. She insisted that she was not hurt; nevertheless her side was sore the following morning and Bob Baxter expressed the opinion that she had cracked a rib.

In the meantime two new mouths to feed had been added, just as Rod found himself with three on the sick list. But one of the new mouths was a big, grinning one belonging to Caroline Mshiyeni; Rod picked her as his hunting partner.

Jackie looked sour. She got Rod aside and whispered, "You haven't any reason to do this to me. I can hunt. My side is all right, just a little stiff."

"It is, huh? So it slows you down when I need you. I can't chance it, Jack."

She glanced at Caroline, stuck out her lip and looked stubborn. Rod said urgently, "Jack, remember what I said about petty jealousies? So help me, you make trouble and I'll paddle you."

"You aren't big enough!"

"I'll get help. Now, look—are we partners?"

"Well, I *thought* so."

"Then be one and don't cause trouble."

She shrugged. "All right. Don't rub it in—I'll stay home."

"I want you to do more than that. Take that old bandage of mine—it's around somewhere—and let Bob Baxter strap your ribs."

"No!"

"Then let Carmen do it. They're both quack doctors, sort of." He raised his voice. "Ready, Carol?"

"Quiverin' and bristlin'."

Rod told Caroline how he and Jacqueline hunted, explained what he expected of her. They located, and avoided, two family herds; old bulls were tough and poor eating and attempting to kill anything but the bull was foolishly dangerous. About noon they found a yearling herd upwind; they split and placed themselves cross wind for the kill. Rod waited for Caroline to flush the game, drive it to him.

He continued to wait. He was getting fidgets when Caroline showed up, moving silently. She motioned for him to follow. He did so, hard put to keep up with her and still move quietly. Presently she stopped; he caught up and saw that she had already made a kill. He looked at it and fought down the anger he felt.

Caroline spoke. "Nice tender one, I think. Suit you, Rod?"

He nodded. "Couldn't be better. A clean kill, too. Carol?"

"Huh?"

"I think you are better at this than I am."

"Oh, shucks, it was just luck." She grinned and looked sheepish.

"I don't believe in luck. Any time you want to lead the hunt, let me know. But be darn sure you let me know."

She looked at his unsmiling face, said slowly, "By any chance are you bawling me out?"

"You could call it that. I'm saying that any time you want to lead the hunt, you tell me. Don't switch in the middle. Don't ever. I mean it."

"What's the matter with you, Rod? Getting your feelings hurt just because I got there first—that's silly!"

Rod sighed. "Maybe that's it. Or maybe I don't like having a girl take the kill away from me. But I'm dead sure about one thing: I don't like having a partner on a hunt who can't be depended on. Too many ways to get hurt. I'd rather hunt alone."

"Maybe I'd rather hunt alone! I don't need any help."

"I'm sure you don't. Let's forget it, huh, and get this carcass back to camp."

Caroline did not say anything while they butchered. When they had the waste trimmed away and were ready to pack as much as possible back to the others Rod said, "You lead off. I'll watch behind."

"Rod?"

"Huh?"

"I'm sorry."

"What? Oh, forget it."

"I won't ever do it again. Look, I'll tell everybody you made the kill."

He stopped and put a hand on her arm. "Why tell anybody anything? It's nobody's business how we organize our hunt as long as we bring home the meat."

"You're still angry with me."

"I never was angry," he lied. "I just don't want us to get each other crossed up."

"Roddie, I'll never cross you up again! Promise."

Girls stayed in the majority to the end of the week. The cave, comfortable for three, adequate for twice that number, was crowded for the number that was daily accumulating. Rod decided to make it a girls' dormitory and moved the males out into the open on the field at the foot of the path up the shale. The spot was unprotected against weather and animals but it did guard the only access to the cave. Weather was no problem; protection against animals was set up as well as could be managed by organizing a night watch whose duty it was to keep fires burning between the bluff and the creek on the upstream side and in the bottleneck downstream.

Rod did not like the arrangements, but they were the best he could do at the time. He sent Bob Baxter and Roy Kilroy downstream to scout for caves and Caroline and Margery Chung upstream for the same purpose. Neither party was successful in the one-day limit he had imposed; the two girls brought back another straggler.

A group of four boys came in a week after Jim's shirt had been requisitioned; it brought the number up to twenty-five and shifted the balance to more boys than girls. The four newcomers could have been classed as men rather than boys, since they were two or three years older than the average. Three of the four classes in this survival-test area had been about to graduate from secondary schools; the fourth class, which included these four, came from Outlands Arts College of Teller University.

"Adult" is a slippery term. Some cultures have placed adult age as low as eleven years, others as high as thirty-five—and some have not recognized any such age as long as an ancestor remained alive. Rod did not think of these new arrivals as senior to him. There were already a few from Teller U. in the group, but Rod was only vaguely aware which ones they were—they fitted in. He was too busy with the snowballing problems of his growing colony to worry about their backgrounds on remote Terra.

The four were Jock McGowan, a brawny youth who seemed all hands and feet, his younger brother Bruce, and Chad Ames and Dick Burke. They had arrived late in the day and Rod had not had time to get acquainted, nor was there time the following morning, as a group of four girls and five boys poured in on them unexpectedly. This had increased his administrative problems almost to the breaking point; the cave would hardly sleep four more females. It was necessary to find, or build, more shelter.

Rod went over to the four young men lounging near the cooking fire. He squatted on his heels and asked, "Any of you know anything about building?"

He addressed them all, but the others waited for Jock McGowan to speak. "Some," Jock admitted. "I reckon I could build anything I wanted to."

"Nothing hard," Rod explained. "Just stone walls. Ever tried your hand at masonry?"

"Sure. What of it?"

"Well, here's the idea. We've got to have better living arrangements right away—we've got people pouring out of our ears. The first thing we are going to do is to throw a wall from the bluff to the creek across this flat area. After that we will build huts, but the first thing is a kraal to stop dangerous animals."

McGowan laughed. "That will be some wall. Have you seen this dingus that looks like an elongated cougar? One of those babies would go over your wall before you could say 'scat.' "

"I know about them," Rod admitted, "and I don't like them." He rubbed the long white scars on his left arm. "They probably could go over any wall we could build. So we'll rig a surprise for them." He picked up a twig and started drawing in the dirt. "We build the wall . . . and bring it around to here. Then, inside for about six meters, we set up sharpened poles. Anything comes over the wall splits its gut on the poles."

Jock McGowan looked at the diagram. "Futile."

"Silly," agreed his brother.

Rod flushed but answered, "Got a better idea?"

"That's beside the point."

"Well," Rod answered slowly, "unless somebody comes down with a better scheme, or unless we find really good caves, we've got to fortify this spot the best we can . . . so we'll do this. I'm going to set the girls to cutting and sharpening stakes. The rest of us will start on the wall. If we tear into it we ought to have a lot of it built before dark. Do you four want to work together? There will be one party collecting rock and another digging clay and making clay mortar. Take your choice."

Again three of them waited. Jock McGowan lay back and laced his hands under his head. "Sorry. I've got a date to hunt today."

Rod felt himself turning red. "We don't need a kill today," he said carefully.

"Nobody asked you, youngster."

Rod felt the cold tenseness he always felt in a hunt. He was uncomfortably aware that an audience had gathered. He tried to keep his voice steady and said, "Maybe I've made a mistake. I—"

"You have."

"I thought you four had teamed with the rest of us. Well?"

"Maybe. Maybe not."

"You'll have to fish or cut bait. If you join, you work like anybody else. If not—well, you're welcome to breakfast and stop in again some time. But be on your way. I won't have you lounging around while everybody else is working."

Jock McGowan sucked his teeth, dug at a crevice with his tongue. His hands were still locked back of his head. "What you don't understand, sonny boy, is that nobody gives the McGowans orders. Nobody. Right, Bruce?"

"Right, Jock."

"Right, Chad? Dick?"

The other two grunted approval. McGowan continued to stare up at the sky. "So," he said softly, "I go where I want to go and stay as long as I like. The question is not whether we are going to join up with you, but what ones I am going to let team with us. But not you, sonny boy; you are still wet behind your ears."

"Get up and get out of here!" Rod started to stand up. He was wearing Colonel Bowie, as always, but he did not reach for it. He began to straighten up from squatting.

Jock McGowan's eyes flicked toward his brother. Rod was hit low . . . and found himself flat on his face with his breath knocked out. He felt the sharp kiss of a knife against his ribs; he held still. Bruce called out, "How about it, Jock?"

Rod could not see Jock McGowan. But he heard him answer, "Just keep him there."

"Right, Jock."

Jock McGowan was wearing both gun and knife. Rod now heard him say, "Anybody want to dance? Any trouble out of the rest of you lugs?"

Rod still could not see Jock, but he could figure from the naked, startled expression of a dozen others that McGowan must have rolled to his feet and covered them with his gun. Everybody in camp carried knives; most had guns as well and Rod could see that Roy Kilroy was wearing his—although most guns were kept when not in use in the cave in a little arsenal which Carmen superintended.

But neither guns nor knives were of use; it had happened too fast, shifting from wordy wrangling to violence with no warning. Rod could see none of his special friends from where he was; those whom he could see did not seem disposed to risk death to rescue him.

Jock McGowan said briskly, "Chad—Dick—got 'em all covered?"

"Right, Skipper."

"Keep 'em that way while I take care of this cholo." His hairy legs appeared in front of Rod's face. "Pulled his teeth, Bruce?"

"Not yet."

"I'll do it. Roll over, sonny boy, and let me at your knife. Let him turn over, Bruce."

Bruce McGowan eased up on Rod and Jock bent down. As he reached for Rod's knife a tiny steel flower blossomed in Jock's side below his ribs. Rod heard nothing, not even the small sound it must have made when it struck. Jock straightened up with a shriek, clutched at his side.

Bruce yelled, "Jock! What's the matter?"

"They got me." He crumpled to the ground like loose clothing.

Rod still had a man with a knife on his back but the moment was enough; he rolled and grabbed in one violent movement and the situation was reversed, with Bruce's right wrist locked in Rod's fist, with Colonel Bowie threatening Bruce's face.

A loud contralto voice sang out, "Take it easy down there! We got you covered."

Rod glanced up. Caroline stood on the shelf at the top of the path to the cave, with a rifle at her shoulder. At the downstream end of the shelf Jacqueline sat with her little dart gun in her lap; she was frantically pumping up again. She raised it, drew a bead on some one past Rod's shoulder.

Rod called out, "Don't shoot!" He looked around. "Drop it, you two!"

Chad Ames and Dick Burke dropped their guns. Rod added, "Roy! Grant Cowper! Gather up their toys. Get their knives, too." He turned back to Bruce McGowan, pricked him under the chin. "Let's have your knife." Bruce turned it loose; Rod took it and got to his feet.

Everyone who had been up in the cave was swarming down, Caroline in the lead. Jock McGowan was writhing on the ground, face turned blue and gasping in the sort of paralysis induced by the poison used on darts. Bob Baxter hurried up, glanced at him, then said to Rod, "I'll take care of that cut in your ribs in a moment." He bent over Jock McGowan.

Caroline said indignantly, "You aren't going to try to save him?"

"Of course."

"Why? Let's chuck him in the stream."

Baxter glanced at Rod. Rod felt a strong urge to order Caroline's suggestion carried out. But he answered, "Do what you can for him, Bob. Where's Jack? Jack—you've got antidote for your darts, haven't you? Get it."

Jacqueline looked scornfully at the figure on the ground. "What for? He's not hurt."

"Huh?"

"Just a pin prick. A practice dart—that's all I keep in Betsey. My hunting darts are put away so that nobody can hurt themselves—and I didn't have time to get them." She prodded Jock with a toe. "He's not poisoned. He's scaring himself to death."

Caroline chortled and waved the rifle she carried. "And this one is empty. Not even a good club."

Baxter said to Jackie, "Are you sure? The reactions look typical."

"Sure I'm sure! See the mark on the end sticking out? A target dart."

Baxter leaned over his patient, started slapping his face. "Snap out of it, McGowan! Stand up. I want to get that dart out of you."

McGowan groaned and managed to stand. Baxter took the dart between thumb and forefinger, jerked it free, Jock yelled. Baxter slapped him again. "Don't you faint on me," he growled. "You're lucky. Let it drain and you'll be all right." He turned to Rod. "You're next."

"Huh? There's nothing the matter with *me.*"

"That stuff on your ribs is paint, I suppose." He looked around. "Carmen, get my kit."

"I brought it down."

"Good. Rod, sit down and lean forward. This is going to hurt a little."

It did hurt. Rod tried to chat to avoid showing that he minded it. "Carol," he asked, "I don't see how you and Jackie worked out a plan so fast. That was smooth."

"Huh? We didn't work out a plan; we both just did what we could and did it fast." She turned to Jacqueline and gave her a clap on the shoulder that nearly knocked her over. "This kid is solid, Roddie, solid!"

Jacqueline recovered, looked pleased and tried not to show it. "Aw, Carol!"

"Anyway I thank you both."

"A pleasure. I wish that pea shooter had been loaded. Rod, what are you going to do with them?"

"Well . . . ummph!"

"Whoops!" said Baxter, behind him. "I said it was going to hurt. I had better put one more clip in. I'd like to put a dressing on that, but we can't, so you lay off heavy work for a while and sleep on your stomach."

"Unh!" said Rod.

"That's the last. You can get up now. Take it easy and give it a chance to scab."

"I still think," Caroline insisted, "that we ought to make them swim the creek. We could make bets on whether or not any of 'em make it across."

"Carol, you're uncivilized."

"I never claimed to be civilized. But I know which end wags and which end bites."

Rod ignored her and went to look at the prisoners. Roy Kilroy had caused them to lie down one on top of the other; it rendered them undignified and helpless. "Let them sit up."

Kilroy and Grant Cowper had been guarding them. Cowper said, "You heard the Captain. Sit up." They unsnarled and sat up, looking glum.

Rod looked at Jock McGowan. "What do you think we ought to do with you?"

McGowan said nothing. The puncture in his side was oozing blood and he was pale. Rod said slowly, "Some think we ought to chuck you in the stream. That's the same as condemning you to death—but if we are going to, we ought to shoot you or hang you. I don't favor letting anybody be eaten alive. Should we hang you?"

Bruce McGowan blurted out, "We haven't done anything!"

"No. But you sure tried. You aren't safe to have around other people."

Somebody called out, "Oh, let's shoot them and get it over with!" Rod ignored it. Grant Cowper came close to Rod and said, "We ought to vote on this. They ought to have a trial."

Rod shook his head. "No." He went on to the prisoners, "I don't favor punishing you—this is personal. But we can't risk having you around either." He turned to Cowper. "Give them their knives."

"Rod? You're not going to fight them?"

"Of course not." He turned back. "You can have your knives; we're keeping your guns. When we turn you loose, head downstream and keep going. Keep going for at least a week. If you ever show your faces again, you won't get a chance to explain. Understand me?"

Jock McGowan nodded. Dick Burke gulped and said, "But turning us out with just knives is the same as killing us."

"Nonsense! No guns. And remember, if you turn back this way, even to hunt, it's once too many. There may be somebody trailing you—with a gun."

"Loaded this time!" added Caroline. "Hey, Roddie, I want that job. Can I? Please?"

"Shut up, Carol. Roy, you and Grant start them on their way."

As exiles and guards, plus sightseers, moved off they ran into Jimmy Throxton coming back into camp. He stopped and stared. "What's the procession? Rod . . . what have you done to your ribs, boy? Scratching yourself again?"

Several people tried to tell him at once. He got the gist of it and shook his head mournfully. "And there I was, good as gold, looking for pretty rocks for our garden wall. Every time there's a party people forget to ask *me*. Discrimination."

"Stow it, Jim. It's not funny."

"That's what I said. It's discrimination."

Rod got the group started on the wall with an hour or more of daylight wasted. He tried to work on the wall despite Bob Baxter's medical orders, but found that he was not up to it; not only was his wound painful but also he felt shaky with reaction.

Grant Cowper looking him up during the noon break. "Skipper, can I talk with you? Privately?"

Rod moved aside with him. "What's on your mind?"

"Mmm . . . Rod, you were lucky this morning. You know that, don't you? No offense intended."

"Sure, I know. What about it?"

"Uh, do you know *why* you had trouble?"

"What? Of course I know—now. I trusted somebody when I should not have."

Cowper shook his head. "Not at all. Rod, what do you know about theory of government?"

Rod looked surprised. "I've had the usual civics courses. Why?"

"I doubt if I've mentioned it, but the course I'm majoring in at Teller U. is colonial administration. One thing we study is how authority comes about in human society and how it is maintained. I'm not criticizing . . . but to be blunt, you almost lost your life because you've never studied such things."

Rod felt annoyed. "What are you driving at?"

"Take it easy. But the fact remains that you didn't have any authority. McGowan knew it and wouldn't take orders. Everybody else knew it, too. When it came to a showdown, nobody knew whether to back you up or not. Because you don't have a milligram of real authority."

"Just a moment! Are you saying I'm not leader of this team?"

"You are *de facto* leader, no doubt about it. But you've never been elected to the job. That's your weakness."

Rod chewed this over. "I know," he said slowly. "It's just that we have been so confounded busy."

"Sure, I know. I'd be the last person to criticize. But a captain ought to be properly elected."

Rod sighed. "I meant to hold an election but I thought getting the wall built was more urgent. All right, let's call them together."

"Oh, you don't need to do it this minute."

"Why not? The sooner the better, apparently."

"Tonight, when it's too dark to work, is soon enough."

"Well . . . okay."

When they stopped for supper Rod announced that there would be an organization and planning meeting. No one seemed surprised, although he himself had mentioned it to no one. He felt annoyed and had to remind himself that there was nothing secret about it; Grant had been under no obligation to keep it quiet. He set guards and fire tenders, then came back into the circle of firelight and called out, "Quiet, everybody! Let's get started. If you guys on watch can't hear, be sure to speak up." He hesitated. "We're going to hold an election. Somebody pointed out that I never have been elected captain of this survival team. Well, if any of you have your noses out of joint, I'm sorry. I was doing the best I could. But you are entitled to elect a captain. All right, any nominations?"

Jimmy Throxton shouted, "I nominate Rod Walker!"

Caroline's voice answered, "I second it! Move the nominations be closed."

Rod said hastily, "Carol, your motion is out of order."

"Why?"

Before he could answer Roy Kilroy spoke up. "Rod, can I have the floor a moment? Privileged question."

Rod turned, saw that Roy was squatting beside Grant Cowper. "Sure. State your question."

"Matter of procedure. The first thing is to elect a temporary chairman."

Rod thought quickly. "I guess you're right. Jimmy, your nomination is thrown out. Nominations for temporary chairman are in order."

"Rod Walker for temporary chairman!"

"Oh, shut up, Jimmy! I don't want to be temporary chairman."

Roy Kilroy was elected. He took the imaginary gavel and announcement, "The chair recognizes Brother Cowper for a statement of aims and purposes of this meeting."

Jimmy Throxton called out, "What do we want any speeches for? Let's elect Rod and go to bed. I'm tired—and I've got a two-hour watch coming up."

"Out of order. The chair recognizes Grant Cowper."

Cowper stood up. The firelight caught his handsome features and curly, short beard. Rod rubbed the scraggly growth on his own chin and wished that he looked like Cowper. The young man was dressed only in walking shorts and soft bush shoes but he carried himself with the easy dignity of a distinguished speaker before some important body. "Friends," he said, "brothers and sisters, we are gathered here tonight not to elect a survival-team captain, but to found a new nation."

He paused to let the idea sink in. "You know the situation we are in. We fervently hope to be rescued, none more so than I. I will even go so far as to say that I think we will be rescued . . . eventually. But we have no way of knowing, we have no data on which to base an intelligent guess, as to *when* we will be rescued.

"It might be tomorrow . . . it might be our descendants a thousand years from now." He said the last very solemnly.

"But when the main body of our great race reestablishes contact with us, it is up to us, this little group here tonight, whether they find a civilized society . . . or flea-bitten animals without language, without arts, with the light of reason grown dim . . . or no survivors at all, nothing but bones picked clean."

"Not mine!" called out Caroline. Kilroy gave her a dirty look and called for order.

"Not yours, Caroline," Cowper agreed gravely. "Nor mine. Not any of us. Because tonight we will take the step that will keep this colony alive. We are poor in things; we will make what we need. We are rich in knowledge; among us we hold the basic knowledge of our great race. We must preserve it . . . we *will!*"

Caroline cut through Cowper's dramatic pause with a stage whisper. "Talks pretty, doesn't he? Maybe I'll marry him."

He did not try to fit this heckling into his speech. "What is the prime knowledge acquired by our race? That without which the rest is useless? What flame must we guard like vestal virgins?"

Some one called out, "Fire." Cowper shook his head.

"Writing!"

"The decimal system."

"Atomics!"

"The wheel, of course."

"No, none of those. They are all important, but they are not the keystone. The greatest invention of mankind is government. It is also the hardest of all. More individualistic than cats, nevertheless we have learned to cooperate more efficiently than ants or bees or termites. Wilder, bloodier, and more deadly than sharks, we have learned to live together as peacefully as lambs. But these things are not easy. That is why that which we do tonight will decide our future . . . and perhaps the future of our children, our children's children, our descendants far into the womb of time. We are not picking a temporary survival leader; we are setting up a government. We must do it with care. We must pick a chief executive for our new nation, a mayor of our city-state. But we must draw up a constitution, sign articles binding us together. We must organize and plan."

"Hear, hear!"

"Bravo!"

"We must establish law, appoint judges, arrange for orderly administration of our code. Take for example, this morning—" Cowper turned to Rod and gave him a friendly smile. "Nothing personal, Rod, you understand that. I think you acted with wisdom and I was happy that you tempered justice with mercy. Yet no one could have criticized if you had yielded to your impulse and killed all four of those, uh . . . antisocial individuals. But justice should not be subject to the whims of a dictator. We can't stake our lives on your temper . . . good or bad. You see that, don't you?"

Rod did not answer. He felt that he was being accused of bad temper, of being a tyrant and dictator, of being a danger to the group. But he could not put his finger on it. Grant Cowper's remarks had been friendly . . . yet they felt intensely personal and critical.

Cowper insisted on an answer. "You do see that, Rod? Don't you? You don't want to continue to have absolute power over the lives and persons of our community? You don't want *that?* Do you?" He waited.

"Huh? Oh, yeah, sure! I mean, I agree with you."

"Good! I was sure you would understand. And I must say that *I* think you have done a very good job in getting us together. I don't agree with any who have criticized you. You were doing your best and we should let bygones be bygones." Cowper grinned that friendly grin and Rod felt as if he were being smothered with kisses.

Cowper turned to Kilroy. "That's all I have to say, Mr. Chairman." He flashed his grin and added as he sat down, "Sorry I talked so long, folks. I had to get it off my chest."

Kilroy clapped his hands once. "The chair will entertain nominations for— Hey, Grant, if we don't call it 'captain,' then what should we call it?"

"Mmm . . ." Cowper said judicially. " 'President' seems a little pompous. I think 'mayor' would be about right—mayor of our city-state, our village."

"The chair will entertain nominations for mayor."

"Hey!" demanded Jimmy Throxton. "Doesn't anybody else get to shoot off his face?"

"Out of order."

"No," Cowper objected, "I don't think you should rule Jimmy out of order, Roy. Anyone who has something to contribute should be encouraged to speak. We mustn't act hastily."

"Okay, Throxton, speak your piece."

"Oh, I didn't want to sound off. I just didn't like the squeeze play."

"All right, the chair stands corrected. Anybody else? If not, we will entertain—"

"One moment, Mr. Chairman!"

Rod saw that it was Arthur Nielsen, one of the Teller University group. He managed to look neat even in these circumstances but he had strayed into camp bereft of all equipment, without even a knife. He had been quite hungry.

Kilroy looked at him. "You want to talk, Waxie?"

"Nielsen is the name. Or Arthur. As you know. Yes."

"Okay. Keep it short."

"I shall keep it as short as circumstances permit. Fellow associates, we have here a unique opportunity, probably one which has not occurred before in history. As Cowper pointed out, we must proceed with care. But, already we have set out on the wrong foot. Our object should be to found the first truly scientific community. Yet what do I find? You are proposing to select an executive by counting noses! Leaders should not be chosen by popular whim; they should be determined by rigorous scientific criteria. Once selected, those leaders must have full scientific freedom to direct the bio-group in accordance with natural law, unhampered by such artificial anachronisms as statutes, constitutions, and courts of law. We have here an adequate supply of healthy females; we have the means to breed scientifically a new race, a super race, a race which, if I may say so—"

A handful of mud struck Nielsen in the chest; he stopped suddenly. "I saw who did that!" he said angrily. "Just the sort of nincompoop who always—"

"Order, order, please!" Kilroy shouted. "No mudslinging, or I'll appoint a squad of sergeants-at-arms. Are you through, Waxie?"

"I was just getting started."

"Just a moment," put in Cowper. "Point of order Mr. Chairman. Arthur has a right to be heard. But I think he is speaking before the wrong body. We're going to have a constitutional committee, I'm sure. He should present his arguments to them. Then, if we like them, we can adopt his ideas."

"You're right, Grant. Sit down, Waxie."

"Huh? I appeal!"

Roy Kilroy said briskly, "The chair has ruled this out of order at this time and the speaker has appealed to the house, a priority motion not debatable. All in favor of supporting the chair's ruling, which is for Waxie to shut up, make it known by saying 'Aye.' "

There was a shouted chorus of assent. "Opposed: 'No.' Sit down, Waxie."

Kilroy looked around. "Anybody else?"

"Yes."

"I can't see. Who is it?"

"Bill Kennedy, Ponce de Leon class. I don't agree with Nielsen except on one point: we are fiddling around with the wrong things. Sure, we need a group captain but, aside from whatever it takes to eat, we shouldn't think about anything but how to get back. I don't want a scientific society; I'd settle for a hot bath and decent food."

There was scattered applause. The chairman said, "I'd like a bath, too . . . and I'd fight anybody for a dish of cornflakes. But, Bill, how do you suggest that we go about it?"

"Huh? We set up a crash-priority project and build a gate. Everybody works on it."

There was silence, then several talked at once: "Crazy! No uranium."—"We might *find* uranium."—"Where do we get the tools? Shucks, I don't even have a screwdriver."—"But where are we?"—"It is just a matter of—"

"Quiet!" yelled Kilroy. "Bill, do you know how to build a gate?"

"No."

"I doubt if anybody does."

"That's a defeatist attitude. Surely some of you educated blokes from Teller have studied the subject. You should get together, pool what you know, and put us to work. Sure, it may take a long time. But that's what we ought to do."

Cowper said, "Just a minute, Roy. Bill, I don't dispute what you say; every idea should be explored. We're bound to set up a planning committee. Maybe we had better elect a mayor, or a captain, or whatever you want to call him—and then dig into your scheme when we can discuss it in detail. I think it has merit and should be discussed at length. What do you think?"

"Why, sure, Grant. Let's get on with the election. I just didn't want that silly stuff about breeding a superman to be the last word."

"Mr. Chairman! I protest—"

"Shut up, Waxie. Are you ready with nominations for mayor? If there is no objection, the chair rules debate closed and will entertain nominations."

"I nominate Grant Cowper!"

"Second!"

"I second the nomination."

"Okay, I third it!"

"Let's make it unanimous! Question, question!"

Jimmy Throxton's voice cut through the shouting, "I NOMINATE ROD WALKER!"

Bob Baxter stood up. "Mr. Chairman?"

"Quiet, everybody. Mr. Baxter."

"I second Rod Walker."

"Okay. Two nominations, Grant Cowper and Rod Walker. Are there any more?"

There was a brief silence. Then Rod spoke up. "Just a second, Roy." He found that his voice was trembling and he took two deep breaths before he went on. "I don't want it. I've had all the grief I want for a while and I'd like a rest. Thanks anyhow, Bob. Thanks, Jimmy."

"Any further nominations?"

"Just a sec, Roy . . . point of personal privilege." Grant Cowper stood up. "Rod, I know how you feel. Nobody in his right mind seeks public office . . . except as a duty, willingness to serve. If you withdraw, I'm going to exercise the same privilege; I don't want the headaches any more than you do."

"Now wait a minute, Grant. You—"

"*You* wait a minute. I don't think either one of us should withdraw; we ought to perform any duty that is handed to us, just as we stand a night watch when it's our turn. But I think we ought to have more nominations." He looked around. "Since that mix-up this morning we have as many girls as men . . . yet both of the candidates are male. That's not right. Uh, Mr. Chairman, I nominate Caroline Mshiyeni."

"Huh? Hey, Grant, don't be silly. I'd look good as a lady mayoress, wouldn't I? Anyhow, I'm for Roddie."

"That's your privilege, Caroline. But you ought to let yourself be placed before the body, just like Rod and myself."

"Nobody's going to vote for *me!*"

"That's where you're wrong. I'm going to vote for you. But we still ought to have more candidates."

"Three nominations before the house," Kilroy announced. "Any more? If not, I declare the—"

"Mr. Chairman!"

"Huh? Okay, Waxie, you want to nominate somebody?"

"Yes."

"Who?"

"Me."

"You want to nominate *yourself?*"

"I certainly do. What's funny about that? I am running on a platform of strict scientific government. I want the rational minds in this group to have someone to vote for."

Kilroy looked puzzled. "I'm not sure that is correct parliamentary procedure. I'm afraid I'll have to over—"

"Never mind, never mind!" Caroline chortled. "*I* nominate him. But I'm going to vote for Roddie," she added.

Kilroy sighed. "Okay, four candidates. I guess we'll have to have a show of hands. We don't have anything for ballots."

Bob Baxter stood up. "Objection, Mr. Chairman. I call for a secret ballot. We can find some way to do it."

A way was found. Pebbles would signify Rod, a bare twig was a note for Cowper, a green leaf meant Caroline, while one of Jimmy's ceramic attempts was offered as a ballot box. "How about Nielsen?" Kilroy asked.

Jimmy spoke up. "Uh, maybe this would do: I made another pot the same time I made this one, only it busted. I'll get chunks of it and all the crackpots are votes for Waxie."

"Mr. Chairman, I resent the insinua—"

"Save it, Waxie. Pieces of baked clay for you, pebbles for Walker, twigs for Grant, leaves for Carol. Get your votes, folks, then file past and drop them in the ballot box. Shorty, you and Margery act as tellers."

The tellers solemnly counted the ballots by firelight. There were five votes for Rod, one for Nielsen, none for Caroline, and twenty-two for Cowper. Rod shook hands with Cowper and faded back into the darkness so that no one would see his face. Caroline looked at the results and said, "Hey, Grant! You promised to vote for me. What happened? Did you vote for yourself? Huh? How about that?"

Rod said nothing. He had voted for Cowper and was certain that the new mayor had not returned the compliment . . . he was sure who his five friends were. Dog take it!—he had seen it coming; why hadn't Grant let him bow out?

Grant ignored Caroline's comment. He briskly assumed the chair and said, "Thank you. Thank you all. I know you want to get to sleep, so I will limit myself tonight to appointing a few committees—"

Rod did not get to sleep at once. He told himself that there was no disgrace in losing an election—shucks, hadn't his old man lost the time he had run for community corporation board? He told himself, too, that trying to ride herd on those apes was enough to drive a man crazy and he was well out of it—he had never *wanted* the job! Nevertheless there was a lump in his middle and a deep sense of personal failure.

It seemed that he had just gone to sleep . . . his father was looking at him saying, "You know we are proud of you, son. Still, if you had had the foresight to—" when someone touched his arm.

He was awake, alert, and had Colonel Bowie out at once.

"Put away that toothpick," Jimmy whispered, "before you hurt somebody. Me, I mean."

"What's up?"

"I'm up, I've got the fire watch. You're about to be, because we are holding a session of the inner sanctum."

"Huh?"

"Shut up and come along. Keep quiet, people are asleep."

The inner sanctum turned out to be Jimmy, Caroline, Jacqueline,

Bob Baxter, and Carmen Garcia. They gathered inside the ring of fire but as far from the sleepers as possible. Rod looked around at his friends. "What's this all about?"

"It's about this," Jimmy said seriously. "You're our Captain. And we like that election as much as I like a crooked deck of cards."

"That's right," agreed Caroline. "All that fancy talk!"

"Huh? Everybody got to talk. Everybody got to vote."

"Yes," agreed Baxter. "Yes . . . and no."

"It was all proper. I have no kick."

"I didn't expect you to kick, Rod. Nevertheless . . . well, I don't know how much politicking you've seen, Rod. I haven't seen much myself, except in church matters and we Quakers don't do things that way; we wait until the Spirit moves. But, despite all the rigamarole, that was a slick piece of railroading. This morning you would have been elected overwhelmingly; tonight you did not stand a chance."

"The point is," Jimmy put in, "do we stand for it?"

"What can we do?"

"What can we do? We don't have to stay here. We've still got our own group; we can walk out and find another place . . . a bigger cave maybe."

"Yes, sir!" agreed Caroline. "Right tonight."

Rod thought about it. The idea was tempting; they didn't need the others . . . guys like Nielsen—and Cowper. The discovery that his friends were loyal to him, loyal to the extent that they would consider exile rather than let him down choked him up. He turned to Jacqueline. "How about you, Jackie?"

"We're partners, Rod. Always."

"Bob—do you want to do this? You and Carmen?"

"Yes. Well . . ."

" 'Well' what?"

"Rod, we're sticking with you. This election is all very well—but you took us in when we needed it and teamed with us. We'll never forget it. Furthermore I think that you make a sounder team captain than Cowper is likely to make. But there is one thing."

"Yes."

"If you decide that we leave, Carmen and I will appreciate it if you put it off a day."

"Why?" demanded Caroline. "Now is the time."

"Well—they've set this up as a formal colony, a village with a mayor. Everybody knows that a regularly elected mayor can perform weddings."

"Oh!" said Caroline. "Pardon my big mouth."

"Carmen and I can take care of the religious end—it's not very complicated in our church. But, just in case we ever are rescued, we would like it better and our folks would like it if the civil requirements were all perfectly regular and legal. You see?"

Rod nodded. "I see."

"But if you say to leave tonight . . ."

"I don't," Rod answered with sudden decision. "We'll stay and get you two properly married. Then—"

"Then we all shove off in a shower of rice," Caroline finished.

"Then we'll see. Cowper may turn out to be a good mayor. We won't leave just because I lost an election." He looked around at their faces. "But . . . but I certainly do thank you. I—"

He could not go on. Carmen stepped forward and kissed him quickly. "Goodnight, Rod. Thanks."

9

"A Joyful Omen"

MAYOR COWPER GOT OFF TO A GOOD START. HE APPROVED, TOOK OVER, and embellished a suggestion that Carmen and Bob should have their own quarters. He suspended work on the wall and set the whole village to constructing a honeymoon cottage. Not until his deputy, Roy Kilroy, reminded him did he send out hunting parties.

He worked hard himself, having set the wedding for that evening and having decreed that the building must be finished by sundown. Finished it was by vandalizing part of the wall to supply building stone when the supply ran short. Construction was necessarily simple since they had no tools, no mortar but clay mud, no way to cut timbers. It was a stone box as tall as a man and a couple of meters square, with a hole for a door. The roof was laid up from the heaviest poles that could be cut from a growth upstream of giant grass much like bamboo—the colonists simply called it "bamboo." This was thatched and plastered with mud; it sagged badly.

But it was a house and even had a door which could be closed—a woven grass mat stiffened with bamboo. It neither hinged nor locked but it filled the hole and could be held in place with a stone and a pole. The floor was clean sand covered with fresh broad leaves.

As a doghouse for a St. Bernard it would have been about right; as a dwelling for humans it was not much. But it was better than that which most human beings had enjoyed through the history and prehistory of the race. Bob and Carmen did not look at it critically.

When work was knocked off for lunch Rod self-consciously sat down near a group around Cowper. He had wrestled with his conscience for a long time in the night and had decided that the only thing to do was to eat sour grapes and pretend to like them. He could start by not avoiding Cowper.

Margery Chung was cook for the day; she cut Rod a chunk of scorched meat. He thanked her and started to gnaw it. Cowper was talking. Rod was not trying to overhear but there seemed to be no reason not to listen.

"—which is the only way we will get the necessary discipline into the group. I'm sure you agree." Cowper glanced up, caught Rod's eye, looked annoyed, then grinned. "Hello, Rod."

"Hi, Grant."

"Look, old man, we're having an executive committee meeting. Would you mind finding somewhere else to eat lunch?"

Rod stood up blushing. "Oh! Sure."

Cowper seemed to consider it. "Nothing private, of course—just getting things done. On second thought maybe you should sit in and give us your advice."

"Huh? Oh, no! I didn't know anything was going on." Rod started to move away.

Cowper did not insist. "Got to keep working, lots to do. See you later, then. Any time." He grinned and turned away.

Rod wandered off, feeling conspicuous. He heard himself hailed and turned gratefully, joined Jimmy Throxton. "Come outside the wall," Jimmy said quietly. "The Secret Six are having a picnic. Seen the happy couple?"

"You mean Carmen and Bob?"

"Know any other happy couples? Oh, there they are—staring hungrily at their future mansion. See you outside."

Rod went beyond the wall, found Jacqueline and Caroline sitting near the water and eating. From habit he glanced around, sizing up possible cover for carnivores and figuring escape routes back into the kraal, but his alertness was not conscious as there seemed no danger in the open so near other people. He joined the girls and sat down on a rock. "Hi, kids."

"Hello, Rod."

"H'lo, Roddie," Caroline seconded. "What news on the Rialto?"

"None, I guess. Say, did Grant appoint an executive committee last night?"

"He appointed about a thousand committees but no executive committee unless he did it after we adjourned. Why an executive committee? This gang needs one the way I need a bicycle."

"Who is on it, Rod?" asked Jacqueline.

Rod thought back and named the faces he had seen around Cowper.

She looked thoughtful. "Those are his own special buddies from Teller U."

"Yes, I guess so."

"I don't like it," she answered.

"What's the harm?"

"Maybe none . . . maybe. It is about what we could expect. But I'd feel better if all the classes were on it, not just that older bunch. You know."

"Shucks, Jack, you've got to give him some leeway."

"I don't see why," put in Caroline. "That bunch you named are the same ones Hizzonor appointed as chairmen of the other committees. It's a tight little clique. You notice none of us unsavory characters got named to any important committee—I'm on waste disposal and camp sanitation, Jackie is on food preparation, and you aren't on any. You should have been on the constitution, codification, and organization committee, but he made himself chairman and left you out. Add it up."

Rod did not answer. Caroline went on, "I'll add it if you won't. First thing you know there will be a nominating committee. Then we'll find that only those of a certain age, say twenty-one, can hold office. Pretty soon that executive committee will turn into a senate (called something else, probably) with a veto that can be upset only by a three-quarters majority that we will never get. That's the way my Uncle Phil would have rigged it."

"Your Uncle Phil?"

"Boy, there was a politician! I never liked him—he had kissed so many babies his lips were puckered. I used to hide when he came into our house. But I'd like to put him up against Hizzonor. It'ud be a battle of dinosaurs. Look, Rod, they've got us roped and tied; I say we should fade out right after the wedding." She turned to Jacqueline. "Right, pardner?"

"Sure . . . if Rod says so."

"Well, I don't say so. Look, Carol, I don't like the situation. To tell the truth . . . well, I was pretty sour at being kicked out of the captaincy. But I can't let the rest of you pull out on that account. There aren't enough of us to form another colony, not safely."

"Why, Roddie, there are three times as many people still back in those trees as there are here in camp. This time we'll build up slowly and be choosy about whom we take. Six is a good start. We'll get by."

"Not six, Carol. Four."

"Huh? Six! We shook on it last night before Jimmy woke you."

Rod shook his head. "Carol, how can we expect Bob and Carmen to walk out . . . right after the rest have made them a wedding present of a house of their own?"

"Well . . . darn it, we'd build them another house!"

"They would go with us, Carol—but it's too much to ask."

"I think," Jacqueline said grudgingly, "that Rod has something, Carol."

The argument was ended by the appearance of Bob, Carmen, and Jimmy. They had been delayed, explained Jimmy, by the necessity of inspecting the house. "As if I didn't know every rock in it. Oh, my back!"

"I appreciate it, Jim," Carmen said softly. "I'll rub your back."

"Sold!" Jimmy lay face down.

"Hey!" protested Caroline. "I carried more rocks than he did. Mostly he stood around and bossed."

"Supervisory work is exceptionally tiring," Jimmy said smugly. "You get Bob to rub your back."

Neither got a back rub as Roy Kilroy called to them from the wall. "Hey! You down there—lunch hour is over. Let's get back to work."

"Sorry, Jimmy. Later." Carmen turned away.

Jimmy scrambled to his feet. "Bob, Carmen—don't go 'way yet. I want to say something."

They stopped. Rod waved to Kilroy. "With you in a moment!" He turned back to the others.

Jimmy seemed to have difficulty in choosing words. "Uh, Carmen . . . Bob. The future Baxters. You know we think a lot of you. We think it's swell that you are going to get married—every family ought to have a marriage. But . . . well, shopping isn't what it might be around here and we didn't know what to get you. So we talked it over and decided to give you this. It's from all of us. A wedding present." Jimmy jammed a hand in his pocket, hauled out his dirty, dog-eared playing cards and handed them to Carmen.

Bob Baxter looked startled. "Gosh, Jimmy, we can't take your cards—your *only* cards."

"I—we want you to have them."

"But—"

"Be quiet, Bob!" Carmen said and took the cards. "Thank you, Jimmy. Thank you very much. Thank you all." She looked around. "Our getting married isn't going to make any difference, you know. It's still one family. We'll expect you all . . . to come play cards . . . at our house just as—" She stopped suddenly and started to cry, buried her head on Bob's shoulder. He patted it. Jimmy looked as if he wanted to cry and Rod felt nakedly embarrassed.

They started back, Carmen with an arm around Jimmy and the other around her betrothed. Rod hung back with the other two. "Did Jimmy," he whispered, "say anything to either of you about this?"

"No," Jacqueline answered.

"Not me," Caroline agreed. "I was going to give 'em my stew pan, but now I'll wait a day or two." Caroline's "bag of rocks" had turned out to contain an odd assortment for survival—among other things, a thin-page diary, a tiny mouth organ, and a half-litre sauce pan. She produced other unlikely but useful items from time to time. Why she had picked them and how she had managed to hang on to them after she discarded the bag were minor mysteries, but, as Deacon Matson had often told the class: "Each to his own methods. Survival is an art, not a science." It was undeniable that she had appeared at the cave healthy, well fed, and with her clothing surprisingly neat and clean in view of the month she had been on the land.

"They won't expect you to give up your stew pan, Caroline."

"I can't use it now that the crowd is so big, and they can set up housekeeping with it. Anyhow, I want to."

"I'm going to give her two needles and some thread. Bob made her leave her sewing kit behind in favor of medical supplies. But I'll wait a while, too."

"I haven't anything I can give them," Rod said miserably.

Jacqueline turned gentle eyes on him. "You can make them a water skin for their house, Rod," she said softly. "They would like that. We can use some of my Kwik-Kure so that it will last."

Rod cheered up at once. "Say, that's a swell idea!"

"We are gathered here," Grant Cowper said cheerfully, "to join these two people in the holy bonds of matrimony. I won't give the usual warning because we all know that no impediment exists to this union. In fact it is the finest thing that could happen to our little community, a joyful omen of things to come, a promise for the future, a guarantee that we are firmly resolved to keep the torch of civilization, now freshly lighted on this planet, forever burning in the future. It means that—"

Rod stopped listening. He was standing at the groom's right as best man. His duties had not been onerous but now he found that he had an overwhelming desire to sneeze. He worked his features around, then in desperation rubbed his upper lip violently and overcame it. He sighed silently and was glad for the first time that Grant Cowper had this responsibility. Grant seemed to know the right words and he did not.

The bride was attended by Caroline Mshiyeni. Both girls carried bouquets of a flame-colored wild bloom. Caroline was in shorts and shirt as usual and the bride was dressed in the conventional blue denim trousers and overshirt. Her hair was arranged *en brosse*; her scrubbed face shone in the firelight and she was radiantly beautiful.

"Who giveth this woman?"

Jimmy Throxton stepped forward and said hoarsely, "I do!"

"The ring, please."

Rod had it on his little finger; with considerable fumbling he got it off. It was a Ponce de Leon senior-class ring, borrowed from Bill Kennedy. He handed it to Cowper.

"Carmen Eleanora, do you take this man to be your lawfully wedded husband, to have and to hold, for better and for worse, in sickness and in health, till death do you part?"

"I do."

"Robert Edward, do you take this woman to be your lawfully wedded wife? Will you keep her and cherish her, cleaving unto her only, until death do you part?"

"I do. I mean, I will. Both."

"Take her hand in yours. Place the ring on her finger. Repeat after me—"

Rod's sneeze was coming back again; he missed part of it.

"—so, by authority vested in me as duly elected Chief Magistrate of this sovereign community, I pronounce you man and wife! Kiss her, chum, before I beat you to it."

Carol and Jackie both were crying; Rod wondered what had gone wrong. He missed his turn at kissing the bride, but she turned to him presently, put an arm around his neck and kissed him. He found himself shaking hands with Bob very solemnly. "Well, I guess that does it. Don't forget you are supposed to carry her through the door."

"I won't forget."

"Well, you told me to remind you. Uh, may the Principle bless you both."

10

"I So Move"

THERE WAS NO MORE TALK OF LEAVING. EVEN CAROLINE DROPPED THE subject.

But on other subjects talk was endless. Cowper held a town meeting every evening. These started with committee reports—the committee on food resources and natural conservation, the committees on artifacts and inventory, on waste disposal and camp sanitation, on exterior security, on human resources and labor allotment, on recruitment and immigration, on conservation of arts and sciences, on constitution, codification, and justice, on food preparation, on housing and city planning—

Cowper seemed to enjoy the endless talk and Rod was forced to admit that the others appeared to have a good time, too—he surprised himself by discovering that he too looked forward to the evenings. It was the village's social life, the only recreation. Each session produced wordy battles, personal remarks and caustic criticisms; what was lacking in the gentlemanly formality found in older congresses was made up in spice. Rod liked to sprawl on the ground with his ear near Jimmy Throxton and listen to Jimmy's slanderous asides about the intelligence, motives, and ancestry of each speaker. He waited for Caroline's disorderly heckling.

But Caroline was less inclined to heckle now; Cowper had appointed her Historian on discovering that she owned a diary and could take shorthand. "It is extremely important," he informed her in the presence of the village, "that we have a full record of these pioneer days for posterity. You've been writing in your diary every day?"

"Sure. That's what it's for."

"Good! From here on it will be an official account. I want you to record the important events of each day."

"All right. It doesn't make the tiniest bit of difference, I do anyhow."

"Yes, yes, but in greater detail. I want you to record our proceedings, too. Historians will treasure this document, Carol."

"I'll bet!"

Cowper seemed lost in thought. "How many blank leaves left in your diary?"

"Couple of hundred, maybe."

"Good! That solves a problem I had been wondering about. Uh, we will have to requisition half of that supply for official use—public notices, committee transactions, and the like. You know."

Caroline looked wide-eyed. "That's a lot of paper, isn't it? You had better send two or three big husky boys to carry it."

Cowper looked puzzled. "You're joking."

"Better make it *four* big huskies. I could probably manage three . . . and somebody is likely to get hurt."

"Now, see here, Caroline, it is just a temporary requisition, in the public interest. Long before you need all of your diary we will devise other writing materials."

"Go ahead and devise! That's *my* diary."

Caroline sat near Cowper, diary in her lap and style in her hand, taking notes. Each evening she opened proceedings by reading the minutes of the previous meeting. Rod asked her if she took down the endless debates.

"Goodness no!"

"I wondered. It seemed to me that you would run out of paper. Your minutes are certainly complete."

She chuckled. "Roddie, want to know what I really write down? Promise not to tell."

"Of course I won't."

"When I 'read the minutes' I just reach back in my mind and recall what the gabble was the night before—I've got an awfully good memory. But what I actually dirty the paper with . . . well, here—" She took her diary from a pocket. "Here's last night: 'Hizzoner called us to disorder at half-past burping time. The committee on cats and dogs reported. No cats, no dogs. The shortage was discussed. We adjourned and went to sleep, those who weren't already.' "

Rod grinned. "A good thing Grant doesn't know shorthand."

"Of course, if anything *real* happens, I put it down. But not the talk, talk, talk."

Caroline was not adamant about not sharing her supply of paper when needed. A marriage certificate, drawn up in officialese by Howard

Goldstein, a Teller law student, was prepared for the Baxters and signed by Cowper, the couple themselves, and Rod and Caroline as witnesses. Caroline decorated it with flowers and turtle doves before delivering it.

There were others who seemed to feel that the new government was long on talk and short on results. Among them was Bob Baxter, but the Quaker couple did not attend most of the meetings. But when Cowper had been in office a week, Shorty Dumont took the floor after the endless committee reports:

"Mr. Chairman!"

"Can you hold it, Shorty? I have announcements to make before we get on to new business."

"This is still about committee reports. When does the committee on our constitution report?"

"Why, I made the report myself."

"You said that a revised draft was being prepared and the report would be delayed. That's no report. What I want to know is: when do we get a permanent set-up? When do we stop floating in air, getting along from day to day on 'temporary executive notices'?"

Cowper flushed. "Do you object to my executive decisions?"

"Won't say that I do, won't say that I don't. But Rod was let out and you were put in on the argument that we needed constitutional government, not a dictatorship. That's why I voted for you. All right, where's our laws? When do we vote on them?"

"You must understand," Cowper answered carefully, "that drawing up a constitution is not done overnight. Many considerations are involved."

"Sure, sure—but it's time we had some notion of what sort of a constitution you are cooking up. How about a bill of rights? Have you drawn up one?"

"All in due time."

"Why wait? For a starter let's adopt the Virginia Bill of Rights as article one. I so move."

"You're out of order. Anyhow we don't even have a copy of it."

"Don't let that bother you; I know it by heart. You ready, Carol? Take this down . . ."

"Never mind," Caroline answered. "I know it, too. I'm writing it."

"You see? These things aren't any mystery, Grant; most of us could quote it. So let's quit stalling."

Somebody yelled, "Whoopee! That's telling him, Shorty. I second the motion."

Cowper shouted for order. He went on, "This is not the time nor the place. When the committee reports, you will find that all proper democratic freedoms and safeguards have been included—modified only by the stern necessities of our hazardous position." He flashed his smile. "Now let's get on with business. I have an announcement about hunting parties. Hereafter each hunting party will be expected to—"

Dumont was still standing. "I said no more stalling, Grant. You argued that what we needed was laws, not a captain's whim. You've been throwing your weight around quite a while now and I don't see any laws. What are your duties? How much authority do you have? Are you both the high and the low justice? Or do the rest of us have rights?"

"Shut up and sit down!"

"How long is your term of office?"

Cowper made an effort to control himself. "Shorty, if you have suggestions on such things, you must take them up with the committee."

"Oh, slush! Give me a straight answer."

"You are out of order."

"I am *not* out of order. I'm insisting that the committee on drawing up a constitution tell us what they are doing. I won't surrender the floor until I get an answer. This is a town meeting and I have as much right to talk as anybody."

Cowper turned red. "I wouldn't be too sure," he said ominously. "Just how old are you, Shorty?"

Dumont stared at him. "Oh, so *that's* it? And the cat is out of the bag!" He glanced around. "I see quite a few here who are younger than I am. See what he's driving at, folks? Second-class citizens. He's going to stick an age limit in that so-called constitution. Aren't you, Grant? Look me in the eye and deny it."

"Roy! Dave! Grab him and bring him to order."

Rod had been listening closely; the show was better than usual. Jimmy had been adding his usual flippant commentary. Now Jimmy whispered, "That tears it. Do we choose up sides or do we fade back and watch the fun?"

Before he could answer Shorty made it clear that he needed no immediate help. He set his feet wide and snapped, "Touch me and somebody gets hurt!" He did not reach for any weapon but his attitude showed that he was willing to fight.

He went on, "Grant, I've got one thing to say, then I'll shut up." He turned and spoke to all. "You can see that we don't have any rights and we don't know where we stand—but we are already organized like a straitjacket. Committees for this, committees for that—and what good has it done? Are we better off than we were before all these half-baked committees were appointed? The wall is still unfinished, the camp is dirtier than ever, and nobody knows what he is supposed to do. Why, we even let the signal fire go out yesterday. When a roof leaks, you don't appoint a committee; you fix the leak. I say give the job back to Rod, get rid of these silly committees, and get on with fixing the leaks. Anybody with me? Make some noise!"

They made plenty of noise. The shouts may have come from less than half but Cowper could see that he was losing his grip on them. Roy Kilroy dropped behind Shorty Dumont and looked questioningly at Cowper; Jimmy jabbed Rod in the ribs and whispered, "Get set, boy."

But Cowper shook his head at Roy. "Shorty," he said quietly, "are you through making your speech?"

"That wasn't a speech, that was a motion. And you had better not tell me it's out of order."

"I did not understand your motion. State it."

"You understood it. I'm moving that we get rid of you and put Rod back in."

Kilroy interrupted. "Hey, Grant, he can't do that. That's not according to—"

"Hold it, Roy. Shorty, your motion is not in order."

"I thought you would say that!"

"And it is really two motions. But I'm not going to bother with trifles. You say people don't like the way I'm doing things, so we'll find out." He went on briskly, "Is there a second to the motion?"

"Second!"

"I second it."

"Moved and seconded. The motion is to recall me and put Rod in office. Any remarks?"

A dozen people tried to speak. Rod got the floor by outshouting the others. "Mr. Chairman, *Mr. Chairman!* Privileged question!"

"The chair recognizes Rod Walker."

"Point of personal privilege. I have a statement to make."

"Well? Go ahead."

"Look, Grant, I didn't know Shorty planned to do this. Tell him, Shorty."

"That's right."

"Okay, okay," Cowper said sourly. "Any other remarks? Don't yell, just stick up your hands."

"I'm not through," insisted Rod.

"Well?"

"I not only did not know, I'm not for it. Shorty, I want you to withdraw your motion."

"No!"

"I think you should. Grant has only had a week; you can't expect miracles in that time—I *know*; I've had grief enough with this bunch of wild men. You may not like the things he's done—I don't myself, a lot of them. That's to be expected. But if you let that be an excuse to run him out of office, then sure as daylight this gang will break up."

"I'm not busting it up—he is! He may be older than I am but if he thinks that makes the least difference when it comes to having a say—well . . . he'd better think twice. I'm warning him. You hear that, Grant?"

"I heard it. You misunderstood me."

"Like fun I did!"

"Shorty," Rod persisted, "will you drop this idea? I'm asking you *please.*"

Shorty Dumont looked stubborn. Rod looked helplessly at Cowper, shrugged and sat down. Cowper turned away and growled, "Any more debate? You back there . . . Agnes? You've got the floor."

Jimmy whispered, "Why did you pull a stunt like that, Rod? Nobility doesn't suit you."

"I wasn't being noble. I knew what I was doing," Rod answered in low tones.

"You messed up your chances to be re-elected."

"Stow it." Rod listened; it appeared that Agnes Fries had more than one grievance. "Jim?"

"Huh?"

"Jump to your feet and move to adjourn."

"What? Ruin this when it's getting good? There is going to be some hair pulled . . . I hope."

"Don't argue; do it!—or I'll bang your heads together."

"Oh, all right. Spoilsport." Jimmy got reluctantly to his feet, took a breath and shouted, "I move we adjourn!"

Rod bounced to his feet. "SECOND THE MOTION!"

Cowper barely glanced at them. "Out of order. Sit down."

"It is *not* out of order," Rod said loudly. "A motion to adjourn is always in order, it takes precedence, and it cannot be debated. I call for the question."

"I never recognized you. This recall motion is going to be voted on if it is the last thing I do." Cowper's face was tense with anger. "Are you through, Agnes? Or do you want to discuss my table manners, too?"

"You *can't* refuse a motion to adjourn," Rod insisted. "Question! Put the question."

Several took up the shout, drowning out Agnes Fries, preventing Cowper from recognizing another speaker. Boos and catcalls rounded out the tumult.

Cowper held up both hands for silence, then called out, "It has been moved and seconded that we adjourn. Those in favor say, 'Aye.'"

"AYE!!"

"Opposed?"

"No," said Jimmy.

"The meeting is adjourned." Cowper strode out of the circle of firelight.

Shorty Dumont came over, planted himself in front of Rod and looked up. "A fine sort of a pal you turned out to be!" He spat on the ground and stomped off.

"Yeah," agreed Jimmy, "what gives? Schizophrenia? Your nurse drop you on your head? That noble stuff in the right doses might have put us back in business. But you didn't know when to stop."

Jacqueline had approached while Jimmy was speaking. "I wasn't pulling any tricks," Rod insisted. "I meant what I said. Kick a captain out when he's had only a few days to show himself and you'll bust us up into a dozen little groups. *I* wouldn't be able to hold them together. Nobody could."

"Bosh! Jackie, tell the man."

She frowned. "Jimmy, you're sweet, but you're not bright."

"*Et tu,* Jackie?"

"Never mind, Jackie will take care of you. A good job, Rod. By tomorrow everybody will realize it. Some of them are a little stirred up tonight."

"What I don't see," Rod said thoughtfully, "is what got Shorty stirred up in the first place?"

"Hadn't you heard? Maybe it was while you were out hunting. I didn't see it, but he got into a row with Roy, then Grant bawled him out in front of everybody. I think Shorty is self-conscious about his height," she said seriously. "He doesn't like to take orders."

"Does anybody?"

The next day Grant Cowper acted as if nothing had happened. But his manner had more of King Log and less of King Stork. Late in the afternoon he looked up Rod. "Walker? Can you spare me a few minutes?"

"Why not?"

"Let's go where we can talk." Grant led him to a spot out of earshot. They sat on the ground and Rod waited. Cowper seemed to have difficulty in finding words.

Finally he said, "Rod, I think I can depend on you." He threw in his grin, but it looked forced.

"Why?" asked Rod.

"Well . . . the way you behaved last night."

"So? Don't bank on it, I didn't do it for you." Rod paused, then added, "Let's get this straight. I don't like you."

For once Cowper did not grin. "That makes it mutual. I don't like you a little bit. But we've got to get along . . . and I think I can trust you."

"Maybe."

"I'll risk it."

"I agree with every one of Shorty's gripes. I just didn't agree with his solution."

Cowper gave a wry smile unlike his usual expression. For an instant Rod found himself almost liking him. "The sad part is that I agree with his gripes myself."

"Huh?"

"Rod, you probably think I'm a stupid jerk but the fact is I do know quite a bit about theory of government. The hard part is to apply it in a . . . a transitional period like this. We've got fifty people here and not a one with any practical experience in government—not even myself. But every single one considers himself an expert. Take that bill-of-rights motion; I couldn't let that stand. I know enough about such things to know that the rights and duties needed for a co-operative colony like this can't be taken over word for word from an agrarian democracy, and they are still different from those necessary for an industrial republic." He looked worried. "It is true that we had considered limiting the franchise."

"You do and they'll toss you in the creek!"

"I know. That's one reason why the law committee hasn't made a report. Another reason is—well, confound it, how can you work out things like a constitution when you practically haven't any writing paper? It's exasperating. But about the franchise: the oldest one of us is around twenty-two and the youngest is about sixteen. The worst of it is that the youngest are the most precocious, geniuses or near-geniuses." Cowper looked up. "I don't mean you."

"Oh, no," Rod said hastily. "I'm no genius!"

"You're not sixteen, either. These brilliant brats worry me. 'Bush lawyers,' every blessed one, with always a smart answer and no sense. We thought with an age limit—a reasonable one—the older heads could act as ballast while they grow up. But it won't work."

"No. It won't."

"But what am I to *do?* That order about hunting teams not being mixed—that wasn't aimed at teams like you and Carol, but she thought it was and gave me the very deuce. I was just trying to take care of these kids. Confound it, I wish they were all old enough to marry and settle down—the Baxters don't give me trouble."

"I wouldn't worry. In a year or so ninety per cent of the colony will be married."

"I hope so! Say . . . are *you* thinking about it?"

"Me?" Rod was startled. "Farthest thing from my mind."

"Um? I thought— Never mind; I didn't get you out here to ask about your private affairs. What Shorty had to say was hard to swallow—but I'm going to make some changes. I'm abolishing most of the committees."

"So?"

"Yes. Blast them, they don't *do* anything; they just produce reports. I'm going to make one girl boss cook—and one man boss hunter. I want you to be chief of police."

"Huh? Why in Ned do you want a chief of police?"

"Well . . . somebody has to see that orders are carried out. You know, camp sanitation and such. Somebody has to keep the signal smoking—we haven't accounted for thirty-seven people, aside from known dead. Somebody has to assign the night watch and check on it. The kids run hog wild if you don't watch them. You are the one to do it."

"Why?"

"Well . . . let's be practical, Rod. I've got a following and so have you. We'll have less trouble if everybody sees that we two stand together. It's for the good of the community."

Rod realized, as clearly as Grant did, that the group had to pull together. But Cowper was asking him to shore up his shaky administration, and Rod not only resented him but thought that Cowper was all talk and no results.

It was not just the unfinished wall, he told himself, but a dozen things. Somebody ought to search for a salt lick, every day. There ought to be a steady hunt for edible roots and berries and things, too—he, for one, was tired of an all-meat diet. Sure, you could stay healthy if you didn't stick just to lean meat, but who wanted to eat nothing but meat, maybe for a lifetime? And there were those stinking hides . . . Grant had ordered every kill skinned, brought back for use.

"What are you going to do with those green hides?" he asked suddenly.

"Huh? Why?"

"They stink. If you put me in charge, I'm going to chuck them in the creek."

"But we're going to need them. Half of us are in rags now."

"But we're not short on hides; tanning is what we need. Those hides won't sun-cure this weather."

"We haven't got tannin. Don't be silly, Rod."

"Then send somebody out to chew bark till they find some. You can't mistake the puckery taste. And get rid of those hides!"

"If I do, will you take the job?"

"Maybe. You said, 'See that orders are carried out.' Whose orders? Yours? Or Kilroy's?"

"Well, both. Roy is my deputy."

Rod shook his head. "No, thanks. You've got him, so you don't need me. Too many generals, not enough privates."

"But, Rod, I *do* need you. Roy doesn't get along with the younger kids. He rubs them the wrong way."

"He rubs me the wrong way, too. Nothing doing, Grant. Besides, I don't like the title anyhow. It's silly."

"Pick your own. Captain of the Guard . . . City Manager. I don't care what you call it; I want you to take over the night guard and see that things run smoothly around camp—and keep an eye on the younger kids. You can do it and it's your duty."

"What will you be doing?"

"I've got to whip this code of laws into shape. I've got to think about long-range planning. Heavens, Rod, I've got a thousand things on my mind. I can't stop to settle a quarrel just because some kid has been teasing the cook. Shorty was right; we can't wait. When I give an order I want a law to back it and not have to take lip from some young snotty. But I can't do it all, I need help."

Cowper put it on grounds impossible to refuse, nevertheless . . . "What about Kilroy?"

"Eh? Confound it, Rod, you can't ask me to kick out somebody else to make room for *you.*"

"I'm not *asking* for the job!" Rod hesitated. He needed to say that it was a matter of stubborn pride to him to back up the man who had beaten him, it was that more than any public-spiritedness. He could not phrase it, but he did know that Cowper and Kilroy were not the same case.

"I won't pull Kilroy's chestnuts out of the fire. Grant, I'll stooge for you; you were elected. But I won't stooge for a stooge."

"Rod, be reasonable! If you got an order from Roy, it would be *my* order. He would simply be carrying it out."

Rod stood up. "No deal."

Cowper got angrily to his feet and strode away.

* * *

There was no meeting that night, for the first time. Rod was about to visit the Baxters when Cowper called him aside. "You win. I've made Roy chief hunter."

"Huh?"

"You take over as City Manager, or Queen of the May, or whatever you like. Nobody has set the night watch. So get busy."

"Wait a minute! I never said I would take the job."

"You made it plain that the only thing in your way was Roy. Okay, you get your orders directly from me."

Rod hesitated. Cowper looked at him scornfully and said, "So you can't co-operate even when you have it all your own way?"

"Not that, but—"

"No 'buts.' Do you take the job? A straight answer: yes, or no."

"Uh . . . yes."

"Okay." Cowper frowned and added, "I almost wish you had turned it down."

"That makes two of us."

Rod started to set the guard and found that every boy he approached was convinced that he had had more than his share of watches. Since the exterior security committee had kept no records—indeed, had had no way to—it was impossible to find out who was right and who was shirking. "Stow it!" he told one. "Starting tomorrow we'll have an alphabetical list, straight rotation. I'll post it even if we have to scratch it on a rock." He began to realize that there was truth in what Grant had said about the difficulty of getting along without writing paper.

"Why don't you put your pal Baxter on watch?"

"Because the Mayor gave him two weeks honeymoon, as you know. Shut up the guff. Charlie will be your relief; make sure you know where he sleeps."

"I think I'll get married. I could use two weeks of loafing."

"I'll give you five to one you can't find a girl that far out of her mind. You're on from midnight to two."

Most of them accepted the inevitable once they were assured of a square deal in the future, but Peewee Schneider, barely sixteen and youngest in the community, stood on his "rights"—he had stood a watch the night before, he did not rate another for at least three nights, and nobody could most colorfully make him.

Rod told Peewee that he would either stand his watch, or Rod would slap his ears loose—and then he would still stand his watch. To which he added that if he heard Peewee use that sort of language around camp again he would wash Peewee's mouth out with soap.

Schneider shifted the argument. "Yah! Where are you going to find soap?"

"Until we get some, I'll use sand. You spread that word, Peewee: no more rough language around camp. We're going to be civilized if it kills us. Four to six, then, and show Kenny where you sleep." As he left Rod made a mental note that they should collect wood ashes and fat; while he had only a vague idea of how to make soap probably someone knew how . . . and soap was needed for other purposes than curbing foul-mouthed pip-squeaks. He had felt a yearning lately to be able to stand upwind of himself . . . he had long ago thrown away his socks.

Rod got little sleep. Everytime he woke he got up and inspected the guard, and twice he was awakened by watchmen who thought they saw something prowling outside the circle of firelight. Rod was not sure, although it did seem once that he could make out a large, long shape drifting past in the darkness. He stayed up a while each time, another gun in case the prowler risked the wall or the fires in the gap. He felt great temptation to shoot at the prowling shadows, but suppressed it. To carry the attack to the enemy would be to squander their scanty ammunition without making a dent in the dangerous beasts around them. There were prowlers every night; they had to live with it.

He was tired and cranky the next morning and wanted to slip away after breakfast and grab a nap in the cave. He had not slept after four in the morning, but had checked on Peewee Schneider at frequent intervals. But there was too much to do; he promised himself a nap later and sought out Cowper instead. "Two or three things on my mind, Grant."

"Spill it."

"Any reason not to put girls on watch?"

"Eh? I don't think it's a good idea."

"Why not? These girls don't scream at a mouse. Every one of them stayed alive by her own efforts at least a month before she joined up here. Ever seen Caroline in action?"

"Mmm . . . no."

"You should. It's a treat. Sudden death in both hands, and eyes in the back of her head. If she were on watch, I would sleep easy. How many men do we have now?"

"Uh, twenty-seven, with the three that came in yesterday."

"All right, out of twenty-seven who doesn't stand watch?"

"Why, everybody takes his turn."

"You?"

"Eh? Isn't that carrying it pretty far? I don't expect *you* to take a watch; you run it and check on the others."

"That's two off. Roy Kilroy?"

"Uh, look, Rod, you had better figure that he is a department head as chief hunter and therefore exempt. You know why—no use looking for trouble."

"I know, all right. Bob Baxter is off duty, too."

"Until next week."

"But this is this week. The committee cut the watch down to one at a time; I'm going to boost it to two again. Besides that I want a sergeant of the guard each night. He will be on all night and sleep all next day . . . then I don't want to put him on for a couple of days. You see where that leaves me? I need twelve watchstanders every night; I have less than twenty to draw from."

Cowper looked worried. "The committee didn't think we had to have more than one guard at a time."

"Committee be hanged!" Rod scratched his scars and thought about shapes in the dark. "Do you want me to run this the way I think it has to be run? Or shall I just go through the motions?"

"Well . . ."

"One man alone either gets jittery and starts seeing shadows—or he dopes off and is useless. I had to wake one last night—I won't tell you who; I scared him out of his pants; he won't do it again. I say we need a real guard, strong enough in case of trouble to handle things while the camp has time to wake up. But if you want it your way, why not relieve me and put somebody else in?"

"No, no, you keep it. Do what you think necessary."

"Okay, I'm putting the girls on. Bob and Carmen, too. And *you.*"

"Huh?"

"And me. And Roy Kilroy. Everybody. That's the only way you will get people to serve without griping; that way you will convince them that it is serious, a first obligation, even ahead of hunting."

Cowper picked at a hangnail, "Do you honestly think I should stand watch? And you?"

"I do. It would boost morale seven hundred per cent. Besides that, it would be a good thing, uh, politically."

Cowper glanced up, did not smile. "You've convinced me. Let me know when it's my turn."

"Another thing. Last night there was barely wood to keep two fires going."

"Your problem. Use anybody not on the day's hunting or cooking details."

"I will. You'll hear some beefs. Boss, those were minor items; now I come to the major one. Last night I took a fresh look at this spot. I don't like it, not as a permanent camp. We've been lucky."

"Eh? Why?"

"This place is almost undefendable. We've got a stretch over fifty meters long between shale and water on the upstream side. Downstream isn't bad, because we build a fire in the bottleneck. But upstream we have walled off less than half and we need a lot more stakes behind the wall. Look," Rod added, pointing, "you could drive an army through there—and last night I had only two little bitty fires. We ought to finish that wall."

"We will."

"But we ought to make a real drive to find a better place. This is makeshift at best. Before you took over I was trying to find more caves—but I didn't have time to explore very far. Ever been to Mesa Verde?"

"In Colorado? No."

"Cliff dwellings, you've seen pictures. Maybe somewhere up or down stream—more likely down—we will find pockets like those at Mesa Verde where we can build homes for the whole colony. You ought to send a team out for two weeks or more, searching. I volunteer for it."

"Maybe. But you can't go; I need you."

"In a week I'll have this guard duty lined up so that it will run itself. Bob Baxter can relieve me; they respect him. Uh . . ." He thought for a moment. Jackie? Jimmy? "I'll team with Carol."

"Rod, I told you I want you here. But are you and Caroline planning to marry?"

"Huh? What gave you that notion?"

"Then you can't team with her in any case. We are trying to re-introduce amenities around here."

"Now see here, Cowper!"

"Forget it."

"Unh . . . all right. But the first thing—the very first—is to finish that wall. I want to put everybody to work right away."

"Mmm . . ." Cowper said. "I'm sorry. You can't."

"Why not?"

"Because we are going to build a house today. Bill Kennedy and Sue Briggs are getting married tonight."

"Huh? I hadn't heard."

"I guess you are the first to hear. They told me about it privately, at breakfast."

Rod was not surprised, as Bill and Sue preferred each other's company. "Look, do they have to get married tonight? That wall is urgent, Grant; I'm telling you."

"Don't be so intense, Rod. You can get along a night or two with bigger fires. Remember, there are human values more important than material values."

11

The Beach of Bones

"*July 29*—Bill and Sue got married tonight. Hizzoner never looked lovelier. He made a mighty pretty service out of it—I cried and so did the other girls. If that boy could *do* the way he can talk! I played Mendelssohn's Wedding March on my harmonica with tears running down my nose and gumming up the reeds—that's a touch I wanted to put into darling Carmen's wedding but I couldn't resist being bridesmaid. The groom got stuck carrying his lady fair over the threshold of their 'house'—if I may call it that—and had to put her down and shove her in ahead of him. The ceiling is lower than it ought to be which is why he got stuck, because we ran out of rock and Roddie raised Cain when we started to use part of the wall. Hizzoner was leading the assault on the wall and both of them got red in the face and shouted at each other. But Hizzoner backed down after Roddie got him aside and said something—Bill was pretty sore at Roddie but Bob sweet-talked him and offered to swap houses and Roddie promised Bill that we would take the roof off and bring the walls up higher as soon as the wall is finished. That might not be as soon as he thinks, though—usable rock is getting hard to find. I've broken all my nails trying to pry out pieces we could use. But I agree with Roddie that we ought to finish that wall and I sleep a lot sounder now that he is running the watch and I'll sleep sounder yet when that wall is tight and the pin-cushion back of it finished. Of course we girls sleep down at the safe end but who wants to wake up and find a couple of our boys missing? It is not as if we had them to spare, bless their silly little hearts. Nothing like a man around the house, Mother always said, to give a home that lived-in look.

"*July 30*—I'm not going to write in this unless something happens. Hizzoner talks about making papyrus like the Egyptians but I'll believe it when I see it.

"*Aug 5*—I was sergeant of the guard last night and Roddie was awake practically all night. I turned in after breakfast and slept until late afternoon—when I woke up there was Roddie, red-eyed and cross, yelling for more rocks and more firewood. Sometimes Roddie is a little hard to take.

"*Aug 9*—the salt lick Alice found is closer than the one Shorty found last week, but not as good.

"*Aug 14*—Jackie finally made up her mind to marry Jim and I think Roddie is flabbergasted—but I could have told him a month ago. Roddie is stupid about such things. I see another house & wall crisis coming and Roddie will get a split personality because he will want Jimmy and Jacqueline to have a house right away and the only decent stone within reach is built into the wall.

"*Aug 15*—Jimmy and Jackie, Agnes and Curt, were married today in a beautiful double ceremony. The Throxtons have the Baxter house temporarily and the Pulvermachers have the Kennedy's doll house while we partition the cave into two sets of married quarters and a storeroom.

"*Sep 1*—the roots I dug up didn't poison me, so I served a mess of them tonight. The shield from power pack of that Thunderbolt gun we salvaged—Johann's, it must have been—made a big enough boiler to cook a little helping for everybody. The taste was odd, maybe because Agnes had been making soap in it—it wasn't very good soap, either. I'm going to call these things yams because they look like yams although they taste more like parsnips. There are a lot of them around. Tomorrow I'm going to try boiling them with greens, a strip of side meat, and plenty of salt. Yum, yum! I'm going to bake them in ashes, too.

"*Sep 16*—Chad Ames and Dick Burke showed up with their tails tucked in; Hizzoner got soft-hearted and let them stay. They say Jock McGowan is crazy. I can believe it.

"*Sep 28*—Philip Schneider died today, hunting. Roy carried him in, but he was badly clawed and lost a lot of blood and was D.O.A. Roy resigned as boss hunter and Hizzoner appointed Cliff. Roy is broken up about it and nobody blames him. The Lord giveth and the Lord taketh away. Blessed be the Name of the Lord.

"*Oct 7*—I've decided to marry M.

"*Oct 10*—seems I was mistaken—M. is going to marry Margery Chung. Well, they are nice kids and if we ever get out of this I'll be glad I'm single since I want to buck for a commission in the Amazons. Note: be a little more standoffish, Caroline. Well, *try!*

"*Oct 20*—Carmen????

"*Oct 21*—Yes.

"*Nov 1*—well Glory be! I'm the new *City Manager*. Little Carol, the girl with two left feet. Just a couple of weeks, temporary and acting while Roddie is away, but say 'sir' when you speak to me. Hizzoner finally let Roddie make the down-river survey he has been yipping about, accompanying it with a slough of advice and injunctions that Roddie will pay no attention to once he is out of sight—if I know Roddie. It's a two-man team and Roddie picked Roy as his teamer. They left this morning.

"*Nov 5*—being City Manager is not all marshmallow sundae. I wish Roddie would get back.

"*Nov 11*—Hizzoner wants me to copy off in here the 'report of the artifacts committee'! Mick Mahmud has been keeping it in his head which strikes me as a good place. But Hizzoner has been very jumpy since Roddie and Roy left, so I guess I will humor him—here it is:

"12 spare knives (besides one each for everybody)

"53 firearms and guns of other sorts—but only about half of them with even one charge left.

"6 Testaments

"2 Peace of the Flame

"1 Koran

"1 Book of Mormon

"1 Oxford Book of English Verse, Centennial Edition

"1 steel bow and 3 hunting arrows

"1 boiler made from a wave shield and quite a bit of metal and plastic junk (worth its weight in uranium, I admit) from the Thunderbolt Jackie salvaged.
"1 stew pan (Carmen's)
"1 pack playing cards with the nine of hearts missing
"13 matches, any number of pocket flamers no longer working, and 27 burning glasses
"1 small hand ax
"565 meters climbing line, some of it chopped up for other uses
"91 fishhooks (and no fish fit to eat!)
"61 pocket compasses, some of them broken
"19 watches that still run (4 of them adjusted to our day)
"2 bars of scented soap that Theo has been hoarding
"2 boxes Kwik-Kure and part of a box of Tan-Fast
"Several kilos of oddments that I suppose we will find a use for but I won't list. Mick has a mind like a pack rat.

"Lots of things we have made and can make more of—pots, bows and arrows, hide scrapers, a stone-age mortar & pestle we can grind seeds on if you don't mind grit in your teeth, etc. Hizzoner says the Oxford Verse is the most valuable thing we have and I agree, but not for his reasons. He wants me to cover all the margins with shorthand, recording all special knowledge that any of us have—everything from math to pig-raising. Cliff says go ahead as long as we don't deface the verses. I don't see when I'm going to find time. I've hardly been out of the settlement since Roddie left and sleep is something I just hear about.

"*Nov 13*—only two more days. 'For this relief, much thanks . . .'

"*Nov 16*—I didn't think they would be on time.

"*Nov 21*—We finally adopted our constitution and basic code today, the first town meeting we've had in weeks. It covers the flyleaves of two Testaments, Bob's and Georgia's. If anybody wants to refer to it, which I doubt, that's where to look.

"*Nov 29*—Jimmy says old Rod is too tough to kill. I hope he's right. Why, oh, why didn't I twist Hizzoner's arm and make him let me go?

"*Dec 15*—there's no use kidding ourselves any longer.

"Dec 21—the Throxtons and Baxters and myself and Grant gathered privately in the Baxter house tonight and Grant recited the service for the dead. Bob said a prayer for both of them and then we sat quietly for a long time, Quaker fashion. Roddie always reminded me of my brother Rickie, so I privately asked Mother to take care of him, and Roy, too—Mother had a lap big enough for three, any time.

"Grant hasn't made a public announcement; officially they are just 'overdue.'

"Dec 25—Christmas"

Rod and Roy traveled light and fast downstream, taking turns leading and covering. Each carried a few kilos of salt meat but they expected to eat off the land. In addition to game they now knew of many edible fruits and berries and nuts; the forest was a free cafeteria to those who knew it. They carried no water since they expected to follow the stream. But they continued to treat the water with respect; in addition to ichthyosaurs that sometimes pulled down a drinking buck there were bloodthirsty little fish that took very small bites—but they traveled in schools and could strip an animal to bones in minutes.

Rod carried both Lady Macbeth and Colonel Bowie; Roy Kilroy carried his Occam's Razor and a knife borrowed from Carmen Baxter. Roy had a climbing rope wrapped around his waist. Each had a hand gun strapped to his hip but these were for extremity; one gun had only three charges. But Roy carried Jacqueline Throxton's air pistol, with freshly envenomed darts; they expected it to save hours of hunting, save time for travel.

Three days downstream they found a small cave, found living in it a forlorn colony of five girls. They powwowed, then headed on down as the girls started upstream to find the settlement. The girls had told them of a place farther down where the creek could be crossed. They found it, a wide rocky shallows with natural stepping stones . . . then wasted two days on the far side before crossing back.

By the seventh morning they had found no cave other than one the girls had occupied. Rod said to Roy, "Today makes a week. Grant said to be back in two weeks."

"That's what the man said. Yes, sir!"

"No results."

"Nope. None."

"We ought to start back."

Roy did not answer. Rod said querulously, "Well, what do you think?"

Kilroy was lying down, watching the local equivalent of an ant. He seemed in no hurry to do anything else. Finally he answered, "Rod, you are bossing this party. Upstream, downstream—just tell me."

"Oh, go soak your head."

"On the other hand, a bush lawyer like Shorty might question Grant's authority to tell us to return at a given time. He might use words like 'free citizen' and 'sovereign autonomy.' Maybe he's got something—this neighborhood looks awfully far 'West of the Pecos.' "

"Well . . . we could stretch it a day, at least. We won't be taking that side trip going back."

"Obviously. Now, if I were leading the party—but I'm not."

"Cut the double talk! I asked for advice."

"Well, I say we are here to find caves, not to keep a schedule."

Rod quit frowning. "Up off your belly. Let's go."

They headed downstream.

The terrain changed from forest valley to canyon country as the stream cut through a plateau. Game became harder to find and they used some of their salt meat. Two days later they came to the first of a series of bluffs carved eons earlier into convolutions, pockets, blank dark eyes. "This looks like it."

"Yes," agreed Roy. He looked around. "It might be even better farther down."

"It might be."

They went on.

In time the stream widened out, there were no more caves, and the canyons gave way to a broad savannah, treeless except along the banks of the river. Rod sniffed. "I smell salt."

"You ought to. There's ocean over there somewhere."

"I don't think so." They went on.

They avoided the high grass, kept always near the trees. The colonists had listed more than a dozen predators large enough to endanger a man, from a leonine creature twice as long as the biggest African lion down to a vicious little scaly thing which was dangerous if cornered. It was generally agreed that the leonine monster was the "stobor" they had been warned against, although a minority favored a smaller carnivore which was faster, trickier, and more likely to attack a man.

One carnivore was not considered for the honor. It was no larger than a jack rabbit, had an oversize head, a big jaw, front legs larger than hind, and no tail. It was known as "dopy joe" from the silly golliwog expression it had and its clumsy, slow movements when disturbed. It was believed to live by waiting at burrows of field rodents for supper to come out. Its skin cured readily and made a good water bag. Grassy fields such as this savannah often were thick with them.

They camped in a grove of trees by the water. Rod said, "Shall I waste a match, or do it the hard way?"

"Suit yourself. I'll knock over something for dinner."

"Watch yourself. Don't go into the grass."

"I'll work the edges. Cautious Kilroy they call me, around the insurance companies."

Rod counted his three matches, hoping there would be four, then started making fire by friction. He had just succeeded, delayed by moss that was not as dry as it should have been, when Roy returned and dropped a small carcass. "The durnedest thing happened."

The kill was a dopy joe; Rod looked at it with distaste. "Was that the best you could do? They taste like kerosene."

"Wait till I tell you. I wasn't hunting him; he was hunting *me.*"

"Don't kid me!"

"Truth. I had to kill him to keep him from snapping my ankles. So I brought him in."

Rod looked at the small creature. "Never heard the like. Must be insanity in his family."

"Probably." Roy started skinning it.

Next morning they reached the sea, a glassy body untouched by tide, unruffled by wind. It was extremely briny and its shore was crusted with salt. They concluded that it was probably a dead sea, not a true ocean. But their attention was not held by the body of water. Stretching away along the shore apparently to the horizon were millions on heaping millions of whitened bones. Rod stared. "Where did they all come from?"

Roy whistled softly. "Search me. But if we could sell them at five pence a metric ton, we'd be millionaires."

"Billionaires, you mean."

"Let's not be fussy." They walked out along the beach, forgetting to be cautious, held by the amazing sight. There were ancient bones, cracked by sun and sea, new bones with gristle clinging, big bones of the giant antelope the colonists never hunted, tiny bones of little buck no larger than terriers, bones without number of all sorts. But there were no carcasses.

They inspected the shore for a couple of kilometers, awed by the mystery. When they turned they knew that they were turning back not just to camp but to head home. This was as far as they could go.

On the trip out they had not explored the caves. On their way back Rod decided that they should try to pick the best place for the colony, figuring game, water supply, and most importantly, shelter and ease of defense.

They were searching a series of arched galleries water-carved in sandstone cliff. The shelf of the lowest gallery was six or seven meters above the sloping stand of soil below. The canyon dropped rapidly here; Rod could visualize a flume from upstream, bringing running water right to the caves . . . not right away, but when they had time to devise tools and cope with the problems. Someday, someday—but in the meantime here was plenty of room for the colony in a spot which almost defended itself. Not to mention, he added, being in out of the rain.

Roy was the better Alpinist; he inched up, flat to the rock, reached the shelf and threw down his line to Rod—snaked him up quickly. Rod got an arm over the edge, scrambled to his knees, stood up—and gasped, "What the deuce!"

"That," said Roy, "is why I kept quiet. I thought you would think I was crazy."

"I think we both are." Rod stared around. Filling the depth of the gallery, not seen from below, was terrace on terrace of cliff dwellings.

They were not inhabited, nor had they ever been by men. Openings which must have been doors were no higher than a man's knee, not wide enough for shoulders. But it was clear that they were dwellings, not merely formations carved by water. There were series of rooms arranged in half a dozen low stories from floor to ceiling of the gallery. The material was a concrete of dried mud, an adobe, used with wood.

But there was nothing to suggest what had built them. Roy started to stick his head into an opening; Rod shouted, "Hey! Don't do that!"

"Why not? It's abandoned."

"You don't know what might be inside. Snakes, maybe."

"There are no snakes. Nobody's ever seen one."

"No . . . but take it easy."

"I wish I had a torch light."

"I wish I had eight beautiful dancing girls and a Cadillac copter. Be careful. I don't want to walk back alone."

They lunched in the gallery and considered the matter. "Of course they were intelligent," Roy declared. "We may find them elsewhere. Maybe really civilized now—these look like ancient ruins."

"Not necessarily intelligent," Rod argued. "Bees make more complicated homes."

"Bees don't combine mud and wood the way these people did. Look at that lintel."

"Birds do. I'll concede that they were bird-brained, no more."

"Rod, you won't look at the evidence."

"Where are their artifacts? Show me one ash tray marked 'Made in Jersey City.' "

"I might find some if you weren't so jumpy."

"All in time. Anyhow, the fact that *they* found it safe shows that we can live here."

"Maybe. What killed them? Or why did they go away?"

They searched two galleries after lunch, found more dwellings. The dwellers had apparently formed a very large community. The fourth gallery they explored was almost empty, containing a beginning of a hive in one corner. Rod looked it over. "We can use this. It may not be the best, but we can move the gang in and then find the best at our leisure."

"We're heading back?"

"Uh, in the morning. This is a good place to sleep and tomorrow we'll travel from 'can' to 'can't'—I wonder what's up there?" Rod was looking at a secondary shelf inside the main arch.

Roy eyed it. "I'll let you know in a moment."

"Don't bother. It's almost straight up. We'll build ladders for spots like that."

"My mother was a human fly, my father was a mountain goat. Watch me."

The shelf was not much higher than his head. Roy had a hand over—when a piece of rock crumbled away. He did not fall far.

Rod ran to him. "You all right, boy?"

Roy grunted, "I guess so," then started to get up. He yelped.

"What's the matter?"

"My right leg. I think . . . ow! I think it's broken."

Rod examined the break, then went down to cut splints. With a piece of the line Roy carried, used economically, for he needed most of it as a ladder, he bound the leg, padding it with leaves. It was a simple break of the tibia, with no danger of infection.

They argued the whole time. "Of course you will," Roy was saying. "Leave me a fresh kill and what salt meat there is. You can figure some way to leave water."

"Come back and find your chawed bones!"

"Not at all. Nothing can get at me. If you hustle, you can make it in three days."

"Four, or five more likely. Six days to lead a party back. Then you want to go back in a stretcher? How would you like to be helpless when a stobor jumps us?"

"But I wouldn't go back. The gang would be moving down here."

"Suppose they do? Eleven days, more likely twelve—Roy, you didn't just bang your shin; you banged your head, too."

The stay in the gallery while Roy's leg repaired was not difficult nor dangerous; it was merely tedious. Rod would have liked to explore all the caves, but the first time he was away longer than Roy thought necessary to make a kill Rod returned to find his patient almost hysterical. He had let his imagination run away, visioning Rod as dead and thinking about his own death, helpless, while he starved or died of thirst. After that Rod left him only to gather food and water. The gallery was safe from all dangers; no watch was necessary, fire was needed only for cooking. The weather was getting warmer and the daily rains dropped off.

They discussed everything from girls to what the colony needed, what could have caused the disaster that had stranded them, what they would have to eat if they could have what they wanted, and back to girls again. They did not discuss the possibility of rescue; they took it for granted that they were there to stay. They slept much of the time and often did nothing, in animal-like torpor.

Roy wanted to start back as soon as Rod removed the splints, but it took him only seconds to discover that he no longer knew how to walk. He exercised for days, then grew sulky when Rod still insisted that he was not able to travel; the accumulated irritations of invalidism spewed out in the only quarrel they had on the trip.

Rod grew as angry as he was, threw Roy's climbing rope at him and shouted, "Go ahead! See how far you get on that gimp leg!"

Five minutes later Rod was arranging a sling, half dragging Roy, white and trembling and thoroughly subdued, back up onto the shelf. Thereafter they spent ten days getting Roy's muscles into shape, then started back.

Shorty Dumont was the first one they ran into as they approached the settlement. His jaw dropped and he looked scared, then he ran to greet them, ran back to alert those in camp. "Hey, everybody! They're *back!*"

Caroline heard the shout, outdistanced the others in great flying leaps, kissed and hugged them both. "Hi, Carol," Rod said. "What are you bawling about?"

"Oh, Roddie, you bad, *bad* boy!"

12

"It Won't Work, Rod"

IN THE MIDST OF JUBILATION ROD HAD TIME TO NOTICE MANY CHANGES. There were more than a dozen new buildings, including two long shed-like affairs of bamboo and mud. One new hut was of sunbaked brick; it had windows. Where the cooking fire had been was a barbecue pit and by it a Dutch oven. Near it a stream of water spilled out of bamboo pipe, splashed through a rawhide net, fell into a rock bowl, and was led away to the creek . . . he hardly knew whether to be pleased or irked at this anticipation of his own notion.

He caught impressions piecemeal, as their triumphal entry was interrupted by hugs, kisses, and bone-jarring slaps on the back, combined with questions piled on questions. "No, no trouble—except that Roy got mad and busted his leg . . . yeah, sure, we found what we went after; wait till you *see* . . . no . . . yes . . . Jackie! . . . Hi, Bob!—it's good to see you, too, boy! Where's Carmen . . . Hi, Grant!"

Cowper was grinning widely, white teeth splitting his beard. Rod noticed with great surprise that the man looked *old*—why, shucks, Grant wasn't more than twenty-two, twenty-three at the most. Where did he pick up those lines?

"Rod, old boy! I don't know whether to have you two thrown in the hoosegow or decorate your brows with laurel."

"We got held up."

"So it seems. Well, there is more rejoicing for the strayed lamb than for the ninety and nine. Come on up to the city hall."

"The what?"

Cowper looked sheepish. "They call it that, so I do. Better than 'Number Ten, Downing Street' which it started off with. It's just the hut where I sleep—it doesn't belong to me," he added. "When they elect somebody else, I'll sleep in bachelor hall." Grant led them toward a little building apart from the others and facing the cooking area.

The wall was gone.

Rod suddenly realized what looked strange about the upstream end of the settlement; the wall was gone completely and in its place was a thornbush barricade. He opened his mouth to make a savage comment—then realized that it really did not matter. Why kick up a row when the colony would be moving to the canyon of the Dwellers? They would never need walls again; they would be up high at night, with their ladders pulled up after them. He picked another subject.

"Grant, how in the world did you guys get the inner partitions out of those bamboo pipes?"

"Eh? Nothing to it. You tie a knife with rawhide to a thinner bamboo pole, then reach in and whittle. All it takes is patience. Waxie worked it out. But you haven't seen anything yet. We're going to have *iron.*"

"Huh?"

"We've got ore; now we are experimenting. But I do wish we could locate a seam of coal. Say, you didn't spot any, did you?"

Dinner was a feast, a *luau*, a celebration to make the weddings look pale. Rod was given a real plate to eat on—unglazed, lopsided, ungraceful, but a plate. As he took out Colonel Bowie, Margery Chung Kinksi put a wooden spoon in his hand. "We don't have enough to go around, but the guests of honor rate them tonight." Rod looked at it curiously. It felt odd in his hand.

Dinner consisted of boiled greens, some root vegetables new to him, and a properly baked haunch served in thin slices. Roy and Rod were served little unleavened cakes like tortillas. No one else had them, but Rod decided that it was polite not to comment on that. Instead he made a fuss over eating bread again.

Margery dimpled. "We'll have plenty of bread some day. Maybe next year."

There were tart little fruits for dessert, plus a bland, tasteless sort which resembled a dwarf banana with seeds. Rod ate too much.

Grant called them to order and announced that he was going to ask the travelers to tell what they had experienced. "Let them get it all told—then they won't have to tell it seventy times over. Come on, Rod. Let's see your ugly face."

"Ah, let Roy. He talks better than I do."

"Take turns. When your voice wears out, Roy can take over."

Between them they told it all, interrupting and supplementing each other. The colonists were awed by the beach of a billion bones, still more interested in the ruins of the Dwellers. "Rod and I are still arguing," Roy told them. "I say that it was a civilization. He says that it could be just instinct. He's crazy with the heat; the Dwellers were *people*. Not humans, of course, but people."

"Then where are they now?"

Roy shrugged. "Where are the Selenites, Dora? What became of the Mithrans?"

"Roy is a romanticist," Rod objected. "But you'll be able to form your own opinions when we get there."

"That's right, Rod," Roy agreed.

"That covers everything," Rod went on. "The rest was just waiting while Roy's leg healed. But it brings up the main subject. How quickly can we move? Grant, is there any reason not to start at once? Shouldn't we break camp tomorrow and start trekking? I've been studying it—how to make the move, I mean—and I would say to send out an advance party at daybreak. Roy or I can lead it. We go downstream an easy day's journey, pick a spot, make a kill, and have fire and food ready when the rest arrive. We do it again the next day. I think we can be safe and snug in the caves in five days."

"Dibs on the advance party!"

"Me, too!"

There were other shouts but Rod could not help but realize that the response was not what he had expected. Jimmy did not volunteer and Caroline merely looked thoughtful. The Baxters he could not see; they were in shadow.

He turned to Cowper. "Well, Grant? Do you have a better idea?"

"Rod," Grant said slowly, "your plan is okay . . . but you've missed a point."

"Yes?"

"Why do you assume that we are going to move?"

"*Huh?* Why, that's what we were sent for! To find a better place to live. We found it—you could hold those caves against an army. What's the hitch? Of *course* we move!"

Cowper examined his nails. "Rod, don't get sore. I don't see it and I doubt if other people do. I'm not saying the spot you and Roy found is not good. It may be better than here—the way this place used to be. But we are doing all right here—and we've got a lot of time and effort invested. Why move?"

"Why, I told you. The caves are safe, completely safe. This spot is exposed . . . it's *dangerous.*"

"Maybe. Rod, in the whole time we've been here, nobody has been hurt inside camp. We'll put it to a vote, but you can't expect us to abandon our houses and everything we have worked for to avoid a danger that may be imaginary."

"Imaginary? Do you think that a stobor couldn't jump that crummy barricade?" Rod demanded, pointing.

"I think a stobor would get a chest full of pointed stakes if he tried it," Grant answered soberly. "That 'crummy barricade' is a highly efficient defense. Take a better look in the morning."

"Where we were you wouldn't need it. You wouldn't need a night watch. Shucks, you wouldn't need houses. Those caves are better than the best house here!"

"Probably. But, Rod, you haven't seen all we've done, how much we would have to abandon. Let's look it over in the daylight, fellow, and then talk."

"Well . . . no, Grant, there is only one issue: the caves are safe; this place isn't. I call for a vote."

"Easy now. This isn't a town meeting. It's a party in your honor. Let's not spoil it."

"Well . . . I'm sorry. But we're all here; let's vote."

"No." Cowper stood up. "There will be a town meeting on Friday as usual. Goodnight, Rod. Goodnight, Roy. We're awfully glad you're back. Goodnight all."

The party gradually fell apart. Only a few of the younger boys seemed to want to discuss the proposed move. Bob Baxter came over, put a hand on Rod and said, "See you in the morning, Rod. Bless you." He left before Rod could get away from a boy who was talking to him.

Jimmy Throxton stayed, as did Caroline. When he got the chance Rod said, "Jimmy? Where do you stand?"

"Me? You know me, pal. Look, I sent Jackie to bed; she wasn't feeling well. But she told me to tell you that we were back of you a hundred per cent, always."

"Thanks. I feel better."

"See you in the morning? I want to check on Jackie."

"Sure. Sleep tight."

He was finally left with Caroline. "Roddie? Want to inspect the guard with me? You'll do it after tonight, but we figured you could use a night with no worries."

"Wait a minute. Carol . . . you've been acting funny."

"Me? Why, Roddie!"

"Well, maybe not. What do you think of the move? I didn't hear you pitching in."

She looked away. “Roddie,” she said, “if it was just me, I’d say start tomorrow. I’d be on the advance party.”

“Good! What’s got into these people? Grant has them buffaloed but I can’t see why.” He scratched his head. “I’m tempted to make up my own party—you, me, Jimmy and Jack, the Baxters, Roy, the few who were rarin’ to go tonight, and anybody else with sense enough to pound sand.”

She sighed. “It won’t work, Roddie.”

“Huh? Why not?”

“I’ll go. Some of the youngsters would go for the fun of it. Jimmy and Jack would go if you insisted . . . but they would beg off if you made it easy for them. The Baxters should not and I doubt if Bob would consent. Carmen isn’t really up to such a trip.”

13

Unkillable

THE MATTER NEVER CAME TO A VOTE. LONG BEFORE FRIDAY ROD KNEW how a vote would go—about fifty against him, less than half that for him, with his friends voting with him through loyalty rather than conviction . . . or possibly against him in a showdown.

He made an appeal in private to Cowper. "Grant, you've got me licked. Even Roy is sticking with you now. But you could swing them around."

"I doubt it. What you don't see, Rod, is that we have taken root. You may have found a better place . . . but it's too late to change. After all, you picked this spot."

"Not exactly, it . . . well, it just sort of happened."

"Lots of things in life just sort of happen. You make the best of them."

"That's what I'm *trying* to do! Grant, admitted that the move is hard; we could manage it. Set up way stations with easy jumps, send our biggest huskies back for what we don't want to abandon. Shucks, we could move a person on a litter if we had to—using enough guards."

"If the town votes it, I'll be for it. But I won't try to argue them into it. Look, Rod, you've got this fixed idea that this spot is dangerously exposed. The facts don't support you. On the other hand see what we have. Running water from upstream, waste disposal downstream, quarters comfortable and adequate for the climate. Salt—do you have salt there?"

"We didn't look for it—but it would be easy to bring it from the seashore."

"We've got it closer here. We've got prospects of metal. You haven't seen that ore outcropping yet, have you? We're better equipped every day; our standard of living is going up. We have a colony nobody need be ashamed of and we did it with bare hands; we were never meant to be a colony. Why throw up what we have gained to squat in caves like savages?"

Rod sighed. "Grant, this bank may be flooded in the rainy season—aside from its poor protection now."

"It doesn't look it to me, but if so, we'll see it in time. Right now we are going into the dry season. So let's talk it over a few months from now."

Rod gave up. He refused to resume as "City Manager" nor would Caroline keep it when Rod turned it down. Bill Kennedy was appointed and Rod went to work under Cliff as a hunter, slept in the big shed upstream with the bachelors, and took his turn at night watch. The watch had been reduced to one man, whose duty was simply to tend fires. There was talk of cutting out the night fires, as fuel was no longer easy to find nearby and many seemed satisfied that the thorn barrier was enough.

Rod kept his mouth shut and stayed alert at night.

Game continued to be plentiful but became skittish. Buck did not come out of cover the way they had in rainy weather; it was necessary to search and drive them out. Carnivores seemed to have become scarcer. But the first real indication of peculiar seasonal habits of native fauna came from a very minor carnivore. Mick Mahmud returned to camp with a badly chewed foot; Bob Baxter patched him up and asked about it.

"You wouldn't believe it."

"Try me."

"Well, it was just a dopy joe. I paid no attention to it, of course. Next thing I knew I was flat on my back and trying to shake it loose. He did all that to me before I got a knife into him. Then I had to cut his jaws loose."

"Lucky you didn't bleed to death."

When Rod heard Mick's story, he told Roy. Having had one experience with a dopy joe turned aggressive, Roy took it seriously and had Cliff warn all hands to watch out; they seemed to have turned nasty.

Three days later the migration of animals started.

At first it was just a drifting which appeared aimless except that it was always downstream. Animals had long since ceased to use the watering place above the settlement and buck rarely appeared in the little valley; now they began drifting into it, would find themselves baffled by the thorn fence, and would scramble out. Nor was it confined to antelope types; wingless birds with great "false faces," rodents, rooters, types nameless to humans, all joined the migration. One of the monstrous leonine predators they called stobor approached the barricade in broad daylight, looked at it, lashed his tail, then clawed his way up the bluff and headed downstream again.

Cliff called off his hunting parties; there was no need to hunt when game walked into camp.

Rod found himself more edgy than usual that night as it grew dark. He left his seat near the barbecue pit and went over to Jimmy and Jacqueline. "What's the matter with this place? It's spooky."

Jimmy twitched his shoulders. "I feel it. Maybe it's the funny way the animals are acting. Say, did you hear they killed a joe inside camp?"

"I know what it is," Jacqueline said suddenly. "No 'Grand Opera.' "

"Grand Opera" was Jimmy's name for the creatures with the awful noises, the ones which had turned Rod's first night into a siege of terror. They serenaded every evening for the first hour of darkness. Rod's mind had long since blanked them out, heeded them no more than chorusing cicadas. He had not consciously heard them for weeks.

Now they failed to wail on time; it upset him.

He grinned sheepishly. "That's it, Jack. Funny how you get used to a thing. Do you suppose they are on strike?"

"More likely a death in the family," Jimmy answered. "They'll be back in voice tomorrow."

Rod had trouble getting to sleep. When the night watch gave an alarm he was up and out of bachelors' barracks at once, Colonel Bowie in hand. "What's up?"

Arthur Nielsen had the watch. "It's all right now," he answered nervously. "A big buffalo buck crashed the fence. And this got through." He indicated the carcass of a dopy joe.

"You're bleeding."

"Just a nip."

Others gathered around. Cowper pushed through, sized the situation and said, "Waxie, get that cut attended to. Bill . . . where's Bill? Bill, put somebody else on watch. And let's get that gap fixed as soon as it's light."

It was greying in the east. Margery suggested, "We might as well stay up and have breakfast. I'll get the fire going." She left to borrow flame from a watch fire.

Rod peered through the damaged barricade. A big buck was down on the far side and seemed to have at least six dopy joes clinging to it. Cliff was there and said quietly, "See a way to get at them?"

"Only with a gun."

"We can't waste ammo on that."

"No." Rod thought about it, then went to a pile of bamboo poles, cut for building. He selected a stout one a head shorter than himself, sat down and began to bind Lady Macbeth to it with rawhide, forming a crude pike spear.

Caroline came over and squatted down. "What are you doing?"

"Making a joe-killer."

She watched him. "I'm going to make me one," she said suddenly and jumped up.

By daylight the animals were in full flight downstream as if chased by forest fire. As the creek had shrunk with the dry season a miniature beach, from a meter to a couple of meters wide, had been exposed below the bank on which the town had grown. The thorn kraal had been extended to cover the gap, but the excited animals crushed through this weak point and now streamed along the water past the camp.

After a futile effort no attempt was made to turn them back. They were pouring into the valley; they had to go somewhere, and the route between water and bank made a safety valve. It kept them from shoving the barricade aside by sheer mass. The smallest animals came through it anyhow, kept going, paid no attention to humans.

Rod stayed at the barricade, ate breakfast standing up. He had killed six joes since dawn while Caroline's score was still higher. Others were making knives into spears and joining them. The dopy joes were not coming through in great numbers; most of them continued to chase buck along the lower route past camp. Those who did seep through were speared; meeting them with a knife gave away too much advantage.

Cowper and Kennedy, inspecting defenses, stopped by Rod; they looked worried. "Rod," said Grant, "how long is this going to last?"

"How should I know? When we run out of animals. It looks like—get him, Shorty! It looks as if the joes were driving the others, but I don't think they are. I think they've *all* gone crazy."

"But what would cause that?" demanded Kennedy.

"Don't ask me. But I think I know where all those bones on that beach came from. But don't ask why. Why does a chicken cross the road? Why do lemmings do what they do? What makes a plague of locusts? Behind you! *Jump!*"

Kennedy jumped, Rod finished off a joe, and they went on talking. "Better detail somebody to chuck these into the water, Bill, before they stink. Look, Grant, we're okay now, but I know what I would do."

"What? Move to your caves? Rod, you were right—but it's too late."

"No, no! That's spilt milk; forget it. The thing that scares me are these mean little devils. They are no longer dopy; they are fast as can be and nasty . . . and they can slide through the fence. We can handle them now—but how about when it gets dark? We've got to have a solid line of fire inside the fence and along the bank. Fire is one thing they can't go through . . . I hope."

"That'll take a lot of wood." Grant looked through the barricade and frowned.

"You bet it will. But it will get us through the night. See here, give me the ax and six men with spears. I'll lead the party."

Kennedy shook his head. "It's my job."

"No, Bill," Cowper said firmly. "I'll lead it. You stay here and take care of the town."

Before the day was over Cowper took two parties out and Bill and Rod led one each. They tried to pick lulls in the spate of animals but Bill's party was caught on the bluff above, where it had been cutting wood and throwing it down past the cave. They were treed for two hours. The little valley had been cleaned out of dead wood months since; it was necessary to go into the forest above to find wood that would burn.

Cliff Pawley, hunter-in-chief, led a fifth party in the late afternoon, immediately broke the handle of the little ax. They returned with what they could gather with knives. While they were away one of the giant buck they called buffalo stampeded off the bluff, fell into camp, broke its neck. Four dopy joes were clinging to it. They were easy to kill as they would not let go.

Jimmy and Rod were on pike duty at the barricade. Jimmy glanced back at where a couple of girls were disposing of the carcasses. "Rod," he said thoughtfully, "we got it wrong. *Those* are stobor . . . the *real* stobor."

"Huh?"

"The big babies we've been calling that aren't 'stobor.' *These* things are what the Deacon warned us against."

"Well . . . I don't care what you call them as long as they're dead. On your toes, boy; here they come again."

Cowper ordered fires laid just before dark and was studying how to arrange one stretch so as not to endanger the flume when the matter was settled; the structure quivered and water ceased to flow. Upstream something had crashed into it and broken the flimsy pipe line.

The town had long since abandoned waterskins. Now they were caught with only a few litres in a pot used by the cooks, but it was a hardship rather than a danger; the urgent need was to get a ring of fire around them. There had already been half a dozen casualties—no deaths but bites and slashings, almost all from the little carnivores contemptuously known as dopy joes. The community's pool of antiseptics, depleted by months of use and utterly irreplaceable, had sunk so low that Rob Baxter used it only on major wounds.

When fuel had been stretched ready to burn in a long arc inside the barricade and down the bank to where it curved back under the cave, the results of a hard day's work looked small; the stockpile was not much greater than the amount already spread out. Bill Kennedy looked at it. "It won't last the night, Grant."

"It's *got* to, Bill. Light it."

"If we pulled back from the fence and the bank, then cut over to the bluff— What do you think?"

Cowper tried to figure what might be saved by the change. "It's not much shorter. Uh, don't light the downstream end unless they start curving back in on us. But let's move; it's getting dark." He hurried to the cooking fire, got a brand and started setting the chain of fire. Kennedy helped and soon the townsite was surrounded on the exposed sides by blaze. Cowper chucked his torch into the fire and said, "Bill, better split the men into two watches and get the women up into the cave—they can crowd in somehow."

"You'll have trouble getting thirty-odd women in there, Grant."

"They can sit up all night. But send them up. Yes, and the wounded men, too."

"Can do." Kennedy started passing the word. Caroline came storming up, spear in hand.

"Grant, what's this nonsense about the girls having to go up to the cave? If you think you're going to cut me out of the fun you had better think again!"

Cowper looked at her wearily. "Carol, I haven't time to monkey. Shut your face and do as you are told."

Caroline opened her mouth, closed it, and did as she was told. Bob Baxter claimed Cowper's attention; Rod noticed that he looked very upset. "Grant? You ordered all the women up to the cave?"

"Yes."

"I'm sorry but Carmen can't."

"You'll have to carry her. She is the one I had most on my mind when I decided on the move."

"But—" Baxter stopped and urged Grant away from the others. He spoke insistently but quietly. Grant shook his head.

"It's not safe, Grant," Baxter went on, raising his voice. "I don't dare risk it. The interval is nineteen minutes now."

"Well . . . all right. Leave a couple of women with her. Use Caroline, will you? That'll keep her out of my hair."

"Okay." Baxter hurried away.

Kennedy took the first watch with a dozen men spread out along the fire line; Rod was on the second watch commanded by Cliff Pawley. He went to the Baxter house to find out how Carmen was doing, was told to beat it by Agnes. He then went to the bachelors' shed and tried to sleep.

He was awakened by yells, in time to see one of the leonine monsters at least five meters long go bounding through the camp and disappear downstream. It had jumped the barrier, the stakes behind it, and the fire behind that, all in one leap.

Rod called out, "Anybody hurt?"

Shorty Dumont answered. "No. It didn't even stop to wave." Shorty was bleeding from a slash in his left calf; he seemed unaware of it. Rod crawled back inside, tried again to sleep.

He was awakened again by the building shaking. He hurried out. "What's up?"

"That you, Rod? I didn't know anybody was inside. Give me a hand; we're going to burn it." The voice was Baxter's; he was prying at a corner post and cutting rawhide strips that held it.

Rod put his spear where it would not be stepped on, resheathed Colonel Bowie, and started to help. The building was bamboo and leaves, with a mud-and-thatch roof; most of it would burn. "How's Carmen?"

"Okay. Normal progress. I can do more good here. Besides they don't *want* me." Baxter brought the corner of the shed down with a crash, gathered a double armful of wreckage and hurried away. Rod picked up a load and followed him.

The reserve wood pile was gone; somebody was tearing the roof off the "city hall" and banging pieces on the ground to shake clay loose. The walls were sun-baked bricks, but the roof would burn. Rod came closer, saw that it was Cowper who was destroying this symbol of the sovereign community. He worked with the fury of anger. "Let me do that, Grant. Have you had any rest?"

"Huh? No."

"Better get some. It's going to be a long night. What time is it?"

"I don't know. Midnight, maybe." Fire blazed up and Cowper faced it, wiping his face with his hand. "Rod, take charge of the second watch and relieve Bill. Cliff got clawed and I sent him up."

"Okay. Burn everything that will burn—right?"

"Everything but the roof of the Baxter house. But don't use it up too fast; it's got to last till morning."

"Got it." Rod hurried to the fire line, found Kennedy. "Okay, Bill,

I'll take over—Grant's orders. Get some sleep. Anything getting through?"

"Not much. And not far." Kennedy's spear was dark with blood in the firelight. "I'm not going to sleep, Rod. Find yourself a spot and help out."

Rod shook his head. "You're groggy. Beat it. Grant's orders."

"No!"

"Well . . . look, take your gang and tear down the old maids' shack. That'll give you a change, at least."

"Uh—all right." Kennedy left, almost staggering. There was a lull in the onrush of animals; Rod could see none beyond the barricade. It gave him time to sort out his crew, send away those who had been on duty since sunset, send for stragglers. He delegated Doug Sanders and Mick Mahmud as firetenders, passed the word that no one else was to put fuel on the fires.

He returned from his inspection to find Bob Baxter, spear in hand, holding his place at the center of the line. Rod put a hand on his shoulder. "The medical officer doesn't need to fight. We aren't that bad off."

Baxter shrugged. "I've got my kit, what there is left of it. This is where I use it."

"Haven't you enough worries?"

Baxter grinned wanly. "Better than walking the floor. Rod, they're stirring again. Hadn't we better build up the fires?"

"Mmm . . . not if we're going to make it last. I don't think they can come through that."

Baxter did not answer, as a joe came through at that instant. It ploughed through the smouldering fire and Baxter speared it. Rod cupped his hands and shouted, "Build up the fires! But go *easy.*"

"Behind you, Rod!"

Rod jumped and whirled, got the little devil. "Where did that one come from? I didn't see it."

Before Bob could answer Caroline came running out of darkness. "Bob! Bob Baxter! I've got to find Bob Baxter!"

"Over here!" Rod called.

Baxter was hardly able to speak. "Is she—is she?" His face screwed up in anguish.

"No, no!" yelled Caroine. "She's all right, she's fine. *It's a girl!*"

Baxter quietly fainted, his spear falling to the ground. Caroline grabbed him and kept him from falling into the fire. He opened his eyes and said, "Sorry. You scared me. You're sure Carmen is all right?"

"Right as rain. The baby, too. About three kilos. Here, give me that sticker—Carmen wants you."

Baxter stumbled away and Caroline took his place. She grinned at Rod. "I feel *swell!* How's business, Roddie? Brisk? I feel like getting me eight or nine of these vermin."

Cowper came up a few minutes later. Caroline called out, "Grant, did you hear the good news?"

"Yes. I just came from there." He ignored Caroline's presence at the guard line but said to Rod, "We're making a stretcher out of pieces of the flume and they're going to haul Carmen up. Then they'll throw the stretcher down and you can burn it."

"Good."

"Agnes is taking the baby up. Rod, what's the very most we can crowd into the cave?"

"Gee!" Rod glanced up at the shelf. "They must be spilling off the edge now."

"I'm afraid so. But we've just *got* to pack them in. I want to send up all married men and the youngest boys. The bachelors will hold on here."

"I'm a bachelor!" Caroline interrupted.

Cowper ignored her. "As soon as Carmen is safe we'll do it—we can't keep fires going much longer." He turned away, headed up to the cave.

Caroline whistled softly. "Roddie, we're going to have fun."

"Not my idea of fun. Hold the fort, Carol. I've got to line things up." He moved down the line, telling each one to go or to stay.

Jimmy scowled at him. "I won't go, not as long as anybody stays. I couldn't look Jackie in the face."

"You'll button your lip and do as Grant says—or I'll give you a mouthful of teeth. Hear me?"

"I hear you. I don't like it."

"You don't have to like it, just do it. Seen Jackie? How is she?"

"I snuck up a while ago. She's all right, just queasy. But the news about Carmen makes her feel so good she doesn't care."

Rod used no age limit to determine who was expendable. With the elimination of married men, wounded, and all women he had little choice; he simply told those whom he considered too young or not too skilled that they were to leave when word was passed. It left him with half a dozen, plus himself, Cowper, and—possibly—Caroline. Trying to persuade Caroline was a task he had postponed.

He returned and found Cowper. "Carmen's gone up," Cowper told him. "You can send the others up now."

"Then we can burn the roof of the Baxter house."

"I tore it down while they were hoisting her." Cowper looked around. "Carol! Get on up."

She set her feet. "I won't!"

Rod said softly, "Carol, you heard him. Go up—*right now!*"

She scowled, stuck out her lip, then said, "All right for *you*, Roddie Walker!"—turned and fled up the path.

Rod cupped his hands and shouted, "All right, everybody! All hands up but those I told to stay. Hurry!"

About half of those leaving had started up when Agnes called down, "Hey! Take it slow! Somebody will get pushed over the edge if you don't quit shoving."

The queue stopped. Jimmy called out, "Everybody exhale. That'll do it."

Somebody called back, "Throw Jimmy off . . . *that* will do it." The line moved again, slowly. In ten minutes they accomplished the sardine-packing problem of fitting nearly seventy people into a space comfortable for not more than a dozen. It could not even be standing room since a man could stand erect only on the outer shelf. The girls were shoved inside, sitting or squatting, jammed so that they hardly had air to breathe. The men farthest out could stand but were in danger of stepping off the edge in the dark, or of being elbowed off.

Grant said, "Watch things, Rod, while I have a look." He disappeared up the path, came back in a few minutes. "Crowded as the bottom of a sack," he said. "Here's the plan. They can scrunch back farther if they have to. It will be uncomfortable for the wounded and Carmen may have to sit up—she's lying down—but it can be done. When the fires die out, we'll shoehorn the rest in. With spears poking out under the overhang at the top of the path we ought to be able to hold out until daylight. Check me?"

"Sounds as good as can be managed."

"All right. When the time comes, you go up next to last, I go up last."

"Unh . . . I'll match you."

Cowper answered with surprising vulgarity and added, "I'm boss; I go last. We'll make the rounds and pile anything left on the fires, then gather them all here. You take the bank, I take the fence."

It did not take long to put the remnants on the fires, then they gathered around the path and waited—Roy, Kenny, Doug, Dick, Charlie, Howard, and Rod and Grant. Another wave of senseless migration was rolling but the fires held it, bypassed it around by the water.

Rod grew stiff and shifted his spear to his left hand. The dying fires were only glowing coals in spots. He looked for signs of daylight in the east. Howard Goldstein said, "One broke through at the far end."

"Hold it, Goldie," Cowper said. "We won't bother it unless it comes here." Rod shifted his spear back to his right hand.

The wall of fire was now broken in many places. Not only could joes get through, but worse, it was hard to see them, so little light did the embers give off. Cowper turned to Rod and said, "All right, everybody up. You tally them." Then he shouted, "Bill! Agnes! Make room, I'm sending them up."

Rod threw a glance at the fence, then turned. "Okay, Kenny first. Doug next, don't crowd. Goldie and then Dick. Who's left? Roy—" He turned, uneasily aware that something had changed.

Grant was no longer behind him. Rod spotted him bending over a dying fire. "Hey, Grant!"

"Be right with you." Cowper selected a stick from the embers, waved it into flame. He hopped over the coals, picked his way through sharpened stakes, reached the thornbush barrier, shoved his torch into it. The dry branches flared up. He moved slowly away, picking his way through the stake trap.

"I'll help you!" Rod shouted. "I'll fire the other end."

Cowper turned and light from the burning thorn showed his stern, bearded face. "Stay back. Get the others up. That's an order!"

The movement upward had stopped. Rod snarled, "Get on up, you lunkheads! Move!" He jabbed with the butt of his spear, then turned around.

Cowper had set the fire in a new place. He straightened up, about to move farther down, suddenly turned and jumped over the dying line of fire. He stopped and jabbed at something in the darkness . . . then screamed.

"Grant!" Rod jumped down, ran toward him. But Grant was down before he reached him, down with a joe worrying each leg and more coming. Rod thrust at one, jerked his spear out, and jabbed at the other, trying not to stab Grant. He felt one grab his leg and wondered that it did not hurt.

Then it did hurt, terribly, and he realized that he was down and his spear was not in his hand. But his hand found his knife without asking; Colonel Bowie finished off the beast clamped to his ankle.

Everything seemed geared to nightmare slowness. Other figures were thrusting leisurely at shapes that hardly crawled. The thornbush, flaming high, gave him light to see and stab a dopy joe creeping toward him. He got it, rolled over and tried to get up.

* * *

He woke with daylight in his eyes, tried to move and discovered that his left leg hurt. He looked down and saw a compress of leaves wrapped with a neat hide bandage. He was in the cave and there were others lying parallel to him. He got to one elbow. "Say, what—"

"Sssh!" Sue Kennedy crawled over and knelt by him. "The baby is asleep."

"Oh . . ."

"I'm on nurse duty. Want anything?"

"I guess not. Uh, what did they name her?"

"Hope. Hope Roberta Baxter. A pretty name. I'll tell Caroline you are awake." She turned away.

Caroline came in, squatted and looked scornfully at his ankle. "That'll teach you to have a party and not invite *me.*"

"I guess so. Carol, what's the situation?"

"Six on the sick list. About twice that many walking wounded. Those not hurt are gathering wood and cutting thorn. We fixed the ax."

"Yes, but . . . we're not having to fight them off?"

"Didn't Sue tell you? A few buck walking around as if they were dazed. That's all."

"They may start again."

"If they do, we'll be ready."

"Good." He tried to raise up. "Where's Grant? How bad was he hurt?"

She shook her head. "Grant didn't make it, Roddie."

"Huh?"

"Bob took off both legs at the knee and would have taken off one arm, but he died while he was operating." She made a very final gesture. "In the creek."

Rod started to speak, turned his head and buried his face. Caroline put a hand on him. "Don't take it hard, Roddie. Bob shouldn't have tried to save him. Grant is better off."

Rod decided that Carol was right—no frozen limb banks on *this* planet. But it did not make him feel better. "We didn't appreciate him," he muttered.

"Stow it!" Caroline whispered fiercely. "He was a fool."

"Huh? Carol, I'm ashamed of you."

He was surprised to see tears rolling down her cheeks. "You *know* he was a fool, Roddie Walker. Most of us knew . . . but we loved him anyhow. I would 'uv *married* him, but he never asked me." She wiped at tears. "Have you seen the baby?"

"No."

Her face lit up. "I'll fetch her. She's beautiful."

"Sue said she was asleep."

"Well . . . all right. But what I came up for is this: what do you want us to do?"

"Huh?" He tried to think. Grant was dead. "Bill was his deputy. Is Bill laid up?"

"Didn't Sue tell you?"

"Tell me what?"

"You're the mayor. We elected you this morning. Bill and Roy and I are just trying to hold things together."

Rod felt dizzy. Caroline's face kept drawing back, then swooping in; he wondered if he were going to faint.

"—plenty of wood," she was saying, "and we'll have the kraal built by sundown. We don't need meat; Margery is butchering that big fellow that fell off the bluff and busted his neck. We can't trek out until you and Carmen and the others can walk, so we're trying to get the place back into shape temporarily. Is there anything you want us to do now?"

He considered it. "No. Not now."

"Okay. You're supposed to rest." She backed out, stood up. "I'll look in later." Rod eased his leg and turned over. After a while he quieted and went to sleep.

Sue brought broth in a bowl, held his head while he drank, then fetched Hope Baxter and held her for him to see. Rod said the usual inanities, wondering if all new babies looked that way.

Then he thought for a long time.

Caroline showed up with Roy. "How's it going, Chief?" Roy said.

"Ready to bite a rattlesnake."

"That's a nasty foot, but it ought to heal. We boiled the leaves and Bob used sulfa."

"Feels all right. I don't seem feverish."

"Jimmy always said you were too mean to die," added Caroline. "Want anything, Roddie? Or to tell us anything?"

"Yes."

"What?"

"Get me out of here. Help me down the path."

Roy said hastily, "Hey, you can't do that. You're not in shape."

"Can't I? Either help, or get out of my way. And get everybody together. We're going to have a town meeting."

They looked at each other and walked out on him. He had made it to the squeeze at the top when Baxter showed up. "Now, Rod! Get back and lie down."

"Out of my way."

"Listen, boy, I don't like to get rough with a sick man. But I will if you make me."

"Bob . . . how bad is my ankle?"

"It's going to be all right . . . *if* you behave. If you don't—well, have you ever seen gangrene? When it turns black and has that sweetish odor?"

"Quit trying to scare me. Is there any reason not to put a line under my arms and lower me?"

"Well . . ."

They used two lines and a third to keep his injured leg free, with Baxter supervising. They caught him at the bottom and carried him to the cooking space, laid him down. "Thanks," he grunted. "Everybody here who can get here?"

"I think so, Roddie. Shall I count?"

"Never mind. I understand you folks elected me cap—I mean 'mayor'—this morning?"

"That's right," agreed Kennedy.

"Uh, who else was up? How many votes did I get?"

"Huh? It was unanimous."

Rod sighed. "Thanks. I'm not sure I would have held still for it if I'd been here. I gathered something else. Do I understand that you expect me to take you down to the caves Roy and I found? Caroline said something . . ."

Roy looked surprised. "We didn't vote it, Rod, but that was the idea. After last night everybody knows we can't stay here."

Rod nodded. "I see. Are you all where I can see you? I've got something to say. I hear you adopted a constitution and things while Roy and I were away. I've never read them, so I don't know whether this is legal or not. But if I'm stuck with the job, I expect to run things. If somebody doesn't like what I do and we're both stubborn enough for a showdown, then you will vote. You back me up, or you turn me down and elect somebody else. Will that work? How about it, Goldie? You were on the law committee, weren't you?"

Howard Goldstein frowned. "You don't express it very well, Rod."

"Probably not. Well?"

"But what you have described is the parliamentary vote-of-confidence. That's the backbone of our constitution. We did it that way to keep it simple and still democratic. It was Grant's notion."

"I'm glad," Rod said soberly. "I'd hate to think that I had torn up Grant's laws after he worked so hard on them. I'll study them, I promise, first chance I get. But about moving to the caves—we'll have a vote of confidence right now."

Goldstein smiled. "I can tell you how it will come out. We're convinced."

Rod slapped the ground. "You don't understand! If you want to move, move . . . but get somebody else to lead you. Roy can do it. Or Cliff, or Bill. But if you leave it to me, no dirty little beasts, all teeth and no brains, are going to drive us out. We're *men* . . . and men don't *have* to be driven out, not by the likes of those. Grant paid for this land—and I say stay here and keep it for him!"

14

Civilization

THE HONORABLE RODERICK L. WALKER, MAYOR OF COWPERTOWN, Chief of State of the sovereign planet GO-73901-II (Lima Catalog), Commander-in-Chief of the Armed Forces, Chief Justice, and Defender of Freedoms, was taking his ease in front of the Mayor's Palace. He was also scratching and wondering if he should ask somebody to cut his hair again—he suspected lice . . . only this planet did not have lice.

His Chief of Government, Miss Caroline Beatrice Mshiyeni, squatted in front of him. "Roddie, I've told them and told them and told them . . . and it does no good. That family makes more filth than everybody else put together. You should have seen it this morning. Garbage in front of their door . . . flies!"

"I saw it."

"Well, what do I do? If you would let me rough him up a little. But you're too soft."

"I guess I am." Rod looked thoughtfully at a slab of slate erected in the village square. It read:

To the Memory of
ULYSSES GRANT COWPER,
First Mayor
—who died for his city

The carving was not good; Rod had done it.

"Grant told me once," he added, "that government was the art of getting along with people you don't like."

"Well, I sure don't like Bruce and Theo!"

"Neither do I. But Grant would have figured out a way to keep them in line without getting rough."

"You figure it out, I can't. Roddie, you should never have let Bruce come back. That was bad enough. But when he married that little . . . well!"

"They were made for each other," Rod answered. "Nobody else would have married either of them."

"It's no joke. It's almost—*Hope!* Quit teasing Grantie!" She bounced up.

Miss Hope Roberta Baxter, sixteen months, and Master Grant Roderick Throxton, thirteen months, stopped what they were doing, which was, respectively, slapping and crying. Both were naked and very dirty. It was "clean" dirt; each child had been bathed by Caroline an hour earlier, and both were fat and healthy.

Hope turned up a beaming face. " '*Ood* babee!" she asserted.

"I *saw* you." Caroline upended her, gave her a spat that would not squash a fly, then picked up Grant Throxton.

"Give her to me," Rod said.

"You're welcome to her," Caroline said. She sat down with the boy in her lap and rocked him. "Poor baby! Show Auntie Carol where it hurts."

"You shouldn't talk like that. You'll make a sissy of him."

"Look who's talking! Wishy-Washy Walker."

Hope threw her arms around Rod, part way, and cooed, "Woddie!" adding a muddy kiss. He returned it. He considered her deplorably spoiled; nevertheless he contributed more than his share of spoiling.

"Sure," agreed Carol. "Everybody loves Uncle Roddie. He hands out the medals and Aunt Carol does the dirty work."

"Carol, I've been thinking."

"Warm day. Don't strain any delicate parts."

"About Bruce and Theo. I'll talk to them."

"Talk!"

"The only real punishment is one we never use—and I hope we never have to. Kicking people out, I mean. The McGowans do as they please because they don't think we would. But I would love to give them the old heave-ho . . . and if it comes to it, I'll make an issue of it before the town—either kick them out or I quit."

"They'd back you. Why, I bet he hasn't taken a bath this week!"

"I don't care whether they back me or not. I've ridden out seven confidence votes; someday I'll be lucky and retire. But the problem is to convince Bruce that I am willing to face the issue, for then I won't have to. Nobody is going to chance being turned out in the woods, not when they've got it soft here. But he's got to be convinced."

"Uh, maybe if he thought you were carrying a grudge about that slice in the ribs he gave you?"

"And maybe I am. But I can't let it be personal, Carol; I'm too stinkin' proud."

"Uh . . . Turn it around. Convince him that the town is chompin' at the bit—which isn't far wrong—and you are trying to restrain them."

"Um, that's closer. Yes, I think Grant would have gone for that. I'll think it over."

"Do that." She stood up. "I'm going to give these children another bath. I declare I don't know where they find so much dirt."

She swung away with a child on each hip, heading for the shower sheds. Rod watched her lazily. She was wearing a leather bandeau and a Maori grass skirt, long leaves scraped in a pattern, curled, and dried. It was a style much favored and Caroline wore it around town, although when she treated herself to a day's hunting she wore a leather breech-clout such as the men wore.

The same leaf fibre could be retted and crushed, combed and spun, but the cloth as yet possessed by the colony was not even enough for baby clothes. Bill Kennedy had whittled a loom for Sue and it worked, but neither well nor fast and the width of cloth was under a half meter. Still, Rod mused, it was progress, it was civilization. They had come a long way.

The town was stobor-tight now. An adobe wall too high and sheer for any but the giant lions covered the upstream side and the bank, and any lion silly enough to jump it landed on a bed of stakes too wide now for even their mighty leaps—the awning under which Rod lolled was the hide of one that had made that mistake. The wall was pierced by stobor traps, narrow tunnels just big enough for the vicious little beasts and which gave into deep pits, where they could chew on each other like Kilkenny cats—which they did.

It might have been easier to divert them around the town, but Rod wanted to kill them; he would not be content until their planet was rid of those vermin.

In the meantime the town was safe. Stobor continued to deserve the nickname "dopy joe" except during the dry season and then they did not become dangerous until the annual berserk migration—the last of which had passed without loss of blood; the colony's defenses worked, now that they understood what to defend against. Rod had required mothers and children to sit out the stampede in the cave; the rest sat up two nights and stayed on guard . . . but no blade was wet.

Rod thought sleepily that the next thing they needed was paper; Grant had been right . . . even a village was hard to run without writing paper. Besides, they must avoid losing the habit of writing. He wanted to follow up Grant's notion of recording every bit of knowledge the gang possessed. Take logarithms—logarithms might not be used for generations, but when it came time to log a couple of rhythms, then . . . he went to sleep.

"You busy, Chief?"

Rod looked up at Arthur Nielsen. "Just sleeping . . . a practice I heartily recommend on a warm Sabbath afternoon. What's up, Art? Are Shorty and Doug pushing the bellows alone?"

"No. Confounded plug came out and we lost our fire. The furnace is ruined." Nielsen sat down wearily. He was hot, very red in the face, and looked discouraged. He had a bad burn on a forearm but did not seem to know it. "Rod, what are we doing wrong? Riddle me that."

"Talk to one of the brains. If you didn't know more about it than I do, we'd swap jobs."

"I wasn't really asking. I know two things that are wrong. We can't build a big enough installation and we don't have coal. Rod, we've *got* to have coal; for cast iron or steel we need coal. Charcoal won't do for anything but spongy wrought iron."

"What do you expect to accomplish overnight, Art? Miracles? You are years ahead of what anybody could ask. You've turned out metal, whether it's wrought iron or uranium. Since you made that spit for the barbecue pit, Margery thinks you are a genius."

"Yes, yes, we've made iron—but it ought to be lots better and more of it. This ore is wonderful . . . the real Lake Superior hematite. Nobody's seen such ore in commercial quantity on Terra in centuries. You ought to be able to breathe on it and make steel. And I could, too, if I had coal. We've got clay, we've got limestone, we've got this lovely ore—but I *can't* get a hot enough fire."

Rod was not fretted; the colony was getting metal as fast as needed. But Waxie was upset. "Want to knock off and search for coal?"

"Uh . . . no, I don't. I want to rebuild that furnace." Nielsen gave a bitter description of the furnace's origin, habits, and destination.

"Who knows most about geology?"

"Uh, I suppose I do."

"Who knows next most?"

"Why, Doug I guess."

"Let's send him out with a couple of boys to find coal. You can have Mick in his place on the bellows—no, wait a minute. How about Bruce?"

"Bruce? *He* won't work."

"Work him. If you work him so hard he runs away and forgets to come back, we won't miss him. Take him, Art, as a favor to me."

"Well . . . okay, if you say so."

"Good. You get one bonus out of losing your batch. You won't miss the dance tonight. Art, you shouldn't start a melt so late in the week; you need your day of rest . . . and so do Shorty and Doug."

"I know. But when it's ready to go I want to fire it off. Working the way we do is discouraging; before you can make anything you have to make the thing that makes it—and usually you have to make something else to make that. Futile!"

"You don't know what 'futile' means. Ask our 'Department of Agriculture.' Did you take a look at the farm before you came over the wall?"

"Well, we walked through it."

"Better not let Cliff catch you, or he'll scalp you. I might hold you for him."

"Humph! A lot of silly grass! Thousands of hectares around just like it."

"That's right. Some grass and a few rows of weeds. The pity is that Cliff will never live to see it anything else. Nor little Cliff. Nevertheless our great grandchildren will eat white bread, Art. But you yourself will live to build precision machinery—you know it can be done, which, as Bob Baxter says, is two-thirds of the battle. Cliff *can't* live long enough to eat a slice of light, tasty bread. It doesn't stop him."

"You should have been a preacher, Rod." Art stood up and sniffed himself. "I'd better get a bath, or the girls won't dance with me."

"I was just quoting. You've heard it before. Save me some soap."

Caroline hit two bars of *Arkansas Traveler,* Jimmy slapped his drum, and Roy called, "Square 'em up, folks!" He waited, then started in high, nasal tones:

"Honor y'r *part*ners!

"Honor y'r *cor*ners!

"Now *all* jump *up* and *when* y' come *down*—"

Rod was not dancing; the alternate set would be his turn. The colony formed eight squares, too many for a caller, a mouth organ, and a primitive drum all unassisted by amplifying equipment. So half of them babysat and gossiped while the other half danced. The caller and the orchestra were relieved at each intermission to dance the other sets.

Most of them had not known how to square-dance. Agnes Pulvermacher had put it over almost single-handed, in the face of kidding and resistance—training callers, training dancers, humming tunes to Caroline, cajoling Jimmy to carve and shrink a jungle drum. Now she had nine out of ten dancing.

Rod had not appreciated it at first (he was not familiar with the history of the Mormon pioneers) and had regarded it as a nuisance which interfered with work. Then he saw the colony, which had experienced a bad letdown after the loss in one night of all they had built, an apathy he had not been able to lift—he saw this same colony begin to smile and joke and work hard simply from being exposed to music and dancing.

He decided to encourage it. He had trouble keeping time and could not carry a tune, but the bug caught him, too; he danced not well but with great enthusiasm.

The village eventually limited dances to Sabbath nights, weddings, and holidays—and made them "formal" . . . which meant that women wore grass skirts. Leather shorts, breechclouts, and slacks (those not long since cut up for rags) were not acceptable. Sue talked about making a real square dance dress as soon as she got far enough ahead in her weaving, and a cowboy shirt for her husband . . . but the needs of the colony made this a distant dream.

Music stopped, principals changed, Caroline tossed her mouth organ to Shorty, and came over. "Come on, Roddie, let's kick some dust."

"I asked Sue," he said hastily and truthfully. He was careful not to ask the same girl twice, never to pay marked attention to any female; he had promised himself long ago that the day he decided to marry should be the day he resigned and he was not finding it hard to stay married to his job. He liked to dance with Caroline; she was a popular partner—except for a tendency to swing her partner instead of letting him swing her—but he was careful not to spend much social time with her because she was his right hand, his alter ego.

Rod went over and offered his arm to Sue. He did not think about it; the stylized amenities of civilization were returning and the formal politenesses of the dance made them seem natural. He led her out and assisted in making a botch of *Texas Star*.

Later, tired, happy, and convinced that the others in his square had made the mistakes and he had straightened them out, Rod returned Sue to Bill, bowed and thanked him, and went back to the place that was always left for him. Margery and her assistants were passing out little brown somethings on wooden skewers. He accepted one. "Smells good, Marge. What are they?"

"Mock Nile birds. Smoked baby-buck bacon wrapped around hamburger. Salt and native sage, pan broiled. You'd better like it; it took us *hours.*"

"Mmmm! I do! How about another?"

"Wait and see. Greedy."

"But I need more. I work hardest. I have to keep up my strength."

"That was *work* I saw you doing this afternoon?" She handed him another.

"I was planning. The old brain was buzzing away."

"I heard the buzzing. Pretty loud, when you lie on your back."

He snagged a third as she turned away, looked up to catch Jacqueline smiling; he winked and grinned.

"Happy, Rod?"

"Yes indeedy. How about you, Jackie?"

"I've never been happier," she said seriously.

Her husband put an arm around her. "See what the love of a good man can do, Rod?" Jimmy said. "When I found this poor child she was beaten, bedraggled, doing your cooking and afraid to admit her name. Now look at her!—fat and sassy."

"I'm not *that* fat!"

"Pleasingly plump."

Rod glanced up at the cave. "Jackie, remember the night I showed up?"

"I'm not likely to forget."

"And the silly notion I had that this was Africa? Tell me—if you had it to do over, would you rather I had been right?"

"I never thought about it. I knew it was not."

"Yes, but 'if'? You would have been home long ago."

Her hand took her husband's. "I would not have met James."

"Oh, yes, you would. You had already met me. You could not have avoided it—my best friend."

"Possibly. But I would not change it. I have no yearning to go 'home,' Rod. *This* is home."

"Me neither," asserted Jimmy. "You know what? This colony gets a little bigger—and it's getting bigger fast—Goldie and I are going to open a law office. We won't have any competition and can pick our clients. He'll handle the criminal end, I'll specialize in divorce, and we'll collaborate on corporate skulduggery. We'll make *millions.* I'll drive a big limousine drawn by eight spanking buck, smoking a big cigar and sneering at the peasants." He called out, "Right, Goldie?"

"Precisely, colleague. I'm making us a shingle: 'Goldstein & Throxton—Get bailed, not jailed!' "

"Keerect. But make that: 'Throxton & Goldstein.' "

"I'm senior. I've got two more years of law."

"A quibble. Rod, are you going to let this Teller U. character insult an old Patrick Henry man?"

"Probably. Jimmy, I don't see how you are going to work this. I don't think we have a divorce law. Let's ask Caroline."

"A trifle. You perform the marriages, Rod; I'll take care of the divorces."

"Ask Caroline what?" asked Caroline.

"Do we have a divorce law?"

"Huh? We don't even have a getting-married law."

"Unnecessary," explained Goldstein. "Indigenous in the culture. Besides, we ran out of paper."

"Correct, Counselor," agreed Jimmy.

"Why ask?" Caroline demanded. "Nobody is thinking about divorce or I would know before they would."

"We weren't talking about that," Rod explained. "Jackie said that she had no wish to go back to Terra and Jimmy was elaborating. Uselessly, as usual."

Caroline stared. "Why would anybody want to go back?"

"Sure," agreed Jimmy. "This is the place. No income tax. No traffic, no crowds, no commercials, no telephones. Seriously, Rod, every one here was aiming for the Outlands or we wouldn't have been taking a survival test. So what difference does it make? Except that we've got everything sooner." He squeezed his wife's hand. "I was fooling about that big cigar; I'm rich now, boy, rich!"

Agnes and Curt had drawn into the circle, listening. Agnes nodded and said, "For once you aren't joking, Jimmy. The first months we were here I cried myself to sleep every night, wondering if they would ever find us. Now I know they never will—and I don't care! I wouldn't go back if I could; the only thing I miss is lipstick."

Her husband's laugh boomed out. "There you have the truth, Rod. The fleshpots of Egypt . . . put a cosmetics counter across this creek and every woman here will walk on water."

"That's not fair, Curt! Anyhow, you promised to make lipstick."

"Give me time."

Bob Baxter came up and sat down by Rod. "Missed you at the meeting this morning, Rod."

"Tied up. I'll make it next week."

"Good." Bob, being of a sect which did not require ordination, had made himself chaplain as well as medical officer simply by starting to hold meetings. His undogmatic ways were such that Christian, Jew, Monist, or Moslem felt at ease; his meetings were well attended.

"Bob, would *you* go back?"

"Go where, Caroline?"

"Back to Terra."

"Yes."

Jimmy looked horrified. "Boil me for breakfast! *Why?*"

"Oh, I'd want to come back! But I need to graduate from medical school." He smiled shyly. "I may be the best surgeon in the neighborhood, but that isn't saying much."

"Well . . ." admitted Jimmy, "I see your point. But you already suit us. Eh, Jackie?"

"Yes, Jimmy."

"It's my only regret," Bob went on. "I've lost ones I should have saved. But it's a hypothetical question. 'Here we rest.' "

The question spread. Jimmy's attitude was overwhelmingly popular, even though Bob's motives were respected. Rod said goodnight; he heard them still batting it around after he had gone to bed; it caused him to discuss it with himself.

He had decided long ago that they would never be in touch with Earth; he had not thought of it for—how long?—over a year. At first it had been mental hygiene, protection of his morale. Later it was logic: a delay in recall of a week might be a power failure, a few weeks could be a technical difficulty—but months on months was cosmic disaster; each day added a cipher to the infinitesimal probability that they would ever be in touch again.

He was now able to ask himself: was this what he wanted?

Jackie was right; this was home. Then he admitted that he *liked* being big frog in a small puddle, he loved his job. He was not meant to be a scientist, nor a scholar, he had never wanted to be a businessman—but what he was doing suited him . . . and he seemed to do it well enough to get by.

" 'Here we rest!' "

He went to sleep in a warm glow.

Cliff wanted help with the experimental crops. Rod did not take it too seriously; Cliff always wanted something; given his head he would have everybody working dawn to dark on his farm. But it was well to find out what he wanted—Rod did not underrate the importance of domesticating plants; that was basic for all colonies and triply so for them. It was simply that he did not know much about it.

Cliff stuck his head into the mayor's hut. "Ready?"

"Sure." Rod got his spear. It was no longer improvised but bore a point patiently sharpened from steel salvaged from Braun's Thunderbolt.

Rod had tried wrought iron but could not get it to hold an edge. "Let's pick up a couple of boys and get a few stobor."

"Okay."

Rod looked around. Jimmy was at his potter's wheel, kicking the treadle and shaping clay with his thumb. "Jim! Quit that and grab your pike. We're going to have some fun."

Throxton wiped at sweat. "You've talked me into it."

They added Kenny and Mick, then Cliff led them upstream. "I want you to look at the animals."

"All right," agreed Rod. "Cliff, I had been meaning to speak to you. If you are going to raise those brutes inside the wall, you'll have to be careful about their droppings. Carol has been muttering."

"Rod, I can't do everything! And you can't put them outside, not if you expect them to live."

"Sure, sure! Well, we'll get you more help, that's the only— Just a second!"

They were about to pass the last hut; Bruce McGowan was stretched in front of it, apparently asleep. Rod did not speak at once; he was fighting down rage. He wrestled with himself, aware that the next moment could change his future, damage the entire colony. But his rational self was struggling in a torrent of anger, bitter and self-righteous. He wanted to do away with this parasite, destroy it. He took a deep breath and tried to keep his mouth from trembling.

"Bruce!" he called softly.

McGowan opened his eyes. "Huh?"

"Isn't Art working his plant today?"

"Could be," Bruce admitted.

"Well?"

" 'Well' what? I've had a week and it's not my dish. Get somebody else."

Bruce wore his knife, as did each of them; a colonist was more likely to be caught naked than without his knife. It was the all-purpose tool, for cutting leather, preparing food, eating, whittling, building, basketmaking, and as make-do for a thousand other tools; their wealth came from knives, arrows were now used to hunt—but knives shaped the bows and arrows.

But a knife had not been used by one colonist against another since that disastrous day when Bruce's brother had defied Rod. Over the same issue, Rod recalled; the wheel had turned full circle. But today he would have immediate backing if Bruce reached for his knife.

But he knew that this must not be settled by five against one; he alone must make this dog come to heel, or his days as leader were numbered.

It did not occur to Rod to challenge Bruce to settle it with bare hands. Rod had read many a historical romance in which the hero invited someone to settle it "man to man," in a stylized imitation fighting called "boxing." Rod had enjoyed such stories but did not apply them to himself any more than he considered personally the sword play of *The Three Musketeers;* nevertheless, he knew what "boxing" meant—they folded their hands and struck certain restricted blows with fists. Usually no one was hurt.

The fighting that Rod was trained in was not simply strenuous athletics. It did not matter whether they were armed; if he and Bruce fought bare hands or otherwise, someone would be killed or badly hurt. The *only* dangerous weapon was man himself.

Bruce stared sullenly. "Bruce," Rod said, striving to keep his voice steady, "a long time ago I told you that people worked around here or got out. You and your brother didn't believe me so we had to chuck you out. Then you crawled back with a tale about how Jock had been killed and could you please join up? You were a sorry sight. Remember?"

McGowan scowled. "You promised to be a little angel," Rod went on. "People thought I was foolish—and I was. But I thought you might behave."

Bruce pulled a blade of grass, bit it. "Bub, you remind me of Jock. He was always throwing his weight around, too."

"Bruce, get up and get out of town! I don't care where, but if you are smart, you will shag over and tell Art you've made a mistake—then start pumping that bellows. I'll stop by later. If sweat isn't pouring off you when I arrive . . . then you'll never come back. You'll be banished for life."

McGowan looked uncertain. He glanced past Rod, and Rod wondered what expressions the others wore. But Rod kept his eyes on Bruce. "Get moving. Get to work, or don't come back."

Bruce got a sly look. "You can't order me kicked out. It takes a majority vote."

Jimmy spoke up. "Aw, quit taking his guff, Rod. Kick him out now."

Rod shook his head. "No. Bruce, if that is your answer, I'll call them together and we'll put you in exile before lunch—and I'll bet my best knife that you won't get three votes to let you stay. Want to bet?"

Bruce sat up and looked at the others, sizing his chances. He looked back at Rod. "Runt," he said slowly, "you aren't worth a hoot without stooges . . . or a couple of girls to do your fighting."

Jimmy whispered, "Watch it, Rod!" Rod licked dry lips, knowing that it was too late for reason, too late for talk. He would have to try to take him . . . he was not sure he could.

"I'll fight you," he said hoarsely. "Right now!"

Cliff said urgently, "Don't, Rod. We'll manage him."

"No. Come on, McGowan." Rod added one unforgivable word.

McGowan did not move. "Get rid of that joe sticker."

Rod said, "Hold my spear, Cliff."

Cliff snapped, "Now wait! I'm not going to stand by and watch this. He might get lucky and kill you, Rod."

"Get out of the way, Cliff."

"No." Cliff hesitated, then added, "Bruce, throw your knife away. Go ahead—or so help me I'll poke a joe-sticker in your belly myself. Give me your knife, Rod."

Rod looked at Bruce, then drew Colonel Bowie and handed it to Cliff. Bruce straightened up and flipped his knife at Cliff's feet. Cliff rasped, "I still say not to, Rod. Say the word and we'll take him apart."

"Back off. Give us room."

"Well—no bone breakers. You hear me, Bruce? Make a mistake and you'll never make another."

" 'No bone breakers,' " Rod repeated, and knew dismally that the rule would work against him; Bruce had him on height and reach and weight.

"Okay," McGowan agreed. "Just cat clawing. I am going to show this rube that one McGowan is worth two of him."

Cliff sighed. "Back off, everybody. Okay—get going!"

Crouched, they sashayed around, not touching. Only the preliminaries could use up much time; the textbook used in most high schools and colleges listed twenty-seven ways to destroy or disable a man hand to hand; none of the methods took as long as three seconds once contact was made. They chopped at each other, feinting with their hands, too wary to close.

Rod was confused by the injunction not to let the fight go to conclusion. Bruce grinned at him. "What's the matter? Scared? I've been waiting for this, you loud-mouthed pimple—now you're going to get it!" He rushed him.

Rod gave back, ready to turn Bruce's rush into his undoing. But Bruce did not carry it through; it had been a feint and Rod had reacted too strongly. Bruce laughed. "Scared silly, huh? You had better be."

Rod realized that he *was* scared, more scared than he had ever been.

The conviction flooded over him that Bruce intended to kill him . . . the agreement about bonebreakers meant nothing; this ape meant to finish him.

He backed away, more confused than ever . . . knowing that he must forget rules if he was to live through it . . . but knowing, too, that he *had* to abide by the silly restriction even if it meant the end of him. Panic shook him; he wanted to run.

He did not quite do so. From despair itself he got a cold feeling of nothing to lose and decided to finish it. He exposed his groin to a *savate* attack.

He saw Bruce's foot come up in the expected kick; with fierce joy he reached in the proper *shinobi* counter. He showed the merest of hesitation, knowing that a full twist would break Bruce's ankle.

Then he was flying through air; his hands had never touched Bruce. He had time for sick realization that Bruce had seen the gambit, countered with another—when he struck ground and Bruce was on him.

"Can you move your arm, Rod?"

He tried to focus his eyes, and saw Bob Baxter's face floating over him. "I licked him?"

Baxter did not answer. An angry voice answered, "Cripes, no! He almost chewed you to pieces."

Rod stirred and said thickly, "Where is he? I've got to whip him."

Baxter said sharply, "Lie still!" Cliff added, "Don't worry, Rod. We fixed him." Baxter insisted, "Shut up. See if you can move your left arm."

Rod moved the arm, felt pain shoot through it, jerked and felt pain everywhere. "It's not broken," Baxter decided. "Maybe a green-stick break. We'll put it in sling. Can you sit up? I'll help."

"I want to stand." He made it with help, stood swaying. Most of the villagers seemed to be there; they moved jerkily. It made him dizzy and he blinked.

"Take it easy, boy," he heard Jimmy say. "Bruce pretty near ruined you. You were crazy to give him the chance."

"I'm all right," Rod answered and winced. "Where is he?"

"Behind you. Don't worry, we fixed him."

"Yes," agreed Cliff. "We worked him over. Who does he think he is? Trying to shove the Mayor around!" He spat angrily.

Bruce was face down, features hidden in one arm; he was sobbing. "How bad is he hurt?" Rod asked.

"Him?" Jimmy said scornfully. "He's not hurt. I mean, he hurts all right—but he's not hurt. Carol wouldn't let us."

Caroline squatted beside Bruce, guarding him. She got up. "I should have let 'em," she said angrily. "But I knew you would be mad at me if I did." She put hands on hips. "Roddie Walker, when are you going to get sense enough to yell for me when you're in trouble? These four dopes stood around and let it happen."

"Wait a minute, Carol," Cliff protested. "I tried to stop it. We all tried, but—"

"But I wouldn't listen," Rod interrupted. "Never mind, Carol, I flubbed it."

"If you would listen to me—"

"Never mind!" Rod went to McGowan, prodded him. "Turn over."

Bruce slowly rolled over. Rod wondered if he himself looked as bad. Bruce's body was dirt and blood and bruises; his face looked as if someone had tried to file the features off. "Stand up."

Bruce started to speak, then got painfully to his feet. Rod said, "I told you to report to Art, Bruce. Get over the wall and get moving."

McGowan looked startled. "Huh?"

"You heard me. I can't waste time playing games. Check in with Art and get to work. Or keep moving and don't come back. Now *move!*"

Bruce stared, then hobbled toward the wall. Rod turned and said, "Get back to work, folks. The fun is over. Cliff, you were going to show me the animals."

"Huh? Look Rod, it'll keep."

"Yes, Rod," Baxter agreed. "I want to put a sling on that arm. Then you should rest."

Rod moved his arm gingerly. "I'll try to get along without it. Come on, Cliff. Just you and me—we'll skip the stobor hunt."

He had trouble concentrating on what Cliff talked about . . . something about gelding a pair of fawns and getting them used to harness. What use was harness when they had no wagons? His head ached, his arm hurt and his brain felt fuzzy. What would Grant have done? He had failed . . . but what should he have said, or not said? Some days it wasn't worth it.

"—so we've got to. You see, Rod?"

"Huh? Sure, Cliff." He made a great effort to recall what Cliff had been saying. "Maybe wooden axles would do. I'll see if Bill thinks he can build a cart."

"But besides a cart, we need—"

Rod stopped him. "Cliff, if you say so, we'll try it. I think I'll take a shower. Uh, we'll look at the field tomorrow."

A shower made him feel better and much cleaner, although the water spilling milk-warm from the flume seemed too hot, then icy cold.

He stumbled back to his hut and lay down. When he woke he found Shorty guarding his door to keep him from being disturbed.

It was three days before he felt up to inspecting the farm. Nielsen reported that McGowan was working, although sullenly. Caroline reported that Theo was obeying sanitary regulations and wearing a black eye. Rod was self-conscious about appearing in public, had even considered one restless night the advisability of resigning and letting someone who had not lost face take over the responsibility. But to his surprise his position seemed firmer than ever. A minority from Teller University, which he had thought of wryly as "loyal opposition," now no longer seemed disposed to be critical. Curt Pulvermacher, their unofficial leader, looked Rod up and offered help. "Bruce is a bad apple, Rod. Don't let him get down wind again. Let me know instead."

"Thanks, Curt."

"I mean it. It's hard enough to get anywhere around here if we all pull together. We can't have him riding roughshod over us. But don't stick your chin out. We'll teach him."

Rod slept well that night. Perhaps he had not handled it as Grant would have, but it had worked out. Cowpertown was safe. Oh, there would be more troubles but the colony would sweat through them. Someday there would be a city here and this would be Cowper Square. Upstream would be the Nielsen Steel Works. There might even be a Walker Avenue . . .

He felt up to looking over the farm the next day. He told Cliff so and gathered the same party, Jimmy, Kent, and Mick. Spears in hand they climbed the stile at the wall and descended the ladder on the far side. Cliff gathered up a handful of dirt, tasted it. "The soil is all right. A little acid, maybe. We won't know until we can run soil chemistry tests. But the structure is good. If you tell that dumb Swede that the next thing he has to make is a plough . . ."

"Waxie isn't dumb. Give him time. He'll make you ploughs and tractors, too."

"I'll settle for a hand plough, drawn by a team of buck. Rod, my notion is this. We weed and it's an invitation to the buck to eat the crops. If we built another wall, all around and just as high—"

"A wall! Any idea how many man-hours that would take, Cliff?"

"That's not the point."

Rod looked around the alluvial flat, several times as large as the land enclosed in the city walls. A thorn fence, possibly, but not a wall, not yet . . . Cliff's ambitions were too big. "Look, let's comb the field for stobor, then send the others back. You and I can figure out afterwards what can be done."

"All right. But tell them to watch where they put their big feet."

Rod spread them in skirmish line with himself in the center. "Keep dressed up," he warned, "and don't let any get past you. Remember, every one we kill now means six less on S-Day."

They moved forward. Kenny made a kill, Jimmy immediately made two more. The stobor hardly tried to escape, being in the "dopy joe" phase of their cycle.

Rod paused to spear one and looked up to speak to the man on his right. But there was no one there. "Hold it! Where's Mick?"

"Huh? Why, he was right here a second ago."

Rod looked back. Aside from a shimmer over the hot field, there was nothing where Mick should have been. Something must have sneaked up in the grass, pulled him down— "Watch it, everybody! Something's wrong. Close in . . . and keep your eyes peeled." He turned back, moved diagonally toward where Mick had disappeared.

Suddenly two figures appeared in front of his eyes—Mick and a stranger.

A stranger in coveralls and shoes . . . The man looked around, called over his shoulder, "Okay, Jake! Put her on automatic and clamp it." He glanced toward Rod but did not seem to see him, walked toward him, and disappeared.

With heart pounding Rod began to run. He turned and found himself facing into an open gate . . . and down a long, closed corridor.

The man in the coveralls stepped into the frame. "Everybody back off," he ordered. "We're going to match in with the Gap. There may be local disturbance."

15

In Achilles' Tent

It had been a half hour since Mick had stumbled through the gate as it had focused, fallen flat in the low gravity of Luna. Rod was trying to bring order out of confusion, trying to piece together his own wits. Most of the villagers were out on the field, or sitting on top of the wall, watching technicians set up apparatus to turn the locus into a permanent gate, with controls and communications on both sides. Rod tried to tell one that they were exposed, that they should not run around unarmed; without looking up the man had said, "Speak to Mr. Johnson."

He found Mr. Johnson, tried again, was interrupted. "Will you kids *please* let us work? We're glad to see you—but we've got to get a power fence around this area. No telling what might be in that tall grass."

"Oh," Rod answered. "Look, I'll set guards. We know what to expect. I'm in ch—"

"Beat it, will you? You kids mustn't be impatient."

So Rod went back inside his city, hurt and angry. Several strangers came in, poked around as if they owned the place, spoke to the excited villagers, went out again. One stopped to look at Jimmy's drum, rapped it and laughed. Rod wanted to strangle him.

"Rod?"

"Uh?" He whirled around. "Yes, Margery?"

"Do I cook lunch, or don't I? All my girls have left and Mel says it's silly because we'll all be gone by lunch time—and I don't know *what* to do."

"Huh? Nobody's leaving . . . that I know of."

"Well, maybe not but that's the talk."

He was not given time to consider this as one of the ubiquitous strangers came up and said briskly, "Can you tell me where to find a lad named Roderick Welker?"

"Walker," Rod corrected. "I'm Rod Walker. What do you want?"

"My name is Sansom, Clyde B. Sansom—Administrative Officer in the Emigration Control Service. Now, Welker, I understand you are group leader for these students. You can—"

"I am Mayor of Cowpertown," Rod said stonily. "What do you want?"

"Yes, yes, that's what the youngster called you. 'Mayor.' " Sansom smiled briefly and went on. "Now, Walker, we want to keep things orderly. I know you are anxious to get out of your predicament as quickly as possible—but we must do things systematically. We are going to make it easy—just delousing and physical examination, followed by psychological tests and a relocation interview. Then you will all be free to return to your homes—after signing a waiver-of-liability form, but the legal officer will take care of that. If you will have your little band line up alphabetically—uh, here in this open space, I think, then I will—" He fumbled with his briefcase.

"Who the deuce are you to give orders around here?"

Sansom looked surprised. "Eh? I told you. If you want to be technical, I embody the authority of the Terran Corporation. I put it as a request—but under field conditions I can compel co-operation, you know."

Rod felt himself turn red. "I don't know anything of the sort! You may be a squad of angels back on Terra . . . but you are in Cowpertown."

Mr. Sansom looked interested but not impressed. "And what, may I ask, is Cowpertown?"

"Huh? *This* is Cowpertown, a sovereign nation, with its own constitution, its own laws—and its own territory." Rod took a breath. "If the Terran Corporation wants anything, they can send somebody and arrange it. But don't tell us to line up alphabetically!"

"Atta boy, Roddie!"

Rod said, "Stick around, Carol," then added to Sansom, "Understand me?"

"Do I understand," Sansom said slowly, "that you are suggesting that the Corporation should appoint an *ambassador* to your group?"

"Well . . . that's the general idea."

"Mmmm . . . an interesting theory, Welker."

" 'Walker.' And until you do, you can darn well clear the sightseers out—and get out yourself. We aren't a zoo."

Sansom looked at Rod's ribs, glanced at his dirty, calloused feet and smiled. Rod said, "Show him out, Carol. Put him out, if you have to."

"Yes, *sir!*" She advanced on Sansom, grinning.

"Oh, I'm leaving," Sansom said quickly. "Better a delay than a mistake in protocol. An ingenious theory, young man. Good-by. We shall see each other later. Uh . . . a word of advice? May I?"

"Huh? All right."

"Don't take yourself too seriously. Ready, young lady?"

Rod stayed in his hut. He wanted badly to see what was going on beyond the wall, but he did not want to run into Sansom. So he sat and gnawed his thumb and thought. Apparently some weak sisters were going back—wave a dish of ice cream under their noses and off they would trot, abandoning their land, throwing away all they had built up. Well, *he* wouldn't! This was home, his place, he had earned it; he wasn't going back and maybe wait half a lifetime for a chance to move to some other planet probably not as good.

Let them go! Cowpertown would be better and stronger without them.

Maybe some just wanted to make a visit, show off grandchildren to grandparents, then come back. Probably . . . in which case they had better make sure that Sansom or somebody gave them written clearance to come back. Maybe he ought to warn them.

But *he* didn't have anyone to visit. Except Sis—and Sis might be anywhere—unlikely that she was on Terra.

Bob and Carmen, carrying Hope, came in to say good-by. Rod shook hands solemnly. "You're coming back, Bob, when you get your degree . . . aren't you?"

"Well, we hope so, if possible. If we are permitted to."

"Who's going to stop you? It's your *right*. And when you do, you'll find us here. In the meantime we'll try not to break legs."

Baxter hesitated. "Have you been to the gate lately, Rod?"

"No. Why?"

"Uh, don't plan too far ahead. I believe some have already gone back."

"How many?"

"Quite a number." Bob would not commit himself further. He gave Rod the addresses of his parents and Carmen's, soberly wished him a blessing, and left.

Margery did not come back and the fire pit remained cold. Rod did not care, he was not hungry. Jimmy came in at what should have been shortly after lunch, nodded and sat down. Presently he said, "I've been out at the gate."

"So?"

"Yup. You know, Rod, a lot of people wondered why you weren't there to say good-by."

"They could come *here* to say good-by!"

"Yes, so they could. But the word got around that you didn't approve. Maybe they were embarrassed."

"Me?" Rod laughed without mirth. "I don't care how many city boys run home to mama. It's a free country." He glanced at Jim. "How many are sticking?"

"Uh, I don't know."

"I've been thinking. If the group gets small, we might move back to the cave—just to sleep, I mean. Until we get more colonists."

"Maybe."

"Don't be so glum! Even if it got down to just you and me and Jackie and Carol, we'd be no worse off than we once were. And it would just be temporary. There'd be the baby, of course—I almost forgot to mention my godson."

"There's the baby," Jimmy agreed.

"What are you pulling a long face about? Jim . . . *you're* not thinking of leaving?"

Jimmy stood up. "Jackie said to tell you that we would stick by whatever you thought was best."

Rod thought over what Jimmy had not said. "You mean she wants to go back? Both of you do."

"Now, Rod, we're partners. But I've got the kid to think about. You see that?"

"Yes. I see."

"Well—"

Rod stuck out his hand. "Good luck, Jim. Tell Jackie good-by for me."

"Oh, she's waiting to say good-by herself. With the kid."

"Uh, tell her not to. Somebody once told me that saying good-by was a mistake. Be seeing you."

"Well—so long, Rod. Take care of yourself."

"You, too. If you see Caroline, tell her to come in."

Caroline was slow appearing; he guessed that she had been at the gate. He said bluntly, "How many are left?"

"Not many," she admitted.

"*How* many?"

"You and me—and a bunch of gawkers."

"*Nobody* else?"

"I checked them off the list. Roddie, what do we do now?"

"Huh? It doesn't matter. Do *you* want to go back?"

"You're boss, Roddie. You're the Mayor."

"Mayor of what? Carol, do you *want* to go back?"

"Roddie, I never thought about it. I was happy here. But—"

"But what?"

"The town is gone, the kids are gone—and I've got only a year if I'm ever going to be a cadet Amazon." She blurted out the last, then added, "But I'll stick if you do."

"No."

"I will so!"

"No. But I want you to do something when you go back."

"What?"

"Get in touch with my sister Helen. Find out where she is stationed. Assault Captain Helen Walker—got it? Tell her I'm okay . . . and tell her I said to help you get into the Corps."

"Uh . . . Roddie, I don't *want* to go!"

"Beat it. They might relax the gate and leave you behind."

"You come, too."

"No. I've got things to do. But you hurry. Don't say good-by. Just go."

"You're mad at me, Roddie?"

"Of course not. But go, *please*, or you'll have me bawling, too."

She gave a choked cry, grabbed his head and smacked his cheek, then galloped away, her sturdy legs pounding. Rod went into his shack and lay face down. After a while he got up and began to tidy Cowpertown. It was littered, dirtier than it had been since the morning of Grant's death.

It was late afternoon before anyone else came into the village. Rod heard and saw them long before they saw him—two men and a woman. The men were dressed in city garb; she was wearing shorts, shirt, and smart sandals. Rod stepped out and said, "What do you want?" He was carrying his spear.

The woman squealed, then looked and added, "Wonderful!"

One man was carrying a pack and tripod which Rod recognized as multi-recorder of the all-purpose sight-smell-sound-touch sort used by news services and expeditions. He said nothing, set his tripod down plugged in cables and started fiddling with dials. The other man, smaller, ginger haired, and with a terrier mustache, said, "You're Walker? The one the others call 'the Mayor'?"

"Yes."

"Kosmic hasn't been in here?"

"Cosmic what?"

"Kosmic Keynotes, of course. Or anybody? LIFE-TIME-SPACE? Galaxy Features?"

"I don't know what you mean. There hasn't been anybody here since morning."

The stranger twitched his mustache and sighed. "That's all I want to know. Go into your trance, Ellie. Start your box, Mac."

"Wait a minute," Rod demanded. "Who are you and what do you want?"

"Eh? I'm Evans of Empire . . . Empire Enterprises."

"Pulitzer Prize," the other man said and went on working.

"With Mac's help," Evans added quickly. "The lady is Ellie Ellens herself."

Rod looked puzzled. Evans said, "You don't *know?* Son, where have you—never mind. She's the highest paid emotional writer in the system. She'll interpret you so that every woman reader from the *Outlands Overseer* to the *London Times* will cry over you and want to comfort you. She's a *great* artist."

Miss Ellens did not seem to hear the tribute. She wandered around with a blank face, stopping occasionally to look or touch.

She turned and said to Rod, "Is this where you held your primitive dances?"

"What? We held square dances here, once a week."

" 'Square dances' . . . Well, we can change that." She went back into her private world.

"The point is, brother," Evans went on, "we don't want just an interview. Plenty of that as they came through. That's how we found out you were here—and dropped everything to see you. I'm not going to dicker; name your own price—but it's got to be exclusive, news, features, commercial rights, everything. Uh . . ." Evans looked around. "Advisory service, too, when the actors arrive."

"Actors?!"

"Of course. If the Control Service had the sense to sneeze, they would have held you all here until a record was shot. But we can do it better with actors. I want you at my elbow every minute—we'll have somebody play your part. Besides that—"

"Wait a minute!" Rod butted in. "Either I'm crazy or you are. In the first place I don't want your money."

"Huh? You signed with somebody? That guard let another outfit in ahead of us?"

"What guard? I haven't seen anybody."

Evans looked relieved. "We'll work it out. The guard they've got to keep anybody from crossing your wall—I thought he might have both hands out. But don't say you don't need money; that's immoral."

"Well, I don't. We don't use money here."

"Sure, sure . . . but you've got a family, haven't you? Families always need money. Look, let's not fuss. We'll treat you right and you can let it pile up in the bank. I just want you to get signed up."

"I don't see why I should."

"Binder," said Mac.

"Mmm . . . yes, Mac. See here, brother, think it over. Just let us have a binder that you won't sign with anybody else. You can still stick us for anything your conscience will let you. Just a binder, with a thousand plutons on the side."

"I'm not going to sign with anybody else."

"Got that, Mac?"

"Canned."

Evans turned to Rod. "You don't object to answering questions in the meantime, do you? And maybe a few pictures?"

"Uh, I don't care." Rod was finding them puzzling and a little annoying, but they were company and he was bitterly lonely.

"Fine!" Evans drew him out with speed and great skill. Rod found himself telling more than he realized he knew. At one point Evans asked about dangerous animals. "I understand they are pretty rough here. Much trouble?"

"Why, no," Rod answered with sincerity. "We never had real trouble with animals. What trouble we had was with people . . . and not much of that."

"You figure this will be a premium colony?"

"Of course. The others were fools to leave. This place is like Terra, only safer and richer and plenty of land. In a few years—say!"

"Say what?"

"How did it happen that they left us here? We were only supposed to be here ten days."

"Didn't they tell you?"

"Well . . . maybe the others were told. I never heard."

"It was the supernova, of course. Delta, uh—"

"Delta Gamma one thirteen," supplied Mac.

"That's it. Space-time distortion, but I'm no mathematician."

"Fluxion," said Mac.

"Whatever that is. They've been fishing for you ever since. As I understand it, the wave front messed up their figures for this whole region. Incidentally, brother, when you go back—"

"I'm not going back."

"Well, even on a visit. Don't sign a waiver. The Board is trying to call it an 'Act of God' and duck responsibility. So let me put a bug in your ear: don't sign away your rights. A friendly hint, huh?"

"Thanks. I won't—well, thanks anyhow."

"Now how about action pix for the lead stories?"

"Well . . . okay."

"Spear," said Mac.

"Yeah, I believe you had some sort of spear. Mind holding it?"

Rod got it as the great Ellie joined them. "Wonderful!" she breathed. "I can feel it. It shows how thin the line is between man and beast. A hundred cultured boys and girls slipping back to illiteracy, back to the stone age, the veneer sloughing away . . . reverting to savagery. Glorious!"

"Look here!" Rod said angrily. "Cowpertown wasn't that way at all! We had laws, we had a constitution, we kept clean. We—" He stopped; Miss Ellens wasn't listening.

"Savage ceremonies," she said dreamily. "A village witch doctor pitting ignorance and superstition against nature. Primitive fertility rites—" She stopped and said to Mac in a businesslike voice, "We'll shoot the dances three times. Cover 'em a little for 'A' list; cover 'em up a lot for the family list—and peel them down for the 'B' list. Got it?"

"Got it," agreed Mac.

"I'll do three commentaries," she added. "It will be worth the trouble." She reverted to her trance.

"Wait a minute!" Rod protested. "If she means what I think she means, there won't be any pictures, with or without actors."

"Take it easy," Evans advised. "I said you would be technical supervisor, didn't I? Or would you rather we did it without you? Ellie is all right, brother. What you don't know—and *she* does—is that you have to shade the truth to get at the real truth, the underlying truth. You'll see."

"But—"

Mac stepped up to him. "Hold still."

Rod did so, as Mac raised his hand. Rod felt the cool touch of an air brush.

"Hey! What are you doing?"

"Make up." Mac returned to his gear.

"Just a little war paint," Evans explained. "The pic needs color. It will wash off."

Rod opened his mouth and eyes in utter indignation; without knowing it he raised his spear. "Get it, Mac!" Evans ordered.

"Got it," Mac answered calmly.

Rod fought to bring his anger down to where he could talk. "Take that tape out," he said softly. "Throw it on the ground. Then get out."

"Slow down," Evans advised. "You'll like that pic. We'll send you one."

"Take it out. Or I'll bust the box and anybody who gets in my way!" He aimed his spear at the multiple lens.

Mac slipped in front, protected it with his body. Evans called out, "Better look at *this.*"

Evans had him covered with a small but businesslike gun. "We go a lot of funny places, brother, but we go prepared. You damage that recorder, or hurt one of us, and you'll be sued from here to breakfast. It's a serious matter to interfere with a news service, brother. The public has rights, you know." He raised his voice. "Ellie! We're leaving."

"Not yet," she answered dreamily. "I must steep myself in—"

"Right now! It's an 'eight-six' with the Reuben Steuben!"

"Okay!" she snapped in her other voice.

Rod let them go. Once they were over the wall he went back to the city hall, sat down, held his knees and shook.

Later he climbed the stile and looked around. A guard was on duty below him; the guard looked up but said nothing. The gate was relaxed to a mere control hole but a loading platform had been set up and a power fence surrounded it and joined the wall. Someone was working at a control board set up on a flatbed truck; Rod decided that they must be getting ready for major immigration. He went back and prepared a solitary meal, the poorest he had eaten in more than a year. Then he went to bed and listened to the jungle "Grand Opera" until he went to sleep.

"Anybody home?"

Rod came awake instantly, realized that it was morning—and that not all nightmares were dreams. "Who's there?"

"Friend of yours." B. P. Matson stuck his head in the door. "Put that whittler away. I'm harmless."

Rod bounced up. "Deacon! I mean 'Doctor.' "

" 'Deacon,' " Matson corrected. "I've got a visitor for you." He stepped aside and Rod saw his sister.

Some moments later Matson said mildly, "If you two can unwind and blow your noses, we might get this on a coherent basis."

Rod backed off and looked at his sister. "My, you look *wonderful,*

Helen." She was in mufti, dressed in a gay tabard and briefs. "You've lost weight."

"Not much. Better distributed, maybe. You've gained, Rod. My baby brother is a man."

"How did you—" Rod stopped, struck by suspicion. "You didn't come here to talk me into going back? If you did, you can save your breath."

Matson answered hastily. "No, no, no! Farthest thought from our minds. But we heard about your decision and we wanted to see you—so I did a little politicking and got us a pass." He added, "Nominally I'm a temporary field agent for the service."

"Oh. Well, I'm certainly glad to see you . . . as long as that is understood."

"Sure, sure!" Matson took out a pipe, stoked and fired it. "I admire your choice, Rod. First time I've been on Tangaroa."

"On what?"

"Huh? Oh. Tangaroa. Polynesian goddess, I believe. Did you folks give it another name?"

Rod considered it. "To tell the truth, we never got around to it. It . . . well, it just *was.*"

Matson nodded. "Takes two of anything before you need names. But it's lovely, Rod. I can see you made a lot of progress."

"We would have done all right," Rod said bitterly, "if they hadn't jerked the rug out." He shrugged. "Like to look around?"

"I surely would."

"All right. Come on, Sis. Wait a minute—I haven't had breakfast; how about you?"

"Well, when we left the Gap it was pushing lunch time. I could do with a bite. Helen?"

"Yes, indeed."

Rod scrounged in Margery's supplies. The haunch on which he had supped was not at its best. He passed it to Matson. "Too high?"

Matson sniffed it. "Pretty gamy. I can eat it if you can."

"We should have hunted yesterday, but . . . things happened." He frowned. "Sit tight. I'll get cured meat." He ran up to the cave, found a smoked side and some salted strips. When he got back Matson had a fire going. There was nothing else to serve; no fruit had been gathered the day before. Rod was uneasily aware that their breakfasts must have been very different.

But he got over it in showing off how much they had done—potter's wheel, Sue's loom with a piece half finished, the flume with the village fountain and the showers that ran continuously, iron artifacts that Art and Doug had hammered out. "I'd like to take you up to Art's iron works but there is no telling what we might run into."

"Come now, Rod, I'm not a city boy. Nor is your sister helpless."

Rod shook his head. "I know this country; you don't. I can go up there at a trot. But the only way for you would be a slow sneak, because I can't cover you both."

Matson nodded. "You're right. It seems odd to have one of my students solicitous over my health. But you are right. We don't know this set up."

Rod showed them the stobor traps and described the annual berserk migration. "Stobor pour through those holes and fall in the pits. The other animals swarm past, as solid as city traffic for hours."

"Catastrophic adjustment," Matson remarked.

"Huh? Oh, yes, we figured that out. Cyclic catastrophic balance, just like human beings. If we had facilities, we could ship thousands of carcasses back to Earth every dry season." He considered it. "Maybe we will, now."

"Probably."

"But up to now it has been just a troublesome nuisance. These stobor especially—I'll show you one out in the field when—say!" Rod looked thoughtful. "These *are* stobor, aren't they? Little carnivores heavy in front, about the size of a tom cat and eight times as nasty?"

"Why ask me?"

"Well, you warned us against stobor. All the classes were warned."

"I suppose these must be stobor," Matson admitted, "but I did not know what they looked like."

"Huh?"

"Rod, every planet has its 'stobor' . . . all different. Sometimes more than one sort." He stopped to tap his pipe. "You remember me telling the class that every planet has unique dangers, different from every other planet in the Galaxy?"

"Yes . . ."

"Sure, and it meant nothing, a mere intellectual concept. But you have to be afraid of the thing behind the concept, if you are to stay alive. So we personify it . . . but we don't tell you what it is. We do it differently each year. It is to warn you that the unknown and deadly can lurk anywhere . . . and to plant it deep in your guts instead of in your head."

"Well, I'll be a— Then there *weren't* any stobor! There never were!"

"Sure there were. You built these traps for them, didn't you?"

* * *

When they returned, Matson sat on the ground and said, "We can't stay long, you know."

"I realize that. Wait a moment." Rod went into his hut, dug out Lady Macbeth, rejoined them. "Here's your knife, Sis. It saved my skin more than once. Thanks."

She took the knife and caressed it, then cradled it and looked past Rod's head. It flashed by him, went tuck-*spong!* in a corner post. She recovered it, came back and handed it to Rod. "Keep it, dear, wear it always in safety and health."

"Gee, Sis, I shouldn't. I've had it too long now."

"Please. I'd like to know that Lady Macbeth is watching over you wherever you are. And I don't need a knife much now."

"Huh? Why not?"

"Because I married her," Matson answered.

Rod was caught speechless. His sister looked at him and said, "What's the matter, Buddy? Don't you approve?"

"Huh? Oh, sure! It's . . ." He dug into his memory, fell back on quoted ritual: " 'May the Principle make you one. May your union be fruitful.' "

"Then come here and kiss me."

Rod did so, remembered to shake hands with the Deacon. It was all right, he guessed, but—well, how old were they? Sis must be thirtyish and the Deacon . . . why the Deacon was *old*—probably past forty.

It did not seem quite decent.

But he did his best to make them feel that he approved. After he thought it over he decided that if two people, with their lives behind them, wanted company in their old age, why, it was probably a good thing.

"So you see," Matson went on, "I had a double reason to look you up. In the first place, though I am no longer teaching, it is vexing to mislay an entire class. In the second place, when one of them is your brother-in-law it is downright embarrassing."

"You've quit teaching?"

"Yes. The Board and I don't see eye to eye on policy. Secondly, I'm leading a party out . . . and this time your sister and I are going to settle down and prove a farm." Matson looked at him. "Wouldn't be interested, would you? I need a salted lieutenant."

"Huh? Thanks, but as I told you, this is my place. Uh, where are you going?"

"Territa, out toward the Hyades. Nice place—they are charging a stiff premium."

Rod shrugged. "Then I couldn't afford it."

"As my lieutenant, you'd be exempt. But I wasn't twisting your arm; I just thought you ought to have a chance to turn it down. I have to get along with your sister, you know."

Rod glanced at Helen. "Sorry, Sis."

"It's all right, Buddy. We're not trying to live your life."

"Mmm . . . no." Matson puffed hard, then went on. "However, as your putative brother and former teacher I feel obligated to mention a couple of things. I'm not trying to sell you anything, but I'll appreciate it if you'll listen. Okay?"

"Well . . . go ahead."

"This is a good spot. But you might go back to school, you know. Acquire recognized professional status. If you refuse recall, here you stay . . . forever. You won't see the rest of the Outlands. They won't give you free passage back later. But a professional gets around, he sees the world. Your sister and I have been on some fifty planets. School does not look attractive now—you're a man and it will be hard to wear boy's shoes. But—" Matson swept an arm, encompassed all of Cowpertown, "—this counts. You can skip courses, get field credit. I have some drag with the Chancellor of Central Tech. Hmmm?"

Rod sat with stony face, then shook his head. "Okay," said Matson briskly. "No harm done."

"Wait. Let me tell you." Rod tried to think how to explain how he felt . . . "Nothing, I guess," he said gruffly.

Matson smoked in silence. "You were leader here," he said at last.

"Mayor," Rod corrected. "Mayor of Cowpertown. I *was* the Mayor, I mean."

"You *are* the Mayor. Population one, but you are still boss. And even those bureaucrats in the control service wouldn't dispute that you've proved the land. Technically you are an autonomous colony—I hear you told Sansom that." Matson grinned. "You're alone, however. You can't live alone, Rod . . . not and stay human."

"Well, yes—but aren't they going to settle this planet?"

"Sure. Probably fifty thousand this year, four times that many in two years. But, Rod, you would be part of the mob. They'll bring their own leaders."

"*I* don't have to be boss! I just—well, I don't want to give up Cowpertown."

"Rod, Cowpertown is safe in history, along with Plymouth Rock, Botany Bay, and Dakin's Colony. The citizens of Tangaroa will undoubtedly preserve it as a historical shrine. Whether you stay is another matter. Nor am I trying to persuade you. I was simply pointing out alternatives." He stood up. "About time we started, Helen."

"Yes, dear." She accepted his hand and stood up.

"Wait a minute!" insisted Rod. "Deacon . . . Sis! I know I sound like a fool. I know this is gone . . . the town, and the kids, and everything. But I *can't* go back." He added, "It's not that I don't want to."

Matson nodded. "I understand you."

"I don't see how. *I* don't."

"Maybe I've been there. Rod, everyone of us is beset by two things: a need to go home, and the impossibility of doing it. You are at the age when these hurt worst. You've been thrown into a situation that makes the crisis doubly acute. You—don't interrupt me—you've been a man here, the old man of the tribe, the bull of the herd. That is why the others could go back but you can't. Wait, please! I suggested that you might find it well to go back and be an adolescent for a while . . . and it seems unbearable. I'm not surprised. It would be easier to be a small child. Children are another race and adults deal with them as such. But adolescents are neither adult nor child. They have the impossible, unsolvable, tragic problems of all fringe cultures. They don't belong, they are second-class citizens, economically and socially insecure. It is a difficult period and I don't blame you for not wanting to return to it. I simply think it might pay. But you have been king of a whole world; I imagine that term papers and being told to wipe your feet and such are out of the question. So good luck. Coming, dear?"

"Deacon," his wife said, "Aren't you going to *tell* him?"

"It has no bearing. It would be an unfair way to influence his judgment."

"You *men!* I'm glad I'm not male!"

"So am I," Matson agreed pleasantly.

"I didn't mean that. Men behave as if logic were stepping on a crack in a sidewalk. I'm going to tell him."

"On your head be it."

"Tell me *what?"* demanded Rod.

"She means," said Matson, "that your parents are back."

"What?"

"Yes, Buddy. They left stasis a week ago and Daddy came out of the hospital today. He's well. But we haven't told him all about you—we haven't known *what* to say."

The facts were simple, although Rod found them hard to soak up. Medical techniques had developed in two years, not a pessimistic twenty; it had been possible to relax the stasis, operate, and restore Mr. Walker to the world. Helen had known for months that such outcome was likely but their father's physician had not approved until he was sure. It had been mere coincidence that Tangaroa had been located at almost the same time. To Rod one event was as startling as the other; his parents had been dead to him for a long time.

"My dear," Matson said sternly, "now that you have thrown him into a whingding, shall we go?"

"Yes. But I had to tell him." Helen kissed Rod quickly, turned to her husband. They started to walk away.

Rod watched them, his face contorted in an agony of indecision.

Suddenly he called out, "Wait! I'm coming with you."

"All right," Matson answered. He turned his good eye toward his wife and drooped the lid in a look of satisfaction that was not quite a wink. "If you are sure that is what you want to do, I'll help you get your gear together."

"Oh, I haven't any baggage. Let's go."

Rod stopped only long enough to free the penned animals.

16

The Endless Road

MATSON CHAPERONED HIM THROUGH EMIGRANTS' GAP, SAVED FROM possible injury a functionary who wanted to give Rod psychological tests, and saw to it that he signed no waivers. He had him bathed, shaved, and barbered, then fetched him clothes, before he let him be exposed to the Terran world. Matson accompanied them only to Kaibab Gate. "I'm supposed to have a lodge dinner, or something, so that you four can be alone as a family. About nine, dear. See you, Rod." He kissed his wife and left.

"Sis? Dad doesn't know I'm coming?"

Helen hesitated. "He knows. I screened him while Deacon was primping you." She added, "Remember, Rod, Dad has been ill . . . and the time has been only a couple of weeks to him."

"Oh, that's so, isn't it?" Used all his life to Ramsbotham anomalies, Rod nevertheless found those concerned with time confusing—planet-hopping via the gates did not seem odd. Besides, he was extremely edgy without knowing why, the truth being that he was having an attack of fear of crowds. The Matsons had anticipated it but had not warned him lest they make him worse.

The walk through tall trees just before reaching home calmed him. The necessity for checking all cover for dangerous animals and keeping a tree near him always in mind gave his subconscious something familiar to chew on. He arrived home almost cheerful without being aware either that he had been frightened by crowds or soothed by non-existent dangers of an urban forest.

His father looked browned and healthy—but shorter and smaller. He embraced his son and his mother kissed him and wept. "It's good to have you home, son. I understand you had quite a trip."

"It's good to be home, Dad."

"I think these tests are much too strenuous, I really do."

Rod started to explain that it really had not been a test, that it had not been strenuous, and that Cowpertown—Tangaroa, rather—had been a soft touch. But he got mixed up and was disturbed by the presence of "Aunt" Nora Peascoat—no relation but a childhood friend of his mother. Besides, his father was not listening.

But Mrs. Peascoat was listening, and looking—peering with little eyes through folds of flesh. "Why, Roderick Walter, I *knew* that couldn't have been a picture of you."

"Eh?" asked his father. "What picture?"

"Why, that wild-man picture that had Roddie's name on it. You must have seen it; it was on facsimile and Empire Hour both. I knew it wasn't him. I said to Joseph, 'Joseph,' I said, 'that's not a picture of Rod Walker—it's a fake.' "

"I must have missed it. As you know, I—"

"I'll send it to you; I clipped it. I knew it was a fake. It's a horrible thing, a great naked savage with pointed teeth and a fiendish grin and a long spear and war paint all over its ugly face. I said to Joseph—"

"As you know, I returned from hospital just this morning, Nora. Rod, there was no picture of you on the news services, surely?"

"Uh, yes and no. Maybe."

"I don't follow you. Why should there be a picture of you?"

"There wasn't any reason. This bloke just took it."

"Then there *was* a picture?"

"Yes." Rod saw that "Aunt" Nora was eyeing him avidly. "But it was a fake—sort of."

"I still don't follow you."

"Please, Pater," Helen intervened. "Rod had a tiring trip. This can wait."

"Oh, surely. I don't see how a picture can be 'a sort of a fake.' "

"Well, Dad, this man painted my face when I wasn't looking. I—" Rod stopped, realizing that it sounded ridiculous.

"Then it *was* your picture?" "Aunt" Nora insisted.

"I'm not going to say any more."

Mr. Walker blinked. "Perhaps that is best."

"Aunt" Nora looked ruffled. "Well, I suppose *anything* can happen 'way off in those odd places. From the teaser on Empire Hour I understand some *very* strange things did happen . . . not all of them *nice.*"

She looked as if daring Rod to deny it. Rod said nothing. She went on, "I don't know what you were thinking of, letting a boy do such things. My father always said that if the Almighty had intended us to use those gate things instead of rocket ships He would have provided His own holes in the sky."

Helen said sharply, "Mrs. Peascoat, in what way is a rocket ship more natural than a gate?"

"Why, Helen Walker! I've been 'Aunt Nora' all your life. 'Mrs. Peascoat' indeed!"

Helen shrugged. "And *my* name is Matson, not Walker—as you know."

Mrs. Walker, distressed and quite innocent, broke in to ask Mrs. Peascoat to stay for dinner. Mr. Walker added, "Yes, Nora, join us Under the Lamp."

Rod counted to ten. But Mrs. Peascoat said she was *sure* they wanted to be *alone*, they had so *much* to talk about . . . and his father did not insist.

Rod quieted during ritual, although he stumbled in responses and once left an awkward silence. Dinner was wonderfully good, but he was astonished by the small portions; Terra must be under severe rationing. But everyone seemed happy and so he was.

"I'm sorry about this mix-up," his father told him. "I suppose it means that you will have to repeat a semester at Patrick Henry."

"On the contrary, Pater," Helen answered, "Deacon is sure that Rod can enter Central Tech with advanced standing."

"Really? They were more strict in my day."

"All of that group will get special credit. What they learned cannot be learned in classrooms."

Seeing that his father was inclined to argue Rod changed the subject. "Sis, that reminds me. I gave one of the girls your name, thinking you were still in the Corps—she wants to be appointed cadet, you see. You can still help her, can't you?"

"I can advise her and perhaps coach her for the exams. Is this important to you, Buddy?"

"Well, yes. And she is number-one officer material. She's a big girl, even bigger than you are—and she looks a bit like you. She is smart like you, too, around genius, and always good-natured and willing—but strong and fast and incredibly violent when you need it . . . sudden death in all directions."

"Roderick." His father glanced at the lamp.

"Uh, sorry, Dad. I was just describing her."

"Very well. Son . . . when did you start picking up your meat with your fingers?"

Rod dropped the tidbit and blushed. "Excuse me. We didn't have forks."

Helen chuckled. "Never mind, Rod. Pater, it's perfectly natural. Whenever we paid off any of our girls we always put them through reorientation to prepare them for the perils of civil life. And fingers were made before forks."

"Mmm . . . no doubt. Speaking of reorientation there is something we must do, daughter, before this family will be organized again."

"So?"

"Yes. I mean the transfer of guardianship. Now that I am well, by a miracle, I must reassume my responsibilities."

Rod's mind slipped several cogs before it penetrated that Dad was talking about *him*. Guardian? Oh . . . Sis was his guardian, wasn't she? But it didn't mean anything.

Helen hesitated. "I suppose so, Pater," she said, her eyes on Rod, "if Buddy wants to."

"Eh? That is not a factor, daughter. Your husband won't want the responsibility of supervising a young boy—and it is my obligation . . . and privilege."

Helen looked annoyed. Rod said, "I can't see that it matters, Dad. I'll be away at college—and after all I am nearly old enough to vote."

His mother looked startled. "Why, Roddie dear!"

"Yes," agreed his father. "I'm afraid I can't regard a gap of three years as negligible."

"What do you mean, Dad? I'll be of age in January."

Mrs. Walker clasped a hand to her mouth. "Jerome . . . we've forgotten the time lag again. Oh, my baby boy!"

Mr. Walker looked astonished, muttered something about "—very difficult" and gave attention to his plate. Presently he looked up. "You'll pardon me, Rod. Nevertheless, until you are of age I must do what I can; I hardly think I want you to live away from home while at college."

"Sir? Why not?"

"Well—I feel that we have drifted apart, and not all for the best. Take this girl you spoke of in such surprising terms. Am I correct in implying that she was, eh . . . a close chum?"

Rod felt himself getting warm. "She was my city manager," he said flatly.

"Your *what?*"

"My executive officer. She was captain of the guard, chief of police, anything you want to call her. She did everything. She hunted, too, but that was just because she liked to. Carol is, uh—well, Carol is *swell.*"

"Roderick, are you *involved* with this girl?"

"Me? Gosh, no! She was more like a big sister. Oh, Carol was sweet on half a dozen fellows, one time or another, but it never lasted."

"I am very glad to hear that you are not seriously interested in her. She does not sound like desirable companionship for a young boy."

"Dad—you don't know what you are saying!"

"Perhaps. I intend to find out. But what is this other matter? 'City Manager!' What were *you?"*

"I," Rod said proudly, "was Mayor of Cowpertown."

His father looked at him, then shook his head. "We'll speak of this later. Possibly you need, eh—medical help." He looked at Helen. "We'll attend to the change in guardianship tomorrow. I can see that there is much I must take care of."

Helen met his eyes. "Not unless Buddy consents."

"Daughter!"

"The transfer was irrevocable. He will have to agree—or I won't do it!"

Mr. Walker looked shocked, Mrs. Walker looked stricken. Rod got up and left the room . . . the first time anyone had ever done so while the Lamp of Peace was burning. He heard his father call after him but he did not turn back.

He found Matson in his room, smoking and reading. "I grabbed a bite and let myself in quietly," Matson explained. He inspected Rod's face. "I told you," he said slowly, "that it would be rough. Well, sweat it out, son, sweat it out."

"I can't *stand* it!"

"Yes, you can."

In Emigrants' Gap the sturdy cross-country wagons were drawn up in echelon, as they had been so often before and would be so many times again. The gate was not ready; drivers gathered at the booth under Liberty's skirts, drinking coffee and joking through the nervous wait. Their professional captain was with them, a lean, homely young man with deep lines in his face, from sun and laughing and perhaps some from worry. But he did not seem to be worrying now; he was grinning and drinking coffee and sharing a doughnut with a boy child. He was dressed in fringed buckskin, in imitation of a very old style; he wore a Bill Cody beard and rather long hair. His mount was a little pinto, standing patiently by with reins hanging. There was a boot scabbard holding a hunting rifle on the nigh side of the saddle, but the captain carried no guns on his person; instead he wore two knives, one on each side.

A siren sounded and a speaker above the Salvation Army booth uttered: "Captain Walker, ready with gate four."

Rod waved at the control booth and shouted, "Call off!" then turned back to Jim and Jacqueline. "Tell Carol I'm sorry she couldn't get leave. I'll be seeing you."

"Might be sooner than you think," asserted Jim. "My firm is going to bid this contract."

"Your firm? Where do you get that noise? Have they made him a partner, Jackie?"

"No," she answered serenely, "but I'm sure they will as soon as he is admitted to the Outlands bar. Kiss Uncle Rod good-by, Grant."

"No," the youngster answered firmly.

"Just like his father," Jimmy said proudly. "Kisses women only."

The count was running back down; Rod heard it and swung into saddle. "Take it easy, kids." The count passed him, finished with a shouted, *"ONE!"*

"Reins up! Reeeiins *UP!"* He waited with arm raised and glanced through the fully-dilated gate past rolling prairie at snow-touched peaks beyond. His nostrils widened.

The control light turned green. He brought his arm down hard and shouted, "Roll 'em! *Ho!"* as he squeezed and released the little horse with his knees. The pinto sprang forward, cut in front of the lead wagon, and Captain Walker headed out on his long road.

TIME FOR THE STARS

For Bill and Bob Davis

Contents

1

The Long Range Foundation

ACCORDING TO THEIR BIOGRAPHIES, DESTINY'S FAVORED CHILDREN usually had their lives planned out from scratch. Napoleon was figuring on how to rule France when he was a barefoot boy in Corsica, Alexander the Great much the same, and Einstein was muttering equations in his cradle.

Maybe so. Me, I just muddled along.

In an old book that belonged to my great grandfather Lucas I once saw a cartoon of a man in evening clothes, going over a ski jump. With an expression of shocked unbelief he is saying: "How did I get up here?"

I know how he felt. How did I get 'way up here?

I was not even planned on. The untaxed quota for our family was three children, then my brother Pat and I came along in one giant economy package. We were a surprise to everyone, especially to my parents, my three sisters, and the tax adjusters. I don't recall being surprised myself but my earliest recollection is a vague feeling of not being quite welcome, even though Dad and Mum, and Faith, Hope, and Charity treated us okay.

Maybe Dad did not handle the emergency right. Many families get an extra child quota on an exchange basis with another family, or something, especially when the tax-free limit has already been filled with all boys or all girls. But Dad was stubborn, maintaining that the law was unconstitutional, unjust, discriminatory, against public morals, and contrary to the will of God. He could reel off a list of important people who were youngest children of large families, from Benjamin Franklin to the first governor of Pluto, then he would demand to know where the human race would have been without them?—after which Mother would speak soothingly.

Dad was probably accurate as he was a student of almost everything, even his trade, which was micromechanics—but especially of history. He wanted to name us for his two heroes in American history, whereas Mother wanted to name us for her favorite artists. This is how I ended up as Thomas Paine Leonardo da Vinci Bartlett and my twin became Patrick Henry Michelangelo Bartlett. Dad called us Tom and Pat and Mother called us Leo and Michel and our sisters called us Useless and Double-Useless. Dad won by being stubborn.

Dad was stubborn. He could have paid the annual head tax on us supernumeraries, applied for a seven-person flat, and relaxed to the inevitable. Then he could have asked for reclassification. Instead he claimed exemption for us twins each year, always ended by paying our head tax with his check stamped "Paid under Protest!" and we seven lived in a five-person flat. When Pat and I were little we slept in homemade cribs in the bathroom which could not have been convenient for anybody, then when we were bigger we slept on the living-room couch, which was inconvenient for everybody, especially our sisters, who found it cramping to their social life.

Dad could have solved all this by putting in for family emigration to Mars or Venus, or the Jovian moons, and he used to bring up the subject. But this was the one thing that would make Mum more stubborn than he was. I don't know which part of making the High Jump scared her, because she would just settle her mouth and not answer. Dad would point out that big families got preferred treatment for emigration and that the head tax was earmarked to subsidize colonies off Earth and why shouldn't we benefit by the money we were being robbed of? To say nothing of letting our children grow up with freedom and elbow room, out where there wasn't a bureaucrat standing behind every productive worker dreaming up more rules and restrictions? Answer me that?

Mother never answered and we never emigrated.

We were always short of money. Two extra mouths, extra taxes, and no family assistance for the two extras make the stabilized family income law as poor a fit as the clothes Mum cut down for us from Dad's old ones. It was darn' seldom that we could afford to dial for dinner like other people and Dad even used to bring home any of his lunch that he didn't eat. Mum went back to work as soon as we twins were in kindergarten, but the only household robot we had was an obsolete model "Morris Garage" *Mother's Helper* which was always burning out valves and took almost as long to program as the job would have taken. Pat and I got acquainted with dish water and detergents—at least I did; Pat usually insisted on doing the sterilizing or had a sore thumb or something.

Dad used to talk about the intangible benefits of being poor—learning to stand on your own feet, building character, and all that. By the time I was old enough to understand I was old enough to wish they weren't so intangible, but, thinking back, maybe he had a point. We did have fun. Pat and I raised hamsters in the service unit and Mum never objected. When we turned the bath into a chem lab the girls did make unfriendly comments but when Dad put his foot down, they sweet-talked him into picking it up again and after that they hung their laundry somewhere else, and later Mum stood between us and the house manager when we poured acid down the drain and did the plumbing no good.

The only time I can remember when Mum put her foot down was when her brother, Uncle Steve, came back from Mars and gave us some canal worms which we planned to raise and sell at a profit. But when Dad stepped on one in the shower (we had not discussed our plans with him) she made us give them to the zoo, except the one Dad had stepped on, which was useless. Shortly after that we ran away from home to join the High Marines—Uncle Steve was a ballistics sergeant—and when lying about our age did not work and they fetched us back, Mum not only did not scold us but had fed our snakes and our silkworms while we were gone.

Oh, I guess we were happy. It is hard to tell at the time. Pat and I were very close and did everything together but I want to get one thing straight: being a twin is not the Damon-and-Pythias dream that throb writers would have you think. It makes you close to another person to be born with him, share a room with him, eat with him, play with him, work with him, and hardly ever do anything without him as far back as you can remember, and farther according to witnesses. It makes you close; it makes you almost indispensable to each other—but it does not necessarily make you love him.

I want to get this straight because there has been a lot of nonsense talked about it since twins got to be suddenly important. I'm me; I'm not my brother Pat. I could always tell us apart, even if other people couldn't. He is the right-handed one; I'm the left-handed one. And from my point of view I'm the one who almost always got the small piece of cake.

I can remember times when he got both pieces through a fast shuffle. I'm not speaking in general; I'm thinking of a certain white cake with chocolate icing and how he confused things so that he got my piece, too, Mum and Dad thinking he was both of us, despite my protests. Dessert can be the high point of the day when you are eight, which was what we were then.

I am not complaining about these things . . . even though I feel a dull lump of anger even now, after all the years and miles, at the recollection of being punished because Dad and Mum thought *I* was the one who was trying to wangle two desserts. But I'm just trying to tell the truth. Doctor Devereaux said to write it all down and where I have to start is how it feels to be a twin. You aren't a twin, are you? Maybe you are but the chances are forty-four to one that you aren't—not even a fraternal, whereas Pat and I are identicals which is four times as unlikely.

They say that one twin is always retarded—I don't think so. Pat and I were always as near alike as two shoes of a pair. The few times we showed any difference I was a quarter inch taller or a pound heavier, then we would even out. We got equally good marks in school; we cut our teeth together. What he did have was more grab than I had, something the psychologists call "pecking order." But it was so subtle you could not define it and other people could not see it. So far as I know, it started from nothing and grew into a pattern that neither of us could break even if we wanted to.

Maybe if the nurse had picked me up first when we were born *I* would have been the one who got the bigger piece of cake. Or maybe she did—I don't *know* how it started.

But don't think that being a twin is all bad even if you are on the short end; it is mostly good. You go into a crowd of strangers and you are scared and shy—and there is your twin a couple of feet away and you aren't alone any more. Or somebody punches you in the mouth and while you are groggy your twin has punched him and the fight goes your way. You flunk a quiz and your twin has flunked just as badly and you aren't alone.

But do not think that being twins is like having a very close and loyal friend. It isn't like that at all and it is a great deal closer.

Pat and I had our first contact with the Long Range Foundation when this Mr. Geeking showed up at our home. I did not warm to him. Dad didn't like him either and wanted to hustle him out, but he was already seated with coffee at his elbow for Mother's notions of hospitality were firm.

So this Geeking item was allowed to state his business. He was, he said, a field representative of "Genetics Investigations."

"What's that?" Dad said sharply.

" 'Genetics Investigations' is a scientific agency, Mr. Bartlett. This present project is one of gathering data concerning twins. It is in the public interest and we hope that you will cooperate."

Dad took a deep breath and hauled out the imaginary soapbox he always had ready. "More government meddling! I'm a decent citizen; I pay my bills and support my family. My boys are just like other boys and I'm sick and tired of the government's attitude about them. I'm not going to have them poked and prodded and investigated to satisfy some bureaucrat. All we ask is to be left alone—and that the government admit the obvious fact that my boys have as much right to breathe air and occupy space as anyone else!"

Dad wasn't stupid; it was just that he had a reaction pattern where Pat and I were concerned as automatic as the snarl of a dog who has been kicked too often. Mr. Geeking tried to soothe him but Dad can't be interrupted when he has started that tape. "You tell the Department of Population Control that I'm not having their 'genetics investigations.' What do they want to find out? How to keep people from having twins, probably. What's wrong with twins? Where would Rome have been without Romulus and Remus?—answer me that! Mister, do you know how many—"

"*Please*, Mr. Bartlett, I'm not from the government."

"Eh? Well, why didn't you say so? Who are you from?"

"Genetics Investigations is an agency of the Long Range Foundation." I felt Pat's sudden interest. Everybody has heard of the Long Range Foundation, but it happened that Pat and I had just done a term paper on non-profit corporations and had used the Long Range Foundation as a type example.

We got interested in the purposes of the Long Range Foundation. Its coat of arms reads: "Bread Cast Upon the Waters," and its charter is headed: "Dedicated to the Welfare of Our Descendants." The charter goes on with a lot of lawyers' fog but the way the directors have interpreted it has been to spend money only on things that no government and no other corporation would touch. It wasn't enough for a proposed project to be interesting to science or socially desirable; it also had to be so horribly expensive that no one else would touch it and the prospective results had to lie so far in the future that it could not be justified to taxpayers or shareholders. To make the LRF directors light up with enthusiasm you had to suggest something that cost a billion or more and probably wouldn't show results for ten generations, if ever . . . something like how to control the weather (they're working on that) or where does your lap go when you stand up.

The funny thing is that bread cast upon waters does come back seven hundred fold; the most preposterous projects made the LRF embarrassing amounts of money—"embarrassing" to a non-profit corporation that is. Take space travel: it seemed tailor-made, back a couple of hundred years ago, for LRF, since it was fantastically expensive and offered no probable results comparable with the investment. There was a time when governments did some work on it for military reasons, but the Concord of Bayreuth in 1980 put a stop even to that.

So the Long Range Foundation stepped in and happily began wasting money. It came at a time when the corporation unfortunately had made a few billions on the Thompson mass-converter when they had expected to spend at least a century on pure research; since they could not declare a dividend (no stockholders), they had to get rid of the money somehow and space travel looked like a rat hole to pour it down.

Even the kids know what happened to that: Ortega's torch made space travel inside the solar system cheap, fast, and easy, and the one-way energy screen made colonization practical and profitable; the LRF could not unload fast enough to keep from making lots more money.

I did not think all this that evening; LRF was just something that Pat and I happened to know more about than most high school seniors . . . more than Dad knew, apparently, for he snorted and answered, "The Long Range Foundation, eh? I'd almost rather you were from the government. If boondoggles like that were properly taxed, the government wouldn't be squeezing head taxes out of its citizens."

This was not a fair statement, not a "flat-curve relationship" as they call it in Beginning Mathematical Empiricism. Mr. McKeefe had told us to estimate the influence, if any, of LRF on the technology "yeast-form" growth curve; either I should have flunked the course or LRF had kept the curve from leveling off early in the 21st century—I mean to say, the "cultural inheritance," the accumulation of knowledge and wealth that keeps us from being savages, had increased greatly as a result of the tax-free status of such non-profit research corporations. I didn't dream up that opinion; there are figures to prove it. What would have happened if the tribal elders had forced Ugh to hunt with the rest of the tribe instead of staying home and whittling out the first wheel while the idea was bright in his mind?

Mr. Geeking answered, "I can't debate the merits of such matters, Mr. Bartlett. I'm merely an employee."

"And I'm paying your salary. Indirectly and unwillingly, but paying it nevertheless."

I wanted to get into the argument but I could feel Pat holding back. It did not matter; Mr. Geeking shrugged and said, "If so, I thank you. But all I came here for was to ask your twin boys to take a few tests and answer some questions. The tests are harmless and the results will be kept confidential."

"What are you trying to find out?"

I think Mr. Geeking was telling the truth when he answered, "I don't know. I'm merely a field agent; I'm not in charge of the project."

Pat cut in. "I don't see why not, Dad. Do you have the tests in your brief case, Mr. Geeking?"

"Now, Patrick—"

"It's all right, Dad. Let's see the tests, Mr. Geeking."

"Uh, that's not what we had in mind. The Project has set up local offices in the TransLunar Building. The tests take about half a day."

"All the way downtown, huh, and a half day's time . . . what do you pay?"

"Eh? The subjects are asked to contribute their time in the interests of science."

Pat shook his head. "Sorry, Mr. Geeking. This is exam week . . . and my brother and I have part-time school jobs, too."

I kept quiet. Our exams were over, except Analysis of History, which is a snap course involving no math but statistics and pseudospatial calculus, and the school chem lab we worked in was closed for examinations. I was sure Dad did not know these things, or he would have butted in; Dad can shift from prejudice to being a Roman judge at the drop of a hint.

Pat stood up, so I stood up. Mr. Geeking sat tight. "Arrangements can be made," he said evenly.

Pat stuck him as much as we made for a month of washing bottles in the lab, just for one afternoon's work—then upped the ante when it was made clear that we would be obliged to take the tests together (as if we would have done it any other way!). Mr. Geeking paid without a quiver, in cash, in advance.

2

The Natural Logarithm of Two

I NEVER IN MY LIFE SAW SO MANY TWINS AS WERE WAITING ON THE fortieth floor of the TransLunar Building the following Wednesday afternoon. I don't like to be around twins, they make me think I'm seeing double. Don't tell me I'm inconsistent; I *never* saw the twins I am part of—I just saw Pat.

Pat felt the same way; we had never been chummy with other twins. He looked around and whistled. "Tom, did you ever see such a mess of spare parts?"

"Never."

"If I were in charge, I'd shoot half of them." He hadn't spoken loud enough to offend anyone; Pat and I used a prison-yard whisper that no one else could hear although we never had trouble understanding it. "Depressing, isn't it?"

Then he whistled softly and I looked where he was looking. Twins of course, but this was a case of when once is good, twice is better. They were red-headed sisters, younger than we were but not too young—sixteen, maybe—and cute as Persian kittens.

Those sisters had the effect on us that a light has on a moth. Pat whispered, "Tom, we owe it to them to grant them a little of our time," and headed toward them, with me in step. They were dressed in fake Scottish outfits, green plaid which made their hair flame like bonfires and to us they looked as pretty as a new fall of snow.

And just as chilly. Pat got halfway through his opening speech when he trailed off and shut up; they were staring through him. I was blushing and the only thing that kept it from being a major embarrassing incident was a loudspeaker that commenced to bray:

"Attention, please! You are requested to report to the door marked with your surname initial." So we went to door A-to-D and the red-headed sisters headed toward the other end of the alphabet without ever having seen us at all. As we queued up Pat muttered, "Is there egg on my chin? Or have they taken a vow to be old maids?"

"Probably both," I answered. "Anyhow, I prefer blondes." This was true, since Maudie was a blonde. Pat and I had been dating Maudie Kauric for about a year—going steady you could call it, though in my case it usually meant that I was stuck with Maudie's chum Hedda Staley, whose notion of dazzling conversation was to ask me if I didn't think Maudie was the cutest thing ever? Since this was true and unanswerable, our talk did not sparkle.

"Well, so do I," Pat agreed, without saying which blonde—Maudie was the only subject on which we were reticent with each other. "But I have never had a closed mind." He shrugged and added cheerfully, "Anyhow, there are other possibilities."

There certainly were, for of the hundreds of twins present maybe a third were near enough our age not to be out of the question and half of them, as near as I could tell without counting, were of the sex that turns a mere crowd into a social event. However, none came up to the high standards of the redheads, so I began looking over the crowd as a whole.

The oldest pair I saw, two grown men, seemed to be not older than the early thirties and I saw one set of little girls about twelve—they had their mother in tow. But most of them were within a loud shout of twenty. I had concluded that "Genetics Investigations" was picking its samples by age groups when I found that we were at the head of the line and a clerk was saying, "Names, please?"

For the next two hours we were passed from one data collector to another, being finger-printed, giving blood samples, checking "yes" or "no" to hundreds of silly questions that can't be answered "yes" or "no." The physical examination was thorough and involved the usual carefully planned nonsense of keeping a person standing in bare feet on a cold floor in a room five degrees too chilly for naked human skin while prodding the victim and asking him rude personal questions.

I was thoroughly bored and was not even amused when Pat whispered that we should strip the clothes off the doctor now and prod *him* in the belly and get the nurse to record how *he* liked it? My only pleasant thought was that Pat had stuck them plenty for their fun. Then they let us get dressed and ushered us into a room where a rather pretty woman sat behind a desk. She had a transparency viewer on her desk and was looking at two personality profiles superimposed on it. They almost matched and I tried to sneak a look to see where they did not.

But I could not tell Pat's from my own and anyhow I'm not a mathematical psychologist.

She smiled and said, "Sit down, boys. I'm Doctor Arnault." She held up the profiles and a bunch of punched cards and added, "Perfect mirror twins, even to dextrocardia. This should be interesting."

Pat tried to look at the papers. "What's our I.Q. this time, Doctor?"

"Never mind." She put the papers down and covered them, then picked up a deck of cards. "Have you ever used these?"

Of course we had, for they were the classic Rhine test cards, wiggles and stars and so forth. Every high school psychology class has a set and a high score almost always means that some bright boy has figured out a way to cold-deck the teacher. In fact Pat had worked out a simple way to cheat when our teacher, with a tired lack of anger, split us up and made us run tests only with other people—whereupon our scores dropped to the limits of standard error. So I was already certain that Pat and I weren't ESP freaks and the Rhine cards were just another boring test.

But I could feel Pat become attentive. "Keep your ears open, kid," I heard him whisper, "and we'll make this interesting." Dr. Arnault did not hear him, of course.

I wasn't sure we ought to but I knew if he could manage to signal to me I would not be able to refrain from fudging the results. But I need not have worried; Dr. Arnault took Pat out and returned without him. She was hooked by microphone to the other test room but there was no chance to whisper through it; it was hot only when she switched it on.

She started right in. "First test run in twenty seconds, Mabel," she said into the mike and switched it off, then turned to me. "Look at the cards as I turn them," she said. "Don't try, don't strain. Just look at them."

So I looked at the cards. This went on with variations for maybe an hour. Sometimes I was supposed to be receiving, sometimes sending. As far as I was concerned nothing happened, for they never told us our scores.

Finally Dr. Arnault looked at a score sheet and said, "Tom, I want to give you a mild injection. It won't hurt you and it'll wear off before you go home. Okay?"

"What sort?" I said suspiciously.

"Don't fret; it is harmless. I don't want to tell you or you might unconsciously show the reaction you expected."

"Uh, what does my brother say? Does he get one, too?"

"Never mind, please. I'm asking you."

I still hesitated. Dad did not favor injections and such unless necessary; he had made a fuss over our taking part in the encephalitis program. "Are you an M.D.?" I asked.

"No, my degree is in science. Why?"

"Then how do you know it's harmless?"

She bit her lip, then answered, "I'll send for a doctor of medicine, if you prefer."

"Uh, no, I guess that won't be necessary." I was remembering something that Dad had said about the sleeping sickness shots and I added, "Does the Long Range Foundation carry liability insurance for this?"

"What? Why, I think so. Yes, I'm sure they do." She looked at me and added, "Tom, how does a boy your age get to be so suspicious?"

"Huh? Why ask me? You're the psychologist, ma'am. Anyhow," I added, "if you had sat on as many tacks as I have, you'd be suspicious too."

"Mmm . . . never mind. I've been studying for years and I still don't know what the younger generation is coming to. Well, are you going to take the injection?"

"Uh, I'll take it—since the LRF carries insurance. Just write out what it is you are giving me and sign it."

She got two bright pink spots in her cheeks. But she took out stationery, wrote on it, folded it into an envelope and sealed it. "Put it in your pocket," she said briskly. "Don't look at it until the experiments are over. Now bare your left forearm."

As she gave me the shot she said sweetly, "This is going to sting a little . . . I hope." It did.

She turned out all the lights except the light in the transparency viewer. "Are you comfortable?"

"Sure."

"I'm sorry if I seemed vexed. I want you to relax and be comfortable." She came over and did something to the chair I was in; it opened out gently until I was practically lying in a hammock. "Relax and don't fight it. If you find yourself getting sleepy, that is to be expected." She sat down and all I could see was her face, illuminated by the viewer. She was awfully pretty, I decided, even though she was too old for it to matter . . . at least thirty, maybe older. And she was nice, too. She spoke for a few minutes in her gentle voice but I don't remember exactly what she said.

I must have gone to sleep, for next it was pitch dark and Pat was right there by me, although I hadn't noticed the light go out nor the door being opened. I started to speak when I heard him whisper:

"Tom, did you ever see such nonsensical rigamarole?"

I whispered back, "Reminds me of the time we were initiated into the Congo Cannibals."

"Keep your voice down; they'll catch on."

"You're the one who is talking too loud. Anyhow, who cares? Let's give 'em the Cannibal war whoop and scare 'em out of their shoes."

"Later, later. Right now my girl friend Mabel wants me to give you a string of numbers. So we'll let them have their fun first. After all, they're paying for it."

"Okay."

"Point six nine three one."

"That's the natural logarithm of two."

"What did you think it was? Mabel's telephone number? Shut up and listen. Just repeat the numbers back. Three point one four one five nine . . ."

It went on quite a while. Some were familiar numbers like the first two; the rest may have been random or even Mabel's phone number, for all of me. I got bored and was beginning to think about sticking in a war whoop on my own when Dr. Arnault said quietly, "End of test run. Both of you please keep quiet and relax for a few minutes. Mabel, I'll meet you in the data comparison room." I heard her go out, so I dropped the war whoop notion and relaxed. Repeating all those numbers in the dark had made me dopey anyhow—and as Uncle Steve says, when you get a chance to rest, do so; you may not get another chance soon.

Presently I heard the door open again, then I was blinking at bright lights. Dr. Arnault said, "That's all today, Tom . . . and thank you very much. We want to see you and your brother at the same time tomorrow."

I blinked again and looked around. "Where's Pat? What does he say?"

"You'll find him in the outer lobby. He told me that you could come tomorrow. You can, can't you?"

"Uh, I suppose so, if it's all right with him." I was feeling sheepish about the trick we had pulled, so I added, "Dr. Arnault? I'm sorry I annoyed you."

She patted my hand and smiled. "That's all right. You were right to be cautious and you were a good subject. You should see the wild ones we sometimes draw. See you tomorrow."

Pat was waiting in the big room where we had seen the redheads. He fell into step and we headed for the drop. "I raised the fee for tomorrow," he whispered smugly.

"You did? Pat, do you think we should do this? I mean, fun is fun, but if they ever twig that we are faking, they'll be sore. They might even make us pay back what they've already paid us."

"How can they? We've been paid to show up and take tests. We've done that. It's up to them to rig tests that can't be beaten. I could, if I were doing it."

"Pat, you're dishonest and crooked, both." I thought about Dr. Arnault . . . she was a nice lady. "I think I'll stay home tomorrow."

I said this just as Pat stepped off the drop. He was ten feet below me all the way down and had forty stories in which to consider his answer. As I landed beside him he answered by changing the subject. "They gave you a hypodermic?"

"Yes."

"Did you think to make them sign an admission of liability, or did you goof?"

"Well, sort of." I felt in my pocket for the envelope; I'd forgotten about it. "I made Dr. Arnault write down what she was giving us."

Pat reached for the envelope. "My apologies, maestro. With my brains and your luck we've got them where we want them." He started to open the envelope. "I bet it was neopentothal—or one of the barbiturates."

I snatched it back. "That's mine."

"Well, open it," he answered, "and don't obstruct traffic. I want to see what dream drug they gave us."

We had come out into the pedestrian level and his advice did have merit. Before opening it I led us across the change strips onto the fast-west strip and stepped behind a wind break. As I unfolded the paper Pat read over my shoulder:

" 'Long Range Fumbling, and so forth—injections given to subjects 7L435 & -6 T. P. Bartlett & P. H. Bartlett (iden-twins)—each one-tenth c.c. distilled water raised to normal salinity,' signed 'Doris Arnault, Sc.D., for the Foundation.' Tom, we've been hoaxed!"

I stared at it, trying to fit what I had experienced with what the paper said. Pat added hopefully, "Or is this the hoax? Were we injected with something else and they didn't want to admit it?"

"No," I said slowly. I was sure Dr. Arnault wouldn't write down "water" and actually give us one of the sleeping drugs—she wasn't that sort of person. "Pat, we weren't drugged . . . we were *hypnotized*."

He shook his head. "Impossible. Granting that I could be hypnotized, you couldn't be. Nothing there to hypnotize. And I wasn't hypnotized, comrade. No spinning lights, no passes with the hands—why, my girl Mabel didn't even stare in my eyes. She just gave me the shot and told me to take it easy and let it take effect."

"Don't be juvenile, Pat. Spinning lights and such is for suckers. I don't care whether you call it hypnotism or salesmanship. They gave us hypos and suggested that we would be sleepy—so we fell asleep."

"So I was sleepy! Anyhow that wasn't quite what Mabel did. She told me not to go to sleep, or if I did, to wake up when she called me. Then when they brought you in, she—"

"Wait a minute. You mean when they moved you back into the room I was in—"

"No, I don't mean anything of the sort. After they brought you in, Mabel gave me this list of numbers and I read them to you and—"

"Wait a minute," I said. "Pat, you're mixed up. How could you *read* them in pitch darkness? She must have read them to you. I mean—" I stopped, for I was getting mixed up myself. Well, she could have read to him from another room. "Were you wearing headphones?"

"What's that got to do with it? Anyhow, it wasn't pitch dark, not after they brought you in. She held up the numbers on a board that was rigged with a light of its own, enough to let me see the numbers and her hands."

"Pat, I wish you wouldn't keep repeating nonsense. Hypnotized or not, I was never so dopey that I couldn't notice anything that happened. I was never moved anywhere; they probably wheeled you in without disturbing you. And the room we were in was pitch dark, not a glimmer."

Pat did not answer right away, which wasn't like him. At last he said, "Tom, are you sure?"

"Sure I'm sure!"

He sighed. "I hate to say this, because I know what you will say. But what are you supposed to do when none of your theories fits?"

"Huh? Is this a quiz? You throw 'em away and try a new one. Basic methodology, freshman year."

"Okay, just slip this on for size, don't mind the pattern: Tom, my boy, brace yourself—we're *mind* readers."

I tried it and did not like it. "Pat, just because you can't explain everything is no reason to talk like the fat old women who go to fortune tellers. We're muddled, I admit, whether it was drugs or hypnosis. But we couldn't have been reading each other's minds or we would have been doing it years ago. We would have noticed."

"Not necessarily. There's never anything much going on in your mind, so why should I notice?"

"But it stands to reason—"

"What's the natural log of two?"

" 'Point six nine three one' is what you said, though I've got very little use for four-place tables. What's that got to do with it?"

"I used four-place because she gave it to me that way. Do you remember what she said just before I gave you that number?"

"Huh? Who?"

"Mabel. Dr. Mabel Lichtenstein. What did she say?"

"Nobody said anything."

"Tom, my senile symbiote, she told me what to do, to wit, read the numbers to you. She told me this in a clear, penetrating soprano. You didn't hear her?"

"No."

"Then you weren't in the same room. You weren't within earshot, even though I was prepared to swear that they had shoved you in right by me. I *knew* you were there. But you weren't. So it was telepathy."

I was confused. I didn't feel telepathic; I merely felt hungry.

"Me, too, on both counts," Pat agreed. "So let's stop at Berkeley Station and get a sandwich."

I followed him off the strips, feeling not quite as hungry and even more confused. Pat had answered a remark I had not made.

3

Project Lebensraum

EVEN THOUGH I WAS TOLD TO TAKE MY TIME AND TELL EVERYTHING, it can't be done. I haven't had time to add to this for days, but even if I didn't have to work I still could not "tell all," because it takes *more* than a day to write down what happens in one day. The harder you try the farther behind you get. So I'm going to quit trying and just hit the high spots.

Anyhow everybody knows the general outline of Project Lebensraum.

We did not say anything to Mum and Dad about that first day. You can't expose parents to that sort of thing; they get jittery and start issuing edicts. We just told them the tests would run a second day and that nobody had told us what the results were.

Dr. Arnault seemed unsurprised when we told her we knew the score, even when I blurted out that we thought we had been faking but apparently weren't. She just nodded and said that it had been necessary to encourage us to think that everything was commonplace, even if there had to be a little fibbing on both sides. "I had the advantage of having your personality analyses to guide me," she added. "Sometimes in psychology you have to go roundabout to arrive at the truth.

"We'll try a more direct way today," she went on. "We'll put you two back to back but close enough together that you unquestionably can hear each other. But I am going to use a sound screen to cut you off partly or completely from time to time without your knowing it."

It was a lot harder the second time. Naturally we tried and naturally we flubbed. But Dr. Arnault was patient and so was Dr. Lichtenstein—Pat's "Dr. Mabel." She preferred to be called Dr. Mabel; she was short and pudgy and younger than Dr. Arnault and about as cute as a female can be and still look like a sofa pillow. It wasn't until later that we found out she was boss of the research team and world famous. "Giggly little fat girl" was an act she used to put ordinary people, meaning Pat and myself, at their ease. I guess this proves you should ignore the package and read the fine print.

So she giggled and Dr. Arnault looked serious and we could not tell whether we were reading minds or not. I could hear Tom's whispers—they told us to go ahead and whisper—and he could hear mine and sometimes they would fade. I was sure we weren't getting anything, not telepathy I mean, for it was just the way Pat and I used to whisper answers back and forth in school without getting caught.

Finally Dr. Mabel giggled sheepishly and said, "I guess that's enough for today. Don't you think so, Doctor?"

Dr. Arnault agreed and Pat and I sat up and faced each other. I said, "I suppose yesterday was a fluke. I guess we disappointed you."

Dr. Mabel looked like a startled kitten. Dr. Arnault answered soberly, "I don't know what you expected, Tom, but for the past hour you and your brother have been cut off from hearing each other during every test run."

"But I *did* hear him."

"You certainly did. But not with your ears. We've been recording each side of the sound barrier. Perhaps we should play back part of it."

Dr. Mabel giggled. "That's a good idea." So they did. It started out with all four voices while they told us what they wanted, then there were just my whispers and Pat's, reading lines back and forth from *The Comedy of Errors*. They must have had parabolic mikes focused on us for our whispers sounded like a wind storm.

Pat's whispers gradually faded out. But mine kept right on going . . . answering a dead silence.

We signed a research contract with the Foundation and Dad countersigned it, after an argument. He thought mind-reading was folderol and we did not dispute him, since the clincher was that money was scarce as always and it was a better-paying job than any summer job we could get, fat enough to insure that we could start college even if our scholarships didn't come through.

But before the summer was over they let us in on the connection between "Genetics Investigations" and "Project Lebensraum." That was a horse of another color—a very dark black, from our parents' standpoint.

Long before that time Pat and I could telepath as easily as we could talk and just as accurately, without special nursing and at any distance. We must have been doing it for years without knowing it—in fact Dr.

Arnault made a surprise recording of our prison-yard whispering (when we weren't trying to telepath, just our ordinary private conversation) and proved that neither one of us could understand our recorded whispers when we were keeping it down low to keep other people from hearing.

She told us that it was theoretically possible that everyone was potentially telepathic, but that it had proved difficult to demonstrate it except with identical twins—and then only with about ten per cent. "We don't know why, but think of an analogy with tuned radio circuits."

"Brain waves?" I asked.

"Don't push the analogy too far. It can't be the brain waves we detect with an encephalograph equipment or we would have been selling commercial telepathic equipment long since. And the human brain is not a radio. But whatever it is, two persons from the same egg stand an enormously better chance of being 'tuned in' than two non-twins do. I can't read your mind and you can't read mine and perhaps we never will. There have been only a few cases in all the history of psychology of people who appeared to be able to 'tune in' on just anyone, and most of those aren't well documented."

Pat grinned and winked at Dr. Mabel. "So we are a couple of freaks."

She looked wide-eyed and started to answer but Dr. Arnault beat her to it. "Not at all, Pat. In you it is normal. But we do have teams in the project who are not identical twins. Some husbands and wives, a few fraternal siblings, even some pairs who were brought together by the research itself. They are the 'freaks.' If we could find out how *they* do it, we might be able to set up conditions to let anyone do it."

Dr. Mabel shivered. "What a terrible thought! There is too little privacy now."

I repeated this to Maudie (with Pat's interruptions and corrections) because the news services had found out what was going on in "Genetics Investigations" and naturally we "mind readers" came in for a lot of silly publicity and just as naturally, under Hedda Staley's mush-headed prodding, Maudie began to wonder if a girl had any privacy? She had, of course; I could not have read her mind with a search warrant, nor could Pat. She would have believed our simple statement if Hedda had not harped on it. She nearly managed to bust us up with Maudie, but we jettisoned her instead and we had threesome dates with Maudie until Pat was sent away.

But that wasn't until nearly the end of the summer after they explained Project Lebensraum.

About a week before our contract was to run out they gathered us twins together to talk to us. There had been hundreds that first day, dozens the second day, but just enough to crowd a big conference room by the end of summer. The redheads were among the survivors but Pat and I did not sit by them even though there was room; they still maintained their icicle attitude and were self-centered as oysters. The rest of us were all old friends by now.

A Mr. Howard was introduced as representing the Foundation. He ladled out the usual guff about being happy to meet us and appreciating the honor and so forth. Pat said to me, *"Hang onto your wallet, Tom. This bloke is selling something."* Now that we knew what we were doing Pat and I talked in the presence of other people even more than we used to. We no longer bothered to whisper since we had had proved to us that we weren't hearing the whispers. But we did subvocalize the words silently, as it helped in being understood. Early in the summer we had tried to do without words and read minds directly but it did not work. Oh, I could latch on to Pat, but the silly, incoherent rumbling that went on in his mind in place of thought was confusing and annoying, as senseless as finding yourself inside another person's dream. So I learned not to listen unless he "spoke" to me and he did the same. When we did, we used words and sentences like anybody else. There was none of this fantastic, impossible popular nonsense about instantly grasping the contents of another person's mind; we simply "talked."

One thing that had bothered me was why Pat's telepathic "voice" sounded like his real one. It had not worried me when I did not know what we were doing, but once I realized that these "sounds" weren't sounds, it bothered me. I began to wonder if I was all there and for a week I could not "hear" him—psychosomatic telepathic-deafness Dr. Arnault called it.

She got me straightened out by explaining what hearing is. You don't hear with your ears, you hear with your brain; you don't see with your eyes, you see with your brain. When you touch something, the sensation is not in your finger, it is inside your head. The ears and eyes and fingers are just data collectors; it is the brain that abstracts order out of a chaos of data and gives it meaning. "A new baby does not really see," she said. "Watch the eyes of one and you can see that it doesn't. Its eyes work but its brain has not yet learned to see. But once the brain has acquired the habits of abstracting as 'seeing' and 'hearing,' the habit persists. How would you expect to 'hear' what your twin says to you telepathically? As little tinkling bells or dancing lights? Not at all. You expect words, your brain 'hears' words; it is a process it is used to and knows how to handle."

I no longer worried about it. I could hear Pat's voice clearer than I could hear the voice of the speaker addressing us. No doubt there were fifty other conversations around us, but I heard no one but Pat and it was obvious that the speaker could not hear anybody (and that he did not know much about telepathy) for he went on:

"Possibly a lot of you wonderful people—" (This with a sickening smile) "—are reading my mind right now. I hope not, or if you are I hope you will bear with me until I have said my say."

"What did I tell you?" Pat put in. *"Don't sign anything until I check it."*

("Shut up,") I told him. ("I want to listen.") His voice used to sound like a whisper; now it tended to drown out real sounds.

Mr. Howard went on, "Perhaps you have wondered why the Long Range Foundation has sponsored this research. The Foundation is always interested in anything which will add to human knowledge. But there is a much more important reason, a supremely important reason . . . and a grand purpose to which you yourselves can be supremely important."

"See? Be sure to count your change."

("Quiet, Pat.")

"Let me quote," Mr. Howard continued, "from the charter of the Long Range Foundation: 'Dedicated to the welfare of our descendants.' " He paused dramatically—I think that was what he intended. "Ladies and gentlemen, what one thing above all is necessary for our descendants?"

"Ancestors!" Pat answered promptly. For a second I thought that he had used his vocal cords. But nobody else noticed.

"There can be only one answer—living room! Room to grow, room to raise families, broad acres of fertile grain, room for parks and schools and homes. We have over five billion human souls on this planet; it was crowded to the point of marginal starvation more than a century ago with only half that number. Yet this afternoon there are a quarter of a million more of us than there were at this same hour yesterday—ninety million more people each year. Only by monumental efforts of reclamation and conservation, plus population control measures that grow daily more difficult, have we been able to stave off starvation. We have placed a sea in the Sahara, we have melted the Greenland ice cap, we have watered the windy steppes, yet each year there is more and more pressure for more and more room for endlessly more people."

I don't care for orations and this was all old stuff. Shucks, Pat and I knew it if anyone did; we were the kittens that should have been drowned; our old man paid a yearly fine for our very existence.

"It has been a century since the inception of interplanetary travel;

man has spread through the Solar System. One would think that nine planets would be ample for a race too fertile for one. Yet you all know that such has not been the case. Of the daughters of Father Sol only fair Terra is truly suited to Man."

"I'll bet he writes advertising slogans."

("Poor ones,") I agreed.

"Colonize the others we have done, but only at a great cost. The sturdy Dutch in pushing back the sea have not faced such grim and nearly hopeless tasks as the colonists of Mars and Venus and Ganymede. What the human race needs and must have are not these frozen or burning or airless discards of creation. We need more planets like this gentle one we are standing on. And there *are* more, many more!" He waved his hands at the ceiling and looked up. "There are dozens, hundreds, thousands, countless hordes of them . . . out there. Ladies and gentlemen, *it is time for the stars!*"

"Here comes the pitch," Pat said quietly. *"A fast curve, breaking inside."*

("Pat, what the deuce is he driving at?")

"He's a real estate agent."

Pat was not far off but I am not going to quote the rest of Mr. Howard's speech. He was a good sort when we got to know him but he was dazzled by the sound of his own voice, so I'll summarize. He reminded us that the Torchship *Avant-Garde* had headed out to Proxima Centauri six years back. Pat and I knew about it not only from the news but because mother's brother, Uncle Steve, had put in for it—he was turned down, but for a while we enjoyed prestige just from being related to somebody on the list—I guess we gave the impression around school that Uncle Steve was certain to be chosen.

Nobody had heard from the *Avant-Garde* and maybe she would be back in fifteen or twenty years and maybe not. The reason we hadn't heard from her, as Mr. Howard pointed out and everybody knows, is that you don't send radio messages back from a ship light-years away and traveling just under the speed of light. Even if you assumed that a ship could carry a power plant big enough to punch radio messages across light-years (which may not be impossible in some cosmic sense but surely is impossible in terms of modern engineering)—even so, what use are messages which travel just barely faster than the ship that sends them? The *Avant-Garde* would be home almost as quickly as any report she could send, even by radio.

Some fuzzbrain asked about messenger rockets. Mr. Howard looked pained and tried to answer and I didn't listen. If radio isn't fast enough, how can a messenger rocket be faster? I'll bet Dr. Einstein spun in his grave.

Mr. Howard hurried on before there were any more silly interruptions. The Long Range Foundation proposed to send out a dozen more starships in all directions to explore Sol-type solar systems for Earth-type planets, planets for colonization. The ships might be gone a long time, for each one would explore more than one solar system.

"And this, ladies and gentlemen, is where you are indispensable to this great project for living room—for *you* will be the means whereby the captains of those ships report back what they have found!"

Even Pat kept quiet.

Presently a man stood up in the back of the room. He was one of the oldest twins among us; he and his brother were about thirty-five. "Excuse me, Mr. Howard, but may I ask a question?"

"Surely."

"I am Gregory Graham; this is my brother Grant Graham. We're physicists. Now we don't claim to be expert in cosmic phenomena but we do know something about communication theory. Granting for the sake of argument that telepathy would work over interstellar distances—I don't think so but I've no proof that it wouldn't—even granting that, I can't see where it helps. Telepathy, light, radio waves, even gravity, are all limited to the speed of light. That is in the very nature of the physical universe, an ultimate limit for all communication. Any other view falls into the ancient philosophical contradiction of action-at-a-distance. It is just possible that you might use telepathy to report findings and let the ship go on to new explorations—but the message would still take light-years to come back. Communication back and forth between a starship and Earth, even by telepathy, is utterly impossible, contrary to the known laws of physics." He looked apologetic and sat down.

I thought Graham had him on the hip. Pat and I got good marks in physics and what Graham had said was the straight word, right out of the book. But Howard did not seem bothered. "I'll let an expert answer. Dr. Lichtenstein? If you please—"

Dr. Mabel stood up and blushed and giggled and looked flustered and said, "I'm terribly sorry, Mr. Graham, I really am, but telepathy isn't like that at all." She giggled again and said, "I shouldn't be saying this, since you are telepathic and I'm not, but telepathy doesn't pay the least bit of attention to the speed of light."

"But it *has* to. The laws of physics—"

"Oh, dear! Have we given you the impression that telepathy is physical?" She twisted her hands. "It probably isn't."

"Everything is physical. I include 'physiological,' of course."

"It is? You do? Oh, I wish I could be sure . . . but physics has always been much too deep for me. But I don't know how you can be sure that telepathy is physical; we haven't been able to make it register on any instrument. Dear me, we don't even know how consciousness hooks into matter. Is consciousness physical? I'm sure I don't know. But we do know that telepathy is faster than light because we measured it."

Pat sat up with a jerk. *"Stick around, kid. I think we'll stay for the second show."*

Graham looked stunned. Dr. Mabel said hastily, "I didn't do it; it was Dr. Abernathy."

"*Horatio* Abernathy?" demanded Graham.

"Yes, that's his first name, though I never dared call him by it. He's rather important."

"Just the Nobel prize," Graham said grimly, "in field theory. Go on. What did he find?"

"Well, we sent this one twin out to Ganymede—such an awfully long way. Then we used simultaneous radio-telephony and telepathy messages, with the twin on Ganymede talking by radio while he was talking directly—telepathically, I mean—to his twin back in Buenos Aires. The telepathic message always beat the radio message by about forty minutes. That would be right, wouldn't it? You can see the exact figures in my office."

Graham managed to close his mouth. "When did this happen? Why hasn't it been published? Who has been keeping it secret? It's the most important thing since the Michelson-Morley experiment—it's terrible!"

Dr. Mabel looked upset and Mr. Howard butted in soothingly. "Nobody has been suppressing knowledge, Mr. Graham, and Dr. Abernathy is preparing an article for publication in the *Physical Review*. However I admit that the Foundation did ask him not to give out an advance release in order to give us time to go ahead with another project—the one you know as 'Genetics Investigations'—on a crash-priority basis. We felt we were entitled to search out and attempt to sign up potential telepathic teams before every psychological laboratory and, for that matter, every ambitious showman, tried to beat us to it. Dr. Abernathy was willing—he doesn't like premature publication."

"If it will make you feel better, Mr. Graham," Dr. Mabel said diffidently, "telepathy doesn't pay attention to the inverse-square law either. The signal strength was as strong at half a billion miles as when the paired telepaths were in adjoining rooms."

Graham sat down heavily. "I don't know whether it does or it doesn't. I'm busy rearranging everything I have ever believed."

The interruption by the Graham brothers had explained some things but had pulled us away from the purpose of the meeting, which was for Mr. Howard to sell us on signing up as spacemen. He did not have to sell me. I guess every boy wants to go out into space; Pat and I had run away from home once to enlist in the High Marines—and this was much more than just getting on the Earth-Mars-Venus run; this meant exploring the stars.

The Stars!

"We've told you about this before your research contracts run out," Mr. Howard explained, "so that you will have time to consider it, time for us to explain the conditions and advantages."

I did not care what the advantages were. If they had invited me to hook a sled on behind, I would have said yes, not worrying about torch blast or space suits or anything.

"Both members of each telepathic team will be equally well taken care of," he assured us. "The starside member will have good pay and good working conditions in the finest of modern torchships in the company of crews selected for psychological compatibility as well as for special training; the earthside member will have his financial future assured, as well as his physical welfare." He smiled. "Most assuredly his physical welfare, for it is necessary that he be kept alive and well as long as science can keep him so. It is not too much to say that signing this contract will add thirty years to your lives."

It burst on me why the twins they had tested had been young people. The twin who went out to the stars would not age very much, not at the speed of light. Even if he stayed away a century it would not seem that long to him—but his twin who stayed behind would grow older. They would have to pamper him like royalty, keep him alive—or their "radio" would break down.

Pat said, *"Milky Way, here I come!"*

But Mr. Howard was still talking. "We want you to think this over carefully; it is the most important decision you will ever make. On the shoulders of you few and others like you in other cities around the globe, all told just a tiny fraction of one per cent of the human race, on you precious few rest the hopes of all humanity. So think carefully and give us a chance to explain anything which may trouble you. Don't act hastily."

The red-headed twins got up and walked out, noses in the air. They did not have to speak to make it clear that they would have nothing to do with anything so unladylike, so rude and crude, as exploring space. In the silence in which they paraded out Pat said to me, *"There go the Pioneer Mothers. That's the spirit that discovered America."* As they passed us he cut loose with a loud razzberry—and I suddenly realized that he was not telepathing when the redheads stiffened and hurried faster. There was an embarrassed laugh and Mr. Howard quickly picked up the business at hand as if nothing had happened while I bawled Pat out.

Mr. Howard asked us to come back at the usual time tomorrow, when Foundation representatives would explain details. He invited us to bring our lawyers, or (those of us who were under age, which was more than half) our parents and their lawyers.

Pat was bubbling over as we left, but I had lost my enthusiasm. In the middle of Mr. Howard's speech I had had a great light dawn: one of us was going to have to stay behind and I knew as certainly as bread falls butter side down which one it would be. A possible thirty more years on my life was no inducement to me. What use is thirty extra years wrapped in cottonwool? There would be no spacing for the twin left behind, not even inside the Solar System . . . and I had never even been to the Moon.

I tried to butt in on Pat's enthusiasm and put it to him fair and square, for I was darned if I was going to take the small piece of cake this time without argument.

"Look, Pat, I'll draw straws with you for it. Or match coins."

"Huh? What are you talking about?"

"You know what I'm talking about!"

He just brushed it aside and grinned. "You worry too much, Tom. They'll pick the teams the way they want to. It won't be up to us."

I knew he was determined to go and I knew I would lose.

4

Half a Loaf

Our parents made the predictable uproar. A conference in the Bartlett family always sounded like a zoo at feeding time but this one set a new high. In addition to Pat and myself, Faith, Hope, and Charity, and our parents, there was Faith's fairly new husband, Frank Dubois, and Hope's brand-new fiancé, Lothar Sembrich. The last two did not count and both of them seemed to me to be examples of what lengths a girl will go to in order to get married, but they used up space and occasionally contributed remarks to confuse the issue. But Mother's brother, Uncle Steve, was there, too, having popped up on Earthside furlough.

It was Uncle Steve's presence that decided Pat to bring it out in the open instead of waiting to tackle Dad and Mum one at a time. Both of them considered Uncle Steve a disturbing influence but they were proud of him; one of his rare visits was always a holiday.

Mr. Howard had given us a sample contract to take home and look over. After dinner Pat said, "By the way, Dad, the Foundation offered us a new contract today, a long-term one." He took it out of his pocket but did not offer it to Dad.

"I trust you told them that you were about to start school again?"

"Sure, we told them that, but they insisted that we take the contract home to show our parents. Okay, we knew what your answer would be." Pat started to put the contract into his pocket.

I said to Pat privately, ("What's the silly idea? You've made him say 'no' and now he can't back down.")

"Not yet he hasn't," Pat answered on our private circuit. *"Don't joggle my elbow."*

Dad was already reaching out a hand. "Let me see it. You should never make up your mind without knowing the facts."

Pat was not quick about passing it over. "Well, there *is* a scholarship clause," he admitted, "but Tom and I wouldn't be able to go to school together the way we always have."

"That's not necessarily bad. You two are too dependent on each other. Some day you will have to face the cold, cruel world alone . . . and going to different schools might be a good place to start."

Pat stuck out the contract, folded to the second page. "It's paragraph ten."

Dad read paragraph ten first, just as Pat meant him to do, and his eyebrows went up. Paragraph ten agreed that the party of the first part, the LRF, would keep the party of the second part in any school of his choice, all expenses, for the duration of the contract, or a shorter time at his option, and agreed to do the same for the party of the third part after the completion of the active period of the contract, plus tutoring during the active period—all of which was a long-winded way of saying that the Foundation would put the one who stayed home through school now and the one who went starside through school when he got back . . . all this in addition to our salaries; see paragraph seven.

So Dad turned to paragraph seven and his eyebrows went higher and his pipe went out. He looked at Pat. "Do I understand that they intend to appoint you two 'communications technicians tenth grade' with no experience?"

Uncle Steve sat up and almost knocked his chair over. "Bruce, did you say 'tenth grade'?"

"So it says."

"Regular LRF pay scales?"

"Yes. I don't know how much that is, but I believe they ordinarily hire skilled ratings beginning at third grade."

Uncle Steve whistled. "I'd hate to tell you how much money it is, Bruce—but the chief electron pusher on Pluto is tenth pay grade . . . and it took him twenty years and a doctor's degree to get there." Uncle Steve looked at us. "Give out, shipmates. Where did they bury the body? Is it a bribe?" Pat did not answer. Uncle Steve turned to Dad and said, "Never mind the fine print, Bruce; just have the kids sign it. Each one of them will make more than you and me together. Never argue with Santa Claus."

But Dad was already reading the fine print, from subparagraph one-A to the penalty clauses. It was written in lawyer language but what it did was to sign us up as crew members for one voyage of an LRF ship, except that one of us was required to perform his duties Earthside. There was lots more to nail it down so that the one who stayed Earthside could not wiggle out, but that was all it amounted to.

The contract did not say where the ship would go or how long the voyage would last.

Dad finally put the contract down and Charity grabbed it. Dad took it from her and passed it over to Mother. Then he said, "Boys, this contract looks so favorable that I suspect there must be a catch. Tomorrow morning I'm going to get hold of Judge Holland and ask him to go over it with me. But if I read it correctly, you are being offered all these benefits—and an extravagant salary—provided one of you makes one voyage in the *Lewis and Clark*."

Uncle Steve said suddenly, "The *Lewis and Clark*, Bruce?"

"The *Lewis and Clark*, or such sister ship as may be designated. Why? You know the ship, Steve?"

Uncle Steve got poker-faced and answered, "I've never been in her. New ship, I understand. Well equipped."

"I'm glad to hear it." Dad looked at Mum. "Well, Molly?"

Mother did not answer. She was reading the contract and steadily getting whiter. Uncle Steve caught my eye and shook his head very slightly. I said to Pat, ("Uncle Steve has spotted the catch in it.")

"He won't hinder."

Mother looked up at last and spoke to Dad in a high voice. "I suppose you are going to consent?" She sounded sick. She put down the contract and Charity grabbed it again just as Hope grabbed it from the other side. It ended with our brother-in-law Frank Dubois holding it while everybody else read over his shoulders.

"Now, my dear," Dad said mildly, "remember that boys do grow up. I would like to keep the family together forever—but it can't be that way and you know it."

"Bruce, you promised that they would not go out into space."

Her brother shot her a glance—his chest was covered with ribbons he had won in space. But Dad went on just as mildly. "Not quite, dear. I promised you that I would not consent to minority enlistment in the peace forces; I want them to finish school and I did not want you upset. But this is another matter . . . and, if we refuse, it won't be long before they can enlist whether we like it or not."

Mother turned to Uncle Steve and said bitterly, "Stephen, you put this idea in their heads."

He looked annoyed then answered as gently as Dad. "Take it easy, Sis. I've been away; you can't pin this on me. Anyhow, you don't put ideas in boys' heads; they grow them naturally."

Frank Dubois cleared his throat and said loudly, "Since this seems to be a family conference, no doubt you would like my opinion."

I said, to Pat only, ("Nobody asked your opinion, you lard head!")

Pat answered, *"Let him talk. He's our secret weapon, maybe."*

"If you want the considered judgment of an experienced businessman, this so-called contract is either a practical joke or a proposition so preposterous as to be treated with contempt. I understand that the twins are supposed to have some freak talent—although I've seen no evidence of it—but the idea of paying them more than a man receives in his mature years, well, it's just not the right way to raise boys. If they were sons of mine, I would forbid it. Of course, they're not—"

"No, they're not," Dad agreed.

Frank looked sharply at him. "Was that sarcasm, Father Bartlett? I'm merely trying to help. But as I told you the other day, if the twins will go to some good business school and work hard, I'd find a place for them in the bakery. If they make good, there is no reason why they should not do as well as I have done." Frank was his father's junior partner in an automated bakery; he always managed to let people know how much money he made. "But as for this notion of going out into space, I've always said that if a man expects to make anything of himself, he should stay home and work. Excuse me, Steve."

Uncle Steve said woodenly, "I'd be glad to excuse you."

"Eh?"

"Forget it, forget it. You stay out of space and I'll promise not to bake any bread. By the way, there's flour on your lapel."

Frank glanced down hastily. Faith brushed at his jacket and said, "Why, that's just powder."

"Of course it is," Frank agreed, brushing at it himself. "I'll have you know, Steve, that I'm usually much too busy to go down on the processing floor. I'm hardly ever out of the office."

"So I suspected."

Frank decided that he and Faith were late for another appointment and got up to go, when Dad stopped them. "Frank? What was that about my boys being freaks?"

"What? I never said anything of the sort."

"I'm glad to hear it."

They left in a sticky silence, except that Pat was humming silently and loudly the *March of the Gladiators*. *"We've got it won, kid!"*

It seemed so to me, too—but Pat had to press our luck. He picked up the contract. "Then it's okay, Dad?"

"Mmm . . . I want to consult Judge Holland—and I'm not speaking for your mother." That did not worry us; Mum wouldn't hold out if

Dad agreed, especially not with Uncle Steve around. "But you could say that the matter has not been disapproved." He frowned. "By the way, there is no time limit mentioned in there."

Uncle Steve fielded that one for us. "That's customary on a commercial ship, Bruce . . . which is what this is, legally. You sign on for the voyage, home planet to home planet."

"Uh, no doubt. But didn't they give you some idea, boys?"

I heard Pat moan, *"There goes the ball game. What'll we tell him, Tom?"* Dad waited and Uncle Steve eyed us.

Finally Uncle Steve said, "Better speak up, boys. Perhaps I should have mentioned that I'm trying to get a billet on one of those ships myself—special discharge and such. So I know."

Pat muttered something. Dad said sharply, "Speak up, son."

"They told us the voyage would probably last . . . about a century."

Mum fainted and Uncle Steve caught her and everybody rushed around with cold compresses getting in each other's way and we were all upset. Once she pulled out of it Uncle Steve said to Dad, "Bruce? I'm going to take the boys out and buy them a tall, strong sarsaparilla and get them out from under foot. You won't want to talk tonight anyhow."

Dad agreed absently that it was a good idea. I guess Dad loved all of us; nevertheless, when the chips were down, nobody counted but Mother.

Uncle Steve took us to a place where he could get something more to his taste than sarsaparilla, then vetoed it when Pat tried to order beer. "Don't try to show off, youngster. You are not going to put me in the position of serving liquor to my sister's kids."

"Beer can't hurt you."

"So? I'm still looking for the bloke who told me it was a soft drink. I'm going to beat him to a pulp with a stein. Pipe down." So we picked soft drinks and he drank some horrible mixture he called a Martian shandy and we talked about Project Lebensraum. He knew more about it than we did even though no press release had been made until that day—I suppose the fact that he had been assigned to the Chief of Staff's office had something to do with it, but he did not say.

Presently Pat looked worried and said, "See here, Uncle Steve, is there any chance that they will let us? Or should Tom and I just forget it?"

"Eh? Of course they are going to let you do it."

"Huh? It didn't look like it tonight. If I know Dad, he would skin us for rugs rather than make Mum unhappy."

"No doubt. And a good idea. But believe me, boys, this is in the bag . . . provided you use the right arguments."

"Which is?"

"Mmm . . . boys, being a staff rating, I've served with a lot of high brass. When you are right and a general is wrong, there is only one way to get him to change his mind. You shut up and don't argue. You let the facts speak for themselves and give him time to figure out a logical reason for reversing himself."

Pat looked unconvinced; Uncle Steve went on, "Believe me. Your pop is a reasonable man and, while your mother is not, she would rather be hurt herself than make anybody she loves unhappy. That contract is all in your favor and they can't refuse—provided you give them time to adjust to the idea. But if you tease and bulldoze and argue the way you usually do, you'll get them united against you."

"Huh? But I never tease, I merely use logical—"

"Stow it, you make me tired. Pat, you were one of the most unlovable brats that ever squawled to get his own way . . . and, Tom, you weren't any better. You haven't mellowed with age; you've simply sharpened your techniques. Now you are being offered something free that I would give my right arm to have. I ought to stand aside and let you flub it. But I won't. Keep your flapping mouths shut, play this easy, and it's yours. Try your usual loathsome tactics and you lose."

We would not take that sort of talk from most people. Anybody else and Pat would have given me the signal and he'd 've hit him high while I hit him low. But you don't argue that way with a man who wears the Ceres ribbon; you listen. Pat didn't even mutter to me about it.

So we talked about Project Lebensraum itself. Twelve ships were to go out, radiating from Sol approximately in axes of a duodecahedron—but only approximately, as each ship's mission would be, not to search a volume of space, but to visit as many Sol-type stars as possible in the shortest time. Uncle Steve explained how they worked out a "minimax" search curve for each ship but I did not understand it; it involved a type of calculus we had not studied. Not that it mattered; each ship was to spend as much time exploring and as little time making the jumps as possible.

But Pat could not keep from coming back to the idea of how to sell the deal to our parents. "Uncle Steve? granting that you are right about playing it easy, here's an argument that maybe they should hear? Maybe you could use it on them?"

"Um?"

"Well, if half a loaf is better than none, maybe they haven't realized that this way one of us stays home." I caught a phrase of what Pat had started to say, which was not "one of us stays home," but "Tom stays home." I started to object, then let it ride. He hadn't said it. Pat went on, "They know we want to space. If they don't let us do this, we'll do it any way we can. If we joined your corps, we might come home on leave—but not often. If we emigrate, we might as well be dead; very few emigrants make enough to afford a trip back to Earth, not while their parents are still alive, at least. So if they keep us home now, as soon as we are of age they probably will never see us again. But if they agree, not only does one stay home, but they are always in touch with the other one—that's the whole purpose in using us telepath pairs." Pat looked anxiously at Uncle Steve. "Shouldn't we point that out? Or will you slip them the idea?"

Uncle Steve did not answer right away, although I could not see anything wrong with the logic. Two from two leaves zero, but one from two still leaves one.

Finally he answered slowly, "Pat, can't you get it through your thick head to leave well enough alone?"

"I don't see what's wrong with my logic."

"Since when was an emotional argument won by logic? You should read about the time King Solomon proposed to divvy up the baby." He took a pull at his glass and wiped his mouth. "What I am about to tell you is strictly confidential. Did you know that the Planetary League considered commissioning these ships as warships?"

"Huh? Why? Mr. Howard didn't say—"

"Keep your voice down. Project Lebensraum is of supreme interest to the Department of Peace. When it comes down to it, the root cause of war is always population pressure no matter what other factors enter in."

"But we've abolished war."

"So we have. So chaps like me get paid to stomp out brush fires before they burn the whole forest. Boys, if I tell you the rest of this, you've *got* to keep it to yourselves now and forever."

I don't like secrets. I'd rather owe money. You can't pay back a secret. But we promised.

"Okay. I saw the estimates the Department of Peace made on this project at the request of LRF. When the *Avant-Garde* was sent out, they gave her one chance in nine of returning. We've got better equipment now; they figure one chance in six for each planetary system visited. Each ship visits an average of six stars on the schedule laid out—so each ship has one chance in thirty-six of coming back. For twelve ships that means one chance in three of maybe *one* ship coming back. That's where you freaks come in."

"Don't call us 'freaks'!" We answered together.

" 'Freaks,' " he repeated. "And everybody is mighty glad you freaks are around, because without you the thing is impossible. Ships and crews are expendable—ships are just money and they can always find people like me with more curiosity than sense to man the ships. But while the ships are expendable, the knowledge they will gather is not expendable. Nobody at the top expects these ships to come back—but we've *got* to locate those earth-type planets; the human race needs them. That is what you boys are for: to report back. Then it won't matter that the ships won't come back."

"I'm not scared," I said firmly.

Pat glanced at me and looked away. I hadn't telepathed but I had told him plainly that the matter was not settled as to which one of us would go. Uncle Steve looked at me soberly and said, "I didn't expect you to be, at your age. Nor am I; I've been living on borrowed time since I was nineteen. By now I'm so convinced of my own luck that if one ship comes back, I'm sure it will be mine. But do you see why it would be silly to argue with your mother that half a set of twins is better than none? Emotionally your argument is all wrong. Go read the Parable of the Lost Sheep. You point out to your mother that one of you will be safe at home and it will simply fix her mind on the fact that the other one *isn't* safe and *isn't* home. If your Pop tries to reassure her, he is likely to stumble onto these facts—for they aren't secret, not the facts on which the statisticians based their predictions; it is just that the publicity about this project will emphasize the positive and play down the negative."

"Uncle Steve," objected Pat, "I don't see how they can be sure that most of the ships will be lost."

"They can't be sure. But these are actually optimistic assumptions based on what experience the race has had with investigating strange places. It's like this, Pat: You can be right over and over again, but when it comes to exploring strange places, the first time you guess wrong is the last guess you make. You're dead. Ever looked at the figures about it in just this one tiny solar system? Exploration is like Russian roulette; you can win and win, but if you keep on, it will kill you, certain. So don't get your parents stirred up on this phase of the matter. *I* don't mind—a man is entitled to die the way he wants to; that's one thing they haven't taxed. But there is no use in drawing attention to the fact that one of you two isn't coming back."

5

The Party of the Second Part

UNCLE STEVE WAS RIGHT ABOUT THE FOLKS GIVING IN; PAT LEFT FOR the training course three weeks later.

I still don't know just how it was that Pat got to be the one. We never matched for it, we never had a knockdown argument, and I never agreed. But Pat went.

I tried to settle it with him several times but he always put me off, telling me not to worry and to wait and see how things worked out. Presently I found it taken for granted that Pat was going and I was staying. Maybe I should have made a stand the day we signed the contract, when Pat hung back and let me sign first, thereby getting me down on paper as the party of the second part who stayed home, instead of party of the third part who went. But it had not seemed worth making a row about, as the two were interchangeable by agreement among the three parties to the contract. Pat pointed this out to me just before we signed; the important thing was to get the contract signed while our parents were holding still—get *their* signatures.

Was Pat trying to put one over on me right then? If so, I didn't catch him wording his thoughts. Contrariwise, would I have tried the same thing on him if I had thought of it? I don't know, I just don't know. In any case, I gradually became aware that the matter was settled; the family took it for granted and so did the LRF people. So I told Pat it was *not* settled. He just shrugged and reminded me that the LRF already had him down to go; it had not been his doing. Maybe I could get them to change their minds . . . if I didn't care whether or not I upset the applecart.

I didn't want to do that. We did not know that the LRF would have got down on its knees and wept rather than let any young and healthy telepath pair get away from them; we thought they had plenty to choose from. I thought that if I made a fuss they might tear up the contract, which they could do up till D-Day by paying a small penalty.

Instead I got Dad alone and talked to him. This shows how desperate I was; neither Pat nor I ever went alone to our parents about the other one. I didn't feel easy about it, but stammered and stuttered and had trouble making Dad understand why I felt swindled.

Dad looked troubled and said, "Tom, I thought you and your brother had settled this between you?"

"That's what I'm trying to tell you! We didn't."

"What do you expect me to do?"

"Why, I want you to make him be fair about it. We ought to match for it, or something. Or you could do it for us and keep it fair and square. Would you?"

Dad gave attention to his pipe the way he does when he is stalling. At last he said, "Tom, I don't see how you can back out now, after everything is settled. Unless you want me to break the contract? It wouldn't be easy but I can."

"But you don't have to break the contract. I just want an even chance. If I lose, I'll shut up. If I win, it won't change anything—except that I would go and Pat would stay."

"Mmm . . ." Dad puffed on his pipe and looked thoughtful. "Tom, have you looked at your mother lately?"

I had, but I hadn't talked with her much. She was moving around like a zombie, looking grief-stricken and hurt. "Why?"

"I can't do this to her. She's already going through the agony of losing your brother; I can't put her through it on your account, too. She couldn't stand it."

I knew she was feeling bad, but I could not see what difference it would make if we swapped. "You're not suggesting that Mum wants it this way? That she would rather have Pat go than me?"

"I am not. Your mother loves you both, equally."

"Then it would be just the same to her."

"It would not. She's undergoing the grief of losing one of her sons. If you swapped now, she would have to go through it afresh for her other son. That wouldn't be fair." He knocked his pipe against an ash tray, which was the same as gaveling that the meeting was adjourned. "No, son, I'm afraid that you will just have to stand by your agreement."

It was hopeless so I shut up. With Dad, bringing Mum's welfare into it was the same as trumping an ace.

Pat left for the training center four days later. I didn't see much of him except the hours we spent down at the TransLunar Building for he was dating Maudie every night and I was not included. He pointed out that this was the last he would see of her whereas I would have plenty of time—so get lost, please. I did not argue; it was not only fair, taken by itself, but I did not want to go along on their dates under the circumstances. Pat and I were farther apart those last few days than we had ever been.

It did not affect our telepathic ability, however, whatever this "tuning" was that some minds could do went right on and we could do it as easily as we could talk . . . and turn it off as easily, too. We didn't have to "concentrate" or "clear our minds" or any of that eastern mysticism nonsense. When we wanted to "talk," we talked.

When Pat left I felt lost. Sure, I was in touch with him four hours a day and any other time I cared to call him, but you can't live your whole life doing things by two's without getting out of joint when you have to do things by one's. I didn't have new habits yet. I'd get ready to go someplace, then I would stop at the door and wonder what I had forgotten. Just Pat. It is mighty lonesome to start off somewhere by yourself when you've always done it with someone.

Besides that, Mum was being brightly cheerful and tender and downright unbearable, and my sleep was all broken up. The training center worked on Switzerland's time zone which meant that I, and all other twins who were staying behind no matter where on Earth they were, worked our practice messages on Swiss time, too. Pat would whistle in my ears and wake me at two in the morning each night and then I would work until dawn and try to catch up on sleep in the daytime.

It was inconvenient but necessary and I was well paid. For the first time in my life I had plenty of money. So did all of our family, for I started paying a fat board bill despite Dad's objections. I even bought myself a watch (Pat had taken ours with him) without worrying about the price, and we were talking about moving into a bigger place.

But the LRF was crowding more and more into my life and I began to realize that the contract covered more than just recording messages from my twin. The geriatrics program started at once. "Geriatrics" is a funny term to use about a person not old enough to vote but it had the special meaning here of making me live as long as possible by starting on me at once. What I ate was no longer my business; I had to follow the diet they ordered, no more sandwiches picked up casually. There was a long list of "special hazard" things I must not do. They gave me shots for everything from housemaid's knee to parrot fever and I had a physical examination so thorough as to make every other one seem like a mere laying on of hands.

The only consolation was that Pat told me they were doing the same to him. We might be common as mud most ways but we were irreplaceable communication equipment to LRF, so we got the treatment a prize race horse or a prime minister gets and which common people hardly ever get. It was a nuisance.

I did not call Maudie the first week or ten days after Pat left; I didn't feel easy about her. Finally she called me and asked if I were angry with her or was she in quarantine? So we made a date for that night. It was not festive. She called me "Pat" a couple of times, which she used to do every now and then and it had never mattered, since Pat and I were used to people mixing up our names. But now it was awkward, because Pat's ghost was a skeleton at the feast.

The second time she did it I said angrily, "If you want to talk to Pat, I can get in touch with him in half a second!"

"What? Why, Tom!"

"Oh, I know you would rather I was Pat! If you think I enjoy being second choice, think again."

She got tears in her eyes and I got ashamed and more difficult. So we had a bitter argument and then I was telling her how I had been swindled.

Her reaction wasn't what I expected. Instead of sympathy she said, "Oh, Tom, Tom! Can't you see that Pat didn't do this to you? You did it to yourself."

"Huh?"

"It's not his fault; it's your own. I used to get so tired of the way you let him push you around. You *liked* having him push you around. You've got a 'will to fail.' "

I was so angry I had trouble answering. "What are you talking about? That sounds like a lot of cheap, chimney-corner psychiatry to me. Next thing you know you'll be telling me I have a 'death wish.' "

She blinked back tears. "No. Maybe Pat has that. He was always kidding about it but, just the same, I know how dangerous it is. I know we won't see him again."

I chewed that over. "Are you trying to say," I said slowly, "that I let Pat do me out of it because I was afraid to go?"

"What? Why, Tom dear, I never said anything of the sort."

"It sounded like it." Then I knew why it sounded like it. Maybe I *was* afraid. Maybe I had struggled just hard enough to let Pat win . . . because I knew what was going to happen to the one who went.

Maybe I was a coward.

We made it up and the date seemed about to end satisfactorily. When I took her home I was thinking of trying to kiss her good night—I never had, what with the way Pat and I were always in each other's hair. I think she expected me to, too . . . when Pat suddenly whistled at me.

"Hey! You awake, mate?"

("Certainly,") I answered shortly. ("But I'm busy.")

"How busy? Are you out with my girl?"

("What makes you think that?")

"You are, aren't you? I figured you were. How are you making out?"

("Mind your own business!")

"Sure, sure! Just say hello to her for me. Hi, Maudie!"

Maudie said, "Tom, what are you so preoccupied about?"

I answered, "Oh, it's just Pat. He says to say hello to you."

"Oh . . . well, hello to him from me."

So I did. Pat chuckled. *"Kiss her good night for me."*

So I didn't, not for either of us.

But I called her again the next day and we went out together regularly after that. Things began to be awfully pleasant where Maudie was concerned . . . so pleasant that I even thought about the fact that college students sometimes got married and now I would be able to afford it, if it happened to work out that way. Oh, I wasn't dead sure I wanted to tie myself down so young, but it is mighty lonely to be alone when you've always had somebody with you.

Then they brought Pat home on a shutter.

It was actually an ambulance craft, specially chartered. The idiot had sneaked off and tried skiing, which he knew as much about as I know about pearl diving. He did not have much of a tumble; he practically fell over his own feet. But there he was, being carried into our flat on a stretcher, numb from the waist down and his legs useless. He should have been taken to a hospital, but he wanted to come home and Mum wanted him to come home, so Dad insisted on it. He wound up in the room Faith had vacated and I went back to sleeping on the couch.

The household was all upset, worse than it had been when Pat went away. Dad almost threw Frank Dubois out of the house when Frank said that now that this space travel nonsense was disposed of, he was still prepared to give Pat a job if he would study bookkeeping, since a bookkeeper could work from a wheelchair. I don't know; maybe Frank had good intentions, but I sometimes think "good intentions" should be declared a capital crime.

But the thing that made me downright queasy was the way Mother took it. She was full of tears and sympathy and she could not do enough for Pat—she spent hours rubbing his legs, until she was ready to collapse. But I could see, even if Dad couldn't, that she was indecently happy—she had her "baby" back. Oh, the tears weren't fake . . . but females seem able to cry and be happy at the same time.

We all knew that the "space travel nonsense" was washed up, but we did not discuss it, not even Pat and I; while he was flat on his back and helpless and no doubt feeling even worse than I did was no time to blame him for hogging things and then wasting our chance. Maybe I was bitter but it was no time to let him know. I was uneasily aware that the fat LRF checks would stop soon and the family would be short of money again when we needed it most and I regretted that expensive watch and the money I had blown in taking Maudie to places we had never been able to afford, but I avoided thinking about even that; it was spilt milk. But I did wonder what kind of a job I could get instead of starting college.

I was taken off guard when Mr. Howard showed up—I had halfway expected that LRF would carry us on the payroll until after Pat was operated, even though the accident was not their fault and was a result of Pat's not obeying their regulations. But with the heaps of money they had I thought they might be generous.

But Mr. Howard did not even raise the question of the Foundation paying for, or not paying for, Pat's disability; he simply wanted to know how soon I would be ready to report to the training center?

I was confused and Mother was hysterical and Dad was angry and Mr. Howard was bland. To listen to him you would have thought that nothing had happened, certainly nothing which involved the slightest idea of letting us out of our contract. The parties of the second part and of the third part were interchangeable; since Pat could not go, naturally I would. Nothing had happened which interfered with our efficiency as a communication team. To be sure, they had let us have a few days to quiet down in view of the sad accident—but could I report at once? Time was short.

Dad got purple and almost incoherent. Hadn't they done enough to his family? Didn't they have any decency? Any consideration?

In the middle of it, while I was trying to adjust to the new situation and wondering what I should say, Pat called me silently. *"Tom! Come here!"*

I excused myself and hurried to him. Pat and I had hardly telepathed at all since he had been hurt. A few times he had called me in the night to fetch him a drink of water or something like that, but we had never really talked, either out loud or in our minds. There was just this black, moody silence that shut me out. I didn't know how to cope with it; it was the first time either of us had ever been ill without the other one.

But when he called I hurried in. "Shut the door."

I did so. He looked at me grimly. "I caught you before you promised anything, didn't I?"

"Yeah."

"Go out there and tell Dad I want to see him right away. Tell Mum I asked her to please quit crying, because she is getting me upset." He smiled sardonically. "Tell Mr. Howard to let me speak to my parents alone. Then you beat it."

"Huh?"

"Get out, don't stop to say good-by and don't say where you are going. When I want you, I'll tell you. If you hang around, Mother will work on you and get you to promise things." He looked at me bleakly. "You never did have any will power."

I let the dig slide off; he was ill. "Look, Pat, you're up against a combination this time. Mother is going to get her own way no matter what and Dad is so stirred up that I'm surprised he hasn't taken a poke at Mr. Howard."

"I'll handle Mother, and Dad, too. Howard should have stayed away. Get going. Split 'em up, then get lost."

"All right," I said uneasily. "Uh . . . look, Pat, I appreciate this."

He looked at me and his lip curled. "Think I'm doing this for you?"

"Why, I thought—"

"You never think . . . and I've been doing nothing else for days. If I'm going to be a cripple, do you fancy I'm going to spend my life in a public ward? Or here, with Mother drooling over me and Dad pinching pennies and the girls getting sick of the sight of me? Not Patrick! If I have to be like this, I'm going to have the best of everything . . . nurses to jump when I lift a finger and dancing girls to entertain me—and you are going to see that the LRF pays for it. We can keep our contract and we're going to. Oh, I know you don't want to go, but now you've *got* to."

"Me? You're all mixed up. You crowded me out. You—"

"Okay, forget it. You're rarin' to go." He reached up and punched me in the ribs, then grinned. "So we'll both go—for you'll take me along every step of the way. Now get out there and break that up."

I left two days later. When Pat handed Mum his reverse-twist whammie, she did not even fight. If getting the money to let her sick baby have proper care and everything else he wanted meant that I had to space, well, it was too bad but that was how it was. She told me how much it hurt to have me go but I knew she was not too upset. But *I* was, rather . . . I wondered what the score would have been if it had been *I* who was in Pat's fix? Would she have let Pat go just as easily simply to get *me* anything I wanted? But I decided to stop thinking about it; parents probably don't know that they are playing favorites even when they are doing it.

Dad got me alone for a man-to-man talk just before I left. He hemmed and hawed and stuck in apologies about how he should have talked things over with me before this and seemed even more embarrassed than I was, which was plenty. When he was floundering I let him know that one of our high school courses had covered most of what he was trying to say. (I didn't let him know that the course had been an anti-climax.) He brightened up and said, "Well, son, your mother and I have tried to teach you right from wrong. Just remember that you are a Bartlett and you won't make too many mistakes. On that other matter, well, if you will always ask yourself whether a girl is the sort you would be proud to bring home to meet your mother, I'll be satisfied."

I promised—it occurred to me that I wasn't going to have much chance to fall into bad company, not with psychologists practically dissecting everybody in Project Lebensraum. The bad apples were never going into the barrel.

When I see how naïve parents are I wonder how the human race keeps on being born. Just the same it was touching and I appreciate the ordeal he put himself through to get me squared away—Dad was always a decent guy and meant well.

I had a last date with Maudie but it wasn't much; we spent it sitting around Pat's bed. She did kiss me good-by—Pat told her to. Oh, well!

6

Torchship *Lewis and Clark*

I WAS IN SWITZERLAND ONLY TWO DAYS. I GOT A QUICK LOOK AT THE lake at Zurich and that was all; the time was jammed with trying to hurry me through all the things Pat had been studying for weeks. It couldn't be done, so they gave me spools of minitape which I was to study after the trip started.

I had one advantage: Planetary League Auxiliary Speech was a required freshman course at our high school—P-L lingo was the working language of Project Lebensraum. I can't say I could speak it when I got there, but it isn't hard. Oh, it seems a little silly to say "goed" when you've always said "gone" but you get used to it, and of course all technical words are Geneva-International and always have been.

Actually, as subproject officer Professor Brunn pointed out, there was not a lot that a telepathic communicator had to know before going aboard ship; the principal purpose of the training center had been to get the crews together, let them eat and live together, so that the psychologists could spot personality frictions which had not been detected through tests.

"There isn't any doubt about you, son. We have your brother's record and we know how close your tests come to matching his. You telepaths have to deviate widely from accepted standards before we would disqualify one of you."

"Sir?"

"Don't you see? We can turn down a ship's captain just for low blood sugar before breakfast and a latent tendency to be short tempered therefrom until he has had his morning porridge. We can fill most billets twenty times over and juggle them until they are matched like a team of acrobats. But not you people. You are so scarce that we must allow you any eccentricity which won't endanger the ship. I wouldn't mind if you believed in astrology—you don't, do you?"

"Goodness, no!" I answered, shocked.

"You see? You're a normal, intelligent boy; you'll do. Why, we would take your twin, on a stretcher, if we had to."

Only telepaths were left when I got to Zurich. The captains and the astrogation and torch crews had joined the ships first, and then the specialists and staff people. All the "idlers" were aboard but us. And I hardly had time to get acquainted even with my fellow mind readers.

They were an odd bunch and I began to see what Professor Brunn meant by saying that we freaks had to be allowed a little leeway. There were a dozen of us—just for the *Lewis and Clark*, I mean; there were a hundred and fifty for the twelve ships of the fleet, which was every telepathic pair that LRF had been able to sign up. I asked one of them, Bernhard van Houten, why each ship was going to carry so many telepaths?

He looked at me pityingly. "Use your head, Tom. If a radio burns out a valve, what do you do?"

"Why, you replace it."

"There's your answer. We're spare parts. If either end of a telepair dies or anything, that 'radio' is burned out, permanently. So they plug in another one of us. They want to be sure they have at least one telepair still working right up to the end of the trip . . . they hope."

I hardly had time to learn their names before we were whisked away. There was myself and Bernhard van Houten, a Chinese-Peruvian girl named Mei-Ling Jones (only she pronounced it "Hone-Ace"), Rupert Hauptman, Anna Horoshen, Gloria Maria Antonita Docampo, Sam Rojas, and Prudence Mathews. These were more or less my age. Then there was Dusty Rhodes who looked twelve and claimed to be fourteen. I wondered how LRF had persuaded his parents to permit such a child to go. Maybe they hated him; it would have been easy to do.

Then there were three who were older than the rest of us: Miss Gamma Furtney, Cas Warner, and Alfred McNeil. Miss Gamma was a weirdie, the sort of old maid who never admits to more than thirty; she was our triplet. LRF had scraped up four sets of triplets who were m-r's and could be persuaded to go; they were going to be used to tie the twelve ships together into four groups of three, then the groups could be hooked with four sets of twins.

Since triplets are eighty-six times as scarce as twins it was surprising that they could find enough who were telepathic and would go, without worrying about whether or not they were weirdies. I suspect that the Misses Alpha, Beta, and Gamma Furtney were attracted by the

Einstein time effect; they could get even with all the men who had not married them by not getting older while those men died of old age.

We were a "corner" ship and Cas Warner was our sidewise twin, who would hook us through his twin to the *Vasco da Gama*, thus linking two groups of three. Other sidewise twins tied the other corners. The ones who worked ship-to-ship did not have to be young, since their twins (or triplets) were not left back on Earth, to grow older while their brothers or sisters stayed young through relativity. Cas Warner was forty-five, a nice quiet chap who seemed to enjoy eating with us kids.

The twelfth was Mr. ("Call me 'Uncle Alfred' ") McNeil, and he was an old darling. He was a black man, his age was anything from sixty-five on up (I couldn't guess), and he had the saintliness that old people get when they don't turn sour and self-centered instead . . . to look at him you would bet heavy odds that he was a deacon in his church.

I got acquainted with him because I was terribly homesick the first night I was in Zurich and he noticed it and invited me to his room after supper and sort of soothed me. I thought he was one of the Foundation psychologists, like Professor Brunn—but no, he was half of a telepair himself . . . and not even a sidewise twin; his partner was staying on Earth.

I couldn't believe it until he showed me a picture of his pair partner—a little girl with merry eyes and pigtails—and I finally got it through my thick head that here was that rarity, a telepathic pair who were not twins. She was Celestine Regina Johnson, his great-niece—only he called her "Sugar Pie" after he introduced me to the photograph and had told her who I was.

I had to pause and tell Pat about it, not remembering that he had already met them.

Uncle Alfred was retired and had been playmate-in-chief to his baby great-niece, for he had lived with his niece and her husband. He had taught the baby to talk. When her parents were both killed in an accident he had gone back to work rather than let the child be adopted. "I found out that I could keep tabs on Sugar Pie even when I couldn't see her. She was always a good baby and it meant I could watch out for her even when I had to be away. I knew it was a gift; I figured that the Lord in His infinite mercy had granted what I needed to let me take care of my little one."

The only thing that had worried him was that he might not live long enough, or, worse still, not be able to work long enough, to permit him to bring up Sugar Pie and get her started right. Then Project Lebensraum had solved everything. No, he didn't mind being away from her because he was *not* away from her; he was with her every minute.

I gathered an impression that he could actually see her but I didn't want to ask. In any case, with him stone walls did not a prison make nor light-years a separation. He knew that the Infinite Mercy that had kept them together this long would keep them together long enough for him to finish his appointed task. What happened after that was up to the Lord.

I had never met anybody who was so quietly, serenely happy. I didn't feel homesick again until I left him and went to bed. So I called Pat and told him about getting acquainted with Uncle Alfred. He said sure, Uncle Alf was a sweet old codger . . . and now I should shut up and go to sleep, as I had a hard day ahead of me tomorrow.

Then they zoomed us out to the South Pacific and we spent one night on Canton Atoll before we went aboard. They wouldn't let us swim in the lagoon even though Sam had arranged a picnic party of me and himself and Mei-Ling and Gloria; swimming was one of the unnecessary hazards. Instead we went to bed early and were awakened two hours before dawn—a ghastly time of day, particularly when your time sense has been badgered by crossing too many time zones too fast. I began to wonder what I was doing there and why?

The *Lewis and Clark* was a few hundred miles east of there in an unused part of the ocean. I had not realized how much water there was until I took a look at it from the air—and at that you see just the top. If they could figure some way to use all those wet acres as thoroughly as they use the Mississippi Valley they wouldn't need other planets.

From the air the *Lewis and Clark* looked like a basketball floating in water; you could not see that it was really shaped like a turnip. It floated with the torch down; the hemispherical upper part was all that showed. I got one look at her, with submersible freighters around her looking tiny in comparison, then our bus was hovering over her and we were being told to mind our step on the ladder and not leave anything behind in the bus. It occurred to me that it wouldn't do any good to write to Lost-and-Found if we did. It was a chilly thought . . . I guess I was still homesick, but mostly I was excited.

I got lost a couple of times and finally found my stateroom just as the speaker system was booming: "All hands, prepare for acceleration. Idlers strap down. Boost stations report in order. Minus fourteen minutes." The man talking was so matter of fact that he might as well have been saying, "Local passengers change at Birmingham."

The stateroom was big enough, with a double wardrobe and a desk with a built-in viewer-recorder and a little washstand and two pull-down beds. They were down, which limited the floor space. Nobody else was around so I picked one, lay down and fastened the three safety belts. I had just done so when that little runt Dusty Rhodes stuck his head in. "Hey! You got my bed!"

I started to tell him off, then decided that just before boost was no time for an argument. "Suit yourself," I answered, unstrapped, and moved into the other one, strapped down again.

Dusty looked annoyed; I think he wanted an argument. Instead of climbing into the one I had vacated, he stuck his head out the door and looked around. I said, "Better strap down. They already passed the word."

"Tripe," he answered without turning. "There's plenty of time. I'll take a quick look up in the control room."

I was going to suggest that he go outside while he was about it when a ship's officer came through, checking the rooms. "In you get, son," he said briskly, using the no-nonsense tone in which you tell a dog to heel. Dusty opened his mouth, closed it, and climbed in. Then the officer "baby-strapped" him, pulling the buckles around so that they could not be reached by the person in the bunk. He even put the chest strap around Dusty's arms.

He then checked my belts. I had my arms outside the straps but all he said was, "Keep your arms on the mattress during boost," and left.

A female voice said, "All special communicators link with your telepartners."

I had been checking with Pat ever since I woke up and had described the *Lewis and Clark* to him when we first sighted her and then inside as well. Nevertheless I said, ("Are you there, Pat?")

"Naturally. I'm not going anyplace. What's the word?"

("Boost in about ten minutes. They just told us to link with out partners during boost.")

"You had better stay linked, or I'll beat your ears off! I don't want to miss anything."

("Okay, okay, don't race your engine. Pat? This isn't quite the way I thought it would be.")

"Huh? How?"

("I don't know. I guess I expected brass bands and speeches and such. After all, this is a big day. But aside from pictures they took of us last night at Canton Atoll, there was more fuss made when we started for Scout camp.")

Pat chuckled. *"Brass bands would get wet where you are—not to mention soaked with neutrons."*

("Sure, sure.") I didn't have to be told that a torchship needs elbow room for a boost. Even when they perfected a way to let them make direct boost from Earth-zero instead of from a space station, they still needed a few thousand square miles of ocean—and at that you heard ignorant prattle about how the back wash was changing the climate and the government ought to do something.

"Anyhow, there are plenty of brass bands and speeches. We are watching one by the Honorable J. Dillberry Egghead . . . shall I read it back?"

("Uh, don't bother. Who's 'we'?")

"All of us. Faith and Frank just came in."

I was about to ask about Maudie when a new voice came over the system: "Welcome aboard, friends. This is the Captain. We will break loose at an easy three gravities; nevertheless, I want to warn you to relax and keep your arms inside your couches. The triple boost will last only six minutes, then you will be allowed to get up. We take off in number-two position, just after the *Henry Hudson*."

I repeated to Pat what the Captain was saying practically as fast as he said it; this was one of the things we had practiced while he was at the training center: letting your directed thoughts echo what somebody else was saying so that a telepair acted almost like a microphone and a speaker. I suppose he was doing the same at the other end, echoing the Captain's words to the family a split second behind me—it's not hard with practice.

The Captain said, "The *Henry* is on her final run-down . . . ten seconds . . . five seconds . . . *now!*"

I saw something like heat lightning even though I was in a closed room. For a few seconds there was a sound over the speaker like sleet on a window, soft and sibilant and far away. Pat said, *"Boy!"*

("What is it, Pat?")

"She got up out of there as if she had sat on a bee. Just a hole in the water and a flash of light. Wait a sec—they're shifting the view pick-up from the space station to Luna."

("You've got a lot better view than I have. All I can see is the ceiling of this room.")

The female voice said, "Mr. Warren! Miss Furtney! Tween-ships telepairs start recording."

The Captain said, "All hands, ready for boost. Stand by for count down," and another voice started in, "Sixty seconds . . . fifty-five . . . fifty . . . forty-five . . . holding on forty-five . . . holding forty-five . . . holding . . . holding . . ."—until I was ready to scream.

"Tom, what's wrong?"

("How should I know?")

"Forty . . . thirty-five . . . thirty . . ."

"Tom, Mum wants me tell you to be very careful."

("What does she think I can do? I'm just lying here, strapped down.")

"I know." Tom chuckled. *"Hang on tight to the brush, you lucky stiff; they are about to take away the ladder."*

". . . four! . . . three! . . . two! . . . ONE!"

I didn't see a flash, I didn't hear anything. I simply got very heavy—like being on the bottom of a football pile-up.

"There's nothing but steam where you were."

I didn't answer, I was having trouble breathing.

"They've shifted the pick-up. They're following you with a telephoto now. Tom, you ought to see this . . . you look just like a sun. It burns the rest of the picture right out of the tank."

("How can I see it?") I said crossly. ("I'm *in* it.")

"You sound choked up. Are you all right?"

("You'd sound choked, too, if you had sand bags piled across your chest.")

"Is it bad?"

("It's not good. But it's all right, I guess.")

Pat let up on me and did a right good job of describing what he was seeing by television. The *Richard E. Byrd* took off just after we did, before we had finished the high boost to get escape velocity from Earth; he told me all about it. I didn't have anything to say anyhow; I couldn't see anything and I didn't feel like chattering. I just wanted to hold still and feel miserable.

I suppose it was only six minutes but it felt more like an hour. After a long, long time, when I had decided the controls were jammed and we were going to keep on at high boost until we passed the speed of light, the pressure suddenly relaxed and I felt light as a snowflake . . . if it hadn't been for the straps I would have floated up to the ceiling.

"We have reduced to one hundred and ten per cent of one gravity," the Captain said cheerfully. "Our cruising boost will be higher, but we will give the newcomers among us a while to get used to it." His tone changed and he said briskly, "All stations, secure from blast-off and set space watches, third section."

I loosened my straps and sat up and then stood up. Maybe we were ten percent heavy, but it did not feel like it; I felt fine. I started for the door, intending to look around more than I had been able to when I came aboard.

Dusty Rhodes yelled at me. "Hey! Come back here and unstrap me! That moron fastened the buckles out of my reach."

I turned and looked at him. "Say 'please.' "

What Dusty answered was not "please." Nevertheless I let him loose. I should have made him say it; it might have saved trouble later.

7

19,900 Ways

THE FIRST THING THAT HAPPENED IN THE *L.C.* MADE ME THINK I WAS dreaming—I ran into Uncle Steve.

I was walking along the circular passageway that joined the staterooms on my deck and looking for the passage inboard, toward the axis of the ship. As I turned the corner I bumped into someone. I said, "Excuse me," and started to go past when the other person grabbed my arm and clapped me on the shoulder. I looked up and it was Uncle Steve, grinning and shouting at me. "Hi, shipmate! Welcome aboard!"

"Uncle Steve! What are *you* doing here?"

"Special assignment from the General Staff . . . to keep *you* out of trouble."

"Huh?"

There was no mystery when he explained. Uncle Steve had known for a month that his application for special discharge to take service with the LRF for Project Lebensraum had been approved; he had not told the family but had spent the time working a swap to permit him to be in the same ship as Pat—or, as it turned out, the one I was in.

"I thought your mother might take it easier if she knew I was keeping an eye on her boy. You can tell her about it the next time you are hooked in with your twin."

"I'll tell her now," I answered and gave a yell in my mind for Pat. He did not seem terribly interested; I guess a reaction was setting in and he was sore at me for being where he had expected to be. But Mother was there and he said he would tell her. "Okay, she knows."

Uncle Steve looked at me oddly. "Is it as easy as that?"

I explained that it was just like talking . . . a little faster, maybe, since you can think words faster than you can talk, once you are used to it. But he stopped me. "Never mind. You're trying to explain color to a blind man. I just wanted Sis to know."

"Well, okay." Then I noticed that his uniform was different. The ribbons were the same and it was an LRF company uniform, like my own, which did not surprise me—but his chevrons were gone. "Uncle Steve . . . you're wearing major's leaves!"

He nodded. "Home town boy makes good. Hard work, clean living, and so on."

"Gee, that's swell!"

"They transferred me at my reserve rank, son, plus one bump for exceptionally neat test papers. Fact is, if I had stayed with the Corps, I would have retired as a ship's sergeant at best—there's no promotion in peacetime. But the Project was looking for certain men, not certain ranks, and I happened to have the right number of hands and feet for the job."

"Just what is your job, Uncle?"

"Commander of the ship's guard."

"Huh? What have we got to guard?"

"That's a good question. Ask me in a year or two and I can give you a better answer. Actually, 'Commander Landing Force' would be a better title. When we locate a likely looking planet—'when and if,' I mean—I'm the laddie who gets to go out and check the lay of the land and whether the natives are friendly while you valuable types stay safe and snug in the ship." He glanced at his wrist. "Let's go to chow."

I wasn't hungry and wanted to look around, but Uncle Steve took me firmly by the arm and headed for the mess room. "When you have soldiered as long as I have, lad, you will learn that you sleep when you get a chance and that you are never late for chow line."

It actually was a chow line, cafeteria style. The *L.C.* did not run to table waiters nor to personal service of any sort, except for the Captain and people on watch. We went through the line and I found that I was hungry after all. That meal only, Uncle Steve took me over to the heads-of-departments table. "Ladies and gentlemen, this is my nephew with two heads, Tom Bartlett. He left his other head dirtside—he's a telepair twin. If he does anything he shouldn't, don't tell me, just clobber him." He glanced at me; I was turning red. "Say 'howdy,' son . . . or just nod if you can't talk."

I nodded and sat down. A sweet old girl with the sort of lap babies like to sit on was next to me. She smiled and said, "Glad to have you with us, Tom." I learned that she was the Chief Ecologist. Her name was Dr. O'Toole, only nobody called her that, and she was married to one of the relativists.

Uncle Steve went around the table, pointing out who was who and what they did: the Chief Engineer, the Relativist (Uncle Steve called him the "Astrogator" as the job would be called in an ordinary ship), Chief Planetologist Harry Gates and the Staff Xenologist, and so forth—I couldn't remember the names at the time—and Reserve Captain Urqhardt. I didn't catch the word "reserve" and was surprised at how young he was. But Uncle Steve corrected me: "No, no! He's not *the* Captain. He's the man who will be captain if it turns out we need a spare. Across from you is the Surgeon—don't let that fool you, either; he never does surgery himself. Dr. Devereaux is the boss head-shrinker."

I looked puzzled and Uncle Steve went on, "You don't savvy? Psychiatrist. Doc Dev is watching every move we make, trying to decide how quick he will have to be with the straitjacket and the needle. Correct, Doc?"

Dr. Devereaux buttered a roll. "Essentially, Major. But finish your meal; we're not coming for you until later in the day." He was a fat little toad, ugly as could be, and with a placid, unbreakable calm. He went on, "I just had an upsetting thought, Major."

"I thought that thoughts never upset you?"

"Consider. Here I am charged with keeping quaint characters like you sane . . . but they forgot to assign anybody to keep *me* sane. What should I do?"

"Mmm . . ." Uncle Steve seemed to study it. "I didn't know that head-shrinkers were supposed to be sane, themselves?"

Dr. Devereaux nodded. "You've put your finger on it. As in your profession, Major, being crazy is an asset. Pass the salt, please."

Uncle Steve shut up and pretended to wipe off blood.

A man came in and sat down; Uncle Steve introduced me and said, "Staff Commander Frick, the Communications Officer. Your boss, Tom."

Commander Frick nodded and said, "Aren't you third section, young man?"

"Uh, I don't know, sir."

"I do . . . and you should have known. Report to the communications office."

"Uh, you mean now, sir?"

"Right away. You are a half hour late."

I said, "Excuse me," and got up in a hurry, feeling silly. I glanced at Uncle Steve but he wasn't looking my way; he seemed not to have heard it.

The communications office was two decks up, right under the control room; I had trouble finding it. Van Houten was there and Mei-Ling and a man whose name was Travers, who was communicator-of-the-watch. Mei-Ling was reading a sheaf of papers and did not look up; I knew that she was telepathing. Van said, "Where the deuce have you been? I'm hungry."

"I didn't know," I protested.

"You're supposed to know."

He left and I turned to Mr. Travers. "What do you want me to do?"

He was threading a roll of tape into an autotransmitter; he finished before he answered me. "Take that stack of traffic as she finishes it, and do whatever it is you do with it. Not that it matters."

"You mean read it to my twin?"

"That's what I said."

"Do you want him to record?"

"Traffic is always recorded. Didn't they teach you anything?"

I thought about explaining that they really hadn't because there had not been time, when I thought, oh what's the use? He probably thought I was Pat and assumed that I had had the full course. I picked up papers Mei-Ling was through with and sat down.

But Travers went on talking. "I don't know what you freaks are up here for now anyhow. You're not needed; we're still in radio range."

I put the papers down and stood up. "Don't call us 'freaks.' "

He glanced at me and said, "My, how tall you've grown. Sit down and get to work."

We were about the same height but he was ten years older and maybe thirty pounds heavier. I might have passed it by if we had been alone, but not with Mei-Ling present. "I said not to call us 'freaks.' It's not polite."

He looked tired and not amused but he didn't stand up. I decided he didn't want a fight and felt relieved. "All right, all right," he answered. "Don't be so touchy. Get busy on that traffic."

I sat down and looked over the stuff I had to send, then called Pat and told him to start his recorder; this was not a practice message.

He answered, *"Call back in half an hour. I'm eating dinner."*

("I was eating lunch but I didn't get to finish. Quit stalling, Pat. Take a look at that contract you were so anxious to sign.")

"You were just as anxious. What's the matter, kid? Cold feet already?"

("Maybe, maybe not. I've got a hunch that this isn't going to be one long happy picnic. But I've learned one thing already; when the Captain sends for a bucket of paint, he wants a full bucket and no excuses. So switch on that recorder and stand by to take down figures.")

Pat muttered and gave in, then announced that he was ready after a delay that was almost certainly caused by Mother insisting that he finish dinner. *"Ready."*

The traffic was almost entirely figures (concerning the take-off, I suppose) and code. Being such, I had to have Pat repeat back everything. It was not hard, but it was tedious. The only message in clear was one from the Captain, ordering roses sent to a Mrs. Detweiler in Brisbane and charged to his LRF account, with a message: "Thanks for a wonderful farewell dinner."

Nobody else sent personal messages; I guess they had left no loose ends back on Earth.

I thought about sending some roses to Maudie, but I didn't want to do it through Pat. It occurred to me that I could do it through Mei-Ling, then I remembered that, while I had money in the bank, I had appointed Pat my attorney; if I ordered them, he would have to okay the bill.

I decided not to cross any bridges I had burned behind me.

Life aboard the *L.C.*, or the *Elsie* as we called her, settled into a routine. The boost built up another fifteen per cent which made me weigh a hundred and fifty-eight pounds; my legs ached until I got used to it—but I soon did; there are advantages in being kind of skinny. We freaks stood a watch in five, two at a time—Miss Gamma and Cas Warner were not on our list because they hooked sidewise with other ships. At first we had a lot of spare time, but the Captain put a stop to that.

Knowing that the LRF did not really expect us to return, I had not thought much about that clause in the contract which provided for tutoring during the trip but I found out that the Captain did not intend to forget it. There was school for everybody, not just for us telepaths who were still of school age. He appointed Dr. Devereaux, Mrs. O'Toole, and Mr. Krishnamurti a school board and courses were offered in practically everything, from life drawing to ancient history. The Captain himself taught that last one; it turned out he knew Sargon the Second and Socrates like brothers.

Uncle Alfred tried to sign up for everything, which was impossible, even if he didn't eat, sleep, nor stand watch. He had never, he told me, had time for all the schooling he wanted and now at last he was going to get it. Even my real uncle, Steve, signed up for a couple of courses. I guess I showed surprise at this, for he said, "Look, Tom, I found out my first cruise that the only way to make space bearable is to have something to learn and learn it. I used to take correspondence courses. But this bucket has the finest assemblage of really bright minds you are ever likely to see. If you don't take advantage of it, you are an idiot. Mama O'Toole's cooking course, for example: where else can you find a *Cordon Bleu* graduate willing to teach you her high art free? I ask you!"

I objected that I would never need to know how to cook high cuisine.

"What's that got to do with it? Learning isn't a means to an end; it is an end in itself. Look at Uncle Alf. He's as happy as a boy with a new slingshot. Anyhow, if you don't sign up for a stiff course, old Doc Devereaux will find some way to keep you busy, even if it is counting rivets. Why do you think the Captain made him chairman of the board of education?"

"I hadn't thought about it."

"Well, think about it. The greatest menace in space is going coffin crazy. You are shut up for a long time in a small space and there is nothing outside but some mighty thin vacuum . . . no street lights, no bowling alleys. Inside are the same old faces and you start hating them. So a smart captain makes sure you have something to keep you interested and tired—and ours is the smartest you'll find or he wouldn't be on this trip."

I began to realize that a lot of arrangements in the *Elsie* were simply to see that we stayed healthy and reasonably happy. Not just school, but other things. Take the number we had aboard, for example—almost two hundred. Uncle Steve told me that the *Elsie* could function as a ship with about ten: a captain, three control officers, three engineer officers, one communicator, one farmer, and a cook. Shucks, you could cut that to five: two control officers (one in command), two torch watchstanders, and a farmer-cook.

Then why two hundred?

In the first place there was room enough. The *Elsie* and the other ships had been rebuilt from the enormous freighters the LRF use to haul supplies out to Pluto and core material back to Earth. In the second place they needed a big scientific staff to investigate the planets we hoped to find. In the third place some were spare parts, like Reserve Captain Urqhardt and, well, me myself. Some of us would die or get killed; the ship had to go on.

But the real point, as I found out, is that no small, isolated social group can be stable. They even have a mathematics for it, with empirical formulas and symbols for "lateral pressures" and "exchange valences" and "exogamic relief." (That last simply means that the young men of a small village should find wives outside the village.)

Or look at it this way. Suppose you had a one-man space ship which could cruise alone for several years. Only a man who was already nutty a certain way could run it—otherwise he would soon go squirrelly some other way and start tearing the controls off the panels. Make it a two-man ship: even if you used a couple as fond of each other as Romeo and Juliet, by the end of the trip even Juliet would start showing black-widow blood.

Three is as bad or worse, particularly if they gang up two against one. Big numbers are much safer. Even with only two hundred people there are exactly nineteen thousand nine hundred ways to pair them off, either as friends or enemies, so you see that the social possibilities shoot up rapidly when you increase the numbers. A bigger group means more chances to find friends and more ways to avoid people you don't like. This is terribly important aboard ship.

Besides elective courses we had required ones called "ship's training"—by which the Captain meant that everybody had to learn at least one job he had not signed up for. I stood two watches down in the damping room, whereupon Chief Engineer Roch stated in writing that he did not think that I would ever make a torcher as I seemed to have an innate lack of talent for nuclear physics. As a matter of fact it made me nervous to be that close to an atomic power plant and to realize the unleashed hell that was going on a few feet away from me.

I did not make out much better as a farmer, either. I spent two weeks in the air-conditioning plant and the only thing I did right was to feed the chickens. When they caught me cross-pollinating the wrong way some squash plants which were special pets of Mrs. O'Toole she let me go, more in sorrow than in anger. "Tom," she said, "what do you do well?"

I thought about it. "Uh, I can wash bottles . . . and I used to raise hamsters."

So she sent me over to the research department and I washed beakers in the chem lab and fed the experimental animals. The beakers were unbreakable. They wouldn't let me touch the electron microscope. It wasn't bad—I could have been assigned to the laundry.

Out of the 19,900 combinations possible in the *Elsie* Dusty Rhodes and I were one of the wrong ones. I hadn't signed up for the life sketching class because he was teaching it; the little wart really was a fine draftsman. I know, I'm pretty good at it myself and I would have liked to have been in that class. What was worse, he had an offensively high I.Q., genius plus, much higher than mine, and he could argue rings around me. Along with that he had the manners of a pig and the social graces of a skunk—a bad go, any way you looked at it.

"Please" and "Thank you" weren't in his vocabulary. He never made his bed unless someone in authority stood over him, and I was likely as not to come in and find him lying on mine, wrinkling it and getting the cover dirty. He never hung up his clothes, he always left our wash basin filthy, and his best mood was complete silence.

Besides that, he didn't bathe often enough. Aboard ship that is a crime.

First I was nice to him, then I bawled him out, then I threatened him. Finally I told him that the next thing of his I found on my bed was going straight into the mass converter. He just sneered and the next day I found his camera on my bed and his dirty socks on my pillow.

I tossed the socks into the wash basin, which he had left filled with dirty water, and locked his camera in my wardrobe, intending to let him stew before I gave it back.

He didn't squawk. Presently I found his camera gone from my wardrobe, in spite of the fact that it was locked with a combination which Messrs. Yale & Towne had light-heartedly described as "Invulnerable." My clean shirts were gone, too . . . that is, they weren't clean; somebody had carefully dirtied every one of them.

I had not complained about him. It had become a point of pride to work it out myself; the idea that I could not cope with somebody half my size and years my junior did not appeal to me.

But I looked at the mess he had made of my clothes and I said to myself, "Thomas Paine, you had better admit that you are licked and holler for help—else your only chance will be to plead justifiable homicide."

But I did not have to complain. The Captain sent for me; Dusty had complained about me instead.

"Bartlett, young Rhodes tells me you are picking on him. What's the situation from your point of view?"

I started to swell up and explode. Then I let out my breath and tried to calm down; the Captain really wanted to know.

"I don't think so, sir, though it is true that we have not been getting along."

"Have you laid hands on him?"

"Uh . . . I haven't smacked him, sir. I've jerked him off my bed more than once—and I wasn't gentle about it."

He sighed. "Maybe you should have smacked him. Out of my sight, of course. Well, tell me about it. Try to tell it straight—and complete."

So I told him. It sounded trivial and I began to be ashamed of myself . . . the Captain had more important things to worry about than whether or not I had to scrub out a hand basin before I could wash my face. But he listened.

Instead of commenting, maybe telling me that I should be able to handle a younger kid better, the Captain changed the subject.

"Bartlett, you saw that illustration Dusty had in the ship's paper this morning?"

"Yes, sir. A real beauty," I admitted. It was a picture of the big earthquake in Santiago, which had happened after we left Earth.

"Mmm . . . we have to allow you special-talent people a little leeway. Young Dusty is along because he was the only m-r available who could receive and transmit pictures."

"Uh, is that important, sir?"

"It could be. We won't know until we need it. But it could be crucially important. Otherwise I would never have permitted a spoiled brat to come aboard this ship." He frowned. "However, Dr. Devereaux is of the opinion that Dusty is not a pathological case."

"Uh, I never said he was, sir."

"Listen, please. He says that the boy has an unbalanced personality—a brain that would do credit to a grown man but with greatly retarded social development. His attitudes and evaluations would suit a boy of five, combined with this clever brain. Furthermore Dr. Devereaux says that he will force the childish part of Dusty's personality to grow up, or he'll turn in his sheepskin."

"So? I mean, 'Yes, sir?' "

"So you should have smacked him. The only thing wrong with that boy is that his parents should have walloped him, instead of telling him how bright he was." He sighed again. "Now I've got to do it. Dr. Devereaux tells me I'm the appropriate father image."

"Yes, sir."

" 'Yes, sir,' my aching head. This isn't a ship; it's a confounded nursery. Are you having any other troubles?"

"No, sir."

"I wondered. Dusty also complained that the regular communicators call you people 'freaks.' " He eyed me.

I didn't answer. I felt sheepish about it.

"In any case, they won't again. I once saw a crewman try to knife another one, just because the other persisted in calling him 'skin head.' My people are going to behave like ladies and gentlemen or I'll bang some heads together." He frowned. "I'm moving Dusty into the room across from my cabin. If Dusty will leave you alone, you let him alone. If he won't . . . well, use your judgment, bearing in mind that you are responsible for your actions—but remember that I don't expect any man to be a doormat. That's all. Good-by."

8

Relativity

I HAD BEEN IN THE *ELSIE* A WEEK WHEN IT WAS DECIDED TO OPERATE on Pat. Pat told me they were going to do it, but he did not talk about it much. His attitude was the old iron-man, as if he meant to eat peanuts and read comics while they were chopping on him. I think he was scared stiff . . . I would have been.

Not that I would have understood if I had known the details; I'm no neural surgeon, nor any sort; removing a splinter is about my speed.

But it meant we would be off the watch list for a while, so I told Commander Frick. He already knew from messages passed between the ship and LRF; he told me to drop off the watch list the day before my brother was operated and to consider myself available for extra duty during his convalescence. It did not make any difference to him; not only were there other telepairs but we were still radio-linked to Earth.

Two weeks after we started spacing and the day before Pat was to be cut on I was sitting in my room, wondering whether to go to the communications office and offer my valuable services in cleaning waste baskets and microfilming files or just sit tight until somebody sent for me.

I had decided on the latter, remembering Uncle Steve's advice never to volunteer, and was letting down my bunk, when the squawker boomed: "T. P. Bartlett, special communicator, report to the Relativist!"

I hooked my bunk up while wondering if there was an Eye-Spy concealed in my room—taking down my bunk during working hours seemed always to result in my being paged. Dr. Babcock was not in the control room and they chased me out, but not before I took a quick look around—the control room was off limits to anyone who did not work there. I found him down in the computation room across from the communications office, where I would have looked in the first place if I hadn't wanted to see the control room.

I said, "T. P. Bartlett, communicator tenth grade, reporting to the Relativist as ordered."

Dr. Babcock swung around in his chair and looked at me. He was a big raw-boned man, all hands and feet, and looked more like a lumberjack than a mathematical physicist. I think he played it up—you know, elbows on the table and bad grammar on purpose. Uncle Steve said Babcock had more honorary degrees than most people had socks.

He stared at me and laughed. "Where did you get that fake military manner, son? Siddown. You're Bartlett?"

I sat. "Yes, sir."

"What's this about you and your twin going off the duty list?"

"Well, my brother is in a hospital, sir. They're going to do something to his spine tomorrow."

"Why didn't you tell me?" I didn't answer because it was so unreasonable; I wasn't even in his department. "Frick never tells me anything, the Captain never tells me anything, now you never tell me anything. I have to hang around the galley and pick up gossip to find out what's going on. I was planning on working you over tomorrow. You know that, don't you?"

"Uh, no, sir."

"Of course you don't, because I never tell anybody anything either. What a way to run a ship! I should have stayed in Vienna. There's a nice town. Ever have coffee and pastries in the Ring?" He didn't wait for an answer. "Nevertheless I was going to work you and your twin over tomorrow—so now we'll have to do it today. Tell him to stand by."

"Uh, what do you want him to do, Doctor? He's already been moved to a hospital."

"Just tell him to stand by. I'm going to calibrate you two, that's what. Figure out your index error."

"Sir?"

"Just tell him."

So I called Pat. I hadn't spoken to him since breakfast; I wondered how he was going to take it.

But he already knew. *"Yes, yes,"* he said in a tired voice. *"They're setting up apparatus in my hospital room right now. Mother made such a fuss I had to send her out."*

("Look, Pat, if you don't want to do this, whatever it is, I'll tell them nothing doing. It's an imposition.")

"What difference does it make?" he said irritably. *"I've got to sweat*

out the next sixteen hours somehow. Anyhow, this may be the last time we work together."

It was the first time he had shown that it was affecting his nerve. I said hastily, ("Don't talk that way, Pat. You're going to get well. You're going to walk again. Shucks, you'll even be able to ski if you want to.")

"Don't give me that Cheerful Charlie stuff. I'm getting more of it from the folks than I can use. It makes me want to throw up."

("Now see here, Pat—")

"Stow it, stow it! Let's get on with what they want us to do."

("Well, all right.") I spoke aloud: "He's ready, Doctor."

"Half a minute. Start your camera, O'Toole." Dr. Babcock touched something on his desk. "Commander Frick?"

"Yes, Doctor," Frick's voice answered.

"We're ready. You coming in?"

"All set here," I heard my boss answer. "We'll come in." A moment later he entered, with Anna Horoshen. In the meantime I took a look around. One whole wall of the computation room was a computer, smaller than the one at Los Alamos but not much. The blinking lights must have meant something to somebody. Sitting at right angles to it at a console was Mr. O'Toole and above the console was a big display scope; at about one-second intervals a flash of light would peak in the center of it.

Anna nodded without speaking; I knew she must be linked. Pat said, *"Tom, you've got a girl named Anna Horoshen aboard. Is she around?"*

("Yes. Why?")

"Say hello to her for me—I knew her in Zurich. Her sister Becky is here." He chuckled and I felt better. *"Good looking babes, aren't they? Maudie is jealous."*

Babcock said to Frick, "Tell them to stand by. First synchronizing run, starting from their end."

"Tell them, Anna."

She nodded. I wondered why they bothered with a second telepair when they could talk through myself and Pat. I soon found out: Pat and I were too busy.

Pat was sounding out ticks like a clock; I was told to repeat them . . . and every time I did another peak of light flashed on the display scope. Babcock watched it, then turned me around so that I couldn't see and taped a microphone to my voice box. "Again."

Pat said, *"Stand by—"* and started ticking again. I did my best to tick right with him but it was the silliest performance possible. I heard Babcock say quietly, "That cut out the feedback and the speed-of-sound lag. I wish there were some way to measure the synaptic rate more closely."

Frick said, "Have you talked to Dev about it?"

I went on ticking.

"A reverse run now, young lady," Babcock said, and slipped headphones on me. I immediately heard a ticking like the ticks Pat had been sending. "That's a spectral metronome you're listening to, young fellow, timed by monochrome light. It was synchronized with the one your brother is using before we left Earth. Now start ticking at him."

So I did. It had a hypnotic quality; it was easier to get into step and tick with it than it was to get out of step. It was impossible to ignore it. I began to get sleepy but I kept on ticking; I couldn't stop.

"End of run," Babcock announced. The ticking stopped and I rubbed my ears.

"Dr. Babcock?"

"Huh?"

"How can you tell one tick from another?"

"Eh? *You* can't. But O'Toole can, he's got it all down on film. Same at the other end. Don't worry about it; just try to stay in time."

This silliness continued for more than an hour, sometimes with Pat sending, sometimes myself. At last O'Toole looked up and said, "Fatigue factor is cooking our goose, Doc. The second differences are running all over the lot."

"Okay, that's all," Babcock announced. He turned to me. "You can thank your brother for me and sign off."

Commander Frick and Anna left. I hung around. Presently Dr. Babcock looked up from his desk and said, "You can go, bub. Thanks."

"Uh, Dr. Babcock?"

"Huh? Speak up."

"Would you mind telling me what this is all about?"

He looked surprised, then said, "Sorry. I'm not used to using people instead of instruments; I forget. Okay, sit down. This is why you m-r people were brought along: for research into the nature of time."

I stared. "Sir? I thought we were along to report back on the planets we expect to find."

"Oh, that— Well, I suppose so, but this is much more important. There are too many people as it is; why encourage new colonies? A mathematician could solve the population problem in jig time—just shoot every other one."

Mr. O'Toole said, without looking up, "The thing I like about you, Chief, is your big warm heart."

"Quiet in the gallery, please. Now today, son, we have been trying to find out what time it is."

I must have looked as puzzled as I felt for he went on, "Oh, we *know* what time it is . . . but too many different ways. See that?" He pointed at the display scope, still tirelessly making a peak every second. "That's the Greenwich time tick, pulled in by radio and corrected for relative speed and change of speed. Then there is the time you were hearing over the earphones; that is the time the ship runs by. Then there is the time you were getting from your brother and passing to us. We're trying to compare them all, but the trouble is that we have to have people in the circuit and, while a tenth of a second is a short time for the human nervous system, a microsecond is a measurably long time in physics. Any radar system splits up a microsecond as easily as you slice a pound of butter. So we use a lot of runs to try to even out our ignorance."

"Yes, but what do you expect to find out?"

"If I 'expected,' I wouldn't be doing it. But you might say that we are trying to find out what the word 'simultaneous' means."

Mr. O'Toole looked up from the console. "If it means anything," he amended.

Dr. Babcock glanced at him. "You still here? 'If it means anything.' Son, ever since the great Doctor Einstein, 'simultaneous' and 'simultaneity' have been dirty words to physicists. We chucked the very concept, denied that it had meaning, and built up a glorious structure of theoretical physics without it. Then you mind readers came along and kicked it over. Oh, don't look guilty; every house needs a housecleaning now and then. If you folks had done your carnival stunt at just the speed of light, we would have assigned you a place in the files and forgotten you. But you rudely insisted on doing it at something enormously greater than the speed of light, which made you as welcome as a pig at a wedding. You've split us physicists into two schools, those who want to class you as a purely psychological phenomenon and no business of physics—these are the 'close your eyes and it will go away' boys—and a second school which realizes that since measurements can be made of whatever this is you do, it is therefore the business of physics to measure and include it . . . since physics is, above all, the trade of measuring things and assigning definite numerical values to them."

O'Toole said, "Don't wax philosophical, Chief."

"You get back to your numbers, O'Toole; you have no soul. These laddies want to measure how fast you do it. They don't care how fast—they've already recovered from the blow that you do it faster than light—but they want to know exactly how fast. They can't accept the idea that you do it 'instantaneously,' for that would require them to go to a different church entirely. They want to assign a definite speed of propagation, such-and-such number of times faster than the speed of light. Then they can modify their old equations and go right on happily doing business at the old stand."

"They will," agreed O'Toole.

"Then there is a third school of thought, the right one . . . my own."

O'Toole, without looking up, made a rude noise.

"Is that your asthma coming back?" Babcock said anxiously. "By the way, you got any results?"

"They're still doing it in nothing flat. Measured time negative as often as positive and never greater than inherent observational error."

"You see, son? That's the correct school. Measure what happens and let the chips fly where they may."

"Hear, hear!"

"Quiet, you renegade Irishman. Besides that, you m-r's give us our first real chance to check another matter. Are you familiar with the relativity transformations?"

"You mean the Einstein equations?"

"Surely. You know the one for time?"

I thought hard. Pat and I had taken first-year physics our freshman year; it had been quite a while. I picked up a piece of paper and wrote down what I thought it was:

$$t_o = t\sqrt{1 - \frac{v^2}{c^2}}$$

"That's it," agreed Dr. Babcock. "At a relative velocity of 'v' time interval at first frame of reference equals time interval at second frame of reference multiplied by the square root of one minus the square of the relative velocity divided by the square of the speed of light. That's just the special case, of course, for constant speeds; it is more complicated for acceleration. But there has been much disagreement as to what the time equations meant, or if they meant anything."

I blurted out, "Huh? But I thought the Einstein theory had been proved?" It suddenly occurred to me that, if the relativity equations were wrong, we were going to be away a mighty long time—Tau Ceti, our first stop, was eleven light-years from the Sun . . . and that was just our first one; the others were a lot farther.

But *everybody* said that once we got up near the speed of light the months would breeze past like days. The equations *said* so.

"Attend me. How do you prove that there are eggs in a bird's nest? Don't strain your gray matter: Go climb the tree and find out. There is no other way. Now we are climbing the tree."

"Fine!" said O'Toole. "Go climb a tree."

"Noisy in here. One school of thought maintained that the equations simply meant that a clock would read differently if you could read it from a passing star . . . which you can't . . . but that there was no real stretching or shrinking of time—whatever 'real' means. Another school pointed to the companion equations for length and mass, maintaining that the famous Michelson-Morley experiment showed that the length transformation was 'real' and pointing out that the increase of mass was regularly computed and used for particle-accelerator ballistics and elsewhere in nuclear physics—for example, in the torch that pushes this ship. So, they reasoned, the change in time rates must be real, because the corollary equations worked in practice. But nobody knew. You have to climb the tree and look."

"When will we know?" I was still worrying. Staying several years, Einstein time, in the ship I had counted on. Getting killed in the course of it, the way Uncle Steve said we probably would, I refused to worry about. But dying of old age in the *Elsie* was not what I had counted on. It was a grim thought, a life sentence shut up inside these steel walls.

"When? Why, we know right now."

"You do? What's the answer?"

"Don't hurry me, son. We've been gone a couple of weeks, at a boost of 124% of one gee; we're up to about 9000 miles per second now. We still haven't come far—call it seven and a half light-hours or about 5,450,000,000 miles. It will be the better part of a year before we are crowding the speed of light. Nevertheless we have reached a sizable percentage of that speed, about five per cent; that's enough to show. Easy to measure, with the aid of you mind readers."

"Well, sir? Is it a real time difference? Or is it just relative?"

"You're using the wrong words. But it's 'real,' so far as the word means anything. The ratio right now is about 99.9%."

"To put it exactly," added Mr. O'Toole, "Bartlett's slippage—that's a technical term I just invented—his 'slippage' in time rate from that of his twin has now reached twelve parts in ten thousand."

"So you would make me a liar for one fiftieth of one percent?" Babcock complained. "O'Toole, why did I let you come along?"

"So you would have some one to work your arithmetic," his assistant answered smugly.

* * *

Pat told me he did not want me around when they operated, but I came anyway. I locked myself in my room so nobody could disturb me and stuck with him. He didn't really object; whenever I spoke he answered and the closer it got to the deadline the more he talked . . . a cheerful babble about nothing and everything. It did not fool me.

When they wheeled him into surgery, he said, *"Tom, you should see my anesthetist. Pretty as a sunny day and just lap size."*

("Isn't her face covered with a mask?")

"Well, not completely. I can see her pretty blue eyes. I think I'll ask her what she's doing tonight."

("Maudie won't like that.")

"You keep Maudie out of this; a sick man is entitled to privileges. Wait a sec, I'll ask her."

("What did she say?")

"She said, 'Nothing much,' and that I would be doing the same for a few days. But I'll get her phone number."

("Two gets you five she won't give it to you.")

"Well, I can try . . . uh uh! Too late, they're starting in . . . Tom, you wouldn't believe this needle; it's the size of an air hose. She says she wants me to count. Okay, anything for a laugh . . . one . . . two . . . three . . ."

Pat got up to seven and I counted with him. All the way through I kept winding up tighter and tighter to unbearable tension and fear. I knew now what he apparently had been sure of all along, that he was not coming out of it. At the count of seven he lost track but his mind did not go silent. Maybe those around the operating table thought they had him unconscious but I knew better; he was trapped inside and screaming to get out.

I called to him and he called back but we couldn't find each other. Then I was as trapped and lost and confused as he was and we groped around in the dark and the cold and the aloneness of the place where you die.

Then I felt the knife whittling at my back and I screamed.

The next thing I remember is a couple of faces floating over me. Somebody said, "I think he's coming around, Doctor." The voice did not belong to anyone; it was a long way off.

Then there was just one face and it said, "Feeling better?"

"I guess so. What happened?"

"Drink this. Here, I'll hold up your head."

When I woke up again I felt fairly wide awake and could see that

I was in the ship's infirmary. Dr. Devereaux was there, looking at me. "You decided to come out of it, young fellow?"

"Out of what, Doctor? What happened?"

"I don't know precisely, but you gave a perfect clinical picture of a patient terminating in surgical shock. By the time we broke the lock on your door, you were far gone—you gave us a bad time. Can you tell me about it?"

I tried to think, then I remembered. Pat! I called him in my mind. ("*Pat!* Where are you, boy?")

He didn't answer. I tried again and he still didn't answer, so I knew. I sat up and managed to choke out, "My brother . . . he *died!*"

Dr. Devereaux said, "Wups! Take it easy. Lie down. He's not dead . . . unless he died in the last ten minutes, which I doubt."

"But I can't reach him!" "How do you know?" "I can't reach him, I tell you!"

"Come down off the ceiling. Because I've been checking on him all morning via the m-r's on watch. He's resting easily under an eighth grain of hypnal, which is why you can't raise him. I may be stupid, son—I *was* stupid, not to warn you to stay out of it—but I've been tinkering with the human mind long enough to figure out approximately what happened to you, given the circumstances. My only excuse is that I have never encountered such circumstances before."

I quieted a little. It made sense that I couldn't wake Pat if they had him under drugs. Under Dr. Devereaux's questions I managed to tell him more or less what had happened—not perfectly, because you can't really tell someone else what goes on inside your head. "Uh, was the operation successful, Doctor?"

"The patient came through in good shape. We'll talk about it later. Now turn over."

"Huh?"

"Turn over. I want to take a look at your back."

He looked at it, then called two of his staff to see it. Presently he touched me. "Does that hurt?"

"Ouch! Uh, yes, it's pretty tender. What's wrong with my back, Doctor?"

"Nothing, really. But you've got two perfect stigmata, just matching the incisions for Macdougal's operation . . . which is the technique they used on your brother."

"Uh, what does that mean?"

"It means that the human mind is complicated and we don't know much about it. Now roll over and go to sleep. I'm going to keep you in bed a couple of days."

I didn't intend to go to sleep but I did. I was awakened by Pat calling me. *"Hey, Tom! Where are you? Snap out of it."*

("I'm right here. What's the matter?")

"Tom . . . I've got my legs back!"

I answered, ("Yeah, I know,") and went back to sleep.

9

Relatives

Once Pat was over his paralysis I should have had the world by the tail, for I had everything I wanted. Somehow it did not work that way. Before he was hurt, I had known why I was down in the dumps: It was because he was going and I wasn't. After he was hurt, I felt guilty because I was getting what I wanted through his misfortune. It didn't seem right to be happy when he was crippled—especially when his crippled condition had got me what I wanted.

So I should have been happy once he was well again.

Were you ever at a party where you were supposed to be having fun and suddenly you realized that you weren't? No reason, just no fun and the whole world gray and tasteless?

Some of the things that were putting me off my feed I could see. First there had been Dusty, but that had been cleared up. Then there had been the matter of other people, especially the electron pushers we stood watch with, calling us freaks and other names and acting as if we were. But the Captain had tromped on that, too, and when we got better acquainted people forgot about such things. One of the relativists, Janet Meers, was a lightning calculator, which made her a freak, too, but everybody took it for granted in her and after a while they took what we did for granted.

After we got out of radio range of Earth the Captain took us out from under Commander Frick and set us up as a department of our own, with "Uncle" Alfred McNeil as head of department and Rupert Hauptman as his assistant—which meant that Rupe kept the watch list while Uncle Alf was in charge of our mess table and sort of kept us in line. We liked old Unc too well to give him much trouble and if somebody did get out of line Unc would look sad and the rest of us would slap the culprit down. It worked.

I think Dr. Devereaux recommended it to the Captain. The fact was that Commander Frick resented us. He was an electrical engineer and had spent his whole life on better and better communication equipment . . . then we came along and did it better and faster with no equipment at all. I don't blame him; I would have been sore, too. But we got along better with Uncle Alf.

I suppose that the *Vasco da Gama* was part of my trouble. The worst thing about space travel is that absolutely nothing happens. Consequently the biggest event in our day was the morning paper. All day long each mind reader on watch (when not busy with traffic, which wasn't much) would copy news. We got the news services free and all the features and Dusty would dress it up by copying pictures sent by his twin Rusty. The communicator on the midwatch would edit it and the m-r and the communicator on the early morning watch would print it and have it in the mess room by breakfast.

There was no limit to the amount of copy we could have; it was just a question of how much so few people could prepare. Besides Solar System news we carried ships' news, not only of the *Elsie* but of the eleven others. Everybody (except myself) knew people in the other ships. Either they had met them at Zurich, or the old spacehands, like the Captain and a lot of others, had friends and acquaintances reaching back for years.

It was mostly social news, but we enjoyed it more than news from Earth and the System, because we felt closer to the ships in the fleet, even though they were billions of miles away and getting farther by the second. When Ray Gilberti and Sumire Watanabe got married in the *Leif Ericsson*, every ship in the fleet held a celebration. When a baby was born in the *Pinta* and our Captain was named godfather, it made us all proud.

We were hooked to the *Vasco da Gama* through Cas Warner, and Miss Gamma Furtney linked us with the *Marco Polo* and the *Santa Maria* through her triplets Miss Alpha and Miss Beta, but we got news from all the ships by pass-down-the-line. Fleet news was never cut, even if dirtside news had to be. As it was, Mama O'Toole complained that if the editions got any larger, she would either have to issue clean sheets and pillow cases only once a week or engineering would have to build her another laundry just to wash newspapers. Nevertheless, the ecology department always had clean paper ready, freshly pressed, for each edition.

We even put out an occasional extra, like the time Lucille LaVonne won "Miss Solar System" and Dusty did a pic of her so perfect you would have sworn it was a photograph. We lost some paper from that as quite a number of people kept their copies for pin-ups instead of turning them back for reclamation—I did myself. I even got Dusty to autograph it. It startled him but pleased him even though he was rude about it—an artist is entitled to credit for his work, I say, even if he is a poisonous little squirt.

What I am trying to say is that the *Elsie Times* was the high point of each day and fleet news was the most important part of it.

I had not been on watch the night before; nevertheless, I was late for breakfast. When I hurried in, everybody was busy with his copy of the *Times* as usual—but nobody was eating. I sat down between Van and Prudence and said, "What's the matter? What's aching everybody?"

Pru silently handed me a copy of the *Times*.

The first page was bordered in black. There were oversize headlines: *VASCO DA GAMA LOST*

I couldn't believe it. The *Vasco* was headed out for Alpha Centauri but she wouldn't get there for another four years, Earth time; she wasn't even close to the speed of light. There was nothing to have any trouble with, out where she was. It must be a mistake.

I turned to see-story-on-page-two. There was a boxed dispatch from the Commodore in the *Santa Maria:* "(Official) At 0334 today Greenwich time TS *Vasco da Gama* (LRF 172) fell out of contact. Two special circuits were operating at the time, one Earthside and one to the *Magellan.* In both cases transmission ceased without warning, in midst of message and at the same apparent instant by adjusted times. The ship contained eleven special communicators; it has not proved possible to raise any of them. It must therefore be assumed that the ship is lost, with no survivors."

The LRF dispatch merely admitted that the ship was out of contact. There was a statement by our Captain and a longer news story which included comments from other ships; I read them but the whole story was in the headlines . . . the *Vasco* was gone wherever it is that ships go when they don't come back.

I suddenly realized something and looked up. Cas Warner's chair was empty. Uncle Alf caught my eye and said quietly, "He knows, Tom. The Captain woke him and told him soon after it happened. The only good thing about it is that he wasn't linked with his brother when it happened."

I wasn't sure that Uncle Alf had the right slant. If Pat got it, I'd want to be with him when it happened, wouldn't I? Well, I thought I would. In any case I was sure that Unc would want to be holding Sugar

Pie's hand if something happened and she had to make the big jump before he did. And Cas and his brother Caleb were close; I knew that.

Later that day the Captain held memorial services and Uncle Alfred preached a short sermon and we all sang the "Prayer for Travelers." After that we pretended that there never had been a ship named the *Vasco da Gama*, but it was all pretense.

Cas moved from our table and Mama O'Toole put him to work as an assistant to her. Cas and his brother had been hotel men before LRF tapped them and Cas could be a lot of help to her; keeping a ship with two hundred people in it in ecological balance is no small job. Goodness, just raising food for two hundred people would be a big job even if it did not have to be managed so as to maintain atmospheric balance; just managing the yeast cultures and the hydroponics took all of the time of nine people.

After a few weeks Cas was supervising catering and housekeeping and Mama O'Toole could give all of her time to the scientific and technical end—except that she continued to keep an eye on the cooking.

But the *Vasco da Gama* should not have made me brood; I didn't know anybody in that ship. If Cas could pull out of it and lead a normal, useful life, I certainly should not have had the mulligrubs. No, I think it was my birthday as much as anything.

The mess room had two big electric clocks in it, controlled from the relativists' computation room, and two bank-style calendars over them. When we started out they were all right together, showing Greenwich time and date. Then, as we continued to accelerate and our speed got closer to that of light, the "slippage" between *Elsie* and the Earth began to show and they got farther and farther out of phase. At first we talked about it, but presently we didn't notice the Greenwich set . . . for what good does it do you to know that it is now three in the morning next Wednesday at Greenwich when it is lunch time in the ship? It was like time zones and the date line back on Earth: not ordinarily important. I didn't even notice when Pat groused about the odd times of day he had to be on duty because I stood watches any time of day myself.

Consequently I was caught flat-footed when Pat woke me with a whistle in the middle of the night and shouted, *"Happy birthday!"*

("Huh? Whose?")

"Yours, dopey. Ours. What's the matter with you? Can't you count?"

("But—")

"Hold it. They are just bringing the cake in and they are going to sing 'Happy Birthday.' I'll echo it for you."

While they were doing so I got up and slipped on a pair of pants and went down to the mess room. It was the middle of "night" for us and there was just a standing light there. But I could see the clocks and calendars—sure enough, the Greenwich date was our birthday and figuring back zone time from Greenwich to home made it about dinner time at home.

But it *wasn't* my birthday. I was on the other schedule and it didn't seem right.

"Blew 'em all out, kid," Pat announced happily. *"That ought to hold us for another year. Mum wants to know if they baked a cake for you there?"*

("Tell her 'yes.' ") They hadn't, of course. But I didn't feel like explaining. Mother got jittery easily enough without trying to explain Einstein time to her. As for Pat, he ought to know better.

The folks had given Pat a new watch and he told me that there was a box of chocolates addressed to me—should he open it and pass it around? I told him to go ahead, not knowing whether to be grateful that I was remembered or to be annoyed at a "present" I couldn't possibly see or touch. After a while I told Pat that I had to get my sleep and please say good night and thank you to everybody for me. But I didn't get to sleep; I lay awake until the passageway lights came on.

The following week they did have a birthday cake for me at our table and everybody sang to me and I got a lot of pleasantly intended but useless presents—you can't give a person much aboard ship when you are eating at the same mess and drawing from the same storerooms. I stood up and thanked them when somebody hollered "Speech!" and I stayed and danced with the girls afterwards. Nevertheless it still did not seem like my birthday because it had already *been* my birthday, days earlier.

It was maybe the next day that my Uncle Steve came around and dug me out in my room. "Where you been keeping yourself, youngster?"

"Huh? Nowhere."

"That's what I thought." He settled in my chair and I lay back down on my bunk. "Every time I look for you, you aren't in sight. You aren't on watch or working all the time. Where are you?"

I didn't say anything. I had been right where I was a lot of the time, just staring at the ceiling. Uncle Steve went on, "When a man takes to crouching in a corner aboard ship, it is usually best, I've found, to let him be. Either he will pull out of it by himself, or he'll go out the airlock one day without bothering with a pressure suit. Either way, he doesn't want to be monkeyed with. But you're my sister's boy and I've got a responsibility toward you. What's wrong? You never show up for fun and games in the evenings and you go around with a long face; what's eating you?"

"There's nothing wrong with me!" I said angrily.

Uncle Steve disposed of that with a monosyllable. "Open up, kid. You haven't been right since the *Vasco* was lost. Is that the trouble? Is your nerve slipping? If it is, Doc Devereaux has synthetic courage in pills. Nobody need know you take 'em and no need to be ashamed—everybody finds a crack in his nerve now and again. I'd hate to tell you what a repulsive form it took the first time I went into action."

"No, I don't think that is it." I thought about it—maybe it was it. "Uncle Steve, what happened to the *Vasco?*"

He shrugged. "Either her torch cut loose, or they bumped into something."

"But a torch *can't* cut loose . . . can it? And there is nothing to bump into out here."

"Correct on both counts. But suppose the torch did blow? The ship would be a pocket-sized *nova* in an umpteenth second. But I can't think of an easier way to go. And the other way would be about as fast, near enough you would never notice. Did you ever think how much kinetic energy we have wrapped up in this bucket at this speed? Doc Babcock says that as we reach the speed of light we'll be just a flat wave front, even though we go happily along eating mashed potatoes and gravy and never knowing the difference."

"But we never quite reach the speed of light."

"Doc pointed that out, too. I should have said 'if.' Is that what is bothering you, kid? Fretting that we might go *boom!* like the *Vasco?* If so, let me point out that almost all the ways of dying in bed are worse . . . particularly if you are silly enough to die of old age—a fate I hope to avoid."

We talked a while longer but did not get anywhere. Then he left, after threatening to dig me out if I spent more than normal sack time in my room. I suppose Uncle Steve reported me to Dr. Devereaux, although both of them claimed not.

Anyhow, Dr. Devereaux tackled me the next day, took me around to his room and sat me down and talked to me. He had a big sloppy-comfortable stateroom; he never saw anybody in the surgery.

I immediately wanted to know why he wanted to talk to me.

He opened his frog eyes wide and looked innocent. "Just happened to get around to you, Tom." He picked up a pile of punched cards. "See these? That's how many people I've had a chat with this week. I've got to pretend to earn my pay."

"Well, you don't have to waste time on me. I'm doing all right."

"But I like to waste time, Tom. Psychology is a wonderful racket. You don't scrub for surgery, you don't have to stare down people's dirty throats, you just sit and pretend to listen while somebody explains that when he was a little boy he didn't like to play with the other little boys. Now you talk for a while. Tell me anything you want to, while I take a nap. If you talk long enough, I can get rested up from the poker party I sat in on last night and still chalk up a day's work."

I tried to talk and say nothing. While I was doing so, Pat called me. I told him to call back; I was busy. Dr. Devereaux was watching my face and said suddenly, "What was on your mind then?"

I explained that it could wait; my twin wanted to talk to me.

"Hmm . . . Tom, tell me about your twin. I didn't have time to get well acquainted with him in Zurich."

Before I knew it I had told him a lot about both of us. He was remarkably easy to talk to. Twice I thought he had gone to sleep but each time I stopped, he roused himself and asked another question that got me started all over again.

Finally he said, "You know, Tom, identical twins are exceptionally interesting to psychologists—not to mention geneticists, sociologists, and biochemists. You start out from the same egg, as near alike as two organic complexes can be. Then you become two different people. Are the differences environmental? Or is there something else at work?"

I thought about this. "You mean the soul, Doctor?"

"Mmm . . . ask me next Wednesday. One sometimes holds personal and private views somewhat different from one's public and scientific opinions. Never mind. The point is that you m-r twins are interesting. I fancy that the serendipitous results of Project Lebensraum will, as usual, be far greater than the intended results."

"The 'Sarah' what, Doctor?"

"Eh? 'Serendipitous.' The adjective for 'Serendipity.' Serendipity means that you dig for worms and strike gold. Happens all the time in science. It is the reason why 'useless' pure research is always so much more practical than 'practical' work. But let's talk about you. I can't help you with your problems—you have to do that yourself. But let's kick it around and pretend that I can, so as to justify my being on the payroll. Now two things stick out like a sore thumb: the first is that you don't like your brother."

I started to protest but he brushed it aside. "Let me talk. Why are you sure that I am wrong? Answer: because you have been told from birth that you love him. Siblings always 'love' each other; that is a foundation of our civilization, like Mom's apple pie. People usually believe anything that they are told early and often. Probably a good thing they believe this one, because brothers and sisters often have more opportunity and more reason to hate each other than anyone else."

"But I *like* Pat. It's just—"

" 'It's just' what?" he insisted gently when I did not finish.

I did not answer and he went on, "It is just that you have every reason to dislike him. He has bossed you and bullied you and grabbed what he wanted. When he could not get it by a straight fight, he used your mother to work on your father to make it come his way. He even got the girl you wanted. Why should you like him? If a man were no relation—instead of being your twin brother—would you like him for doing those things to you? Or would you hate him?"

I didn't relish the taste of it. "I wasn't being fair to him, Doctor. I don't think Pat knew he was hogging things . . . and I'm sure our parents never meant to play favorites. Maybe I'm just feeling sorry for myself."

"Maybe you are. Maybe there isn't a word of truth in it and you are constitutionally unable to see what's fair when you yourself are involved. But the point is that this is the way you do feel about it . . . and you certainly would not like such a person—except that he is your twin brother, so of course you must 'love' him. The two ideas fight each other. So you will continue to be stirred up inside until you figure out which one is false and get rid of it. That's up to you."

"But . . . doggone it, Doctor, I *do* like Pat!"

"Do you? Then you had better dig out of your mind the notion that he has been handing you the dirty end of the stick all these years. But I doubt if you do. You're fond of him—we're all fond of things we are used to, old shoes, old pipes, even the devil we know is better than a strange devil. You're loyal to him. He's necessary to you and you are necessary to him. But 'like' him? It seems most improbable. On the other hand, if you could get it through your head that there is no longer any need to 'love' him, nor even to like him, then you might possibly get to like him a little for what he is. You'll certainly grow more tolerant of him, though I doubt if you will ever like him much. He's a rather unlikeable cuss."

"That's not true! Pat's always been very popular."

"Not with me. Mmm . . . Tom, I cheated. I know your brother better than I let on. Neither one of you is very likeable, matter of fact, and you are very much alike. Don't take offense. I can't abide 'nice' people; 'sweetness and light' turns my stomach. I like ornery people with a good, hard core of self interest—a lucky thing, in view of my profession. You and your brother are about equally selfish, only he is more successful at it. By the way, he likes you."

"Huh?"

"Yes. The way he would a dog that always came when called. He feels protective toward you, when it doesn't conflict with his own interests. But he's rather contemptuous of you; he considers you a weakling—and, in his book, the meek are not entitled to inherit the earth; that's for chaps like himself."

I chewed that over and began to get angry. I did not doubt that Pat felt that way about me—patronizing and willing to see to it that I got a piece of cake . . . provided that he got a bigger one.

"The other thing that stands out," Dr. Devereaux went on, "is that neither you nor your brother wanted to go on this trip."

This was so manifestly untrue and unfair that I opened my mouth and left it open. Dr. Devereaux looked at me. "Yes? You were about to say?"

"Why, that's the silliest thing I ever heard, Doctor! The only real trouble Pat and I ever had was because both of us wanted to go and only one of us could."

He shook his head. "You've got it backwards. Both of you wanted to stay behind and only one of you could. Your brother won, as usual."

"No, he didn't . . . well, yes, he did, but the chance to go; not the other way around. And he would have, too, if it hadn't been for that accident."

" 'That accident.' Mmm . . . yes." Dr. Devereaux held still, with his head dropped forward and his hands folded across his belly, for so long that I thought again that he was asleep. "Tom, I'm going to tell you something that is none of your business, because I think you need to know. I suggest that you never discuss it with your twin . . . and if you do, I'll make you out a liar, net. Because it would be bad for him. Understand me?"

"Then don't tell me," I said surlily.

"Shut up and listen." He picked up a file folder. "Here is a report on your brother's operation, written in the talk we doctors use to confuse patients. You wouldn't understand it and, anyhow, it was sent sidewise, through the *Santa Maria* and in code. You want to know what they found when they opened your brother up?"

"Uh, not especially."

"There was no damage to his spinal cord of any sort."

"Huh? Are you trying to tell me that he was *faking* his legs being paralyzed? I don't believe it!"

"Easy, now. He wasn't faking. His legs *were* paralyzed. He could not possibly fake paralysis so well that a neurologist could not detect it. I examined him myself; your brother was paralyzed. But not from damage to his spinal cord—which I knew and the surgeons who operated on him knew."

"But—" I shook my head. "I guess I'm stupid."

"Aren't we all? Tom, the human mind is not simple; it is very complex. Up at the top, the conscious mind has its own ideas and desires, some of them real, some of them impressed on it by propaganda and training and the necessity for putting up a good front and cutting a fine figure to other people. Down below is the unconscious mind, blind and deaf and stupid and sly, and with—usually—a different set of desires and very different motivations. It wants its own way . . . and when it doesn't get it, it raises a stink until it is satisfied. The trick in easy living is to find out what your unconscious mind really wants and give it to it on the cheapest terms possible, before it sends you through emotional bankruptcy to get its own way. You know what a psychotic is, Tom?"

"Uh . . . a crazy person."

" 'Crazy' is a word we're trying to get rid of. A psychotic is a poor wretch who has had to sell out the shop and go naked to the world to satisfy the demands of his unconscious mind. He's made a settlement, but it has ruined him. My job is to help people make settlements that won't ruin them—like a good lawyer. We never try to get them to evade the settlement, just arrange it on the best terms.

"What I'm getting at is this: your brother managed to make a settlement with his unconscious on fairly good terms, very good terms considering that he did it without professional help. His conscious mind signed a contract and his unconscious said flatly that he must not carry it out. The conflict was so deep that it would have destroyed some people. But not your brother. His unconscious mind elected to have an accident instead, one that could cause paralysis and sure enough it did—*real* paralysis, mind you; no fakery. So your brother was honorably excused from an obligation he could not carry out. Then, when it was no longer possible to go on this trip, he was operated on. The surgery merely corrected minor damage to the bones. But he was encouraged to think that his paralysis would go away—and so it did." Devereaux shrugged.

I thought about it until I was confused. This conscious and unconscious stuff—I'd studied it and passed quizzes in it . . . but I didn't take any stock in it. Doc Devereaux could talk figures of speech until he was blue in the face but it didn't get around the fact that both Pat and I had wanted to go and the only reason Pat had to stay behind was because he had hurt himself in that accident. Maybe the paralysis was hysterical, maybe he had scared himself in to thinking he was hurt worse than he was. But that didn't make any difference.

But Doc Devereaux talked as if the accident wasn't an accident. Well, what of it? Maybe Pat was scared green and had been too proud to show it—I still didn't think he had taken a tumble on a mountainside on purpose.

[cf4] In any case, Doc was dead wrong on one thing: *I* had wanted to go. Oh, maybe I had been a little scared and I knew I had been homesick at first—but that was only natural.

("Then why are you so down in the dumps, stupid?")

That wasn't Pat talking; that was me, talking to myself. Shucks, maybe it was my unconscious mind, talking out loud for once.

"Doc?"

"Yes, Tom."

"You say I didn't really want to come along?"

"It looks that way."

"But you said the unconscious mind always wins. You can't have it both ways."

He sighed. "That isn't quite what I said. You were hurried into this. The unconscious is stupid and often slow; yours did not have time to work up anything as easy as a skiing accident. But it is stubborn. It's demanding that you go home . . . which you can't. But it won't listen to reason. It just keeps on nagging you to give it the impossible, like a baby crying for the moon."

I shrugged. "To hear you tell it, I'm in an impossible mess."

"Don't look so danged sourpuss! Mental hygiene is a process of correcting the correctable and adjusting to the inevitable. You've got three choices."

"I didn't know I had any."

"Three. You can keep on going into a spin until your mind builds up a fantasy acceptable to your unconscious . . . a psychotic adjustment, what you would call 'crazy.' Or you can muddle along as you are, unhappy and not much use to yourself or your shipmates . . . and always with the possibility of skidding over the line. Or you can dig into your own mind, get acquainted with it, find out what it really wants, show it what it can't have and why, and strike a healthy bargain with it on the basis of what is possible. If you've got guts and gumption, you'll try the last one. It won't be easy." He waited, looking at me.

"Uh, I guess I'd better try. But how do I do it?"

"Not by moping in your room about might-have-beens, that's sure."

"My Uncle Steve—Major Lucas, I mean—" I said slowly, "told me

I shouldn't do that. He wants me to stir around and associate with other people. I guess I should."

"Surely, surely. But that's not enough. You can't chin yourself out of the hole you are in just by pretending to be the life of the party. You have to get acquainted with yourself."

"Yes, sir. But *how?*"

"Well, we can't do it by having you talk about yourself every afternoon while I hold your hand. Mmm . . . I suggest that you try writing down who you are and where you've been and how you got from there to here. You make it thorough enough and maybe you will begin to see 'why' as well as 'how.' Keep digging and you may find out who you are and what you want and how much of it you can get."

I must have looked baffled for he said, "Do you keep a diary?"

"Sometimes. I've got one along."

"Use it as an outline. 'The Life and Times of T. P. Bartlett, Gent.' Make it complete and try to tell the truth—all the truth."

I thought that over. Some things you don't want to tell anybody. "Uh, I suppose you'll want to read it, Doctor?"

"Me? Heaven forbid! I get too little rest without reading the amateur literary efforts of two hundred misguided people. This is for *you*, son; you'll be writing to yourself . . . only write it as if you didn't know anything about yourself and had to explain everything. Write it as if you expected to lose your memory and wanted to be sure you could pick up the strings again. Put it all down." He frowned and added grudgingly, "If you feel that you have found out something important and want a second opinion, I suppose I could squeeze in time to read part of it, at least. But I won't promise. Just write it to yourself—to the one with amnesia."

So I told him I would try . . . and I have. I can't see that it has done any special good (I pulled out of the slump anyhow) and there just isn't time to do the kind of a job he told me to do. I've had to hurry over the last part of this because this is the first free evening I've had in a month.

But it's amazing how much you can remember when you really try.

10

Relations

THERE HAVE BEEN A LOT OF CHANGES AROUND THE *ELSIE*. FOR ONE thing we are over the hump now and backing down the other side, decelerating as fast as we boosted; we'll be at Tau Ceti in about six months, ship's time.

But I am getting ahead of myself. It has been about a year, S-time, since I started this, and about twelve years, Earth time, since we left Earth. But forget E-time; it doesn't mean anything. We've been thirteen months in the ship by S-time and a lot has happened. Pat getting married—no, that didn't happen in the ship and it's the wrong place to start.

Maybe the place to start is with another marriage, when Chet Travers married Mei-Ling Jones. It met with wide approval, except on the part of one of the engineers who was sweet on her himself. It caused us freaks and the electron pushers to bury the hatchet to have one of us marry one of them, especially when Commander Frick came down the aisle in the mess room with the bride on his arm, looking as proud and solemn as if she had been his daughter. They were a good match; Chet was not yet thirty and I figure that Mei-Ling is at least twenty-two.

But it resulted in a change in the watch list and Rupe put me on with Prudence Mathews.

I had always liked Pru without paying much attention to her. You had to look twice to know that she was pretty. But she had a way of looking up at you that made you feel important. Up to the time I started standing watches with her I had more or less left the girls alone; I guess I was "being true to Maudie." But by then I was writing this confession story for Doc Devereaux; somehow writing things down gives them finality. I said to myself, "Why not? Tom, old boy, Maudie is as definitely out of your life as if one of you were dead. But life goes on, right here in this bucket of wind."

I didn't do anything drastic; I just enjoyed Pru's company as much as possible . . . which turned out to be a lot.

I've heard that when the animals came aboard the *Ark* two by two, Noah separated them port and starboard. The *Elsie* isn't run that way. Chet and Mei-Ling had found it possible to get well enough acquainted to want to make it permanent. A little less than half of the crew had come aboard as married couples; the rest of us didn't have any obstacles put in our way if we had such things on our minds.

But somehow without its ever showing we were better chaperoned than is usual back dirtside. It didn't seem organized . . . and yet it must have been. If somebody was saying good night a little too long in a passageway after the lights were dimmed, it would just happen that Uncle Alfred had to get up about then and shuffle down the passageway. Or maybe it would be Mama O'Toole, going to make herself a cup of chocolate "to help her get to sleep."

Or it might be the Captain. I think he had eyes in the back of his head for everything that went on in the ship. I'm convinced that Mama O'Toole had. Or maybe Unc was actually one of those hypothetical wide-range telepaths but was too polite and too shrewd to let anybody know it.

Or maybe Doc Devereaux had us all so well analyzed in those punched cards of his that he always knew which way the rabbit would jump and could send his dogs to head him off. I wouldn't put it past him.

But it was always just enough and not too much. Nobody objected to a kiss or two if somebody wanted to check on the taste; on the other hand we never had any of the scandals that pop up every now and then in almost any community. I'm sure we didn't; you can't keep such things quiet in a ship. But nobody seemed to see a little low-pressure lalligagging.

Certainly Pru and I never did anything that would arouse criticism.

Nevertheless we were taking up more and more of each other's time, both on and off watch. I wasn't serious, not in the sense of thinking about getting married; but I was serious in that it was becoming important. She began to look at me privately and a bit possessively, or maybe our hands would touch in passing over a stack of traffic and we could feel the sparks jump.

I felt fine and alive and I didn't have time to write in these memoirs. I gained four pounds and I certainly wasn't homesick.

Pru and I got in the habit of stopping off and raiding the pantry whenever we came off a night watch together. Mama O'Toole didn't mind; she left it unlocked so that anyone who wanted a snack could find one—she said this was our home, not a jail. Pru and I would make a sandwich, or concoct a creative mess, and eat and talk before we turned in. It didn't matter what we talked about; what mattered was the warm glow we shared.

We came off watch at midnight one night and the mess room was deserted; the poker players had broken up early and there wasn't even a late chess game. Pru and I went into the pantry and were just getting set to grill a yeast-cheese sandwich. The pantry is rather cramped; when Pru turned to switch on the small grill, she brushed against me.

I got a whiff of her nice, clean hair and something like fresh clover or violets. Then I put my arms around her.

She didn't make any fuss. She stopped dead for an instant, then she relaxed.

Girls are nice. They don't have any bones and I think they must be about five degrees warmer than we are, even if fever thermometers don't show it. I put my face down and she put her face up and closed her eyes and everything was wonderful.

For maybe half a second she kissed me and I knew she was as much in favor of it as I was, which is as emphatic as I can put it.

Then she had broken out of my arms like a wrestler and was standing pressed against the counter across from me and looking terribly upset. Well, so was I. She wasn't looking at me; she was staring at nothing and seemed to be listening . . . so I knew; it was the expression she wore when she was linked—only she looked terribly unhappy too.

I said, "Pru! What's the matter?"

She did not answer; she simply started to leave. She had taken a couple of steps toward the door when I reached out and grabbed her wrist. "Hey, are you mad at me?"

She twisted away, then seemed to realize that I was still there. "I'm sorry, Tom," she said huskily. "My sister is angry."

I had never met Patience Mathews—and now I hardly wanted to. "Huh? Well, of all the silly ways to behave I—"

"My sister doesn't like you, Tom," she answered firmly, as if that explained everything. "Good night."

"But—"

"Good night, Tom."

Pru was as nice as ever at breakfast but when she passed me the rolls the sparks didn't jump. I wasn't surprised when Rupe reshuffled the watch list that day but I did not ask why. Pru didn't avoid me and she would even dance with me when there was dancing, but the fire was out and neither of us tried to light it again.

A long time later I told Van about it. I got no sympathy. "Think you're the first one to get your finger mashed in the door? Pru is a sweet little trick, take it from Grandfather van Houten. But when Sir Galahad himself comes riding up on a white charger, he's going to have to check with Patience before he can speak to Pru . . . and I'll bet you the answer is 'No!' Pru is willing, in her sweet little half-witted way, but Patience won't okay anything more cozy than 'Pease Porridge Hot.' "

"I think it's a shame. Mind you, it doesn't matter to me now. But her sister is going to ruin her life."

"It's her business. Myself, I reached a compromise with my twin years ago—we beat each other's teeth in and after that we cooperated on a businesslike basis. Anyhow, how do you know that Pru isn't doing the same to Patience? Maybe Pru started it."

It didn't sour me on girls, not even on girls who had twin sisters who were mind readers, but after that I enjoyed the company of all of them. But for a while I saw more of Unc. He liked to play dominoes, then when we had finished all even up for the evening he liked to talk about Sugar Pie—and *to* her, of course. He would look at his big photograph of her and so would I and the three of us would talk, with Unc echoing for both of us. She really was a nice little girl and it was a lot of fun to get to know a little six-year-old girl—it's very quaint what they think about.

One night I was talking with them and looking at her picture, as always, when it occurred to me that time had passed and that Sugar Pie must have changed—they grow up fast at that age. I got a brilliant idea. "Unc, why don't you have Sugar Pie mail a new photograph to Rusty Rhodes? Then he could transmit it to Dusty and Dusty could draw you one as perfect as that one, only it would be up to date, show you what she looks like now, huh? How about it, Sugar Pie? Isn't that a good idea?"

"It isn't necessary."

I was looking at the picture and I nearly popped my fuses. For a moment it wasn't the same picture. Oh, it was the same merry little girl, but she was a little older, she was shy a front tooth, and her hair was different.

And she was alive. Not just a trukolor stereo, but alive. There's a difference.

But when I blinked it was the same old picture.

I said hoarsely, "Unc, who said, 'It isn't necessary?' You? Or Sugar Pie?"

"Why, Sugar Pie did. I echoed."

"Yes, Unc . . . but I didn't hear *you;* I heard *her.*" Then I told him about the photograph.

He nodded. "Yes, that's the way she looks. She says to tell you that her tooth is coming in, however."

"Unc . . . there's no way to get around it. For a moment I crowded in on your private wave length." I was feeling shaky.

"I knew. So did Sugar Pie. But you didn't crowd in, son; a friend is always welcome."

I was still trying to soak it in. The implications were more mind-stretching, even, than when Pat and I found out we could do it. But I didn't know what they were yet. "Uh, Unc, do you suppose we could do it again? Sugar Pie?"

"We can try."

But it didn't work . . . unless I heard her voice as well as Unc's when she said, "Good night, Tommie." I wasn't sure.

After I got to bed I told Pat about it. He was interested after I convinced him that it really had happened. *"This is worth digging into, old son. I'd better record it. Doc Mabel will want to kick it around."*

("Uh, wait until I check with Uncle Alf.")

"Well, all right. I guess it is his baby . . . in more ways than one. Speaking of his baby, maybe I should go see her? With two of us at each end it might be easier to make it click again. Where does his niece live?"

("Uh, Johannesburg.")

"Mmm . . . that's a far stretch down the road, but I'm sure the LRF would send me there if Doc Mabel got interested."

("Probably. But let me talk to Unc.")

But Unc talked to Dr. Devereaux first. They called me in and Doc wanted to try it again at once. He was as near excited as I ever saw him get. I said, "I'm willing, but I doubt if we'll get anywhere; we didn't last night. I think that once was just a fluke."

"Fluke, spook. If it can be done once, it can be done again. We've got to be clever enough to set up the proper conditions." He looked at me. "Any objection to a light dose of hypnosis?"

"Me? Why, no, sir. But I don't hypnotize easily."

"So? According to your record, Dr. Arnault found it not impossible. Just pretend I'm she."

I almost laughed in his face. I look more like Cleopatra than he looks like pretty Dr. Arnault. But I agreed to go along with the gag.

"All either of you will need is a light trance to brush distractions aside and make you receptive."

I don't know what a "light trance" is supposed to feel like. I didn't feel anything and I wasn't asleep.

But I started hearing Sugar Pie again.

I think Dr. Devereaux's interest was purely scientific; any new fact about what makes people tick could rouse him out of his chronic torpor. Uncle Alf suggested that Doc was anxious also to set up a new telepathic circuit, just in case. There was a hint in what Unc said that he realized that he himself would not last forever.

But there was a hint of more than that. Uncle Alf let me know very delicately that, if it should come to it, it was good to know that somebody he trusted would be keeping an eye on his baby. He didn't quite say it, not that baldly, so I didn't have to answer, or I would have choked up. It was just understood—and it was the finest compliment I ever received. I wasn't sure I deserved it so I decided I would just have to manage to deserve it if I ever had to pay off.

I could "talk" to Uncle Alf now, of course, as well as to Sugar Pie. But I didn't, except when all three of us were talking together; telepathy is an imposition when it isn't necessary. I never called Sugar Pie by myself, either, save for a couple of test runs for Doc Devereaux's benefit to establish that I *could* reach her without Unc's help. That took drugs; Unc would wake up from an ordinary sleep if anyone shouted on that "wave length." But otherwise I left her alone; I had no business crowding into a little girl's mind unless she was ready and expecting company.

It was shortly after that that Pat got married.

11

Slippage

My relations with Pat got steadily better all during that first boost, after Dr. Devereaux took me in hand. I found out, after I admitted that I despised and resented Pat, that I no longer did either one. I cured him of bothering me unnecessarily by bothering him unnecessarily—he could shut off an alarm clock but he couldn't shut off me. Then we worked out a live-and-let-live formula and got along better. Presently I found myself looking forward to whatever time we had set for checking with each other and I realized I liked him, not "again" but "at last," for I had never felt that warm toward him before.

But even while we were getting closer we were falling apart; "slippage" was catching up with us. As anyone can see from the relativity formulas, the relationship is not a straight-line one; it isn't even noticeable at the beginning but it builds up like the dickens at the other end of the scale.

At three-quarters the speed of light he complained that I was drawling, while it seemed to me that he was starting to jabber. At nine-tenths of the speed of light it was close to two for one, but we knew what was wrong now and I talked fast and he talked slow.

At 99% of c, it was seven to one and all we could do to make ourselves understood. Later that day we fell out of touch entirely.

Everybody else was having the same trouble. Sure, telepathy is instantaneous, at least the trillions of miles between us didn't cause any lag, not even like the hesitation you get in telephoning from Earth to Luna, nor did the signal strength drop off. But brains are flesh and blood, and thinking takes time . . . and our time rates were out of gear. I was thinking so slowly (from Pat's viewpoint) that he could not slow down and stay with me; as for him, I knew from time to time that he was trying to reach me but it was just a squeal in the earphones so far as making sense was concerned.

Even Dusty Rhodes couldn't make it. His twin couldn't concentrate on a picture for the long hours necessary to let Dusty "see" it.

It was upsetting, to say the least, to all of us. Hearing voices is all right, but not when you can't tell what they are saying and can't shut them off. Maybe some of the odd cases in psychiatry weren't crazy at all; maybe the poor wretches were tuned in on a bad wave length.

Unc took it the worst at first and I sat with him all one evening while we both tried, together. Then he suddenly regained his serenity; Sugar Pie was thinking about him, that he knew; so being, words weren't really necessary.

Pru was the only one who flourished; she was out from under the thumb of her sister. She got really kissed, probably for the first time in her life. No, not by me; I just happened to be wandering down for a drink at the scuttlebutt, then I backed away quietly and let the drink wait. No point in saying who it was, as it didn't mean anything—I think Pru would have kissed the Captain at that point if he had held still. Poor little Pru!

We resigned ourselves to having to wait until we slid back down closer into phase. We were still hooked ship-to-ship because the ships were accelerating to the same schedule, and there was much debate back and forth about the dilemma, one which apparently nobody had anticipated. In one way it was not important, since we would not have anything to report until we slowed down and started checking the stars we were headed for, but in another way it was: The time the *Elsie* spent at the speed of light (minus a gnat's whisker) was going to seem very short to us—but it was going to be ten solid years and a bit over to those back Earthside. As we learned later, Dr. Devereaux and his opposite numbers in the other ships and back in LRF were wondering how many telepathic pairs they would have still functioning (if any) after a lapse of years. They had reason to worry. It had already been established that identical twins were hardly ever telepairs if they had lived apart for years—that was the other reason why most of those picked were young; most twins are separated by adult life.

But up to then, we hadn't been "separated" in Project Lebensraum. Sure, we were an unthinkable distance apart but each pair had been in daily linkage and in constant practice by being required to stand regular watches, even if there was nothing to send but the news.

But what would a few years of being out of touch do to rapport between telepartners?

This didn't bother me; I didn't know about it. I got a sort of an answer out of Mr. O'Toole which caused me to think that a couple of weeks of ship's time would put us back close enough in phase to make ourselves understood. In the meantime, no watches to stand so it wasn't all bad. I went to bed and tried to ignore the squeals inside my head.

I was awakened by Pat.

"Tom . . . answer me, Tom. Can you hear me, Tom? Answer me."

("Hey, Pat, I'm here!") I was wide awake, out of bed and standing on the floor plates, so excited I could hardly talk.

"Tom! Oh, Tom! It's good to hear you, boy—it's been two years since I was last able to raise you."

("But—") I started to argue, then shut up. It had been less than a week to me. But I would have to look at the Greenwich calendar and check with the computation office before I could even guess how long it had been for Pat.

"Let me talk, Tom, I can't keep this up long. They've had me under deep hypnosis and drugs for the past six weeks and it has taken me this long to get in touch with you. They don't dare keep me under much longer."

("You mean they've got you hypped right now?")

"Of course, or I couldn't talk to you at all. Now—" His voice faded out for a second. *"Sorry. They had to stop to give me another shot and an intravenous feeding. Now listen and record this schedule: Van Houten—"* He reeled off precise Greenwich times and dates, to the second, for each of us, and faded out while I was reading them back. I caught a *"So long"* that went up in pitch, then there was silence.

I pulled on pants before I went to wake the Captain but I did not stop for shoes. Then everybody was up and all the daytime lights were turned on even though it was officially night and Mama O'Toole was making coffee and everybody was talking. The relativists were elbowing each other in the computation room and Janet Meers was working out ship's time for Bernie van Houten's appointment with his twin without bothering to put it through the computer because he was first on the list.

Van failed to link with his brother and everybody got jittery and Janet Meers was in tears because somebody suggested that she had made a mistake in the relative times, working it in her head. But Dr. Babcock himself pushed her solution through the computer and checked her to nine decimals. Then he announced in a chilly tone that he would thank everyone not to criticize his staff thereafter; that was his privilege.

Gloria linked with her sister right after that and everybody felt better. The Captain sent a dispatch to the flagship through Miss Gamma and got an answer back that two other ships were back in contact, the *Nautilus* and the *Cristoforo Colombo.*

There was no more straggling up to relieve the watch and stopping to grab a bite as we passed the pantry. If the recomputed time said your opposite number would be ready to transmit at 3:17:06 and a short tick, ship's time, you were waiting for him from three o'clock on and no nonsense, with the recorder rolling and the mike in front of your lips. It was easy for us in the ship, but each one of us knew that his telepair was having to undergo both hypnosis and drastic drugging to stay with us at all—Dr. Devereaux did not seem happy about it.

Nor was there any time for idle chit-chat, not with your twin having to chop maybe an hour out of his life for each word. You recorded what he sent, right the first time and no fumbles; then you transmitted what the Captain had initialed. If that left a few moments to talk, all right. Usually it did not . . . which was how I got mixed up about Pat's marriage.

You see, the two weeks bracketing our change-over from boost to deceleration, during which time we reached our peak speed, amounted to about ten years Earthside. That's 250 to 1 on the average. But it wasn't all average; at the middle of that period the slippage was much greater. I asked Mr. O'Toole what the maximum was and he just shook his head. There was no way to measure it, he told me, and the probable errors were larger than the infinitesimal values he was working with.

"Let's put it this way," he finished. "I'm glad there is no hay fever in this ship, because one hard sneeze would push us over the edge."

He was joking, for, as Janet Meers pointed out, as our speed approached the speed of light, our mass approached infinity.

But we fell out of phase again for a whole day.

At the end of one of those peak "watches" (they were never more than a couple of minutes long, S-time) Pat told me that he and Maudie were going to get married. Then he was gone before I could congratulate him. I started to tell him that I thought Maudie was a little young and wasn't he rushing things, and missed my chance. He was off our band.

I was not exactly jealous. I examined myself and decided that I was not when I found out that I could not remember what Maudie looked like. Oh, I knew what she looked like—blonde, and a little snub nose with a tendency to get freckles across it in the summertime. But I couldn't call up her face the way I could Pru's face, or Janet's. All I felt was a little left out of things.

I did remember to check on the Greenwich, getting Janet to relate it back to the exact time of my last watch. Then I saw that I had been foolish to criticize. Pat was twenty-three and Maudie was twenty-one, almost twenty-two.

I did manage to say, "Congratulations," on my next linkage but Pat did not have a chance to answer. Instead he answered on the next. "Thanks for the congratulations. We've named her after Mother but I think she is going to look like Maudie."

This flabbergasted me. I had to ask for Janet's help again and found that everything was all right—I mean, when a couple has been married two years a baby girl is hardly a surprise, is it? Except to me.

All in all, I had to make quite a few readjustments those two weeks. At the beginning Pat and I were the same age, except for an inconsequential slippage. At the end of that period (I figure the end as being the time when it was no longer necessary to use extreme measures to let us telepairs talk) my twin was more than eleven years older than I was and had a daughter seven years old.

I stopped thinking about Maudie as a girl, certainly not as one I had been sweet on. I decided that she was probably getting fat and sloppy and very, very domestic—she never could resist that second chocolate eclair. As a matter of fact, Pat and I had grown very far apart, for we had little in common now. The minor gossip of the ship, so important to me, bored him; on the other hand, I couldn't get excited about his flexible construction units and penalty dates. We still telecommunicated satisfactorily but it was like two strangers using a telephone. I was sorry, for I had grown to like him before he slipped away from me.

But I did want to see my niece. Knowing Sugar Pie had taught me that baby girls are more fun than puppies and even cuter than kittens. I remembered the idea I had had about Sugar Pie and braced Dusty on the subject.

He agreed to do it; Dusty can't turn down a chance to show how well he can draw. Besides, he had mellowed, for him; he no longer snarled when you tried to pet him even though it might be years before he would learn to sit up and beg.

Dusty turned out a beautiful picture. All Baby Molly lacked was little wings to make her a cherub. I could see a resemblance to myself—to her father, that is. "Dusty, this is a beautiful picture. Is it a good likeness?"

He bristled. "How should I know? But if there is a micron's difference, or a shade or tone off that you could pick up with a spectrophotometer, from the pic your brother mailed to my brother, I'll eat it! But how do I know how the proud parents had the thing prettied up?"

"Sorry, sorry! It's a swell picture. I wish there were some way I could pay you."

"Don't stay awake nights; I'll think of something. My services come high."

I took down my pic of Lucille LaVonne and put Molly in her place. I didn't throw away the one of Lucille, though.

It was a couple of months later that I found out that Dr. Devereaux had seen entirely different possibilities in my being able to use the "wave length" of Uncle Alf and Sugar Pie from the obvious ones I had seen. I had continued to talk with both of them, though not as often as I had at first. Sugar Pie was a young lady now, almost eighteen, in normal school at Witwatersrand and already started practice teaching. Nobody but Unc and I called her "Sugar Pie" and the idea that I might someday substitute for Unc was forgotten—at the rate we were shifting around pretty soon *she* could bring *me* up.

But Doc Devereaux had not forgotten the matter. However the negotiations had been conducted by him with LRF without consulting me. Apparently Pat had been told to keep it to himself until they were ready to try it, for the first I knew of it was when I told him to stand by to record some routine traffic (we were back on regular watches by then). *"Skip it, old son,"* he said. *"Pass the traffic to the next victim. You and I are going to try something fresh."*

("What?")

"LRF orders, all the way down from the top. Molly has an interim research contract all of her own, just like you and I had."

("Huh? She's not a twin.")

"Let me count her. No, there's just one of her—though she sometimes seems like an entire herd of wild elephants. But she's here, and she wants to say hello to Uncle Tom."

("Oh, fine. Hello, Molly.")

"Hello, Uncle Tom."

I almost jumped out of my skin. I had caught it right off, with no fumbling. ("Hey, who was that? Say that again!")

"Hello, Uncle Tom." She giggled. *"I've got a new hair bow."*

I gulped. ("I'll bet you look mighty cute in it, honey. I wish I could see you. Pat! When did this happen?")

"On and off, for the past ten weeks. It took some tough sessions with Dr. Mabel to make it click. By the way, it took some tougher sessions with, uh, the former Miss Kauric before she would agree to let us try it."

"He means Mummy," Molly told me in a conspirator's whisper. *"She didn't like it. But I do, Uncle Tom. I think it's nice."*

"I've got no privacy from either one of them," Pat complained. *"Look, Tom, this is just a test run and I'm signing off. I've got to get the terror back to her mother."*

"She's going to make me take a nap," Molly agreed in a resigned voice, *"and I'm too old for naps. Good-by, Uncle Tom. I love you."*

("I love you, Molly.")

I turned around and Dr. Devereaux and the Captain were standing behind me, ears flapping. "How did it go?" Dr. Devereaux demanded, eagerly—for him.

I tried to keep my face straight. "Satisfactorily. Perfect reception."

"The kid, too?"

"Why, yes, sir. Did you expect something else?"

He let out a long breath. "Son, if you weren't needed, I'd beat your brains out with an old phone list."

I think Baby Molly and I were the first secondary communication team in the fleet. We were not the last. The LRF, proceeding on a hypothesis suggested by the case of Uncle Alfred and Sugar Pie, assumed that it was possible to form a new team where the potential new member was very young and intimately associated with an adult member of an old team. It worked in some cases. In other cases it could not even be tried because no child was available.

Pat and Maude had a second baby girl just before we reached the Tau Ceti system. Maudie put her foot down with respect to Lynette; she said two freaks in her family were enough.

12

Tau Ceti

BY THE TIME WE WERE A FEW LIGHT-HOURS FROM TAU CETI WE KNEW that we had not drawn a blank; by stereo and doppler-stereo Harry Gates had photographed half a dozen planets. Harry was not only senior planetologist; he was boss of the research department. I suppose he had enough degrees to string like beads, but I called him "Harry" because everybody did. He was not the sort you call "Doctor"; he was eager and seemed younger than he was.

To Harry the universe was a complicated toy somebody had given him; he wanted to take it apart and see what made it go. He was delighted with it and willing to discuss it with anybody at any time. I got acquainted with him in the bottle-washing business because Harry didn't treat lab assistants like robots; he treated them like people and did not mind that he knew so much more than they did—he even seemed to think that he could learn something from them.

How he found time to marry Barbara Kuiper I don't know, but Barbara was a torch watchstander, so it probably started as a discussion of physics and drifted over into biology and sociology; Harry was interested in everything. But he didn't find time to be around the night their first baby was born, as that was the night he photographed the planet he named Constance, after the baby. There was objection to this, because everybody wanted to name it, but the Captain decided that the ancient rule applied: Finders of astronomical objects were entitled to name them.

Finding Constance was not an accident. (I mean the planet, not the baby; the baby wasn't lost.) Harry wanted a planet about fifty to fifty-one million miles from Tau, or perhaps I should say that the LRF wanted one at that distance. You see, while Tau Ceti is a close relative of the

Sun, by spectral types, Tau is smaller and gives off only about three-tenths as much sunshine—so, by the same old tired inverse square law you use to plan the lights for a living room or to arrange a photoflash picture, a planet fifty million miles from Tau would catch the same amount of sunlight as a planet ninety-three million miles from Sol, which is where Earth sits. We weren't looking for just any planet, or we would have stayed home in the Solar System; we wanted a reasonable facsimile of Earth or it would not be worth colonizing.

If you go up on your roof on a clear night, the stars look so plentiful you would think that planets very much like Earth must be as common as eggs in a hen yard. Well, they are: Harry estimates that there are between a hundred thousand and a hundred million of them in our own Milky Way—and you can multiply that figure by anything you like for the whole universe.

The hitch is that they aren't conveniently at hand. Tau Ceti was only eleven light-years from Earth; most stars in our own Galaxy average more like fifty thousand light-years from Earth. Even the Long Range Foundation did not think in those terms; unless a star was within a hundred light-years or so it was silly to think of colonizing it even with torchships. Sure, a torchship can go as far as necessary, even across the Galaxy—but who is going to be interested in receiving its real estate reports after a couple of ice ages have come and gone? The population problem would be solved one way or another long before then . . . maybe the way the Kilkenny cats solved theirs.

But there are only fifteen hundred-odd stars within a hundred light-years of Earth and only about a hundred and sixty of these are of the same general spectral type as the Sun. Project Lebensraum hoped to check not more than half of these, say seventy-five at the outside—less since we had lost the *Vasco da Gama*.

If even *one* real Earth-type planet was turned up in the search, the project would pay off. But there was no certainty that it would. A Sol-type star might not have an Earth-type planet; a planet might be too close to the fire, or too far, or too small to hold an atmosphere, or too heavy for humanity's fallen arches, or just too short on the H_2O that figures into everything we do.

Or it might be populated by some rough characters with notions about finders-keepers.

The *Vasco da Gama* had had the best chance to find the first Earth-type planet as the star she had been heading for, Alpha Centauri Able, is the *only* star in this part of the world which really is a twin of the Sun. (Able's companion, Alpha Centauri Baker, is a different sort, spectral type K.) We had the next best chance, even though Tau Ceti is less like the Sun than is Alpha Centauri-B, for the next closest G-type is about thirteen light years from Earth . . . which gave us a two-year edge over the *Magellan* and nearly four over the *Nautilus*.

Provided we found anything, that is. You can imagine how jubilant we were when Tau Ceti turned out to have pay dirt.

Harry was jubilant, too, but for the wrong reasons. I had wandered into the observatory, hoping to get a sight of the sky—one of the *Elsie*'s shortcomings was that it was almost impossible to see out—when he grabbed me and said, "Look at this, pal!"

I looked at it. It was a sheet of paper with figures on it; it could have been Mama O'Toole's crop-rotation schedule. "What is it?"

"Can't you read? It's Bode's Law, that's what it is!"

I thought back. Let me see . . . no, that was Ohm's Law—then I remembered; Bode's Law was a simple geometrical progression that described the distances of the Solar planets from the Sun. Nobody had ever been able to find a reason for it and it didn't work well in some cases, though I seemed to remember that Neptune, or maybe Pluto, had been discovered by calculations that made use of it. It looked like an accidental relationship.

"What of it?" I asked.

" 'What of it?' the man says! Good grief! This is the most important thing since Newton got conked with the apple."

"Maybe so, Harry, but I'm a little slow today. I thought Bode's Law was just an accident. Why couldn't it be an accident here, too?"

"Accident! Look, Tom, if you roll a seven once, that's an accident. When you roll a seven eight hundred times in a row, somebody has loaded the dice."

"But this is only twice."

"It's not the same thing. Get me a big enough sheet of paper and I'll write down the number of zeros it takes to describe how unlikely this 'accident' is." He looked thoughtful. "Tommie, old friend, this is going to be the key that unlocks how planets are made. They'll bury us right alongside Galileo for this. Mmm . . . Tom, we can't afford to spend much time in this neighborhood; we've got to get out and take a look at the Beta Hydri system and make sure it checks the same way—just to convince the mossbacks back Earthside, for it will, it will! I gotta go tell the Captain we'll have to change the schedule." He stuffed the paper in a pocket and hurried away. I looked around but the anti-radiation shutters were over the observatory ports; I didn't get to see out.

Naturally the Captain did not change the schedule; we were out there looking for farm land, not trying to unscrew the inscrutable. A few weeks later we were in orbit around Constance. It put us into free-fall for the first time during the trip, for we had not even been so during acceleration-deceleration change-over but had done it in a skew path instead; chief engineers don't like to shut a torch down unless there is time for an overhaul before starting up again—there was the case of the *Peter the Great* who shut hers off, couldn't light up again, and fell into the Sun.

I didn't like free-fall. But it's all right if you don't overload your stomach.

Harry did not seem disappointed. He had a whole new planet to play with, so he tabled Bode's Law and got busy. We stayed in orbit, a thousand miles up, while research found out everything possible about Connie without actually touching it: direct visual search, radiation survey, absorption-spectra of her atmosphere. She had two moons, one a nice size, though smaller than Luna, so they were able to measure her surface gravity exactly.

She certainly looked like a home from home. Commander Frick had his boys and girls set up a relay tank in the mess room, with color and exaggerated stereo, so that we all could see. Connie looked like the pictures they show of Earth from space stations, green and blue and brown and half covered with clouds and wearing polar ice like skullcaps. Her air pressure was lower than ours but her oxygen ratio was higher; we could breathe it. Absorption spectra showed higher carbon dioxide but not as high as Earth had during the Coal Age.

She was smaller but had a little more land area than Earth; her oceans were smaller. Every dispatch back to Earth carried good news and I even managed to get Pat's mind off his profit-and-loss for a while . . . he had incorporated us as "Bartlett Brothers, Inc." and seemed to expect me to be interested in the bookkeeping simply because my accumulated LRF salary had gone into the capitalization. Shucks, I hadn't touched money for so long I had forgotten anybody used the stuff.

Naturally our first effort was to find out if anybody was already in occupation . . . intelligent animal life I mean, capable of using tools, building things, and organizing. If there was, we were under orders to scoot out of there without landing, find fuel somewhere else in that system, and let a later party attempt to set up friendly relations; the LRF did not want to repeat the horrible mistake that had been made with Mars.

But the electro-magnetic spectrum showed nothing at all, from gamma radiation right up to the longest radio wave lengths. If there were people down there, they didn't use radio and they didn't show city lights and they didn't have atomic power. Nor did they have aircraft, nor roads, nor traffic on the surface of their oceans, nor anything that looked like cities. So we moved down just outside the atmosphere in an "orange slice" pole-to-pole orbit that let us patrol the whole surface, a new sector each half turn.

Then we searched visually, by photography, and by radar. We didn't miss anything more conspicuous than a beaver dam, I'm sure. No cities, no houses, no roads, no bridges, no ships, nobody home. Oh, animals, surely—we could see herds grazing on the plains and we got lesser glimpses of other things. But it looked like a squatter's paradise.

The Captain sent a dispatch: "I am preparing to land."

I promptly volunteered for the reconnaissance party. First I braced my uncle Major Lucas to let me join his guard. He told me to go roll my hoop. "If you think I have any use for an untrained recruit, you're crazier than you apparently think I am. If you wanted to soldier, you should have thought of it as soon as we torched off."

"But you've got men from all the other departments in your guard."

"Every one of 'em trained soldiers. Seriously, Tom, I can't afford it. I need men who will protect *me*; not somebody so green I'll have to protect him. Sorry."

So I tackled Harry Gates to let me join the scientific party the ship's guard would protect. He said, "Certainly, why not? Plenty of dirty work that my gang of prima donnas won't want to do. You can start by checking this inventory."

So I checked while he counted. Presently he said, "How does it feel to be a little green man in a flying saucer?"

"What?"

"An oofoe. We're an oofoe, do you realize that?"

I finally understood him—an U.F.O., an "unidentified flying object." There were accounts of the U.F.O. hysteria in all the histories of space flight. "I suppose we *are* an U.F.O., sort of."

"It's exactly what we are. The U.F.O.'s were survey ships, just as we are. They looked us over, didn't like what they saw, and went away. If they hadn't found Earth crawling with hostile natives, they would have landed and set up housekeeping, just as we are going to do."

"Harry, do you *really* believe the U.F.O.'s were anything but imagination or mistakes in reporting? I thought that theory was exploded long ago."

"Take another look at the evidence, Tom. There was *something* going on up in our sky shortly before we took up space jumping ourselves. Sure, most of the reports were phonies. But some weren't. You have to believe evidence when you have it in front of you, or else the universe is just too fantastic. Surely you don't think that human beings are the only ones who ever built star ships?"

"Well . . . maybe not. But if somebody else has, why haven't they visited us long ago?"

"Simple arithmetic, pal; it's a big universe and we're just one small corner of it. Or maybe they did. That's my own notion; they surveyed us and Earth wasn't what they wanted—maybe us, maybe the climate. So the U.F.O.'s went away." He considered it. "Maybe they landed just long enough to fuel."

That was all I got out of my tenure as a member of the scientific party; when Harry submitted my name on his list, the Captain drew a line through it. "No special communicators will leave the ship."

That settled it; the Captain had a whim of iron. Van got to go, as his brother had been killed in an accident while we were at peak—so I called Pat and told him about Van and suggested that Pat drop dead. He didn't see anything funny in it.

The *Elsie* landed in ocean comfortably deep, then they used the auxiliaries to bring her close to the shore. She floated high out of the water, as two-thirds of her tanks were empty, burned up, the water completely disintegrated in boosting us first up to the speed of light, then backing us down again. The engineers were already overhauling her torch before we reached final anchorage. So far as I know, none of them volunteered for the landing party; I think that to most of the engineers the stop on Constance was just a chance to pick up more boost mass and take care of repairs and overhauls they had been unable to do while underway. They didn't care where they were or where they were going so long as the torch worked and all the machinery ticked. Dr. Devereaux told me that the Staff Metallurgist had been out to Pluto six times and had never set foot on any planet but Earth.

"Is that normal?" I asked, thinking how fussy Doc had been about everybody else, including me.

"For his breed of cat, it's robust mental health. Any other breed I would lock up and feed through the keyhole."

Sam Rojas was as annoyed as I was at the discrimination against us telepaths; he had counted on planting his feet on strange soil, like Balboa and Columbus and Lundy. He came around to see me about it. "Tom, are you going to stand for it?"

"Well, I don't want to—but what can we *do?*"

"I've been talking to some of the others. It's simple. We don't."

"We don't what?"

"Mmm . . . we just don't. Tom, ever since we slowed down, I've detected a falling off in my telepathic ability. It seems to be affecting all of us—those I've talked to. How about yourself?"

"Why, I haven't—"

"Think hard," he interrupted. "Surely you've noticed it. Why, I doubt if I could raise my twin right now. It must have something to do with where we are . . . maybe there is something odd about the radiation of Tau Ceti, or something. Or maybe it comes from Connie. Who knows? And, for that matter, who can check on us?"

I began to get the pattern. I didn't answer, because it was a tempting idea.

"If we can't communicate," he went on, "we ought to be useful for something else . . . like the landing party, for instance. Once we are out of range of this mysterious influence probably we would be able to make our reports back to Earth all right. Or maybe it would turn out that some of the girls who didn't want to go with the landing party could manage to get in touch with Earth and carry the reports . . . provided us freaks weren't discriminated against."

"It's an idea," I admitted.

"Think about it. You'll find your special talent getting weaker and weaker. Me, I'm stone deaf already." He went away.

I toyed with the idea. I knew the Captain would recognize a strike when he saw one . . . but what could he *do?* Call us all liars and hang us by our thumbs until we gave in? How could he be certain that we hadn't all gone sour as m-r's? The answer was that he could not be certain; nobody but a mind reader knows what it feels like, nobody but the mind reader himself can tell that he is doing it. When we slipped out of contact at peak he hadn't doubted us, he had just accepted it. He would have to accept it now, no matter what he thought.

For he had to have us; we were indispensable.

Dad used to be arbitration representative in his guild local; I remembered his saying once that the only strike worth calling was one in which the workers were so badly needed that the strike would be won before a walkout. That was the pinch we had the Captain in; he *had* to have us. No strikebreakers closer than eleven light-years. He wouldn't dare get rough with us.

Except that any one of us could break the strike. Let's see—Van was out of it and so was Cas Warner; they were no longer telepaired, their twins were dead. Pru's sister Patience was still alive, but that telepair had never been mended after peak—her sister had refused the risky drugs and hypnosis routine and they never got back into rapport. Miss Gamma did not count, because the ships her two sisters were in were still peaking, so we were cut off from sidewise relay back to Earth until one of them decelerated. Not counting Sam and myself, whom did that leave? And could they be counted on? There was Rupe, Gloria, Anna, and Dusty . . . and Unc of course. And Mei-Ling.

Yes, they were solid. Making us feel that we were freaks when we first came aboard had consolidated us. Even if one or two didn't feel right about it, nobody would let the others down. Not even Mei-Ling who was married to an outsider. It would work. If Sam could line them up.

I wanted to go dirtside the worst way . . . and maybe this was the worst way, but I still wanted to.

Just the same, there was something sneaky about it, like a kid spending his Sunday School collection money.

Sam had until noon the next day to get it lined up, because we were down to one watch a day. A continuous communication watch was not necessary and there was more ship's work to do now that we were getting ready to explore. I tabled the matter and went down to tag the rats that would be used by the scientific survey.

But I did not have to wait until the following day; Unc called us together that evening and we crowded into his room—all but Miss Gamma and Van and Pru and Cas. Unc looked around, looking horse-faced and sad, and said he was sorry we couldn't all sit down but he wouldn't keep us long. Then he started a meandering speech about how he thought of us all as his children and he had grown to love us and we would always be his children, no matter what. Then he started talking about the dignity of being a human being.

"A man pays his bills, keeps himself clean, respects other people, and keeps his word. He gets no credit for this; he has to do this much just to stay even with himself. A ticket to heaven comes higher."

He paused and added, "Especially he keeps his promises." He looked around and added, "That's all I had to say. Oh, I might as well make one announcement while we are here. Rupe has had to shift the watch list around a little bit." He picked out Sam Rojas with his eyes. "Sam, I want you to take next watch, tomorrow noon. Will you do it?"

There wasn't a sound for about three heart beats. Then Sam said slowly, "Why, I guess so, Unc, if you want me to."

"I'd be much obliged, Sam. One way and another, I don't want to put anybody else on that watch . . . and I wouldn't feel like standing it myself if you couldn't do it. I guess I would just have to tell the Captain there wasn't anybody available. So I'm pleased that you'll do it."

"Uh, why, sure, Unc. Don't worry about it."

And that was the end of the strike.

Unc didn't let us go quite yet. "I thought I'd tell you about the change in the watch list while I had you here and save Rupe from having to take it around to have you initial it. But I called you together to ask you about something else. The landing party will be leaving the ship before long. Nice as Constance looks, I understand that it will be risky . . . diseases that we don't know about, animals that might turn out to be deadly in ways we didn't expect, almost anything. It occurred to me that we might be able to help. We could send one of us with the landing party and keep one of us on watch in the ship—and we could arrange for their telepairs to relay by telephone. That way we'd always be in touch with the landing party, even if radios broke down or no matter what. It would be a lot of extra work and no glory . . . but it would be worth it if it saved the life of one shipmate."

Sam said suddenly, "Who are you figuring on to go with the landing party, Unc?"

"Why, I don't know. It isn't expected of us and we don't rate special-hazard pay, so I wouldn't feel like *ordering* anybody—I doubt if the Captain would back me up. But I was hoping for enough volunteers so that we could rotate the dirtside watch." He blinked and looked unsure of himself. "But nobody is expected to volunteer. I guess you had better let me know privately."

He didn't have to wait; we all volunteered. Even Mei-Ling did and then got mad and cried when Unc pointed out gently that she had better have her husband's consent—which she wasn't going to get; the Travers family was expecting a third.

Unc tackled the Captain the next morning. I wanted to hang around and hear the outcome but there was too much work to do. I was surprised, a half hour later, to be paged by speaker down in the lab; I washed my hands and hurried up to the Old Man's cabin.

Unc was there, looking glum, and the Captain was looking stern. I tried to call Unc on the Sugar-Pie band, to find out where things stood, but for once he ignored me. The Captain looked at me coldly and said, "Bartlett, Mr. McNeil has proposed a plan whereby the people in your department want to help out in the dirtside survey. I'll tell you right off that I have turned it down. The offer is appreciated—but I have no more intention of risking people in your special category in such duty than I would approve of modifying the ship's torch to sterilize the dinner dishes. First things first!"

He drummed on his desk. "Nevertheless, the suggestion has merit. I won't risk your whole department . . . but I might risk one special communicator to increase the safeguards for the landing party. Now it occurred to me that we have one sidewise pair right in this ship, without having to relay through Earth. You and Mr. McNeil. Well? What have you to say?"

I started to say, "Sure!"—then thought frantically. If I got to go after all that had happened, Sam was going to take a very dark view of it . . . and so was everybody. They might think I had framed it.

"Well? Speak up!"

Doggone, no matter what they thought, it wasn't a thing you could refuse. "Captain, you know perfectly well I volunteered for the landing party several days ago."

"So you did. All right, I'll take your consent for granted. But you misunderstood me. You aren't going; that will be Mr. McNeil's job. You'll stay here and keep in touch with him."

I was so surprised that I almost missed the next thing the Captain said. I shot a remark to Unc privately: ("What's this, Unc? Don't you know that all of them will think you swindled them?")

This time he answered me, distress in his voice: *"I know it, son. He took me by surprise."*

("Well, what are you going to do?")

"I don't know. I'm wrong both ways."

Sugar Pie suddenly cut in with, *"Hey! What are you two fussing about?"*

Unc said gently: *"Go away, honey. This is man talk."*

"Well!" But she didn't interrupt again. Perhaps she listened.

The Captain was saying: "—in any doubly-manned position, we will never risk the younger when the elder can serve. That is standard and applies as much to Captain Urqhardt and myself as it does to any other two. The mission comes first. Bartlett, your expected usefulness is at least forty years longer than that of Mr. McNeil. Therefore he must be preferred for a risk task. Very well, gentlemen. You'll receive instructions later."

("Unc—what are you going to tell Sam? Maybe *you* agree—I don't!")

"Don't joggle my elbow, son." He went on aloud: "No, Captain."

The Captain stared. "Why, you old scoundrel! Are you that fond of your skin?"

Unc faced him right back. "It's the only one I have, Captain. But that doesn't have anything to do with the case. And maybe you were a little hasty in calling me names."

"Eh?" The Captain turned red. "I'm sorry, Mr. McNeil. I take that back. But I think you owe me an explanation for your attitude."

"I'm going to give it, sir. We're old men, both of us. I can get along without setting foot on this planet and so can you. But it looks different to young people. You know perfectly well that my people volunteered for the landing party not because they were angels, not scientists, not philanthropists . . . but because they are aching to go ashore. You know that; you told me as much, not ten minutes ago. If you are honest with yourself, you know that most of these children would never have signed up for this trip if they had suspected that they were to be locked up, never permitted to have what they call an 'adventure.' They didn't sign up for money; they signed up for the far horizons. Now you rob them of their reasonable expectations."

The Captain looked grim. He clenched and unclenched a fist, then said, "There may be something in what you say. But I must make the decisions; I can't delegate that. My decision stands. You go and Bartlett stays."

I said: ("Tell him he won't get a darn' message through!")

Unc didn't answer me. "I'm afraid not, Captain. This is a volunteer job . . . and I'm not volunteering."

The Captain said slowly, "I'm not sure that volunteering is necessary. My authority to define a man's duty is broad. I rather think you are refusing duty."

"Not so, Captain. I didn't say I wouldn't take your orders; I just said I was not volunteering. But I'd ask for written orders, I think, and I would endorse them: 'Accepted under protest,' and ask to have a copy transmitted to the Foundation. I don't volunteer."

"But—confound it, man! you volunteered with the rest. That's what you came in here for. And I picked you."

Unc shook his head. "Not quite, Captain. We volunteered as a group. You turned us down as a group. If I gave you the impression that I was volunteering any other way, I am sorry . . . but that's how it is. Now if you will excuse me, sir, I'll go back and tell my people you won't have us."

The Captain turned pink again. Then he suddenly started to roar with laughter. He jumped up and put his arm around Unc's narrow shoulders. "You old scoundrel! You *are* an old scoundrel, a mutinous black-hearted scoundrel. You make me long for the days of bread-and-water and the rope's end. Now sit back down and we'll work this out. Bartlett, you can go."

I left, reluctantly, and then stayed away from the other freaks because I didn't want to answer questions. But Unc was thoughtful; he called me, mind to mind, as soon as he was out of the Captain's cabin and told me the upshot. It was a compromise. He and I and Rupe and Sam would rotate, with the first trick (considered to be the most dangerous) to be his. The girls would take the shipside watch, with Dusty classed with them because of age. But a bone was thrown to them: once medicine and research classed the planet as safe, they would be allowed sightseeing, one at a time. "*I had to twist his arm on that part,*" Unc admitted, "*but he agreed.*"

Then it turned out to be an anticlimax; Connie was about as dangerous as Kansas. Before any human went outside the ship other than encased in a quarantine suit we exposed rats and canaries and hamsters to natural atmosphere; they loved it. When the first party went ashore, still in quarantine suits but breathing Connie's air after it had passed through electrostatic precipitators, two more experimental animals went with them—Bernhard van Houten and Percival the Pig.

Van had been down in the dumps ever since his twin was killed; he volunteered and I think Dr. Devereaux urged the Captain to let him. Somebody had to do it; you can make all the microscopic and chemical tests you like—the day comes when a living man has to expose his skin to a planet to find out if it is friendly. As Dr. Babcock says, eventually you must climb the tree. So Van went ashore without a quarantine suit, wearing shorts and shirt and shoes and looking like a Scoutmaster.

Percival the Pig did not volunteer, but he thought it was a picnic. He was penned in natural bush and allowed to forage, eating anything from Connie's soil that he thought was fit to eat. A pig has advantages as an experimental animal; he eats anything, just as rats and men do, and I understand that his metabolism is much like ours—pigs even catch many of the same diseases. If Percival prospered, it was almost certain that we would, particularly as Percy had not been given the inoculations that we had, not even the wide-spectrum G.A.R. serum which is supposed to give some protection even against diseases mankind has never encountered before.

Percy got fat, eating anything and drinking brook water. Van got a sunburn and then tanned. Both were healthy and the pioneer party took off their quarantine suits. Then almost everybody (even Percy) came down with a three-day fever and a touch of diarrhea, but everybody recovered and nobody caught it twice.

They rotated after that and all but Uncle Steve and Harry and certain ones whom they picked swapped with someone in the ship. Half of the second party were inoculated with serum made from the blood of those who had recovered from three-day fever; most of those did not catch it. But the ones who returned were not allowed back in the ship at once; they were quarantined on a temporary deck rigged above the top bulge of the *Elsie*.

I don't mean to say that the planet was just like a city park—you can get killed, even in Kansas. There was a big, lizardlike carnivore who was no bargain. One of those got Lefty Gomez the first time our people ran into one and the beast would have killed at least two more if Lefty had been the kind of man who insists on living forever. I would never have figured Lefty as a hero—he was assistant pastry cook and dry-stores keeper back in the ship—but Uncle Steve says that ultimate courage is the commonest human virtue and that seven out of ten are Medal of Honor men, given the circumstances.

Maybe so. I must be one of the other three. I don't think I would have stood my ground and kept poking away at the thing's eyes, armed only with a campfire spit.

But *tyrannosaurus ceti* was not dangerous enough to give the planet a down check, once we knew he was there and what he was. Any big cat would have been much more dangerous, because cats are smart and he was stupid. You had to shoot first, but an explosive bullet made him lie down and be a rug. He had no real defense against men and someday men would exterminate him.

The shore party camped within sight of the ship on the edge of beautiful Babcock Bay, where we were anchored. The two helicopters patrolled each day, always together so that one could rescue the men in the other if it went down, and never more than a few hundred miles from base. Patrols on foot never went more than ten miles from base; we weren't trying to conquer the country, but simply trying to find out if men could conquer and hold it. They could . . . at least around Babcock Bay . . . and where men can get a toe hold they usually hang on.

My turn did not come until the fourth rotation and by then they were even letting women go ashore; the worry part was over.

The oddest thing about being outdoors was the sensation of weather; I had been in air-conditioning for two years and I had forgotten rain and wind and sunshine in your face. Aboard the *Elsie* the engineer on watch used to cycle the temperature and humidity and ozone content on a random schedule, which was supposed to be good for our metabolisms. But it wasn't weather; it was more like kissing your sister.

The first drop of rain I felt startled me; I didn't know what it was. Then I was running up and down and dancing like a kid and trying to catch it in my mouth. It was rain, real rain and it was wonderful!

I couldn't sleep that night. A breeze on my face and the sounds of others sleeping around me and the distant noises of live things outside our snooper fences and the lack of perfect darkness all kept me awake. A ship is alive, too, and has its noises, but they are different from those outdoors; a planet is alive in another way.

I got up quietly and tip-toed outside. In front of the men's quarters about fifty feet away I could see the guardsman on watch. He did not notice me, as he had his head bent over dials and displays from the inner and outer fences and from the screen over us. I did not want to talk, so I went around behind the hut, out of sight of even the dim light from his instruments. Then I stopped and looked up.

It was the first good view of the sky I had had since we had left Earth and the night was clear. I stood there, dazzled and a little drunk from it.

Then I started trying to pick out constellations.

It was not hard; eleven light-years is just down the street for most stars. The Dipper was overhead, looking a little more battered than it does from Earth but perfectly recognizable. Orion blazed near the horizon ahead of me but Procyon had moved over a long way and Sirius was not even in sight—skidded below the skyline, probably, for Sirius is even closer to the Earth than is Tau Ceti and our position would shift him right across the sky. I tried to do a spherical triangle backwards in my head to figure where to look for Sirius and got dizzy and gave up.

Then I tried to find Sol. I knew where he would be, in Boötes, between Arcturus and Virgo—but I had to find Boötes, before I could look for Father Sol.

Boötes was behind me, as close to the skyline as Orion was on the other side. Arcturus had shifted a little and spoiled the club shape of Boötes but there was no doubt in my mind.

There it was! A yellow-white star, the color of Capella, but dimmer, about second magnitude, which was right, both position and magnitude. Besides, it had to be the Sun, because there hadn't been any star that bright in that location when Pat and I were studying for our astrogation merit badge. It was the Sun.

I stared at it, in a thoughtful melancholy, warm rather than sad. I wondered what Pat was doing? Walking the baby, maybe. Or maybe not; I couldn't remember what the Greenwich ought to be. There he was, thirty years old and a couple of kids, the best part of his life behind him . . . and here I was, just old enough to be finishing my sophomore year in college if I were home.

No, I wouldn't be; I'd be Pat's age.

But I *wasn't* thirty.

I cheered up and decided that I had the best break after all, even if it had seemed not so good at first. I sighed and walked around a bit, not worrying, for not even one of those lizard brutes could get close to our night defenses without bringing thunder and lightning down around his ears. If he had ears. Percy's pen was not far in that rear direction; he heard me and came to his fence, so I walked up and scratched his snout. "Nice place, eh, boy?" I was thinking that when the *Elsie* did get home—and I no longer believed Uncle Steve's dire predictions—when

I did get back, I would still be in my early twenties, just a good age to emigrate. And Connie looked like a fine place to come back to.

Percy answered with a snuffling grunt which I interpreted to mean: "You didn't bring me anything to eat? A fine way to treat a pal!" Percy and I were old friends; aboard ship I fed him, along with his brothers and the hamsters and the rats.

"Percy, you're a pig."

He did not argue but continued to snuffle into my empty hand. I was thinking that eleven light-years wasn't far; it was about right. The stars were still familiar.

Presently Percy got tired of it and so did I, so I wiped my hand on my pants and went back to bed.

13

Irrelevant Relations

BEYOND BETA HYDRI: I OUGHT TO BRING THIS UP TO DATE, OR ELSE throw it away. I hardly ever have time to write now, since we are so short handed. Whatever it was we picked up on Constance—or, possibly, caught from improperly fumigated stores—has left us with more than enough to do, especially in my department. There are only six left now to handle all the traffic, Unc, myself, Mei-Ling, Anna, Gloria, and Sam. Dusty lived through it but he is out of touch, apparently permanently. His brother had no kids for a secondary team and they just slipped apart on the last peak and never matched in again.

I am dependent on my great-niece Kathleen and on Molly, her mother. Pat and I can still talk, but only with their help; if we try it alone, it's like trying to make yourself understood in a machine shop. You know the other fellow is saying something but the more you strain the less you hear. Pat is fifty-four, now that we have peaked on this leg; we just don't have anything in common. Since Maude's death he isn't interested in anything but business—and I am not interested in that.

Unc is the only one who doesn't feel his original telepartner slipping away. Celestine is forty-two now; they are coming together instead of separating. I still call her "Sugar Pie," just to hear her chuckle. It is hard to realize that she is twice my age; she ought to have braids and a missing front tooth.

All in all, we lost thirty-two people in the Plague. I had it and got well. Doc Devereaux didn't get well and neither did Prudence nor Rupe. We have to fill in and act as if the others had never been with us. Mei-Ling's baby died and for a while we thought we were going to lose Mei-Ling, but now she takes her watch and does her work and even laughs. I guess the one we all miss the most is Mama O'Toole.

What else of importance has happened? Well, what can happen in a ship? Nothing. Beta Hydri was a washout. Not only nothing resembling an Earth-type planet, but no oceans—no water oceans, I mean; it was a choice for fuel between ammonia and methane, and the Chief Engineer and the Captain had long worried conferences before they settled for ammonia. Theoretically the *Elsie* will burn anything; give her mass-converter something to chew on and the old "e equals mc^2" gets to work; the torch spits the mass out as radiation at the speed of light and neutrons at almost the speed of light. But while the converter does not care, all of the torch's auxiliary equipment is built to handle fluid, preferably water.

We had a choice between ammonia, already liquid, and an outer planet that was mostly ice, but ice not much warmer than absolute zero. So they crossed their fingers, put her down in an ocean of ammonia, and filled up the old girl's tanks. The planet we named Inferno and then called it nastier names. We had to sit there four days at two gravities and it was cold, even with the ship's air heaters going full blast.

The Beta Hydri system is one I am not going back to; creatures with other metabolisms can have it and welcome. The only one who was pleased was Harry Gates, because the planetary arrangements followed Bode's Law. I wouldn't care if they had been in Vee formation.

The only other thing that sticks in my mind was (of all things!) political trouble. Our last peak started just as that war broke out between the Afro-European Federation and Estados Unidos de Sud. It shouldn't have meant anything to us—it did not, to most of us, or at least we kept our sympathies to ourselves. But Mr. Roch, our Chief Engineer, is from the Federation and his first assistant was born in Buenos Aires. When Buenos Aires got it, probably including some of Mr. Regato's relatives, he blamed his boss personally. Silly, but what can you expect?

After that, the Captain gave orders that he would check Earthside news before it was printed and he reminded us of the special restrictions on communicators in re security of communications. I think I would have been bright enough to submit that dispatch to the Captain before printing it, but I can't be sure. We'd had always had free press in the *Elsie*.

The only thing that got us out of that mess was that we peaked right after. When we came out of peak, fourteen years had passed and the latest political line-up had Argentina friends with her former enemies and on the outs with the rest of South America. After a while Mr. Roch and Mr. Regato were back playing chess together, just as if the Captain had never had to restrict them to keep them from each other's throats.

Everything that happens back on Earth is a little unreal to me, even though we continue to get the news when we are not at peak. You get your mind adjusted to a new situation; the *Elsie* goes through a peak . . . years have passed and everything has changed. They are calling the Planetary League the "United System" now and they say that the new constitution makes war impossible.

It's still the Planetary League to me—and it was supposed to make war impossible, too. I wonder what they changed besides the names?

Half of the news I don't understand. Kathleen tells me that her class has pooled their eveners to buy a Fardie for their school as a graduation present and that they are going to outswing it for the first time at the commencement exercises—then she had to hurry away because she had been co-opted in charge. That was just last watch. Now what is a "Fardie" and what was wrong with it where it was?

The technical news that reaches us I don't understand, either, but at least I know why and usually somebody aboard does understand it. The relativists are excited about stuff coming in which is so technical that it has to be retransmitted and confirmed before it is released—this with Janet Meers standing behind you and trying to snatch spools out of the recorder. Mr. O'Toole gets excited too, only the way he shows it is for the end of his nose to get pink. Dr. Babcock never shows excitement, but he missed coming in for meals two days running after I copied a monograph called "Sumner on Certain Aspects of Irrelevance." At the end of that time I sent one back to LRF which Dr. Babcock had written. It was just as crammed with indigestible mathematics, but I gathered that Dr. Babcock was politely calling Professor Sumner a fool.

Janet Meers tried to explain it to me, but all that I got out of it was that the concept of simultaneity was forcing a complete new look at physics.

"Up to now," she told me, "we've concentrated on the relative aspects of the space-time continuum. But what you m-r people do is *irrelevant* to space-time. Without time there is no space; without space there can be no time. Without space-time there can be no conservation of energy-mass. Heavens, there's *nothing*. It has driven some of the old-timers out of their minds. But now we are beginning to see how you people may possibly fit into physics—the new physics, I mean; it's all changed."

I had had enough trouble with the old-style physics; having to learn a new one made my head ache just to think about it. "What use is it?" I asked.

She looked shocked. "Physics doesn't have to have any *use*. It just *is*."

"Well, I don't know. The old physics was useful. Take the torch that drives us, for example—"

"Oh, that! That's not physics, that's just engineering"—as if I had mentioned something faintly scandalous.

I will never understand Janet and perhaps it is just as well that she promised to "be a sister to me." She said that she did not mind my being younger than she was, but that she did not think she could look up to a man who could not solve a fourth-degree function in his head. ". . . and a wife should always look up to her husband, don't you think?"

We are making the boosts at 1.5 gravity now. What with slippage, it cuts each up-boost and each down-boost to about four months, S-time, even though the jumps are longer. During boost I weigh 220 pounds and I've started wearing arch supports, but 50% extra weight is all right and is probably good for us, since it is too easy not to get enough exercise aboard ship.

The LRF has stopped using the drug stuff to help communication at peak, which would have pleased Dr. Devereaux since he disapproved of it so. Now your telepartner patches in with the help of hypnosis and suggestion alone, or you don't patch. Kathleen managed to cross the last peak with me that way, but I can see that we are going to lose communication teams all through the fleet, especially those who have not managed to set up tertiary telepartners. I don't know where my own team would be without Kathleen. In the soup, I guess. As it is, the *Niña* and the *Henry Hudson* are each down to two teams and the other four ships still in contact with Earth are not much better off. We are probably in the best shape, although we don't get much fleet news since Miss Gamma fell out of step with her sisters—or lost them, as the case may be; the *Santa Maria* is listed as "missing" but the *Marco Polo* is simply carried as "out of contact" as she was approaching peak when last heard from and won't be out of it for several Greenwich years.

We are headed now for a little G-type star so dim from Earth that it doesn't rate a name, nor even a Greek-letter constellation designation, but just a catalog number. From Earth it lies in Phoenix, between Hydrus the Sea Serpent and Cetus the Whale. ("Hydrus," not "Hydra"—Hydra is six R.A. hours over and farther north.) Unc called it a "Whistle Stop" so that is what we dubbed it, because you can't reel off a Palomar Catalog number each time you speak of where you are going. No doubt it will get an impressive name if it turns out to have a planet half as good as Connie. Incidentally Connie will be colonized in spite of the epidemic we may have picked up there; the first shiploads are on their way. Whatever the bug was that bit us (and it very possibly may have come from Earth), it is no worse than half a dozen other diseases men have had and have fought back at and licked. At least, that is the official view and the pioneer ships are going out on the assumption that they will probably catch it and have to conquer it.

Personally, I figure that one way of dying is as dangerous as another; when you're dead, you're dead—even if you die from "nothing serious." And the Plague, bad at it was, didn't kill me.

"Whistle Stop" wasn't worth a stop. We're on our way to Beta Ceti, sixty-three light-years from Earth.

I wish Dusty were still hooked up to transmit pictures; I would like one of my great grandniece Vicky. I know what she looks like—carroty red hair, freckles across her nose, green eyes, a big mouth and braces on her teeth. At present she is sporting a black eye as well, picked up at school when somebody called her a freak and she resented it—I would love to have seen that fight! Oh, I know what she looks like but I'd like a picture anyhow.

It is funny how our family has run to girls. No, when I add it up, counting all decendants of my sisters as well as my brother, it comes out about even. But Maude and Pat had two girls and no boys, and I went away and did not get married, so the Bartlett name has died out.

I certainly would like to have a picture of Vicky. I know she is homely, but I'll bet she is cute, too—the kind of tomboy who always has scabs on her knees because she won't play the ladylike games. She generally hangs around for a while after we are through transmitting and we talk. Probably she is just being polite, for she obviously thinks of me as being as old as her great-grandfather Bartlett even though her mother has told her that I am not. I suppose it depends on where you sit. I ought to be in my last year in college now, but she knows that I am Pat's twin.

If she wants to put a long white beard on me, that is all right with me, for the sake of her company. She was in a hurry this morning but nice about it. "*Will you excuse me, please, Uncle Tom? I've got to go study for a quiz in algebra.*"

("Realio trulio?") I said.

"Realio trulio, cross my heart. I'd like to stay."

("Run along, Freckle Face. Say hello to the folks.")

" 'Bye! I'll call you a little early tomorrow."

She really is a nice child.

14

Elysia

Beta Ceti is a big star in the main spectral sequence, almost big enough to be classed as a giant—a small giant, thirty-seven times as bright as the Sun. It looks so bright from Earth that it has a name of its own, Deneb Kaitos, but we never call it that because "Deneb" brings to mind the other Deneb, Alpha Cygni, which is a real giant in a different part of the sky almost sixteen hundred light-years away.

Since Beta Ceti is so much brighter than the Sun, the planet we had been looking for, if it existed at all, had to be nearly six hundred million miles out, farther than Jupiter is from Sol.

We've found one, at five hundred and eighty million miles, which is close enough. Better yet, it is the smallest planet in a system that seems to run to outsizes; the one in the next track beyond is bigger than Jupiter.

I scheduled most of the routine skyside survey of Elysia, under Harry Gates' absent-minded supervision. Harry is as eager as a fox terrier to finish his *magnum opus* before he has to knock off and take charge of the ground survey. He wants to transmit it back Earthside and preserve his name in science's hall of fame—not that he puts it that way, for Harry isn't stuck up; nevertheless, he thinks he has worked out a cosmogony for solar systems which includes Bode's Law. He says that if he is right, any star in the main spectral sequence will have planets.

Maybe . . . I would not know. But I can't see what use a star is without planets and I don't believe all this complicated universe got here by accident. Planets are meant to be used.

Acting as Harry's Man Friday has not been difficult. All I had to do was to dig the records of the preliminary survey of Connie out of the microfilms and write up similar schedules for Elysia, modified to allow for our loss of personnel. Everybody was eager to help, because (so far as we know) we are the only ship to draw a lucky number twice and only one of four to hit even once. But we are down now, water-borne, and waiting for medicine to okay Elysia for ground survey; I'm not quite so rushed. I tried to get in touch with Vicky and just chat this evening. But it happens to be evening back home, too, and Vicky is out on a date and politely put me off.

Vicky grew up some when we peaked this last jump; she now takes notice of boys and does not have as much time for her ancient uncle. ("Is it George?") I asked when she wanted to know if my call was important.

"Well, if you must know, it is George!" she blurted out.

("Don't get excited, Freckle Face,") I answered. ("I just asked.")

"Well, I told you."

("Sure, sure. Have a good time, hon, and don't stay out too late.")

"You sound just like Daddy."

I suppose I did. The fact is I don't have much use for George, although I have never seen him, never will, and don't know much about him, except that Vicky says that he is "the tenth power" and "first with the worst" in spite of being "ruffily around the round" if I knew what she meant, but she would equalize that.

I didn't know what she meant, but I interpreted it to mean approval slightly qualified and that she expected him to be perfect, or "ricketty all through" when she got through making him over. I suspect him of being the kind of pimply-faced, ignorant young bore that I used to be myself and have always disliked—something about like Dusty Rhodes at the present without Dusty's amazing mind.

This sounds as if I were jealous of a boy I'll never see over a girl I have never seen, but that is ridiculous. My interest is fatherly, or big-brotherly, even though I am effectively no relation to her; i.e., my parents were two of her sixteen great-great-grandparents—a relationship so distant that most people aren't even aware of relatives of that remote degree.

Or maybe Van's wild theory has something to it and we are all getting to be cranky old men—just our bodies are staying young. But that is silly. Even though seventy-odd Greenwich years have passed, it has been less than four for me since we left Earth. My true time is hunger and sleep; I've slept about fourteen hundred times in the *Elsie* and eaten three meals and a snack or two for each sleep. That is four years, not seventy.

No, I'm just disappointed that on my first free evening in a couple of weeks I have nothing better to do than write in my diary. But, speaking of sleep, I had better get some; the first party will go ashore tomorrow, if medicine approves, and I will be busy. I won't be on it but there is plenty to do to get them off.

We are a sorry mess. I don't know what we can do now.

I had better begin at the beginning. Elysia checked out in all ways on preliminary survey—breathable atmosphere, climate within Earth limits and apparently less extreme; a water, oxygen and carbon dioxide life cycle; no unusual hazards. No signs of intelligent life, or course, or we would have skipped it. It is a watery world even more than Terra is, with over 90% oceans and there was talk of naming it "Aquaria" instead of Elysia, but somebody pointed out that there was no sense in picking a name which might make it unattractive to colonists when there seemed to be nearly as much usable land as Earth had.

So we cuddled up to an island as big as Madagascar—almost a continent for Elysia—with the idea that we could cover the whole island in the detailed survey and be able to report that a colony could settle there as fast as LRF could send a ship—we knew that Connie was already settled and we wanted to get this one settled and make it a clean sweep for the *Elsie*.

I gave Percy a pat and told him to size up the lay of the land and to let me know if he found any lady pigs. Uncle Lucas took the guard ashore and the science party followed the same day. It was clear that Elysia was going to be no more of a problem than Connie had been and almost as big a prize—except for the remote possibility of exotic infection we could not handle.

That was two weeks ago.

It started out routine as breakfast. Percy and the other experimental animals flourished on an Elysian diet; Van failed to catch anything worse than an itch and presently he was trying Elysian food himself—there were awkward looking four-winged birds which broiled nicely; Van said they reminded him of roast turkey with an overtone of cantaloupe. But Percy the Pig would not touch some fish that were caught and the rats that did eat them died, so sea food was put off until further investigation could be made. The fish did not look like ours; they were flat the wrong way, like a flounder, and they had tendrils something like a catfish which ravelled on the ends instead of being spiny. Harry Gates was of the opinion that they were feeling organs and possibly manipulative as well.

The island had nothing like the big-mouthed carnivorous lizards that got Lefty Gomez. However, there was no telling what might be on other islands, since the land masses were so detached that totally different lines of evolution might have been followed in each island group. Our report was going to recommend that Devereaux Island be settled first, then investigate the others cautiously.

I was due to go ashore on third rotation, Unc having taken the first week, then a week of rest, and now would take shipside watch while I linked with him from ashore. But at the last minute I agreed to swap, as Anna was anxious to go. I did not want to swap, but I had been running the department's watch list since Rupe's death and it would have been awkward to refuse. Gloria was going, too, since her husband was on that rotation, but Gloria did not count as her telepartner was on vacation back Earthside.

When they left, I was up on top of the *Elsie,* glumly watching them get into the boats. There was a "monkey island" deck temporarily rigged up there, outside the air lock; it was a good place to watch the boats being loaded at the cargo ports lower down. Engineering had completed inspection and overhaul and had about finished filling the boost-mass tanks; the *Elsie* was low in the water and the cargo ports were not more than ten feet above waterline. It made loading convenient; at the time we put the first party ashore the tanks were empty and the boats had to be lowered nearly a hundred feet and passengers had to go down rope ladders—not easy for people afraid of heights, as so many are. But it was a cinch that day.

The airlock was only large enough for people; anything bigger had to go through the cargo ports. It was possible to rig the cargo ports as airlocks and we had done so on Inferno around Beta Hydri, but when the air was okay we just used them as doors. They were at the cargo deck, underneath the mess deck and over the auxiliary machinery spaces; our three boats and the two helicopters were carried just inside on that deck. The boats could be swung out on gooseneck davits from where they nested but the helicopters had to be hooked onto boat falls, swung out, then a second set of falls hooked to them from the monkey island above, by which a helicopter could be scooted up the *Elsie*'s curved side and onto the temporary top deck, where her jet rotors would be attached.

Mr. Regato cursed the arrangement every time we used it. "Mechanical buffoonery!" was his name for it. "I've never seen a ship's architect who wasn't happy as soon as he had a pretty picture. He never stops to think that some poor fool is going to have to *use* his pretty picture."

As may be, the arrangement did let the helis be unloaded with a minimum of special machinery to get out of order—which, I understand, was a prime purpose in refitting the ships for the Project. But that day the helicopters were outside and ready, one of them at camp and the other tied down near me on the monkey island. All we had to do was to load the boats.

The boats were whale boats molded of glass and teflon and made nonsinkable by plastic foam in all dead spaces. They were so tough that, while you might be able to bash one in, you could not puncture it with anything short of a drill or a torch, yet they were so light that four men could lift one that was empty. It did them no harm to drive them up onto a rocky beach, then they could be unloaded and easily dragged higher. They were driven by alcohol jets, just as the heli's were, but they had oars and sails as well. We never used the oars although all the men had gone through a dry drill under my Uncle Steve's watchful eye.

The boats had come in the night before loaded with specimens for the research department; now they were going back with people who would replace those ashore. From the monkey island I could see, half a mile away, the people who were coming back, waiting on the beach for the boats. Two of the boats were lying off, waiting for the third; each had about eighteen people in it and a few bundles of things requisitioned by Harry Gates for his scientific uses ashore, as well as a week's supplies for the whole party.

I noticed a movement behind me, turned, and saw that it was the Old Man coming up the airlock hatch. "Good morning, Captain."

"Morning, Bartlett." He looked around. "Nice day."

"Yes, sir . . . and a nice place."

"It is indeed." He looked toward the shore. "I'm going to find *some* excuse to hit dirt before we leave here. I've been on steel too long."

"I don't see why not, sir. This place is friendly as a puppy. Not like Inferno."

"Not a bit." He turned away, so I did too; you don't press conversation on the Captain unless he wants it. The third boat was loaded now and cast loose; all three were about fifty yards away and were forming a column to go in together. I waved to Gloria and Anna.

At each boat, a long, wet rope as thick as my waist came up out of the water, passed across it amidships and back into the water on the other side. I yelled, "Hey, Captain! *Look!*"

He turned. The boats rolled sideways and sank—they were *pulled* under. I heard somebody scream and the water was crowded with struggling bodies.

The Captain leaned past me at the rail and looked at the disaster. He said in an ordinary tone, "Can you start that chopper?"

"Uh, I think so, Captain." I was not a helicopter pilot but I knew how it worked.

"Then do it." He leaned far over and yelled, *"Get that cargo door closed!"* He turned and dived down the hatch. I caught a glimpse of what had made him yell as I turned to climb into the helicopter. It was another of those wet ropes slithering up the *Elsie*'s side toward the cargo port.

Starting the helicopter was more complicated than I had realized, but there was a check-off list printed on the instrument panel. I had fumbled my way down to "step four: start impeller" when I was pushed aside by Ace Wenzel, the torchman who was the regular pilot. Ace did something with both hands, the blades started to revolve, making shadows across our faces, and he yelled, "Cast her loose!"

I was shoved out the door as the Surgeon was climbing in; I fell four feet to the deck as the down blast hit me. I picked myself up and looked around.

There was nothing in the water, *nothing*. Not a body, not a person struggling to keep afloat, no sign of the boats. There was not even floating cargo although some of the packages would float. I knew; I had packed some of them.

Janet was standing next to me, shaking with dry sobs. I said stupidly, "What happened?"

She tried to control herself and said shakily, "I don't know. I saw one of them get Otto. It just . . . it just—" She started to bawl again and turned away.

There wasn't anything on the water, but now I saw that there was something *in* the water, under it. From high up you can see down into water if it is fairly smooth; arranged around the ship in orderly ranks were things of some sort. They looked like whales—or what I think a whale would look like in water; I've never seen a whale.

I was just getting it through my confused head that I was looking at the creatures who had destroyed the boats when somebody yelled and pointed. On shore the people who were to return were still on the beach, but they were no longer alone—they were surrounded. The things had come ashore, on each side of them and had flanked them. I could not see well at that distance but I could see the sea creatures because they were so much bigger than we were. They didn't have legs, so far as I could tell, but it did not slow them down—they were *fast*.

And our people were being herded into the water.

There was nothing we could do about it, not *anything*. Under us we had a ship that was the end product of centuries of technical progress; its torch could destroy a city in the blink of an eye. Ashore the guard had weapons by which one man was equal to an army of older times and there were more such weapons somewhere in the ship. But at the time I did not even know where the armory was, except that it was somewhere in the auxiliary deck—you can live a long time in a ship and never visit all her compartments.

I suppose I should have been down in the auxiliary deck, searching for weapons. But what I did was stand there, frozen, with a dozen others, and watch it happen.

But somebody had been more alert than I had been. Two men came bursting up through the hatch; they threw down two ranger guns and started frantically to plug them in and break open packages of ammunition. They could have saved the effort; by the time they were ready to sight in on the enemy, the beach was as empty as the surface of the water. Our shipmates had been pushed and dragged under. The helicopter was hovering over the spot; its rescue ladder was down but there was no one on it.

The helicopter swung around over the island and across our camp site, then returned to the ship.

While it was moving in to touch down, Chet Travers hurried up the ladder. He looked around, saw me and said, "Tom, where's the Captain?"

"In the chopper."

"Oh." He frowned. "Well, give him this. Urgent. I've got to get back down." He shoved a paper at me and disappeared. I glanced at it, saw that it was a message form, saw who it was from, and grabbed the Captain's arm as he stepped out of the heli.

He shrugged me off. "Out of my way!"

"Captain, you've *got* to—it's a message from the island—from Major Lucas."

He stopped then and took it from me, then fumbled for his reading glasses, which I could see sticking out of a pocket. He shoved the despatch form back at me before I could help him and said, "Read it to me, boy."

So I did. " 'From: Commander Ship's Guard—To: Commanding Officer *Lewis and Clark*—Oh nine three one—at oh nine oh five survey camp was attacked by hostile natives, believed to be amphibious. After suffering initial heavy losses the attack was beaten off and I have withdrawn with seven survivors to the hilltop north of the camp. We were forced to abandon survey craft number two. At time of attack, exchange party was waiting on beach; we are cut off from them and their situation is not known but must be presumed to be desperate.

" 'Discussion: The attack was intelligently organized and was armed. Their principal weapon appears to be a jet of sea water at very high pressure but they use also a personal weapon for stabbing and cutting. It must be assumed that they have other weapons. It must be conditionally assumed that they are as intelligent as we are, as well disciplined, and possibly as well armed for the conditions. Their superior numbers give them a present advantage even if they have no better weapons.

" 'Recommendations: My surviving command can hold out where it is against weapons thus far encountered. It is therefore urgently recommended that immediate measures be limited to rescuing beach party. Ship should then be placed in orbit until a plan can be worked out and weapons improvised to relieve my command without hazard to the ship.—S. Lucas, Commandant, oh nine three six.' "

The Captain took the message and turned toward the hatch without speaking. Nobody said anything although there were at least twenty of us crowded up there. I hesitated, then, when I saw that others were going down, I pushed in and followed the Captain.

He stopped two decks down and went into the communications office. I didn't follow him, but he left the door open. Chet Travers was in there, bent over the gear he used to talk with the camp, and Commander Frick was leaning over him with a worried look on his face. The Captain said, "Get me Major Lucas."

Commander Frick looked up. "We're trying to, Captain. Transmission cut off while they were sending us a list of casualties."

The Captain chewed his lip and looked frustrated, then he said, "Keep trying," and turned. He saw me.

"Bartlett!"

"Yes, sir!"

"You have one of your people over there. Raise him."

"I thought rapidly, trying to remember the Greenwich even as I was calling Vicky—if Vicky was home, she could get through on the direct line to LRF and they could hook her with Sam Rojas's telepartner and thence to Sam, and the Captain could talk to Uncle Steve on a four-link relay almost as fast as he could by radio. ("Vicky! Come in, Vicky! Urgent!")

"Yes, Uncle Tom? What is it? I was asleep."

Commander Frick said, "I don't think that will work, Captain. Rojas isn't on the list of survivors. He was scheduled for rotation; he must have been down at the beach."

Of course, of course! Sam would have been down at the beach—I had stood by and must have watched him being herded into the water!

"What is it, Uncle Tom?"

("Just wait, hon. Stay linked.")

"Then get me somebody else," the Captain snapped.

"There isn't anyone else, Captain," Frick answered. "Here's the list of survivors. Rojas was the only fr— the only special communicator we had ashore."

The Captain glanced at the list, said, "Pass the word for all hands not on watch to assemble in the mess room on the double." He turned and walked right through me. I jumped out of the way.

"What's the matter, Uncle Tom? You sound worried."

I tried to control my voice. ("It was a mistake, hon. Just forget it and try to get back to sleep. I'm sorry.")

"All right. But you still sound worried."

I hurried after the Captain. Commander Frick's voice was calling out the order over the ship's system as we hurried down the ladders, yet he was only a moment or two behind me in reaching the mess room. In a matter of seconds we were all there . . . just a handful of those who had left Earth—about forty. The Captain looked around and said to Cas Warner, "Is this all?"

"I think so, Captain, aside from the engineering watch."

"I left Travers on watch," added Frick.

"Very well." The Captain turned and faced us. "We are about to rescue the survivors ashore. Volunteers step forward."

We didn't step, we surged, all together. I would like to say that I was a split second ahead, because of Uncle Steve, but it wouldn't be true. Mrs. Gates was carrying young Harry in her arms and she was as fast as I was.

"Thank you," the Captain said stiffly. "Now will the women please go over there by the pantry so that I can pick the men who will go."

"Captain?"

"Yes, Captain Urqhardt?"

"I will lead the party."

"You'll do nothing of the sort, sir. I will lead. You will now take some women and go down and fetch what we need."

Urqhardt barely hesitated, then said, "Aye, aye, sir."

"That rule—our standing rule for risk—will apply to all of you. In doubly-manned jobs the older man will go. In other jobs, if the job can be dispensed with, the man will go; if it cannot be, the man will stay." He looked around. "Dr. Babcock!"

"Righto, Skipper!"

Mr. O'Toole said, "Just a moment, Captain. I am a widower and Dr. Babcock is much more—"

"Shut *up*."

"But—"

"Confound it, sir, must I debate every decision with every one of you? Must I remind you that every second counts? Get over there with the women."

Red-faced and angry Mr. O'Toole did as he was told. The Captain went on, "Mr. Warner. Mr. Roch. Dr. Severin—" Quickly he picked those he wanted, then waved the rest of us over toward the pantry.

Uncle Alfred McNeil tried to straighten his stooped shoulders. "Captain, you forgot me. I'm the oldest in my department."

The Captain's face softened just a hair. "No, Mr. McNeil, I didn't forget," he said quietly, "but the capacity of the chopper is limited—and we have seven to bring back. So I must omit you."

Unc's shoulders sagged and I thought he was going to cry, then he shuffled over away from the selected few. Dusty Rhodes caught my eye and looked smug and proud; he was one of the chosen. He still did not look more than sixteen and I don't think he had ever shaved; this was probably the first time in his life that he had ever been treated in all respects as a man.

In spite of the way the others had been shut off short I couldn't let it stand. I stepped forward again and touched the Captain's sleeve. "Captain . . . you've *got* to let me go! My uncle is over there."

I thought he was going to explode, but he caught himself. "I see your point. But you are a special communicator and we haven't any to spare. I'll tell Major Lucas that you tried."

"But—"

"Now shut up and do as you are told—before I kick you half across the compartment." He turned away as if I didn't exist.

Five minutes later arms had been issued and we were all crowding up the ladders to see them off. Ace Wenzel started the helicopter at idling speed and jumped out. They filed in, eight of them, with the Captain last. Dusty had a bandolier over each shoulder and a ranger gun in his hands; he was grinning excitedly. He threw me a wink and said, "I'll send you a postcard."

The Captain paused and said, "Captain Urqhardt."

"Yes, sir."

The Captain and the reserve captain conferred for a moment; I couldn't hear them and I don't think we were meant to hear. Then Captain Urqhardt said loudly, "Aye, aye, sir. It shall be done."

"Very good, sir." The Captain stepped in, slammed the door, and took the controls himself. I braced myself against the down blast.

Then we waited.

I alternated between monkey island and the comm office. Chet Travers still could not raise Uncle Steve but he was in touch with the heli Every time I went top side I looked for the sea things but they seemed to have gone away.

Finally I came down again to the comm room and Chet was looking joyful. "They've got 'em!" he announced. "They're off the ground." I started to ask him about it but he was turning to announce the glad news over the ship's system; I ran up to see if I could spot the heli.

I saw it, near the hilltop, about a mile and a half away. It moved rapidly toward the ship. Soon we could see people inside. As it got closer someone opened a window on the side toward us.

The Captain was not really skilled with a helicopter. He tried to make a landing straight in but his judgment of wind was wrong and he had to swing on past and try again. The maneuver brought the craft so close to the ship that we could see the passengers plainly. I saw Uncle Steve and he saw me and waved; he did not call out, he just waved. Dusty Rhodes was beside him and saw me, too. He grinned and waved and shouted, "Hey, Tom, I rescued your buddy!" He reached back and then Percy's head and cloven forehooves showed above the frame, with Dusty holding the pig with one hand and pointing to him with the other. They were both grinning.

"Thanks!" I yelled back. "Hi, Percy!"

The chopper turned a few hundred feet beyond the ship and headed back into the wind.

It was coming straight toward the ship and would have touched down soon when something came out of the water right under it. Some said it was a machine—to me it looked like an enormous elephant's trunk. A stream of water so solid, hard, and bright that it looked like steel shot out of the end of it; it struck a rotor tip and the heli staggered.

The Captain leaned the craft over and it slipped out of contact. The stream followed it, smashed against the fuselage and again caught a rotor; the heli tilted violently and began to fall.

I'm not much in an emergency; it is hours later when I figure out what I should have done. This time I acted without thinking. I dived down the ladder without hitting the treads and was on down in the cargo deck almost at once. The port on that side was closed, as it had been since the Captain ordered it closed earlier; I slapped the switch and it began to grind open. Then I looked around and saw what I needed: the boat falls, coiled loosely on deck, not yet secured. I grabbed a bitter end and was standing on the port as it was still swinging down to horizontal.

The wrecked helicopter was floating right in front of me and there were people struggling in the water. "Uncle Steve!" I yelled. *"Catch!"* I threw the line as far as I could.

I had not even seen him as I yelled. It was just the idea that was in the top of my mind. Then I did see him, far beyond where I had been able to throw the line. I heard him call back, "Coming, Tom!" and he started swimming strongly toward the ship.

I was so much in a daze that I almost pulled the line in to throw it again when I realized that I had managed to throw far enough for some one. I yelled again. "Harry! Right behind you! Grab on!"

Harry Gates rolled over in the water, snatched at the line and got it. I started to haul him in.

I almost lost him as I got him to the ship's skin. One of his arms seemed almost useless and he nearly lost his grasp. But between us we managed to manhandle him up and into the port; we would not have made it if the ship had not been so low in the water. He collapsed inside and lay on his face, gasping and sobbing.

I jerked the fall loose from his still clenched hand and turned to throw it to Uncle Steve.

The helicopter was gone, Uncle Steve was gone, again the water was swept clean—except for Percy, who, with his head high out of water, was swimming with grim determination toward the ship.

I made sure that there were no other people anywhere in the water. Then I tried to think what I could do for Percy.

The poor little porkchop could not grab a line, that was sure. Maybe I could lasso him. I fumbled to get a slip knot in the heavy line. I had just managed it when Percy gave a squeal of terror and I jerked my head around just in time to see him pulled under the water.

It wasn't a mouth that got him. I don't think it was a mouth.

15

"Carry Out Her Mission!"

I DON'T KNOW WHAT I EXPECTED AFTER THE ATTACK BY THE BEHEMOTHS. We just wandered around in a daze. Some of us tried to look out from the monkey island deck until that spouter appeared again and almost knocked one of us off, then Captain Urqhardt ordered all hands to stay inside and the hatch was closed.

I certainly did not expect a message that was brought around after supper (if supper had been served; some made themselves sandwiches) telling me to report at once for heads-of-departments conference. "That's you, isn't it, Tom?" Chet Travers asked me. "They tell me Unc Alfred is on the sick list. His door is closed."

"I suppose it's me." Unc had taken it hard and was in bed with a soporific in him, by order of the one remaining medical man, Dr. Pandit.

"Then you had better shag up there."

First I went to Captain Urqhardt's room and found it dark, then I got smart and went to the Captain's cabin. The door was open and some were already around the table with Captain Urqhardt at the head. "Special communications department, sir," I announced myself.

"Sit down, Bartlett."

Harry came in behind me and Urqhardt got up and shut the door and sat down. I looked around, thinking it was a mighty funny heads-of-departments meeting. Harry Gates was the only boss there who had been such when we left Earth. Mr. Eastman was there instead of Commander Frick. Mama O'Toole was long dead but now Cas was gone too; ecology was represented by Mr. Krishnamurti who had merely been in charge of air-conditioning and hydroponics when we had left. Mr. O'Toole was there in place of Dr. Babcock, Mr. Regato instead of Mr. Roch. Sergeant Andreeli, who was also a machinist in engineering, was here in place of Uncle Steve and he was the only member of the ship's guard left alive—because he had been sent back to the ship with a broken arm two days earlier. Dr. Pandit sat where Dr. Devereaux should have been.

And myself of course but I was just fill-in; Unc was still aboard. Worst of all, there was Captain Urqhardt sitting where the Captain should have been.

Captain Urqhardt started in, "There is no need to detail our situation; you all know it. We will dispense with the usual departmental reports, too. In my opinion our survey of this planet is as complete as we can make it with present personnel and equipment . . . save that an additional report must be made of the hazard encountered today in order that the first colonial party will be prepared to defend itself. Is there disagreement? Dr. Gates, do you wish to make further investigations here?"

Harry looked surprised and answered, "No, Captain. Not under the circumstances."

"Comment?" There was none. "Very well," Urqhardt continued. "I propose to shape course for Alpha Phoenicis. We will hold memorial services at nine tomorrow morning and boost at noon. Comment? Mr. O'Toole."

"Eh? Do you mean can we have the figures ready? I suppose so, if Janet and I get right on it."

"Do so, as soon as we adjourn. Mr. Regato?"

Regato was looking astounded. "I didn't expect this, Captain."

"It is short notice, but can your department be ready? I believe you have boost mass aboard."

"It isn't that, Captain. Surely, the torch will be ready. But I thought we would make one long jump for Earth."

"What led you to assume that?"

"Why, uh . . ." The new Chief Engineer stuttered and almost slipped out of P-L lingo into Spanish. "The shape we are in, sir. The engineering department will have to go on watch-and-watch, heel and toe. I can't speak for other departments, but they can't be in much better shape."

"No, you can't and I am not asking you to. With respect to your own department, is it mechanically ready?"

Regato swallowed. "Yes, sir. But people break down as well as machinery."

"Wouldn't you have to stand watch-and-watch to shape course for Sol?" Urqhardt did not wait for the obvious answer, but went on, "I should not have to say this. We are not here for our own convenience; we are here on an assigned mission . . . as you all know. Earlier today, just before Captain Swenson left, he said to me, 'Take charge of my ship, sir. Carry out her mission.' I answered, 'Aye, aye, sir.' Let n remind you of that mission: we were sent out to conduct the survey w have been making, with orders to continue the search as long as w were in communication with Earth—when we fell out of communica tion, we were free to return to Earth, if possible. Gentlemen, we are sti in touch with Earth; our next assigned survey point is Alpha Phoenici. Could anything be clearer?"

My thoughts were boiling up so that I hardly heard him. I wa thinking: Who does this guy think he is? Columbus? Or the Flyin Dutchman? There were only a little over thirty of us left alive—in ship that had started with two hundred. The boats were gone, the heli' were— I almost missed his next remark.

"Bartlett?"

"Sir?"

"What about your department?"

It dawned on me that *we* were the key department—us freaks. Wher *we* fell out of touch, he *had* to turn back. I was tempted to say that we had all gone deaf, but I knew I couldn't get away with it. So I stalled.

"As you pointed out, sir, we are in touch with Earth."

"Very well." His eyes turned toward Dr. Pandit.

"Just a moment, Captain," I insisted. "There's more to it."

"Eh? State it."

"Well, this next jump is about thirty years, isn't it? Greenwich, I mean."

"Of that order. Somewhat less."

" 'Of that order.' There are three special communicators left, myself, Unc—I mean Mr. McNeil—and Mei-Ling Travers. I think you ought to count Unc out."

"Why?"

"Because he has his original telepartner and she is now as old as he is. Do you think Unc will live another thirty years?"

"But it won't be thirty years for him—oh, sorry! I see your point. She would be well past a hundred if she lived at all. Possibly senile."

"Probably, sir. Or more likely dead."

"Very well, we won't count McNeil. That leaves two of you. Plenty for essential communication."

"I doubt it, sir. Mei-Ling is a poor bet. She has only a secondary linkage and her partner is over thirty, with no children. Based on other telepairs, I would say that it is most unlikely that they will stay in rapport through another peak . . . not a thirty-year one."

"That still leaves yourself."

I thought suddenly that if I had the guts to jump over the side, they could all go home. But it was just a thought; when I die, it won't be suicide. "My own case isn't much better, sir. My telepartner is about—" I had to stop and count up, then the answer did not seem right. "—is about nineteen, sir. No kids. No chance of kids before we peak . . . and I couldn't link in with a brand-new baby anyhow. She'll be fiftyish when we come out. So far as I know, there hasn't been a case in the whole fleet of bridging that long a period out of rapport."

He waited several moments before he answered. "Have you any reason to believe that it is impossible?"

"Well . . . no, sir. But it is extremely unlikely."

"Hmm . . . do you consider yourself an authority in theory of telepathy?"

"Huh? No, sir. I am just a telepath, that's all."

"I think he is probably right," put in Dr. Pandit.

"Are you an authority, Doctor?"

"Me, sir? As you know, my specialty is exotic pathology. But—"

"In that case, we will consult authorities Earthside. Perhaps they can suggest some way to improve our chances. Very probably, under the circumstances, the Foundation will again authorize use of drugs to reduce the possibility that our special communicators might fall out of touch during peak. Or something."

I thought of telling him that Vicky wasn't going to risk dangerous habit-forming drugs. Then I thought better of it. Pat had—and Vicky might.

"That is all, gentlemen. We will boost at noon tomorrow. Uh, one more thing . . . One of you implied that morale is not too high in the ship. That is correct and I am perhaps more aware of it than you are. But morale will shake down to normal and we will best be able to forget the losses we have suffered if we all get quickly back to work. I want only to add that you all, as senior officers of this ship, have most to do with morale by setting an example. I am sure that you will." He stood up.

I don't know how news travels in a ship but by the time I got down to the mess room everybody knew that we were boosting tomorrow . . . and not for home. It was buzz-buzz and yammer all over. I ducked out because I didn't want to discuss it; my thoughts were mixed. I thought the Captain was insisting on one more jump from which he couldn't possibly report his results, if any—and with a nice fat chance that none of us would ever get home. On the other hand I admired the firm way he faced us up to our obligations and brushed aside panic. He had guts.

So did the Flying Dutchman have guts—but at last report he was still trying to round the Cape and not succeeding.

The Captain—Captain Swenson, I corrected—would not have been that bull-headed.

Or would he? According to Urqhardt, the last thing the Captain had said had been to remind Urqhardt that it was up to him to carry out the mission. All of us had been very carefully chosen (except us freaks) and probably the skipper and the relief skipper of each ship were picked primarily for bulldog stubbornness, the very quality that had kept Columbus going on and on when he was running out of water and his crew was muttering mutiny. I remembered Uncle Steve had once suggested as much.

I decided to go talk to Uncle Steve . . . then I remembered I couldn't and I really felt bad. When my parents had died, two peaks back, I had felt bad because I didn't feel as bad as I knew I should have felt. When it happened—or rather, by the time I knew about it—they were long dead, people I had not seen in a long time and just faces in a photograph. But Uncle Steve I had seen every day—I had seen *today*. And I had been in the habit of kicking my troubles around with him whenever they were too much for me.

I felt his loss then, the delayed shock you get when you are hit hard. The hurt doesn't come until you pull yourself together and realize you're hit.

It was just as well that somebody tapped on my door then, or I would have bawled.

It was Mei-Ling and her husband, Chet. I invited them in and they sat down on the bed. Chet got to the point. "Tom, where do you stand on this?"

"On what?"

"This silly business of trying to go on with a skeleton crew."

"It doesn't matter where I stand," I said slowly. "I'm not running the ship."

"Ah, but you are!"

"Huh?"

"I don't mean quite that, but I do mean you can put a stop to the nonsense. Now, look, Tom, everybody knows what you told the Captain and—"

"Who's been talking?"

"Huh? Never mind. If it didn't leak from you, it probably did from everybody else present; it's common knowledge. What you told him made sense. What it comes down to is that Urqhardt is depending on you and you alone to keep him in touch with the home office. So you're the man with the stick. You can stop him."

"Huh? Now wait. I'm not the only one. Granted that he isn't counting on Unc—how about Mei-Ling?"

Chet shook his head. "Mei-Ling isn't going to 'think-talk' for him."

His wife said, "Now, Chet, I haven't said so."

He looked at her fondly. "Don't be super-stupid, my lovely darling. You know that there is no chance at all that you will be any use to him after peak. If our brave Captain Urqhardt hasn't got that through his head now, he will . . . even if I have to explain to him in words of one syllable."

"But I *might* stay linked."

"Oh, no, you won't . . . or I'll bash your pretty head in. Our kids are going to grow up on Earth."

She looked soberly at him and patted his hand. The Travers's were not expecting again, but everybody knew they were hoping; I began to see why Chet was adamant . . . and I became quite sure that Mei-Ling would not link again after peak—not after her husband had argued with her for a while. What Chet wanted was more important to her than what the Captain wanted, or any abstract duty to a Foundation back on Earth.

Chet went on, "Think it over, Tom, and you will see that you can't let your shipmates down. To go on is suicidal and everybody knows it but the Captain. It's up to you."

"Uh, I'll think it over."

"Do that. But don't take too long." They left.

I went to bed but didn't sleep. The deuce of it was that Chet was almost certainly right . . . including the certainty that Mei-Ling would never patch in with her telepair after another peak, for she was beginning to slip even now. I had been transmitting mathematical or technical matter which would have fallen to her ever since last peak, because her linking was becoming erratic. Chet wouldn't have to bash her admittedly-pretty head in; she was falling out of touch.

On the other hand . . .

When I had reached "On the other hand" about eighteen times, I got up and dressed and went looking for Harry Gates; it occurred to me that since he was a head of department and present at the meeting, it was proper to talk to him about it.

He wasn't in his room; Barbara suggested that I try the laboratory. He was there, alone, unpacking specimens that had been sent over the day before. He looked up. "Well, Tom, how is it going?"

"Not too good."

"I know. Say, I haven't had a proper chance to thank you. Shall I write it out, or will you have it right off my chest?"

"Uh, let's take it for granted." I had not understood him at first, for it is the simple truth that I had forgotten about pulling him out of the water; I hadn't had time to think about it.

"As you say. But I won't forget it. You know that, don't you?"

"Okay. Harry, I need advice."

"You do? Well, I've got it in all sizes. All of it free and all of it worth what it costs, I'm afraid."

"You were at the meeting tonight."

"So were you." He looked worried.

"Yes." I told him all that had been fretting me, then thought about it and told him all that Chet had said. "What am I to do, Harry? Chet is right; the chance of doing any good on another jump isn't worth it. Even if we find a planet worth reporting—a chance that is never good, based on what the fleet has done as a whole—even so, we almost certainly won't be able to report it except by going back, two centuries after we left. It's ridiculous and, as Chet says, suicidal, with what we've got left. On the other hand, the Captain is right; this is what we signed up for. The ship's sailing orders say for us to go on."

Harry carefully unpacked a package of specimens before he answered.

"Tommie, you should ask me an easy one. Ask me whether or not to get married and I'll tell you like a shot. Or anything else. But there is one thing no man can tell another man and that is where his duty lies. That you must decide for yourself."

I thought about it. "Doggone it, Harry, how do *you* feel about it?"

"Me?" He stopped what he was doing. "Tom, I just don't know. For myself personally . . . well, I've been happier in this ship than I have ever been before in my life. I've got my wife and kids with me and I'm doing just the work I want to do. With others it may be different."

"How about your kids?"

"Aye, there's the rub. A family man—" He frowned. "I can't advise you, Tom. If I even hint that you should not do what you signed up to do, I'd be inciting to mutiny . . . a capital crime, for both of us. If I tell you that you *must* do what the Captain wants, I'd be on safe legal grounds—but it might mean the death of you and me and my kids and all the rest of us . . . because Chet has horse sense on his side even if the law is against him." He sighed. "Tom, I just missed checking out today—thanks to you—and my judgment isn't back in shape. I can't advise you; I'd be prejudiced."

I didn't answer. I was wishing that Uncle Steve had made it; he always had an answer for everything.

"All I can do," Harry went on, "is to make a weaselly suggestion."

"Huh? What is it?"

"You might go to the Captain privately and tell him just how worried you are. It might affect his decisions. At least he ought to know."

I said I would think about it and thanked him and left. I went to bed and eventually got to sleep. I was awakened in the middle of the night by the ship shaking. The ship always swayed a little when waterborne, but not this way, nor this much, not on Elysia.

It stopped and then it started again . . . and again it stopped . . . and started. I was wondering what . . . when it suddenly quivered in an entirely different way, one that I recognized; it was the way the torch felt when it was just barely critical. The engineers called it "clearing her throat" and was a regular part of overhaul and inspection. I decided that Mr. Regato must be working late, and I quieted down again. The bumping did not start up again.

At breakfast I found out what it was: the behemoths had tried something, nobody knew what, against the ship itself . . . whereupon the Captain had quite logically ordered Mr. Regato to use the torch against them. Now, although we still did not know much about them, we did know one thing: they were not immune to superheated steam and intense radioactivity.

This brush with the sea devils braced my spine; I decided to see the Captain as Harry had suggested.

He let me in without keeping me waiting more than five minutes. Then he kept quiet and let me talk as long as I wanted to. I elaborated the whole picture, as I saw it, without attributing anything to Chet or Harry. I couldn't tell from his face whether I was reaching him or not, so I put it strongly: that Unc and Mei-Ling were both out of the picture and that the chance that I would be of any use after the next peak was so slight that he was risking his ship and his crew on very long odds.

When I finished I still didn't know, nor did he make a direct answer. Instead he said, "Bartlett, for fifty-five minutes yesterday evening you had two other members of the crew in your room with your door closed."

"Huh? Yes, sir."

"Did you speak to them of this?"

I wanted to lie. "Uh . . . yes, sir."

"After that you looked up another member of the crew and remained with him until quite late . . . or quite early, I should say. Did you speak to him on the same subject?"

"Yes, sir."

"Very well. I am holding you for investigation on two counts: suspicion of inciting to mutiny and suspicion of intent to mutiny. You are under arrest. Go to your room and remain there. No visitors."

I gulped. Then something Uncle Steve had told me came to my aid—Uncle had been a jawbone space-lawyer and loved to talk about it. "Aye, aye, sir. But I insist that I be allowed to see counsel of my choice . . . and that I be given a public hearing."

The Captain nodded as if I had told him that it was raining. "Certainly. Your legal rights will be respected. But those matters will have to wait; we are now preparing to get underway. So place yourself under arrest and get to your quarters."

He turned away and left me to confine myself. He didn't even seem angry.

So here I sit, alone in my room. I had to tell Unc he couldn't come in and, later, Chet. I can't believe what has happened to me.

16

"Just a Mathematical Abstraction"

THAT MORNING SEEMED A MILLION YEARS LONG. VICKY CHECKED WITH me at the usual time, but I told her that the watch list was being switched around again and that I would get in touch with her later. *"Is something wrong?"* she asked.

"No, hon, we're just having a little reorganization aboard ship."

"All right. But you sound worried."

I not only didn't tell her that I was in a jam, I didn't tell her anything about the disaster. Time enough later, after it had aged—unless she found out from official news. Meanwhile there was no reason to get a nice kid upset over something she couldn't help.

Twenty minutes later Mr. Eastman showed up. I answered the door when he knocked and told him, "I'm not to have any visitors. Sorry."

He didn't leave. "I'm not a visitor, Tom; I'm here officially, for the Captain."

"Oh." I let him in.

He had a tool kit with him. He set it down and said, "The regular and special communication departments have been consolidated, now that we are so short-handed, so it looks like I'm your boss. It won't make any difference, I'm sure. But I'm to make a reconnection on your recorder, so that you can record directly into the comm office."

"Okay. But why?"

He seemed embarrassed. "Well . . . you were due to go on watch a half hour ago. We're going to fix this so that you can stand your watches conveniently from here. The Captain is annoyed that I didn't arrange it earlier." He started unscrewing the access plate to the recorder.

I was speechless. Then I remembered something Uncle Steve had told me. "Hey, wait a minute!"

"Eh?"

"Oh, go ahead and rewire it, I don't care. But I won't stand any watches."

He straightened up and looked worried. "Don't talk like that, Tom. You're in enough trouble now; don't make it worse. Let's pretend you never said it. Okay?"

Mr. Eastman was a decent sort and the only one of the electronics people who had never called us freaks. I think he was really concerned about me. But I said, "I don't see how it can be worse. You tell the Captain that I said he could take his watches and—" I stopped. That wasn't what Uncle Steve would say. "Sorry. Please tell him this: 'Communicator Bartlett's respects to the Captain and he regrets that he cannot perform duty while under arrest.' Got it?"

"Now look here, Tom, that's not the proper attitude. Surely, there is something in what you say from a standpoint of regulations. But we are short-handed; everybody has to pitch in and help. You can't stand on the letter of the law; it isn't fair to the rest."

"Can't I?" I was breathing hard and exulting in the chance to hit back. "The Captain can't have his cake and eat it too. A man under arrest doesn't perform duty. It's always been that way and it always will be. You just tell him what I said."

He silently finished the reconnection with quick precision. "You're sure that's what you want me to tell him?"

"Quite sure."

"All right. Hooked the way that thing is now—" he added, pointing a thumb at the recorder, "—you can reach me on it if you change your mind. So long."

"One more thing—"

"Eh?"

"Maybe the Captain hasn't thought about it, since his cabin has a bathroom, but I've been in here some hours. Who takes me down the passageway and when? Even a prisoner is entitled to regular policing."

"Oh. I guess I do. Come along."

That was the high point of the morning. I expected Captain Urqhardt to show up five minutes after Mr. Eastman had left me at my room—breathing fire and spitting cinders. So I rehearsed a couple of speeches in my head, carefully phrased to keep me inside the law and quite respectful. I knew I had him.

But nothing happened. The Captain did not show up; nobody showed up. It got to be close to noon. When no word was passed about standing by for boost, I got in my bunk with five minutes to spare and waited.

It was a long five minutes.

About a quarter past twelve I gave up and got up. No lunch either. I heard the gong at twelve-thirty, but still nothing and nobody. I finally decided that I would skip one meal before I complained, because I didn't want to give him the chance to change the subject by pointing out that I had broken arrest. It occurred to me that I could call Unc and tell him about the failure in the beans department, then I decided that the longer I waited, the more wrong the Captain would be.

About an hour after everybody else had finished eating Mr. Krishnamurti showed up with a tray. The fact that he brought it himself instead of sending whoever had pantry duty convinced me that I must be a Very Important Prisoner—particularly as Kris was unanxious to talk to me and even seemed scared of being near me. He just shoved it in and said, "Put it in the passageway when you are through."

"Thanks, Kris."

But buried in the food on the tray was a note: "Bully for you! Don't weaken and we'll trim this bird's wings. Everybody is pulling for you." It was unsigned and I did not recognize the handwriting. It wasn't Krishnamurti's; I knew his from the time when I was fouling up his farm. Nor was it either of the Travers's, and certainly not Harry's.

Finally I decided that I didn't want to guess whose it was and tore it in pieces and chewed it up, just like the Man in the Iron Mask or the Count of Monte Cristo. I don't really qualify as a romantic hero, however, as I didn't swallow it; I just chewed it up and spat it out. But I made darn sure that note was destroyed, for I not only did not want to know who had sent it, I didn't want anybody ever to know.

Know why? That note didn't make me feel good; it worried me. Oh, for two minutes it bucked me up; I felt larger than life, the champion of the downtrodden.

Then I realized what the note meant . . .

Mutiny.

It's the ugliest word in space. Any other disaster is better.

One of the first things Uncle Steve had told me—told Pat and myself, way back when we were kids—was: "The Captain is right even when he is wrong." It was years before I understood it; you have to live in a ship to know why it is true. And I didn't understand it in my heart until I read that encouraging note and realized that somebody was seriously thinking of bucking the Captain's authority . . . and that I was the symbol of their resistance.

A ship is not just a little world; it is more like a human body. You can't have democracy in it, not democratic consent at least, no matter how pleasant and democratic the Captain's manner may be. If you're in a pinch, you don't take a vote from your arms and legs and stomach and gizzard and find out what the majority wants. Darn well you don't! Your brain makes a decision and your whole being carries it out.

A ship in space is like that all the time and has to be. What Uncle Steve meant was that the Captain had *better* be right, you had better pray that he is right even if you disagree with him . . . because it won't save the ship to be right yourself if he is wrong.

But a ship is not a human body; it is people working together with a degree of selflessness that doesn't come easy—not to me, at least. The only thing that holds it together is a misty something called its morale, something you hardly know it has until the ship loses it. I realized then that the *Elsie* had been losing hers for some time. First Doc Devereaux had died and then Mama O'Toole and both of those were body blows. Now we had lost the Captain and most of the rest . . . and the *Elsie* was falling to pieces.

Maybe the new captain wasn't too bright, but he was trying to stop it. I began to realize that it wasn't just machinery breaking down or attacks from hostile natives that lost ships; maybe the worst hazard was some bright young idiot deciding that he was smarter than the captain and convincing enough others that he was right. I wondered how many of the eight ships that were out of contact had died proving that their captains were wrong and that somebody like me was right.

It wasn't nearly enough to be right.

I got so upset that I thought about going to the Captain and telling him I was wrong and what could I do to help? Then I realized that I couldn't do that, either. He had told me to stay in my room—no 'if's' or 'maybe's.' If it was more important to back up the Captain and respect his authority than anything else, then the only thing was to do as I had been ordered and sit tight.

So I did.

Kris brought me dinner, almost on time. Late that evening the speakers blared the usual warning. I lay down and the *Elsie* boosted off Elysia. But we didn't go on, we dropped into an orbit, for we went into free fall right afterwards. I spent a restless night; I don't sleep well when I'm weightless.

I was awakened by the ship going into light boost, about a half gravity. Kris brought me breakfast but I didn't ask what was going on and he didn't offer to tell me. About the middle of the morning the ship's system called out: "Communicator Bartlett, report to the Captain." It was repeated before I realized it meant me . . . then I jumped up, ran my shaver over my face, decided that my uniform would have to do, 'nd hurried up to the Cabin.

He looked up when I reported my presence. "Oh, yes. Bartlett. Upon investigation I find that there is no reason to prefer charges. You are released from arrest and restored to duty. See Mr. Eastman."

He looked back at his desk and I got sore. I had been seesawing between a feeling of consecrated loyalty to the ship and to the Captain as the head thereof, and an equally strong desire to kick Urqhardt in the stomach. One kind word from him and I think I would have been his boy, come what may. As it was, I was sore.

"Captain!"

He looked up. "Yes?"

"I think you owe me an apology."

"You do? I do not think so. I acted in the interest of the whole ship. However, I harbor no ill feelings, if that is of any interest to you." He looked back at his work, dismissing me . . . as if *my* hard feelings, if any, were of no possible importance.

So I got out and reported to Mr. Eastman. There didn't seem to be anything else to do.

Mei-Ling was in the comm office, sending code groups. She glanced up and I noticed that she looked tired. Mr. Eastman said, "Hello, Tom. I'm glad you're here; we need you. Will you raise your telepartner, please?"

One good thing about having a telepath run the special watch list is that other people don't seem to realize that the other end of each pair—the Earthside partner—is not a disembodied spirit. They eat and sleep and work and raise families, and they can't be on call whenever somebody decides to send a message. "Is it an emergency?" I asked, glancing at the Greenwich and then at the ship's clock. Vicky wouldn't check with me for another half hour; she might be at home and free, or she might not be.

"Perhaps not 'emergency' but 'urgent' certainly."

So I called Vicky and she said she did not mind. ("Code groups, Freckle Face,") I told her. ("So set your recorder on 'play back.' ")

"It's quivering, Uncle Tom. Agitate at will."

For three hours we sent code groups, than which there is nothing more tedious. I assumed that it was probably Captain Urqhardt's report of what had happened to us on Elysia, or more likely his second report after the LRF had jumped him for more details. There was no reason to code it so far as I was concerned; I had been there—so it must be to keep it from our telepartners until LRF decided to release it. This suited me as I would not have relished passing all that blood and slaughter, in clear language, to little Vicky.

While we were working the Captain came in and sat down with Mr.

Eastman; I could see that they were cooking up more code groups; the Captain was dictating and Eastman was working the encoding machine. Mei-Ling had long since gone. Finally Vicky said faintly, *"Uncle Tom, how urgent are these anagrams? Mother called me to dinner half an hour ago."*

("Hang on and I'll find out.") I turned to the Captain and Mr. Eastman, not sure of which one to ask. But I caught Eastman's eye and said, "Mr. Eastman, how rush is this stuff? We want to—"

"Don't interrupt us," the Captain cut in. "Just keep on transmitting. The priority is not your concern."

"Captain, you don't understand; I'm not speaking for myself. I was about to say—"

"Carry on with your work."

I said to Vicky, ("Hold on a moment, hon.") Then I sat back and said, "Aye aye, Captain. I'm perfectly willing to keep on spelling eye charts all night. But there is nobody at the other end."

"What do you mean?"

"I mean it is dinner time and way past for my partner. If you want special duty at the Earthside end, you'd better coordinate with the LRF comm office. Seems to me that somebody has the watch list all mixed up."

"I see." As usual he showed no expression. I was beginning to think he was all robot, with wires instead of veins. "Very well. Mr. Eastman, get Mr. McNeil and have him relieve Mr. Bartlett."

"Yes, Captain."

"Excuse me, Captain . . ."

"Yes, Bartlett?"

"Possibly you don't know that Unc's partner lives in Greenwich zone minus-two. It's the middle of the night there—and she is an old lady, past seventy-five. I thought maybe you would want to know."

"Mmm, is that right, Eastman?"

"I believe so, sir."

"Cancel that last order. Bartlett, is your partner willing to go on again after an hour's break for chow? Without clearing it with LRF?"

"I'll see, sir." I spoke to Vicky; she hesitated. I said, ("What is it, Freckle Face? A date with George? Say the word and I'll tell Captain Bligh he can't have you.")

"Oh, it's all right. I'll throw the switch on George. I just wish they would give us something besides alphabet soup. Okay, one hour."

("One hour, sugar plum. Run eat your salad. Mind your waistline.")

"My waistline is just fine, thank you."

"Okay, Captain."

"Very well. Please thank him for me."

He was so indifferent about it that I added a touch of my own. "My partner is a girl, Captain, not a 'him.' Her mother has placed a two-hour curfew on it. Otherwise it must be arranged with LRF."

"So. Very well." He turned to Eastman. "Can't we manage to co-ordinate these communication watches?"

"I'm trying, Captain. But it is new to me . . . and we have only three watchstanders left."

"A watch in three should not be too difficult. Yet there always seems to be some reason why we can't transmit. Comment?"

"Well, sir, you saw the difficulty just now. It's a matter of coordinating with Earth. Uh, I believe the special communicators usually arranged that themselves. Or one of them did."

"Which one? Mr. McNeil?"

"I believe Bartlett usually handled it, sir."

"So. Bartlett?"

"I did, sir."

"Very well, you have the job again. Arrange a continuous watch." He started to get up.

How do you tell the Captain he can't have his bucket of paint? "Aye aye, sir. But just a minute, Captain—"

"Yes?"

"Do I understand you are authorizing me to arrange a continuous watch with LRF? Signed with your release number?"

"Naturally."

"Well, what do I do if they won't agree to such long hours for the old lady? Ask for still longer hours for the other two? In the case of my partner, you'll run into parent trouble; she's a young girl."

"So. I can't see why the home office hired such people."

I didn't say anything. If he didn't know that you don't hire telepaths the way you hire butchers, I wasn't going to explain.

But he persisted. "Comment?"

"I have no comment, sir. You can't get more than three or four hours a day out of any of them, except in extreme emergency. Is this one? If it is, I can arrange it without bothering the home office."

He did not answer directly. Instead he said, "Arrange the best watch list you can. Consult with Mr. Eastman." As he turned to leave I caught a look of unutterable weariness on his face and suddenly felt sorry for him. At least I didn't want to swap jobs with him.

Vicky took a trick in the middle of the night, over Kathleen's objections. Kathleen wanted to take it herself, but the truth was that she and I could no longer work easily without Vicky in the circuit, at least not anything as difficult as code groups.

The Captain did not come in to breakfast and I got there late. I looked around and found a place by Janet Meers. We no longer sat by departments—just one big horseshoe table, with the rest of the mess room arranged to look like a lounge, so that it would not seem so empty.

I was just digging into scrambled yeast on toast when Mr. Eastman stood up and tapped a glass for attention. He looked as if he had not slept for days. "Quiet, please. I have a message from the Captain." He pulled out a sheet and started to read:

" 'Notice to All Hands: By direction of the Long Range Foundation the mission of this ship has been modified. We will remain in the neighborhood of Beta Ceti pending rendezvous with Foundation ship *Serendipity*. Rendezvous is expected in approximately one month. Immediately thereafter we will shape orbit for Earth.

" 'F. X. Urqhardt, commanding *Lewis and Clark*.' "

My jaw dropped. Why, the silent creeper! All the time I had been lambasting him in my mind he had been arguing the home office into canceling our orders . . . no wonder he had used code; you say in clear language that your ship is a mess and your crew has gone to pot. Not if you can help it, you don't. I didn't even resent that he had not trusted us freaks to respect the security of communications; I wouldn't have trusted myself, under the circumstances.

Janet's eyes were shining . . . like a woman in love, or like a relativistic mathematician who has just found a new way to work a transformation. "So they've done it!" she said in a hushed voice.

"Done what?" I asked. She was certainly taking it in a big way; I hadn't realized she was that anxious to get home.

"Tommie, don't you *see?* They've done it, they've done it, they've applied irrelevance. Dr. Babcock was right."

"Huh?"

"Why, it's perfectly plain. What kind of a ship can get here in a month? An *irrelevant* ship, of course. One that is faster than light." She frowned. "But I don't see why it should take even a month. It shouldn't take any time at all. It wouldn't use time."

I said, "Take it easy, Janet. I'm stupid this morning—I didn't have much sleep last night. Why do you say that ship . . . uh, the *Serendipity* . . . is faster than light? That's impossible."

"Tommie, Tommie . . . look, dear, if it was an ordinary ship, in order to rendezvous with us here, it would have had to have left Earth over sixty-three years ago."

"Well, maybe it did."

"Tommie! It couldn't possibly—because that long ago nobody knew that we would be here now. How could they?"

I figured back. Sixty-three Greenwich years ago . . . mmm, that would have been sometime during our first peak. Janet seemed to be right; only an incredible optimist or a fortune teller would have sent a ship from Earth at that time to meet us here now. "I don't understand it."

"Don't you see, Tommie? I've explained it to you, I know I have. Irrelevance. Why, you telepaths were the reason the investigation started; you proved that 'simultaneity' was an admissible concept . . . and the inevitable logical consequence was that time and space do not exist."

I felt my head begin to ache. "They don't? Then what is that we seem to be having breakfast in?"

"Just a mathematical abstraction, dear. Nothing more." She smiled and looked motherly. "Poor 'Sentimental Tommie.' You worry too much."

I suppose Janet was right, for we made rendezvous with F. S. *Serendipity* twenty-nine Greenwich days later. We spent the time moseying out at a half gravity to a locus five billion miles Galactic-north of Beta Ceti, for it appeared that the *Sarah* did not want to come too close to the big star. Still, at sixty-three light-years, five billion miles is close shooting—a *very* near miss. We also spent the time working like mischief to arrange and prepare specimens and in collating data. Besides that, Captain Urqhardt suddenly discovered, now that we were expecting visitors, that lots and lots of things had not been cleaned and polished lately. He even inspected staterooms, which I thought was snoopy.

The *Sarah* had a mind-reader aboard, which helped when it came time to close rendezvous. She missed us by nearly two light-hours; then their m-r and myself exchanged coordinates (referred to Beta Ceti) by relay back Earthside and got each other pin-pointed in a hurry. By radar and radio alone we could have fiddled around for a week—if we had ever made contact at all.

But once that was done, the *Sarah* turned out to be a fast ship, lively enough to bug your eyes out. She was in our lap, showing on our short-range radar, as I was reporting the coordinates she had just had to the Captain. An hour later she was made fast and sealed to our lock. And she was a *little* ship. The *Elsie* had seemed huge when I first joined her; then after a while she was just the right size, or a little cramped for some purposes. But the *Sarah* wouldn't have made a decent Earth-Moon shuttle.

Mr. Whipple came aboard first. He was an incredible character to find in space; he even carried a brief case. But he took charge at once. He had two men with him and they got busy in a small compartment in the cargo deck. They knew just what compartment they wanted; we had to clear potatoes out of it in a hurry. They worked in there half a day, installing something they called a "null-field generator," working in odd clothes made entirely of hair-fine wires, which covered them like mummies. Mr. Whipple stayed in the door, watching while they worked and smoking a cigar—it was the first I had seen in three years and the smell of it made me ill. The relativists stuck close to him, exchanging excited comments, and so did the engineers, except that they looked baffled and slightly disgusted. I heard Mr. Regato say, "Maybe so. But a torch is reliable. You can depend on a torch."

Captain Urqhardt watched it all, Old Stone Face in person.

At last Mr. Whipple put out his cigar and said, "Well, that's that, Captain. Thompson will stay and take you in and Bjorkensen will go on in the *Sarah*. I'm afraid you will have to put up with me, too, for I am going back with you."

Captain Urqhardt's face was a gray-white. "Do I understand, sir, that you are relieving me of my command?"

"What? Good heavens, Captain, what makes you say that?"

"You seem to have taken charge of my ship . . . on behalf of the home office. And now you tell me that this man . . . er, Thompson—will take us in."

"Gracious, no. I'm sorry. I'm not used to the niceties of field work; I've been in the home office too long. But just think of Thompson as a . . . mmm, a sailing master for you. That's it; he'll be your pilot. But no one is displacing you; you'll remain in command until you return home and turn over your ship. Then she'll be scrapped, of course."

Mr. Regato said in a queer, high voice, "Did you say 'scrapped,' Mr. Whipple?" I felt my stomach give a twist. Scrap the *Elsie? No!*

"Eh? I spoke hastily. Nothing has been decided. Possibly she will be kept as a museum. In fact, that is a good idea." He took out a notebook and wrote in it. He put it away and said, "And now, Captain, if you will, I'd like to speak to all your people. There isn't much time."

Captain Urqhardt silently led him back to the mess deck.

When we were assembled, Mr. Whipple smiled and said, "I'm not much at speechmaking. I simply want to thank you all, on behalf of the Foundation, and explain what we are doing. I won't go into detail, as I am not a scientist; I am an administrator, busy with the liquidation of Project Lebensraum, of which you are part. Such salvage and rescue operations as this are necessary; nevertheless, the Foundation is anxious to free the *Serendipity,* and her sister ships, the *Irrelevant,* the *Infinity,* and *Zero,* for their proper work, that is to say, their survey of stars in the surrounding space."

Somebody gasped. "But that's what *we* were doing!"

"Yes, yes, of course. But times change. One of the null-field ships can visit more stars in a year than a torch ship can visit in a century. You'll be happy to know that the *Zero* working alone has located seven Earth-type planets this past month."

It didn't make me happy.

Uncle Alfred McNeil leaned forward and said in a soft, tragic voice that spoke for all of us, "Just a moment, sir. Are you telling us that what we did . . . *wasn't necessary?*"

Mr. Whipple looked startled. "No, no, no! I'm terribly sorry if I gave that impression. What you did was utterly necessary, or there would not be any null ships today. Why, that's like saying that what Columbus did wasn't necessary, simply because we jump across oceans as if they were mud puddles nowadays."

"Thank you, sir," Unc said quietly.

"Perhaps no one has told you just how indispensably necessary Project Lebensraum has been. Very possibly—things have been in a turmoil around the Foundation for some time—I know I've had so little sleep myself that I don't know what I've done and left undone. But you realize, don't you, that without the telepaths among you, all this progress would not have taken place?" Whipple looked around. "Who are they? I'd like to shake hands with them. In any case—I'm not a scientist, mind you; I'm a lawyer—in any case, if we had not had it proved beyond doubt that telepathy is truly instantaneous, proof measured over many light-years, our scientists might still be looking for errors in the sixth decimal place and maintaining that telepathic signals do not propagate instantaneously but simply at a speed so great that its exact order was concealed by instrumental error. So I understand, so I am told. So you see, your great work has produced wondrous results, much greater than expected, even if they were not quite the results you were looking for."

I was thinking that if they had told us just a few days sooner, Uncle Steve would still be alive.

But he never did want to die in bed.

"But the fruition of your efforts," Whipple went on, "did not show at once. Like so many things in science, the new idea had to grow for a long time, among specialists . . . then the stupendous results burst suddenly on the world. For myself, if anyone had told me six months ago that I would be out here among the stars today, giving a popular lecture on the new physics, I wouldn't have believed him. I'm not sure that I believe it now. But here I am. Among other things, I am here to help you get straightened away when we get back home." He smiled and bowed.

"Uh, Mr. Whipple," Chet Travers asked, "just when will we get home?"

"Oh, didn't I tell you? Almost immediately . . . say soon after lunch."

17

Of Time and Change

I MIGHT AS WELL FINISH THIS OFF AND GIVE IT A DECENT BURIAL. I'LL never have time to write again.

They held us in quarantine for a week at Rio. If it had not been for the LRF man with us, they might have been holding us yet. But they were nice to us. Emperor Dom Pedro III of Brazil presented us each with the Richardson Medal on behalf of the United System and made a speech which showed that he was not quite sure who we were or where we had been, but nevertheless our services were appreciated.

But not as much attention was paid to us as I had expected. Oh, I don't mean that the news services ignored us; they did take our pictures and they interviewed each of us. But the only news story I saw was headed: THIRD LOAD OF RIP VAN WINKLES ARRIVE TODAY.

The reporter or whoever it was who wrote the piece had fun with it and I hope he chokes. It seems that our clothes were quaint and our speech was quaint and we were all deliciously old-fashioned and a bit simple-minded. The picture was captioned: "Off Hats, Chuckies! Grandpa Towncomes."

I didn't look at the other stories.

It didn't worry Unc; I doubt if he noticed. He was simply eager to see Celestine. "I do hope," he said to me half seriously, "that child can cook the way her mother could."

"You'll be living with her?" I asked.

"Of course. Haven't we always?"

That was so logical that I had no answer. Then we exchanged addresses. That was logical, too, but it seemed odd—all the address any of us had had was the *Elsie*. But I exchanged addresses with everybody and made a note to look up Dusty's twin, if he was still alive, and tell him he could be proud of his brother—perhaps I could locate him through the Foundation.

When they turned us loose and Celestine Johnson did show up I did not recognize her. I saw this tall, handsome old lady rush up and put her arms around Unc, almost lifting him off his feet, and I wondered if I should rescue him.

But then she looked up and caught my eye and smiled and I yelled, "Sugar Pie!"

She smiled still more and I felt myself washed through with sweetness and love. *"Hello, Tommie. It's good to see you again."*

Presently I promised to visit them at my very first chance and left them; they didn't need me for their homecoming. Nobody had come to meet me; Pat was too old and no longer traveled, Vicky was too young to be allowed to travel alone, and as for Molly and Kathleen, I think their husbands didn't see any reason for it. Neither of them liked me, anyhow. I don't blame them, under the circumstances . . . even though it had been a long time (years to them) since I had mind-talked to their wives other than with Vicky's help. But I repeat, I don't blame them. If telepathy ever becomes common, such things could cause a lot of family friction.

Besides, I was in touch with Vicky whenever I wanted to be. I told her to forget it and not make a fuss; I preferred not to be met.

In fact, save for Unc, almost none of us was met other than by agents of LRF. After more than seventy-one years there was simply no one to meet them. But Captain Urqhardt was the one I felt sorriest for. I saw him standing alone while we were all waiting outside quarantine for our courier-interpreters. None of the rest was alone; we were busy saying good-by. But he didn't have any friends—I suppose he couldn't afford to have any friends aboard ship, even while he was waiting to become Captain.

He looked so bleak and lonely and unhappy that I walked up and stuck out my hand. "I want to say good-by, Captain. It's been an honor to serve with you . . . and a pleasure." The last was not a lie; right then I meant it.

He looked surprised, then his face broke into a grin that I thought would crack it; his face wasn't used to it. He grabbed my hand and said, "It's been my pleasure, too, Bartlett. I wish you all the luck in the world. Er . . . what are your plans?"

He said it eagerly and I suddenly realized he wanted to chat, just to visit. "I don't have any firm plans, Captain. I'm going home first, then I suppose I'll go to school. I want to go to college, but I suppose I'll have some catching up to do. There have been some changes."

"Yes, there have been changes," he agreed solemnly. "We'll all have catching up to do."

"Uh, what are your plans, sir?"

"I don't have any. I don't know what I can do."

He said it simply, a statement of fact; with sudden warm pity I realized that it was true. He was a torchship captain, as specialized a job as ever existed . . . and now there were no more torchships. It was as if Columbus had come back from his first voyage and found nothing but steamships. Could he go to sea again? He wouldn't even have been able to find the bridge, much less know what to do when he got there.

There was no place for Captain Urqhardt; he was an anachronism. One testimonial dinner and then thank you, good night.

"I suppose I could retire," he went on, looking away. "I've been figuring my back pay and it comes to a preposterous sum."

"I suppose it would, sir." I hadn't figured my pay; Pat had collected it for me.

"Confound it, Bartlett! I'm too young to retire."

I looked at him. I had never thought of him as especially old and he was not, not compared with the Captain—with Captain Swenson. But I decided that he must be around forty, ship's time. "Say, Captain, why don't you go back to school, too? You can afford it."

He looked unhappy. "Perhaps I should. I suppose I ought to. Or maybe I should just chuck it and emigrate. They say there are a lot of places to choose from now."

"I'll probably do that myself, eventually. If you ask me, things have become too crowded around here. I've been thinking about Connie, and how pretty Babcock Bay looked." I really had been thinking about it during the week we had spent in quarantine. If Rio was a sample, Earth didn't have room enough to fall down; we were clear down in the Santos District and yet they said it was Rio. "If we went back to Babcock Bay, we'd be the oldest settlers."

"Perhaps I will. Yes, perhaps I will." But he still looked lost.

Our courier-interpreters had instructions to take us all home, or wherever we wanted to go, but I let mine leave once I had my ticket for home. She was awfully nice but she bothered me. She treated me as a cross between grandfather who must be watched over in traffic and a little boy who must be instructed. Not but what I needed instruction.

But once I had clothes that would not be stared at, I wanted to be on my own. She had taught me enough System Speech in a week so that I could get by in simple matters and I hoped that my mistakes would be charged up to a local accent from somewhere. Actually, I found that System Speech, when it wasn't upgained to tears, was just P-L lingo with more corners knocked off and some words added. English, in other words, trimmed and stretched to make a trade lingo.

So I thanked Senhorita Guerra and told her good-by and waved my ticket at a sleepy gatekeeper. He answered in Portuguese and I looked stupid, so he changed it to, "Outdowngo rightwards. Ask from allone." I was on my way.

Somehow everybody in the ship seemed to know that I was a Rip Van Winkle and the hostess insisted on helping me make the change at White Sands. But they were friendly and did not laugh at me. One chap wanted to know about the colony being opened up on Capella VIII and did not understand why I hadn't been there if I had spaced all that time. I tried to explain that Capella was clear across the sky and more than a hundred light-years from where I had been, but I didn't put the idea across.

But I did begin to see why we had not made a big splash in the news. Colony planets were the rage and there was a new one every day, so why should anyone be excited over one that we had found sixty years back? Or even over one just a few months back which did not compare with ones being turned up now? As for starships—see the latest news for current departures.

We were going to be a short paragraph in history and a footnote in science books; there wasn't room for us in the news. I decided that even a footnote averaged well and forgot it.

Instead I started thinking about my re-education which, I was beginning to realize, was going to have to be extensive; the changes had been more than I had bargained for. Take female styles, for example—look, I'm no Puritan, but they didn't dress, if you want to call it that, this way when I was a kid. Girls running around without a thing on their heads, not even on top . . . heads bare-naked, like an animal.

It was a good thing that Dad hadn't lived to see it. He never let our sisters come to the table without a hat, even if Pat and I were the only unmarried males present.

Or take the weather. I had known that LRF was working on it, but I never expected them to get anywhere. Don't people find it a little dull to have it rain only at night? Or take trucks. Of course, all you expect of a truck is that it haul things from here to there. But the lack of wheels does make them look unstable.

I wonder how long it will be before there is not a wheel on Earth?

I had decided that I would just have to get used to it all, when the hostess came by and put something in my lap and when I picked it up, it *spoke* to me. It was just a souvenir of the trip.

Pat's town house was eight times as big as the flat seven of us used to live in; I decided that he had managed to hang onto at least some of the money. His robutler took my cape and boots and ushered me in to see him.

He didn't get up. I wasn't sure he could get up. I had known that he was old but I hadn't realized that he was *old!* He was—let me see, eighty-nine. Yes, that was right; we had our ninetieth birthday coming up.

I tried to keep it casual. "Hi, Pat."

"Hi, Tom." He touched the arm of his chair and it rolled toward me. "Don't move. Stand there and let me look at you." He looked me up and down, then said wonderingly, "I knew intellectually that you would not have changed with the years. But to see it, to realize it, is quite another thing, eh? 'The Picture of Dorian Gray.' "

His voice was old.

"Where is the family?" I said uncomfortably.

"I've told the girls to wait. I wanted to see my brother alone at first. If you mean Gregory and Hans as well, no doubt you will meet them at dinner tonight. But never mind them, lad; just let me visit with you a while. It's been a long time." I could see tears, the ready tears of old age, in his eyes and it embarrassed me.

"Yes, I guess it has."

He leaned forward and gripped the arms of his chair. "Tell me just one thing. Was it fun?"

I thought about it. Doc Devereaux . . . Mama O'Toole . . . poor little Pru who had never lived to grow up, not really. Uncle Steve. Then I switched it off and gave him the answer he wanted. "Yes, it was fun, lots of fun."

He sighed. "That's good. I quit regretting years ago. But if it hadn't been fun, it would have been such a terrible waste."

"It was."

"That's all I wanted to hear you say. I'll call the girls down in a moment. Tomorrow I'll show you around the plant and introduce you to the key men. Not that I expect you to take hold right away. Take a long vacation if you like. But not too long, Tom . . . for I guess I'm getting old. I can't look ahead the way I used to."

I suddenly realized that Pat had everything planned out, just as he always had. "Wait a minute, Pat. I'll be pleased to have you show me around your plant—and honored. But don't count on anything. First I'm going to school. After that—well, we'll see."

"Eh? Don't be silly. And don't call it 'my' plant; it's 'Bartlett Brothers, Incorporated.' It always has been. It's your responsibility as much as mine."

"Now, take it easy, Pat. I was just—"

"Quiet!" His voice was thin and shrill but it still had the sound of command. "I won't have any nonsense out of you, young man. You've had your own way and you've been off on a long picnic—I won't criticize how you managed it. That's by-gones. But now you must buckle down and assume your responsibilities in the family business." He stopped and breathed heavily, then went on more softly, almost to himself. "I had no sons, I have no grandsons; I've had to carry the burden alone. To have my brother, to have my own brother . . ." His voice faded out.

I went up and took him by the shoulder—then I let go; it felt like match sticks. But I decided that I might as well settle it once and all; I told myself it would be kinder. "Listen to me, Pat. I don't want to seem ungrateful, but you must get this straight. I'm going to live my own life. Understand me. It might include 'Bartlett Brothers'; it might not. Probably not. But *I* will decide. I'll never be told again."

He brushed it aside. "You don't know your own mind; you're just a boy. Never mind, we'll speak of it tomorrow. Today is a day of gladness."

"No, Pat. I am not a boy, I am a man. You'll have to accept that. I'll make my own mistakes and I'll not be told."

He wouldn't look at me. I insisted, "I mean it, Pat. I mean it so much that if you can't accept it and abide by it, I'm walking out right now. Permanently."

Then he looked up. "You wouldn't do that to me."

"I would."

He searched my eyes. "I believe you would. You always were a mean one. You gave me a lot of trouble."

"I'm still mean . . . if you want to call it that."

"Uh . . . but you wouldn't do it to the girls? Not to little Vicky?"

"I will if you force my hand."

He held my eyes for a second, then his shoulders sagged and he buried his face in his hands. I thought he was going to cry and I felt like a villain, bullying an old man like that. I patted his shoulders, wishing that I had stalled, rather than forcing the issue.

I remembered that this frail old man had risked his health and his sanity to get in touch with me at first peak, and I thought: if he wants it so badly, maybe I should humor him. After all, he did not have long to live.

No!

It wasn't right for one person to impose his will on another, through strength or even through weakness. I was myself . . . and I was going out to the stars again. Suddenly I knew it. Oh, college perhaps, first—but I was going. I owed this old man gratitude . . . but I did not owe him the shape of my life. That was mine.

I took his hand and said, "I'm sorry, Pat."

He said without looking up, "All right, Tom. Have it your own way. I'm glad to have you home anyway . . . on your own terms."

We talked inanities for a few moments, then he had the robutler fetch me coffee—he had milk. At last he said, "I'll call the girls." He touched the arm of his chair, a light glowed and he spoke to it.

Molly came down with Kathleen behind her. I would have known either of them anywhere, though I had never seen them. Molly was a woman in her late sixties, still handsome. Kathleen was fortyish and did not look it—no, she looked her age and wore it regally. Molly stood on tiptoe, holding both my hands, and kissed me. "We're glad you are home, Tommie."

"So we are," Kathleen agreed, and her words echoed in my mind. She kissed me, too, then said just with her voice. "So this is my aged and ageless great uncle. Tom, you make me wish for a son. You aren't uncle-ish and I'll never call you 'uncle' again."

"Well, I don't feel uncle-ish. Except to Molly, maybe."

Molly looked startled, then giggled like a girl. "All right, Uncle Tom. I'll remember your years . . . and treat you with respect."

"Where's Vicky?"

"I'm here, Uncle Tom. Down in a split."

("Hurry, hon.")

Kathleen looked sharply at me, then let it pass—I'm sure she did not mean to listen. She answered, "Vicky will be down in a moment, Tom. She had to get her face just so. You know how girls are."

I wondered if I did. But Vicky was down, almost at once.

There were no freckles on her face, no braces on her teeth. Her mouth wasn't large; it was simply perfectly right for her. And the carrotty hair that had worried her so was a crown of flame.

She did not kiss me; she simply came straight to me as if we had been alone, took my hands and looked up at me.

"Uncle Tom. Tom."

("Freckle Face . . .")

I don't know how long we played statues. Presently she said, *"After we are married, there will be none of this many-light-years-apart stuff . . . Understand me? I go where you go. To Babcock Bay, if that's what you want. But I go."*

("Huh? When did you decide to marry me?")

"You seem to forget that I have been reading your mind since I was a baby—and a lot more thoroughly than you think I have! I'm still doing it."

("But how about George?")

"Nothing about George. He was a mere make-do when I thought you would not be back until I was an old lady. Forget him."

("All right.")

Our "courtship" had lasted all of twenty seconds. Without letting go my hands Vicky spoke aloud. "Tom and I are going downtown and get married. We'd like you all to come along."

So we did.

I saw Pat eyeing me after the ceremony, sizing up the new situation and mulling over how he would use it. But Pat doesn't understand the new setup; if I get bossed, it won't be by him. Vicky says that she will soon have me "ricketty all through." I hope not but I suppose she will. If so, I trust I'll be able to adjust to it . . . I've adjusted to stranger things.

CITIZEN OF THE GALAXY

To Fritz Leiber

1

"LOT NINETY-SEVEN," THE AUCTIONEER ANNOUNCED. "A BOY."

The boy was dizzy and half sick from the feel of ground underfoot. The slave ship had come more than forty light-years; it carried in its holds the stink of all slave ships, a reek of crowded unwashed bodies, of fear and vomit and ancient grief. Yet in it the boy had been someone, a recognized member of a group, entitled to his meal each day, entitled to fight for his right to eat it in peace. He had even had friends.

Now he was again nothing and nobody, again about to be sold.

A lot had been knocked down on the auction block, matched blonde girls, alleged to be twins; the bidding had been brisk, the price high. The auctioneer turned with a smile of satisfaction and pointed at the boy. "Lot ninety-seven. Shove him up here."

The boy was cuffed and prodded onto the block, stood tense while his feral eyes darted around, taking in what he had not been able to see from the pen. The slave market lies on the spaceport side of the famous Plaza of Liberty, facing the hill crowned by the still more famous Praesidium of the Sargon, capitol of the Nine Worlds. The boy did not recognize it; he did not even know what planet he was on. He looked at the crowd.

Closest to the slave block were beggars, ready to wheedle each buyer as he claimed his property. Beyond them, in a semi-circle, were seats for the rich and privileged. On each flank of this elite group waited their slaves, bearers, and bodyguards and drivers, idling near the ground cars of the rich and the palanquins and sedan chairs of the still richer. Behind the lords and ladies were commoners, idlers and curious, freedmen and pickpockets and vendors of cold drinks, an occasional commoner merchant not privileged to sit but alert for a bargain in a porter, a clerk, a mechanic, or even a house servant for his wives.

"Lot ninety-seven," the auctioneer repeated. "A fine, healthy lad, suitable as page or tireboy. Imagine him, my lords and ladies, in the livery of your house. Look at—" His words were lost in the scream of a ship, doppling in at the spaceport behind him.

The old beggar Baslim the Cripple twisted his half-naked body and squinted his one eye over the edge of the block. The boy did not look like a docile house servant to Baslim; he looked a hunted animal, dirty, skinny, and bruised. Under the dirt, the boy's back showed white scar streaks, endorsements of former owners' opinions.

The boy's eyes and the shape of his ears caused Baslim to guess that he might be of unmutated Earth ancestry, but not much could be certain save that he was small, scared, male, and still defiant. The boy caught the beggar staring at him and glared back.

The din died out and a wealthy dandy seated in front waved a kerchief lazily at the auctioneer. "Don't waste our time, you rascal. Show us something like that last lot."

"Please, noble sir. I must dispose of the lots in catalog order."

"Then get on with it! Or cuff that starved varmint aside and show us merchandise."

"You are kind, my lord." The auctioneer raised his voice. "I have been asked to be quick and I am sure my noble employer would agree. Let me be frank. This beautiful lad is young; his new owner must invest instruction in him. Therefore—" The boy hardly listened. He knew only a smattering of this language and what was said did not matter anyhow. He looked over the veiled ladies and elegant men, wondering which one would be his new problem.

"—a low starting price and a quick turnover. A bargain! Do I hear twenty stellars?"

The silence grew awkward. A lady, sleek and expensive from sandaled feet to lace-veiled face, leaned toward the dandy, whispered and giggled. He frowned, took out a dagger and pretended to groom his nails. "I said to get on with it," he growled.

The auctioneer sighed. "I beg you to remember, gentlefolk, that I must answer to my patron. But we'll start still lower. Ten stellars—yes, I said, 'Ten.' Fantastic!"

He looked amazed. "Am I growing deaf? Did someone lift a finger and I fail to see it? Consider, I beg you. Here you have a fresh young lad like a clean sheet of paper; you can draw any design you like. At this unbelievably low price you can afford to make a mute of him, or alter him as your fancy pleases."

"Or feed him to the fish!"

" 'Or feed him—' Oh, you are witty, noble sir!"

"I'm bored. What makes you think that sorry item is worth anything? Your son, perhaps?"

The auctioneer forced a smile. "I would be proud if he were. I wish I were permitted to tell you this lad's ancestry—"

"Which means you don't know."

"Though my lips must be sealed, I can point out the shape of his skull, the perfectly rounded curve of his ears." The auctioneer nipped the boy's ear, pulled it.

The boy twisted and bit his hand. The crowd laughed.

The man snatched his hand away. "A spirited lad. Nothing a taste of leather won't cure. Good stock, look at his ears. The best in the Galaxy, some say."

The auctioneer had overlooked something; the young dandy was from Syndon IV. He removed his helmet, uncovering typical Syndonian ears, long, hairy, and pointed. He leaned forward and his ears twitched. *"Who is your noble protector?"*

The old beggar Baslim scooted near the corner of the block, ready to duck. The boy tensed and looked around, aware of trouble without understanding why. The auctioneer went white—no one sneered at Syndonians face to face . . . not more than once. "My lord," he gasped, "you misunderstood me."

"Repeat that crack about 'ears' and 'the best stock.' "

Police were in sight but not close. The auctioneer wet his lips. "Be gracious, gentle lord. My children would starve. I quoted a common saying—not *my* opinion. I was trying to hasten a bid for this chattel . . . as you yourself urged."

The silence was broken by a female voice saying, "Oh, let him go, Dwarol. It's not his fault how the slave's ears are shaped; he has to sell him."

The Syndonian breathed heavily. "Sell him, then!"

The auctioneer took a breath. "Yes, my lord." He pulled himself together and went on, "I beg my lords' and ladies' pardons for wasting time on a minor lot. I now ask for any bid at all."

He waited, said nervously, "I hear no bid, I see no bid. No bid once . . . if you do not bid, I am required to return this lot to stock and consult my patron before continuing. No bid twice. There are many beautiful items to be offered; it would be a shame not to show them. No bid three—"

"There's your bid," the Syndonian said.

"Eh?" The old beggar was holding up two fingers. The auctioneer stared. "Are *you* offering a bid?"

"Yes," croaked the old man, "if the lords and ladies permit."

The auctioneer glanced at the seated circle. Someone in the crowd shouted, "Why not? Money is money."

The Syndonian nodded; the auctioneer said quickly, "You offer two stellars for this boy?"

"No, no, no, no, no!" Baslim screamed. "Two *minims!*"

The auctioneer kicked at him; the beggar jerked his head aside. The auctioneer shouted, "Get out! I'll teach you to make fun of your betters!"

"Auctioneer!"

"Sir? Yes, my lord?"

The Syndonian said, "Your words were 'any bid at all.' Sell him the boy."

"But—"

"You heard me."

"My lord, I *cannot* sell on one bid. The law is clear; one bid is not an auction. Nor even two unless the auctioneer has set a minimum. With no minimum, I am not allowed to sell with less than three bids. Noble sir, this law was given to protect the owner, not my unhappy self."

Someone shouted, "That's the law!"

The Syndonian frowned. "Then declare the bid."

"Whatever pleases my lords and ladies." He faced the crowd. "For lot ninety-seven: I heard a bid of two minims. Who'll make it four?"

"Four," stated the Syndonian.

"Five!" a voice called out.

The Syndonian motioned the beggar to him. Baslim moved on hands and one knee, with the stump of the other leg dragging and was hampered by his alms bowl. The auctioneer started droning, "Going at five minims once . . . five minims twice . . ."

"Six!" snapped the Syndonian, glanced into the beggar's bowl, reached in his purse and threw him a handful of change.

"I hear six. Do I hear seven?"

"Seven," croaked Baslim.

"I'm bid seven. You, over there, with your thumb up. You make it eight?"

"Nine!" interposed the beggar.

The auctioneer glared but put the bid. The price was approaching one stellar, too expensive a joke for most of the crowd. The lords and ladies neither wanted the worthless slave nor wished to queer the Syndonian's jest.

The auctioneer chanted, "Going once at nine . . . going twice at nine . . . going three times—*sold* at nine minims!" He shoved the boy off the block almost into the beggar's lap. "Take him and get out!"

"Softly," cautioned the Syndonian. "The bill of sale."

Restraining himself, the auctioneer filled in price and new owner on a form already prepared for lot ninety-seven. Baslim paid over nine minims—then had to be subsidized again by the Syndonian, as the stamp tax was more than the selling price. The boy stood quietly by. He knew that he had been sold again and he was getting it through his head that the old man was his new master—not that it mattered; he wanted neither of them. While all were busy with the tax, he made a break.

Without appearing to look the old beggar made a long arm, snagged an ankle, pulled him back. Then Baslim heaved himself erect, placed an arm across the boy's shoulders and used him for a crutch. The boy felt a bony hand clutch his elbow in a strong grip and relaxed himself to the inevitable—another time; they always got careless if you waited.

Supported, the beggar bowed with great dignity. "My lord," he said huskily, "I and my servant thank you."

"Nothing, nothing." The Syndonian flourished his kerchief in dismissal.

From the Plaza of Liberty to the hole where Baslim lived was less than a li, no more than a half mile, but it took them longer than such distance implies. The hopping progress the old man could manage using the boy as one leg was even slower than his speed on two hands and one knee, and it was interrupted frequently by rests for business—not that business ceased while they shuffled along, as the old man required the boy to thrust the bowl under the nose of every pedestrian.

Baslim accomplished this without words. He had tried Interlingua, Space Dutch, Sargonese, half a dozen forms of patois, thieves' kitchen, cant, slave lingo, and trade talk—even System English—without result, although he suspected that the boy had understood him more than once. Then he dropped the attempt and made his wishes known by sign language and a cuff or two. If the boy and he had no words in common, he would teach him—all in good time, all in good time. Baslim was in no hurry. Baslim was never in a hurry; he took the long view.

Baslim's home lay under the old amphitheater. When Sargon Augustus of imperial memory decreed a larger circus only part of the old one was demolished; the work was interrupted by the Second Cetan War and never resumed. Baslim led the boy into these ruins. The going was rough and it was necessary for the old man to resume crawling.

But he never let go his grip. Once he had the boy only by breechclout; the boy almost wriggled out of his one bit of clothing before the beggar snatched a wrist. After that they went more slowly.

They went down a hole at the dark end of a ruined passage, the boy being forced to go first. They crawled over shards and rubble and came into a night-black but smooth corridor. Down again . . . and they were in the performers' barracks of the old amphitheater, under the old arena.

They came in the dark to a well-carpentered door. Baslim shoved the boy through, followed him and closed it, pressed his thumb to a personal lock, touched a switch; light came on. "Well, lad, we're home."

The boy stared. Long ago he had given up having expectations of any sort. But what he saw was not anything he could have expected. It was a modest decent small living room, tight, neat, and clean. Ceiling panels gave pleasant glareless light. Furniture was sparse but adequate. The boy looked around in awe; poor as it was, it was better than anything he remembered having lived in.

The beggar let go his shoulder, hopped to a stack of shelves, put down his bowl, and took up a complicated something. It was not until the beggar shucked his clout and strapped the thing in place that the boy figured out what it was: an artificial leg, so well articulated that it rivaled the efficiency of flesh and blood. The man stood up, took trousers from a chest, drew them on, and hardly seemed crippled. "Come here," he said, in Interlingua.

The boy did not move. Baslim repeated it in other languages, shrugged, took the boy by an arm, led him into a room beyond. It was small, both kitchen and wash room; Baslim filled a pan, handed the boy a bit of soap and said, "Take a bath." He pantomimed what he wanted.

The boy stood in mute stubbornness. The man sighed, picked up a brush suitable for floors and started as if to scrub the boy. He stopped with stiff bristles touching skin and repeated, "Take a bath. Wash yourself," saying it in Interlingua and System English.

The boy hesitated, took off his clout and started slowly to lather himself.

Baslim said, "That's better," picked up the filthy breech clout, dropped it in a waste can, laid out a towel, and, turning to the kitchen side, started preparing a meal.

A few minutes later he turned and the boy was gone.

Unhurriedly he walked into the living room, found the boy naked and wet and trying very hard to open the door. The boy saw him but redoubled his futile efforts. Baslim tapped him on the shoulder, hooked a thumb toward the smaller room. "Finish your bath."

He turned away. The boy slunk after him.

When the boy was washed and dry, Baslim put the stew he had been freshening back on the burner, turned the switch to "simmer" and opened a cupboard, from which he removed a bottle and daubs of vegetable flock. Clean, the boy was a pattern of scars and bruises, unhealed sores and cuts and abrasions, old and new. "Hold still."

The stuff stung; the boy started to wiggle. "Hold still!" Baslim repeated in a pleasant firm tone and slapped him. The boy relaxed, tensing only as the medicine touched him. The man looked carefully at an old ulcer on the boy's knee, then, humming softly, went again to the cupboard, came back and injected the boy in one buttock—first acting out the idea that he would slap his head off his shoulders if he failed to take it quietly. That done, he found an old cloth, motioned the boy to wrap himself a clout, turned back to his cooking.

Presently Baslim placed big bowls of stew on the table in the living room, first moving chair and table so that the boy might sit on the chest while eating. He added a handful of fresh green lentils and a couple of generous chunks of country bread, black and hard. "Soup's on, lad. Come and get it."

The boy sat down on the edge of the chest but remained poised for flight and did not eat.

Baslim stopped eating. "What's the matter?" He saw the boy's eyes flick toward the door, then drop. "Oh, so that's it." He got up, steadying himself to get his false leg under him, went to the door, pressed his thumb in the lock. He faced the boy. "The door is unlocked," he announced. "Either eat your dinner, or leave." He repeated it several ways and was pleased when he thought that he detected understanding on using the language he surmised might be the slave's native tongue.

But he let the matter rest, went back to the table, got carefully into his chair and picked up his spoon.

The boy reached for his own, then suddenly was off the chest and out the door. Baslim went on eating. The door remained ajar, light streaming into the labyrinth.

Later, when Baslim had finished a leisurely dinner, he became aware that the boy was watching him from the shadows. He avoided looking, lounged back, and started picking his teeth. Without turning, he said in the language he had decided might be the boy's own, "Will you come eat your dinner? Or shall I throw it away?"

The boy did not answer. "All right," Baslim went on, "if you won't, I'll have to close the door. I can't risk leaving it open with the light on." He slowly got up, went to the door, and started to close it. "Last call," he announced. "Closing up for the night."

As the door was almost closed the boy squealed, "Wait!" in the language Baslim expected, and scurried inside.

"Welcome," Baslim said quietly. "I'll leave it unlocked, in case you change your mind." He sighed. "If I had my way, no one would ever be locked in."

The boy did not answer but sat down, huddled himself over the food and began wolfing it as if afraid it might be snatched away. His eyes flicked from right to left. Baslim sat down and watched.

The extreme pace slowed but chewing and gulping never ceased until the last bit of stew had been chased with the last hunk of bread, the last lentil crunched and swallowed. The final bites appeared to go down by sheer will power, but swallow them he did, sat up, looked Baslim in the eye and smiled shyly. Baslim smiled back.

The boy's smile vanished. He turned white, then a light green. A rope of drool came willy-nilly from a corner of his mouth—and he was disastrously sick.

Baslim moved to avoid the explosion. "Stars in heaven, I'm an idiot!" he exclaimed, in his native language. He went into the kitchen, returned with rags and pail, wiped the boy's face and told him sharply to quiet down, then cleaned the stone floor.

After a bit he returned with a much smaller ration, only broth and a small piece of bread. "Soak the bread and eat it."

"I better not."

"Eat it. You won't be sick again. I should have known better, seeing your belly against your backbone, than to give you a man-sized meal. But eat slowly."

The boy looked up and his chin quivered. Then he took a small spoonful. Baslim watched while he finished the broth and most of the bread.

"Good," Baslim said at last. "Well, I'm for bed, lad. By the way, what's your name?"

The boy hesitated. "Thorby."

" 'Thorby'—a good name. You can call me 'Pop.' Good night." He unstrapped his leg, hopped to the shelf and put it away, hopped to his bed. It was a peasant bed, a hard mattress in a corner. He scrunched close to the wall to leave room for the boy and said, "Put out the light before you come to bed." Then he closed his eyes and waited.

There was long silence. He heard the boy go to the door; the light went out. Baslim waited, listening for noise of the door opening. It did not come; instead he felt the mattress give as the boy crawled in. "Good night," he repeated.

"G'night."

He had almost dozed when he realized that the boy was trembling violently. He reached behind him, felt skinny ribs, patted them; the boy broke into sobs.

He turned over, eased his stump into a comfortable position, put an arm around the boy's shaking shoulders and pulled his face against his own chest. "It's all right, Thorby," he said gently, "it's all right. It's over now. It'll never happen again."

The boy cried out loud and clung to him. Baslim held him, speaking softly until the spasms stopped. Then he held still until he was sure that Thorby was asleep.

2

THORBY'S WOUNDS HEALED, THOSE OUTSIDE QUICKLY, THOSE INSIDE slowly. The old beggar acquired another mattress and stuck it in the other corner. But Baslim would sometimes wake to find a small warm bundle snuggled against his spine and know thereby that the boy had had another nightmare. Baslim was a light sleeper and hated sharing a bed. But he never forced Thorby to go back to his own bed when this happened.

Sometimes the boy would cry out his distress without waking. Once Baslim was jerked awake by hearing Thorby wail, "Mama, Mama!" Without making a light he crawled quickly to the boy's pallet and bent over him. "There, there, son, it's all right."

"Papa?"

"Go back to sleep, son. You'll wake Mama." He added, "I'll stay with you—you're safe. Now be quiet. We don't want to wake Mama . . . do we?"

"All right, Papa."

The old man waited, almost without breathing, until he was stiff and cold and his stump ached. When he was satisfied that the boy was asleep he crawled to his own bed.

That incident caused the old man to try hypnosis. A long time earlier, when Baslim had had two eyes, two legs, and no reason to beg, he had learned the art. But he had never liked hypnosis, even for therapy; he had an almost religious concept of the dignity of the individual; hypnotizing another person did not fit his basic evaluation.

But this was an emergency.

He was sure that Thorby had been taken from his parents so young that he had no conscious memory of them. The boy's notion of life was a jumbled recollection of masters, some bad, some worse, all of whom had tried to break the spirit of a "bad" boy. Thorby had explicit memories of some of these masters and described them in gutter speech vivid and violent. But he was never sure of time or place—"place" was some estate, or household, or factor's compound, never a particular planet or sun (his notions of astronomy were mostly wrong and he was innocent of galactography) and "time" was simply "before" or "after," "short" or "long." While each planet has its day, its year, its own method of dating, while they are reconciled for science in terms of the standard second as defined by radioactive decay, the standard year of the birthplace of mankind, and a standard reference date, the first jump from that planet, Sol III, to its satellite, it was impossible for an illiterate boy to date anything that way. Earth was a myth to Thorby and a "day" was the time between two sleeps.

Baslim could not guess the lad's age. The boy looked like unmutated Earth stock and was pre-adolescent, but any guess would be based on unproved assumption. Vandorians and Italo-Glyphs look like the original stock, but Vandorians take three times as long to mature—Baslim recalled the odd tale about the consular agent's daughter whose second husband was the great grandson of her first and she had outlived them both. Mutations do not necessarily show up in appearance.

It was conceivable that this boy was "older" in standard seconds than Baslim himself; space is deep and mankind adapted itself in many ways to many conditions. Never mind!—he was a youngster and he needed help.

Thorby was not afraid of hypnosis; the word meant nothing to him, nor did Baslim explain. After supper one evening the old man simply said, "Thorby, I want you to do something."

"Sure, Pop. What?"

"Lie down on your bed. Then I'm going to make you sleepy and we'll talk."

"Huh? You mean the other way around, don't you?"

"No. This is a different sort of sleep. You'll be able to talk."

Thorby was dubious but willing. The old man lighted a candle, switched off the glow plates. Using the flame to focus attention he started the ancient routines of monotonous suggestion, of relaxation, drowsiness . . . sleep.

"Thorby, you are asleep but you can hear me. You can answer."

"Yes, Pop."

"You will stay asleep until I tell you to wake. But you will be able to answer any question I ask."

"Yes, Pop."

"You remember the ship that brought you here. What was its name?"

"The *Merry Widow*. Only that wasn't what we called it."

"You remember getting into that ship. Now you are in it—you can see it. You remember all about it. Now go back to where you were when you went aboard."

The boy stiffened without waking. "I don't want to!"

"I'll be right with you. You'll be safe. Now what is the name of the place? Go back to it. Look at it."

An hour and a half later Baslim still squatted beside the sleeping boy. Sweat poured down wrinkles in his face and he felt badly shaken. To get the boy back to the time he wanted to explore it had been necessary to force him back through experiences disgusting even to Baslim, old and hardened as he was. Repeatedly Thorby had fought against it, nor could Baslim blame him—he felt now that he could count the scars on the boy's back and assign a villain to each.

But he had achieved his purpose: to delve farther back than the boy's waking memory ran, back into his very early childhood, and at last to the traumatic moment when the baby manchild had been taken from his parents.

He left the boy in deep coma while he collected his shattered thoughts. The last few moments of the quest had been so bad that the old man doubted his judgment in trying to dig out the source of the trouble.

Well, let's see . . . what had he found out?

The boy was born free. But he had always been sure of that.

The boy's native language was System English, spoken with an accent Baslim could not place; it had been blurred by baby speech. That placed him inside the Terran Hegemony; it was even possible (though not likely) that the boy had been born on Earth. That was a surprise; he had thought the boy's native language was Interlingua, since he spoke it better than he did the other three he knew.

What else? Well, the boy's parents were certainly dead, if the confused and terror-ridden memory he had pried out of the boy's skull could be trusted. He had been unable to dig out their family name nor any way of identifying them—they were just "Papa" and "Mama"—so Baslim gave up a half-formed plan of trying to get word to relatives of the boy.

Well, now to make this ordeal he had put the lad through worth the cost—

"Thorby?"

The boy moaned and stirred. "Yes, Pop?"

"You are asleep. You won't wake up until I tell you to."

"I won't wake up until you tell me to."

"When I tell you, you will wake at once. You will feel fine and you won't remember anything we've talked about."

"Yes, Pop."

"You will forget. But you will feel fine. About half an hour later you will feel sleepy again. I'll tell you to go to bed and you will go to bed and go right to sleep. You'll sleep all night, good sleep and pleasant dreams. You won't have any more bad dreams. Say it."

"I won't have any more bad dreams."

"You won't ever have any more bad dreams. Not ever."

"Not ever."

"Papa and Mama don't want you to have any bad dreams. They're happy and they want you to be happy. When you dream about them, it will always be happy dreams."

"Happy dreams."

"Everything is all right now, Thorby. You are starting to wake. You're waking up and you can't remember what we've been talking about. But you'll never have bad dreams again. Wake up, Thorby."

The boy sat up, rubbed his eyes, yawned, and grinned. "Gee, I fell asleep. Guess I played out on you, Pop. Didn't work, huh?"

"Everything's all right, Thorby."

It took more than one session to lay those ghosts, but the nightmares dwindled and stopped. Baslim was not technician enough to remove the bad memories; they were still there. All he did was to implant suggestions to keep them from making Thorby unhappy. Nor would Baslim have removed memories had he been skilled enough; he had a stiff-necked belief that a man's experiences belonged to him and that even the worst should not be taken from him without his consent.

Thorby's days were as busy as his nights had become peaceful. During their early partnership Baslim kept the boy always with him. After breakfast they would hobble to the Plaza of Liberty, Baslim would sprawl on the pavement and Thorby would stand or squat beside him, looking starved and holding the bowl. The spot was always picked to obstruct foot traffic, but not enough to cause police to do more than growl. Thorby learned that none of the regular police in the Plaza would ever do more than growl; Baslim's arrangements with them were beneficial to underpaid police.

Thorby learned the ancient trade quickly—learned that men with women were generous but that the appeal should be made to the woman, that it was usually a waste of time to ask alms of unaccompanied women (except unveiled women), that it was an even bet between a kick and a gift in bracing a man alone, that spacemen hitting dirt gave handsomely. Baslim taught him to keep a little money in the bowl, neither smallest change nor high denominations.

At first Thorby was just right for the trade; small, half-starved, covered with sores, his appearance alone was enough. Unfortunately he soon looked better. Baslim repaired that with make-up, putting shadows under his eyes and hollows in his cheeks. A horrible plastic device stuck on his shinbone provided a realistic large "ulcer" in place of the sores he no longer had; sugar water made it attractive to flies—people looked away even as they dropped coins in the bowl.

His better-fed condition was not as easy to disguise but he shot up fast for a year or two and continued skinny, despite two hearty meals a day and a bed to doss on.

Thorby soaked up a gutter education beyond price. Jubbulpore, capital of Jubbul and of the Nine Worlds, residence in chief of the Great Sargon, boasts more than three thousand licensed beggars, twice that number of street vendors, more grog shops than temples and more temples than any other city in the Nine Worlds, plus numbers uncountable of sneak thieves, tattoo artists, griva pushers, doxies, cat burglars, back-alley money changers, pickpockets, fortune tellers, muggers, assassins, and grifters large and small. Its inhabitants brag that within a li of the pylon at the spaceport end of the Avenue of Nine anything in the explored universe can be had by a man with cash, from a starship to ten grains of stardust, from the ruin of a reputation to the robes of a senator with the senator inside.

Technically Thorby was not part of the underworld, since he had a legally recognized status (slave) and a licensed profession (beggar). Nevertheless he was in it, with a worm's-eye view. There were no rungs below his on the social ladder.

As a slave he had learned to lie and steal as naturally as other children learn company manners, and much more quickly. But he discovered that these common talents were raised to high art in the seamy underside of the city. As he grew older, learned the language and the streets, Baslim began to send him out on his own, to run errands, to shop for food, and sometimes to make a pitch by himself while the old man stayed in. Thus he "fell into evil company" if one can fall from elevation zero.

He returned one day with nothing in his bowl. Baslim made no comment but the boy explained. "Look, Pop, I did all right!" From under his clout he drew a fancy scarf and proudly displayed it.

Baslim did not smile and did not touch it. "Where did you get that?"

"I inherited it!"

"Obviously. But from whom?"

"A lady. A nice lady, pretty."

"Let me see the house mark. Mmm . . . probably Lady Fascia. Yes, she is pretty, I suppose. But why aren't you in jail?"

"Why, gee, Pop, it was easy! Ziggie has been teaching me. He knows all the tricks. He's smooth—you should see him work."

Baslim wondered how one taught morals to a stray kitten? He did not consider discussing it in abstract ethical terms; there was nothing in the boy's background, nothing in his present environment, to make it possible to communicate on such a level.

"Thorby, why do you want to change trades? In our business you pay the police their commission, pay your dues to the guild, make an offering at the temple on holy day, and you've no worries. Have we ever gone hungry?"

"No, Pop—but look at it! It must have cost almost a stellar!"

"At least two stellars, I'd say. But a fence would give you two minims—if he was feeling generous. You should have brought more than that back in your bowl."

"Well . . . I'll get better at it. And it's more fun than begging. You ought to see how Ziggie goes about it."

"I've seen Ziggie work. He's skillful."

"He's the best!"

"Still, I suppose he could do better with two hands."

"Well, maybe, though you only use one hand. But he's teaching me to use either hand."

"That's good. You might need to know—some day you might find yourself short one, the way Ziggie is. You know how Ziggie lost his hand?"

"Huh?"

"You know the penalty? If they catch you?"

Thorby did not answer. Baslim went on, "One hand for the first offense—that's what it cost Ziggie to learn his trade. Oh, he's good, for he's still around and plying his trade. You know what the second offense carries? Not just the other hand. You know?"

Thorby gulped. "I'm not sure."

"I think you must have heard; you don't want to remember." Baslim drew his thumb across his throat. "That's what Ziggie gets next time—they shorten him. His Serenity's justices figure that a boy who can't learn once won't learn twice, so they shorten him."

"But, Pop, I won't be caught! I'll be awful careful . . . just like today. I promise!"

Baslim sighed. The kid still believed that it couldn't happen to him. "Thorby, get your bill of sale."

"What for, Pop?"

"Get it."

The boy fetched it; Baslim examined it—"one male child, registered number (left thigh) 8XK40367"—nine minims and get out of here, you! He looked at Thorby and noted with surprise that he was a head taller than he had been that day. "Get my stylus. I'm going to free you. I've always meant to, but there didn't seem to be any hurry. But we'll do it now and tomorrow you go to the Royal Archives and register it."

Thorby's jaw dropped. "What for, Pop?"

"Don't you want to be free?"

"Uh . . . well . . . Pop, I *like* belonging to *you.*"

"Thanks, lad. But I've got to do it."

"You mean you're kicking me out?"

"No. You can stay. But only as a freedman. You see, son, a master is responsible for his bondservant. If I were a noble and you did something, I'd be fined. But since I'm not . . . well, if I were shy a hand, as well as a leg and an eye, I don't think I could manage. So if you're going to learn Ziggie's trade, I had better free you; I can't afford the risk. You'll have to take your own chances; I've lost too much already. Any more and I'd be better off shortened."

He put it brutally, never mentioning that the law in application was rarely so severe—in practice, the slave was confiscated, sold, and his price used in restitution, if the master had no assets. If the master were a commoner, he might also get a flogging if the judge believed him to be actually as well as legally responsible for the slave's misdeed. Nevertheless Baslim had stated the law: since a master exercised high and low justice over a slave, he was therefore liable in his own person for his slave's acts, even to capital punishment.

Thorby started to sob, for the first time since the beginning of their relationship. "Don't turn me loose, Pop—please don't! I've *got* to belong to you."

"I'm sorry, son. I told you you don't have to go away."

"*Please,* Pop. I won't ever swipe another thing!"

Baslim took his shoulder. "Look at me, Thorby. I'll make you a bargain."

"Huh? Anything you say, Pop. As long as—"

"Wait till you hear it. I won't sign your papers now. But I want you to promise two things."

"Huh? Sure! What?"

"Don't rush. The first is that you promise never again to steal anything, from anybody. Neither from fine ladies in sedan chairs, nor from poor people like ourselves—one is too dangerous and the other . . . well, it's disgraceful, though I don't expect you know what that means. The second is to promise that you will never lie to me about anything . . . *not anything*."

Thorby said slowly, "I promise."

"I don't mean just lying about the money you've been holding out on me, either. I mean *anything*. By the way, a mattress is no place to hide money. Look at me, Thorby. You know I have connections throughout the city."

Thorby nodded. He had delivered messages for the old man to odd places and unlikely people. Baslim went on, "If you steal, I'll find out . . . eventually. If you lie to me, I'll catch you . . . eventually. Lying to other people is your business, but I tell you this: once a man gets a reputation as a liar, he might as well be struck dumb, for people do not listen to the wind. Never mind. The day I learn that you have stolen anything . . . or the day I catch you lying to me . . . I sign your papers and free you."

"Yes, Pop."

"That's not all. I'll kick you out with what you had when I bought you—a breechclout and a set of bruises. You and I will be finished. If I set eyes on you again, I'll spit on your shadow."

"Yes, Pop. Oh, I never will, Pop!"

"I hope not. Go to bed."

Baslim lay awake, worrying, wondering if he had been too harsh. But, confound it, it was a harsh world; he had to teach the kid to live in it.

He heard a sound like a rodent gnawing; he held still and listened. Presently he heard the boy get up quietly and go to the table; there followed a muted jingle of coins being placed on wood and he heard the boy return to his pallet.

When the boy started to snore he was able to drop off to sleep himself.

3

BASLIM HAD LONG SINCE TAUGHT THORBY TO READ AND WRITE Sargonese and Interlingua, encouraging him with cuffs and other inducements since Thorby's interest in matters intellectual approached zero. But the incident involving Ziggie and the realization that Thorby was growing up reminded Baslim that time did not stand still, not with kids.

Thorby was never able to place the time when he realized that Pop was not exactly (or not entirely) a beggar. The extremely rigorous instruction he now received, expedited by such unlikely aids as a recorder, a projector, and a sleep instructor, would have told him, but by then nothing Pop could do or say surprised him—Pop knew everything and could manage anything. Thorby had acquired enough knowledge of other beggars to see discrepancies; he was not troubled by them—Pop was Pop, like the sun and the rain.

They never mentioned outside their home anything that happened inside, nor even where it was; no guest was ever there. Thorby acquired friends and Baslim had dozens or even hundreds and seemed to know the whole city by sight. No one but Thorby had access to Baslim's hideaway. But Thorby was aware that Pop had activities unconnected with begging. One night they went to sleep as usual; Thorby awakened about dawn to hear someone stirring and called out sleepily, "Pop?"

"Yes. Go back to sleep."

Instead the boy got up and switched on the glow plates. He knew it was hard for Baslim to get around in the dark without his leg; if Pop wanted a drink of water or anything, he'd fetch it. "You all right, Pop?" he asked, turning away from the switch.

Then he gasped in utter shock. This was a stranger, a *gentleman!*

"It's all right, Thorby," the stranger said with Pop's voice. "Take it easy, son."

"Pop?"

"Yes, son. I'm sorry I startled you—I should have changed before I came back. Events pushed me." He started stripping off fine clothing.

When Baslim removed the evening head dress, he looked more like Pop . . . except for one thing. "Pop . . . your eye."

"Oh, that. It comes out as easily as it went in. I look better with two eyes, don't I?"

"I don't know." Thorby stared at it worriedly. "I don't think I like it."

"So? Well, you won't often see me wear it. As long as you are awake you can help."

Thorby was not much help; everything Pop did was new to him. First Baslim dug tanks and trays from a food cupboard which appeared to have an extra door in its back. Then he removed the false eye and, handling it with great care, unscrewed it into two parts and removed a tiny cylinder, using tweezers.

Thorby watched the processing that followed but did not understand, except that he could see that Pop was working with extreme care and exact timing. At last Baslim said, "All done. Now we'll see if I got any pictures."

Baslim inserted the spool in a microviewer, scanned it, smiled grimly and said, "Get ready to go out. Skip breakfast. You can take along a piece of bread."

"Huh?"

"Get moving. No time to waste."

Thorby put on his make-up and clout and dirtied his face. Baslim was waiting with a photograph and a small flat cylinder about the size of a half-minim bit. He shoved the photo at Thorby. "Look at it. Memorize it."

"Why?"

Baslim pulled it back. "Would you recognize that man?"

"Uh . . . let me see it again."

"You've *got* to know him. Look at it well this time."

Thorby did so, then said, "All right, I'll know him."

"He'll be in one of the taprooms near the port. Try Mother Shaum's first, then the Supernova and the Veiled Virgin. If you don't hit, work both sides of Joy Street until you do. You've *got* to find him before the third hour."

"I'll find him, Pop."

"When you do, put this thing in your bowl along with a few coins.

Then tell him the tale but be sure to mention that you are the son of Baslim the Cripple."

"Got it, Pop."

"Get going."

Thorby wasted no time getting down to the port. It was the morning following the Feast of the Ninth Moon and few were stirring; he did not bother to pretend to beg en route, he simply went the most direct way, through back courts, over fences, or down streets, avoiding only the sleepy night patrol. But, though he reached the neighborhood quickly, he had the Old One's luck in finding his man; he was in none of the dives Baslim had suggested, nor did the rest of Joy Street turn him up. It was pushing the deadline and Thorby was getting worried when he saw the man come out of a place he had already tried.

Thorby ducked across the street, came up behind him. The man was with another man—not good. But Thorby started in:

"Alms, gentle lords! Alms for mercy on your souls!"

The wrong man tossed him a coin; Thorby caught it in his teeth. "Bless you, my lord!" He turned to the other. "Alms, gentle sir. A small gift for the unfortunate. I am the son of Baslim the Cripple and—"

The first man aimed a kick at him. "Get out."

Thorby rolled away from it. "—son of Baslim the Cripple. Poor old Baslim needs soft foods and medicines. I am all alone—"

The man of the picture reached for his purse. "Don't do it," his companion advised. "They're all liars and I've paid him to let us alone."

" 'Luck for the jump,' " the man answered. "Now let me see . . ." He fumbled in his purse, glanced into the bowl, placed something in it.

"Thank you, my lords. May your children be sons." Thorby moved on before he looked. The tiny flat cylinder was gone.

He worked on up Joy Street, doing fairly well, and checked the Plaza before heading home. To his surprise Pop was in his favorite pitch, by the auction block and facing the port. Thorby slipped down beside him. "Done."

The old man grunted.

"Why don't you go home, Pop? You must be tired. I've made us a few bits already."

"Shut up. Alms, my lady! Alms for a poor cripple."

At the third hour a ship took off with a *whoosh!* that doppplered away into subsonics; the old man seemed to relax. "What ship was that?" Thorby asked. "Not the Syndon liner."

"Free Trader *Romany Lass,* bound for the Rim . . . and your friend was in her. You go home now and get your breakfast. No, go buy your breakfast, for a treat."

Baslim no longer tried to hide his extraprofessional activities from Thorby, although he never explained the why or how. Some days only one of them would beg, in which case the Plaza of Liberty was always the pitch, for it appeared that Baslim was especially interested in arrivals and departures of ships and most especially movements of slave ships and the auction that always followed the arrival of one.

Thorby was more use to him after his education had progressed. The old man seemed to think that everyone had a perfect memory and he was stubborn enough to impress his belief despite the boy's grumbles.

"Aw, Pop, how do you expect me to remember? You didn't give me a chance to *look* at it!"

"I projected that page at least three seconds. Why didn't you read it?"

"Huh? There wasn't time."

"I read it. You can, too. Thorby, you've seen jugglers in the Plaza. You've seen old Mikki stand on his head and keep nine daggers in the air while he spins four hoops with his feet?"

"Uh, sure."

"Can you do that?"

"No."

"Could you learn to?"

"Uh . . . I don't know."

"*Anyone* can learn to juggle . . . with enough practice and enough beatings." The old man picked up a spoon, a stylus, and a knife and kept them in the air in a simple fountain. Presently he missed and stopped. "I used to do a little, just for fun. This is juggling with the mind . . . and anyone can learn *it,* too."

"Show me how you did that, Pop."

"Another time, if you behave yourself. Right now you are learning to use your eyes. Thorby, this mind-juggling was developed a long time ago by a wise man, a Doctor Renshaw, on the planet Earth. You've heard of Earth."

"Well . . . sure, I've heard of it."

"Mmm . . . meaning you don't believe in it?"

"Uh, I don't know . . . but all that stuff about frozen water falling from the sky, and cannibals ten feet tall, and towers higher than the Praesidium, and little men no bigger than dolls that live in trees—well, I'm not a fool, Pop."

Baslim sighed and wondered how many thousands of times he had sighed since saddling himself with a son. "Stories get mixed up. Someday—when you've learned to read—I'll let you view books you can trust."

"But I can read now."

"You just think you can. Thorby, there is such a place as Earth and it truly is strange and wonderful—a most unlikely planet. Many wise men have lived and died there—along with the usual proportion of fools and villains—and some of their wisdom has come down to us. Samuel Renshaw was one such wise man. He proved that most people go all their lives only half awake; more than that, he showed how a man could wake up and live—see with his eyes, hear with his ears, taste with his tongue, think with his mind, and remember perfectly what he saw, heard, tasted, thought." The old man shoved his stump out. "This doesn't make me a cripple. I see more with my one eye than you do with two. I am growing deaf . . . but not as deaf as you are, because what I hear, I remember. Which one of us is the cripple? But, son, you aren't going to stay crippled, for I am going to renshaw you if I have to beat your silly head in!"

As Thorby learned to use his mind, he found that he liked to; he developed an insatiable appetite for the printed page, until, night after night, Baslim would order him to turn off the viewer and go to bed. Thorby didn't see any use in much of what the old man forced him to learn—languages, for example, that Thorby had never heard. But they were not hard, with his new skill in using his mind, and when he discovered that the old man had spools and reels which could be read or listened to only in these "useless" tongues, he suddenly found them worth knowing. History and galactography he loved; his personal world, light-years wide in physical space, had been in reality as narrow as a slave factor's pen. Thorby reached for wider horizons with the delight of a baby discovering its fist.

But mathematics Thorby saw no use in, other than the barbaric skill of counting money. But presently he learned that mathematics need not have use; it was a game, like chess but more fun.

The old man wondered sometimes what use it all was? That the boy was even brighter than he had thought, he now knew. But was it fair to the boy? Was he simply teaching him to be discontented with his lot? What chance on Jubbul had the slave of a beggar? Zero raised to the *n*th power remained zero.

"Thorby."

"Yeah, Pop. Just a moment, I'm in the middle of a chapter."

"Finish it later. I want to talk with you."

"Yes, my lord. Yes, master. Right away, boss."

"And keep a civil tongue in your head."

"Sorry, Pop. What's on your mind?"

"Son, what are you going to do when I'm dead?"

Thorby looked stricken. "Are you feeling bad, Pop?"

"No. So far as I know, I'll last for years. On the other hand, I may not wake up tomorrow. At my age you never know. If I don't, what are you going to do? Hold down my pitch in the Plaza?"

Thorby didn't answer; Baslim went on, "You can't and we both know it. You're already so big that you can't tell the tale convincingly. They don't give the way they did when you were little."

Thorby said slowly, "I haven't meant to be a burden, Pop."

"Have I complained?"

"No." Thorby hesitated. "I've thought about it . . . some. Pop, you could hire me out to a labor company."

The old man made an angry gesture. "That's no answer! No, son, I'm going to send you away."

"Pop! You promised you wouldn't."

"I promised nothing."

"But I don't want to be freed, Pop. If you free me—well, if you do, I won't leave!"

"I didn't exactly mean that."

Thorby was silent for a long moment. "You're going to sell me, Pop?"

"Not exactly. Well . . . yes and no."

Thorby's face held no expression. At last he said quietly, "It's one or the other, so I know what you mean . . . and I guess I oughtn't to kick. It's your privilege and you've been the best . . . master . . . I ever had."

"I'm not your master!"

"Paper says you are. Matches the number on my leg."

"Don't talk that way! Don't *ever* talk that way."

"A slave had better talk that way, or else keep his mouth shut."

"Then, for Heaven's sake, keep it shut! Listen, son, let me explain. There's nothing here for you and we both know it. If I die without freeing you, you revert to the Sargon—"

"They'll have to catch me!"

"They will. But manumission solves nothing. What guilds are open to freedmen? Begging, yes—but you'd have to poke out your eyes to do well at it, after you're grown. Most freedmen work for their former masters, as you know, for the free-born commoners leave mighty slim pickings. They resent an ex-slave; they won't work with him."

"Don't worry, Pop. I'll get by."

"I do worry. Now you listen. I'm going to arrange to sell you to a man I know, who will ship you away from here. Not a slave ship, just a ship. But instead of shipping you where the bill of lading reads, you'll—"

"No!"

"Hold your tongue. You'll be dropped on a planet where slavery is against the law. I can't tell you which one, because I am not sure of the ship's schedule, nor even what ship; the details have to be worked out. But in any free society I have confidence you can get by." Baslim stopped to mull a thought he had had many times. Should he send the kid to Baslim's own native planet? No, not only would it be extremely difficult to arrange but it was not a place to send a green immigrant . . . get the lad to any frontier world, where a sharp brain and willingness to work were all a man needed; there were several within trading distance of the Nine Worlds. He wished tiredly that there were some way of knowing the boy's own home world. Possibly he had relatives there, people who would help him. Confound it, there ought to be a galaxy-wide method of identification!

Baslim went on, "That's the best I can do. You'll have to behave as a slave between the sale and being shipped out. But what's a few weeks against a chance—"

"No!"

"Don't be foolish, son."

"Maybe I am. But I won't do it. I'm staying."

"So? Son . . . I hate to remind you—but you can't stop me."

"Huh?"

"As you pointed out, there's a paper that says I can."

"Oh."

"Go to bed, son."

Baslim did not sleep. About two hours after they had put out the light he heard Thorby get up very quietly. He could follow every move the lad made by interpreting muffled sounds. Thorby dressed (a simple matter of wrapping his clout), he went into the adjoining room, fumbled in the bread safe, drank deeply, and left. He did not take his bowl; he did not go near the shelf where it was kept.

After he was gone, Baslim turned over and tried to sleep, but the ache inside him would not permit. It had not occurred to him to speak the word that would keep the boy; he had too much self-respect not to respect another person's decision.

Thorby was gone four days. He returned in the night and Baslim heard him but again said nothing. Instead he went quietly and deeply asleep for the first time since Thorby had left. But he woke at the usual time and said, "Good morning, son."

"Uh, good morning, Pop."

"Get breakfast started. I have something to attend to."

They sat down presently over bowls of hot mush. Baslim ate with his usual careful disinterest; Thorby merely picked at his. Finally he blurted out, "Pop, when are you going to sell me?"

"I'm not."

"Huh?"

"I registered your manumission at the Archives the day you left. You're a free man, Thorby."

Thorby looked startled, then dropped his eyes to his food. He busied himself building little mountains of mush that slumped as soon as he shaped them. Finally he said, "I wish you hadn't."

"If they picked you up, I didn't want you to have 'escaped slave' against you."

"Oh." Thorby looked thoughtful. "That's 'F&B,' isn't it? Thanks, Pop. I guess I acted kind of silly."

"Possibly. But it wasn't the punishment I was thinking of. Flogging is over quickly, and so is branding. I was thinking of a possible second offense. It's better to be shortened than to be caught again after a branding."

Thorby abandoned his mush entirely. "Pop? Just what does a lobotomy do to you?"

"Mmm . . . you might say it makes the thorium mines endurable. But let's not go into it, not at meal times. Speaking of such, if you are through, get your bowl and let's not dally. There's an auction this morning."

"You mean I can stay?"

"This is your home."

Baslim never again suggested that Thorby leave him. Manumission made no difference in their routine or relationship. Thorby did go to the Royal Archives, paid the fee and the customary gift and had a line tattooed through his serial number, the Sargon's seal tattooed beside it with book and page number of the record which declared him to be a free subject of the Sargon, entitled to taxes, military service, and starvation without let or hindrance. The clerk who did the tattooing looked at Thorby's serial number and said, "Doesn't look like a birthday job, kid. Your old man go bankrupt? Or did your folks sell you just to get shut of you?"

"None of your business!"

"Don't get smart, kid, or you'll find that this needle can hurt even more. Now give me a civil answer. I see it's a factor's mark, not a private owner's, and from the way it has spread and faded, you were maybe five or six. When and where was it?"

"I don't know. Honest I don't."

"So? That's what I tell my wife when she asks personal questions. Quit wiggling; I'm almost through. There . . . congratulations and welcome to the ranks of free men. I've been free a parcel of years now and I predict that you will find it looser but not always more comfortable."

4

THORBY'S LEG HURT FOR A COUPLE OF DAYS; OTHERWISE MANUMISSION left his life unchanged. But he really was becoming inefficient as a beggar; a strong healthy youth does not draw the alms that a skinny child can. Often Baslim would have Thorby place him on his pitch, then send him on errands or tell him to go home and study. However, one or the other was always in the Plaza. Baslim sometimes disappeared, with or without warning; when this happened it was Thorby's duty to spend daylight hours on the pitch, noting arrivals and departures, keeping mental notes of slave auctions, and picking up information about both traffics through contacts around the port, in the wineshops, and among the unveiled women.

Once Baslim was gone for a double nineday; he was simply missing when Thorby woke up. It was much longer than he had ever been away before; Thorby kept telling himself that Pop could look out for himself, while having visions of the old man dead in a gutter. But he kept track of the doings at the Plaza, including three auctions, and recorded everything that he had seen and had been able to pick up.

Then Baslim returned. His only comment was, "Why didn't you memorize it instead of recording?"

"Well, I did. But I was afraid I would forget something, there was so much."

"Hummph!"

After that Baslim seemed even quieter, more reserved, than he had always been. Thorby wondered if he had displeased him, but it was not the sort of question Baslim answered. Finally one night the old man said, "Son, we never did settle what you are to do after I'm gone."

"Huh? But I thought we had decided that, Pop. It's my problem."

"No, I simply postponed it . . . because of your thickheaded stubbornness. But I can't wait any longer. I've got orders for you and you are going to carry them out."

"Now, wait a minute, Pop! If you think you can bully me into leaving you—"

"Shut up! I said, 'After I'm gone.' When I'm dead, I mean; not one of these little business trips . . . you are to look up a man and give him a message. Can I depend on you? Not goof off and forget it?"

"Why, of course, Pop. But I don't like to hear you talk that way. You're going to live a long time—you might even outlive me."

"Possibly. But will you shut up and listen, then do as I tell you?"

"Yes, sir."

"You'll find this man—it may take a while—and deliver this message. Then he will have something for you to do . . . I think. If he does, I want you to do exactly what he tells you to. Will you do that also?"

"Why, of course, Pop, if that's what you want."

"Count it as one last favor to an old man who tried to do right by you and would have done better had he been able. It's the very last thing I want from you, son. Don't bother to burn an offering for me at the temple, just do these two things: deliver a message and one more thing, whatever the man suggests that you do."

"I will, Pop," Thorby answered solemnly.

"All right. Let's get busy."

The "man" turned out to be any one of five men. Each was skipper of a starship, a tramp trader, not of the Nine Worlds but occasionally picking up cargoes from ports of the Nine Worlds. Thorby thought over the list. "Pop, there's only one of these ships I recall ever putting down here."

"They all have, one time or another."

"It might be a long time before one showed up."

"It might be years. But when it happens, I want the message delivered exactly."

"To any of them? Or all of them?"

"The first one who shows up."

The message was short but not easy, for it was in three languages, depending on who was to receive it, and none of the languages was among those Thorby knew. Nor did Baslim explain the words; he wanted it learned by rote in all three.

After Thorby had stumbled through the first version of the message for the seventh time Baslim covered his ears. "No, no! It won't do, son. That accent!"

"I'm doing my best," Thorby answered sullenly.

"I know. But I want the message understood. See here, do you remember a time when I made you sleepy and talked to you?"

"Huh? I get sleepy every night. I'm sleepy now."

"So much the better." Baslim put him into a light trance—with difficulty as Thorby was not as receptive as he had been as a child. But Baslim managed it, recorded the message in the sleep instructor, set it running and let Thorby listen, with post-hypnotic suggestion that he would be able to say it perfectly when he awakened.

He was able to. The second and third versions were implanted in him the following night. Baslim tested him repeatedly thereafter, using the name of a skipper and a ship to bring each version forth.

Baslim never sent Thorby out of the city; a slave required a travel permit and even a freedman was required to check in and out. But he did send him all over the metropolis. Three ninedays after Thorby had learned the messages Baslim gave him a note to deliver in the shipyard area, which was a reserve of the Sargon rather than part of the city. "Carry your freedman's tag and leave your bowl behind. If a policeman stops you, tell him you're looking for work in the yards."

"He'll think I'm crazy."

"But he'll let you through. They do use freedmen, as sweepers and such. Carry the message in your mouth. Who are you looking for?"

"A short, red-haired man," Thorby repeated, "with a big wart on the left side of his nose. He runs a lunch stand across from the main gate. No beard. I'm to buy a meat pie and slip him the message with the money."

"Right."

Thorby enjoyed the outing. He did not wonder why Pop didn't viewphone messages instead of sending him a half day's journey; people of their class did not use such luxuries. As for the royal mails, Thorby had never sent or received a letter and would have regarded the mails as a most chancy way to send a note.

His route followed one arc of the spaceport through the factory district. He relished that part of the city; there was always so much going on, so much life and noise. He dodged traffic, with truck drivers cursing him and Thorby answering with interest; he peered in each open door, wondering what all the machines were for and why commoners would stand all day in one place, doing the same thing over and over—or were they slaves? No, they couldn't be; slaves weren't allowed to touch power machinery except on plantations—that was what the riots had been about last year and the Sargon had lifted his hand in favor of the commoners.

Was it true that the Sargon never slept and that his eye could see anything in the Nine Worlds? Pop said that was nonsense, the Sargon was just a man, like anybody. But if so, how did he get to be Sargon?

He left the factories and skirted the shipyards. He had never been this far before. Several ships were in for overhaul and two small ships were being built, cradled in lacy patterns of steel. Ships made his heart lift and he wished he were going somewhere. He knew that he had traveled by starship twice—or was it three times?—but that was long ago and he didn't mean traveling in the hold of a slaver, that wasn't traveling!

He got so interested that he almost walked past the lunch stand. The main gate reminded him; it was twice as big as the others, had a guard on it, and a big sign curving over it with the seal of the Sargon on top. The lunch stand was across from it; Thorby dodged traffic pouring through the gate and went to it.

The man behind the counter was not the right man; what little hair he had was black and his nose had no wart.

Thorby walked up the road, killed a half-hour and came back. There was still no sign of his man. The counterman noticed the inspection, so Thorby stepped forward and said, "Do you have sunberry crush?"

The man looked him over. "Money?"

Thorby was used to being required to prove his solvency; he dug out the coin. The man scooped it up, opened a bottle for him. "Don't drink at the counter, I need the stools."

There were plenty of stools, but Thorby was not offended; he knew his social status. He stood back but not so far as to be accused of trying to abscond with the bottle, then made the drink last a long time. Customers came and went; he checked each, on the chance that the red-headed man might have picked this time to eat. He kept his ears cocked.

Presently the counterman looked up. "You trying to wear that bottle out?"

"Just through, thanks." Thorby came up to put the bottle down and said, "Last time I was over this way a red-headed chap was running this place."

The man looked at him. "You a friend of Red?"

"Well, not exactly. I just used to see him here, when I'd stop for a cold drink, or—"

"Let's see your permit."

"What? I don't need—" The man grabbed at Thorby's wrist. But Thorby's profession had made him adept at dodging kicks, cuffs, canes, and such; the man clutched air.

The man came around the counter, fast; Thorby ducked into traffic. He was halfway across the street and had had two narrow escapes before he realized that he was running toward the gate—and that the counterman was shouting for the guard there.

Thorby turned and started dodging traffic endwise. Fortunately it was dense; this road carried the burden of the yards. He racked up three more brushes with death, saw a side street that dead-ended into the throughway, ducked between two trucks, down the side street as fast as he could go, turned into the first alley, ran down it, hid behind an outbuilding and waited.

He heard no pursuit.

He had been chased many times before, it did not panic him. A chase was always two parts: first breaking contact, second the retiring action to divorce oneself from the incident. He had accomplished the first; now he had to get out of the neighborhood without being spotted—slow march and no suspicious moves. In losing himself he had run away from the city, turned left into the side street, turned left again into the alley; he was now almost behind the lunch stand—it had been a subconscious tactic. The chase always moved away from the center; the lunch stand was one place where they would not expect him to be. Thorby estimated that in five minutes, or ten, the counterman would be back at his job and the guard back at the gate; neither one could leave his post unwatched. Shortly, Thorby could go on through the alley and head home.

He looked around. The neighborhood was commercial land not yet occupied by factories, jumble of small shops, marginal businesses, hovels, and hopeless minor enterprise. He appeared to be in back of a very small hand laundry; there were poles and lines and wooden tubs and steam came out a pipe in the outbuilding. He knew his location now—two doors from the lunch stand; he recalled a homemade sign: "MAJESTIC HOME LAUNDRY—*Lowest Prices.*"

He could cut around this building and—but better check first. He dropped flat and stuck an eye around the corner of the outbuilding, sighted back down the alley.

Oh, oh!—two patrolmen moving up the alley . . . he had been wrong, wrong! They hadn't dropped the matter, they had sent out the alarm. He pulled back and looked around. The laundry? No. The outbuilding? The patrol would check it. Nothing but to run for it—right into the arms of another patrol. Thorby knew how fast the police could put a cordon around a district. Near the Plaza he could go through their nets, but here he was in strange terrain.

His eye lit on a worn-out washtub . . . then he was under it. It was a tight fit, with knees to his chin and splinters in his spine. He was afraid that his clout was sticking out but it was too late to correct it; he heard someone coming.

Footsteps came toward the tub and he stopped breathing. Someone stepped on the tub and stood on it.

"Hi there, mother!" It was a man's voice. "You been out here long?"

"Long enough. Mind that pole, you'll knock the clothes down."

"See anything of a boy?"

"What boy?"

"Youngster, getting man-tall. Fuzz on his chin. Breech clout, no sandals."

"Somebody," the woman's voice above him answered indifferently, "came running through here like his ghost was after him. I didn't really see him—I was trying to get this pesky line up."

"That's our baby! Where'd he go?"

"Over that fence and between those houses."

"Thanks, mother! Come on, Juby."

Thorby waited. The woman continued whatever she was doing; her feet moved and the tub creaked. Then she stepped down and sat on the tub. She slapped it gently. "Stay where you are," she said softly. A moment later he heard her go away.

Thorby waited until his bones ached. But he resigned himself to staying under that tub until dark. It would be chancy, as the night patrol questioned everyone but nobles after curfew, but leaving this neighborhood in daylight had become impossible. Thorby could not guess why he had been honored by a turn-out of the guard, but he did not want to find out. He heard someone—the woman?—moving around the yard from time to time.

At least an hour later he heard the creak of ungreased wheels. Someone tapped on the tub. "When I lift the tub, get into the cart, fast. It's right in front of you."

Thorby did not answer. Daylight hit his eyes, he saw a small pushcart—and was in it and trying to make himself small. Laundry landed on him. But before that blanked out his sight he saw that the tub was no longer nakedly in the open; sheets had been hung on lines so that it was screened.

Hands arranged bundles over him and a voice said, "Hold still until I tell you to move."

"Okay . . . and thanks a million! I'll pay you back someday."

"Forget it." She breathed heavily. "I had a man once. Now he's in the mines. I don't care what you've done—I don't turn anybody over to the patrol."

"Oh. I'm sorry."

"Shut up."

The little cart bumped and wobbled and presently Thorby felt the change to pavement. Occasionally they stopped; the woman would remove a bundle, be gone a few minutes, come back and dump dirty clothes into the cart. Thorby took it with the long patience of a beggar.

A long time later the cart left pavement. It stopped and the woman said in a low voice, "When I tell you, get out the righthand side and keep going. Make it fast."

"Okay. And thanks again!"

"Shut up." The cart bumped along a short distance, slowed without stopping, and she said, "Now!"

Thorby threw off his covering, bounced out and landed on his feet, all in one motion. He was facing a passage between two buildings, a serviceway from alley to street. He started down it fast but looked back over his shoulder.

The cart was just disappearing. He never did see her face.

Two hours later he was back in his own neighborhood. He slipped down beside Baslim. "No good."

"Why not?"

"Snoopies. Squads of 'em."

"Alms, gentle sir! You swallowed it? Alms for the sake of your parents!"

"Of course."

"Take the bowl." Baslim got to hands and knee, started away.

"Pop! Don't you want me to help you?"

"You stay here."

Thorby stayed, irked that Pop had not waited for a full report. He hurried home as soon as it was dark, found Baslim in the kitchen-washroom, paraphernalia spread around him and using both recorder and book projector. Thorby glanced at the displayed page, saw that he could not read it and wondered what language it was—an odd one; the words were all seven letters, no more, no less. "Hi, Pop. Shall I start supper?"

"No room . . . and no time. Eat some bread. What happened today?"

Thorby told him, while munching bread. Baslim simply nodded. "Lie down. I've got to use hypnosis on you again. We've got a long night ahead."

The material Baslim wanted him to memorize consisted of figures, dates, and endless three-syllable nonsense words. The light trance felt dreamily pleasant and the droning of Baslim's voice coming out of the recorder was pleasant, too.

During one of the breaks, when Baslim had commanded him to wake up, he said, "Pop, who's this message for?"

"If you ever get a chance to deliver it, you'll know; you won't have any doubts. If you have trouble remembering it, tell him to put you into a light trance; it'll come back."

"Tell whom?"

"Him. Never mind. You are going to sleep. You are asleep." Baslim snapped his fingers.

While the recorder was droning Thorby was vaguely aware once that Baslim had just come in. He was wearing his false leg, which affected Thorby with dreamy surprise; Pop ordinarily wore it only indoors. Once Thorby smelled smoke and thought dimly that something must be burning in the kitchen and he should go check. But he was unable to move and the nonsense words kept droning into his ears.

He became aware that he was droning back to Pop the lesson he had learned. "Did I get it right?"

"Yes. Now go to sleep. Sleep the rest of the night."

Baslim was gone in the morning. Thorby was not surprised; Pop's movements had been even less predictable than usual lately. He ate breakfast, took his bowl and set out for the Plaza. Business was poor—Pop was right; Thorby now looked too healthy and well fed for the profession. Maybe he would have to learn to dislocate his joints like Granny the Snake. Or buy contact lenses with cataracts built into them.

Midafternoon an unscheduled freighter grounded at the port. Thorby started the usual inquiries, found that it was the Free Trader *Sisu,* registered home port New Finlandia, Shiva III.

Ordinarily this would have been a minor datum, to be reported to Pop when he saw him. But Captain Krausa of the *Sisu* was one of the five persons to whom Thorby was someday to deliver a message, if and when.

It fretted Thorby. He knew that he was not to look up Captain Krausa—that was the distant future, for Pop was alive and well. But maybe Pop would be anxious to know that this ship had arrived. Tramp freighters came and went, nobody knew when, and sometimes they were in port only a few hours.

Thorby told himself that he could get home in five minutes—and Pop might thank him. At worst he would bawl him out for leaving the Plaza, but, shucks, he could pick up anything he missed, through gossip.

Thorby left.

The ruins of the old amphitheater extend around one third of the periphery of the new. A dozen holes lead down into the labyrinth which had served the old slave barracks; an unlimited number of routes ran underground from these informal entrances to that part which Baslim had preempted as a home. Thorby and he varied their route in random fashion and avoided being seen entering or leaving.

This time, being in a hurry, Thorby went to the nearest—and on past; there was a policeman at it. He continued as if his destination had been a tiny greengrocer's booth on the street rimming the ruins. He stopped and spoke to the proprietress. "Howdy, Inga. Got a nice ripe melon you're going to have to throw away?"

"No melons."

He displayed money. "How about that big one? Half price and I won't notice the rotten spot." He leaned closer. "What's burning?"

Her eyes flicked toward the patrolman. "Get lost."

"Raid?"

"Get lost, I said."

Thorby dropped a coin on the counter, picked up a bell-fruit and walked away, sucking the juice. He did not hurry.

A cautious reconnaissance showed him that police were staked out all through the ruins. At one entrance a group of ragged troglodytes huddled sadly under the eye of a patrolman. Baslim had estimated that at least five hundred people lived in the underground ruins. Thorby had not quite believed it, as he had rarely seen anyone else enter or heard them inside. He recognized only two faces among the prisoners.

A half-hour later and more worried every minute Thorby located an entrance which the police did not seem to know. He scanned it for several minutes, then darted from behind a screen of weeds and was down it. Once inside he got quickly into total darkness, then moved cautiously, listening. The police were supposed to have spectacles which let them see in the dark. Thorby wasn't sure this was true as he had always found darkness helpful in evading them. But he took no chances.

There were indeed police down below; he heard two of them and saw them by hand torches they carried—if snoopies could see in the dark these two did not seem equipped for it. They were obviously searching, stun guns drawn. But they were in strange territory whereas Thorby was playing his home field. A specialized speleologist, he knew these corridors the way his tongue knew his teeth; he had been finding his way through them in utter blackness twice a day for years.

At the moment they had him trapped; he kept just far enough ahead to avoid their torches, skirted a hole that reached down into the next level, went beyond it, ducked into a doorway and waited.

They reached the hole, eyed the narrow ledge Thorby had taken so casually in the dark, and one of them said, "We need a ladder."

"Oh, we'll find stairs or a chute." They turned back. Thorby waited, then went back and down the hole.

A few minutes later he was close to his home doorway. He looked and listened and sniffed and waited until he was certain that no one was close, then crept to the door and reached for the thumbhole in the lock. Even as he reached he knew that something was wrong.

The door was gone; there was just a hole.

He froze, straining every sense. There was an odor of strangers but it wasn't fresh and there was no sound of breathing. The only sound was a faint drip-drip in the kitchen.

Thorby decided that he just had to see. He looked behind him, saw no glimmer, reached inside for the light switch and turned it to "dim."

Nothing happened. He tried the switch in all positions, still no light. He went inside, avoided something cluttering Baslim's neat living room, on into the kitchen, and reached for candles. They were not where they belonged but his hand encountered one nearby; he found the match safe and lit the candle.

Ruin and wreckage!

Most of the damage seemed the sort that results from a search which takes no account of cost, aiming solely at speed and thoroughness. Every cupboard, every shelf had been spilled, food dumped on the floor. In the large room the mattresses had been ripped open, stuffing spilled out. But some of it looked like vandalism, unnecessary, pointless.

Thorby looked around with tears welling up and his chin quivering. But when he found, near the door, Pop's false leg, lying dead on the floor with its mechanical perfection smashed as if trampled by boots, he broke into sobs and had to put the candle down to keep from dropping it. He picked up the shattered leg, held it like a doll, sank to the floor and cradled it, rocking back and forth and moaning.

5

THORBY SPENT THE NEXT SEVERAL HOURS IN THE BLACK CORRIDORS outside their ruined home, near the first branching, where he would hear Pop if he came back but where Thorby would have a chance to duck if police showed up.

He caught himself dozing, woke with a start, and decided that he had to find out what time it was; it seemed as if he had been keeping vigil a week. He went back into their home, found a candle and lit it. But their only clock, a household "Eternal," was smashed. No doubt the radioactive capsule was still reckoning eternity but the works were mute. Thorby looked at it and forced himself to think in practical terms.

If Pop were free, he would come back. But the police had taken Pop away. Would they simply question him and turn him loose?

No, they would not. So far as Thorby knew, Pop had never done anything to harm the Sargon—but he had known for a long time that Pop was not simply a harmless old beggar. Thorby did not know why Pop had done the many things which did not fit the idea of "harmless old beggar" but it was clear that the police knew or suspected. About once a year the police had "cleaned out" the ruins by dropping a few retch-gas bombs down the more conspicuous holes; it simply meant having to sleep somewhere else for a couple of nights. But this was a raid in force. They had intended to arrest Pop and they had been searching for something.

The Sargon's police operated on a concept older than justice; they assumed that a man was guilty, they questioned him by increasingly strong methods until he talked . . . methods so notorious that an arrested person was usually anxious to tell all before questioning started. But

Thorby was certain that the police would get nothing out of Pop which the old man did not wish to admit.

Therefore the questioning would go on a long time.

They were probably working on Pop this very minute. Thorby's stomach turned over.

He had to get Pop away from them.

How? How does a moth attack the Praesidium? Thorby's chances were not much better. Baslim might be in a back room of the district police barracks, the logical place for a petty prisoner. But Thorby had an unreasoned conviction that Pop was not a petty prisoner . . . in which case he might be anywhere, even in the bowels of the Praesidium.

Thorby could go to the district police office and ask where his patron had been taken—but such was the respect in which the Sargon's police were held that this solution did not occur to him; had he presented himself as next of kin of a prisoner undergoing interrogation Thorby would have found himself in another closed room being interviewed by the same forceful means as a check on the answers (or lack of them) which were being wrung out of Baslim.

Thorby was not a coward; he simply knew that one does not dip water with a knife. Whatever he did for Pop would have to be done indirectly. He could not demand his "rights" because he had none; the idea never entered his head. Bribery was possible—for a man with a poke full of stellars. Thorby had less than two minims. Stealth was all that was left and for that he needed information.

He reached this conclusion as soon as he admitted that there was no reasonable chance that the police would turn Pop loose. But, on the wild chance that Baslim might talk his way free, Thorby wrote a note, telling Pop that he would check back the next day, and left it on a shelf they used as a mail drop. Then he left.

It was night when he stuck his head above ground. He could not decide whether he had been down in the ruins for half a day or a day and a half. It forced him to change plans; he had intended to go first to Inga the greengrocer and find out what she knew. But at least there were no police around now; he could move freely as long as he evaded the night patrol. But where? Who could, or would, give him information?

Thorby had dozens of friends and knew hundreds by sight. But his acquaintances were subject to curfew; he saw them only in daylight and in most cases did not know where they slept. But there was one neighborhood which was not under curfew; Joy Street and its several adjoining courts never closed. In the name of commerce and for the accommodation of visiting spacemen taprooms and gaming halls and other places of hospitality to strangers in that area near the spaceport never closed their doors. A commoner, even a freedman, might stay up all night there, although he could not leave between curfew and dawn without risking being picked up.

This risk did not bother Thorby; he did not intend to be seen and, although it was patrolled inside, he knew the habits of the police there. They traveled in pairs and stayed on lighted streets, leaving their beats only to suppress noisy forms of lawbreaking. But the virtue of the district, for Thorby's purpose, was that the gossip there was often hours ahead of the news as well as covering matters ignored or suppressed by licensed news services.

Someone on Joy Street would know what had happened to Pop.

Thorby got into the honky-tonk neighborhood by scrambling over roof tops. He went down a drain into a dark court, moved along it to Joy Street, stopped short of the street lights, looked up and down for police and tried to spot someone he knew. There were many people about but most of them were strangers on the town. Thorby knew every proprietor and almost every employee up and down the street but he hesitated to walk into one of the joints; he might walk into the arms of police. He wanted to spot someone he trusted, whom he could motion into the darkness of the court.

No police but no friendly faces, either—just a moment; there was Auntie Singham.

Of the many fortunetellers who worked Joy Street Auntie Singham was the best; she never purveyed anything but good fortune. If these things failed to come to pass, no customer ever complained; Auntie's warm voice carried conviction. Some whispered that she improved her own fortunes by passing information to the police, but Thorby did not believe it because Pop did not. She was a likely source of news and Thorby decided to chance it—the most she could tell the police was that he was alive and on the loose . . . which they knew.

Around the corner to Thorby's right was the Port of Heaven cabaret; Auntie was spreading her rug on the pavement there, anticipating customers spilling out at the end of a performance now going on.

Thorby glanced each way and hurried along the wall almost to the cabaret. "Psst! Auntie!"

She looked around, looked startled, then her face became expressionless. Through unmoving lips she said, loud enough to reach him, "Beat it, son! Hide! Are you crazy?"

"Auntie . . . *where have they got him?*"

"Crawl in a hole and pull it in after you. There's a reward out!"

"For *me?* Don't be silly, Auntie; nobody would pay a reward for me. Just tell me where they're holding him. Do you know?"

"They're not."

" 'They're not' what?"

"You don't know? Oh, poor lad! They've shortened him."

Thorby was so shocked that he was speechless. Although Baslim had talked of the time when he would be dead, Thorby had never really believed in it; he was incapable of imagining Pop dead and gone.

He missed her next words; she had to repeat. "Snoopers! Get out!"

Thorby glanced over his shoulder. Two patrolmen, moving this way—time to leave! But he was caught between street and blank wall, with no bolt hole but the entrance to the cabaret . . . if he ducked in there, dressed as he was, being what he was, the management would simply shout for the patrol.

But there was nowhere else to go. Thorby turned his back on the police and went inside the narrow foyer of the cabaret. There was no one there; the last act was in progress and even the hawker was not in sight. But just inside was a ladder-stool and on it was a box of transparent letters used to change signs billing the entertainers. Thorby saw them and an idea boiled up that would have made Baslim proud of his pupil—Thorby grabbed the box and stool and went out again.

He paid no attention to the approaching policemen, placed the ladder-stool under the little lighted marquee that surmounted the entrance and jumped up on it, with his back to the patrolmen. It placed most of his body in bright light but his head and shoulders stuck up into the shadow above the row of lights. He began methodically to remove letters spelling the name of the star entertainer.

The two police reached a point right behind him. Thorby tried not to tremble and worked with the steady listlessness of a hired hand with a dull job. He heard Auntie Singham call out, "Good evening, Sergeant."

"Evening, Auntie. What lies are you telling tonight?"

"Lies indeed! I see a sweet young girl in your future, with hands graceful as birds. Let me see your palm and perhaps I can read her name."

"What would my wife say? No time to chat tonight, Auntie." The sergeant glanced at the workman changing the sign, rubbed his chin and said, "We've got to stay on the prowl for Old Baslim's brat. You haven't seen him?" He looked again at the work going on above him and his eyes widened slightly.

"Would I sit here swapping gossip if I had?"

"Hmm . . ." He turned to his partner. "Roj, move along and check Ace's Place, and don't forget the washroom. I'll keep an eye on the street."

"Okay, Sarge."

The senior patrolman turned to the fortuneteller as his partner moved away. "It's a sad thing, Auntie. Who would have believed that old Baslim could have been spying against the Sargon and him a cripple?"

"Who indeed?" She rocked forward. "Is it true that he died of fright before they shortened him?"

"He had poison ready, knowing what was coming. But dead he was, before they pulled him out of his hole. The captain was furious."

"If he was dead already, why shorten him?"

"Come, come, Auntie, the law must be served. Shorten him they did, though it's not a job I'd relish." The sergeant sighed. "It's a sad world, Auntie. Think of that poor boy, led astray by that old rascal . . . and now the captain and the commandant both want to ask the lad questions they meant to ask the old man."

"What good will that do them?"

"None, likely." The sergeant poked gutter filth with the butt of his staff. "But if I were the lad, knowing the old man is dead and not knowing any answers to difficult questions, I'd be far, far from here already. I'd find me a farmer a long way from the city, one who needed willing hands cheap and took no interest in the troubles of the city. But since I'm not, why then, as soon as I clap eyes on him, if I do, I'll arrest him and haul him up before the captain."

"He's probably hiding between rows in a bean field this minute, trembling with fright."

"Likely. But that's better than walking around with no head on your shoulders." The police sergeant looked down the street, called out, "Okay, Roj. Right with you." As he started away he glanced again at Thorby and said, "Night, Auntie. If you see him, shout for us."

"I'll do that. Hail to the Sargon."

"Hail."

Thorby continued to pretend to work and tried not to shake, while the police moved slowly away. Customers trickled out of the cabaret and Auntie took up her chant, promising fame, fortune, and a bright glimpse of the future, all for a coin. Thorby was about to get down, stick the gear back into the entranceway and get lost, when a hand grabbed his ankle.

"What are you doing!"

Thorby froze, then realized it was just the manager of the place, angry at finding his sign disturbed. Without looking down Thorby said, "What's wrong? You paid me to change this blinker."

"*I* did?"

"Why, sure, you did. You told me—" Thorby glanced down, looked amazed and blurted, "You're not the one."

"I certainly am not. Get down from there."

"I can't. You've got my ankle."

The man let go and stepped back as Thorby climbed down. "I don't know what silly idiot could have told you—" He broke off as Thorby's face came into light. "Hey, it's that beggar boy!"

Thorby broke into a run as the man grabbed for him. He went ducking in and out between pedestrians as the shout of, "Patrol! Patrol! *Police!*" rose behind him. Then he was in the dark court again and, charged with adrenaline, was up a drainpipe as if it had been level pavement. He did not stop until he was several dozen roofs away.

He sat down against a chimney pot, caught his breath and tried to think.

Pop was dead. He couldn't be but he was. Old Poddy wouldn't have said so if he hadn't known. Why . . . why, Pop's head must be on a spike down at the pylon this minute, along with the other losers. Thorby had one grisly flash of visualization, and at last collapsed, wept uncontrollably.

After a long time he raised his head, wiped his face with knuckles, and straightened up.

Pop was dead. All right, what did he do now?

Anyhow, Pop had beat them out of questioning him. Thorby felt bitter pride. Pop was always the smart one; they had caught him but Pop had had the last laugh.

Well, what *did* he do now?

Auntie Singham had warned him to hide. Poddy had said, plain as anything, to get out of town. Good advice—if he wanted to stay as tall as he was, he had better be outside the city before daylight. Pop would expect him to put up a fight, not sit still and wait for the snoopies, and there was nothing left that he could do for Pop, now that Pop was dead—*hold it!*

"When I'm dead, you are to look up a man and give him a message. Can I depend on you? Not goof off and forget it?"

Yes, Pop, you can! I didn't forget—I'll deliver it! Thorby recalled for the first time in more than a day why he had come home early: Starship *Sisu* was in port; her skipper was on Pop's list. *"The first one who shows up"*—that's what Pop had said. I didn't goof, Pop; I almost did but I remembered. I'll do it, I'll do it! Thorby decided with fierce resurgence that this message must be the final, important thing that Pop had to get out—since they said he was a spy. All right, he'd help Pop finish his job. I'll do it, Pop. You'll have the best of them yet!

Thorby felt no twinge at the "treason" he was about to attempt; shipped in as a slave against his will, he felt no loyalty to the Sargon and Baslim had never tried to instill any. His strongest feeling toward the Sargon was superstitious fear and even that washed away in the violence of his need for revenge. He feared neither police nor Sargon himself; he simply wanted to evade them long enough to carry out Baslim's wishes. After that . . . well, if they caught him, he hoped to have finished the job before they shortened him.

If the *Sisu* were still in port . . .

Oh, she had to be! But the first thing was to find out for sure that the ship had not left, then—no, the *first* thing was to get out of sight before daylight. It was a million times more important to stay clear of the snoopies now that he had it through his thick head that there was something he could do for Pop.

Get out of sight, find out if the *Sisu* was still dirtside, get a message to her skipper . . . and do all this with every patrolman in the district looking for him—

Maybe he had better work his way over to the shipyards, where he was not known, sneak inside and back the long way to the port and find the *Sisu*. No, that was silly; he had almost been caught over that way just from not knowing the layout. Here, at least, he knew every building, most of the people.

But he had to have help. He couldn't go on the street, stop spacemen and ask. Who was a close enough friend to help . . . at risk of trouble with police? Ziggie? Don't be silly; Ziggie would turn him in for the reward, for two minims Ziggie would sell his own mother—Ziggie thought that anyone who didn't look out for number one first, last, and always was a sucker.

Who else? Thorby came up against the hard fact that most of his friends were around his age and as limited in resources. Most of them he did not know how to find at night, and he certainly could not hang around in daylight and wait for one to show up. As for the few who lived with their families at known addresses, he could not think of one who could both be trusted and could keep parents concerned from tipping off the police. Most honest citizens at Thorby's level went to great lengths to mind their own business and stay on the right side of the police.

It had to be one of Pop's friends.

He ticked off this list almost as quickly. In most cases he could not be sure how binding the friendship was, blood brotherhood or merely acquaintance. The only one whom he could possibly reach and who might possibly help was Mother Shaum. She had sheltered them once when they were driven out of their cave with retch gas and she had always had a kind word and a cold drink for Thorby.

He got moving; daylight was coming.

Mother Shaum's place was a taproom and lodging house, on the other side of Joy Street and near the crewmen's gate to the spaceport. Half an hour later, having crossed many roofs, twice been up and down in side courts and once having ducked across the lighted street, Thorby was on the roof of her place. He had not dared walk in her door; too many witnesses would force her to call the patrol. He had considered the back entrance and had squatted among garbage cans before deciding that there were too many voices in the kitchen.

But when he did reach her roof, he was almost caught by daylight; he found the usual access to the roof but he found also that its door and lock were sturdy enough to defy bare-handed burglary.

He went to the rear with the possibility in mind of going down, trying the back door anyhow; it was almost dawn and becoming urgent to get under cover. As he looked down the back he noticed ventilation holes for the low attic, one at each side. They were barely as wide as his shoulders, as deep as his chest—but they led inside.

They were screened but a few minutes and many scratches later he had one kicked in. Then he tried the unlikely task of easing himself over the edge feet first and snaking into the hole. He got in as far as his hips, his clout caught on raw edges of screening and he stuck like a cork, lower half inside the house, chest and head and arms sticking out like a gargoyle. He could not move and the sky was getting lighter.

With a drag from his heels and sheer force of will the cloth parted and he moved inside, almost knocking himself out by banging his head. He lay still and caught his breath, then pushed the screening untidily back into place. It would no longer stop vermin but it might fool the eye from four stories down. It was not until then that he realized that he had almost fallen those four stories.

The attic was no more than a crawl space; he started to explore on hands and knees for the fixture he believed must be here: a scuttle hole for repairs or inspection. Once he started looking and failed to find it, he was not sure that there was such a thing—he knew that some houses had them but he did not know much about houses; he had not lived in them much.

He did not find it until sunrise striking the vent holes gave illumination. It was all the way forward, on the street side.

And it was bolted from underneath.

But it was not as rugged as the door to the roof. He looked around, found a heavy spike dropped by a workman and used it to dig at the wooden closure. In time he worked a knot loose, stopped and peered through the knothole.

There was a room below; he saw a bed with one figure in it.

Thorby decided that he could not expect better luck; only one person to cope with, to persuade to find Mother Shaum without raising an alarm. He took his eye away, put a finger through and felt around; he touched the latch, then gladly broke a fingernail easing the bolt back. Silently he lifted the trap door.

The figure in the bed did not stir.

He lowered himself, hung by his fingertips, dropped the remaining short distance and collapsed as noiselessly as possible.

The person in bed was sitting up with a gun aimed at him. "It took you long enough," she said. "I've been listening to you for the past hour."

"Mother Shaum! Don't shoot!"

She leaned forward, looked closely. "Baslim's kid!" She shook her head. "Boy, you're a mess . . . and you're hotter than a fire in a mattress, too. What possessed you to come here?"

"I didn't know where else to go."

She frowned. "I suppose that's a compliment . . . though I had ruther have had a plague of boils, if I'd uv had my druthers." She got out of bed in her nightdress, big bare feet slapping on the floor, and peered out the window at the street below. "Snoopies here, snoopies there, snoopies checking every joint in the street three times in one night and scaring my customers . . . boy, you've caused more hooraw than I've seen since the factory riots. Why didn't you have the kindness to drop dead?"

"You won't hide me, Mother?"

"Who said I wouldn't? I've never gone out of my way to turn anybody in yet. But I don't have to like it." She glowered at him. "When did you eat last?"

"Uh, I don't remember."

"I'll scare you up something. I don't suppose you can pay for it?" She looked at him sharply.

"I'm not hungry. Mother Shaum, is the *Sisu* still in port?"

"Huh? I don't know. Yes, I do; she is—a couple of her boys were in earlier tonight. Why?"

"I've got to get a message to her skipper. I've got to see him, I've just *got* to!"

She gave a moan of utter exasperation. "First he wakes a decent working woman out of her first sleep of the night, he plants himself on her at rare risk to her life and limb and license. He's filthy dirty and scratched and bloody and no doubt will be using my clean towels with laundry prices the way they are. He hasn't eaten and can't pay for his tucker . . . and now he adds insult to injury by demanding that I run *errands* for him!"

"I'm not hungry . . . and it doesn't matter whether I wash or not. But I've *got* to see Captain Krausa."

"Don't be giving me orders in my own bedroom. Overgrown and unspanked, you are, if I knew that old scamp you lived with. You'll have to wait until one of the *Sisu*'s lads shows up later in the day, so's I can get a note out to the Captain." She turned toward the door. "Water's in the jug, towel's on the rack. Mind you get clean." She left.

Washing did feel good and Thorby found astringent powder on her dressing table, dusted his scratches. She came back, slapped two slices of bread with a generous slab of meat between them in front of him, added a bowl of milk, left without speaking. Thorby hadn't thought that it was possible to eat, with Pop dead, but found that it was—he had quit worrying when he first saw Mother Shaum.

She came back. "Gulp that last bite and in you go. The word is they're going to search every house."

"Huh? Then I'll get out and run for it."

"Shut up and do as I say. In you go now."

"In where?"

"In there," she answered, pointing.

"In *that?*" It was a built-in window seat and chest, in a corner; its shortcoming lay in its size, it being as wide as a man but less than a third as long. "I don't think I can fold up that small."

"And that's just what the snoopies will think. Hurry." She lifted the lid, dug out some clothing, lifted the far end of the box at the wall adjoining the next room as if it were a sash, and disclosed thereby that a hole went on through the wall. "Scoot your legs through—and don't think you are the only one who has ever needed to lie quiet."

Thorby got into the box, slid his legs through the hole, lay back; the lid when closed would be a few inches above his face. Mother Shaum threw clothing on top of him, concealing him. "You okay?"

"Yeah, sure. Mother Shaum? Is he really dead?"

Her voice became almost gentle. "He is, lad. A great shame it is, too."

"You're sure?"

"I was bothered by the same doubt, knowing him so well. So I took a walk down to the pylon to see. He is. But I can tell you this, lad, he's got a grin on his face like he'd outsmarted them . . . and he had, too. They don't like it when a man doesn't wait to be questioned." She sighed again. "Cry now, if you need, but be quiet. If you hear anyone, don't even breathe."

The lid slammed. Thorby wondered whether he would be able to breathe at all, but found that there must be air holes; it was stuffy but bearable. He turned his head to get his nose clear of cloth resting on it.

Then he did cry, after which he went to sleep.

He was awakened by voices and footsteps, recalled where he was barely in time to keep from sitting up. The lid above his face opened, and then slammed, making his ears ring; a man's voice called out, "Nothing in this room, Sarge!"

"We'll see." Thorby recognized Poddy's voice. "You missed that scuttle up there. Fetch the ladder."

Mother Shaum's voice said, "Nothing up there but the breather space, Sergeant."

"I said, 'We'd see.' "

A few minutes later he added, "Hand me the torch. Hmm . . . you're right, Mother . . . but he has been here."

"Huh?"

"Screen broken back at the end of the house and dust disturbed. I think he got in this way, came down through your bedroom, and out."

"Saints and devils! I could have been murdered in my bed! Do you call that police protection?"

"You're not hurt. But you'd better have that screen fixed, or you'll have snakes and all their cousins living with you." He paused. "It's my thought he tried to stay in the district, found it too hot, and went back to the ruins. If so, no doubt we'll gas him out before the day is over."

"Do you think I'm safe to go back to my bed?"

"Why should he bother an old sack of suet like you?"

"What a nasty thing to say! And just when I was about to offer you a drop to cut the dust."

"You were? Let's go down to your kitchen, then, and we'll discuss it. I may have been wrong." Thorby heard them leave, heard the ladder being removed. At last he dared breathe.

Later she came back, grumbling, and opened the lid. "You can stretch your legs. But be ready to jump back in. Three pints of my best. Policemen!"

6

THE SKIPPER OF THE *SISU* SHOWED UP THAT EVENING. CAPTAIN KRAUSA was tall, fair, rugged and had the worry wrinkles and grim mouth of a man used to authority and responsibility. He was irked with himself and everyone for having allowed himself to be lured away from his routine by nonsense. His eye assayed Thorby unflatteringly. "Mother Shaum, is *this* the person who insisted that he had urgent business with me?"

The captain spoke Nine Worlds trade lingo, a degenerate form of Sargonese, uninflected and with a rudimentary positional grammar. But Thorby understood it. He answered, "If you are Captain Fjalar Krausa, I have a message for you, noble sir."

"Don't call me 'noble sir'; I'm Captain Krausa, yes."

"Yes, nob—yes, Captain."

"If you have a message, give it to me."

"Yes, Captain." Thorby started reciting the message he had memorized, using the Suomish version to Krausa. " 'To Captain Fjalar Krausa, master of Starship *Sisu* from Baslim the Cripple: Greetings, old friend! Greetings to your family, clan, and sib, and my humblest respects to your revered mother. I am speaking to you through the mouth of my adopted son. He does not understand Suomic; I address you privately. When you receive this message, I am already dead—"

Krausa had started to smile; now he let out an exclamation. Thorby stopped. Mother Shaum interrupted with, "What's he saying? What language is that?"

Krausa brushed it aside. "It's my language. Is what he says true?"

"Is what true? How would I know? I don't understand that yammer."

"Uh . . . sorry, sorry! He tells me that an old beggar who used to hang around the Plaza—'Baslim' he called himself—is dead. Is this true?"

"Eh? Of course it is. I could have told you, if I had known you were interested. Everybody knows it."

"Everybody but me, apparently. What happened to him?"

"He was shortened."

"Shortened? *Why?*"

She shrugged. "How would I know? The word is, he died or poisoned himself, or something, before they could question him—so how would I know? I'm just a poor old woman, trying to make an honest living, with prices getting higher every day. The Sargon's police don't confide in *me*."

"But if—never mind. He managed to cheat them, did he? It sounds like him." He turned to Thorby. "Go on. Finish your message."

Thorby, thrown off stride, had to go back to the beginning. Krausa waited impatiently until he reached: "—I am already dead. My son is the only thing of value of which I die possessed; I entrust him to your care. I ask that you succor and admonish him as if you were I. When opportunity presents, I ask that you deliver him to the commander of any vessel of the Hegemonic Guard, saying that he is a distressed citizen of the Hegemony and entitled as such to their help in locating his family. If they will bestir themselves, they can establish his identity and restore him to his people. All the rest I leave to your good judgment. I have enjoined him to obey you and I believe that he will; he is a good lad, within the limits of his age and experience, and I entrust him to you with a serene heart. Now I must depart. My life has been long and rich; I am content. Farewell."

The Captain chewed his lip and his face worked in the fashion of a grown man who is busy not crying. Finally he said gruffly, "That's clear enough. Well, lad, are you ready?"

"Sir?"

"You're coming with me. Or didn't Baslim tell you?"

"No, sir. But he told me to do whatever you told me to. I'm to come with you?"

"Yes. How soon can you leave?"

Thorby gulped. "Right now, sir."

"Then come on. I want to get back to my ship." He looked Thorby up and down. "Mother Shaum, can we put some decent clothes on him? That outlandish rig won't do to come aboard in. Or never mind; there's a slop shop down the street; I'll pick him up a kit."

She had listened with growing amazement. Now she said, "You're taking him to your ship?"

"Any objections?"

"Huh? Not at all . . . if you don't care if they rack him apart."

"What do you mean?"

"Are you crazy? There are six snoopers between here and the spaceport gate . . . and each one anxious to pick up the reward."

"You mean he's wanted?"

"Why do you think I've hidden him in my own bedroom? He's as hot as bubbling cheese."

"But why?"

"Again, how would I know? He is."

"You don't really think that a lad like this would know enough about what old Baslim was doing to make it worth—"

"Let's not speak of what Baslim was doing or did. I'm a loyal subject of the Sargon . . . with no wish to be shortened. You say you want to take the boy into your ship. I say, 'Fine!' I'll be happy to be quit of the worry. But *how?*"

Krausa cracked his knuckles one by one. "I had thought," he said slowly, "that it would be just a matter of walking him down to the gate and paying his emigration tax."

"It's not, so forget it. Is there any way to get him aboard without passing him through the gate?"

Captain Krausa looked worried. "They're so strict about smuggling here that if they catch you, they confiscate the ship. You're asking me to risk my ship . . . and myself . . . and my whole crew."

"I'm not asking you to risk anything. I've got myself to worry about. I was just telling you the straight score. If you ask me, I'd say you were crazy to attempt it."

Thorby said, "Captain Krausa—"

"Eh? What is it, lad?"

"Pop told me to do as you said . . . but I'm sure he never meant you to risk your neck on my account." He swallowed. "I'll be all right."

Krausa sawed the air impatiently. "No, no!" he said harshly. "Baslim wanted this done . . . and debts are paid. Debts are always paid!"

"I don't understand."

"No need for you to. But Baslim wanted me to take you with me, so that's how it's got to be." He turned to Mother Shaum. "The question is, how? Any ideas?"

"Mmm . . . possibly. Let's go talk it over." She turned. "Get back in your hide-away, Thorby, and be careful. I may have to go out for a while."

* * *

Shortly before curfew the next day a large sedan chair left Joy Street. A patrolman stopped it and Mother Shaum stuck her head out. He looked surprised. "Going out, Mother? Who'll take care of your customers?"

"Mura has the keys," she answered. "But keep an eye on the place, that's a good friend. She's not as firm with them as I am." She put something in his hand and he made it disappear.

"I'll do that. Going to be gone all night?"

"I hope not. Perhaps I had better have a street pass, do you think? I'd like to come straight home if I finish my business."

"Well, now, they've tightened up a little on street passes."

"Still looking for the beggar's boy?"

"As a matter of fact, yes. But we'll find him. If he's fled to the country, they'll starve him out; if he's still in town, we'll run him down."

"Well, you could hardly mistake me for him. So how about a short pass for an old woman who needs to make a private call?" She rested her hand on the door; the edge of a bill stuck out.

He glanced at it and glanced away. "Is midnight late enough?"

"Plenty, I should think."

He took out his book and started writing, tore out the form and handed it to her. As she accepted it the money disappeared. "Don't make it later than midnight."

"Earlier, I hope."

He glanced inside the sedan chair, then looked over her entourage. The four bearers had been standing patiently, saying nothing—which was not surprising, since they had no tongues. "Zenith Garage?"

"I always trade there."

"I thought I recognized them. Well matched."

"Better look them over. One of them might be the beggar's boy."

"Those great hairy brutes! Get along with you, Mother."

"Hail, Shol."

The chair swung up and moved away at a trot. As they rounded the corner she slowed them to a walk and drew all curtains. Then she patted the cushions billowing around her. "Doing all right?"

"I'm squashed," a voice answered faintly.

"Better squashed than shortened. I'll ease over a bit. Your lap is bony."

For the next mile she was busy modifying her costume, and putting on jewels. She veiled her face until only her live, black eyes showed. Finished, she stuck her head out and called instructions to the head porter; the chair swung right toward the spaceport. When they reached the road girdling its high, impregnable fence it was almost dark.

The gate for spacemen is at the foot of Joy Street, the gate for passengers is east of there in the Emigration Control Building. Beyond that, in the warehouse district, is Traders' Gate—freight and outgoing customs. Miles beyond are shipyard gates. But between the shipyards and Traders' Gate is a small gate reserved for nobles rich enough to own space yachts.

The chair reached the spaceport fence short of Traders' Gate, turned and went along the fence toward it. Traders' Gate is several gates, each a loading dock built through the barrier, so that a warehouse truck can back up, unload; the Sargon's inspectors can weigh, measure, grade, prod, open, and ray the merchandise, as may be indicated, before it slides across the dock into spaceport trucks on the other side, to be delivered to waiting ships.

This night dock-three of the gate had its barricade open; Free Trader *Sisu* was finishing loading. Her master watched, arguing with inspectors, and oiling their functioning in the immemorial fashion. A ship's junior officer helped him, keeping tally with pad and pencil.

The sedan chair weaved among waiting trucks and passed close to the dock. The master of the *Sisu* looked up as the veiled lady in the chair peered out at the activity. He glanced at his watch and spoke to his junior officer. "One more load, Jan. You go in with the loaded truck and I'll follow with the last one."

"Aye aye, sir." The young man climbed on the tail of the truck and told the driver to take it away. An empty truck pulled into its place. It loaded quickly as the ship's master seemed to find fewer things to argue about with the inspectors. Then he was not satisfied and demanded that it be done over. The boss stevedore was pained but the master soothed him, glanced at his watch again and said, "There's time. I don't want these crates cracked before we get them into the ship; the stuff costs money. So let's do it right."

The sedan chair had moved on along the fence. Shortly it was dark; the veiled lady looked at the glowing face of her finger watch and urged her bearers into a trot.

They came at last to the gate reserved for nobles. The veiled lady leaned her head out and snapped, "Open up!"

There were two guards on the gate, one in a little watch room, the other lounging outside. The one outside opened the gate, but placed his staff across it when the sedan chair started to go through. Stopped, the bearers lowered it to the ground with the righthand or door side facing into the gate.

The veiled lady called out, "Clear the way, you! Lord Marlin's yacht."

The guard blocking the gate hesitated. "My lady has a pass?"

"Are you a fool?"

"If my lady has no pass," he said slowly, "perhaps my lady will suggest some way to assure the guard that My Lord Marlin is expecting her?"

The veiled lady was a voice in the dark—the guard had sense enough not to shine the light in her face; he had long experience with nobles and fumed. "If you insist on being a fool, call my lord at his yacht! Phone him—and I trust you'll find you've pleased him!"

The guard in the watch room came out. "Trouble, Sean?"

"Uh, no." They held a whispered consultation. The junior went inside to phone Lord Marlin's yacht, while the other waited outside.

But it appeared that the lady had had all the nonsense she was willing to endure. She threw open the door of the chair, burst out, and stormed into the watch room with the other startled guard after her. The one making the call stopped punching keys with connection uncompleted and looked up . . . and felt sick. This was even worse than he had thought. This was no flighty young girl, escaped from her chaperones; this was an angry dowager, the sort with enough influence to break a man to common labor or worse—with a temper that made her capable of it. He listened open-mouthed to the richest tongue-lashing it had been his misfortune to endure in all the years he had been checking lords and ladies through their gate.

While the attention of both guards was monopolized by Mother Shaum's rich rhetoric, a figure detached itself from the sedan chair, faded through the gate and kept going, until it was lost in the gloom of the field. As Thorby ran, even as he expected the burning tingle of a stun gun bolt in his guts, he watched for a road on the right joining the one from the gate. When he came to it he threw himself down and lay panting.

Back at the gate, Mother Shaum stopped for breath. "My lady," one of them said placatingly, "if you will just let us complete the call—"

"Forget it! No, *remember* it!—for tomorrow you'll hear from My Lord Marlin." She flounced back to her chair.

"Please, my lady!"

She ignored them, spoke sharply to the slaves; they swung the chair up, broke into a trot. One guard's hand went to his belt, as a feeling of something badly wrong possessed him. But his hand stopped. Right or wrong, knocking down a lady's bearer was not to be risked, no matter what she might be up to.

And, after all, she hadn't actually done anything wrong.

When the master of the *Sisu* finally okayed the loading of the last truck, he climbed onto its bed, waved the driver to start, then worked his way forward. "Hey, there!" He knocked on the back of the cab.

"Yes, Captain?" The driver's voice came through faintly.

"There's a stop sign where this road joins the one out to the ships. I notice most of you drivers don't bother with it."

"That one? There's never any traffic on that road. That road is a stop just because the nobles use it."

"That's what I mean. One of them might pop up and I'd miss my jump time just for a silly traffic accident with one of your nobles. They could hold me here for many ninedays. So come to a full stop, will you?"

"Whatever you say, Captain. You're paying the bill."

"So I am." A half-stellar note went through a crack in the cab.

When the truck slowed, Krausa went to the tail gate. As it stopped he reached down and snaked Thorby inside. "Quiet!" Thorby nodded and trembled. Krausa took tools from his pockets, attacked one of the crates. Shortly he had one side open, burlap pulled back, and he started dumping verga leaves, priceless on any other planet. Soon he had a largish hole and a hundred pounds of valuable leaves were scattered over the plain. "Get in!"

Thorby crawled into the space, made himself small. Krausa pulled burlap over him, sewed it, crimped slats back into place, and finished by strapping it and sealing it with a good imitation of the seal used by the inspectors—it was a handcrafted product of his ship's machine shop. He straightened up and wiped sweat from his face. The truck was turning into the loading circle for the *Sisu*.

He supervised the final loads himself, with the Sargon's field inspector at his elbow, checking off each crate, each bale, each carton as it went into the sling. Then Krausa thanked the inspector appropriately and rode the sling up instead of the passenger hoist. Since a man was riding it, the hoist man let down the sling with more than usual care. The hold was almost filled and stowed for jump; there was very little head room. Crewmen started wrestling crates free of the sling and even the Captain lent a hand, at least to the extent of one crate. Once the sling was dragged clear, they closed the cargo door and started dogging it for space. Captain Krausa reached into his pocket again and started tearing open that crate.

Two hours later Mother Shaum stood at her bedroom window and looked out across the spaceport. She glanced at her watch. A green rocket rose from the control tower; seconds later a column of white light climbed to the sky. When the noise reached her, she smiled grimly and went downstairs to supervise the business—Mura couldn't really handle it properly alone.

7

INSIDE THE FIRST FEW MILLION MILES THORBY WAS UNHAPPILY CONvinced that he had made a mistake.

He passed out from inhaling fumes of verga leaves and awakened in a tiny, one-bunk stateroom. Waking was painful; although the *Sisu* maintained one standard gravity of internal field throughout a jump his body had recognized both the slight difference from Jubbul-surface gravity and the more subtle difference between an artificial field and the natural condition. His body decided that he was in the hold of a slaver and threw him into the first nightmare he had had in years.

Then his tired, fume-sodden brain took a long time struggling up out of the horror.

At last he was awake, aware of his surrounding, and concluded that he was aboard the *Sisu* and safe. He felt a glow of relief and gathering excitement that he was traveling, going somewhere. His grief over Baslim was pushed aside by strangeness and change. He looked around.

The compartment was a cube, only a foot or so higher and wider than his own height. He was resting on a shelf that filled half the room and under him was a mattress strangely and delightfully soft, of material warm and springy and smooth. He stretched and yawned in surprised wonder that traders lived in such luxury. Then he swung his feet over and stood up.

The bunk swung noiselessly up and fitted itself into the bulkhead. Thorby could not puzzle out how to open it again. Presently he gave up. He did not want a bed then; he did want to look around.

When he woke the ceiling was glowing faintly. When he stood up it glowed brightly and remained so. But the light did not show where the door was. There were vertical metal panels on three sides, any of which might have been a door, save that none displayed thumb slot, hinge, or other familiar mark.

He considered the possibility that he had been locked in, but was not troubled. Living in a cave, working in the Plaza, he was afflicted neither with claustrophobia nor agoraphobia; he simply wanted to find the door and was annoyed that he could not recognize it. If it were locked, he did not think that Captain Krausa would let it stay locked unduly long. But he could not find it.

He did find a pair of shorts and a singlet, on the deck. When he woke he had been bare, the way he usually slept. He picked up these garments, touched them timidly, wondered at their magnificence. He recognized them as being the sort of thing most spacemen wore and for a moment let himself be dazzled at the thought of wearing such luxuries. But his mind shied away from such impudence.

Then he recalled Captain Krausa's distaste at his coming aboard in the clothes he normally wore—why, the Captain had even intended to take him to a tailoring shop in Joy Street which catered to spacemen! He had *said* so.

Thorby concluded that these clothes must be for him. For *him!* His breech clout was missing and the Captain certainly had not intended him to appear in the *Sisu* naked. Thorby was not troubled by modesty; the taboo was spotty on Jubbul and applied more to the upper classes. Nevertheless clothes were worn.

Marveling at his own daring, Thorby tried them on. He got the shorts on backwards, figured out his mistake, and put them on properly. He got the pullover shirt on backwards, too, but the error was not as glaring; he left it that way, thinking that he had it right. Then he wished mightily that he could see himself.

Both garments were of simple cut, undecorated light green, and fashioned of strong, cheap material; they were working clothes from the ship's slop chest, a type of garment much used by both sexes on many planets through many centuries. Yet Solomon in all his glory was not arrayed as Thorby! He smoothed the cloth against his skin and wanted someone to see him in his finery. He set about finding the door with renewed eagerness.

It found him. While running his hands over the panels on one bulkhead he became aware of a breeze, turned and found that one panel had disappeared. The door let out into a passageway.

A young man dressed much as Thorby was (Thorby was overjoyed to find that he had dressed properly for the occasion) was walking down the curved corridor toward Thorby. Thorby stepped out and spoke a greeting in Sargonese trade talk.

The man's eyes flicked toward Thorby, then he marched on past as if no one was there. Thorby blinked, puzzled and a little hurt. Then he called out to the receding back in Interlingua.

No answer and the man disappeared before he could try other languages.

Thorby shrugged and let it roll off; a beggar does not gain by being touchy. He set out to explore.

In twenty minutes he discovered many things. First, the *Sisu* was much larger than he had imagined. He had never before seen a starship close up, other than from the doubtful vantage of a slaver's hold. Ships in the distance, sitting on the field of Jubbul's port, had seemed large but not this enormous. Second, he was surprised to find so many people. He understood that the Sargon's freighters operating among the Nine Worlds were usually worked by crews of six or seven. But in his first few minutes he encountered several times that number of both sexes and all ages.

Third, he became dismally aware that he was being snubbed. People did not look at him, nor did they answer when he spoke; they walked right through him if he did not jump. The nearest he accomplished to social relations was with a female child, a toddler who regarded him with steady, grave eyes in answer to his overtures—until snatched up by a woman who did not even glance at Thorby.

Thorby recognized the treatment; it was the way a noble treated one of Thorby's caste. A noble could not see him, he did not exist—even a noble giving alms usually did so by handing it through a slave. Thorby had not been hurt by such treatment on Jubbul; that was natural, that was the way things had always been. It had made him neither lonely nor depressed; he had had plenty of warm company in his misery and had not known that it was misery.

But had he known ahead of time that the entire ship's company of the *Sisu* would behave like nobles he would never have shipped in her, snoopies or not. But he had not expected such treatment. Captain Krausa, once Baslim's message had been delivered, had been friendly and gruffly paternal; Thorby had expected the crew of the *Sisu* to reflect the attitude of her master.

He wandered the steel corridors, feeling like a ghost among living, and at last decided sadly to go back to the cubicle in which he had awakened. Then he discovered that he was lost. He retraced what he thought was the route—and in fact was; Baslim's renshawing had not been wasted—but all he found was a featureless tunnel. So he set out again, uncomfortably aware that whether he found his own room or not, he must soon find where they hid the washroom, even if he had to grab someone and shake him.

He blundered into a place where he was greeted by squeals of female indignation; he retreated hastily and heard a door slam behind him.

Shortly thereafter he was overtaken by a hurrying man who spoke to him, in Interlingua: "What the dickens are you doing wandering around and butting into things?"

Thorby felt a wave of relief. The grimmest place in the world, lonelier than being alone, is Coventry, and even a reprimand is better than being ignored. "I'm lost," he said meekly.

"Why didn't you stay where you were?"

"I didn't know I was supposed to—I'm sorry, noble sir—and there wasn't any washroom."

"Oh. But there is, right across from your bunkie."

"Noble sir, I did not know."

"Mmm . . . I suppose you didn't. I'm not 'noble sir'; I'm First Assistant Power Boss—see that you remember it. Come along." He grabbed Thorby by an arm, hurried him back through the maze, stopped in the same tunnel that had stumped Thorby, ran his hand down a seam in the metal. "Here's your bunkie." The panel slid aside.

The man turned, did the same on the other side. "Here's the starboard bachelors' washroom." The man advised him scornfully when Thorby was confused by strange fixtures, then chaperoned him back to his room. "Now stay here. Your meals will be fetched."

"First Assistant Power Boss, sir?"

"Eh?"

"Could I speak with Captain Krausa?"

The man looked astonished. "Do you think the Skipper has nothing better to do than talk to *you?*"

"But—"

The man had left; Thorby was talking to a steel panel.

Food appeared eventually, served by a youngster who behaved as if he were placing a tray in an empty room. More food appeared later and the first tray was removed. Thorby almost managed to be noticed; he hung onto the first tray and spoke to the boy in Interlingua. He detected a flicker of understanding, but he was answered by one short word. The word was "Fraki!" and Thorby did not recognize it . . . but he could recognize the contempt with which it was uttered. A fraki is a small, shapeless, semi-saurian scavenger of Alpha Centaura Prime III, one of the first worlds populated by men. It is ugly, almost mindless, and has disgusting habits. Its flesh can be eaten only by a starving man. Its skin is unpleasant to touch and leaves a foul odor.

But "fraki" means more than this. It means a groundhog, an earth-crawler, a dirt dweller, one who never goes into space, not of our tribe, not human, a goy, an auslander, a savage, beneath contempt. In Old Terran cultures almost every animal name has been used as an insult: pig, dog, sow, cow, shark, louse, skunk, worm—the list is endless. No such idiom carries more insult than "fraki."

Fortunately all Thorby got was the fact that the youngster did not care for him . . . which he knew.

Presently Thorby became sleepy. But, although he had mastered the gesture by which doors were opened, he still could not find any combination of swipes, scratches, punches, or other actions which would open the bed; he spent that night on the floorplates. His breakfast appeared next morning but he was unable to detain the person serving it, even to be insulted again. He did encounter other boys and young men in the washroom across the corridor; while he was still ignored, he learned one thing by watching—he could wash his clothing there. A gadget would accept a garment, hold it a few minutes, spew it forth dry and fresh. He was so delighted that he laundered his new finery three times that day. Besides, he had nothing else to do. He again slept on the floor that night.

He was squatting in his bunkie, feeling a great aching loneliness for Pop and wishing that he had never left Jubbul, when someone scratched at his door. "May I come in?" a voice inquired in careful, badly-accented Sargonese.

"Come in!" Thorby answered eagerly and jumped up to open the door. He found himself facing a middle-aged woman with a pleasant face. "Welcome," he said in Sargonese, and stood aside.

"I thank you for your gracious—" she stumbled and said quickly, "Do you speak Interlingua?"

"Certainly, madam."

She muttered in System English, "Thank goodness for that—I've run out of Sargonese," then went on in Interlingua, "Then we will speak it, if you don't mind."

"As you wish, madam," Thorby answered in the same language, then added in System English, "unless you would rather use another language."

She looked startled. "How many languages do you speak?"

Thorby thought. "Seven, ma'am. I can puzzle out some others, but I cannot say that I speak them."

She looked even more surprised and said slowly, "Perhaps I have made a mistake. But—correct me if I am wrong and forgive my ignorance—I was told that you were a beggar's son in Jubbulpore."

"I am the son of Baslim the Cripple," Thorby said proudly, "a licensed beggar under the mercy of the Sargon. My late father was a learned man. His wisdom was famous from one side of the Plaza to the other."

"I believe it. Uh . . . are all beggars on Jubbul linguists?"

"What, ma'am? Most of them speak only gutter argot. But my father did not permit me to speak it . . . other than professionally, of course."

"Of course." She blinked. "I wish I could have met your father."

"Thank you, ma'am. Will you sit down? I am ashamed that I have nothing but the floor to offer . . . but what I have is yours."

"Thank you." She sat on the floor with more effort than did Thorby, who had remained thousands of hours in lotus seat, shouting his plea for alms.

Thorby wondered whether to close the door, whether this lady—in Sargonese he thought of her as "my lady" even though her friendly manner made her status unclear—had left it open on purpose. He was floundering in a sea of unknown customs, facing a social situation totally new to him. He solved it with common sense; he asked, "Do you prefer the door open or closed, ma'am?"

"Eh? It doesn't matter. Oh perhaps you had better leave it open; these are bachelor quarters of the starboard moiety and I'm supposed to live in port purdah, with the unmarried females. But I'm allowed some of the privileges and immunities of . . . well, of a pet dog. I'm a tolerated 'fraki.' " She spoke the last word with a wry smile.

Thorby had missed most of the key words. "A 'dog'? That's a wolf creature?"

She looked at him sharply. "You learned this language on Jubbul?"

"I have never been off Jubbul, ma'am—except when I was very young. I'm sorry if I do not speak correctly. Would you prefer Interlingua?"

"Oh, no. You speak System English beautifully . . . a better Terran accent than mine—I've never been able to get my birthplace out of my vowels. But it's up to me to make myself understood. Let me introduce myself. I'm not a trader; I'm an anthropologist they are allowing to travel with them. My name is Doctor Margaret Mader."

Thorby ducked his head and pressed his palms together. "I am honored. My name is Thorby, son of Baslim."

"The pleasure is mine, Thorby. Call me 'Margaret.' My title doesn't count here anyhow, since it is not a ship's title. Do you know what an anthropologist is?"

"Uh, I am sorry, ma'am—Margaret."

"It's simpler than it sounds. An anthropologist is a scientist who studies how people live together."

Thorby looked doubtful. "This is a science?"

"Sometimes I wonder. Actually, Thorby, it is a complicated study, because the patterns that men work out to live together seem unlimited. There are only six things that all men have in common with all other men and not with animals—three of them part of our physical makeup, the way our bodies work, and three of them are learned. Everything else that a man does, or believes, all his customs and economic practices, vary enormously. Anthropologists study those variables. Do you understand 'variable'?"

"Uh," Thorby said doubtfully, "the *x* in an equation?"

"Correct!" she agreed with delight. "We study the *x*'s in the human equations. That's what I'm doing. I'm studying the way the Free Traders live. They have worked out possibly the oddest solutions to the difficult problem of how to be human and survive of any society in history. They are unique." She moved restlessly. "Thorby, would you mind if I sat in a chair? I don't bend as well as I used to."

Thorby blushed. "Ma'am . . . I have none. I am dis—"

"There's one right behind you. And another behind me." She stood up and touched the wall. A panel slid aside; an upholstered armchair unfolded from the space disclosed.

Seeing his face she said, "Didn't they show you?" and did the same on the other wall; another chair sprang out.

Thorby sat down cautiously, then let his weight relax into cushions as the chair felt him out and adjusted itself to him. A big grin spread over his face. "Gosh!"

"Do you know how to open your work table?"

"Table?"

"Good heavens, didn't they show you anything?"

"Well . . . there was a bed in here once. But I've lost it."

Doctor Mader muttered something, then said, "I might have known it. Thorby, I admire these Traders. I even like them. But they can be the most stiff-necked, self-centered, contrary, self-righteous, uncooperative—but I should not criticize our hosts. Here." She reached out both hands, touched two spots on the wall and the disappearing bed swung down. With the chairs open, there remained hardly room for one person to stand. "I'd better close it. You saw what I did?"

"Let me try."

She showed Thorby other built-in facilities of what had seemed to be a bare cell: two chairs, a bed, clothes cupboards. Thorby learned that he owned, or at least had, two more work suits, two pairs of soft ship's shoes, and minor items, some of which were strange, bookshelf and spool racks (empty, except for the Laws of *Sisu*), a drinking fountain, a bed reading light, an intercom, a clock, a mirror, a room thermostat, and gadgets which were useless to him as his background included no need. "What's that?" he asked at last.

"That? Probably the microphone to the Chief Officer's cabin. Or it may be a dummy with the real one hidden. But don't worry; almost no one in this ship speaks System English and she isn't one of the few. They talk their 'secret language'—only it isn't secret; it's just Finnish. Each Trader ship has its own language—one of the Terran tongues. And the culture has an over-all 'secret' language which is merely degenerate Church Latin—and at that they don't use it; 'Free Ships' talk to each other in Interlingua."

Thorby was only half listening. He had been excessively cheered by her company and now, in contrast, he was brooding over his treatment from others. "Margaret . . . why won't they *speak* to people?"

"Eh?"

"You're the first person who's spoken to me!"

"Oh." She looked distressed. "I should have realized it. You've been ignored."

"Well . . . they feed me."

"But they don't talk with you. Oh, you poor dear! Thorby, they don't speak to you because you are *not* 'people.' Nor am I."

"They don't talk to you either?"

"They do now. But it took direct orders from the Chief Officer and much patience on my part." She frowned. "Thorby, every excessively clannish culture—and I know of none more clannish than this—every such culture has the same key word in its language . . . and the word is 'people' however they say it. It means themselves. 'Me and my wife, son John and his wife, us four and no more'—cutting off their group from all others and denying that others are even human. Have you heard the word 'fraki' yet?"

"Yes. I don't know what it means."

"A fraki is just a harmless, rather repulsive little animal. But when they say it, it means 'stranger.' "

"Uh, well, I guess I am a stranger."

"Yes, but it also means you can never be anything else. It means that you and I are subhuman breeds outside the law—*their* law."

Thorby looked bleak. "Does that mean I have to stay in this room and never, ever talk to anybody?"

"Goodness! I don't know. *I'll* talk to you—"

"Thanks!"

"Let me see what I can find out. They're not cruel; they're just pig-headed and provincial. The fact that you have feelings never occurs to them. I'll talk to the Captain; I have an appointment with him as soon as the ship goes irrational." She glanced at her anklet. "Heavens, look at the time! I came here to talk about Jubbul and we haven't said a word about it. May I come back and discuss it with you?"

"I wish you would."

"Good. Jubbul is a well-analyzed culture, but I don't think any student has ever had opportunity to examine it from the perspective you had. I was delighted when I heard that you were a professed mendicant."

"Excuse me?"

"A beggar. Investigators who have been allowed to live there have all been guests of the upper classes. That forces them to see . . . well, the way slaves live for example, from the outside, not the inside. You see?"

"I guess so." Thorby added, "If you want to know about slaves, I was one."

"You *were?*"

"I'm a freedman. Uh, I should have told you," he added uncomfortably, afraid that his new-found friend would scorn him, now that she knew his class.

"No reason to, but I'm overjoyed that you mentioned it. Thorby, you're a treasure trove! Look, dear, I've got to run; I'm late now. But may I come back soon?"

"Huh? Why, surely, Margaret." He added honestly, "I really don't have much else to do."

Thorby slept in his wonderful new bed that night. He was left alone the next morning but he was not bored, as he had so many toys to play with. He opened things out and caused them to fold up again, delighted at how each gadget folded in on itself to occupy minimum space. He concluded that it must be witchcraft. Baslim had taught him that magic and witchcraft were nonsense but the teaching had not fully stuck—Pop had known everything but just the same, how could you fly in the face of experience? Jubbul had plenty of witches and if they weren't practicing magic, what were they doing?

He had just opened his bed for the sixth time when he was almost shocked out of the shoes he had dared to try on by an unholy racket. It was the ship's alarm, calling all hands to General Quarters, and it was merely a drill, but Thorby did not know that. When he reswallowed his heart, he opened the door and looked out. People were running at breakneck speed.

Shortly the corridors were empty. He went back into his bunkie, waited and tried to understand. Presently his sharp ears detected the absence of the soft sigh of the ventilation system. But there was nothing he could do about it. He should have mustered in the innermost compartment, along with children and other noncombatants, but he did not know.

So he waited.

The alarm rang again, in conjunction with a horn signal, and again there were running people in the passageways. Again it was repeated, until the crew had run through General Quarters, Hull Broach, Power Failure, Air Hazard, Radiation Hazard, and so forth—all the general drills of a taut ship. Once the lights went out and once for frightening moments Thorby experienced the bewildering sensation of free fall as the ship's artificial field cut off.

After a long time of such inexplicable buffoonery he heard the soothing strains of recall and the ventilation system whispered back to normal. No one bothered to look for him; the old woman who mustered nonparticipants hadn't noticed the absence of the fraki although she had counted the animal pets aboard.

Immediately thereafter Thorby was dragged up to see the Chief Officer.

A man opened his door, grabbed his shoulder and marched him away. Thorby put up with it for a short distance, then he rebelled; he had his bellyful of such treatment.

The gutter fighting he had learned in order to survive in Jubbulpore was lacking in rules. Unfortunately this man had learned in a school equally cold-blooded but more scientific; Thorby got in one swipe, then found himself pinned against the bulkhead with his left wrist in danger of breaking. "Cut out the nonsense!"

"Quit pushing me around!"

"I said, 'Cut out the nonsense.' You're going up to see the Chief Officer. Don't give me trouble, Fraki, or I'll stuff your head in your mouth."

"I want to see Captain Krausa!"

The man relaxed the pressure and said, "You'll see him. But the Chief Officer has ordered you to report . . . and she can't be kept waiting. So will you go quietly? Or shall I carry you there in pieces?"

Thorby went quietly. Pressure on a wrist joint combined with pressure on a nerve between the bones of the palm carries its own rough logic. Several decks up he was shoved through an open door. "Chief Officer, here's the fraki."

"Thank you, Third Deck Master. You may go."

Thorby understood only the word "fraki." He picked himself up and found himself in a room many times as large as his own. The most prominent thing in it was an imposing bed, but the small figure in the bed dominated the room. Only after he had looked at her did he notice that Captain Krausa stood silent on one side of the bed and that a woman perhaps the Captain's age stood on the other.

The woman in bed was shrunken with age but radiated authority. She was richly dressed—the scarf over her thin hair represented more money than Thorby had ever seen at one time—but Thorby noticed only her fierce, sunken eyes. She looked at him. "So! Oldest Son, I have much trouble believing it." She spoke in Suomic.

"My Mother, the message could not have been faked."

She sniffed.

Captain Krausa went on with humble stubbornness, "Hear the message yourself, My Mother." He turned to Thorby and said in Interlingua, "Repeat the message from your father."

Obediently, not understanding but enormously relieved to be in the presence of Pop's friend, Thorby repeated the message by rote. The old woman heard him through, then turned to Captain Krausa. "What is this? He speaks our language! A *fraki!*"

"No, My Mother, he understands not a word. That is Baslim's voice."

She looked back at Thorby, spilled a stream of Suomic on him. He looked questioningly at Captain Krausa. She said, "Have him repeat it again."

The Captain gave the order; Thorby, confused but willing, did so. She lay silent after he had concluded while the other waited. Her face screwed up in anger and exasperation. At last she rasped, "Debts must be paid!"

"That was my thought, My Mother."

"But why should the draft be drawn on us?" she answered angrily.

The Captain said nothing. She went on more quietly, "The message is authentic. I thought surely it must be faked. Had I known what you intended I would have forbidden it. But, Oldest Son, stupid as you are, you were right. And debts must be paid." Her son continued to say nothing; she added angrily, "Well? Speak up! What coin do you propose to tender?"

"I have been thinking, My Mother," Krausa said slowly. "Baslim demands that we care for the boy only a limited time . . . until we can turn him over to a Hegemonic military vessel. How long will that be? A year, two years. But even that presents problems. However, we have a precedent—the fraki female. The Family has accepted her—oh, a little grumbling, but they are used to her now, even amused by her. If My Mother intervened for this lad in the same way—"

"Nonsense!"

"But, My Mother, we are obligated. Debts must—"

"Silence!"

Krausa shut up.

She went on quietly, "Did you not listen to the wording of the burden Baslim placed on you? '—succor and admonish him as if you were I.' What was Baslim to this fraki?"

"Why, he speaks of him as his adopted son. I thought—"

"You didn't think. If you take Baslim's place, what does that make *you?* Is there more than one way to read the words?"

Krausa looked troubled. The ancient went on, "*Sisu* pays debts in full. No half-measures, no short weights—in *full.* The fraki must be adopted . . . by you."

Krausa's face was suddenly blank. The other woman, who had been moving around quietly with make-work, dropped a tray.

The Captain said, "But, My Mother, what will the Family—"

"*I* am the Family!" She turned suddenly to the other woman. "Oldest Son's Wife, have all my senior daughters attend me."

"Yes, Husband's Mother." She curtsied and left.

The Chief Officer looked grimly at the overhead, then almost smiled. "This is not all bad, Oldest Son. What will happen at the next Gathering of the People?"

"Why, we will be thanked."

"Thanks buy no cargo." She licked her thin lips. "The People will be in debt to *Sisu* . . . and there will be a change in status of ships. We won't suffer."

Krausa smiled slowly. "You always were a shrewd one, My Mother."

"A good thing for *Sisu* that I am. Take the fraki boy and prepare him. We'll do this quickly."

8

THORBY HAD TWO CHOICES: BE ADOPTED QUIETLY, OR MAKE A FUSS and be adopted anyhow. He chose the first, which was sensible, as opposing the will of the Chief Officer was unpleasant and almost always futile. Besides, while he felt odd and rather unhappy about acquiring a new family so soon after the death of Pop, nevertheless he could see that the change was to his advantage. As a fraki, his status had never been lower. Even a slave has equals.

But most important, Pop had told him to do what Captain Krausa said for him to do.

The adoption took place in the dining saloon at the evening meal that day. Thorby understood little of what went on and none of what was said, since the ceremonies were in the "secret language," but the Captain had coached him in what to expect. The entire ship's company was there, except those on watch. Even Doctor Mader was there, inside the main door and taking no part but where she could see and hear.

The Chief Officer was carried in and everyone stood. She was settled on a lounge at the head of the officers' table, where her daughter-in-law, the Captain's wife attended her. When she was comfortable, she made a gesture and they sat down, the Captain seating himself on her right. Girls from the port moiety, the watch with the day's duty, then served all hands with bowls of thin mush. No one touched it. The Chief Officer banged her spoon on her bowl and spoke briefly and emphatically.

Her son followed her. Thorby was surprised to discover that he recognized a portion of the Captain's speech as being identical with part of the message Thorby had delivered; he could spot the sequence of sounds.

The Chief Engineer, a man older than Krausa, answered, then several older people, both men and women, spoke. The Chief Officer asked a question and was answered in chorus—a unanimous assent. The old woman did not ask for dissenting votes.

Thorby was trying to catch Doctor Mader's eye when the Captain called to him in Interlingua. Thorby had been seated on a stool alone and was feeling conspicuous, especially as persons he caught looking at him did not seem very friendly.

"Come here!"

Thorby looked up, saw both the Captain and his mother looking at him. She seemed irritated or it may have been the permanent set of her features. Thorby hurried over.

She dipped her spoon in his dish, barely licked it. Feeling as if he were doing something horribly wrong but having been coached, he dipped his spoon in her bowl, timidly took a mouthful. She reached up, pulled his head down and pecked him with withered lips on both cheeks. He returned the symbolic caress and felt gooseflesh.

Captain Krausa ate from Thorby's bowl; he ate from the Captain's. Then Krausa took a knife, held the point between thumb and forefinger and whispered in Interlingua, "Mind you don't cry out." He stabbed Thorby in his upper arm.

Thorby thought with contempt that Baslim had taught him to ignore ten times that much pain. But blood flowed freely. Krausa led him to a spot where all might see, said something loudly, and held his arm so that a puddle of blood formed on the deck. The Captain stepped on it, rubbed it in with his foot, spoke loudly again—and a cheer went up. Krausa said to Thorby in Interlingua, "Your blood is now in the steel; our steel is in your blood."

Thorby had encountered sympathetic magic all his life and its wild, almost reasonable logic he understood. He felt a burst of pride that he was now part of the ship.

The Captain's wife slapped a plaster over the cut. Then Thorby exchanged food and kisses with her, after which he had to do it right around the room, every table, his brothers and his uncles, his sisters and his cousins and his aunts. Instead of kissing him, the men and boys grasped his hands and then clapped him across the shoulders. When he came to the table of unmarried females he hesitated—and discovered that they did not kiss him; they giggled and squealed and blushed and hastily touched forefingers to his forehead.

Close behind him, girls with the serving duty cleared away the bowls of mush—purely ritualistic food symbolizing the meager rations on which the People could cross space if necessary—and were serving a feast. Thorby would have been clogged to his ears with mush had he not caught onto the trick: don't eat it, just dip the spoon, then barely taste it. But when at last he was seated, an accepted member of the Family, at the starboard bachelors' table, he had no appetite for the banquet in his honor. Eighty-odd new relatives were too much. He felt tired, nervous, and let down.

But he tried to eat. Presently he heard a remark in which he understood only the word "fraki." He looked up and saw a youth across the table grinning unpleasantly.

The president of the table, seated on Thorby's right, rapped for attention. "We'll speak nothing but Interlingua tonight," he announced, "and thereafter follow the customs in allowing a new relative gradually to acquire our language." His eye rested coldly on the youngster who had sneered at Thorby. "As for you, Cross-Cousin-in-Law by Marriage, I'll remind you—just once—that my Adopted Younger Brother is senior to you. And I'll see you in my bunkie after dinner."

The younger boy looked startled. "Aw, Senior Cousin, I was just saying—"

"Drop it." The young man said quietly to Thorby, "Use your fork. People do not eat meat with fingers."

"Fork?"

"Left of your plate. Watch me; you'll learn. Don't let them get you riled. Some of these young oafs have yet to learn that when Grandmother speaks, she means business."

Thorby was moved from his bunkie into a less luxurious larger room intended for four bachelors. His roommates were Fritz Krausa, who was his eldest unmarried foster brother and president of the starboard bachelor table, Chelan Krausa-Drotar, Thorby's foster ortho-second-cousin by marriage, and Jeri Kingsolver, his foster nephew by his eldest married brother.

It resulted in his learning Suomic rapidly. But the words he needed first were not Suomish; they were words borrowed or invented to describe family relationships in great detail. Languages reflect cultures; most languages distinguish brother, sister, father, mother, aunt, uncle, and link generations by "great" or "grand." Some languages make no distinction between (for example) "father" and "uncle" and the language reflects tribal custom. Contrariwise, some languages (e.g., Norwegian) split "uncle" into maternal and paternal ("morbror" and "farbror").

The Free Traders can state a relationship such as "my maternal foster half-stepuncle by marriage, once removed and now deceased" in *one* word, one which means that relationship and no other. The relation between any spot on a family tree and any other spot can be so stated. Where most cultures find a dozen titles for relatives sufficient the Traders use more than two thousand. The languages name discreetly and quickly such variables as generation, lineal or collateral, natural or adopted, age within generation, sex of speaker, sex of relative referred to, sexes of relatives forming linkage, consanguinity or affinity, and vital status.

Thorby's first task was to learn the word and the relationship defined by it with which he must address each of more than eighty new relatives; he had to understand the precise flavor of relationship, close or distant, senior or junior; he had to learn other titles by which he would be addressed by each of them. Until he had learned all this, he could not talk because as soon as he opened his mouth he would commit a grave breach in manners.

He had to associate five things for each member of the *Sisu*'s company, a face, a full name (his own name was now Thorby Baslim-Krausa), a family title, that person's family title for him, and that person's ship's rank (such as "Chief Officer" or "Starboard Second Assistant Cook"). He learned that each person must be addressed by family title in family matters, by ship's rank concerning ship's duties, and by given names on social occasions if the senior permitted it—nicknames hardly existed, since the nickname could be used only down, *never* up.

Until he grasped these distinctions, he could not be a functioning member of the family even though he was legally such. The life of the ship was a caste system of such complex obligations, privileges and required reactions to obligatory actions, as to make the stratified, protocol-ridden society of Jubbul seem like chaos. The Captain's wife was Thorby's "mother" but she was also Deputy Chief Officer; how he addressed her depended on what he had to say. Since he was in bachelor quarters, the mothering phase ceased before it started; nevertheless she treated him warmly as a son and offered her cheek for his kiss just as she did for Thorby's roommate and elder brother Fritz.

But as Deputy Chief Officer she could be as cold as a tax collector.

Not that her status was easier; she would not be Chief Officer until the old woman had the grace to die. In the meantime she was hand and voice and body servant for her mother-in-law. Theoretically senior officers were elective; practically it was a one-party system with a single slate. Krausa was captain because his father had been; his wife was deputy chief officer because she was his wife, and she would someday become chief officer—and boss him and his ship as his mother did—for the same reason. Meanwhile his wife's high rank carried with it the worst job in the ship, with no respite, for senior officers served for life

. . . unless impeached, convicted, and expelled—onto a planet for unsatisfactory performance, into the chilly thinness of space for breaking the ancient and pig-headed laws of *Sisu*.

But such an event was as scarce as a double eclipse; Thorby's mother's hope lay in heart failure, stroke, or other hazard of old age.

Thorby as adopted youngest son of Captain Krausa, senior male of the Krausa sept, titular head of *Sisu* clan (the Captain's mother being the real head), was senior to three-fourths of his new relatives in clan status (he had not yet acquired ship's rank). But seniority did not make life easier. With rank goeth privileges—so it ever shall be. But also with it go responsibility and obligation, always more onerous than privileges are pleasant.

It was easier to learn to be a beggar.

He was swept up in his new problems and did not see Doctor Margaret Mader for days. He was hurrying down the trunk corridor of fourth deck—he was always hurrying now—when he ran into her.

He stopped. "Hello, Margaret."

"Hello, Trader. I thought for a moment that you were no longer speaking to fraki."

"Aw, Margaret!"

She smiled. "I was joking. Congratulations, Thorby. I'm happy for you—it's the best solution under the circumstances."

"Thanks. I guess so."

She shifted to System English and said with motherly concern, "You seem doubtful, Thorby. Aren't things going well?"

"Oh, things are all right." He suddenly blurted the truth. "Margaret, I'm never going to understand these people!"

She said gently, "I've felt the same way at the beginning of every field study and this one has been the most puzzling. What is bothering you?"

"Uh . . . I don't know. I never know. Well, take Fritz—he's my elder brother. He's helped me a lot—then I miss something that he expects me to understand and he blasts my ears off. Once he hit me. I hit back and I thought he was going to explode."

"Peck rights," said Margaret.

"What?"

"Never mind. It isn't scientifically parallel; humans aren't chickens. What happened?"

"Well, just as quickly he went absolutely cold, told me he would forget it, wipe it out, because of my ignorance."

"Noblesse oblige."

"Huh?"

"Sorry. My mind is a junk yard. And did he?"

"Completely. He was sweet as sugar. I don't know why he got sore . . . and I don't know why he quit being sore when I hit him." He spread his hands. "It's not natural."

"No, it isn't. But few things are. Mmm . . . Thorby, I might be able to help. It's possible that I know how Fritz works better than he knows. Because I'm *not* one of the 'People.' "

"I don't understand."

"I do, I think. It's my job to. Fritz was born into the People; most of what he knows—and he is a very sophisticated young man—is subconscious. He can't explain it because he doesn't know he knows it; he simply functions. But what I have learned these past two years I have learned consciously. Perhaps I can advise you when you are shy about asking one of them. You can speak freely with me; I have no status."

"Gee, Margaret, would you?"

"Whenever you have time. I haven't forgotten that you promised to discuss Jubbul with me, either. But don't let me hold you; you seemed in a hurry."

"I wasn't, not really." He grinned sheepishly. "When I hurry I don't have to speak to as many people . . . and I usually don't know *how*."

"Ah, yes. Thorby, I have photographs, names, family classification, ship's job, on everyone. Would it help?"

"Huh? I should say so! Fritz thinks it's enough just to point somebody out once and say who he is."

"Then come to my room. It's all right; I have a dispensation to interview anyone there. The door opens into a public corridor; you don't cross purdah line."

Arranged by case cards with photographs, the data Thorby had had trouble learning piecemeal he soaked up in half an hour—thanks to Baslim's training and Doctor Mader's orderliness. In addition, she had prepared a family tree for the *Sisu*; it was the first he had seen; his relatives did not need diagrams, they simply knew.

She showed him his own place. "The plus mark means that while you are in the direct sept, you were not born there. Here are a couple more, transferred from collateral branches to sept . . . to put them into line of command I suspect. You people call yourselves a 'family' but the grouping is a phratry."

"A what?"

"A related group without a common ancestor which practices exogamy—that means marrying outside the group. The exogamy taboo holds, modified by rule of moiety. You know how the two moieties work?"

"They take turns having the day's duty."

"Yes, but do you know why the starboard watch has more bachelors and the port watch more single women?"

"Uh, I don't think so."

"Females adopted from other ships are in port moiety; native bachelors are starboard. Every girl in your side must be exchanged . . . unless she can find a husband among a very few eligible men. You should have been adopted on this side, but that would have required a different foster father. See the names with a blue circle-and-cross? One of those girls is your future wife . . . unless you find a bride on another ship."

Thorby felt dismayed at the thought. "Do I *have* to?"

"If you gain ship's rank to match your family rank, you'll have to carry a club to beat them off."

It fretted him. Swamped with family, he felt more need for a third leg than he did for a wife.

"Most societies," she went on, "practice both exogamy and endogamy—a man must marry outside his family but inside his nation, race, religion, or some large group, and you Free Traders are no exception; you must cross to another moiety but you can't marry fraki. But your rules produce an unusual setup; each ship is a patrilocal matriarchy."

"A what?"

" 'Patrilocal' means that wives join their husbands' families; a matriarchy . . . well, who bosses this ship?"

"Why, the Captain."

"He does?"

"Well, Father listens to Grandmother, but she is getting old and—"

"No 'buts.' The Chief Officer is boss. It surprised me; I thought it must be just this ship. But it extends all through the People. Men do the trading, conn the ship and mind its power plant—but a woman always is boss. It makes sense within its framework; it makes your marriage customs tolerable."

Thorby wished she would not keep referring to marriage.

"You haven't seen ships trade daughters. Girls leaving weep and wail and almost have to be dragged . . . but girls arriving have dried their eyes and are ready to smile and flirt, eyes open for husbands. If a girl catches the right man and pushes him, someday she can be sovereign of an independent state. Until she leaves her native ship, she isn't anybody—which is why her tears dry quickly. But if men were boss, girl-swapping would be slavery; as it is, it's a girl's big chance."

Doctor Mader turned away from the chart. "Human customs that help people live together are almost never planned. But they *are* useful, or they don't survive. Thorby, you have been fretted about how to behave toward your relatives."

"I certainly have!"

"What's the most important thing to a Trader?"

Thorby thought. "Why, the Family. Everything depends on who you are in the Family."

"Not at all. His ship."

"Well, when you say 'ship' you mean 'family.' "

"Just backwards. If a Trader becomes dissatisfied, where can he go? Space won't have him without a ship around him; nor can he imagine living on a planet among fraki, the idea is disgusting. His ship is his life, the air he breathes comes from his ship; somehow he must learn to live in it. But the pressure of personalities is almost unbearable and there is no way to get away from each other. Pressure could build up until somebody gets killed . . . or until the ship itself is destroyed. But humans devise ways to adjust to any conditions. You people lubricate with rituals, formalism, set patterns of speech, obligatory actions and responses. When things grow difficult you hide behind a pattern. That's why Fritz didn't stay angry."

"Huh?"

"He couldn't. You had done something wrong . . . but the fact itself showed that you were ignorant. Fritz had momentarily forgotten, then he remembered and his anger disappeared. The People do not permit themselves to be angry with a child; instead they set him back on the proper path . . . until he follows your complex customs as automatically as Fritz does."

"Uh, I think I see." Thorby sighed. "But it isn't easy."

"Because you weren't born to it. But you'll learn and it will be no more effort than breathing—and as useful. Customs tell a man who he is, where he belongs, what he must do. Better illogical customs than none; men cannot live together without them. From an anthropologist's view, 'justice' is a search for workable customs."

"My father—my other father, I mean; Baslim the Cripple—used to say the way to find justice is to deal fairly with other people and not worry about how they deal with you."

"Doesn't that fit what I said?"

"Uh, I guess so."

"I think Baslim the Cripple would regard the People as just." She patted his shoulder. "Never mind, Thorby. Do your best and one day you'll marry one of those nice girls. You'll be happy."

The prophecy did not cheer Thorby.

9

BY THE TIME *SISU* APPROACHED LOSIAN THORBY HAD A BATTLE STAtion worthy of a man. His first assignment had been to assist in the central dressing station, an unnecessary job. But his background in mathematics got him promoted.

He had been attending the ship's school. Baslim had given him a broad education, but this fact did not stand out to his instructors, since most of what they regarded as necessary—the Finnish language as they spoke it, the history of the People and of *Sisu*, trading customs, business practices, and export and import laws of many planets, hydroponics and ship's economy, ship safety and damage control—were subjects that Baslim had not even touched; he had emphasized languages, science, mathematics, galactography and history. The new subjects Thorby gobbled with a speed possible only to one renshawed by Baslim's strenuous methods. The Traders needed applied mathematics—bookkeeping and accounting, astrogation, nucleonics for a hydrogen-fusion-powered n-ship. Thorby splashed through the first, the second was hardly more difficult, but as for the third, the ship's schoolmaster was astounded that this ex-fraki had already studied multi-dimensional geometries.

So he reported to the Captain that they had a mathematical genius aboard.

This was not true. But it got Thorby reassigned to the starboard fire-control computer.

The greatest hazard to trading ships is in the first and last legs of each jump, when a ship is below speed-of-light. It is theoretically possible to detect and intercept a ship going many times speed-of-light, when it is irrational to the four-dimensional space of the senses; in practice it is about as easy as hitting a particular raindrop with a bow and arrow during a storm at midnight. But it is feasible to hunt down a ship moving below speed-of-light if the attacker is fast and the victim is a big lumbering freighter.

The *Sisu* had acceleration of one hundred standard gravities and used it all to cut down the hazard time. But a ship which speeds up by a kilometer per second each second will take three and one half standard days to reach speed-of-light.

Half a week is a long, nervous time to wait. Doubling acceleration would have cut danger time by half and made the *Sisu* as agile as a raider—but it would have meant a hydrogen-fission chamber eight times as big with parallel increase in radiation shielding, auxiliary equipment, and paramagnetic capsule to contain the hydrogen reaction; the added mass would eliminate cargo capacity. Traders are working people; even if there were no parasites preying on them they could not afford to burn their profits in the inexorable workings of an exponential law of multi-dimensional physics. So the *Sisu* had the best legs she could afford—but not long enough to outrun a ship unburdened by cargo.

Nor could *Sisu* maneuver easily. She had to go precisely in the right direction when she entered the trackless night of n-space, else when she came out she would be too far from market; such a mistake could turn the ledger from black to red. Still more hampering, her skipper had to be prepared to cut power entirely, or risk having his in-ship artificial gravity field destroyed—and thereby make strawberry jam of the Family as soft bodies were suddenly exposed to one hundred gravities.

This is why a captain gets stomach ulcers; it isn't dickering for cargoes, figuring discounts and commissions, and trying to guess what goods will show the best return. It's not long jumps through the black—that is when he can relax and dandle babies. It is starting and ending a jump that kills him off, the long aching hours when he may have to make a split-second decision involving the lives—or freedom—of his family.

If raiders wished to destroy merchant ships, *Sisu* and her sisters would not stand a chance. But the raider wants loot and slaves; it gains nothing simply to blast a ship.

Merchantmen are limited by no qualms; an attacking ship's destruction is the ideal outcome. Atomic target-seekers are dreadfully expensive, and using them up is rough on profit-and-loss—but there is no holding back if the computer says the target can be reached—whereas a raider will use destruction weapons only to save himself. His tactic is to blind the trader, burn out her instruments so that he can get close enough to paralyze everyone aboard—or, failing that, kill without destroying ship and cargo.

The trader runs if she can, fights if she must. But when she fights, she fights to kill.

Whenever *Sisu* was below speed-of-light, she listened with artificial senses to every disturbance in multi-space, the whisper of n-space communication or the "white" roar of a ship boosting at many gravities. Data poured into the ship's astrogational analog of space and the questions were: Where is this other ship? What is its course? speed? acceleration? Can it catch us before we reach n-space?

If the answers were threatening, digested data channeled into port and starboard fire-control computers and *Sisu* braced herself to fight. Ordnancemen armed A-bomb target seekers, caressed their sleek sides and muttered charms; the Chief Engineer unlocked the suicide switch which could let the power plant become a hydrogen bomb of monstrous size and prayed that, in final extremity, he would have the courage to deliver his people into the shelter of death; the Captain sounded the clangor calling the ship from watch-and-watch to General Quarters. Cooks switched off fires; auxiliary engineers closed down air circulation; farmers said good-by to their green growing things and hurried to fighting stations; mothers with babies mustered, then strapped down and held those babies tightly.

Then the waiting started.

But not for Thorby—not for those assigned to fire-control computers. Sweating into their straps, for the next minutes or hours the life of *Sisu* is in their hands. The fire-control computer machines, chewing with millisecond meditation data from the analog, decide whether or not torpedoes can reach the target, then offer four answers: ballistic "possible" or "impossible" for projected condition, yes or no for condition changed by one ship, or the other, or both, through cutting power. These answers automatic circuits could handle alone, but machines do not think. Half of each computer is designed to allow the operator to ask what the situation might be in the far future of five minutes or so from now if variables change . . . and whether the target might be reached under such changes.

Any variable can be shaded by human judgment; an intuitive projection by a human operator can save his ship—or lose it. A paralysis beam travels at speed-of-light; torpedoes never have time to get up to more than a few hundred kilometers per second—yet it is possible for a raider to come within beaming range, have his pencil of paralyzing radiation on its way, and the trader to launch a target-seeker before the beam strikes . . . and still be saved when the outlaw flames into atomic mist a little later.

But if the operator is too eager by a few seconds, or overly cautious by the same, he can lose his ship. Too eager, the missile will fail to reach target; too cautious, it will never be launched.

Seasoned oldsters are not good at these jobs. The perfect firecontrolman is an adolescent, or young man or woman, fast in thought and action, confident, with intuitive grasp of mathematical relations beyond rote and rule, and not afraid of death he cannot yet imagine.

The traders must be always alert for such youngsters; Thorby seemed to have the feel for mathematics; he might have the other talents for a job something like chess played under terrific pressure and a fast game of spat ball. His mentor was Jeri Kingsolver, his nephew and roommate. Jeri was junior in family rank but appeared to be older; he called Thorby "Uncle" outside the computer room; on the job Thorby called him "Starboard Senior Firecontrolman" and added "Sir."

During long weeks of the dive through dark toward Losian, Jeri drilled Thorby. Thorby was supposed to be training for hydroponics and Jeri was the Supercargo's Senior Clerk, but the ship had plenty of farmers and the Supercargo's office was never very busy in space; Captain Krausa directed Jeri to keep Thorby hard at it in the computer room.

Since the ship remained at battle stations for half a week while boosting to speed-of-light, each fighting station had two persons assigned watch-and-watch. Jeri's junior controlman was his younger sister Mata. The computer had twin consoles, either of which could command by means of a selector switch. At General Quarters they sat side by side, with Jeri controlling and Mata ready to take over.

After a stiff course in what the machine could do Jeri put Thorby at one console, Mata at the other and fed them problems from the ship's control room. Each console recorded; it was possible to see what decisions each operator had made and how these compared with those made in battle, for the data were from records, real or threatened battles in the past.

Shortly Thorby became extremely irked; Mata was enormously better at it than he was.

So he tried harder and got worse. While he sweated, trying to outguess a slave raider which had once been on *Sisu*'s screens, he was painfully aware of a slender, dark, rather pretty girl beside him, her swift fingers making tiny adjustments among keys and knobs, changing a bias or modifying a vector, herself relaxed and unhurried. It was humiliating afterwards to find that his pacesetter had "saved the ship" while he had failed.

Worse still, he was aware of her as a girl and did not know it—all he knew was that she made him uneasy.

After one run Jeri called from ship's control, "End of drill. Stand by." He appeared shortly and examined their tapes, reading marks on sensitized paper as another might read print. He pursed his lips over Thorby's record. "Trainee, you fired three times . . . and not a one of your beasts got within fifty thousand kilometers of the enemy. We don't mind expense—it's merely Grandmother's blood. But the object is to blast him, not scare him into a fit. You have to wait until you can hit."

"I did my best!"

"Not good enough. Let's see yours, Sis."

The nickname irritated Thorby still more. Brother and sister were fond of each other and did not bother with titles. So Thorby had tried using their names . . . and had been snubbed; he was "Trainee," they were "Senior Controlman" and "Junior Controlman." There was nothing he could do; at drill he was junior. For a week, Thorby addressed Jeri as "Foster Ortho-Nephew" outside of drills and Jeri had carefully addressed him by family title. Then Thorby decided it was silly and went back to calling him Jeri. But Jeri continued to call him "Trainee" during drill, and so did Mata.

Jeri looked over his sister's record and nodded. "Very nice, Sis! You're within a second of post-analyzed optimum, and three seconds better than the shot that got the so-and-so. I have to admit that's sweet shooting . . . because the real run is my own. That raider off Ingstel . . . remember?"

"I certainly do." She glanced at Thorby.

Thorby felt disgusted. "It's not fair!" He started hauling at safety-belt buckles.

Jeri looked surprised. "What, Trainee?"

"I said it's not fair! You send down a problem, I tackle it cold—and get bawled out because I'm not perfect. But all she had to do is to fiddle with controls to get an answer she already knows . . . to make me look cheap!"

Mata was looking stricken. Thorby headed for the door. "I never asked for this! I'm going to the Captain and ask for another job."

"Trainee!"

Thorby stopped. Jeri went on quietly. "Sit down. When I'm through, you can see the Captain—if you think it's advisable."

Thorby sat down.

"I've two things to say," Jeri continued coldly. "First—" He turned to his sister. "Junior Controlman, did you know what problem this was when you were tracking?"

"No, Senior Controlman."

"Have you worked it before?"

"I don't think so."

"How was it you remembered it?"

"What? Why, you said it was the raider off Ingstel. I'll never forget because of the dinner afterwards—you sat with Great Grandmo—with the Chief Officer."

Jeri turned to Thorby. "You see? She tracked it cold . . . as cold as I had to when it happened. And she did even better than I did; I'm proud to have her as my junior tracker. For your information, Mister Stupid Junior Trainee, this engagement took place before the Junior Controlman became a trainee. She hasn't even run it in practice. She's just better at it than you are."

"All right," Thorby said sullenly. "I'll probably never be any good. I said I wanted to quit."

"I'm talking. Nobody asks for this job; it's a headache. Nobody quits it, either. After a while the job quits him, when post-analysis shows that he is losing his touch. Maybe I'm beginning to. But I promise you this: you'll either learn, or *I* will go to the Captain and tell him you don't measure up. In the meantime . . . if I have any lip out of you, I'll haul you before the Chief Officer!" He snapped, "Extra drill run. Battle stations. Cast loose your equipment." He left the room.

Moments later his voice reached them. "Bogie! Starboard computer room, report!"

The call to dinner sounded; Mata said gravely, "Starboard tracker manned. Data showing, starting run." Her fingers started caressing keys. Thorby bent over his own controls; he wasn't hungry anyhow. For days Thorby spoke with Jeri only formally. He saw Mata at drill, or across the lounge at meals; he treated her with cold correctness and tried to do as well as she did. He could have seen her at other times; young people associated freely in public places. She was taboo to him, both as his niece and because they were of the same moiety, but that was no bar to social relations.

Jeri he could not avoid; they ate at the same table, slept in the same room. But Thorby could and did throw up a barrier of formality. No one said anything—these things happened. Even Fritz pretended not to notice.

But one afternoon Thorby dropped into the lounge to see a story film with a Sargonese background; Thorby sat through it to pick it to pieces. But when it was over he could not avoid noticing Mata because she walked over, stood in front of him, addressed him humbly as her uncle and asked if he would care for a game of spat ball before supper?

He was about to refuse when he noticed her face; she was watching him with tragic eagerness. So he answered, "Why, thanks, Mata. Work up an appetite."

She broke into smiles. "Good! I've got Ilsa holding a table. Let's!"

Thorby beat her three games and tied one . . . a remarkable score, since she was female champion and was allowed only one point handicap when playing the male champion. But he did not think about it; he was enjoying himself.

His performance picked up, partly through the grimness with which he worked, partly because he did have feeling for complex geometry, and partly because the beggar's boy had had his brain sharpened by an ancient discipline. Jeri never again compared aloud the performances of Mata and Thorby and gave only brief comments on Thorby's results: "Better," or "Coming along," and eventually, "You're getting there." Thorby's morale soared; he loosened up and spent more time socially, playing spat ball with Mata rather frequently.

Toward the end of journey through darkness they finished the last drill one morning and Jeri called out, "Stand easy! I'll be a few minutes." Thorby relaxed from pleasant strain. But after a moment he fidgeted; he had a hunch that he had been in tune with his instruments. "Junior Controlman . . . do you suppose he would mind if I looked at my tape?"

"I don't think so," Mata answered. "I'll take it out; then it's my responsibility."

"I don't want to get you in trouble."

"You won't," Mata answered serenely. She reached back of Thorby's console, pulled out the strip record, blew on it to keep it from curling, and examined it. Then she pulled her own strip, compared the two.

She looked at him gravely. "That's a very good run, Thorby."

It was the first time she had ever spoken his name. But Thorby hardly noticed. "Really? You mean it?"

"It's a *very* good run . . . Thorby. We both got hits. But yours is optimum between 'possible' and 'critical limit'—whereas mine is too eager. See?"

Thorby could read strips only haltingly, but he was happy to take her word for it. Jeri came in, took both strips, looked at Thorby's, then looked more closely. "I dug up the post-analysis before I came down," he said.

"Yes, sir?" Thorby said eagerly.

"Mmm . . . I'll check it after chow—but it looks as if your mistakes had cancelled out."

Mata said, "Why, Bud, that's a perfect run and you know it!"

"Suppose it is?" Jeri grinned. "You wouldn't want our star pupil to get a swelled head, would you?"

"Pooh!"

"Right back to you, small and ugly sister. Let's go to chow."

They went through a narrow passage into trunk corridor of second deck, where they walked abreast. Thorby gave a deep sigh.

"Trouble?" his nephew asked.

"Not a bit!" Thorby put an arm around each of them. "Jeri, you and Mata are going to make a marksman out of me yet."

It was the first time Thorby had addressed his teacher by name since the day he had received the scorching. But Jeri accepted his uncle's overture without stiffness. "Don't get your hopes up, bunkmate. But I think we've got it licked." He added, "I see Great Aunt Tora is giving us her famous cold eye. If anybody wants my opinion, I think Sis can walk unassisted—I'm sure Great Aunt thinks so."

"Pooh to her, too!" Mata said briskly. "Thorby just made a perfect run."

Sisu came out of darkness, dropping below speed-of-light. Losian's sun blazed less than fifty billion kilometers away; in a few days they would reach their next market. The ship went to watch-and-watch battle stations.

Mata took her watch alone; Jeri required the trainee to stand watches with him. The first watch was always free from strain; even if a raider had accurate information via n-space communicator of *Sisu*'s time of departure and destination, it was impossible in a jump of many light-years to predict the exact time and place where she would poke her nose out into rational space.

Jeri settled in his chair some minutes after Thorby had strapped down with that age-old tense feeling that this time it was not practice. Jeri grinned at him. "Relax. If you get your blood stream loaded, your back will ache, and you'll never last."

Thorby grinned feebly. "I'll try."

"That's better. We're going to play a game." Jeri pulled a boxlike contrivance out of a pocket, snapped it open.

"What is that?"

"A 'killjoy.' It fits here." Jeri slipped it over the switch that determined which console was in command. "Can you see the switch?"

"Huh? No."

"Hand the man the prize." Jeri fiddled with the switch behind the screen. "Which of us is in control in case we have to launch a bomb now?"

"How can I tell? Take that off, Jeri; it makes me nervous."

"That's the game. Maybe I'm controlling and you are just going through motions; maybe *you* are the man at the trigger and I'm asleep in my chair. Every so often I'll fiddle with the switch—but you won't know how I've left it. So when a flap comes—and one will; I feel it in my bones—you can't assume that good old Jeri, the man with the micrometer fingers, has the situation under control. You might have to save the firm. *You.*"

Thorby had a queasy vision of waiting men and bombs in the missile room below—waiting for him to solve precisely an impossible problem of life and death, of warped space and shifting vectors and complex geometry. "You're kidding," he said feebly. "You wouldn't leave me in control. Why, the Captain would skin you alive."

"Ah, that's where you're wrong. There always comes a day when a trainee makes his first real run. After that, he's a controlman . . . or an angel. But we don't let you worry at the time. Oh no! we just keep you worried all the time. Now here's the game. Any time I say, 'Now!' you guess who has control. You guess right, I owe you one dessert; you guess wrong, you owe me one. *Now!*"

Thorby thought quickly. "I guess I've got it."

"Wrong." Jeri lifted the killjoy. "You owe me one dessert—and it's berry tart tonight; my mouth is watering. But faster; you're supposed to make quick decisions. Now!"

"You've still got it!"

"So I have. Even. Now!"

"You!"

"Nope. See? And I eat your tart—I ought to quit while I'm ahead. Love that juice! Now!"

When Mata relieved them, Jeri owned Thorby's desserts for the next four days. "We start again with that score," Jeri said, "except that I'm going to collect that berry tart. But I forgot to tell you the big prize."

"Which is?"

"Comes the real thing, we bet three desserts. After it's over, you guess and we settle. Always bet more on real ones."

Mata sniffed. "Bud, are you trying to make him nervous?"

"Are you nervous, Thorby?"

"Nope!"

"Quit fretting, Sis. Got it firmly in your grubby little hands?"

"I relieve you, sir."

"Come on, Thorby; let's eat. Berry tarts—aaah!"

Three days later the score stood even, but only because Thorby had missed most of his desserts. *Sisu* was enormously slowed, almost to planetary speeds, and Losian's sun loomed large on the screens. Thorby decided, with mildest regret, that his ability to fight would not be tested this jump.

Then the general alarm made him rear up against safety belts. Jeri had been talking; his head jerked around, he looked at displays, and his hands moved to his controls. "Get on it!" he yelped. "This one's real."

Thorby snapped out of shock and bent over his board. The analog globe was pouring data to them; the ballistic situation had built up. Good heavens, it was *close!* And matching in fast! How had anything moved in so close without being detected? Then he quit thinking and started investigating answers . . . no, not yet . . . before long though . . . could the bandit turn a little at that boost and reduce his approach? . . . try a projection at an assumed six gravities of turning . . . would a missile reach him? . . . would it still reach him if he did not—

He hardly felt Mata's gentle touch on his shoulder. But he heard Jeri snap, "Stay out, Sis! We're on it, we're on it!"

A light blinked on Thorby's board; the squawk horn sounded, "Friendly craft, friendly craft! Losian planetary patrol, identified. Return to watch-and-watch."

Thorby took a deep breath, felt a great load lift.

"Continue your run!" screamed Jeri.

"Huh?"

"*Finish your run!* That's no Losian craft; *that's a raider!* Losians can't maneuver that way! You've got it, boy, you've got it! *Nail him!*"

Thorby heard Mata's frightened gasp, but he was again at his problem. Change anything? Could he reach him? Could he still reach him in the cone of possible maneuver? *Now!* He armed his board and let the computer give the order, on projection.

He heard Jeri's voice faintly; Jeri seemed to be talking very slowly. "Missile away. I think you got him . . . but you were eager. Get off another one before their beam hits us."

Automatically Thorby complied. Time was too short to try another solution; he ordered the machine to send another missile according to projection. He then saw by his board that the target was no longer under power and decided with a curiously empty feeling that his first missile had destroyed it.

"That's all!" Jeri announced. "Now!"

"What?"

"Who had it? You or me? Three desserts."

"*I* had it," Thorby said with certainty. In another level he decided that he would never really be a Trader—to Jeri that target had been—just fraki. Or three desserts.

"Wrong. That puts me three up. I turned coward and kept control myself. Of course the bombs were disarmed and the launchers locked as soon as the Captain gave the word . . . but I didn't have the nerve to risk an accident with a friendly ship."

"*Friendly* ship!"

"Of course. But for you, Assistant Junior Controlman, it was your first real one . . . as I intended."

Thorby's head floated. Mata said, "Bud, you're mean to collect. You cheated."

"Sure I cheated. But he's a blooded controlman now, just the same. And I'm going to collect, just the very same. Ice cream tonight!"

10

THORBY DID NOT STAY AN ASSISTANT JUNIOR FIRECONTROLMAN; JERI moved up to astrogation trainee; Mata took charge of the starboard room, and Thorby was officially posted as the new Starboard Junior Firecontrolman, with life and death in his forefinger. He was not sure that he liked it.

Then that arrangement tumbled almost as quickly.

Losian is a "safe" planet. Inhabited by civilized non-humans, it is a port safe from ground raids; no dirtside defensive watches were necessary. Men could leave the ship for pleasure and even women could do so. (Some of the women aboard had not left the ship, save at Gatherings of the People, since being exchanged to *Sisu* as girls.)

Losian was to Thorby his "first" foreign land, Jubbul being the only planet clear in his memory. So he was very eager to see it. But work came first. When he was confirmed as a firecontrolman, he was transferred from hydroponics into the junior vacancy among the Supercargo's clerks. It increased Thorby's status; business carried more prestige than housekeeping. Theoretically he was now qualified to check cargo; in fact a senior clerk did that while Thorby sweated, along with junior male relatives from every department. Cargo was an all-hands operation, as *Sisu* never permitted stevedores inside, even if it meant paying for featherbedding.

The Losians have never invented tariff; crated bales of verga leaves were turned over to purchaser right outside the ship. In spite of blowers the hold reeked of their spicy, narcotic fragrance and reminded Thorby of months past and light-years away when he had huddled, a fugitive in danger of being shortened, into a hole in one crate while a friendly stranger smuggled him through the Sargon's police.

It didn't seem possible. *Sisu* was home. Even as he mused, he thought in the Family's language.

He realized with sudden guilt that he had not thought about Pop very often lately. Was he forgetting Pop? No, no! He could never forget, not anything . . . Pop's tones of voice, the detached look when he was about to comment unfavorably, his creaking movements on chilly mornings, his unfailing patience no matter what—why, in all those years Pop had never been angry with him—yes, he had, once.

" *'I am not your master!'* "

Pop had been angry that once. It had scared Thorby; he hadn't understood.

Now, across long space and time, Thorby suddenly understood. Only one thing could make Pop angry: Pop had been explosively insulted at the assertion that Baslim the Cripple was master to a slave. Pop, who maintained that a wise man could not be insulted, since truth could not insult and untruth was not worthy of notice.

Yet Pop had been insulted by the truth, for certainly Pop had been his master; Pop had bought him off the block. No, that was nonsense! He hadn't been Pop's slave; he had been Pop's son . . . Pop was never his master, even the times he had given him a quick one across the behind for goofing. Pop . . . was just 'Pop.'

Thorby knew then that the one thing that Pop hated was slavery.

Thorby was not sure why he was sure, but he was. He could not recall that Pop had ever said a word about slavery, as such; all Thorby could remember Pop saying was that a man need never be other than free in his own mind.

"Hey!"

The Supercargo was looking at him. "Sir?"

"Are you moving that crate, or making a bed of it?"

Three local days later Thorby had finished showering, about to hit dirt with Fritz, when the deckmaster stuck his head in the washroom, spotted him, and said, "Captain's compliments and Clerk Thorby Baslim-Krausa will attend him."

"Aye aye, Deckmaster," Thorby answered and added something under his breath. He hurried into clothes, stuck his head into his bunkie, gave the sad word to Fritz and rushed to the Cabin, hoping that the Deckmaster had told the Captain that Thorby had been showering.

The door was open. Thorby started to report formally when the Captain looked up. "Hello, Son. Come in."

Thorby shifted gears from Ship to Family. "Yes, Father."

"I'm about to hit dirt. Want to come along?"

"Sir? I mean, 'Yes, Father!' that 'ud be swell!"

"Good. I see you're ready. Let's go." He reached in a drawer and handed Thorby some twisted bits of wire. "Here's pocket money; you may want a souvenir."

Thorby examined it. "What's this stuff worth, Father?"

"Nothing—once we're off Losian. So give me back what you have left so I can turn it in for credit. They pay us off in thorium and goods."

"Yes, but how will I know how much to pay for a thing?"

"Take their word for it. They won't cheat and won't bargain. Odd ones. Not like Lotarf . . . on Lotarf, if you buy a beer without an hour's dickering you're ahead."

Thorby felt that he understood Lotarfi better than he did Losians. There was something indecent about a purchase without a polite amount of dickering. But fraki had barbaric customs; you had to cater to them—*Sisu* prided herself on never having trouble with fraki.

"Come along. We can talk as we go."

As they were being lowered Thorby looked at the ship nearest them, Free Trader *El Nido*, Garcia clan. "Father, are we going to visit with them?"

"No, I exchanged calls the first day."

"I didn't mean that. Will there be any parties?"

"Oh. Captain Garcia and I agreed to dispense with hospitality; he's anxious to jump. No reason why you shouldn't visit them though, subject to your duties." He added, "Hardly worth it; she's like *Sisu*, only not as modern."

"Thought I might look at her computer rooms."

They hit ground and stepped off. "Doubt if they'd let you. They're a superstitious lot." As they stepped clear of the hoist a baby Losian came streaking up, circled and sniffed their legs. Captain Krausa let the little thing investigate him, then said mildly, "That's enough," and gently pushed it away. Its mother whistled it back, picked it up and spanked it. Captain Krausa waved to her, called out, "Hello, friend!"

"Hello, Trader Man," she answered in Interlingua shrill and sibilant. She was two-thirds Thorby's height, on four legs with forelimbs elevated—the baby had been on all six. Both were sleek and pretty and sharp-eyed. Thorby was amused by them and only slightly put off by the double mouth arrangement—one for eating, one for breathing and talking.

Captain Krausa continued talking. "That was a nice run you made on that Losian craft."

Thorby blushed. "You knew about that, Father?"

"What kind of a captain am I if I don't? Oh, I know what's worrying you. Forget it. If I give you a target, you burn it. It's up to me to kill your circuits if we make friendly identification. If I slap the God-be-thanked switch, you can't get your computer to fire, the bombs are disarmed, the launching gear is locked, the Chief can't move the suicide switch. So even if you hear me call off the action—or you get excited and don't hear—it doesn't matter. Finish your run; it's good practice."

"Oh. I didn't know, Father."

"Didn't Jeri tell you? You must have noticed the switch; it's the big red one, under my right hand."

"Uh, I've never been in the Control Room, Father."

"Eh? I must correct that; it might belong to you someday. Remind me . . . right after we go irrational."

"I will, Father." Thorby was pleased at the prospect of entering the mysterious shrine—he was sure that half of his relatives had never visited it—but he was surprised at the comment. Could a former fraki be eligible for command? It was legal for an adopted son to succeed to the worry seat; sometimes captains had no sons of their own. But an ex-fraki?

Captain Krausa was saying, "I haven't given you the attention I should, Son . . . not the care I should give Baslim's son. But it's a big family and my time is so taken up. Are they treating you all right?"

"Why, sure, Father!"

"Mmm . . . glad to hear it. It's—well, you weren't born among the People, you know."

"I know. But everybody has treated me fine."

"Good. I've had good reports about you. You seem to learn fast, for a—you learn fast."

Thorby sourly finished the phrase in his mind. The Captain went on, "Have you been in the Power Room?"

"No, sir. Just the practice room once."

"Now is a good time, while we're grounded. It's safer and the prayers and cleansing aren't so lengthy." Krausa paused. "No, we'll wait until your status is clear—the Chief is hinting that you are material for his department. He has some silly idea that you will never have children anyway and he might regard a visit as an opportunity to snag you. Engineers!"

Thorby understood this speech, even the last word. Engineers were regarded as slightly balmy; it was commonly believed that radiations from the artificial star that gave *Sisu* her life ionized their brain tissues. True or not, engineers could get away with outrageous breaches of etiquette—"not guilty by reason of insanity" was an unspoken defense for them once they had been repeatedly exposed to the hazards of their trade. The Chief Engineer even talked back to Grandmother.

But junior engineers were not allowed to stand power room watches until they no longer expected to have children; they took care of auxiliary machinery and stood training watches in a dummy power room. The People were cautious about harmful mutations, because they were more exposed to radiation hazards than were planet dwellers. One never saw overt mutation among them; what happened to babies distorted at birth was a mystery so taboo that Thorby was not even aware of it; he simply knew that power watchstanders were old men.

Nor was he interested in progeny; he simply saw in the Captain's remarks a hint that the Chief Engineer considered that Thorby could reach the exalted status of power watchstander quickly. The idea dazzled him. The men who wrestled with the mad gods of nuclear physics held status just below astrogators . . . and, in their own opinion, higher. Their opinion was closer to fact than was the official one; even a deputy captain who attempted to pull rank on a man standing power room watches was likely to wind up counting stores while the engineer rested in sick bay, then went back to doing as he pleased. Was it possible that an ex-fraki could aspire to such heights? Perhaps someday be Chief Engineer and sass the Chief Officer with impunity? "Father," Thorby said eagerly, "the Chief Engineer thinks I can learn power room rituals?"

"Wasn't that what I said?"

"Yes, sir. Uh . . . I wonder why he thought so?"

"Are you dense? Or unusually modest? Any man who can handle firecontrol mathematics can learn nuclear engineering. But he can learn astrogation, too, which is just as important."

Engineers never handled cargo; the only work they did in port was to load tritium and deuterium, or other tasks strictly theirs. They did no housekeeping. They . . . "Father? I think I might like to be an engineer."

"So? Well, now that you've thought so, forget it."

"But—"

" 'But' what?"

"Nothing, sir. Yes, sir."

Krausa sighed. "Son, I have obligations toward you; I'm carrying them out as best I can." Krausa thought over what he could tell the lad. Mother had pointed out that if Baslim had wanted the boy to know the message he had carried, Baslim would have put it in Interlingua. On the other hand, since the boy now knew the Family language perhaps he had translated it himself. No, more likely he had forgotten it. "Thorby, do you know who your family is?"

Thorby was startled. "Sir? My family is *Sisu.*"

"Certainly! I mean your family before that."

"You mean Pop? Baslim the Cripple?"

"No, no! He was your foster father, just as I am now. Do you know what family you were born in?"

Thorby said bleakly, "I don't think I had one."

Krausa realized that he had poked a scar, said hastily, "Now, Son, you don't have to copy all the attitudes of your messmates. Why, if it weren't for fraki, with whom would we trade? How would the People live? A man is fortunate to be born People, but there is nothing to be ashamed of in being born fraki. Every atom has its purpose."

"I'm not ashamed!"

"Take it easy!"

"Sorry sir. I'm not ashamed of my ancestors. I simply don't know who they were. Why, for all I know, they may have been People."

Krausa was startled. "Why, so they could have been," he said slowly. Most slaves were purchased on planets that respectable traders never visited, or were born on estates of their owners . . . but a tragic percentage were *People,* stolen by raiders. This lad— Had any ship of the People been lost around the necessary time? He wondered if, at the next Gathering, he might dig up identification from the Commodore's files?

But even that would not exhaust the possibilities; some chief officers were sloppy about sending in identifications at birth, some waited until a Gathering. Mother, now, never grudged the expense of a long n-space message; she wanted her children on record at once—*Sisu* was never slack.

Suppose the boy were born People and his record had never reached the Commodore? How unfair to lose his birthright!

A thought tip-toed through his brain: a slip could be corrected in more ways than one. If any Free Ship had been lost— He could not remember.

Nor could he talk about it. But what a wonderful thing to give the lad an ancestry! If he could . . .

He changed the subject. "In a way, lad, you were always of the People."

"Huh? Excuse me, Father?"

"Son, Baslim the Cripple was an honorary member of the People."

"*What?* How, Father? What ship?"

"All ships. He was elected at a Gathering. Son, a long time ago a shameful thing happened. Baslim corrected it. It put all the People in debt to him. I have said enough. Tell me, have you thought of getting married?"

Marriage was the last thing on Thorby's mind; he was blazing anxious to hear more about what Pop had done that had made him incredibly one of the People. But he recognized the warning with which an elder closed a taboo subject.

"Why, no, Father."

"Your Grandmother thinks that you have begun to notice girls seriously."

"Well, sir, Grandmother is never wrong . . . but I hadn't been aware of it."

"A man isn't complete without a wife. But I don't think you're old enough. Laugh with all the girls and cry with none—and remember our customs." Krausa was thinking that he was bound by Baslim's injunction to seek aid of the Hegemony in finding where the lad had come from. It would be awkward if Thorby married before the opportunity arose. Yet the boy had grown taller in the months he had been in *Sisu*. Adding to Krausa's fret was an uneasy feeling that his half-conceived notion of finding (or faking) an ancestry for Thorby conflicted with his unbreakable obligations to Baslim.

Then he had a cheerful idea. "Tell you what, Son! It's possible that the girl for you isn't aboard. After all, there are only a few in port side purdah—and picking a wife is a serious matter. She can gain you status or ruin you. So why not take it easy? At the Great Gathering you will meet hundreds of eligible girls. If you find one you like and who likes you, I'll discuss it with your Grandmother and if she approves, we'll dicker for her exchange. We won't be stingy either. How does that sound?"

It put the problem comfortably in the distance. "It sounds fine, Father!"

"I have said enough." Krausa thought happily that he would check the files while Thorby was meeting those "hundreds of girls"—and he need not review his obligation to Baslim until he had done so. The lad might be a born member of the People—in fact his obvious merits made fraki ancestry almost unthinkable. If so, Baslim's wishes would be carried out in the spirit more than if followed to the letter. In the meantime—forget it!

They completed the mile to the edge of the Losian community. Thorby stared at sleek Losian ships and thought uneasily that he had tried to burn one of those pretty things out of space. Then he reminded himself that Father had said it was not a firecontrolman's business to worry about what target was handed him.

When they got into city traffic he had no time to worry. Losians do not use passenger cars, nor do they favor anything as stately as a sedan chair. On foot, they scurry twice as fast as a man can run; in a hurry, they put on a vehicle which makes one think of jet propulsion. Four and sometimes six limbs are encased in sleeves which end in something like skates. A framework fits the body and carries a bulge for the power plant (what sort Thorby could not imagine). Encased in this mechanical clown suit, each becomes a guided missile, accelerating with careless abandon, showering sparks, filling the air with earsplitting noises, cornering in defiance of friction, inertia, and gravity, cutting in and out, never braking until the last minute.

Pedestrians and powered speed maniacs mix democratically, with no perceptible rules. There seems to be no age limit for driver's licenses and the smallest Losians are simply more reckless editions of their elders.

Thorby wondered if he would ever get out into space alive.

A Losian would come zipping toward Thorby on the wrong side of the street (there was no right side), squeal to a stop almost on Thorby's toes, zig aside while snatching breath off his face and heart out of his mouth—and never touch him. Thorby would jump. After a dozen escapes he tried to pattern himself after his foster father. Captain Krausa plowed stolidly ahead, apparently sure that the wild drivers would treat him as a stationary object. Thorby found it hard to live by that faith, but it seemed to work.

Thorby could not make out how the city was organized. Powered traffic and pedestrians poured through any opening and the convention of private land and public street did not seem to hold. At first they proceeded along an area which Thorby classified as a plaza, then they went up a ramp, through a building which had no clear limits—no vertical walls, no defined roof—out again and down, through an arch which skirted a hole. Thorby was lost.

Once he thought they must be going through a private home—they pushed through what must have been a dinner party. But the guests merely pulled in their feet.

Krausa stopped. "We're almost there. Son, we're visiting the fraki who bought our load. This meeting heals the trouble between us caused by buying and selling. He has offended me by offering payment; now we have to become friends again."

"We don't get paid?"

"What would your Grandmother say? We've already been paid—but now I'll give it to him free and he'll give me the thorium just because he likes my pretty blue eyes. Their customs don't allow anything as crass as selling."

"They don't trade with each other?"

"Of course they do. But the theory is that one fraki gives another anything he needs. It's sheer accident that the other happens to have money that he is anxious to press on the other as a gift—and that the two gifts balance. They are shrewd merchants, Son; we never pick up an extra credit here."

"Then why this nonsense?"

"Son, if you worry about why fraki do what they do, you'll drive yourself crazy. When you're on their planet, do it their way . . . it's good business. Now listen. We'll have a meal of friendship . . . only they can't, or they'll lose face. So there will be a screen between us. You have to be present, because the Losian's son will be there—only it's a daughter. And the fraki I'm going to see is the mother, not the father. Their males live in purdah . . . I think. But notice that when I speak through the interpreter, I'll use masculine gender."

"Why?"

"Because they know enough about our customs to know that masculine gender means the head of the house. It's logical if you look at it correctly."

Thorby wondered. Who was head of the Family? Father? Or Grandmother? Of course, when the Chief Officer issued an order, she signed it "By Order of the Captain," but that was just because . . . no. Well, anyhow—

Thorby suddenly suspected that the customs of the Family might be illogical in spots. But the Captain was speaking. "We don't actually eat with them; that's another fiction. You'll be served a green, slimy liquid. Just raise it to your lips; it would burn out your gullet. Otherwise—" Captain Krausa paused while a Losian scorcher avoided the end of his nose. "Otherwise listen so that you will know how to behave next time. Oh yes!—after I ask how old my host's son is, you'll be asked how old you are. You answer 'forty.' "

"Why?"

"Because that is a respectable age, in their years, for a son who is assisting his father."

They arrived and seemed still to be in public. But they squatted down opposite two Losians while a third crouched nearby. The screen between them was the size of a kerchief; Thorby could see over it. Thorby tried to look, listen, and learn, but the traffic never let up. It shot around and cut between them, with happy, shrill racket.

Their host started by accusing Captain Krausa of having lured him into a misdeed. The interpreter was almost impossible to understand, but he showed surprising command of scurrilous Interlingua. Thorby could not believe his ears and expected that Father would either walk out, or start trouble.

But Captain Krausa listened quietly, then answered with real poetry—he accused the Losian of every crime from barratry to mopery and dopery in the spaceways.

This put the meeting on a friendly footing. The Losian made them a present of the thorium he had already paid, then offered to throw in his sons and everything he possessed.

Captain Krausa accepted and gave away *Sisu,* with all contents.

Both parties generously gave back the gifts. They ended at status quo, each to retain as a symbol of friendship what each now had: the Losian many hundredweight of verga leaf, the Trader slugs of thorium. Both agreed that the gifts were worthless but valuable for reasons of sentiment. In a burst of emotion the Losian gave away his son and Krausa made him (her) a present of Thorby. Inquiries followed and it was discovered that each was too young to leave the nest.

They got out of this dilemma by having the sons exchange names and Thorby found himself owner of a name he did not want and could not pronounce. Then they "ate."

The horrid green stuff was not only not fit to drink, but when Thorby inhaled, he burned his nostrils and choked. The Captain gave him a reproving glance.

After that they left. No good-bys, they just walked off. Captain Krausa said meditatively while proceeding like a sleepwalker through the riot of traffic, "Nice people, for fraki. Never any sharp dealing and absolutely honest. I often wonder what one of them would do if I took him up on one of those offers. Pay up, probably."

"Not really!"

"Don't be sure. I might hand you in on that half-grown Losian."

Thorby shut up.

Business concluded, Captain Krausa helped Thorby shop and sightsee, which relieved Thorby, because he did not know what to buy, nor even how to get home. His foster father took him to a shop where Interlingua was understood. Losians manufacture all sorts of things of extreme complexity, none of which Thorby recognized. On Krausa's advice Thorby selected a small polished cube which, when shaken, showed endless Losian scenes in its depths. Thorby offered the shopkeeper his tokens; the Losian selected one and gave him change from a necklace of money. Then he made Thorby a present of shop and contents.

Thorby, speaking through Krausa, regretted that he had nothing to offer save his own services the rest of his life. They backed out of the predicament with courteous insults.

Thorby felt relieved when they reached the spaceport and he saw the homely, familiar lines of old *Sisu*.

When Thorby reached his bunkie, Jeri was there, feet up and hands back of his head. He looked up and did not smile.

"Hi, Jeri!"

"Hello, Thorby."

"Hit dirt?"

"No."

"I did. Look what I bought!" Thorby showed him the magic cube. "You shake it and every picture is different."

Jeri looked at one picture and handed it back. "Very nice."

"Jeri, what are you glum about? Something you ate?"

"No."

"Spill it."

Jeri dropped his feet to the deck, looked at Thorby. "I'm back in the computer room."

"Huh?"

"Oh, I don't lose status. It's just while I train somebody else."

Thorby felt a cold wind. "You mean I've been busted?"

"No."

"Then what *do* you mean?"

"Mata has been swapped."

11

Mata swapped? Gone forever? Little Mattie with the grave eyes and merry giggle? Thorby felt a burst of sorrow and realized to his surprise that it mattered.

"I don't believe it!"

"Don't be a fool."

"When? Where has she gone? Why didn't you tell me?"

"To *El Nido*, obviously; it's the only ship of the People in port. About an hour ago. I didn't tell you because I had no idea it was coming . . . until I was summoned to Grandmother's cabin to say good-by." Jeri frowned. "It had to come someday . . . but I thought Grandmother would let her stay as long as she kept her skill as a tracker."

"Then why, Jeri? *Why?*"

Jeri stood up, said woodenly, "Foster Ortho-Uncle, I have said enough."

Thorby pushed him back into his chair. "You can't get away with that, Jeri. I'm your 'uncle' only because they said I was. But I'm still the ex-fraki you taught to use a tracker and we both know it. Now talk man to man. Spill it!"

"You won't like it."

"I don't like it now! Mattie gone . . . Look, Jeri, there is nobody here but us. Whatever it is, tell me. I promise you, on *Sisu*'s steel, that I won't make an uncle-and-nephew matter of it. Whatever you say, the Family will never know."

"Grandmother might be listening."

"If she is, I've ordered you to talk and it's my responsibility. But she won't be; it's time for her nap. So talk."

"Okay." Jeri looked at him sourly. "You asked for it. You mean to say you haven't the dimmest idea why Grandmother hustled my Sis out of the ship?"

"Huh? None . . . or I wouldn't ask."

Jeri made an impatient noise. "Thorby, I knew you were thick-witted. I didn't know you were deaf, dumb, and blind."

"Never mind the compliments! Tell me the score."

"You're the reason Mata got swapped. *You.*" Jeri looked at Thorby with disgust.

"Me?"

"Who else? Who pairs off at spat ball? Who sits together at story films? What new relative is always seen with a girl from his own moiety? I'll give you a hint—the name starts with 'T.' "

Thorby turned white. "Jeri, I never had the slightest idea."

"You're the only one in the ship who didn't." Jeri shrugged. "I'm not blaming you. It was her fault. She was chasing you, you stupid clown! What I can't figure out is why you didn't know. I tried to give you hints."

Thorby was as innocent of such things as a bird is of ballistics. "I don't believe it."

"It doesn't matter whether you do or don't . . . everybody else saw it. But you both could have gotten away with it, as long as you kept it open and harmless—and I was watching too closely for anything else—if Sis hadn't lost her head."

"Huh? How?"

"Sis did something that made Grandmother willing to part with a crack firecontrolman. She went to Grandmother and asked to be adopted across moiety line. In her simple, addled-pated way she figured that since you were adopted in the first place, it didn't really matter that she was your niece—just shift things around and she could marry you." Jeri grunted. "If you had been adopted on the other side, she could have wangled it. But she must have been clean off her head to think that Grandmother—*Grandmother!*—would agree to anything so scandalous."

"But . . . well, I'm not actually any relation to her. Not that I had any idea of marrying her."

"Oh, beat it! You make me tired."

Thorby moped around, unwilling to go back and face Jeri. He felt lost and alone and confused; the Family seemed as strange, their ways as difficult to understand, as the Losians.

He missed Mata. He had never missed her before. She had been something pleasant but routine—like three meals a day and the other comforts he had learned to expect in *Sisu*. Now he missed her.

Well, if that was what she wanted, why hadn't they let her? Not that he had thought about it . . . but as long as you had to get married some day, Mata would be as tolerable as any. He liked her.

Finally he remembered that there was one person with whom he could talk. He took his troubles to Doctor Mader.

He scratched at her door, received a hurried, "Come in!" He found her down on her knees, surrounded by possessions. She had a smudge on her nose and her neat hair was mussed. "Oh. Thorby. I'm glad you showed up. They told me you were dirtside and I was afraid I would miss you."

She spoke System English; he answered in it. "You wanted to see me?"

"To say good-by. I'm going home."

"Oh." Thorby felt again the sick twinge he had felt when Jeri had told about Mata. Suddenly he was wrenched with sorrow that Pop was gone. He pulled himself together and said, "I'm sorry. I'll miss you."

"I'll miss you, Thorby. You're the only one in this big ship that I felt at home with . . . which is odd, as your background and mine are about as far apart as possible. I'll miss our talks."

"So will I," Thorby agreed miserably. "When are you leaving?"

"*El Nido* jumps tomorrow. But I should transfer tonight; I don't dare miss jump, or I might not get home for years."

"*El Nido* is going to your planet?" A fantastic scheme began to shape in his mind.

"Oh, no! She's going to Thaf Beta VI. But a Hegemonic mail ship calls there and I can get home. It is too wonderful a chance to miss." The scheme died in Thorby's brain; it was preposterous, anyhow—he might be willing to chance a strange planet, but Mata was no fraki.

Doctor Mader went on, "The Chief Officer arranged it." She smiled wryly. "She's glad to get rid of me. I hadn't had any hope that she could put it over, in view of the difficulty in getting me aboard *Sisu*; I think your grandmother must have some bargaining point that she did not mention. In any case I'm to go . . . with the understanding that I remain in strict purdah. I shan't mind; I'll use the time on my data."

Mention of purdah reminded Thorby that Margaret would see Mata. He started with stumbling embarrassment to explain what he had come to talk about. Doctor Mader listened gravely, her fingers busy with packing. "I know, Thorby. I probably heard the sad details sooner than you did."

"Margaret, did you ever hear of anything so silly?"

She hesitated. "Many things . . . much sillier."

"But there wasn't anything to it! And if that was what Mata wanted, why didn't Grandmother let her . . . instead of shipping her out among strangers. I . . . well, I wouldn't have minded. After I got used to it."

The fraki woman smiled. "That's the oddest gallant speech I ever heard, Thorby."

Thorby said, "Could you get a message to her for me?"

"Thorby, if you want to send her your undying love or something, then don't. Your Grandmother did the best thing for her great granddaughter, did it quickly with kindness and wisdom. Did it in Mata's interests against the immediate interests of *Sisu*, since Mata was a valuable fighting man. But your Grandmother measured up to the high standards expected of a Chief Officer; she considered the long-range interests of everyone and found them weightier than the loss of one firecontrolman. I admire her at last—between ourselves, I've always detested the old girl." She smiled suddenly. "And fifty years from now Mata will make the same sort of wise decisions; the sept of *Sisu* is sound."

"I'll be flogged if I understand it!"

"Because you are almost as much fraki as I am . . . and haven't had my training. Thorby, most things are right or wrong only in their backgrounds; few things are good or evil in themselves. But things that are right or wrong according to their culture, really *are* so. This exogamy rule the People live by, you probably think it's just a way to outsmart mutations—in fact that's the way it is taught in the ship's school."

"Of course. That's why I can't see—"

"Just a second. So you can't see why your Grandmother should object. But it's essential that the People marry back and forth among ships, not just because of genes—that's a side issue—but because a ship is too small to be a stable culture. Ideas and attitudes have to be cross-germinated, too, or *Sisu* and the whole culture will die. So the custom is protected by strongest possible taboo. A 'minor' break in this taboo is like a 'minor' break in the ship, disastrous unless drastic steps are taken. Now . . . do you understand that?"

"Well . . . no, I don't think so."

"I doubt if your Grandmother understands it; she just knows what's right for her family and acts with forthrightness and courage. Do you still want to send a message?"

"Uh, well, could you tell Mata that I'm sorry I didn't get to say good-by?"

"Mmm, yes. I may wait a while."

"All right."

"Feeling better yourself?"

"Uh, I guess so . . . since you say it's best for Mata." Thorby suddenly burst out, "But, Margaret, I don't know what is the matter with me! I thought I was getting the hang of things. Now it's all gone to pieces. I feel like a fraki and I doubt if I'll ever learn to be a Trader."

Her face was suddenly sad. "You were free once. It's a hard habit to get over."

"Huh?"

"You've had violent dislocations, Thorby. Your foster father—your first one, Baslim the Wise—bought you as a slave and made you his son, as free as he was. Now your second foster father, with the best of intentions, adopted you as his son, and thereby made you a slave."

"Why, Margaret!" Thorby protested. "How can you say such a thing?"

"If you aren't a slave, what are you?"

"Why, I'm a Free Trader. At least that's what Father intended, if I can ever get over my fraki habits. But I'm not a slave. The People are *free*. All of us."

"All of you . . . but not each of you."

"What do you mean?"

"The People are free. It's their proudest boast. Any of them can tell you that freedom is what makes them People and not fraki. The People are free to roam the stars, never rooted to any soil. So free that each ship is a sovereign state, asking nothing of anyone, going anywhere, fighting against any odds, asking no quarter, not even cooperating except as it suits them. Oh, the People are free; this old Galaxy has never seen such freedom. A culture of less than a hundred thousand people spread through a quarter of a billion cubic light-years and utterly free to move anywhere at any time. There has never been a culture like it and there may never be again. Free as the sky . . . more free than the stars, for the stars go where they must. Ah, yes, the People are free." She paused. "But at what price was this freedom purchased?"

Thorby blinked.

"I'll tell you. Not with poverty. The People enjoy the highest average wealth in history. The profits of your trading are fantastic. Nor has it been with cost to health or sanity. I've never seen a community with less illness. Nor have you paid in happiness or self-respect. You're a smugly happy lot, and your pride is something sinful—of course you do have a lot to be proud of. But what you *have* paid for your unparalleled freedom . . . is freedom itself. No, I'm not talking riddles. The People are free . . . at the cost of loss of individual freedom for each of you—and I don't except the Chief Officer or Captain; they are the least free of any."

Her words sounded outrageous. "How can we be both free and not free?" he protested.

"Ask Mata. Thorby, you live in a steel prison; you are allowed out perhaps a few hours every few months. You live by rules more stringent than any prison. That those rules are intended to make you all happy—and do—is beside the point; they are orders you have to obey. You sleep where you are told, you eat when you are told and what you are offered—it's unimportant that it is lavish and tasty; the point is you have no choice. You are told what to do ninety percent of the time. You are so bound by rules that much of what you say is not free speech but required ritual; you could go through a day and not utter a phrase not found in the Laws of *Sisu*. Right?"

"Yes, but—"

"Yes, with no 'buts.' Thorby, what sort of people have so little freedom? Slaves? Can you think of a better word?"

"But we can't be sold!"

"Slavery has often existed where slaves were never bought and sold, but simply inherited. As in *Sisu*. Thorby, being a slave means having someone as your master, with no hope of changing it. You slaves who call yourselves the 'People' can't even hope for manumission."

Thorby scowled. "You figure that's what's wrong with me?"

"I think your slave's collar is chafing you, in a fashion that does not trouble your shipmates—because they were born with theirs and you were once free." She looked at her belongings. "I've got to get this stuff into *El Nido*. Will you help me?"

"I'd be glad to."

"Don't expect to see Mata."

"I wasn't," Thorby fibbed. "I want to help you. I hate to see you leave."

"Truthfully, I don't hate to leave . . . but I hate to say good-by to you." She hesitated. "I want to help you, too. Thorby, an anthropologist should never interfere. But I'm leaving and you aren't really part of the culture I was studying. Could you use a hint from an old woman?"

"Why, you aren't old!"

"That's two gallant speeches. I'm a grandmother, though the Chief Officer might be startled to hear me claim that status. Thorby, I thought you would become adjusted to this jail. Now I'm not sure. Freedom is a hard habit to break. Dear, if you decide that you can't stand it, wait until the ship calls at a planet that is democratic and free and human—then hit dirt and run! But, Thorby, do this before Grandmother decides to marry you to someone, because if you wait that long—you're lost!"

12

Losian to Finster, Finster to Thoth IV, Thoth IV to Woolamurra, *Sisu* went skipping around a globe of space nine hundred light-years in diameter, the center of which was legendary Terra, cradle of mankind. *Sisu* had never been to Terra; the People operate out where pickings are rich, police protection non-existent, and a man can dicker without being hampered by finicky regulations.

Ship's history alleged that the original *Sisu* had been built on Terra and that the first Captain Krausa had been born there, a (whisper it) fraki. But that was six ships ago and ship's history was true in essence, rather than fiddlin' fact. The *Sisu* whose steel now protected the blood was registered out of New Finlandia, Shiva III . . . another port she had never visited but whose fees were worth paying in order to have legal right to go about her occasions whenever, in pursuit of profit, *Sisu* went inside the globe of civilization. Shiva III was very understanding of the needs of Free Traders, not fussy about inspections, reports, and the like as long as omissions were repaired by paying penalties; many ships found her registration convenient.

On Finster Thorby learned another method of trading. The native fraki, known to science by a pseudo-Latin name and called "Those confounded slugs!" by the People, live in telepathic symbiosis with lemur-like creatures possessed of delicate, many-boned hands—"telepathy" is a conclusion; it is believed that the slow, monstrous, dominant creatures supply the brains and the lemuroids the manipulation.

The planet offers beautifully carved gem stones, raw copper, and a weed from which is derived an alkaloid used in psychotherapy. What else it could supply is a matter of conjecture; the natives have neither speech nor writing, communication is difficult.

This occasions the method of trading new to Thorby—the silent auction invented by the trading Phoenicians when the shores of Africa ran beyond the known world.

Around *Sisu* in piles were placed what the traders had to offer: heavy metals the natives needed, everlasting clocks they had learned to need, and trade goods the Family hoped to teach them to need. Then the humans went inside.

Thorby said to Senior Clerk Arly Krausa-Drotar, "We just leave that stuff lying around? If you did that on Jubbul, it would disappear as you turned your back."

"Didn't you see them rig the top gun this morning?"

"I was down in the lower hold."

"It's rigged and manned. These creatures have no morals but they're smart. They'll be as honest as a cashier with the boss watching."

"What happens now?"

"We wait. They look over the goods. After a while . . . a day, maybe two . . . they pile stuff by our piles. We wait. Maybe they make their piles higher. Maybe they shift things around and offer us something else—and possibly we have outsmarted ourselves and missed something we would like through holding out. Or maybe we take one of our piles and split it into two, meaning we like the stuff but not the price.

"Or maybe we don't want it at any price. So we move our piles close to something they have offered that we do like. But we still don't touch their stuff; we wait.

"Eventually nobody has moved anything in quite a while. So, where the price suits us, we take in what they offer and leave our stuff. They come and take our offering away. We take in any of our own stuff where the price isn't right; they take away the stuff we turn down.

"But that doesn't end it. Now both sides know what the other one wants and what he will pay. They start making the offers; we start bidding with what we know they will accept. More deals are made. When we are through this second time, we have unloaded anything they want for stuff of theirs that we want at prices satisfactory to both. No trouble. I wonder if we do better on planets where we can talk."

"Yes, but doesn't this waste a lot of time?"

"Know anything we've got more of?"

The slow-motion auction moved without a hitch on goods having established value; deals were spottier on experimental offerings—gadgets which had seemed a good buy on Losian mostly failed to interest the Finstera. Six gross of folding knives actually intended for Woolamurra brought high prices. But the star item was not properly goods of any sort.

Grandmother Krausa, although bedfast, occasionally insisted on being carried on inspection tours; somebody always suffered. Shortly before arrival at Finster her ire had centered on nursery and bachelor quarters. In the first her eye lit on a stack of lurid picture books. She ordered them confiscated; they were "fraki trash."

The bachelors were inspected when word had gone out that she intended to hit only nursery, purdah, and galley; Grandmother saw their bunkies before they could hide their pin-up pictures.

Grandmother was shocked! Not only did pin-up pictures follow comic books, but a search was made for the magazines from which they had been clipped. The contraband was sent to auxiliary engineering, there to give up identities into elemental particles.

The Supercargo saw them there and got an idea; they joined the offerings outside the ship.

Strangely carved native jewels appeared beside the waste paper—chrysoberyl and garnet and opal and quartz.

The Supercargo blinked at the gauds and sent word to the Captain.

The booklets and magazines were redistributed, each as a separate offering. More jewels—

Finally each item was broken down into pages; each sheet was placed alone. An agreement was reached: one brightly colored sheet, one jewel. At that point bachelors who had managed to hide cherished pin-ups found patriotism and instinct for trade out-weighing possessiveness—after all they could restock at the next civilized port. The nursery was combed for more adventure comics.

For the first time in history comic books and pin-up magazines brought many times their weights in fine jewelry.

Thoth IV was followed by Woolamurra and each jump zig-zagged closer to the coming Great Gathering of the People; the ship was seized with carnival fever. Crew members were excused from work to practice on musical instruments, watches were rearranged to permit quartets to sing together, a training table was formed for athletes and they were excused from all watches save battle stations in order to train themselves into exhausted sleep. Headaches and tempers developed over plans for hospitality fit to support the exalted pride of *Sisu*.

Long messages flitted through n-space and the Chief Engineer protested the scandalous waste of power with sharp comments on the high price of tritium. But the Chief Officer cheerfully okayed the charge vouchers. As the time approached, she developed a smile that creased her wrinkles in unaccustomed directions, as if she knew something but wasn't talking. Twice Thorby caught her smiling at him and it worried him; it was better not to catch Grandmother's attention. He had had her full attention once lately and had not enjoyed it—he had been honored by eating with her, for having burned a raider.

The bogie had appeared on *Sisu*'s screens during the lift from Finster—an unexpected place to be attacked since there was not much traffic there. The alarm had come only four hours out, when *Sisu* had attained barely 5% of speed-of-light and had no hope of running for it.

The matter landed in Thorby's lap; the portside computer was disabled—it had a "nervous breakdown" and the ship's electronics men had been sweating over it since jump. Thorby's nephew Jeri had returned to astrogation, the new trainee having qualified on the long jump from Losian—he was a stripling in whom Thorby had little confidence, but Thorby did not argue when Jeri decided that Kenan Drotar was ready for a watch even though he had never experienced a "real one." Jeri was anxious to go back to the control room for two reasons, status, and an unmentioned imponderable: the computer room was where Jeri had served with his missing kid sister.

So when the raider popped up, it was up to Thorby.

He felt shaky when he first started to test the problem, being acutely aware that the portside computer was out. The greatest comfort to a firecontrolman is faith in the superman abilities of the team on the other side, a feeling of "Well, even if I goof, those bulging brains will nail him," while that team is thinking the same thing. It helps to produce all-important relaxation.

This time Thorby did not have that spiritual safety net. Nor any other. The Finstera are not a spacefaring people; there was no possibility that the bogie would be identified as theirs. Nor could he be a trader; he had too many gravities in his tail. Nor a Hegemonic Guard; Finster was many light-years outside civilization. Thorby knew with sick certainty that sometime in the next hour his guesses must produce an answer; he must launch and hit—or shortly thereafter he would be a slave again and all his family with him.

It spoiled his timing, it slowed his thoughts.

But presently he forgot the portside computer, forgot the Family, forgot even the raider as such. The raider's movements became just data pouring into his board and the problem something he had been trained to do. His teammate slammed in and strapped himself into the other chair while General Quarters was still clanging, demanded to know the score. Thorby didn't hear him, nor did he hear the clanging stop. Jeri came in thereafter, having been sent down by the Captain; Thorby never saw him. Jeri motioned the youngster out of the twin seat, got into it himself, noted that the switch had Thorby's board in control, did not touch it. Without speaking he glanced over Thorby's setup and began working alternate solutions, ready to back him up by slapping the selector switch as soon as Thorby launched and then launch again, differently. Thorby never noticed.

Presently Krausa's strong bass came over the squawk line. "Starboard tracker . . . can I assist you by maneuvering?"

Thorby never heard it. Jeri glanced at him and answered, "I do not advise it, Captain."

"Very well."

The Senior Portside Firecontrolman, in gross violation of regulations, came in and watched the silent struggle, sweat greasing his face. Thorby did not know it. Nothing existed but knobs, switches, and buttons, all extensions of his nervous system. He became possessed of an overwhelming need to sneeze—repressed it without realizing it.

Thorby made infinitesimal adjustments up to the last moment, then absent-mindedly touched the button that told the computer to launch as the projected curve maximized. Two heartbeats later an atomic missile was on its way.

Jeri reached for the selector switch—stopped as he saw Thorby go into frenzied activity, telling his board to launch again on the assumption that the target had cut power. Then incoming data stopped as the ship went blind. Paralysis hit them.

Post-analysis showed that the paralyzing beam was on them seventy-one seconds. Jeri came out of it when it ceased; he saw Thorby looking dazedly at his board . . . then become violently active as he tried to work a new solution based on the last data.

Jeri put a hand on him. "The run is over, Thorby."

"Huh?"

"You got him. A sweet run. Mata would be proud of you."

Sisu was blind for a day, while repairs were made in her n-space eyes. The Captain continued to boost; there was nothing else to do. But presently she could see again and two days later she plunged into the comforting darkness of multi-space. The dinner in Thorby's honor was that night.

Grandmother made the usual speech, giving thanks that the Family was again spared, and noting that the son of *Sisu* beside her was the instrument of that happy but eminently deserved outcome. Then she lay back and gobbled her food, with her daughter-in-law hovering over her.

Thorby did not enjoy the honor. He had no clear recollection of the run; it felt as if he were being honored by mistake. He had been in semi-shock afterwards, then his imagination started working.

They were only pirates, he knew that. Pirates and slavers, they had tried to steal *Sisu*, had meant to enslave the Family. Thorby had hated slavers before he could remember—nothing so impersonal as the institution of slavery, he hated slavers in his baby bones before he knew the word.

He was sure that Pop approved of him; he knew that Pop, gentle as he was, would have shortened every slaver in the Galaxy without a tear.

Nevertheless Thorby did not feel happy. He kept thinking about a live ship—suddenly all dead, gone forever in a burst of radiance. Then he would look at his forefinger and wonder. He was caught in the old dilemma of the man with unintegrated values, who eats meat but would rather somebody else did the butchering.

When the dinner in his honor arrived he was three nights short on sleep and looked it. He pecked at his food.

Midway in the meal he became aware that Grandmother was glaring; he promptly spilled food on his dress jacket. "Well!" she snarled. "Have a nice nap?"

"Uh, I'm sorry, Grandmother. Did you speak to me?"

He caught his Mother's warning look but it was too late; Grandmother was off. "I was waiting for *you* to say something to *me!*"

"Uh . . . it's a nice day."

"I had not noticed that it was unusual. It rarely rains in space."

"I mean it's a nice party. Yes, a real nice party. Thank you for giving it, Grandmother."

"That's better. Young man, it is customary, when a gentleman dines with a lady, to offer her polite conversation. This may not be the custom among fraki, but it is invariable among People."

"Yes, Grandmother. Thank you, Grandmother."

"Let's start again. It's a nice party, yes. We try to make everyone feel equal, while recognizing the merits of each. It is gratifying to have a chance—at last—to join with our Family in noting a virtue in you . . . one commendable if not exceptional. Congratulations. Now it's your turn."

Thorby slowly turned purple.

She sniffed and said, "What are you doing to get ready for the Gathering?"

"Uh, I don't know, Grandmother. You see, I don't sing, or play, or dance—and the only games I know are chess and spat ball and . . . well, I've never seen a Gathering. I don't know what they're like."

"Hmmph! So you haven't."

Thorby felt guilty. He said, "Grandmother . . . you must have been to lots of Gatherings. Would you tell me about them?"

That did it. She relaxed and said in hushed voice, "They don't have the Gatherings nowadays that they had when I was a girl . . ." Thorby did not have to speak again, other than sounds of awed interest. Long after the rest were waiting for Grandmother's permission to rise, she was saying, ". . . and I had my choice of a hundred ships, let me tell you. I was a pert young thing, with a tiny foot and a saucy nose, and my Grandmother got offers for me throughout the People. But I knew *Sisu* was for me and I stood up to her. Oh, I was a lively one! Dance all night and as fresh for the games next day as a—"

While it was not a merry occasion, it was not a failure.

Since Thorby had no talent he became an actor.

Aunt Athena Krausa-Fogarth, Chief of Commissary and superlative cook, had the literary disease in its acute form; she had written a play. It was the life of the first Captain Krausa, showing the sterling nobility of the Krausa line. The first Krausa had been a saint with heart of steel. Disgusted with the evil ways of fraki, he had built *Sisu* (single-handed), staffed it with his wife (named Fogarth in draft, changed to Grandmother's maiden name before the script got to her; and with their remarkable children. As the play ends they jump off into space, to spread culture and wealth through the Galaxy.

Thorby played the first Krausa. He was dumbfounded, having tried out because he was told to. Aunt Athena seemed almost as surprised; there was a catch in her voice when she announced his name. But Grandmother seemed pleased. She showed up for rehearsals and made suggestions which were happily adopted.

The star playing opposite Thorby was Loeen Garcia, late of *El Nido*. He had not become chummy with Mata's exchange; he had nothing against her but had not felt like it. But he found Loeen easy to know. She was a dark, soft beauty, with an intimate manner. When Thorby was required to ignore taboo and *kiss* her, in front of Grandmother and everybody, he blew his lines.

But he tried. Grandmother snorted in disgust. "What are you trying to do! Bite her? And don't let go as if she were radioactive. She's your wife, stupid. You've just carried her into your ship. You're alone with her, you love her. Now do it . . . no, no, no! Athena!"

Thorby looked wildly around. It did not help to catch sight of Fritz with eyes on the overhead, a beatific smile on his face.

"Athena! Come here, Daughter, and show this damp young hulk how a woman should be kissed. Kiss him yourself and then have him try again. Places, everyone."

Aunt Athena, twice Thorby's age, did not upset him so much. He complied clumsily with her instructions, then managed to kiss Loeen without falling over her feet.

It must have been a good play; it satisfied Grandmother. She looked forward to seeing it at the Gathering.

But she died on Woolamurra.

13

WOOLAMURRA IS A LUSH PIONEER PLANET BARELY INSIDE THE TERRAN Hegemony; it was *Sisu*'s last stop before diving deeper for the Gathering. Rich in food and raw materials, the fraki were anxious to buy manufactured articles. *Sisu* sold out of Losian artifacts and disposed of many Finsteran jewels. But Woolamurra offered little which would bring a profit and money was tight in terms of power metal—Woolamurra had not prospected much and was anxious to keep what radioactives it had for its infant industry.

So *Sisu* accepted a little uranium and a lot of choice meats and luxury foods. *Sisu* always picked up gourmet delicacies; this time she stocked tons more than the Family could consume, but valuable for swank at the Gathering.

The balance was paid in tritium and deuterium. A hydrogen-isotopes plant is maintained there for Hegemonic ships but it will sell to others. *Sisu* had last been able to fuel at Jubbul-Losian ships use a different nuclear reaction.

Thorby was taken dirtside by his Father several times in New Melbourne, the port. The local language is System English, which Krausa understood, but the fraki spoke it with clipped haste and an odd vowel shift; Captain Krausa found it baffling. It did not sound strange to Thorby; it was as if he'd heard it before. So Krausa took him to help out.

This day they went out to complete the fuel transaction and sign a waiver required for private sales. The commercial tenders accepted by *Sisu* had to be certified by the central bank, then be taken to the fuel plant. After papers were stamped and fees paid, the Captain sat and chatted with the director. Krausa could be friendly with a fraki on terms of complete equality, never hinting at the enormous social difference between them.

While they chatted, Thorby worried. The fraki was talking about Woolamurra. "Any cobber with strong arms and enough brain to hold his ears apart can go outback and make a fortune."

"No doubt," agreed the Captain. "I've seen your beef animals. Magnificent."

Thorby agreed. Woolamurra might be short on pavement, arts, and plumbing; the planet was bursting with opportunity. Besides that, it was a pleasant, decent world, comfortably loose. It matched Doctor Mader's recipe: "—wait until your ship calls at a planet that is democratic, free, and human . . . then run!"

Life in *Sisu* had become more pleasant even though he was now conscious of the all-enveloping, personally-restricting quality of life with the Family. He was beginning to enjoy being an actor; it was fun to hold the stage. He had even learned to handle the clinch in a manner to win from Grandmother a smile; furthermore, even though it was play-acting, Loeen was a pleasant armful. She would kiss him and murmur: "My husband! My noble husband! We will roam the Galaxy together."

It gave Thorby goose bumps. He decided that Loeen was a great actress.

They became quite friendly. Loeen was curious about what a fire-controlman did, so under the eye of Great Aunt Tora, Thorby showed her the computer room. She looked prettily confused. "Just what is n-space? Length, breadth, and thickness are all you see . . . how about these other dimensions?"

"By logic. You see four dimensions . . . those three, and time. Oh, you can't *see* a year, but you can measure it."

"Yes, but how can logic—"

"Easy as can be. What is a point? A location in space. But suppose there isn't any space, not even the four ordinary dimensions. No space. Is a point conceivable?"

"Well, I'm thinking about one."

"Not without thinking about space. If you think about a point, you think about it *somewhere*. If you have a line, you can imagine a point somewhere on it. But a point is just a location and if there isn't anywhere for it to be located, it's nothing. Follow me?"

Great Aunt Tora interrupted. "Could you children continue this in the lounge? My feet hurt."

"Sorry, Great Aunt. Will you take my arm?"

Back in the lounge Thorby said, "Did you soak up that about a point needing a line to hold it?"

"Uh, I think so. Take away its location and it isn't there at all."

"Think about a line. If it isn't in a surface, does it exist?"

"Uh, that's harder."

"If you get past that, you've got it. A line is an ordered sequence of points. But where does the order come from? From being in a surface. If a line isn't held by a surface, then it could collapse into itself. It hasn't any width. You wouldn't even know it had collapsed . . . nothing to compare it with. But every point would be just as close to every other point, no 'ordered sequence.' Chaos. Still with me?"

"Maybe."

"A point needs a line. A line needs a surface. A surface has to be part of solid space, or its structure vanishes. And a solid needs hyper-space to hold it . . . and so on up. Each dimension demands one higher, or geometry ceases to exist. The universe ceases to exist." He slapped the table. "But it's here, so we know that multi-space still functions . . . even though we can't see it, any more than we can see a passing second."

"But where does it all stop?"

"It can't. Endless dimensions."

She shivered. "It scares me."

"Don't worry. Even the Chief Engineer only has to fret about the first dozen dimensions. And—look, you know we turn inside out when the ship goes irrational. Can you feel it?"

"No. And I'm not sure I believe it."

"It doesn't matter, because we aren't equipped to feel it. It can happen while eating soup and you never spill a drop, even though the soup turns inside out, too. So far as we are concerned it's just a mathematical concept, like the square root of minus one—which we tangle with when we pass speed-of-light. It's that way with all multi-dimensionality. You don't have to feel it, see it, understand it; you just have to work logical symbols about it. But it's real, if 'real' means anything. Nobody has ever seen an electron. Nor a thought. You can't see a thought, you can't measure, weigh, nor taste it—but thoughts are the most real things in the Galaxy." Thorby was quoting Baslim.

She looked at him admiringly. "You must be awfully brainy, Thorby. 'Nobody ever saw a thought.' I like that."

Thorby graciously accepted the praise.

When he went to his bunkie, he found Fritz reading in bed. Thorby was feeling the warm glow that comes from giving the word to an eager mind. "Hi, Fritz! Studying? Or wasting your youth?"

"Hi. Studying. Studying art."

Thorby glanced over. "Don't let Grandmother catch you."

"Got to have something to trade those confounded slugs next time we touch Finster." Woolamurra was "civilization"; the bachelors had replenished their art. "You look as if you had squeezed a bonus out of a Losian. What clicks?"

"Oh, just talking with Loeen. I was introducing her to n-space . . . and darn if she didn't catch on fast."

Fritz looked judicial. "Yes, she's bright." He added, "When is Grandmother posting the banns?"

"What are you talking about!"

"No banns?"

"Don't be silly."

"Mmm . . . you find her good company. Bright, too. Want to know how bright?"

"Well?"

"So bright that she taught in *El Nido*'s school. Her specialty was math. Multi-dimensional geometry, in fact."

"I don't believe it!"

"Happens I transcribed her record. But ask her."

"I shall! Why isn't she teaching math here?"

"Ask Grandmother. Thorby, my skinny and retarded brother—I think you were dropped on your head. But, sorry as you are, I love you for the fumbling grace with which you wipe drool off your chin. Want a hint from an older and wiser head?"

"Go ahead. You will anyhow."

"Thanks. Loeen is a fine girl and it might be fun to solve equations with her for life. But I hate to see a man leap into a sale before he checks the market. If you just hold off through this next jump, you'll find that the People have several young girls. Several thousand."

"I'm not looking for a wife!"

"Tut, tut! It's a man's duty. But wait for the Gathering, and we'll shop. Now shut up, I want to study art."

"Who's talking?"

Thorby did not ask Loeen what she had done in *El Nido*, but it did open his eyes to the fact that he was playing the leading role in a courtship without having known it. It scared him. Doctor Mader's words haunted his sleep "—before Grandmother decides to marry you to someone . . . if you wait that long—you're lost!"

Father and the Woolamurra official gossiped while Thorby fretted. Should he leave *Sisu?* If he wasn't willing to be a trader all his life he had to get out while still a bachelor. Of course, he could stall—look at

Fritz. Not that he had anything against Loeen, even if she had made a fool of him.

But if he was going to leave—and he had doubts as to whether he could stand the custom-ridden monotonous life forever—then Woolamurra was the best chance he might have in years. No castes, no guilds, no poverty, no immigration laws—why, they even accepted mutants! Thorby had seen hexadactyls, hirsutes, albinos, lupine ears, giants, and other changes. If a man could work, Woolamurra could use him.

What should he do? Say, "Excuse me, please," leave the room—then start running? Stay lost until *Sisu* jumped? He couldn't do *that!* Not to father, not to *Sisu;* he owed them too much.

What, then? Tell Grandmother he wanted off? If she let him off, it would probably be some chilly spot between stars! Grandmother would regard ingratitude to *Sisu* as the unforgivable sin.

And besides . . . The Gathering was coming. He felt a great itch to see it. And it wouldn't be right to walk out on the play. He was not consciously rationalizing; although stage-struck, he still thought that he did not want to play the hero in a melodrama—whereas he could hardly wait.

So he avoided his dilemma by postponing it.

Captain Krausa touched his shoulder. "We're leaving."

"Oh. Sorry, Father. I was thinking."

"Keep it up, it's good exercise. Good-by, Director, and thanks. I look forward to seeing you next time we call."

"You won't find me, Captain. I'm going to line me out a station, as far as eye can reach. Land of me own. If you ever get tired of steel decks, there's room here for you. And your boy."

Captain Krausa's face did not show his revulsion. "Thanks. But we wouldn't know which end of a plow to grab. We're traders."

"Each cat his own rat."

When they were outside Thorby said, "What did he mean, Father? I've seen cats, but what is a rat?"

"A rat is a sorci, only thinner and meaner. He meant that each man has his proper place."

"Oh." They walked in silence. Thorby was wondering if he had as yet found his proper place.

Captain Krausa was wondering the same thing. There was a ship just beyond *Sisu;* its presence was a reproach. It was a mail courier, an official Hegemonic vessel, crewed by Guardsmen. Baslim's words rang accusingly in his mind: "—when opportunity presents, I ask that you deliver him to the commander of any Hegemonic military vessel."

This was not a "military" vessel. But that was a quibble; Baslim's intentions were plain and this ship would serve. Debts must be paid. Unfortunately Mother interpreted the words strictly. Oh, he knew why; she was determined to show off the boy at the Gathering. She intended to squeeze all possible status out of the fact that *Sisu* had paid the People's debt. Well, that was understandable.

But it wasn't fair to the boy!

Or was it? For his own reasons Krausa was anxious to take the lad to the Gathering. He was certain now that Thorby's ancestry must be of the People—and in the Commodore's files he expected to prove it.

On the other hand—He had agreed with Mother over Mata Kingsolver; a minx should not be allowed to back a taboo lad into a corner, better to ship her at once. But didn't Mother think he could see what she was up to now?

He wouldn't permit it! By *Sisu*, he wouldn't! The boy was too young and he would forbid it . . . at least until he proved that the boy was of the People, in which case the debt to Baslim was paid.

But that mail courier out there whispered that he was being as unwilling to acknowledge honest debt as he was accusing Mother of being.

But it was for the lad's own good!

What is justice?

Well, there was one fair way. Take the lad and have a showdown with Mother. Tell the lad *all* of Baslim's message. Tell him that he could take passage in the courier to the central worlds, tell him how to go about finding his family. But tell him, too, that he, the Krausa, believed that Thorby was of the People and that the possibility could and should be checked first. Yes, and tell him bluntly that Mother was trying to tie him down with a wife. Mother would scream and quote the Laws—but this was not in the Chief Officer's jurisdiction; Baslim had laid the injunction on *him*. And besides, it was right; the boy himself should choose.

Spine stiffened but quaking, Captain Krausa strode back to face his Mother.

As the hoist delivered them up the Deck Master was waiting. "Chief Officer's respects and she wishes to see the Captain, sir."

"That's a coincidence," Krausa said grimly. "Come, Son. We'll both see her."

"Yes, Father."

They went around the passageway, reached the Chief Officer's cabin. Krausa's wife was outside. "Hello, my dear. The Decker said that Mother had sent for me."

"I sent for you."

"He got the message garbled. Whatever it is, make it quick, please. I am anxious to see Mother anyhow."

"He did not get it garbled; the Chief Officer did send for you."

"Eh?"

"Captain, your Mother is dead."

Krausa listened with blank face, then it sank in and he slapped the door aside, ran to his Mother's bed, threw himself down, clutched the tiny, wasted form laid out in state, and began to weep racking, terrible sounds, the grief of a man steeled against emotion, who cannot handle it when he breaks.

Thorby watched with awed distress, then went to his bunkie and thought. He tried to figure out why he felt so badly. He had not loved Grandmother—he hadn't even *liked* her.

Then why did he feel so lost?

It was almost like when Pop died. He loved Pop—but not her.

He found that he was not alone; the entire ship was in shock. There was not one who could remember, or imagine, *Sisu* without her. She was *Sisu.* Like the undying fire that moved the ship, Grandmother had been an unfailing force, dynamic, indispensable, basic. Now suddenly she was gone.

She had taken her nap as usual, grumbling because Woolamurra's day fitted their schedule so poorly—typical fraki inefficiency. But she had gone to sleep with iron discipline that had adapted itself to a hundred time schedules.

When her daughter-in-law went to wake her, she could not be waked.

Her bedside scratch pad held many notes: Speak to Son about this. Tell Tora to do that. Jack up the C.E. about temperature control. Go over banquet menus with Athena. Rhoda Krausa tore out the page, put it away for reference, straightened her, then ordered the Deck Master to notify her husband.

The Captain was not at dinner. Grandmother's couch had been removed; the Chief Officer sat where it had been. In the Captain's absence the Chief Officer signalled the Chief Engineer; he offered the prayer for the dead, she gave the responses. Then they ate in silence. No funeral would be held until Gathering.

The Chief Officer stood up presently. "The Captain wishes to announce," she said quietly, "that he thanks those who attempted to call on him. He will be available tomorrow." She paused. " 'The atoms come out of space and to space they return. The spirit of *Sisu* goes on.' "

Thorby suddenly no longer felt lost.

14

THE GREAT GATHERING WAS EVEN MORE THAN THORBY HAD IMAGINED. Mile after mile of ships, more than eight hundred bulky Free Traders arranged in concentric ranks around a circus four miles across . . . *Sisu* in the innermost circle—which seemed to please Thorby's Mother—then more ships than Thorby knew existed: *Kraken, Deimos, James B. Quinn, Firefly, Bon Marché, Dom Pedro, Cee Squared, Omega, El Nido*—Thorby resolved to see how Mata was doing—*Saint Christopher, Vega, Vega Prime, Galactic Banker, Romany Lass* . . . Thorby made note to get a berthing chart . . . *Saturn, Chiang, Country Store, Joseph Smith, Aloha* . . .

There were too many. If he visited ten ships a day, he might see most of them. But there was too much to do and see; Thorby gave up the notion.

Inside the circle was a great temporary stadium, larger than the New Amphitheatre at Jubbulpore. Here elections would be held, funerals and weddings, athletic contests, entertainments, concerts—Thorby recalled that *Spirit of Sisu* would be performed there and trembled with stage fright.

Between stadium and ships was a midway—booths, rides, games, exhibits educational and entertaining, one-man pitches, dance halls that never closed, displays of engineering gadgets, fortunetellers, gambling for prizes and cash, open-air bars, soft drink counters offering anything from berry juices of the Pleiades worlds to a brown brew certified to be the ancient, authentic Terran *Coca-Cola* as licensed for bottling on Hekate.

When he saw this maelstrom Thorby felt that he had wandered into Joy Street—bigger, brighter, and seven times busier than Joy Street with the fleet in. This was the fraki's chance to turn a fairly honest credit while making suckers of the shrewdest businessmen in the Galaxy; this was the day, with the lid off and the Trader without his guards up—they'd sell you your own hat if you laid it on the counter.

Fritz took Thorby dirtside to keep him out of trouble, although Fritz's sophistication was hardly complete, since he had seen just one Great Gathering. The Chief Officer lectured the young people before granting hit-dirt, reminding them that *Sisu* had a reputation for proper behavior, and then issued each a hundred credits with a warning that it must last throughout the Gathering.

Fritz advised Thorby to cache most of it. "When we go broke, we can sweet-talk Father out of pocket money. But it's not smart to take it all."

Thorby agreed. He was not surprised when he felt the touch of a pickpocket; he grabbed a wrist to find out what he had landed.

First he recovered his wallet. Then he looked at the thief. He was a dirty-faced young fraki who reminded Thorby poignantly of Ziggie, except that this kid had two hands. "Better luck next time," he consoled him. "You don't have the touch yet."

The kid seemed about to cry. Thorby started to turn him loose, then said, "Fritz, check your wallet."

Fritz did so, it was gone. "Well, I'll be—"

"Hand it over, kid."

"I didn't take it! You let me go!"

"Cough up . . . before I unscrew your skull."

The kid surrendered Fritz's wallet; Thorby turned him loose. Fritz said, "Why did you do that? I was trying to spot a cop."

"That's why."

"Huh? Talk sense."

"I tried to learn that profession once. It's not easy."

"You? A poor joke, Thorby."

"Remember me? The ex-fraki, the beggar's boy? That clumsy attempt to equalize the wealth made me homesick. Fritz, where I come from, a pickpocket has status. I was merely a beggar."

"Don't let Mother hear that."

"I shan't. But I am what I am and I know what I was and I don't intend to forget. I never learned the pickpocket art, but I was a good beggar, I was taught by the best. My Pop. Baslim the Cripple. I'm not ashamed of him and all the Laws of *Sisu* can't make me."

"I did not intend to make you ashamed," Fritz said quietly.

They walked on, savoring the crowd and the fun. Presently Thorby said, "Shall we try that wheel? I've spotted the gimmick."

Fritz shook his head. "Look at those so-called prizes."

"Okay. I was interested in how it was rigged."

"Thorby—"

"Yeah? Why the solemn phiz?"

"You know who Baslim the Cripple really was?"

Thorby considered it. "He was my Pop. If he had wanted me to know anything else, he would have told me."

"Mmm . . . I suppose so."

"But you know?"

"Some."

"Uh, I am curious about one thing. What was the debt that made Grandmother willing to adopt me?"

"Uh, 'I have said enough.' "

"You know best."

"Oh, confound it, the rest of the People know! It's bound to come up at this Gathering."

"Don't let me talk you into anything, Fritz."

"Well . . . look, Baslim wasn't always a beggar."

"So I long since figured out."

"What he was is not for me to say. A lot of People kept his secret for years; nobody has told me that it is all right to talk. But one fact is no secret among the People . . . and you're one of the People. A long time ago, Baslim saved a whole Family. The People have never forgotten it. The *Hansea*, it was . . . the *New Hansea* is sitting right over there. The one with the shield painted on her. I can't tell you more, because a taboo was placed on it—the thing was so shameful that we never talk about it. I have said enough. But you could go over to the *New Hansea* and ask to look through her old logs. If you identified yourself—who you are in relation to Baslim—they couldn't refuse. Though the Chief Officer might go to her cabin afterwards and have weeping hysterics."

"Hmm . . . I don't want to know badly enough to make a lady cry. Fritz? Let's try this ride." So they did—and after speeds in excess of light and accelerations up to one hundred gravities, Thorby found a roller coaster too exciting. He almost lost his lunch.

A Great Gathering, although a time of fun and renewed friendships, has its serious purposes. In addition to funerals, memorial services for lost ships, weddings, and much transferring of young females, there is also business affecting the whole People and, most important, the paramount matter of buying ships.

Hekate has the finest shipyards in the explored Galaxy. Men and women have children; ships spawn, too. *Sisu* was gravid with people, fat with profit in uranium and thorium; it was time that the Family split up. At least a third of the families had the same need to trade wealth for living room; fraki shipbrokers were rubbing their hands, mentally figuring commissions. Starships do not sell like cold drinks; ship-brokers and salesmen often live on dreams. But perhaps a hundred ships would be sold in a few weeks.

Some would be new ships from the yards of Galactic Transport, Ltd., daughter corporation of civilization-wide Galactic Enterprises, or built by Space Engineers Corporation, or Hekate Ships, or Propulsion, Inc., or Hascomb & Sons—all giants in the trade. But there was cake for everyone. The broker who did not speak for a builder might have an exclusive on a second-hand ship, or a line to a rumor of a hint that the owners of a suitable ship might listen if the price was right—a man could make a fortune if he kept his eyes open and his ear to the ground. It was a time to by-pass mails and invest in expensive n-space messages; the feast would soon be over.

A family in need of space had two choices: either buy another ship, split and become two families, or a ship could join with another in purchasing a third, to be staffed from each. Twinning gave much status. It was proof that the family which managed it were master traders, able to give their kids a start in the world without help. But in practice the choice usually dwindled to one: join with another ship and split the expense, and even then it was often necessary to pledge all three ships against a mortgage on the new one.

It had been thirty years since *Sisu* had split up. She had had three decades of prosperity; she should have been able to twin. But ten years ago at the last Great Gathering Grandmother had caused *Sisu* to guarantee along with parent ships the mortgage against a ship newly born. The new ship gave a banquet honoring *Sisu*, then jumped off into dark and never came back. Space is vast. Remember her name at Gathering.

The result was that *Sisu* paid off one-third of forty percent of the cost of the lost ship; the blow hurt. The parent ships would reimburse *Sisu*—debts are always paid—but they had left the last Gathering lean from having spawned; coughing up each its own liability had left them skin and bones. You don't dun a sick man; you wait.

Grandmother had not been stupid. The parent ships, *Caesar Augustus* and *Dupont*, were related to *Sisu*; one takes care of one's own. Besides, it was good business; a trader unwilling to lend credit will discover that he has none. As it was, *Sisu* could write a draft on any Free Trader anywhere and be certain that it would be honored.

But it left *Sisu* with less cash than otherwise at a time when the Family should split.

Captain Krausa hit dirt the first day and went to the Commodore's Flag, *Norbert Wiener*. His wife stayed aboard but was not idle; since her succession to Chief Officer, she hardly slept. Today she worked at her desk, stopping for face-to-face talks with other chief officers via the phone exchange set up by city services for the Gathering. When her lunch was fetched, she motioned to put it down; it was still untouched when her husband returned. He came in and sat down wearily. She was reading a slide rule and checked her answer on a calculator before she spoke. "Based on a Hascomb F-two ship, the mortgage would run just over fifty percent."

"Rhoda, you know *Sisu* can't finance a ship unassisted."

"Don't be hasty, dear. Both *Gus* and *Dupont* would co-sign . . . in their case, it's the same as cash."

"If their credit will stretch."

"And *New Hansea* would jump at it—under the circumstances—and—"

"Rhoda! You were young, two Gatherings ago, but you are aware that the debt lies equally on all . . . not just *Hansea*. That was unanimous."

"I was old enough to be your wife, Fjalar. Don't read the Laws to me. But *New Hansea* would jump at the chance . . . under a secrecy taboo binding till the end of time. Nevertheless the carrying charges would eat too much. Did you get to see a *Galactic Lambda?*"

"I don't need to; I've seen the specs. No legs."

"You men! I wouldn't call eighty gravities 'no legs.' "

"You would if you had to sit in the worry seat. *Lambda* class were designed for slow freight inside the Hegemonic sphere; that's all they're good for."

"You're too conservative, Fjalar."

"And I'll continue to be where safety of a ship is concerned."

"No doubt. And I'll have to find solutions that fit your prejudices. However, *Lambda* class is just a possibility. There is also you-know-which. She'll go cheap."

He frowned. "An unlucky ship."

"It will take powerful cleansing to get those bad thoughts out. But think of the price."

"It's more than bad thoughts in you-know-which-ship. I never heard of a chief officer suiciding before. Or a captain going crazy. I'm surprised they got here."

"So am I. But she's here and she'll be up for sale. And any ship can be cleansed."

"I wonder."

"Don't be superstitious, dear. It's a matter of enough care with the rituals, which is my worry. However, you can forget the you-know-which-one. I think we'll split with another ship."

"I thought you were set on doing it alone?"

"I've merely been exploring our strength. But there are things more important than setting up a new ship single-handed."

"There certainly are! Power, a good weapons system, working capital, blooded officers in key spots—why, we can't man two ships. Take firecontrolmen alone. If—"

"Stop fretting. We could handle those. Fjalar, how would you like to be Deputy Commodore?"

He braked at full power. "Rhoda! Are you feverish?"

"No."

"There are dozens of skippers more likely to be tapped. I'll never be Commodore—and what's more, I don't want it."

"I may settle for Reserve Deputy, since Commodore Denbo intends to resign after the new deputy is elected. Never mind; you will be Commodore at the next Gathering."

"Preposterous!"

"Why are men so impractical? Fjalar, all you think about is your control room and business. If I hadn't kept pushing, you would never have reached deputy captain."

"Have you ever gone hungry?"

"I'm not complaining, dear. It was a great day for me when I was adopted by *Sisu*. But listen. We have favors coming from many sources, not just *Gus* and *Dupont*. Whatever ship we join with will help. I intend to leave the matter open until after election—and I've had tentative offers all morning, strong ships, well connected. And finally, there's *New Hansea*."

"What about *New Hansea?*"

"Timed properly, with the Hanseatics proposing your name, you'll be elected by acclamation."

"Rhoda!"

"You won't have to touch it. And neither will Thorby. You two will simply appear in public and be your charming, male, non-political selves. I'll handle it. By the way, it's too late to pull Loeen out of the play but I'm going to break that up fast. Your Mother did not see the whole picture. I want my sons married—but it is essential that Thorby *not* be married, nor paired off, until *after* the election. Now . . . did you go to the flagship?"

"Certainly."

"What ship was he born in? It could be important."

Krausa gave a sigh. "Thorby was not born of the People."

"What? Nonsense! You mean that identification is not certain. Mmm . . . which missing ships are possibilities?"

"I said he was not of the People! There is a not a ship missing, nor a child missing from a ship, which can be matched with his case. He would have to be much older, or much younger, than he is."

She shook her head. "I don't believe it."

"You mean you don't want to!"

"I *don't* believe it. He's People. You can tell it in his walk, his manner, his good mind, everything about him. Hmm . . . I'll look at the files myself."

"Go ahead. Since you don't believe *me*."

"Now, Fjalar, I didn't say—"

"Oh, yes, you did. If I told you it was raining dirtside, and you didn't want rain, you—"

"Please, dear! You know it never rains this time of year on Hekate. I was just—"

"Sky around us!"

"There's no need to lose your temper. It doesn't become a captain."

"It doesn't become a captain to have his word doubted in his own ship, either!"

"I'm sorry, Fjalar." She went on quietly, "It won't hurt to look. If I widened the search, or looked through unfiled material—you know how clerks are with deadfile data. Mmm . . . it would help if I knew who Thorby's parents were—before election. While I shan't permit him to marry before then, I might line up important support if it was assumed that immediately after, a wedding could be expec—"

"Rhoda."

"What, dear? The entire *Vega* group could be swayed, *if* a presumption could be established about Thorby's birth . . . *if* an eligible daughter of theirs—"

"Rhoda!"

"I was talking, dear."

"For a moment, I'll talk. The Captain. Wife, he's fraki blood. Furthermore, Baslim knew it . . . and laid a strict injunction on me to help him find his family. I had hoped—yes, and believed—that the files would show that Baslim was mistaken." He frowned and chewed his lip. "A Hegemonic cruiser is due here in two weeks. That ought to give you time to assure yourself that I can search files as well as any clerk."

"What do you mean?"

"Is there doubt? Debts are always paid . . . and there is one more payment due."

She stared. "Husband, are you out of your mind?"

"I don't like it any better than you do. He's not only a fine boy; he's the most brilliant tracker we've ever had."

"Trackers!" she said bitterly. "Who cares about that? Fjalar, if you think that I will permit one of my sons to be turned over to *fraki*—" She choked up.

"He *is* fraki."

"He is *not*. He is *Sisu*, just as I am. I was adopted, so was he. We are both *Sisu*, we will always be."

"Have it your way. I hope he will always be *Sisu* in his heart. But the last payment must be made."

"That debt was paid in full, long ago!"

"The ledger doesn't show it."

"Nonsense! Baslim wanted the boy returned to his family. Some fraki family—if fraki have families. So we gave him a family—our own, clan and sept. Is that not better payment than some flea-bitten fraki litter? Or do you think so little of *Sisu?*"

She glared up at him, and the Krausa thought bitterly that there must be something to the belief that the pure blood of the People produced better brains. In dickering with fraki he never lost his temper. But Mother—and now Rhoda—could always put him in the wrong.

At least Mother, hard as she had been, had never asked the impossible. But Rhoda . . . well, Wife was new to the job. He said tensely, "Chief Officer, this injunction was laid on me personally, not on *Sisu*. I have no choice."

"So? Very well, Captain—we'll speak of it later. And now, with all respect to you, sir, I have work to do."

Thorby had a wonderful time at the Gathering but not as much fun as he expected; repeatedly Mother required him to help entertain chief officers of other ships. Often a visitor brought a daughter or granddaughter along and Thorby had to keep the girl busy while the elders talked. He did his best and even acquired facility in the half-insulting small talk of his age group. He learned something that he called dancing which would have done credit to any man with two left feet and knees that bent backwards. He could now put his arm around a girl when music called for it without chills and fever.

Mother's visitors quizzed him about Pop. He tried to be polite but it annoyed him that everyone knew more about Pop than he did—except the things that were important.

But it did seem that duty could be shared. Thorby realized that he was junior son, but Fritz was unmarried, too. He suggested that if Fritz were to volunteer, the favor could be returned later.

Fritz gave a raucous laugh. "What can you offer that can repay me for dirtside time at Gathering?"

"Well . . ."

"Precisely. Seriously, old knucklehead, Mother wouldn't listen, even if I were insane enough to offer. She says you, she means you." Fritz yawned. "Man, am I dead! Little red-head off the *Saint Louis* wanted to dance all night. Get out and let me sleep before the banquet."

"Can you spare a dress jacket?"

"Do your own laundry. And cut the noise."

But on this morning one month after grounding Thorby was hitting dirt with Father, with no chance that Mother would change their minds; she was out of the ship. It was the Day of Remembrance. Services did not start until noon but Mother left early for something to do with the election tomorrow.

Thorby's mind was filled with other matters. The services would end with a memorial to Pop. Father had told him that he would coach him in what to do, but it worried him, and his nerves were not soothed by the fact that *Spirit of Sisu* would be staged that evening.

His nerves over the play had increased when he discovered that Fritz had a copy and was studying it. Fritz had said gruffly, "Sure, I'm learning your part! Father thought it would be a good idea in case you fainted or broke your leg. I'm not trying to steal your glory; it's intended to let you relax—if you can relax with thousands staring while you smooch Loeen."

"Well, could you?"

Fritz looked thoughtful. "I could try. Loeen looks cuddly. Maybe I should break your leg myself."

"Bare hands?"

"Don't tempt me. Thorby, this is just precaution, like having two trackers. But nothing less than a broken leg can excuse you from strutting your stuff."

Thorby and his Father left *Sisu* two hours before the services. Captain Krausa said, "We might as well enjoy ourselves. Remembrance is a happy occasion if you think of it the right way—but those seats are hard and it's going to be a long day."

"Uh, Father . . . just what is it I'll have to do when it comes time for Pop—for Baslim?"

"Nothing much. You sit up front during the sermon and give responses in the Prayer for the Dead. You know how, don't you?"

"I'm not sure."

"I'll write it out for you. As for the rest . . . well, you'll see me do the same for my Mother—your Grandmother. You watch and when it comes your turn, you do the same."

"All right, Father."

"Now let's relax."

To Thorby's surprise Captain Krausa took a slideway outside the Gathering, then whistled down a ground car. It seemed faster than those Thorby had seen on Jubbul and almost as frantic as the Losians. They reached the rail station with nothing more than an exchange of compliments between their driver and another, but the ride was so exciting that Thorby saw little of the City of Artemis.

He was again surprised when Father bought tickets. "Where are we going?"

"A ride in the country." The Captain glanced at his watch. "Plenty of time."

The monorail gave a fine sensation of speed. "How fast are we going, Father?"

"Two hundred kilometers an hour, at a guess." Krausa had to raise his voice.

"It seems faster."

"Fast enough to break your neck. That's as fast as a speed can be."

They rode for half an hour. The countryside was torn up by steel mills and factories for the great yards, but it was new and different; Thorby stared and decided that the Sargon's reserve was a puny enterprise compared with this. The station where they got off lay outside a long, high wall; Thorby could see space ships beyond it. "Where are we?"

"Military field. I have to see a man—and today there is just time." They walked toward a gate. Krausa stopped, looked around; they were alone. "Thorby—"

"Yes, Father?"

"Do you remember the message from Baslim you delivered to me?"

"Sir?"

"Can you repeat it?"

"Huh? Why, I don't know, Father. It's been a long time."

"Try it. Start in: 'To Captain Fjalar Krausa, master of Starship *Sisu*, from Baslim the Cripple: Greetings, old friend!—' "

" ' "Greetings, old friend," ' " Thorby repeated. " 'Greetings to your family, clan, and sib, and'—why, I understand it!"

"Of course," the Krausa said gently, "this is the Day of Remembrance. Go on."

Thorby went on. Tears started down his cheeks as he heard Pop's voice coming from his own throat: " '—and my humblest respects to your revered mother. I am speaking to you through the mouth of my adopted son. He does not understand Suomic'—oh, but I *do!*"

"Go on."

When Thorby reached: " 'I am already dead—' " he broke down. Krausa blew his nose vigorously, told him to proceed. Thorby managed to get to the end, though his voice was shaking. Then Krausa let him cry a moment before telling him sternly to wipe his face and brace up. "Son . . . you heard the middle part? You understood it?"

"Yes . . . uh, yes. I guess so."

"Then you know what I have to do."

"You mean . . . I have to leave *Sisu?*"

"What did Baslim say? 'When opportunity presents—' This is the first opportunity I've had . . . and I've had to squeeze to get it. It's almost certainly the last. Baslim didn't make me a gift of you, Son—just a loan. And now I must pay back the loan. You see that, don't you?"

"Uh . . . I guess so."

"Then let's get on with it." Krausa reached inside his jacket, pulled out a sheaf of bills and shoved them at Thorby. "Put this in your pocket. I would have made it more, but it was all I could draw without attracting your Mother's suspicions. Perhaps I can send you more before you jump."

Thorby held it without looking at it, although it was more money than he had ever touched before. "Father . . . you mean I've *already left Sisu?*"

Krausa had turned. He stopped. "Better so, Son. Good-bys are not comfort; only remembrance is a comfort. Besides, it has to be this way."

Thorby swallowed. "Yes, sir."

"Let's go."

They walked quickly toward the guarded gate. They were almost there when Thorby stopped. "Father . . . I don't want to go!"

Krausa looked at him without expression. "You don't have to."

"I thought you said I did have to?"

"No. The injunction laid on me was to deliver you and to pass on the message Baslim sent to me. But there my duty ends, my debt is paid. I won't order you to leave the Family. The rest was Baslim's idea . . . conceived, I am sure, with the best of intentions for your welfare.

But whether or not you are obligated to carry out his wishes is something between you and Baslim. I can't decide it for you. Whatever debt you may or may not owe Baslim, it is separate from the debt the People owed to him."

Krausa waited while Thorby stood mute, trying to think. What had Pop expected of him? What had he told him to do? *"Can I depend on you? You won't goof off and forget it?"* Yes, but *what*, Pop? *"Don't burn any offerings . . . just deliver a message, and then one thing more: do whatever this man suggests."* Yes, Pop, but the man won't *tell* me!

Krausa said urgently, "We haven't much time. I have to get back. But, Son, whatever you decide, it's final. If you don't leave *Sisu* today, you won't get a second chance. I'm sure of that."

"It's the very last thing that I want from you, son . . . can I depend on you?" Pop said urgently, inside his head.

Thorby sighed. "I guess I have to, Father."

"I think so, too. Now let's hurry."

The gate pass office could not be hurried, especially as Captain Krausa, although identifying himself and son by ship's papers, declined to state his business with the commander of Guard Cruiser *Hydra* other than to say that it was "urgent and official."

But eventually they were escorted by a smart, armed fraki to the cruiser's hoist and turned over to another. They were handed along inside the ship and reached an office marked "Ship's Secretary—Enter Without Knocking." Thorby concluded that *Sisu* was smaller than he had thought and he had never seen so much polished metal in his life. He was rapidly regretting his decision.

The Ship's Secretary was a polite, scrubbed young man with the lace orbits of a lieutenant. He was also very firm. "I'm sorry, Captain, but you will have to tell me your business . . . if you expect to see the Commanding Officer."

Captain Krausa said nothing and sat tight.

The nice young man colored, drummed on his desk. He got up. "Excuse me a moment."

He came back and said tonelessly, "The Commanding Officer can give you five minutes." He led them into a larger office and left them. An older man was there, seated at a paper-heaped desk. He had his blouse off and showed no insignia of rank. He got up, put out his hand, and said, "Captain Krausa? Of Free Trader . . . *Seezoo*, is it? I'm Colonel Brisby, commanding."

"Glad to be aboard, Skipper."

"Glad to have you. How's business?" He glanced at Thorby. "One of your officers?"

"Yes and no."

"Eh?"

"Colonel? May I ask in what class you graduated?"

"What? Oh-Eight. Why do you ask?"

"I think you can answer that. This lad is Thorby Baslim, adopted son of Colonel Richard Baslim. The Colonel asked me to deliver him to you."

15

"WHAT?"

"The name means something to you?"

"Of course it does." He stared at Thorby. "There's no resemblance."

" 'Adopted' I said. The Colonel adopted him on Jubbul."

Colonel Brisby closed the door. Then he said to Krausa, "Colonel Baslim is dead. Or 'missing and presumed dead,' these past two years."

"I know. The boy has been with me. I can report some details of the Colonel's death, if they are not known."

"You were one of his couriers?"

"Yes."

"You can prove it?"

"X three oh seven nine code FT."

"That can be checked. We'll assume it is for the moment. By what means do you identify . . . Thorby Baslim?"

Thorby did not follow the conversation. There was a buzzing in his ears, as if the tracker was being fed too much power, and the room was swelling and then growing smaller. He did figure out that this officer knew Pop, which was good . . . but what was this about Pop being a colonel? Pop was Baslim the Cripple, licensed mendicant under the mercy of . . . under the mercy . . .

Colonel Brisby told him sharply to sit down, which he was glad to do. Then the Colonel speeded up the air blower. He turned to Captain Krausa. "All right, I'm sold. I don't know what regulation I'm authorized to do it under . . . we are required to give assistance to 'X' Corps people, but this is not quite that. But I can't let Colonel Baslim down."

" 'Distressed citizen,' " suggested Krausa.

"Eh? I don't see how that can be stretched to fit a person on a planet under the Hegemony, who is obviously not distressed—other than a little white around the gills, I mean. But I'll do it."

"Thank you, Skipper." Krausa glanced at his watch. "May I go? In fact I must."

"Just a second. You're simply leaving him with me?"

"I'm afraid that's the way it must be."

Brisby shrugged. "As you say. But stay for lunch. I want to find out more about Colonel Baslim."

"I'm sorry, I can't. You can reach me at the Gathering, if you need to."

"I will. Well, coffee at least." The ship commander reached for a button.

"Skipper," Krausa said with distress, looking again at his watch, "I must leave *now*. Today is our Remembrance . . . and my Mother's funeral is in fifty minutes."

"What? Why didn't you say so? Goodness, man! You'll never make it."

"I'm very much afraid so . . . but I *had* to do this."

"We'll fix that." The Colonel snatched open the door. "Eddie! An air car for Captain Krausa. Speed run. Take him off the top and put him down where he says. Crash!"

"Aye aye, Skipper!"

Brisby turned back, raised his eyebrows, then stepped into the outer office. Krausa was facing Thorby, his mouth working painfully. "Come here, Son."

"Yes, Father."

"I have to go now. Maybe you can manage to be at a Gathering . . . some day."

"I'll try, Father!"

"If not . . . well, the blood stays in the steel, the steel stays in the blood. You're still *Sisu*."

" 'The steel stays in the blood.' "

"Good business, Son. Be a good boy."

"Good . . . business! Oh, Father!"

"Stop it! You'll have me doing it. Listen, I'll take your responses this afternoon. You must not show up."

"Yes, sir."

"Your Mother loves you . . . and so do I."

Brisby tapped on the open door. "Your car is waiting, Captain."

"Coming, Skipper." Krausa kissed Thorby on both cheeks and turned suddenly away, so that all Thorby saw was his broad back.

* * *

Colonel Brisby returned presently, sat down, looked at Thorby and said, "I don't know quite what to do with you. But we'll manage." He touched a switch. "Have someone dig up the berthing master-at-arms, Eddie." He turned to Thorby. "We'll make out, if you're not too fussy. You traders live pretty luxuriously, I understand."

"Sir?"

"Yes?"

"Baslim was a colonel? Of your service?"

"Well . . . yes."

Thorby had now had a few minutes to think—and old memories had been stirred mightily. He said hesitantly, "I have a message for you—I think."

"From Colonel Baslim?"

"Yes, sir. I'm supposed to be in a light trance. But I think I can start it." Carefully, Thorby recited a few code groups. "Is this for you?"

Colonel Brisby again hastily closed the door. Then he said earnestly, "Don't *ever* use that code unless you are certain everyone in earshot is cleared for it and the room has been debugged."

"I'm sorry, sir."

"No harm done. But anything in that code is hot. I just hope that it hasn't cooled off in two years." He touched the talker switch again. "Eddie, cancel the master-at-arms. Get me the psych officer. If he's out of the ship, have him chased down." He looked at Thorby. "I still don't know what to do with you. I ought to lock you in the safe."

The long message was squeezed out of Thorby in the presence only of Colonel Brisby, his Executive Officer Vice Colonel "Stinky" Stancke, and the ship's psychologist Medical-Captain Isadore Krishnamurti. The session went slowly; Dr. Kris did not often use hypnotherapy. Thorby was so tense that he resisted, and the Exec had a blasphemous time with recording equipment. But at last the psychologist straightened up and wiped his face. "That's all, I think," he said wearily. "But what is it?"

"Forget you heard it, Doc," advised Brisby. "Better yet, cut your throat."

"Gee, thanks, Boss."

Stancke said, "Pappy, let's run him through again. I've got this mad scientist's dream working better. His accent may have garbled it."

"Nonsense. The kid speaks pure Terran."

"Okay, so it's my ears. I've been exposed to bad influences—been aboard too long."

"If," Brisby answered calmly, "that is a slur on your commanding officer's pure speech, I consider the source. Stinkpot, is it true that you Riffs write down anything you want understood?"

"Only with Araleshi . . . sir. Nothing personal, you asked. Well, how about it? I've got the noise filtered out."

"Doc?"

"Hmm . . . The subject is fatigued. Is this your only opportunity?"

"Eh? He'll be with us quite a while. All right, wake him."

Shortly Thorby was handed over to the berthing P.O. Several liters of coffee, a tray of sandwiches, and one skipped meal later the Colonel and his second in command had recorded in clear the thousands of words of old Baslim the Beggar's final report. Stancke sat back and whistled. "You can relax, Pappy. This stuff didn't cool off—a half-life of a century, on a guess."

Brisby answered soberly, "Yes, and a lot of good boys will die before it does."

"You ain't foolin'. What gets me is that trader kid—running around the Galaxy with all that 'burn-before-reading' between his ears. Shall I slide down and poison him?"

"What, and have to fill out all those copies?"

"Well, maybe Kris can wipe it out of his tender gray matter without resorting to a trans-orbital."

"Anybody touches that kid and Colonel Baslim will rise up out of his grave and strangle him, is my guess. Did you know Baslim, Stinky?"

"One course under him in psychological weapons, my last year at the Academy. Just before he went 'X' Corps. Most brilliant mind I've ever met—except yours, of course, Pappy, sir, boss."

"Don't strain yourself. No doubt he was a brilliant teacher—he would be tops at anything. But you should have known him before he was on limited duty. I was privileged to serve under him. Now that I have a ship of my own I just ask myself: 'What would Baslim do?' He was the best commanding officer a ship ever had. It was during his second crack at colonel—he had been up to wing marshal and put in for reduction to have a ship again, to get away from a desk."

Stancke shook his head. "I can't wait for a nice cushy desk, where I can write recommendations nobody will read."

"You aren't Baslim. If it wasn't hard, he didn't like it."

"I'm no hero. I'm more the salt of the earth. Pappy, were you with him in the rescue of the *Hansea?*"

"You think I would fail to wear the ribbon? No, thank goodness; I had been transferred. That was a hand-weapons job. Messy."

"Maybe you would have had the sense not to volunteer."

"Stinky, even you would volunteer, fat and lazy as you are—if Baslim asked for volunteers."

"I'm not lazy, I'm efficient. But riddle me this: what was a C.O. doing leading a landing party?"

"The Old Man followed regulations only when he agreed with them. He wanted a crack at slavers with his own hands—he hated slavers with a cold passion. So he comes back a hero and what can the Department do? Wait until he gets out of the hospital and court-martial him? Stinky, even top brass can be sensible when they have their noses rubbed in it. So they cited him for above-and-beyond under unique circumstances and put him on limited duty. But from here on, when 'unique circumstances' arise, every commanding officer knows that he can't thumb through the book for an alibi. It'll be up to him to continue the example."

"Not me," Stancke said firmly.

"You. When you're a C.O. and comes time to do something unpleasant, there you'll be, trying to get your tummy in and your chest out, with your chubby little face set in hero lines. You won't be able to help it. The Baslim conditioned-reflex will hit you."

Around dawn they got to bed. Brisby intended to sleep late but long habit took him to his desk only minutes late. He was not surprised to find his professedly-lazy Exec already at work.

His Paymaster-Lieutenant was waiting. The fiscal officer was holding a message form; Brisby recognized it. The night before, after hours of dividing Baslim's report into phrases, then recoding it to be sent by split routes, he had realized that there was one more chore before he could sleep: arrange for identification search on Colonel Baslim's adopted son. Brisby had no confidence that a waif picked up on Jubbul could be traced in the vital records of the Hegemony—but if the Old Man sent for a bucket of space, that was what he wanted and no excuses. Toward Baslim, dead or not, Colonel Brisby maintained the attitudes of a junior officer. So he had written a despatch and left word with the duty officer to have Thorby finger-printed and the prints coded at reveille. Then he could sleep.

Brisby looked at the message. "Hasn't this gone out?" he demanded.

"The photo lab is coding the prints now, Skipper. But the Comm Office brought it to me for a charge, since it is for service outside the ship."

"Well, assign it. Do I have to be bothered with every routine matter?"

The Paymaster decided that the Old Man had been missing sleep again. "Bad news, Skipper."

"Okay, spill it."

"I don't know of a charge to cover it. I doubt if there is an appropriation to fit even if we could figure out a likely-sounding charge."

"I don't care what charge. Pick one and get that message moving. Use that general one. Oh-oh-something."

" 'Unpredictable Overhead, Administrative.' It won't work, Skipper. Making an identity search on a civilian cannot be construed as ship's overhead. Oh, I can put that charge number on and you'll get an answer. But—"

"That's what I want. An answer."

"Yes, sir. But eventually it reaches the General Accounting Office and the wheels go around and a card pops out with a red tag. Then my pay is checked until I pay it back. That's why they make us blokes study law as well as accounting."

"You're breaking my heart. Okay, Pay, if you're too sissy to sign it, tell me what charge number that overhead thing is; I'll write it in and sign my name and rank. Okay?"

"Yes, sir. But, Skipper—"

"Pay, I've had a hard night."

"Yes, sir. I'm required by law to advise you. You don't have to take it, of course."

"Of course," Brisby agreed grimly.

"Skipper, have you any notion how expensive an identification search can be?"

"It can't be much. I can't see why you are making such an aching issue of it. I want a clerk to get off his fundament and look in the files. I doubt if they'll bill us. Routine courtesy."

"I wish I thought so, sir. But you've made this an unlimited search. Since you haven't named a planet, first it will go to Tycho City, live files and dead. Or do you want to limit it to live files?"

Brisby thought. If Colonel Baslim had believed that this young man had come from inside civilization, then it was likely that the kid's family thought he was dead. "No."

"Too bad. Dead files are three times as big as the live. So they search at Tycho. It takes a while, even with machines—over twenty billion entries. Suppose you get a null result. A coded inquiry goes to vital bureaus on all planets, since Great Archives are never up to date and some planetary governments don't send in records anyhow. Now the cost mounts, especially if you use n-space routing; exact coding on a fingerprint set is a fair-sized book. Of course if you take one planet at a time and use mail—"

"No."

"Well . . . Skipper, why not put a limit on it? A thousand credits, or whatever you can afford if—I mean *'when'*—they check your pay."

"A thousand credits? Ridiculous!"

"If I'm wrong, the limitation won't matter. If I'm right—and I am, a thousand credits could just be a starter—then your neck isn't out too far."

Brisby scowled. "Pay, you aren't working for me to tell me I can't do things."

"Yes, sir."

"You're here to tell me how I *can* do what I'm going to do anyhow. So start digging through your books and find out how. Legally. And free."

"Aye aye, sir."

Brisby did not go right to work. He was fuming—some day they would get the service so fouled up in red tape they'd never get a ship off the ground. He bet that the Old Man had gone into the Exotic Corps with a feeling of relief—"X" Corps agents didn't have red tape; one of 'em finds it necessary to spend money, he just did so, ten credits or ten million. That was how to operate—pick your men, then trust them. No regular reports, no forms, no nothing—just do what needs to be done.

Whereupon he picked up the ship's quarterly fuel and engineering report. He put it down, reached for a message form, wrote a follow-up on Baslim'sreport, informing Exotic Bureau that the unclassified courier who had delivered report was still in jurisdiction of signer and in signer's opinion additional data could be had if signer were authorized to discuss report with courier at discretion.

He decided not to turn it over to the code and cipher group; he opened his safe and set about coding it. He had just finished when the Paymaster knocked. Brisby looked up. "So you found the paragraph."

"Perhaps, Skipper. I've been talking with the Executive Officer."

"Shoot."

"I see we have subject person aboard."

"Now don't tell me I need a charge for that!"

"Not at all, Skipper. I'll absorb his ration in the rush. You keep him aboard forever and I won't notice. Things don't get awkward until they get on the books. But how long do you expect to keep him? It must be more than a day or two, or you wouldn't want an identity search."

The Commanding Officer frowned. "It may be quite a while. First I've got to find out who he is, where he's from. Then, if we're going that way, I intend to give him an unlogged lift. If we aren't—well, I'll pass him along to a ship that is. Too complicated to explain, Pay—but necessary."

"Okay. Then why not enlist him?"

"Huh?"

"It would clear up everything."

Brisby frowned. "I see. I could take him along legally . . . and arrange a transfer. And it would give you a charge number. But . . . well, suppose Shiva III is the spot—and his enlistment is not up. Can't just tell him to desert. Besides I don't know that he wants to enlist."

"You can ask him. How old is he?"

"I doubt if he knows. He's a waif."

"So much the better. You ship him. Then when you find out where he has to go, you discover an error in his age . . . and correct it. It turns out that he reaches his majority in time to be paid off on his home planet."

Brisby blinked. "Pay, are all paymaster dishonest?"

"Only the good ones. You don't like it, sir?"

"I love it. Okay, I'll check. And I'll hold up that despatch. We'll send it later."

The Paymaster looked innocent. "Oh, no, sir, we won't ever send it."

"How's that?"

"It won't be necessary. We enlist him to fill vacancy in complement. We send in records to BuPersonnel. They make the routine check, name and home planet—Hekate, I suppose, since we got him here. By then we're long gone. They don't find him registered here. Now they turn it over to Bu-Security, who sends us a priority telling us not to permit subject personnel to serve in sensitive capacity. But that's all, because it's possible that this poor innocent citizen never got registered. But they can't take chances, so they start the very search you want, first Tycho, then everywhere else, security priority. So they identify him and unless he's wanted for murder it's a routine muddle. Or they can't identify him and have to make up their minds whether to register him, or give him twenty-four hours to get out of the Galaxy—seven to two they decide to forget it—except that someone aboard is told to watch him and report suspicious behavior. But the real beauty of it is that the job carries a BuSecurity cost charge."

"Pay, do you think that Security has agents in this vessel I don't know about?"

"Skipper, what do you think?"

"Mmm . . . I don't know—but if I were Chief of Security I would have! Confound it, if I lift a civilian from here to the Rim, that'll be reported too—no matter what I log."

"Shouldn't be surprised, sir."

"Get out of here! I'll see if the lad will buy it." He flipped a switch. "Eddie!" Instead of sending for Thorby, Brisby directed the Surgeon to examine him, since it was pointless to pressure him to enlist without determining whether or not he could. Medical-Major Stein, accompanied by Medical-Captain Krishnamurti, reported to Brisby before lunch.

"Well?"

"No physical objection, Skipper. I'll let the Psych Officer speak for himself."

"All right. By the way, how old is he?"

"He doesn't know."

"Yes, yes," Brisby agreed impatiently, "but how old do you think he is?"

Dr. Stein shrugged. "What's his genetic picture? What environment? Any age-factor mutations? High or low gravity planet? Planetary metabolic index? He could be as young as ten standard years, as old as thirty, on physical appearance. I can assign a fictional adjusted age, on the assumption of no significant mutations and Terra-equivalent environment—an unjustified assumption until they build babies with data plates—an adjusted age of not less than fourteen standard years, not more than twenty-two."

"Would an adjusted age of eighteen fit?"

"That's what I said."

"Okay, make it just under that—minority enlistment."

"There's a tattoo on him," Dr. Krishnamurti offered, "which might give a clue. A slave mark."

"The deuce you say!" Colonel Brisby reflected that his follow-up despatch to "X" Corps was justified. "Dated?"

"Just a manumission—a Sargonese date which fits his story. The mark is a factor's mark. No date."

"Too bad. Well, now that he is clear with Medical, I'll send for him."

"Colonel."

"Eh? Yes, Kris?"

"I cannot recommend enlistment."

"Huh? He's as sane as you are."

"Surely. But he is a poor risk."

"Why?"

"I interviewed subject under light trance this morning Colonel, did you ever keep a dog?"

"No. Not many where I come from."

"Very useful laboratory animals, they parallel many human characteristics. Take a puppy, abuse him, kick him mistreat him—he'll revert to feral carnivore. Take his litter brother, pet him, talk to him, let him sleep with you, but train him—he's a happy, well-behaved house pet. Take another from that same litter, pet him on even days and kick him on odd days. You'll have him so confused that he'll be ruined for either role; he can't survive as a wild animal and he doesn't understand what is expected of a pet. Pretty soon he won't eat, he won't sleep, he can't control his functions; he just cowers and shivers."

"Hmm . . . do you psychologists do such things often?"

"I never have. But it's in the literature . . . and this lad's case parallels it. He's undergone a series of traumatic experiences in his formative years, the latest of which was yesterday. He's confused and depressed. Like that dog, he may snarl and bite at any time. He ought not to be exposed to new pressures; he should be cared for where he can be given psychotherapy."

"Phooey!"

The psychological officer shrugged. Colonel Brisby added, "I apologize, Doctor. But I know something about this case, with all respect to your training. This lad has been in good environment the past couple of years." Brisby recalled the farewell he had unwillingly witnessed. "And before that, he was in the hands of Colonel Richard Baslim. Heard of him?"

"I know his reputation."

"If there is any fact I would stake my ship on, it is that Colonel Baslim would *never* ruin a boy. Okay, so the kid has had a rough time. But he has also been succored by one of the toughest, sanest, most humane men ever to wear our uniform. You bet on your dogs; I'll back Colonel Richard Baslim. Now . . . are you advising me not to enlist him?"

The psychologist hesitated. Brisby said, "Well?"

Major Stein interrupted. "Take it easy, Kris; I'm overriding you."

Brisby said, "I want a straight answer, then *I'll* decide."

Dr. Krishnamurti said slowly, "Suppose I record my opinions but state that there are no certain grounds for refusing enlistment?"

"Why?"

"Obviously you want to enlist this boy. But if he gets into trouble—well, my endorsement could get him a medical discharge instead of a sentence. He's had enough bad breaks."

Colonel Brisby clapped him on the shoulder. "Good boy, Kris! That's all, gentlemen."

Thorby spent an unhappy night. The master-at-arms billeted him in senior P.O.s quarters and he was well treated, but embarrassingly aware of the polite way in which those around him did not stare at his gaudy *Sisu* dress uniform. Up till then he had been proud of the way *Sisu*'s dress stood out; now he was learning painfully that clothing has its proper background. That night he was conscious of snores around him . . . strangers . . . fraki—and he yearned to be back among People, where he was known, understood, recognized.

He tossed on a harder bed than he was used to and wondered who would get his own?

He found himself wondering whether anyone had ever claimed the hole he still thought of as "home." Would they repair the door? Would they keep it clean and decent the way Pop liked? *What would they do with Pop's leg?*

Asleep, he dreamt of Pop and of *Sisu*, all mixed up. At last, with Grandmother shortened and a raider bearing down, Pop whispered, *"No more bad dreams, Thorby. Never again, son. Just happy dreams."*

He slept peacefully then—and awoke in this forbidding place with gabbling fraki all around him. Breakfast was substantial but not up to Aunt Athena's high standards; however he was not hungry.

After breakfast he was quietly tasting his misery when he was required to undress and submit to indignities. It was his first experience with medical men's offhand behavior with human flesh—he loathed the poking and prodding.

When the Commanding Officer sent for him Thorby was not even cheered by seeing the man who knew Pop. This room was where he had had to say a last "good-business" to Father; the thoughts lingering there were not good.

He listened listlessly while Brisby explained. He woke up a little when he understood that he was being offered status—not much, he gathered. But status. The fraki had status among themselves. It had never occurred to him that fraki status could matter even to fraki.

"You don't have to," Colonel Brisby concluded, "but it will make simpler the thing Colonel Baslim wanted me to do—find your family, I mean. You would like that, wouldn't you?"

Thorby almost said that he knew where his Family was. But he knew what the Colonel meant: his own sib, whose existence he had never quite been able to imagine. Did he really have blood relatives somewhere?

"I suppose so," he answered slowly. "I don't know."

"Mmm . . ." Brisby wondered what it was like to have no frame to your picture. "Colonel Baslim was anxious to have me locate your family. I can handle it easier if you are officially one of us. Well? It's

Guardsman third class . . . thirty credits a month, all you can eat and not enough sleep. And glory. A meager amount."

Thorby looked up. "This is the same Fam—service my Pop—Colonel Baslim, you call him—was in? He really was?"

"Yes. Senior to what you will be. But the same service. I think you started to say 'family.' We like to think of the Service as one enormous family. Colonel Baslim was one of the more distinguished members of it."

"Then I want to be adopted."

"Enlisted."

"Whatever the word is."

16

Fraki weren't bad when you got to know them.

They had their secret language, even though they thought they talked Interlingua. Thorby added a few dozen verbs and a few hundred nouns as he heard them; after that he tripped over an occasional idiom. He learned that his light-years as a trader were respected, even though the People were considered odd. He didn't argue; fraki couldn't know better.

H.G.C. *Hydra* lifted from Hekate, bound for the Rim worlds. Just before jump a money order arrived accompanied by a supercargo's form which showed the draft to be one eighty-third of *Sisu*'s appreciation from Jubbulpore to Hekate—as if, thought Thorby, he were a girl being swapped. It was an uncomfortably large sum and Thorby could find no entry charging him interest against a capital share of the ship—which he felt should be there for proper accounting; it wasn't as if he had been born in the ship. Life among the People had made the beggar boy conscious of money in a sense that alms never could—books must balance and debts must be paid.

He wondered what Pop would think of all that money. He felt easier when he learned that he could deposit it with the Paymaster.

With the draft was a warm note, wishing him good business wherever he went and signed: "Love, Mother." It made Thorby feel better and much worse.

A package of belongings arrived with a note from Fritz: "Dear Brother, Nobody briefed me about recent mysterious happenings, but things were crisp around the old ship for a few days. If such were not unthinkable, I would say there had been a difference of opinion at highest level. Me, I have no opinions, except that I miss your idle chatter and blank expressions. Have fun and be sure to count your change.

"Fritz

"P.S. The play was an artistic success—and Loeen *is* cuddly."

Thorby stored his *Sisu* belongings; he was trying to be a Guardsman and they made him uncomfortable. He discovered that the Guard was not the closed corporation the People were; it required no magic to make a Guardsman if a man had what it took, because nobody cared where a man came from or what he had been. The *Hydra* drew its company from many planets; there were machines in BuPersonnel to ensure this. Thorby's shipmates were tall and short, bird-boned and rugged, smooth and hairy, mutated and superficially unmutated. Thorby hit close to norm and his Free Trader background was merely an acceptable eccentricity; it made him a spaceman of sorts even though a recruit.

In fact, the only hurdle was that he was a raw recruit. "Guardsman 3/c" he might be but a boot he would remain until he proved himself, most especially since he had not had boot training.

But he was no more handicapped than any recruit in a military outfit having proud *esprit de corps*. He was assigned a bunk, a mess, a working station, and a petty officer to tell him what to do. His work was compartment cleaning, his battle station was runner for the Weapons Officer in case phones should fail—it meant that he was available to fetch coffee.

Otherwise he was left in peace. He was free to join a bull session as long as he let his seniors sound off, he was invited into card games when a player was needed, he was not shut out of gossip, and he was privileged to lend jumpers and socks to seniors who happened to be short. Thorby had had experience at being junior; it was not difficult.

The *Hydra* was heading out for patrol duty; the mess talk centered around "hunting" prospects. The *Hydra* had fast "legs," three hundred gravities; she sought action with outlaws where a merchantman such as the *Sisu* would avoid it if possible. Despite her large complement and heavy weapons, the *Hydra* was mostly power plant and fuel tanks.

Thorby's table was headed by his petty officer, Ordnanceman 2/c Peebie, down as "Decibel." Thorby was eating one day with his ears tuned down, while he debated visiting the library after dinner or attending the stereo show in the messroom, when he heard his nickname: "Isn't that right, Trader?"

Thorby was proud of the nickname. He did not like it in Peebie's mouth but Peebie was a self-appointed wit—he would greet Thorby with the nickname, inquire solicitously, "How's business?" and make gestures of counting money. So far, Thorby had ignored it.

"Isn't what right?"

"Why'n't y'keep y'r ears open? Can't you hear anything but rustle and clink? I was telling 'em what I told the Weapons Officer: the way to rack up more kills is to go after 'em, not pretend to be a trader, too scared to fight and too fat to run."

Thorby felt a simmer. "Who," he said, "told you that traders were scared to fight?"

"Quit pushin' that stuff! Whoever heard of a trader burning a bandit?"

Peebie may have been sincere; kills made by traders received no publicity. But Thorby's burn increased. "I have."

Thorby meant that he had heard of traders' burning raiders; Peebie took it as a boast. "Oh, you did, did you? Listen to that, men—our peddler is a hero. He's burned a bandit all by his own little self! Tell us about it. Did you set fire to his hair? Or drop potassium in his beer?"

"I used," Thorby stated, "a Mark XIX one-stage target-seeker, made by Bethlehem-Antares and armed with a 20 megaton plutonium warhead. I launched a timed shot on closing to beaming range on a collision-curve prediction."

There was silence. Finally Peebie said coldly, "Where did you read that?"

"It's what the tape showed after the engagement. I was senior starboard firecontrolman. The portside computer was out—so I know it was my shot that burned him."

"Now he's a weapons officer! Peddler, don't peddle it here."

Thorby shrugged. "I used to be. A weapons control officer, rather. I never learned much about ordnance."

"Modest, isn't he? Talk is cheap, Trader."

"You should know, Decibel."

Peebie was halted by his nickname; Thorby did not rate such familiarity. Another voice cut in, saying sweetly, "Sure, Decibel, talk is cheap. Now you tell about the big kills you've made. Go ahead." The speaker was non-rated but was a clerk in the executive office and immune to Peebie's displeasure.

Peebie glowered. "Enough of this prattle," he growled. "Baslim, I'll see you at oh eight hundred in combat control—we'll find out how much you know about firecontrol."

Thorby was not anxious to be tested; he knew nothing about the *Hydra*'s equipment. But an order is an order; he was facing Peebie's smirk at the appointed time.

The smirk did not last. *Hydra*'s instruments bore no resemblance to those in the *Sisu*, but the principles were the same and the senior gunnery sergeant (cybernetics) seemed to find nothing unlikely in an ex-trader knowing how to shoot. He was always looking for talent; people to handle ballistic trackers for the preposterous problems of combat at sub-light-speed were as scarce among Guardsmen as among the People.

He questioned Thorby about the computer he had handled. Presently he nodded. "I've never seen anything but schematics on a Dusseldorf tandem rig; that approach is obsolete. But if you can get a hit with that junk, we can use you." The sergeant turned to Peebie. "Thanks, Decibel. I'll mention it to the Weapons Officer. Stick around, Baslim."

Peebie looked astonished. "He's got work to do, Sarge."

Sergeant Luter shrugged. "Tell your leading P.O. that I need Baslim here."

Thorby had been shocked to hear *Sisu*'s beautiful computers called "junk." But shortly he knew what Luter meant; the massive brain that fought for the *Hydra* was a genius among computers. Thorby would never control it alone—but soon he was an acting ordnanceman 3/c (cybernetics) and relatively safe from Peebie's wit. He began to feel like a Guardsman—very junior but an accepted shipmate.

Hydra was cruising above speed-of-light toward the Rim world Ultima Thule, where she would refuel and start prowling for outlaws. No query had reached the ship concerning Thorby's identity. He was contented with his status in Pop's old outfit; it made him proud to feel that Pop would be proud of him. He did miss *Sisu*, but a ship with no women was simpler to live in; compared with *Sisu* the *Hydra* had no restrictive regulations.

But Colonel Brisby did not let Thorby forget why he had been enlisted. Commanding officers are many linkages away from a recruit; a non-rated man might not lay eyes on his skipper except at inspections. But Brisby sent for Thorby repeatedly.

Brisby received authorization from the Exotic Corps to discuss Colonel Baslim's report with Baslim's courier, bearing in mind the critical classification of the subject. So Brisby called Thorby in.

Thorby was first warned of the necessity of keeping his mouth shut. Brisby told him that the punishment for blabbing would be as heavy as a court-martial could hand out. "But that's not the point. We have to be sure that the question never arises. Otherwise we can't discuss it."

Thorby hesitated. "How can I know that I'll keep my mouth shut when I don't know what it is?"

Brisby looked annoyed. "I can order you to."

"Yes, sir. And I'll say, 'Aye aye, sir.' But does that make you certain that I wouldn't risk a court-martial?"

"But— This is ridiculous! I want to talk about Colonel Baslim's work. But you're to keep your yap shut, you understand me? If you don't, I'll tear you to pieces with my bare hands. No young punk is going to quibble with me where the Old Man's work is concerned!"

Thorby looked relieved. "Why didn't you say it was that, Skipper? I wouldn't blab about anything of Pop's—why, that was the first thing he taught me."

"Oh." Brisby grinned. "I should have known. Okay."

"I suppose," Thorby added thoughtfully, "that it's all right to talk to *you*."

Brisby looked startled. "I hadn't realized that this cuts two ways. But it does. I can show you a despatch from his corps, telling me to discuss his report with you. Would that convince you?"

Brisby found himself showing a "Most Secret" despatch to his most junior, acting petty officer, to convince said junior that his C.O. was entitled to talk with him. At the time it seemed reasonable; it was not until later that the Colonel wondered.

Thorby read the translated despatch and nodded. "Anything you want, Skipper. I'm sure Pop would agree."

"Okay. You know what he was doing?"

"Well . . . yes and no. I saw some of it. I know what sort of things he was interested in having me notice and remember. I used to carry messages for him and it was always very secret. But I never knew why." Thorby frowned. "They said he was a spy."

"Intelligence agent sounds better."

Thorby shrugged. "If he was spying, he'd call it that. Pop never minced words."

"No, he never minced words," Brisby agreed, wincing as he recalled being scorched right through his uniform by a dressing-down. "Let me explain. Mmm . . . know any Terran history?"

"Uh, not much."

"It's a miniature history of the race. Long before space travel, when we hadn't even filled up Terra, there used to be dirtside frontiers. Every time new territory was found, you always got three phenomena: traders ranging out ahead and taking their chances, outlaws preying on the honest men—and a traffic in slaves. It happens the same way today, when we're pushing through space instead of across oceans and prairies. Frontier traders are adventurers taking great risks for great profits. Outlaws, whether hill bands or sea pirates or the raiders in space, crop up in any area not under police protection. Both are temporary. But slavery is another matter—the most vicious habit humans fall into and the hardest to break. It starts up in every new land and it's terribly hard to root out. After a culture falls ill of it, it gets rooted in the economic system and laws, in men's habits and attitudes. You abolish it; you drive it underground—there it lurks, ready to spring up again, in the minds of people who think it is their 'natural' right to own other people. You can't reason with them; you can kill them but you can't change their minds."

Brisby sighed. "Baslim, the Guard is just the policeman and the mailman; we haven't had a major war in two centuries. What we do work at is the impossible job of maintaining order on the frontier, a globe three thousand light-years in circumference—no one can understand how big that is; the mind can't swallow it.

"Nor can human beings police it. It gets bigger every year. Dirtside police eventually close the gaps. But with us, the longer we try the more there is. So to most of us it's a job, an honest job, but one that can never be finished.

"But to Colonel Richard Baslim it was a passion. Especially he hated the slave trade, the thought of it could make him sick at his stomach—I've seen. He lost his leg and an eye—I suppose you know—while rescuing a shipload of people from a slaving compound.

"That would satisfy most officers—go home and retire. Not old Spit-and-Polish! He taught a few years, then he went to the one corps that might take him, chewed up as he was, and presented a plan.

"The Nine Worlds are the backbone of the slave trade. The Sargony was colonized a long time ago, and they never accepted Hegemony after they broke off as colonies. The Nine Worlds don't qualify on human rights and don't want to qualify. So we can't travel there and they can't visit our worlds.

"Colonel Baslim decided that the traffic could be rendered uneconomic if we knew how it worked in the Sargony. He reasoned that slavers had to have ships, had to have bases, had to have markets, that it was not just a vice but a business. So he decided to go there and study it.

"This was preposterous—one man against a nine-planet empire . . . but the Exotic Corps deals in preposterous notions. Even they would probably not have made him an agent if he had not had a scheme to get his reports out. An agent couldn't travel back and forth, nor could he use the mails—there aren't any between us and them—and he certainly couldn't set up an n-space communicator; that would be as conspicuous as a brass band.

"But Baslim had an idea. The *only* people who visit both the Nine Worlds and our own are Free Traders. But they avoid politics like poison, as you know better than I, and they go to great lengths not to offend local customs. However Colonel Baslim had a personal 'in' to them.

"I suppose you know that those people he rescued were Free Traders. He told 'X' Corps that he could report back through his friends. So they let him try. It's my guess that no one knew that he intended to pose as a beggar—I doubt if he planned it; he was always great at improvising. But he got in and for years he observed and got his reports out.

"That's the background and now I want to squeeze every possible fact out of you. You can tell us about methods—the report I forwarded never said a word about methods. Another agent might be able to use his methods."

Thorby said soberly, "I'll tell you anything I can. I don't know much."

"You know more than you think you do. Would you let the psych officer put you under again and see if we can work total recall?"

"Anything is okay if it'll help Pop's work."

"It should. Another thing—" Brisby crossed his cabin, held up a sheet on which was the silhouette of a spaceship. "What ship is this?"

Thorby's eyes widened. "A Sargonese cruiser."

Brisby snatched up another one. "This?"

"Uh, it looks like a slaver that called at Jubbulpore twice a year."

"Neither one," Brisby said savagely, "is anything of the sort. These are recognition patterns out of my files—of ships built by our biggest shipbuilder. If you saw them in Jubbulpore, they were either copies, or bought from us!"

Thorby considered it. "They build ships there."

"So I've been told. But Colonel Baslim reported ships' serial numbers—how he got them I couldn't guess; maybe you can. He claims that the slave trade is getting help from our own worlds!" Brisby looked unbearably disgusted.

Thorby reported regularly to the Cabin, sometimes to see Brisby, sometimes to be interviewed under hypnosis by Dr. Krishnamurti. Brisby always mentioned the search for Thorby's identity and told him not to be discouraged; such a search took a long time. Repeated mention changed Thorby's attitude about it from something impossible to something which was going to be true soon; he began thinking about his family, wondering who he was?—it was going to be nice to know, to be like other people.

Brisby was reassuring himself; he had been notified to keep Thorby off sensitive work the very day the ship jumped from Hekate when he had hoped that Thorby would be identified at once. He kept the news to himself, holding fast to his conviction that Colonel Baslim was never wrong and that the matter would be cleared up.

When Thorby was shifted to Combat Control, Brisby worried when the order passed across his desk—that was a "security" area, never open to visitors—then he told himself that a man with no special training couldn't learn anything there that could really affect security and that he was already using the lad in much more sensitive work. Brisby felt that he was learning things of importance—that the Old Man, for example, had used the cover personality of a one-legged beggar to hide two-legged activities . . . but had actually been a beggar; he and the boy had lived only on alms. Brisby admired such artistic perfection—it should be an example to other agents.

But the Old Man always had been a shining example.

So Brisby left Thorby in combat control. He omitted to make permanent Thorby's acting promotion in order that the record of change in rating need not be forwarded to BuPersonnel. But he became anxious to receive the despatch that would tell him who Thorby was.

His executive was with him when it came in. It was in code, but Brisby recognized Thorby's serial number; he had written it many times in reports to "X" Corps. "Look at this, Stinky! This tells us who our foundling is. Grab the machine; the safe is open."

Ten minutes later they had processed it; it read:

—"NULL RESULT FULL IDENTSEARCH BASLIM THORBY GDS-MN THIRD. AUTH & DRT TRANSFER ANY RECEIVING STATION RETRANSFER HEKATE INVESTIGATION DISPOSITION—CHFBUPERS."

"Stinky, ain't that a mess?"

Stancke shrugged. "It's how the dice roll, boss."

"I feel as if I had let the Old Man down. He was sure the kid was a citizen."

"I misdoubt there are millions of citizens who would have a bad time proving who they are. Colonel Baslim may have been right—and still it can't be proved."

"I hate to transfer him. I feel responsible."

"Not your fault."

"You never served under Colonel Baslim. He was easy to please . . . all he wanted was one-hundred-percent perfection. And this doesn't feel like it."

"Quit blaming yourself. You have to accept the record."

"Might as well get it over with. Eddie! I want to see Ordnanceman Baslim."

Thorby noticed that the Skipper looked grim—but then he often did. "Acting Ordnanceman Third Class Baslim reporting, sir."

"Thorby . . ."

"Yes, sir?" Thorby was startled. The Skipper sometimes used his first name because that was what he answered to under hypnosis—but this was not such a time.

"The identification report on you came."

"Huh?" Thorby was startled out of military manners. He felt a surge of joy—he was going to know who he was!

"They can't identify you." Brisby waited, then said sharply, "Did you understand?"

Thorby swallowed. "Yes, sir. They don't know who I am. I'm not . . . anybody."

"Nonsense! You're still yourself."

"Yes, sir. Is that all, sir? May I go?"

"Just a moment. I have to transfer you back to Hekate." He added hastily, seeing Thorby's expression, "Don't worry. They'll probably let you serve out your enlistment if you want to. In any case, they can't do anything to you; you haven't done anything wrong."

"Yes, sir," Thorby repeated dully.

Nothing and nobody—He had a blinding image of an old, old nightmare . . . standing on the block, hearing an auctioneer chant his description, while cold eyes stared at him. But he pulled himself together and was merely quiet the rest of the day. It was not until the compartment was dark that he bit his pillow and whispered brokenly, "Pop . . . oh, *Pop!*"

The Guards uniform covered Thorby's legs, but in the showers the tattoo on his left thigh could be noticed. When this happened, Thorby explained without embarrassment what it signified. Responses varied from curiosity, through half-disbelief, to awed surprise that here was a man who had been through it—capture, sale, servitude, and miraculously, free again. Most civilians did not realize that slavery still existed; Guardsmen knew better.

No one was nasty about it.

But the day after the null report on identification Thorby encountered "Decibel" Peebie in the showers. Thorby did not speak; they had not spoken much since Thorby had moved out from under Peebie, even though they sat at the same table. But now Peebie spoke. "Hi, Trader!"

"Hi." Thorby started to bathe.

"What's on your leg? Dirt?"

"Where?"

"On your thigh. Hold still. Let's see."

"Keep your hands to yourself!"

"Don't be touchy. Turn around to the light. What is it?"

"It's a slaver's mark," Thorby explained curtly.

"No foolin'? So you're a slave?"

"I used to be."

"They put chains on you? Make you kiss your master's foot?"

"Don't be silly!"

"Look who's talking! You know what, Trader boy? I heard about that mark—and I think you had it tattooed yourself. To make big talk. Like that one about how you blasted a bandit ship."

Thorby cut his shower short and got out.

At dinner Thorby was helping himself from a bowl of mashed potatoes. He heard Peebie call out something but his ears filtered out "Decibel's" endless noise.

Peebie repeated it. "Hey, Slave! Pass the potatoes! You know who I mean! Dig the dirt out of your ears!"

Thorby passed him the potatoes, bowl and all, in a flat trajectory, open face of the bowl plus potatoes making perfect contact with the open face of Decibel.

The charge against Thorby was "Assaulting a Superior Officer, the Ship then being in Space in a Condition of Combat Readiness." Peebie appeared as complaining witness.

Colonel Brisby stared over the mast desk and his jaw muscles worked. He listened to Peebie's account: "I asked him to pass the potatoes . . . and he hit me in the face with them."

"That was all?"

"Well, sir, maybe I didn't say please. But that's no reason—"

"Never mind the conclusions. The fight go any farther?"

"No, sir. They separated us."

"Very well. Baslim, what have you to say for yourself?"

"Nothing, sir."

"Is that what happened?"

"Yes, sir."

Brisby stopped to think, while his jaw muscles twitched. He felt angry, an emotion he did not permit himself at mast—he felt let down. Still, there must be more to it.

Instead of passing sentence he said, "Step aside. Colonel Stancke—"

"Yes, sir?"

"There were other men present. I want to hear from them."

"I have them standing by, sir."

"Very well."

Thorby was convicted—three days bread & water, solitary, sentence suspended, thirty days probation; acting rank stricken.

Decibel Peebie was convicted (court trial waived when Brisby pointed out how the book could be thrown at him) of "Inciting to Riot, specification: using derogatory language with reference to another Guardsman's Race, Religion, Birthplace, or Condition previous to entering Service, the Ship then being etc."—sentence three days B & W, sol., suspended, reduction one grade, ninety days probation in ref. B & W, sol., only.

The Colonel and Vice Colonel went back to Brisby's office. Brisby was looking glum; mast upset him at best. Stancke said, "Too bad you had to clip the Baslim kid. I think he was justified."

"Of course he was. But 'Inciting to riot' is no excuse for riot. Nothing is."

"Sure, you had to. But I don't like that Peebie character. I'm going to make a careful study of his efficiency marks."

"Do that. But, confound it, Stinky—I have a feeling I started the fight myself."

"*Huh?*"

"Two days ago I had to tell Baslim that we hadn't been able to identify him. He walked out in a state of shock. I should have listened to my psych officer. The lad has scars that make him irresponsible under the right—I mean the 'wrong'—stimulus. I'm glad it was mashed potatoes and not a knife."

"Oh, come now, boss! Mashed potatoes are hardly a deadly weapon."

"You weren't here when he got the bad news. Not knowing who he is hurts him."

Stancke's pudgy face pouted in thought. "Boss? How old was this kid when he was captured?"

"Eh? Kris thinks he was about four."

"Skipper, that backwoods place where you were born: at what age were you fingerprinted, blood-typed, retina-photographed and so forth?"

"Why, when I started school."

"Me, too. I'll bet they wait that long most places."

Brisby blinked. "That's why they wouldn't have anything on him!"

"Maybe. But on Riff they take identity on a baby before he leaves the delivery room."

"My people, too. But—"

"Sure, sure! It's common practice. But *how?*"

Brisby looked blank, then banged the desk. "*Footprints!* And we didn't send them in." He slapped the talkie. "Eddie! Get Baslim here on the double!"

Thorby was glumly removing the chevron he had worn by courtesy for so short a time. He was scared by the peremptory order; it boded ill. But he hurried. Colonel Brisby glared at him. "Baslim, take off your shoes!"

"Sir?"

"Take off your shoes!"

Brisby's despatch questioning failure to identify and supplying BuPers with footprints was answered in forty-eight hours. It reached the *Hydra* as she made her final approach to Ultima Thule. Colonel Brisby decoded it when the ship had been secured dirtside.

It read: "—GUARDSMAN THORBY BASLIM IDENTIFIED MISS ING PERSON THOR BRADLEY RUDBEK TERRA NOT HEKATE TRANSFER RUDBEK FASTEST MILORCOM TERRA DISCHARGE ARRIVAL NEXTKIN NOTIFIED REPEAT FASTEST CHFBUPERS."

Brisby was chuckling. "Colonel Baslim is *never* wrong. Dead or alive, he's never wrong!"

"Boss . . ."

"Huh?"

"Read it again. Notice who he is."

Brisby reread the despatch. Then he said in a hushed voice, "Why do things like this always happen to *Hydra*?" He strode over and snatched the door. "Eddie!"

Thorby was on beautiful Ultima Thule for two hours and twenty-seven minutes; what he saw of the famous scenery after coming three hundred light-years was the field between the *Hydra* and Guard Mail Courier *Ariel*. Three weeks later he was on Terra. He felt dizzy.

17

Lovely Terra, Mother of Worlds! What poet, whether or not he has been privileged to visit her, has not tried to express the homesick longing of men for mankind's birthplace . . . her cool green hills, cloud-graced skies, restless oceans, her warm maternal charm.

Thorby's first sight of legendary Earth was by view screen of G.M.C. *Ariel.* Guard Captain N'Gangi, skipper of the mail ship, stepped up the gain and pointed out arrow-sharp shadows of the Egyptian Pyramids. Thorby didn't realize the historical significance and was looking in the wrong place. But he enjoyed seeing a planet from space; he had never been thus privileged before.

Thorby had a dull time in the *Ariel.* The mail ship, all legs and tiny payload, carried a crew of three engineers and three astrogators, all of whom were usually on watch or asleep. He started off badly because Captain N'Gangi had been annoyed by a "hold for passenger" despatch from the *Hydra*—mail ships don't like to hold; the mail must go through.

But Thorby behaved himself, served the precooked meals, and spent his time plowing through the library (a drawer under the skipper's bunk); by the time they approached Sol the commanding officer was over his pique . . . to have the feeling brought back by orders to land at Galactic Enterprises' field instead of Guard Base. But N'Gangi shook hands as he gave Thorby his discharge and the paymaster's draft.

Instead of scrambling down a rope ladder (mail couriers have no hoists), Thorby found that a lift came up to get him. It leveled off opposite the hatch and offered easy exit. A man in spaceport uniform of Galactic Enterprises met him. "Mr. Rudbek?"

"That's me—I guess."

"This way, Mr. Rudbek, if you please."

The elevator took them below ground and into a beautiful lounge. Thorby, mussed and none too clean from weeks in a crowded steel box, was uneasy. He looked around.

Eight or ten people were there, two of whom were a gray-haired, self-assured man and a young woman. Each was dressed in more than a year's pay for a Guardsman. Thorby did not realize this in the case of the man but his Trader's eye spotted it in the female; it took money to look that demurely provocative.

In his opinion the effect was damaged by her high-fashion hairdo, a rising structure of green blending to gold. He blinked at the cut of her clothes; he had seen fine ladies in Jubbulpore where the climate favored clothing only for decoration, but the choice in skin display seemed different here. Thorby realized uneasily that he was again going to have to get used to new customs.

The important-looking man met him as he got out of the lift. "Thor! Welcome home, lad!" He grabbed Thorby's hand. "I'm John Weemsby. Many is the time I've bounced you on my knee. Call me Uncle Jack. And this is your cousin Leda."

The girl with green hair placed hands on Thorby's shoulders and kissed him. He did not return it; he was much too startled. She said, "It's wonderful to have you home, Thor."

"Uh, thanks."

"And now you must greet your grandparents," Weemsby announced. "Professor Bradley . . . and your Grandmother Bradley."

Bradley was older than Weemsby, slight and erect, a paunch, neatly trimmed beard; he was dressed like Weemsby in daytime formal jacket, padded tights and short cape, but not as richly. The woman had a sweet face and alert blue eyes; her clothing did not resemble that of Leda but seemed to suit her. She pecked Thorby on the cheek and said gently, "It's like having my son come home."

The elderly man shook hands vigorously. "It's a miracle, son! You look just like our boy—your father. Doesn't he, dear?"

"He does!"

There was chitchat which Thorby answered as well as he could. He was confused and terribly self-conscious; it was more embarrassing to meet these strangers who claimed him as their blood than it had been to be adopted into *Sisu*. These old people—they were his grandparents? Thorby couldn't believe it even though he supposed they were.

To his relief the man—Weemsby?—who claimed to be his Uncle Jack said with polite authority, "We had better go. I'll bet this boy is tired. So I'll take him home. Eh?"

The Bradleys murmured agreement; the party moved toward the exit. Others in the room, all men none of whom had been introduced, went with them. In the corridor they stepped on a glideway which picked up speed until walls were whizzing past. It slowed as they neared the end—miles away, Thorby judged—and was stationary for them to step off.

This place was public; the ceiling was high and the walls were lost in crowds; Thorby recognized the flavor of a transport station. The silent men with them moved into blocking positions and their party proceeded in a direct line regardless of others. Several persons tried to break through and one man managed it. He shoved a microphone at Thorby and said rapidly, "Mr. Rudbek, what is your opinion of the—"

A guard grabbed him. Mr. Weemsby said quickly, "Later, later! Call my office; you'll get the story."

Lenses were trained on them, but from high up and far away. They moved into another passageway, a gate closed behind them. Its glideway deposited them at an elevator which took them to a small enclosed airport. A craft was waiting and beyond it a smaller one, both sleek, smooth, flattened ellipsoids. Weemsby stopped. "You'll be all right?" he asked Mrs. Bradley.

"Oh, surely," answered Professor Bradley.

"The car was satisfactory?"

"Excellent. A nice hop—and, I'm sure, a good one back."

"Then we'll say good-by. I'll call you—when he's had a chance to get oriented. You understand?"

"Oh, surely. We'll be waiting." Thorby got a peck from his grandmother, a clap on the shoulder from his grandfather. Then he embarked with Weemsby and Leda in the larger car. Its skipper saluted Mr. Weemsby, then saluted Thorby—Thorby managed to return it.

Mr. Weemsby paused in the central passage. "Why don't you kids go forward and enjoy the hop? I've got calls waiting."

"Certainly, Daddy."

"You'll excuse me, Thor? Business goes on—it's back to the mines for Uncle Jack."

"Of course . . . Uncle Jack."

Leda led him forward and they sat down in a transparent bubble on the forward surface. The car rose straight up until they were several thousand feet high. It made a traffic-circle sweep over a desert plain, then headed north toward mountains.

"Comfy?" asked Leda.

"Quite. Uh, except that I'm dirty and mussed."

"There's a shower abaft the lounge. But we'll be home shortly—so why not enjoy the trip?"

"All right." Thorby did not want to miss any of fabulous Terra. It looked, he decided, like Hekate—no, more like Woolamurra, except that he had never seen so many buildings. The mountains—

He looked again. "What's that white stuff? Alum?"

Leda looked. "Why, that's snow. Those are the Sangre de Cristos."

" 'Snow,' " Thorby repeated. "That's frozen water."

"You haven't seen snow before?"

"I've heard of it. It's not what I expected."

"It *is* frozen water—and yet it isn't exactly; it's more feathery." She reminded herself of Daddy's warning; she must not show surprise at anything.

"You know," she offered, "I think I'll teach you to ski."

Many miles and some minutes were used explaining what skiing was and why people did it. Thorby filed it away as something he might try, more likely not. Leda said that a broken leg was "all that could happen." This is fun? Besides, she had mentioned how cold it could be. In Thorby's mind cold was linked with hunger, beatings, and fear. "Maybe I could learn," he said dubiously, "but I doubt it."

"Oh, sure you can!" She changed the subject. "Forgive my curiosity, Thor, but there is a faint accent in your speech."

"I didn't know I had an accent—"

"I didn't mean to be rude."

"You weren't. I suppose I picked it up in Jubbulpore. That's where I lived longest."

" 'Jubbulpore' . . . let me think. That's—"

"Capital of the Nine Worlds."

"Oh, yes! One of our colonies, isn't it?"

Thorby wondered what the Sargon would think of that. "Uh, not exactly. It is a sovereign empire now—their tradition is that they were never anything else. They don't like to admit that they derive from Terra."

"What an odd point of view."

A steward came forward with drinks and dainty nibbling foods. Thor accepted a frosted tumbler and sipped cautiously. Leda continued, "What were you doing there, Thor? Going to school?"

Thorby thought of Pop's patient teaching, decided that was not what she meant. "I was begging."

"What?"

"I was a beggar."

"Excuse me?"

"A beggar. A licensed mendicant. A person who asks for alms."

"That's what I thought you said," she answered. "I know what a beggar is; I've read books. But—excuse me, Thor; I'm just a home girl—I was startled."

She was not a "home girl"; she was a sophisticated woman adjusted to her environment. Since her mother's death she had been her father's hostess and could converse with people from other planets with aplomb, handling small talk of a large dinner party with gracious efficiency in three languages. Leda could ride, dance, sing, swim, ski, supervise a household, do arithmetic slowly, read and write if necessary, and make the proper responses. She was an intelligent, pretty, well-intentioned woman, culturally equivalent to a superior female head-hunter—able, adjusted and skilled.

But this strange lost-found cousin was a new bird to her. She said hesitantly, "Excuse my ignorance, but we don't have anything like that on Earth. I have trouble visualizing it. Was it terribly unpleasant?"

Thorby's mind flew back; he was squatting in lotus seat in the great Plaza with Pop sprawled beside him, talking. "It was the happiest time of my life," he said simply.

"Oh." It was all she could manage.

But Daddy had left them so that she could get to work. Asking a man about himself never failed. "How does one get started, Thor? I wouldn't know where to begin."

"I was taught. You see, I was up for sale and—" He thought of trying to explain Pop, decided to let it wait. "—an old beggar bought me."

" 'Bought' you?"

"I was a slave."

Leda felt as if she had stepped off into water over her head. Had he said "cannibal," "vampire," or "warlock" she could have been no more shocked. She came up, mentally gasping. "Thor—if I have been rude, I'm sorry—but we all are curious about the time—goodness! it's been over fifteen years—that you have been missing. But if you don't want to answer, just say so. You were a nice little boy and I was fond of you—please don't slap me down if I ask the wrong question."

"You don't believe me?"

"How could I? There haven't been slaves for centuries."

Thorby wished that he had never had to leave the *Hydra*, and gave up. He had learned in the Guard that the slave trade was something many fraki in the inner worlds simply hadn't heard of. "You knew me when I was little?"

"Oh, yes!"

"Why can't I remember you? I can't remember anything back before I was a—I can't remember Terra."

She smiled. "I'm three years older than you. When I saw you last, I was six—so I remember—and you were three, so you've forgotten."

"Oh." Thorby decided that here was a chance to find out his own age. "How old are you now?"

She smiled wryly. "Now I'm the same age you are—and I'll stay that age until I'm married. Turn about, Thorby—when you ask the wrong question, I shan't be offended. You don't ask a lady her age on Terra; you assume that she is younger than she is."

"So?" Thorby pondered this curious custom. Among People a female claimed the highest age she could, for status.

"So. For example, your mother was a lovely lady but I never knew her age. Perhaps she was twenty-five when I knew her, perhaps forty."

"You knew my parents?"

"Oh, yes! Uncle Creighton was a darling with a boomy voice. He used to give me handfuls of dollars to buy candy sticks and balloons with my own sweaty little hand." She frowned. "But I can't remember his face. Isn't that silly? Never mind, Thor; tell me anything you want to. I'd be happy to hear anything you don't mind telling."

"I don't mind," Thorby answered, "but, while I must have been captured, I don't remember it. As far as I remember, I never had parents; I was a slave, several places and masters—until I reached Jubbulpore. Then I was sold again and it was the luckiest thing that ever happened to me."

Leda lost her company smile. She said in a still voice, "You *really* mean it. Or do you?"

Thorby suffered the ancient annoyance of the returned traveler. "If you think that slavery has been abolished . . . well, it's a big galaxy. Shall I roll up my trouser leg and show you?"

"Show me what, Thor?"

"My slave's mark. The tattoo a factor uses to identify merchandise." He rolled up his left trouser. "See? The date is my manumission—it's Sargonese, a sort of Sanskrit; I don't suppose you can read it."

She stared, round-eyed. "How horrible! How perfectly horrible!"

He covered it. "Depends on your master. But it's not good."

"But why doesn't somebody *do* something?"

He shrugged. "It's a long way off."

"But—" She stopped as her father came out.

"Hi, kids. Enjoying the hop, Thor?"

"Yes, sir. The scenery is wonderful."

"The Rockies aren't a patch on the Himalayas. But our Tetons are pretty wonderful . . . and there they are. We'll be home soon." He pointed. "See? There's Rudbek."

"That city is named Rudbek?"

"It used to be Johnson's Hole, or some such, when it was a village. But I wasn't speaking of Rudbek City; I meant our home—your home—'Rudbek.' You can see the tower above the lake . . . with the Grand Tetons behind it. Most magnificent setting in the world. You're Rudbek of Rudbek at Rudbek . . . 'Rudbek Cubed,' your father called it . . . but he married into the name and wasn't impressed by it. I like it; it has a rolling thunder, and it's good to have a Rudbek back in residence."

Thorby wallowed in his bath, from needle shower, through hot pool whose sides and bottom massaged him with a thousand fingers, to lukewarm swimming plunge that turned cooler while he was in it. He was cautious in the last, having never learned to swim.

And he had never had a valet. He had noticed that Rudbek had dozens of people in it—not many for its enormous size, but he began to realize that most of them were servants. This impressed him not as much as it might have; he knew how many, many slaves staffed any rich household on Jubbul; he did not know that a living servant on Terra was the peak of ostentatious waste, greater than sedan chairs on Jubbul, much greater than the lavish hospitality at the Gatherings. He simply knew that valets made him nervous and now he had a squad of three. Thorby refused to let anyone bathe him; he gave in to being shaved because the available razor was a classic straight-edge and his own would not work on Rudbek's power supply. Otherwise he merely accepted advice about unfamiliar clothing.

The clothing waiting for him in wardrobe loads did not fit perfectly; the chief valet snipped and rewelded, muttering apologies. He had Thorby attired, ruffled jabot to tights, when a footman appeared. "Mr. Weemsby sends greetings to Rudbek and asks that he come to the great hall."

Thorby memorized the route as he followed.

Uncle Jack, in midnight and scarlet, was waiting with Leda, who was wearing . . . Thorby was at loss; colors kept changing and some it was hardly there. But she looked well. Her hair was now iridescent. He spotted among her jewels a bauble from Finster and wondered if it had shipped in *Sisu*—why, it was possible that he had listed it himself!

Uncle Jack said jovially, "There you are, lad! Refreshed? We won't wear you out, just a family dinner."

The dinner included twelve people and started with a reception in the great hall, drinks, appetizers, passed by soft-footed servants, music, while others were presented. "Rudbek of Rudbek, Lady Wilkes—your Aunt Jennifer, lad, come from New Zealand to welcome you"—"Rudbek of Rudbek, Judge Bruder and Mrs. Bruder—Judge is Chief Counsel," and so on. Thorby memorized names, linked them with faces, thinking that it was like the Family—except that relationship titles were not precise definitions; he had trouble estimating status. He did not know which of eighty-odd relations "cousin" meant with respect to Leda, though he supposed that she must be a first cross-cousin, since Uncle Jack had a surname not Rudbek; so he thought of her as taboo—which would have dismayed her.

He did realize that he must be in the sept of a wealthy family. But what his status was nobody mentioned, nor could he figure out status of others. Two of the youngest women dropped him curtseys. He thought the first had stumbled and tried to help her. But when the second did it, he answered by pressing his palms together.

The older women seemed to expect him to treat them with respect. Judge Bruder he could not classify. He hadn't been introduced as a relative—yet this was a family dinner. He fixed Thorby with an appraising eye and barked, "Glad to have you back, young man! There should be a Rudbek at Rudbek. Your holiday has caused trouble—hasn't it, John?"

"More than a bit," agreed Uncle Jack, "but we'll get straightened out. No hurry. Give the lad a chance to find himself."

"Surely, surely. Thumb in the dike."

Thorby wondered what a dike was, but Leda came up and placed her hand on his elbow. She steered him to the banquet hall; others followed. Thorby sat at one end of a long table with Uncle Jack at the other; Aunt Jennifer was on Thorby's right and Leda on his left. Aunt Jennifer started asking questions and supplying answers. He admitted that he had just left the Guard, she had trouble understanding that he had not been an officer; he let it ride and mentioned nothing about Jubbulpore—Leda had made him wary of the subject. It did not matter; he asked a question about New Zealand and received a guidebook lecture.

Then Leda turned from Judge Bruder and spoke to Thorby; Aunt Jennifer turned to the man on her right.

The tableware was in part strange, especially chop tongs and skewers. But spoons were spoons and forks were forks; by keeping his eye on Leda he got by. Food was served formally, but he had seen Grandmother so served; table manners were not great trouble to a man coached by Fritz's sharp-tongued kindness.

Not until the end was he stumped. The Butler-in-Chief presented him with an enormous goblet, splashed wetness in it and waited. Leda said softly, "Taste it, nod, and put it down." He did so; as the butler moved away, she whispered, "Don't drink it, it's bottled lightning. By the way, I told Daddy, 'No toasts.' "

At last the meal was over. Leda again cued him. "Stand up." He did and everyone followed.

The "family dinner" was just a beginning. Uncle Jack was in evidence only at dinners, and not always then. He excused his absences with, "Someone has to keep the fires burning. Business won't wait." As a trader Thorby understood that Business was Business, but he looked forward to a long talk with Uncle Jack, instead of so much social life. Leda was helpful but not informative. "Daddy is awfully busy. Different companies and things. It's too complicated for me. Let's hurry; the others are waiting."

Others were always waiting. Dancing, skiing—Thorby loved the flying sensation but considered it a chancy way to travel, particularly when he fetched up in a snow bank, having barely missed a tree—card parties, dinners with young people at which he took one end of the table and Leda the other, more dancing, hops to Yellowstone to feed the bears, midnight suppers, garden parties. Although Rudbek estate lay in the lap of the Tetons with snow around it, the house had an enormous tropical garden under a dome so pellucid that Thorby did not realize it was there until Leda had him touch it. Leda's friends were fun and Thorby gradually became sophisticated in small talk. The young men called him "Thor" instead of "Rudbek" and called Leda "Slugger." They treated him with familiar respect, and showed interest in the fact that he had been in the Guard and had visited many worlds, but they did not press personal questions. Thorby volunteered little, having learned his lesson.

But he began to tire of fun. A Gathering was wonderful but a working man expects to work.

The matter came to a head. A dozen of them were skiing and Thorby was alone on the practice slope. A man glided down and snowplowed to a stop. People hopped in and out at the estate's field day and night; this newcomer was Joel de la Croix.

"Hi, Thor."

"Hi, Joe."

"I've been wanting to speak to you. I've an idea I would like to discuss, after you take over. Can I arrange to see you, without being baffled by forty-'leven secretaries?"

"When I take over?"

"Or later, at your convenience. I want to talk to the boss; after all, you're the heir. I don't want to discuss it with Weemsby . . . even if he would see me." Joe looked anxious. "All I want is ten minutes. Say five if I don't interest you at once. 'Rudbek's promise.' Eh?"

Thorby tried to translate. Take over? Heir? He answered carefully, "I don't want to make any promises now, Joel."

De la Croix shrugged. "Okay. But think about it. I can prove it's a moneymaker."

"I'll think about it," Thorby agreed. He started looking for Leda. He got her alone and told her what Joe had said.

She frowned slightly. "It probably wouldn't hurt, since you aren't promising anything. Joel is a brilliant engineer. But better ask Daddy."

"That's not what I meant. What did he mean: 'take over'?"

"Why, you will, eventually."

"Take over *what?*"

"Everything. After all, you're Rudbek of Rudbek."

"What do you mean by 'everything'?"

"Why, why—" She swept an arm at mountain and lake, at Rudbek City beyond. "All of it, Rudbek. Lots of things. Things personally yours, like your sheep station in Australia and the house in Majorca. And business things. Rudbek Associates is many things—here and other planets. I couldn't begin to describe them. But they're yours, or maybe 'ours' for the whole family is in it. But you are the Rudbek of Rudbek. As Joe said, the heir."

Thorby looked at her, while his lips grew dry. He licked them and said, "Why wasn't I told?"

She looked distressed. "Thor dear! We've let you take your time. Daddy didn't want to worry you."

"Well," he said, "I'm worried now. I had better talk to Uncle Jack."

John Weemsby was at dinner but so were many guests. As they were leaving Weemsby motioned Thorby aside. "Leda tells me you're fretting."

"Not exactly. I want to know some things."

"You shall—I was hoping that you would tire of your vacation. Let's go to my study."

They went there; Weemsby dismissed his second-shift secretary and said, "Now what do you want to know?"

"I want to know," Thorby said slowly, "what it means to be 'Rudbek of Rudbek.' "

Weemsby spread his hands. "Everything . . . and nothing. You are titular head of the business, now that your father is dead . . . if he is."

"Is there any doubt?"

"I suppose not. Yet you turned up."

"Supposing he is dead, what am I? Leda seems to think I own just about everything. What did she mean?"

Weemsby smiled. "You know girls. No head for business. The ownership of our enterprises is spread around—most of it is in our employees. But, if your parents are dead, you come into stock in Rudbek Associates, which in turn has an interest in—sometimes a controlling interest—in other things. I couldn't describe it now. I'll have the legal staff do it—I'm a practical man, too busy making decisions to worry about who owns every share. But that reminds me . . . you haven't had a chance to spend much money, but you might want to." Weemsby opened a drawer, took out a pad. "There's a megabuck. Let me know if you run short."

Thorby thumbed through it. Terran currency did not bother him: a hundred dollars to the credit—which he thought of as five loaves of bread, a trick the Supercargo taught him—a thousand credits to the supercredit, a thousand supercredits to the megabuck. So simple that the People translated other currencies into it, for accounting.

But each sheet was ten thousand credits . . . and there were a hundred sheets. "Did I . . . inherit this?"

"Oh, that's just spending money—checks, really. You convert them at dispensers in stores or banks. You know how?"

"No."

"Don't get a thumbprint on the sensitized area until you insert it in the dispenser. Have Leda show you—if that girl could make money the way she spends it, neither you nor I would have to work. But," Weemsby added, "since we do, let's do a little." He took out a folder and spread papers. "Although this isn't hard. Just sign at the bottom of each, put your thumbprint by it, and I'll call Beth in to notarize. Here, we can open each one to the last page. I had better hold 'em—the consarned things curl up."

Weemsby held one for Thorby's signature. Thorby hesitated, then instead of signing, reached for the document. Weemsby held on. "What's the trouble?"

"If I'm going to sign, I ought to read it." He was thinking of something Grandmother used to be downright boring about.

Weemsby shrugged. "They are routine matters that Judge Bruder prepared for you." Weemsby placed the document on the others, tied the stack, and closed the folder. "These papers tell me to do what I have to do anyway. Somebody has to do the chores."

"Why do I have to sign?"

"This is a safety measure."

"I don't understand."

Weemsby sighed. "The fact is, you don't understand business. No one expects you to; you haven't had any chance to learn. But that's why I have to keep slaving away; business won't wait." He hesitated. "Here's the simplest way to put it. When your father and mother went on a second honeymoon, they had to appoint someone to act while they were gone. I was the natural choice, since I was their business manager and your grandfather's before that—he died before they went away. So I was stuck with it while they went jaunting. Oh, I'm not complaining; it's not a favor one would refuse a member of the family. Unfortunately they did not come back, so I was left holding the baby.

"But now *you* are back and we must make sure everything is orderly. First it is necessary for your parents to be declared legally dead—that must be done before you can inherit. That will take a while. So here I am, *your* business manager, too—manager for all the family—and I don't have anything from you telling me to act. These papers do that."

Thorby scratched his cheek. "If I haven't inherited yet, why do you need anything from me?"

Weemsby smiled. "I asked that myself. Judge Bruder thinks it is best to tie down all possibilities. Now since you are of legal age—"

" 'Legal age'?" Thorby had never heard the term; among the People, a man was old enough for whatever he could do.

Weemsby explained. "So, since the day you passed your eighteenth birthday, you have been of legal age, which simplifies things—it means you don't have to become a ward of a court. We have your parents' authorization; now we add yours—and then it doesn't matter how long it takes the courts to decide that your parents are dead, or to settle their wills. Judge Bruder and I and the others who have to do the work can carry on without interruption. A time gap is avoided . . . one that might cost the business many megabucks. Now do you understand?"

"I think so."

"Good. Let's get it done." Weemsby started to open the folder.

Grandmother always said to read before signing—then think it over. "Uncle Jack, I want to read them."

"You wouldn't understand them."

"Probably not." Thorby picked up the folder. "But I've got to learn."

Weemsby reached for the folder. "It isn't necessary."

Thorby felt a surge of obstinacy. "Didn't you say Judge Bruder prepared these for me?"

"Yes."

"Then I want to take them to my apartment and try to understand them. If I'm 'Rudbek of Rudbek' I ought to know what I'm doing."

Weemsby hesitated, then shrugged. "Go ahead. You'll find that I'm simply trying to do for you what I have always been doing."

"But I still ought to understand what I'm doing."

"Very well! Good night."

Thorby read till he fell asleep. The language was baffling but the papers did seem to be what Uncle Jack said they were—instructions to John Weemsby to continue the routine business of a complex setup. He fell asleep full of terms like "full power of attorney," "all manner of business," "receive and pay monies," "revocable only by mutual consent," "waiver of personal appearance," "full faith and credence," and "voting proxy in all stockholding and/or directorial meetings, special or annual."

As he dozed off it occurred to him that he had not asked to see the authorizations given by his parents.

Sometime during the night he seemed to hear Grandmother's impatient voice: "*—then think it over! If you don't understand it, and the laws under which it will be executed, then don't sign it!—no matter how much profit may appear to be in store. Too lazy and too eager can ruin a trader.*"

He stirred restlessly.

18

HARDLY ANYONE CAME DOWN FOR BREAKFAST IN RUDBEK. BUT BREAKfast in bed was not in Thorby's training; he ate alone in the garden, luxuriating in hot mountain sunshine and lush tropical flowers while enjoying the snowy wonderland around him. Snow fascinated him—he had never dreamed that anything could be so beautiful.

But the following morning Weemsby came into the garden only moments after Thorby sat down. A chair was placed under Weemsby; a servant quickly laid a place. He said, "Just coffee. Good morning, Thor."

"Good morning, Uncle Jack."

"Well, did you get your studying done?"

"Sir? Oh, yes. That is, I fell asleep reading."

Weemsby smiled. "Lawyerese is soporific. Did you satisfy yourself that I had told you correctly what they contained?"

"Uh, I think so."

"Good." Weemsby put down his coffee and said to a servant, "Hand me a house phone. Thor, you irritated me last night."

"I'm sorry, sir."

"But I realize you were right. You should read what you sign—I wish I had time to! I have to accept the word of my staff in routine matters or I would never have time for policy . . . and I assumed that you would do the same with me. But caution is commendable." He spoke into the phone. "Carter, fetch those papers from Rudbek's apartment. The garden."

Thorby wondered if Carter could find the stuff—there was a safe in his study but he had not learned to use it, so he had hidden the papers behind books. He started to mention it but Uncle Jack was talking.

"Here is something you will want to see . . . an inventory of real property you own—or will own, when the wills are settled. These holdings are unconnected with the business."

Thorby looked through it with amazement. Did he really own an island named Pitcairn at fifteen something south and a hundred and thirty west—whatever that meant? A domehouse on Mars? A shooting lodge in Yukon—where was "Yukon" and why shoot there? You ought to be in free space to risk shooting. And what were all these other things?

He looked for one item. "Uncle Jack? How about Rudbek?"

"Eh? You're sitting on it."

"Yes . . . but do I own it? Leda said I did."

"Well, yes. But it's entailed—that means your great-great-grandfather decided that it should never be sold . . . so that there would always be a Rudbek at Rudbek."

"Oh."

"I thought you might enjoy looking over your properties. I've ordered a car set aside for you. Is that one we hopped here in satisfactory?"

"What? Goodness, yes!" Thorby blinked.

"Good. It was your mother's and I've been too sentimental to dispose of it. But it has had all latest improvements added. You might persuade Leda to hop with you; she is familiar with most of that list. Take some young friends along and make a picnic of it, as long as you like. We can find a congenial chaperone."

Thorby put the list down. "I probably will, Uncle Jack . . . presently. But I ought to get to work."

"Eh?"

"How long does it take to learn to be a lawyer here?"

Weemsby's face cleared. "I see. Lawyers' quaint notions of language can shock a man. It takes four or five years."

"It does?"

"The thing for you is two or three years at Harvard or some other good school of business."

"I need that?"

"Definitely."

"Unh . . . you know more about it than I do—"

"I should! By now."

"—but couldn't I learn something about the business before I go to school? I haven't any idea what it is."

"Plenty of time."

"But I want to learn *now*."

Weemsby started to cloud, then smiled and shrugged. "Thor, you have your mother's stubbornness. All right, I'll order a suite for you at the main office in Rudbek City—and staff it with people to help you. But I warn you, it won't be fun. Nobody owns a business; the business owns him. You're a slave to it."

"Well . . . I ought to try."

"Commendable spirit." The phone by Weemsby's cup blinked; he picked it up, frowned, said, "Hold on." He turned to Thorby. "That idiot can't find those papers."

"I meant to tell you. I hid them—I didn't want to leave them out."

"I see. Where are they?"

"Uh, I'll have to dig them out."

Weemsby said in the phone, "Forget it." He tossed the phone to a servant and said to Thorby, "Then fetch them, if you don't mind."

Thorby did mind. So far he had had four bites; it annoyed him to be told to run an errand while eating. Besides . . . was he "Rudbek of Rudbek"? or still messenger for the weapons officer? "I'll be going up after breakfast."

Uncle Jack looked vexed. But he answered, "I beg your pardon. If you can't tear yourself away, would you please tell *me* where to find them? I have a hard day ahead and I would like to dispose of this triviality and go to work. *If* you don't mind."

Thorby wiped his mouth. "I would rather not," he said slowly, "sign them now."

"What? You told me that you had satisfied yourself."

"No, sir, I told you that I had read them. But I don't understand them. Uncle Jack, where are the papers that my parents signed?"

"Eh?" Weemsby looked at him sharply. "Why?"

"I want to see them."

Weemsby considered. "They must be in the vault at Rudbek City."

"All right. I'll go there."

Weemsby suddenly stood up. "If you will excuse me, I'll go to work," he snapped. "Young man, some day you will realize what I have done for you! In the meantime, since you choose to be uncooperative, I still must get on with my duties."

He left abruptly. Thorby felt hurt—he didn't want to be uncooperative . . . but if they had waited for years, why couldn't they wait a little longer and give him a chance?

He recovered the papers, then phoned Leda. She answered, with vision switched off. "Thor dear, what are you doing up in the middle of the night?"

He explained that he wanted to go to the family's business offices. "I thought maybe you could direct me."

"You say Daddy said to?"

"He's going to assign me an office."

"I won't just direct you; I'll take you. But give a girl a chance to get a face on and swallow orange juice."

He discovered that Rudbek was connected with their offices in Rudbek City by high-speed sliding tunnel. They arrived in a private foyer guarded by an elderly receptionist. She looked up. "Hello, Miss Leda! How nice to see you!"

"You, too, Aggie. Will you tell Daddy we're here?"

"Of course." She looked at Thorby.

"Oh," said Leda. "I forgot. This is Rudbek of Rudbek."

Aggie jumped to her feet. "Oh, dear me! I didn't *know*—I'm sorry, sir!"

Things happened quickly. In minutes Thorby found himself with an office of quiet magnificence, with a quietly magnificent secretary who addressed him by his double-barreled title but expected him to call her "Dolores." There seemed to be unlimited genies ready to spring out of walls at a touch of her finger.

Leda stuck with him until he was installed, then said, "I'll run along, since you insist on being a dull old businessman." She looked at Dolores. "Or will it be dull? Perhaps I should stay." But she left.

Thorby was intoxicated with being immensely wealthy and powerful. Top executives called him "Rudbek," junior executives called him "Rudbek of Rudbek," and those still more junior crowded their words with "sirs"—he could judge status by how he was addressed.

While he was not yet active in business—he saw Weemsby rarely and Judge Bruder almost never—anything he wanted appeared quickly. A word to Dolores and a respectful young man popped in to explain legal matters; another word and an operator appeared to show moving stereocolor of business interests anywhere, even on other planets. He spent days looking at such pictures, yet still did not see them all.

His office became so swamped with books, spools, charts, brochures, presentations, file jackets, and figures, that Dolores had the office next door refitted as a library. There were figures on figures, describing in fiscal analog enterprises too vast to comprehend otherwise. There were so many figures, so intricately related, that his head ached. He began to have misgivings about the vocation of tycoon. It wasn't all just being treated with respect, going through doors first and always getting what you asked for. What was the point if you were so snowed under that you could not enjoy it? Being a Guardsman was easier.

Still, it was nice to be important. Most of his life he had been nobody, and at best he had been very junior.

If only Pop could see him now!—surrounded by lavish furnishings, a barber to trim his hair while he worked (Pop used to cut it under a bowl), a secretary to anticipate his wishes, and dozens of people eager to help. But Pop's face in this dream was wearing Pop's reproving expression; Thorby wondered what he had done wrong, and dug harder into the mess of figures.

Eventually a pattern began to emerge. The business was Rudbek & Associates, Ltd. So far as Thorby could tell this firm did nothing. It was chartered as a private investment trust and just owned things. Most of what Thorby would own, when his parents' wills were proved, was stock in this company. Nor would he own it all; he felt almost poverty-stricken when he discovered that mother and father together held only eighteen percent of many thousand shares.

Then he found out about "voting" and "non-voting"; the shares coming to him were eighteen-fortieths of the voting shares; the remainder was split between relatives and non-relatives.

Rudbek & Assocs. owned stock in other companies—and here it got complicated. Galactic Enterprises, Galactic Acceptance Corporation, Galactic Transport, Interstellar Metals, Three Planets Fiscal (which operated on twenty-seven planets), Havermeyer Laboratories (which ran barge lines and bakeries as well as research stations)—the list looked endless. These corporations, trusts, cartels, and banking houses seemed as tangled as spaghetti. Thorby learned that he owned (through his parents) an interest in a company called "Honace Bros., Pty." through a chain of six companies—18% of 31% of 43% of 19% of 44% of 27%, a share so microscopic that he lost track. But his parents owned directly seven per cent of Honace Brothers—with the result that his indirect interest of one-twentieth of one per cent controlled it utterly but paid little return, whereas seven per cent owned directly did not control—but paid one hundred and forty times as much.

It began to dawn on him that control and ownership were only slightly related; he had always thought of "ownership" and "control" as being the same thing; you owned a thing, a begging bowl, or a uniform jacket—of course you controlled it!

The converging, diverging, and crossing of corporations and companies confused and disgusted him. It was as complex as a firecontrol computer without a computer's cool logic. He tried to draw a chart and could not make it work. The ownership of each entity was tangled in common stocks, preferred stocks, bonds, senior and junior issues, securities with odd names and unknown functions; sometimes one company owned a piece of another directly and another piece through a third, or two companies might each own a little of the other, or sometimes a company owned part of itself in a tail-swallowing fashion. It didn't make sense.

This wasn't "business"—what the People did was *business* . . . buy, sell, make a profit. But this was a silly game with wild rules.

Something else fretted him. He had not known that Rudbek built spaceships. Galactic Enterprises controlled Galactic Transport, which built ships in one of its many divisions. When he realized it he felt a glow of pride, then discovered gnawing uneasiness—something Colonel Brisby had said . . . something Pop had proved: that the "largest" or it might have been "one of the largest" builders of starships was mixed up in the slave trade.

He told himself he was being silly—this beautiful office was about as far from the dirty business of slave traffic as anything could be. But as he was dropping to sleep one night he came wide awake with the black, ironic thought that one of those slave ships in whose stinking holds he had ridden might have been, at that very time, the property of the scabby, frightened slave he was then.

It was a nightmare notion; he pushed it away. But it took the fun out of what he was doing.

One afternoon he sat studying a long memorandum from the legal department—a summary, so it said, of Rudbek & Assocs.' interests—and found that he had dragged to a halt. It seemed as if the writer had gone out of his way to confuse things. It would have been as intelligible in ancient Chinese—more so; Sargonese included many Mandarin words.

He sent Dolores out and sat with his head in his hands. Why, oh, why hadn't he been left in the Guard? He had been happy there; he had understood the world he was in.

Then he straightened up and did something he had been putting off; he returned a vuecall from his grandparents. He had been expected to visit them long since, but he had felt compelled to try to learn his job first.

Indeed he was welcome! "Hurry, son—we'll be waiting." It was a wonderful hop across prairie and the mighty Mississippi (small from that height) and over city-pocked farm land to the sleepy college town of Valley View, where sidewalks were stationary and time itself seemed slowed. His grandparents' home, imposing for Valley View, was homey after the awesome halls of Rudbek.

But the visit was not relaxing. There were guests at dinner, the president of the college and department heads, and many more after dinner—some called him "Rudbek of Rudbek," others addressed him uncertainly as "Mr. Rudbek," and still others, smug with misinformation as to how the nabob was addressed by familiars, simply as "Rudbek." His grandmother twittered around, happy as only a proud hostess can be, and his grandfather stood straight and addressed him loudly as "Son."

Thorby did his best to be a credit to them. He soon realized that it was not what he said but the fact of talking to Rudbek that counted.

The following night, which his grandmother reluctantly kept private, he got a chance to talk. He wanted advice.

First information was exchanged. Thorby learned that his father, on marrying the only child of his grandfather Rudbek, had taken his wife's family name. "It's understandable," Grandfather Bradley told him. "Rudbek has to have a Rudbek. Martha was heir but Creighton had to preside—board meetings and conferences and at the dinner table for that matter. I had hoped that my son would pursue the muse of history, as I have. But when this came along, what could I do but be happy for him?"

His parents and Thorby himself had been lost as a consequence of his father's earnest attempt to be in the fullest sense Rudbek of Rudbek—he had been trying to inspect as much of the commercial empire as possible. "Your father was always conscientious and when your Grandfather Rudbek died before your father completed his apprenticeship, so to speak, Creighton left John Weemsby in charge—John is, I suppose you know, the second husband of your other grandmother's youngest sister Aria—and Leda, of course, is Aria's daughter by her first marriage."

"No, I hadn't known." Thorby translated the relationships into *Sisu* terms . . . and reached the startling conclusion that Leda was in the other moiety!—if they had such things here, which they didn't. And Uncle Jack—well, he wasn't "uncle"—but how would you say it in English?

"John had been a business secretary and factotum to your other grandfather and he was the perfect choice, of course; he knew the inner workings better than anyone, except your grandfather himself. After we got over the shock of our tragic loss we realized that the world must go on and that John could handle it as well as if he had been Rudbek himself."

"He's been simply wonderful!" grandmother chirped.

"Yes, he has. I must admit that your grandmother and I became used to a comfortable scale of living after Creighton married. College salaries are never what they should be; Creighton and Martha were very generous. Your grandmother and I might have found it difficult after we realized that our son was gone, never to come back, had not John told us not to worry. He saw to it that our benefit continued just as before."

"And increased it," Grandmother Bradley added emphatically.

"Well, yes. All the family—we think of ourselves as part of Rudbek family even though we bear a proud name of our own—all of the family have been pleased with John's stewardship."

Thorby was interested in something other than "Uncle Jack's" virtues. "You told me that we left Akka, jumping for Far-Star, and never made it? That's a long, long way from Jubbul."

"I suppose it is. The College has only a small Galactovue and I must admit that it is hard to realize that what appears to be an inch or so is actually many light-years."

"About a hundred and seventy light-years, in this case."

"Let me see, how much would that be in miles?"

"You don't measure it that way, any more than you measure that couchomat you're on in microns."

"Come now, young man, don't be pedantic."

"I wasn't being, Grandfather. I was thinking that it was a long way from where I was captured to where I was last sold. I hadn't known it."

"I heard you use that term 'sold' once before. You must realize that it is not correct. After all, the serfdom practiced in the Sargony is not chattel slavery. It derives from the ancient Hindu gild or 'caste' system—a stabilized social order with mutal obligations, up and down. You must not call it 'slavery.'"

"I don't know any other word to translate the Sargonese term."

"I could think of several, though I don't know Sargonese . . . it's not a useful tongue in scholarship. But, my dear Thor, you aren't a student of human histories and culture. Grant me a little authority in my own field."

"Well . . ." Thorby felt baffled. "I don't know System English perfectly and there's a lot of history I don't know—there's an awful lot of history."

"So there is. As I am the first to admit."

"But I can't translate any better—I was sold and I was a slave!"

"Now, Son."

"Don't contradict your grandfather, dear, that's a good boy."

Thorby shut up. He had already mentioned his years as a beggar—and discovered that his grandmother was horrified, had felt that he had disgraced himself, though she did not quite say so. And he had already found that while his grandfather knew much about many things, he was just as certain of his knowledge when Thorby's eyes had reported things differently. Thorby concluded glumly that it was part of being senior and nothing could be done about it. He listened while Grandfather Bradley discoursed on the history of the Nine Worlds. It didn't agree with what the Sargonese believed but wasn't too far from what Pop had taught him—other than about slavery. He was glad when the talk drifted back to the Rudbek organization. He admitted his difficulties.

"You can't build Rome in a day, Thor."

"It looks as if I never would learn! I've been thinking about going back into the Guard."

His grandfather frowned. "That would not be wise."

"Why not, sir?"

"If you don't have talent for business, there are other honorable professions."

"Meaning the Guard isn't?"

"Mmm . . . your grandmother and I are philosophical pacifists. It cannot be denied that there is never a moral justification for taking human life."

"Never," agreed grandmother firmly.

Thorby wondered what Pop would think? Shucks, he knew!—Pop cut 'em down like grass to rescue a load of slaves. "What do you do when a raider jumps you?"

"A what?"

"A pirate. You've got a pirate on your tail and closing fast."

"Why, you run, I suppose. It's not moral to stay and do battle. Thor, nothing is ever gained by violence."

"But you *can't* run; he has more legs. It's you or him."

"You mean 'he.' Then you surrender; that defeats his purpose . . . as the immortal Gandhi proved."

Thorby took a deep breath. "Grandfather, I'm sorry but it *doesn't* defeat his purpose. You have to fight. Raiders take slaves. The proudest thing I ever did was to burn one."

"Eh? 'Burn one'?"

"Hit him with a target-seeker. Blast him out of the sky."

Grandmother gasped. At last his grandfather said stiffly, "Thor, I'm afraid you've been exposed to bad influences. Not your fault, perhaps. But you have many misconceptions, both in fact and in evaluation. Now be logical. If you 'burned him' as you say, how do you *know* he intended—again, as you say—to 'take slaves'? What could he do with them? Nothing."

Thorby kept silent. It made a difference which side of the Plaza you saw a thing from . . . and if you didn't have status, you weren't listened to. That was a universal rule.

Grandfather Bradley continued, "So we'll say no more about it. On this other matter I'll give you the advice I would give your departed father: if you feel that you have no head for trade, you don't have to enter it. But to run away and join the Guard, like some childish romantic—no, Son! But you needn't make up your mind for years. John is a very able regent; you don't have a decision facing you." He stood up. "I know, for I've discussed this with John, and he's willing, in all humility, to carry the burden a little farther . . . or much farther, if need be. And now we had all better seek our pillows. Morning comes early."

Thor left the next morning, with polite assurances that the house was his—which made him suspect that it was. He went to Rudbek City, having reached a decision during a restless night. He wanted to sleep with a live ship around him. He wanted to be back in Pop's outfit; being a billionaire boss wasn't his style.

He had to do something first; dig out those papers that father and mother had signed, compare them with the ones prepared for him—since father must have known what was needed—sign them, so that Uncle Jack could get on with the work after he was gone. Grandfather was right about that; John Weemsby knew how to do the job and he didn't. He should be grateful to Uncle Jack. He would thank him before he left. Then off Terra and out to where people talked his language!

He buzzed Uncle Jack's office as soon as he reached his own, was told that he was out of town. He decided that he could write a note and make it sound better—oh yes! Must say good-by to Leda. So he buzzed the legal department and told him to dig his parents' authorizations out of the vault and send them to his office.

Instead of papers, Judge Bruder arrived. "Rudbek, what's this about your ordering certain papers from the vault?"

Thorby explained. "I want to see them."

"No one but officers of the company can order papers from the vault."

"What am I?"

"I'm afraid you are a young man with confused notions. In time, you will have authority. But at the moment you are a visitor, learning something about your parents' affairs."

Thorby swallowed it; it was true, no matter how it tasted. "I've been meaning to ask you about that. What's the progress in the court action to have my parents declared dead?"

"Are you trying to bury them?"

"Of course not. But it has to be done, or so Uncle Jack says. So where are we?"

Bruder sniffed. "Nowhere. Through your doing."

"What do you mean?"

"Young man, do you think that the officers of this company will initiate a process which would throw affairs of the firm into incredible confusion unless you take necessary steps to guard against it? Why, it may take *years* to settle the wills—during which, business would come to a stop . . . simply because you neglected to sign a few simple instruments which I prepared weeks ago."

"You mean nothing will be done until I sign?"

"That is correct."

"I don't understand. Suppose I were dead—or had never been born. Does business stop every time a Rudbek dies?"

"Mmm . . . well, no. A court authorizes matters to proceed. But you *are* here and we must take that into consideration. Now see here, I'm at the very end of my patience. You seem to think, simply because you've read a few balance sheets, that you understand business. You don't. For example your belief that you can order instruments turned over to you that were given to John Weemsby personally and are not even company property. If you were to attempt to take charge of the firm at this time—if we proceeded with your notion to have your parents declared dead—I can see that we would have all sorts of confusion while you were finding your balance. We can't afford it. The company can't afford it. Rudbek can't afford it. So I want those papers signed today and no more shilly-shallying. You understand?"

Thorby lowered his head. "I won't."

"What do you mean, 'You won't'?"

"I won't sign anything until I know what I'm doing. If I can't even see the papers my parents signed, then I certainly won't."

"We'll see about that!"

"I'm going to sit tight until I find out what's going on around here!"

19

THORBY DISCOVERED THAT FINDING OUT WAS DIFFICULT. THINGS WENT on much as before but were not the same. He had vaguely suspected that the help he was being given in learning the business had sometimes been too much not well enough organized; he felt smothered in unrelated figures, verbose and obscure "summaries," "analyses" that did not analyze. But he had known so little that it took time to become even a suspicion.

The suspicion became certainty from the day he defied Judge Bruder. Dolores seemed eager as ever and people still hopped when he spoke but the lavish flow of information trickled toward a stop. He was stalled with convincing excuses but could never quite find out what he wanted to know. A "survey is being prepared" or the man who "has charge of that is out of the city" or "those are vault files and none of the delegated officers are in today." Neither Judge Bruder nor Uncle Jack was ever available and their assistants were politely unhelpful. Nor was he able to corner Uncle Jack at the estate. Leda told him that "Daddy often has to go away on trips."

Things began to be confused in his own office. Despite the library Dolores had set up she could not seem to find, or even recall, papers that he had marked for retention. Finally he lost his temper and bawled her out.

She took it quietly. "I'm sorry, sir. I'm trying very hard."

Thorby apologized. He knew a slow-down when he saw one; he had checked enough stevedores to know. But this poor creature could not help herself; he was lashing out at the wrong person. He added placatingly, "I really am sorry. Take the day off."

"Oh, I couldn't, sir."

"Who says so? Go home."

"I'd rather not, sir."

"Well . . . suit yourself. But go lie down in the ladies' lounge or something. That's an order. I'll see you tomorrow."

She looked worried and left. Thorby sat at his chaste, bare, unpowered executive desk and thought.

It was what he needed: to be left alone without a flood of facts and figures. He started digesting what he had soaked up. Presently he started listing the results.

Item: Judge Bruder and Uncle Jack had put him in Coventry for refusing to sign the proxies.

Item: He might be "Rudbek of Rudbek"—but Uncle Jack would continue to run things until Thorby's parents were legally dead.

Item: Judge Bruder had told him bluntly that no steps would be taken about the above until he admitted his incompetence and signed proxies.

Item: He did not know what his parents had signed. He had tried to force a showdown—and had failed.

Item: "Ownership" and "control" were very different. Uncle Jack controlled everything that Thorby owned; Uncle Jack owned merely a nominal one share to qualify him as acting chairman of the board. (Leda owned a chunk as she was a Rudbek while Uncle Jack wasn't—but Uncle Jack probably controlled her stock too; Leda paid no attention to business.)

Conclusions:—

What conclusions? Was Uncle Jack doing something crooked and didn't dare let him find out? Well, it didn't look like it. Uncle Jack had salary and bonuses so large that only a miser would want more money simply as money. His parents' accounts seemed in order—they showed a huge balance; the megabuck Uncle Jack had handed him hardly made a dent. The only other withdrawals were for Grandfather and Grandmother Bradley, plus a few sums around the family or charge to the estates—nothing important, another couple of megabucks.

Conclusion: Uncle Jack was boss, liked being boss, and meant to go on being boss if possible.

"Status" . . . Uncle Jack had high status and was fighting to keep it. Thorby felt that he understood him at last. Uncle Jack put up with the overwork he complained about because he *liked* being boss—just as captains and chief officers worked themselves silly, even though every member of a Free Trader family owned the same share. Uncle Jack was "chief officer" and didn't intend to surrender his supreme status to someone a third of his age who (let's face it!) wasn't competent for the work the status required.

In this moment of insight Thorby felt that he ought to sign those proxies for Uncle Jack, who had earned the job whereas Thorby had merely inherited it. Uncle Jack must have been terribly disappointed when he had turned up alive; it must have seemed an utterly unfair twist of fate.

Well, let him have it! Settle things and join the Guard.

But Thorby was not ready to back down to Judge Bruder. He had been pushed around—and his strongest reflex was resistance to any authority he had not consented to; it had been burned into his soul with whips. He did not know this—he just knew that he was going to be stubborn. He decided that Pop would want him to be.

Thought of Pop reminded him of something. Was Rudbek connected, even indirectly, with the slave trade? He realized now why Pop wanted him to hang on—he could not quit until he knew . . . nor until he had put a stop to it if the unspeakable condition did exist. But how could he find out? He was Rudbek of Rudbek . . . but they had him tied with a thousand threads, like the fellow in that story Pop had told . . . "Gulliver and his Starship," that was it.

Well, let's see, Pop had reported to "X" Corps that there was a tie-up among some big spaceship outfit, the Sargon's government, and the raider-slavetraders. Raiders had to have ships. Ships . . . there was a book he had read last week, Galactic Transport's history of every ship they had built, from #0001 to the latest. He went into his library. Hmm . . . tall red book, not a tape.

Confounded thing was missing . . . like a lot of things lately. But he had almost renshawed the book, being interested in ships. He started making notes.

Most of them were in service inside the Hegemony, some in Rudbek interests, some in others. Some of his ships had been sold to the People, a pleasing thought. But some had wound up registered to owners he could not place . . . and yet he thought he knew the names, at least, of all outfits engaged in legitimate interstellar trade under the Hegemony—and he certainly would recognize any Free Trader clan.

No way to be sure of anything from his desk, even if he had the book. Maybe there was *no* way, from Terra . . . maybe even Judge Bruder and Uncle Jack would not know if something fishy were going on.

He got up and switched on the Galactovue he had had installed. It showed only the explored fraction of the Galaxy—even so, the scale was fantastically small.

He began operating controls. First he lighted in green the Nine

Worlds. Then he added, in yellow, pestholes avoided by the People. He lighted up the two planets between which he and his parents had been captured, then did the same for every missing ship of the People concerning which he happened to know the span of the uncompleted jump.

The result was a constellation of colored lights, fairly close together as star distances go and in the same sector as the Nine Worlds. Thorby looked at it and whistled. Pop had known what he was talking about—yet it would be hard to spot unless displayed like this.

He began thinking about cruising ranges and fueling stations maintained by Galactic Transport out that way . . . then added in orange the banking offices of Galactic Acceptance Corporation in the "neighborhood."

Then he studied it.

It was not certain proof—yet what other outfit maintained such activities facing that sector?

He intended to find out.

20

THORBY FOUND THAT LEDA HAD ORDERED DINNER IN THE GARDEN. They were alone, and falling snow turned the artificial sky into an opalescent bowl. Candles, flowers, a string trio, and Leda herself made the scene delightful but Thorby failed to enjoy it, even though he liked Leda and considered the garden the best part of Rudbek Hall. The meal was almost over when Leda said, "A dollar for your thoughts."

Thorby looked guilty. "Uh, nothing."

"It must be a worrisome nothing."

"Well . . . yes."

"Want to tell Leda?"

Thorby blinked. Weemsby's daughter was the last one he could talk to. His gloom was caused by wonder as to what he could do if he became convinced that Rudbek was mixed up in slavery. "I guess I'm not cut out to be a businessman."

"Why, Daddy says you have a surprising head for figures."

Thorby snorted. "Then why doesn't he—" He stopped.

"Why doesn't he what?"

"Uh . . ." Doggone it, a man had to talk to somebody . . . someone who sympathized—or bawled him out if necessary. Like Pop. Like Fritz. Yeah, like Colonel Brisby. He was surrounded by people, yet utterly alone—except that Leda seemed to want to be friendly. "Leda, how much of what I say to you do you tell your father?"

To his amazement she blushed. "What made you say that, Thor?"

"Well, you are pretty close to him. Aren't you?"

She stood up suddenly. "If you've finished, let's walk."

Thorby stood up. They strolled paths, watched the storm, listened to its soft noises against the dome. She guided them to a spot away from the house and shielded by bushes and there sat down on a boulder. "This is a good spot—for private conversation."

"It is?"

"When the garden was wired, I made sure that there was somewhere I could be kissed without Daddy's snoopers listening in."

Thorby stared. "You mean that?"

"Surely you realize you are monitored almost everywhere but the ski slopes?"

"I didn't. And I don't like it."

"Who does? But it is a routine precaution with anything as big as Rudbek; you mustn't blame Daddy. I just spent some credits to make sure the garden wasn't as well wired as he thought. So if you have anything to say you don't want Daddy to hear, you can talk now. He'll never know. That's a cross-my-heart promise."

Thorby hesitated, then checked the area. He decided that if a microphone were hidden nearby it must be disguised as a flower . . . which was possible. "Maybe I ought to save it for the ski slope."

"Relax, dear. If you trust me at all, trust me that this place is safe."

"Uh, all right." He found himself blurting out his frustrations . . . his conclusion that Uncle Jack was intentionally thwarting him unless he would turn over his potential power. Leda listened gravely. "That's it. Now—am I crazy?"

She said, "Thor, you know that Daddy has been throwing me at you?"

"Huh?"

"I don't see how you could miss it. Unless you are utterly—but then, perhaps you are. Just take it as true. It's one of those obvious marriages that everyone is enthusiastic about . . . except maybe the two most concerned."

Thorby forgot his worries in the face of this amazing statement. "You mean . . . well, uh, that you—" He trailed off.

"Heavens, dear! If I intended to go through with it, would I have told you anything? Oh, I admit I promised, before you arrived, to consider it. But you never warmed to the idea—and I'm too proud to be willing under those circumstances even if the preservation of Rudbek depended on it. Now what's this about Daddy not letting you see the proxies that Martha and Creighton gave him?"

"They won't let me see them; I won't sign until they do."

"But you'll sign if they do?"

"Uh . . . maybe I will, eventually. But I want to see what arrangements my parents made."

"I can't see why Daddy opposes such a reasonable request. Unless . . ." She frowned.

"Unless what?"

"What about your shares? Have those been turned over to you?"

"What shares?"

"Why, *yours.* You know what shares I hold. They were given to me when I was born, by Rudbek—your grandfather, I mean. My uncle. You probably got twice as many, since you were expected to become the Rudbek someday."

"I haven't any shares."

She nodded grimly. "That's one reason Daddy and the Judge don't want you to see those papers. Our personal shares don't depend on anyone; they're ours to do as we please with, since we are both legal age. Your parents voted yours, just as Daddy still votes mine—but any proxy they assigned concerning your shares can't be any good now. You can pound the desk and they'll have to cough up, or shoot you." She frowned. "Not that they would shoot. Thor, Daddy is a good sort, most ways."

"I never said he wasn't."

"I don't love him but I'm fond of him. But when it comes down to it, I'm a Rudbek and he's not. That's silly, isn't it? Because we Rudbeks aren't anything special; we're just shrewd peasants. But I've got a worry, too. You remember Joel de la Croix?"

"He's the one that wanted an interview with me?"

"That's right. Joey doesn't work here any more."

"I don't understand."

"He was a rising star in the engineering department of Galactic—didn't you know? The office says he left to accept other employment; Joey says he was fired for going over their heads to speak to you." She frowned. "I didn't know what to believe. Now I believe Joey. Well, Thor, are you going to take it lying down? Or prove that you are Rudbek of Rudbek?"

Thorby chewed his lip. "I'd like to go back into the Guard and forget the whole mess. I used to wonder what it was like to be rich. Now I *am* and it turns out to be mostly headaches."

"So you'd walk out on it?" Her voice was faintly scornful.

"I didn't say *that.* I'm going to stay and find out what goes on. Only I don't know how to start. You think I should pound Uncle Jack's desk and demand my shares?"

"Unnh . . . not without a lawyer at your side."

"There are too many lawyers in this now!"

"That's why you need one. It will take a sharp one to win a scrap with Judge Bruder."

"How do I find one?"

"Goodness, I don't use lawyers. But I can find out. Now let's stroll and chat—in case anybody is interested."

Thorby spent a glum morning studying corporation law. Just past lunch Leda called. "Thor, how about taking me skiing? The storm is over and the snow is just right." She looked at him eagerly.

"Well—"

"Oh, come on!"

He went. They said nothing until they were far from the house. Then Leda said, "The man you need is James J. Garsch, New Washington."

"I thought that must be why you called. Do you want to ski? I'd like to go back and call him."

"Oh, my!" she shook her head sadly. "Thor, I may have to marry you just to mother you. You go back to the house and call a lawyer outside Rudbek—one whose reputation is sky-high. What happens?"

"What?"

"You might wake up in a quiet place with big muscular nurses around you. I've had a sleepless night and I'm convinced they mean business. So I had to make up my mind. I was willing for Daddy to run things forever . . . but if he fights dirty, I'm on your side."

"Thanks, Leda."

" 'Thanks' he says! Thor, this is for Rudbek. Now to business. You can't grab your hat and go to New Washington to retain a lawyer. If I know Judge Bruder, he has planned what to do if you try. But you can go look at some of your estate . . . starting with your house in New Washington."

"That's smart, Leda."

"I'm so smart I dazzle myself. If you want it to look good, you'll invite me along—Daddy has told me that I ought to show you around."

"Why, sure, Leda. If it won't be too much trouble."

"I'll simply force myself. We'll actually do some sightseeing, in the Department of North America, at least. The only thing that bothers me is how to get away from the guards."

"Guards?"

"Nobody high up in Rudbek ever travels without bodyguards. Why, you'd be run ragged by reporters and crackpots."

"I think," Thorby said slowly, "that you must be mistaken in my case. I went to see my grandparents. There weren't any guards."

"They specialize in being unobtrusive. I'll bet there were always at least two in your grandmother's house while you were there. See that solitary skier? Long odds he's not skiing for fun. So we have to find a way to get them off your neck while you look up Counselor Garsch. Don't worry, I'll think of something."

Thorby was immensely interested in the great capital but still more interested in getting on with his purpose. Leda did not let him hurry. "First we sightsee. We naturally would."

The house, simple compared with Rudbek—twenty rooms, only two of them large—was as ready as if he had stepped out the day before. Two of the servants he recognized as having been at Rudbek. A ground car, with driver and footman in Rudbek livery, was waiting. The driver seemed to know where to take them; they rode around in the semi-tropic winter sunshine and Leda pointed out planetary embassies and consulates. When they passed the immense pile which is headquarters of the Hegemonic Guard, Thorby had the driver slow down while he rubbernecked. Leda said, "That's your alma mater, isn't it?" Then she whispered, "Take a good look. The building opposite its main door is where you are going."

They got out at the Replica Lincoln Memorial, walked up the steps and felt the same hushed awe that millions have felt when looking at that brooding giant figure. Thorby had a sudden feeling that the statue looked like Pop—not that it did, but still it *did*. His eyes filled with tears.

Leda whispered, "This place always gets me—it's like a haunted church. You know who he was? He founded America. Ancient history is awesome."

"He did something else."

"What?"

"He freed slaves."

"Oh." She looked up with sober eyes. "That means something special to you . . . doesn't it?"

"Very special." He considered telling Leda his strongest reason for pushing the fight, since they were alone and this was a place that wouldn't be bugged. But he couldn't. He felt that Pop would not mind—but he had promised Colonel Brisby.

He puzzled over inscriptions on the walls, in letters and spelling used before English became System English. Leda tugged his sleeve and whispered, "Come on. I can never stay here long or I start crying." They tiptoed away.

Leda decided that she just had to see the show at the Milky Way. So they got out and she told the driver to pick them up in three hours and ten minutes, then Thorby paid outrageous scalpers' prices for a double booth and immediate occupancy.

"There!" she sighed as they started inside. "That's half of it. The footman will drop off as they round the corner, but we're rid of the driver for a while; there isn't a place to park around here. But the footman will be right behind us, if he wants to keep his job. He's buying a ticket this minute. Or maybe he's already inside. Don't look."

They started up the escalator. "This gives us a few seconds; he won't get on until we curve out of sight. Now listen. The people holding these seats will leave as soon as we show the tickets—only I'm going to hang onto one, pay him to stay. Let's hope it's a man because our nursemaid is going to spot that booth in minutes . . . seconds, if he was able to get our booth number down below. You keep going. When he finds our booth he'll see me in it with a man. He won't see the man's face in the dark but he'll be certain of me because of this outlandish, night-glow outfit I'm wearing. So he'll be happy. You zip out any exit but the main lobby; the driver will probably wait there. Try to be in the outer lobby a few minutes before the time I told them to have the car. If you don't make it, hire a flea-cab and go home. I'll complain aloud that you didn't like the show and went home."

Thorby decided that the "X" Corps had missed a bet in Leda. "Won't they report that they lost track of me?"

"They'll be so relieved they'll never breathe it. Here we are—keep moving. See you!"

Thorby went out a side exit, got lost, got straightened out by a cop, at last found the building across from Guard SHQ. The building directory showed that Garsch had offices on the 34th terrace; a few minutes later he faced a receptionist whose mouth was permanently pursed in "No."

She informed him frostily that the Counselor never saw anyone except by appointment. Did he care to make an inquiry appointment with one of the Counselor's associates? "Name, please!"

Thorby glanced around, the room was crowded. She slapped a switch. "Speak up!" she snapped. "I've turned on the privacy curtain."

"Please tell Mr. Garsch that Rudbek of Rudbek would like to see him."

Thorby thought that she was about to tell him not to tell fibs. Then she got up hastily and left.

She came back and said quietly, "The Counselor can give you five minutes. This way, sir."

James J. Garsch's private office was in sharp contrast with building and suite; he himself looked like an unmade bed. He wore trousers, not tights, and his belly bulged over his belt. He had not shaved that day; his grizzled beard matched the fringe around his scalp. He did not stand up. "Rudbek?"

"Yes, sir. Mr. James J. Garsch?"

"The same. Identification? Seems to me I saw your face in the news but I don't recollect."

Thorby handed over his ID folder. Garsch glanced at the public ID, studied the rare and more difficult-to-counter-feit ID of Rudbek & Assocs.

He handed it back. "Siddown. What can I do for you?"

"I need advice . . . and help."

"That's what I sell. But Bruder has lawyers running out of his ears. What can *I* do for you?"

"Uh, is this confidential?"

"Privileged, son. The word is 'privileged.' You don't ask a lawyer that; he's either honest or he ain't. Me, I'm middlin' honest. You take your chances."

"Well . . . it's a long story."

"Then make it short. You talk. I listen."

"You'll represent me?"

"You talk, I listen," Garsch repeated. "Maybe I'll go to sleep. I ain't feeling my best today. I never do."

"All right." Thorby launched into it. Garsch listened with eyes closed, fingers laced over his bulge.

"That's all," concluded Thorby, "except that I'm anxious to get straightened out so that I can go back into the Guard."

Garsch for the first time showed interest. "Rudbek of Rudbek? In the Guard? Let's not be silly, son."

"But I'm not really 'Rudbek of Rudbek.' I'm an enlisted Guardsman who got pitched into it by circumstances beyond my control."

"I knew that part of your story; the throb writers ate it up. But we all got circumstances we can't control. Point is, a man doesn't quit his job. Not when it's *his*."

"It's not mine," Thorby answered stubbornly.

"Let's not fiddle. First, we get your parents declared dead. Second, we demand their wills and proxies. If they make a fuss, we get a court order . . . and even the mighty Rudbek folds up under a simple subpoena-or-be-locked-up-for-contempt." He bit a fingernail. "Might be some time before the estate is settled and you are qualified. Court might appoint you to act, or the wills may say who, or the court might appoint somebody else. But it won't be those two, if what you say is correct.

Even one of Bruder's pocket judges wouldn't dare; it would be too raw and he'd know he'd be reversed."

"But what can I do if they won't even start the action to have my parents declared dead?"

"Who told you you had to wait on them? You're the interested party; they might not even qualify as *amicus curiae*. If I recall the gossip, they're hired hands, qualified with one nominal share each. You're the number-one interested party, so you start the action. Other relatives? First cousins, maybe?"

"No first cousins. I don't know what other heirs there may be. There's my grandparents Bradley."

"Didn't know they were alive. Will they fight you?"

Thorby started to say no, changed his mind. "I don't know."

"Cross it when we come to it. Other heirs . . . well, we won't know till we get a squint at the wills—and that probably won't happen until a court forces them. Any objection to hypnotic evidence? Truth drugs? Lie detectors?"

"No. Why?"

"You're the best witness that they are dead, not just long time missing."

"But if a person is missing long enough?"

"Depends. Any term of years is just a guide to the court, not a rule of law. Time was when seven years would do it—but that's no longer true. Things are roomier now."

"How do we start?"

"Got any money? Or have they got you hogtied on that? I come high. I usually charge for each exhale and inhale."

"Well, I've got a megabuck . . . and a few thousand more. About eight."

"Hmm . . . Haven't said I'd take this case. Has it occurred to you that your life may be in danger?"

"Huh! No, it hasn't."

"Son, people do odd things for money, but they'll do still more drastic things for power over money. Anybody sittin' close to a billion credits is in danger; it's like keeping a pet rattlesnake. If I were you and started feeling ill, I'd pick my own doctor. I'd be cautious about going through doors and standing close to open windows." He thought. "Rudbek is not a good place for you now; don't tempt them. Matter of fact, you ought not to be here. Belong to the Diplomatic Club?"

"No, sir."

"You do now. People 'ud be surprised if you didn't. I'm often there, around six. Got a room there, sort of private. Twenty eleven."

" 'Twenty eleven.' "

"I still haven't said I'd take it. Got any idea what I'd have to do if I lose this case?"

"Eh? No, sir."

"What was the place you mentioned? Jubbulpore? That's where I'd have to move." Suddenly he grinned. "But I've been spoiling for a fight. Rudbek, eh? Bruder. You mentioned a megabuck?"

Thorby got out his book of checking certificates, passed them over. Garsch riffled through it, shoved it into a drawer. "We won't convert this now; they're almost certainly noting your withdrawals. Anyhow, it's going to cost you more. G'bye. Say in a couple of days."

Thorby left, feeling bucked up. He had never met a more mercenary, predatory old man—he reminded Thorby of the old, scarred freedmen professionals who swaggerred around the New Amphitheater.

As he came outdoors he saw Guard Headquarters. He looked again—then ducked through murderous traffic and ran up its steps.

21

Thorby found a circle of receptionist booths around the great foyer. He pushed through crowds pouring out and went into one. A contralto voice said, "Punch your name. State department and office into the microphone. Wait until the light appears, then state your business. You are reminded that working hours are over and only emergencies are now handled."

Thorby punched, "Thorby Baslim," into the machine, then said, "Exotic Corps."

He waited. The tape repeated, "Punch your name. State the department and office into—" It suddenly cut off. A man's voice said, "Repeat that."

"Exotic Corps."

"Business?"

"Better check my name in your files."

At last another female voice chanted, "Follow the light immediately over your head. Do not lose it."

He followed it up escalators, down slideways, and into an unmarked door, where a man not in uniform led him through two more. He faced another man in civilian clothes who stood up and said, "Rudbek of Rudbek. I am Wing Marshal Smith."

"Thorby Baslim, please, sir. Not 'Rudbek.' "

"Names aren't important but identities are. Mine isn't 'Smith,' but it will do. I suppose you have identification?"

Thorby produced his ID again. "You probably have my fingerprints."

"They'll be here in a moment. Do you mind supplying them again?"

While Thorby had his prints taken, a print file card popped out onto the Marshal's desk. He put both sets into a comparator, seemed to pay no attention but until it flashed green he spoke only politenesses.

Then he said, "All right, Thorby Baslim . . . Rudbek. What can I do for you?"

"Maybe it's what I can do for you?"

"So?"

"I came here for two reasons," Thorby stated. "The first is, I think I can add something to Colonel Baslim's final report. You know who I mean?"

"I knew him and admired him very much. Go on."

"The second is—I'd like to go back into the Guard and go 'X' Corps." Thorby couldn't recall when he had decided this, but he had—not just Pop's outfit, Pop's own corps. Pop's work.

"Smith" raised his brows. "So? Rudbek of Rudbek?"

"I'm getting that fixed." Thorby sketched rapidly how he must settle his parents' estate, arrange for handling of their affairs. "Then I'm free. I know it's presumptuous of an acting ordnanceman third class—no, I was busted from that; I had a fight—for a boot Guardsman to talk about 'X' Corps, but I think I've got things you could use. I know the People . . . the Free Traders, I mean. I speak several languages. I know how to behave in the Nine Worlds. I've been around a bit, not much and I'm no astrogator . . . but I've traveled a little. Besides that, I've seen how Pop—Colonel Baslim—worked. Maybe I could do some of it."

"You have to love this work to do it. Lots of times it's nasty . . . things a man wouldn't do, for his own self-respect, if he didn't think it was necessary."

"But I do! Uh, I was a slave. You knew that? Maybe it would help if a man knew how a slave feels."

"Perhaps. Though it might make you too emotional. Besides, slave traffic isn't all we are interested in. A man comes here, we don't promise him certain work. He does what he's told. We use him. We usually use him up. Our casualty rate is high."

"I'll do what I'm told. I just happen to be interested in the slave traffic. Why, most people here don't seem to know it exists."

"Most of what we deal in the public wouldn't believe. Can you expect the people you see around you to take seriously unbelievable stories about far-away places? You must remember that less than one percent of the race ever leaves its various planets of birth."

"Uh, I suppose so. Anyhow they don't believe it."

"That's not our worst handicap. The Terran Hegemony is no empire; it is simply leadership in a loose confederation of planets. The difference between what the Guard *could* do and what it is *allowed* to do is very frustrating. If you have come here thinking that you will see slavery abolished in your lifetime, disabuse your mind. Our most optimistic target date is two centuries away—and by that time slavery will have broken out in planets not even discovered today. Not a problem to be solved once and for all. A continuing process."

"All I want to know is, can I help?"

"I don't know. Not because you describe yourself as a junior enlisted man . . . we're all pretty much the same rank in this place. The Exotic Corps is an idea, not an organization chart. I'm not worried about what Thorby Baslim can do; he can do something, even if it's only translating. But Rudbek of Rudbek . . . mmm, I wonder."

"But I told you I was getting rid of that!"

"Well—let's wait until you have. By your own statement you are not presenting yourself for enrollment today. What about the other reason? Something to add to Colonel Baslim's report?"

Thorby hesitated. "Sir, Colonel Brisby, my C.O., told me that P—Colonel Baslim had proved a connection between the slave trade and some big starshipbuilding outfit."

"He told you that?"

"Yes, sir. You could look it up in Colonel Baslim's report."

"I don't need to. Go on."

"Well . . . is it Rudbek he was talking about? Galactic Transport, that is?"

"Smith" considered it. "Why ask me if your company is mixed up in slave trade? You tell us."

Thorby frowned. "Is there a Galactovue around here?"

"Down the hall."

"May I use it?"

"Why not?" The Wing Marshal led him through a private corridor into a conference room dominated by a star-flecked stereo display. It was much the biggest Thorby had ever seen.

He had to ask questions; it had complicated controls. Then he got to work. His face puckering with strain, Thorby painted in colored lights amid fairy stars the solid picture he had built in the Galactovue in his office. He did not explain and the officer watched in silence. Thorby stepped back at last. "That's all I know now."

"You missed a few." The Wing Marshal added some lights in yellow, some in red, then working slowly, added half a dozen missing ships. "But that's quite a feat to do from memory and a remarkable concatenation of ideas. I see you included yourself—maybe it does help to have a personal interest." He stepped back. "Well, Baslim, you asked a question. Are you ready to answer it?"

"I think Galactic Transport is in it up to here! Not everybody, but enough key people. Supplying ships. And repairs and fuel. Financing, maybe."

"Mmm . . ."

"Is all this physically possible otherwise?"

"You know what they would say if you accused them of slave trading—"

"Not the trade itself. At least I don't think so."

"Connected with it. First they would say that they had never heard of any slave trade, or that it was just a wild rumor. Then they would say that, in any case, they just sell ships—and is a hardware dealer who sells a knife responsible if a husband carves his wife?"

"The cases aren't parallel."

"They wouldn't concede that. They would say that they were not breaking any laws and even stipulating that there might be slavery somewhere, how can you expect people to get worked up over a possible evil light-years away? In which they are correct; you can't expect people to, because they *won't*. Then some smarmy well-dressed character will venture the opinion that slavery—when it existed—was not so bad, because a large part of the population is really happier if they don't have the responsibilities of a free man. Then he'll add that if they didn't sell ships, someone else would—it's just business."

Thorby thought of nameless little Thorbys out there in the dark, crying hopelessly with fear and loneliness and hurt, in the reeking holds of slavers—ships that might be *his*. "One stroke of the lash would change his slimy mind!"

"Surely. But we've abolished the lash here. Sometimes I wonder if we should have." He looked at the display. "I'm going to record this; it has facets not yet considered together. Thanks for coming in. If you get more ideas, come in again."

Thorby realized that his notion of joining the corps had not been taken seriously. "Marshal Smith . . . there's one other thing I might do."

"What?"

"Before I join, if you let me . . . or maybe after; I don't know how you do such things . . . I could go out as Rudbeck of Rudbek, in my own ship, and check those places—the red ones, ours. Maybe the boss can dig out things that a secret agent would have trouble getting close to."

"Maybe. But you know that your father started to make an inspection trip once. He wasn't lucky in it." Smith scratched his chin. "We've never quite accounted for that one. Until you showed up alive, we assumed that it was natural disaster. A yacht with three passengers, a crew of eight and no cargo doesn't look like worthwhile pickings for bandits in business for profit—and they generally know what they're doing."

Thorby was shocked. "Are you suggesting that—"

"I'm not suggesting anything. But bosses prying into employees' sidelines have, in other times and places, burned their fingers. And your father was certainly checking."

"About the slave trade?"

"I couldn't guess. Inspecting. In that area. I've got to excuse myself. But do come see me again . . . or phone and someone will come to you."

"Marshal Smith . . . what parts of this, if any, can be talked over with other people?"

"Eh? Any of it. As long as you don't attribute it to this corps, or to the Guard. But facts as you know them—" He shrugged. "—who will believe you? Although if you talk to your business associates about your suspicions, you may arouse strong feelings against you personally . . . some of those feelings sincere and honest. The others? I wish I knew."

Thorby was so late that Leda was both vexed and bursting with curiosity. But she had to contain it not only because of possible monitoring but because of an elderly aunt who had called to pay her respects to Rudbek of Rudbek, and was staying the night. It was not until next day, while examining Aztec relics in the Fifth of May Museum, that they were able to talk.

Thorby recounted what Garsch had said, then decided to tell more. "I looked into rejoining the Guard yesterday."

"Thor!"

"Oh, I'm not walking out. But I have a reason. The Guard is the only organization trying to put a stop to slave traffic. But that is all the more reason why I can't enlist now." He outlined his suspicions about Rudbek and the traffic.

Her face grew pale. "Thor, that's the most horrible idea I ever heard. I *can't* believe it."

"I'd like to prove it isn't true. But somebody builds their ships, somebody maintains them. Slavers are not engineers; they're parasites."

"I still have trouble believing that there is such a thing as slavery."

He shrugged. "Ten lashes will convince anybody."

"Thor! You don't mean they *whipped* you?"

"I don't remember clearly. But the scars are on my back."

She was very quiet on the way home.

Thorby saw Garsch once more, then they headed for the Yukon, in company with the elderly aunt, who had somehow attached herself.

Garsch had papers for Thorby to sign and two pieces of information. "The first action has to be at Rudbek, because that was the legal residence of your parents. The other thing is, I did some digging in newspaper files."

"Yes?"

"Your grandfather did give you a healthy block of stock. It was in stories about the whoop-te-do when you were born. The Bourse Journal listed the shares by serial numbers. So we'll hit 'em with that, too—on the same day. Don't want one to tip off the other."

"You're the doctor."

"But I don't want you in Rudbek until the clerk shouts 'Oyez!' Here's a mail-drop you can use to reach me . . . even phone through, if you have to. And right smartly you set up a way for me to reach you."

Thorby puzzled over that requirement, being hemmed in as he was by bodyguards. "Why don't you, or somebody—a young man, maybe—phone my cousin with a code message? People are always phoning her and most of them are young men. She'll tell me and I'll find a place to phone back."

"Good idea. He'll ask if she knows how many shopping days left till Christmas. All right—see you in court." Garsch grinned. "This is going to be fun. And very, very expensive for you. G'bye."

22

"Have a nice vacation?" Uncle Jack smiled at him. "You've led us quite a chase. You shouldn't do that, boy."

Thorby wanted to hit him but, although the guards let go his arms when they shoved him into the room, his wrists were tied.

Uncle Jack stopped smiling and glanced at Judge Bruder. "Thor, you've never appreciated that Judge Bruder and I worked for your father, and for your grandfather. Naturally we know what's best. But you've given us trouble and now we'll show you how we handle little boys who don't appreciate decent treatment. We teach them. Ready, Judge?"

Judge Bruder smiled savagely and took the whip from behind him. "Bend him over the desk!"

Thorby woke up gasping. Whew, a bad one! He looked around the small hotel room he was in and tried to remember where he was. For days he had moved daily, sometimes half around the planet. He had become sophisticated in the folkways of this planet, enough not to attract attention, and even had a new ID card, quite as good as a real one. It had not been difficult, once he realized that underworlds were much the same everywhere.

He remembered now—this was América de Sud.

The bed alarm sounded—just midnight, time to leave. He dressed and glanced at his baggage, decided to abandon it. He walked down the backstairs, out the back way.

Aunt Lizzie had not liked the Yukon cold but she put up with it. Eventually someone called and reminded Leda that there were few shopping days to Christmas, so they left. At Uranium City Thorby managed to return the call. Garsch grinned. "I'll see you in the district court in-and-for the county of Rudbek, division four, at nine-fifty-nine the morning of January fourth. Now get lost completely."

So at San Francisco Thorby and Leda had a tiff in the presence of Aunt Lizzie; Leda wanted to go to Nice, Thorby insisted on Australia. Thorby said angrily, "Keep the car! I'll go by myself." He flounced out and bought a ticket for Great Sydney.

He pulled a rather old washroom trick, tubed under the Bay, and, convinced that his bodyguard had been evaded, counted the cash Leda had slipped him as privately as they had quarreled publicly. It came to a little under two hundred thousand credits. There was a note saying that she was sorry it wasn't more but she had not anticipated needing money.

While waiting at the South American field Thorby counted what was left of Leda's money and reflected that he had cut it fine, both time and money. Where did it all go?

Photographers and reporters gave him a bad time at Rudbek City; the place swarmed with them. But he pushed through and met Garsch inside the bar at nine-fifty-eight. The old man nodded. "Siddown. Hizzoner will be out soon."

The judge came out and a clerk intoned the ancient promise of justice: "—draw nigh and ye shall be heard!" Garsch remarked, "Bruder has this judge on a leash."

"Huh? Then why are we here?"

"You're paying me to worry. Any judge is a good judge when he knows he's being watched. Look behind you."

Thorby did so. The place was so loaded with press that a common citizen stood no chance. "I did a good job, if I do say so." Garsch hooked a thumb at the front row. "The galoot with the big nose is the ambassador from Proxima. The old thief next to him is chairman of the judiciary committee. And—" He broke off.

Thorby could not spot Uncle Jack but Bruder presided over the other table-he did not look at Thorby. Nor could Thorby find Leda. It made him feel very much alone. But Garsch finished opening formalities, sat down and whispered. "Message for you. Young lady says to say 'Good luck.' "

Thorby was active only in giving testimony and that after many objections, counter objections, and warnings from the bench. While he was being sworn, he recognized in the front row a retired chief justice of the Hegemonic Ultimate Court who had once dined at Rudbek. Then

Thorby did not notice anything, for he gave his testimony in deep trance surrounded by hypnotherapists.

Although every point was chewed endlessly, only once did the hearing approach drama. The court sustained an objection by Bruder in such fashion that a titter of unbelief ran around the room and someone stamped his feet. The judge turned red. "Order! The bailiff will clear the room!"

The move to comply started, over protests of reporters. But the front two rows sat tight and stared at the judge. The High Ambassador from the Vegan League leaned toward his secretary and whispered; the secretary started slapping a Silent-Steno.

The judge cleared his throat. "—unless this unseemly behavior ceases at once! This court will not tolerate disrespect."

Thorby was almost surprised when it ended: "—must therefore be conclusively presumed that Creighton Bradley Rudbek and Martha Bradley Rudbek did each die, are now dead, and furthermore did meet their ends in common disaster. May their souls rest in peace. Let it be so recorded." The court banged his gavel. "If custodians of wills of the decedents, if wills there be, are present in this court, let them now come forward."

There was no hearing about Thorby's own shares; Thorby signed a receipt for certificates thereto in the judge's chambers. Neither Weemsby nor Bruder was present.

Thorby took a deep breath as Garsch and he came out of chambers. "I can hardly believe that we've won."

Garsch grinned. "Don't kid yourself. We won the first round on points. Now it begins to get expensive."

Thorby's mouth sagged. Rudbek guards moved in and started taking them through the crowd.

Garsch had not overstated it. Bruder and Weemsby sat tight, still running Rudbek & Assocs., and continued to fight. Thorby never did see his parents' proxies—his only interest in them now was to see whether, as he suspected, the differences between the papers Bruder had prepared and those of his parents lay in the difference between "revocable" and "revocable only by mutual agreement."

But when the court got around to ordering them produced, Bruder claimed that they had been destroyed in routine clearing from files of expired instruments. He received a ten-day sentence for contempt, suspended, and that ended it.

But, while Weemsby was no longer voting the shares of Martha and Creighton Rudbek, neither was Thorby; the shares were tied up while the wills were being proved. In the meantime, Bruder and Weemsby remained officers of Rudbek & Assocs., with a majority of directors backing them. Thorby was not even allowed in Rudbek Building, much less in his old office.

Weemsby never went back to Rudbek estate; his belongings were sent to him. Thorby moved Garsch into Weemsby's apartment. The old man slept there often; they were very busy.

At one point Garsch told him that there were ninety-seven actions, for or against, moving or pending, relating to the settlement of his estate. The wills were simple in essence; Thorby was the only major heir. But there were dozens of minor bequests; there were relatives who might get something if the wills were set aside; the question of "legally dead" was again raised, the presumption of "common disaster" versus deaths at different times was hashed again; and Thorby's very identity was questioned. Neither Bruder nor Weemsby appeared in these actions; some relative or stockholder was always named as petitioner—Thorby was forced to conclude that Uncle Jack had kept everyone happy.

But the only action that grieved him was brought by his grandparents Bradley, asking that he be made their ward because of incompetence. The evidence, other than the admitted fact that he was new to the complexities of Terran life, was his Guardsman medical record—a Dr. Krishnamurti had endorsed that he was "potentially emotionally unstable and should not be held fully answerable for actions under stress."

Garsch had him examined in blatant publicity by the physician to the Secretary General of the Hegemonic Assembly. Thorby was found legally sane. It was followed by a stockholder's suit asking that Thorby be found professionally unequipped to manage the affairs of Rudbek & Assocs., in private and public interest.

Thorby was badly squeezed by these maneuvers; he was finding it ruinously expensive to be rich. He was heavily in debt from legal costs and running Rudbek estate and had not been able to draw his own accumulated royalties as Bruder and Weemsby continued to contend, despite repeated adverse decisions, that his identity was uncertain.

But a weary time later a court three levels above the Rudbek district court awarded to Thorby (subject to admonitions as to behavior and unless revoked by court) the power to vote his parents' stock until such time as their estates were settled.

Thorby called a general meeting of stockholders, on stockholders' initative as permitted by the bylaws, to elect officers.

The meeting was in the auditorium of Rudbek Building; most stockholders on Terra showed up even if represented by proxy. Even Leda popped in at the last minute, called out merrily, "Hello, everybody!" then turned to her stepfather. "Daddy, I got the notice and decided to see the fun—so I jumped into the bus and hopped over. I haven't missed anything, have I?"

She barely glanced at Thorby, although he was on the platform with the officers. Thorby was relieved and hurt; he had not seen her since they had parted at San Francisco. He knew that she had residence at Rudbek Arms in Rudbek City and was sometimes in town, but Garsch had discouraged him from getting in touch with her—"Man's a fool to chase a woman when she's made it plain she doesn't want to see him."

So he simply reminded himself that he must pay back her loan—with interest—as soon as possible.

Weemsby called the meeting to order, announced that in accordance with the call the meeting would nominate and elect officers. "Minutes and old business postponed by unanimous consent." *Bang!* "Let the secretary call the roll for nominations for chairman of the board." His face wore a smile of triumph.

The smile worried Thorby. He controlled, his own and his parents', just under 45% of the voting stock. From the names used in bringing suits and other indirect sources he thought that Weemsby controlled about 31%; Thorby needed to pick up 6%. He was counting on the emotional appeal of "Rudbek of Rudbek"—but he couldn't be sure, even though Weemsby needed more than three times as many "uncertain" votes . . . uncertain to Thorby; they might be in Weemsby's pocket.

But Thorby stood up and nominated himself, through his own stock. "Thor Rudbek of Rudbek!"

After that it was pass, pass, pass, over and over again—until Weemsby was nominated. There were no other nominations.

"The Secretary will call the roll," Weemsby intoned.

"Announce your votes by shares as owners, followed by votes as proxy. The Clerk will check serial numbers against the Great Record. Thor Rudbek . . . of Rudbek."

Thorby voted all 45%-minus that he controlled, then sat down feeling very weary. But he got out a pocket calculator. There were 94,000 voting shares; he did not trust himself to keep tally in his head. The Secretary read on, the clerk droned his checks on the record. Thorby needed to pick up 5657 votes, to win by one vote.

He began slowly to pick up odd votes—232, 906, 1917—some of them directly, some through proxy. But Weemsby picked up votes also. Some shareholders answered, "Pass to proxy," or failed to respond—as the names marched past and these missing votes did not appear, Thorby was forced to infer that Weemsby held those proxies himself. But still the additional votes for "Rudbek of Rudbek" mounted—2205, 3036, 4309 . . . and there it stuck. The last few names passed.

Garsch leaned toward him. "Just the sunshine twins left."

"I know." Thorby put away his calculator, feeling sick—so Weemsby had won, after all.

The Secretary had evidently been instructed what names to read last. "The Honorable Curt Bruder!"

Bruder voted his one qualifying share for Weemsby. "Our Chairman, Mr. John Weemsby."

Weemsby stood up and looked happy. "In my own person, I vote one share. By proxies delivered to me and now with the Secretary I vote—" Thorby did not listen; he was looking for his hat.

"The tally being complete, I declare—" the Secretary began.

"No!"

Leda was on her feet. "I'm here *myself*. This is my first meeting and *I'm going to vote!*"

Her stepfather said hastily, "That's all right, Leda—mustn't interrupt." He turned to the Secretary. "It doesn't affect the result."

"But it *does!* I cast one thousand eight hundred and eighty votes for Thor, Rudbek of Rudbek!"

Weemsby stared. "Leda Weemsby!"

She retorted crisply, "My legal name is Leda *Rudbek*."

Bruder was shouting, "Illegal! The vote has been recorded. It's too—"

"Oh, nonsense!" shouted Leda. "I'm here and I'm voting. Anyhow, I cancelled that proxy—I registered it in the post office in this very building and saw it delivered and signed for at the 'principal offices of this corporation'—that's the right phrase, isn't it, Judge?—ten minutes before the meeting was called to order. If you don't believe me, send down for it. But what of it?—I'm here. Touch me." Then she turned and smiled at Thorby.

Thorby tried to smile back, and whispered savagely to Garsch, "Why did you keep this a secret?"

"And let 'Honest John' find out that he had to beg, borrow, or buy some more votes? He might have won. She kept him happy, just as I told her to. That's quite a girl, Thorby. Better option her."

Five minutes later Thorby, shaking and white, got up and took the gavel that Weemsby had dropped. He faced the crowd. "We will now elect the rest of the board," he announced, his voice barely under control. The slate that Garsch and Thorby had worked out was passed by acclamation—with one addition: Leda.

Again she stood up. "Oh, no! You can't do this to me."

"Out of order. You've assumed responsibility, now accept it."

She opened her mouth, closed it, sat down.

When the Secretary declared the result, Thorby turned to Weemsby. "You are General Manager also, are you not?"

"Yes."

"You're fired. Your one share reverts. Don't try to go back to your former office; just get your hat and go."

Bruder jumped up. Thorby turned to him. "You, too. Sergeant-at-Arms, escort them out of the building."

23

THORBY LOOKED GLUMLY AT A HIGH STACK OF PAPERS, EACH ITEM flagged "URGENT." He picked up one, started to read—put it down and said, "Dolores, switch control of my screen to me. Then go home."

"I can stay, sir."

"I said, 'Go home.' How are you going to catch a husband with circles under your eyes?"

"Yes, sir." She changed connections. "Good night, sir."

"Good night."

Good girl, there. Loyal, he thought. Well, he hoped. He hadn't dared use a new broom all the way; the administration had to have continuity. He signaled a number.

A voice without a face said, "Scramble Seven."

" 'Prometheus Bound,' " Thorby answered, "and nine makes sixteen."

"Scramble set up."

"Sealed," Thorby agreed.

The face of Wing Marshal "Smith" appeared. "Hi, Thor."

"Jake, I've got to postpone this month's conference again. I hate to—but you should see my desk."

"Nobody expects you to devote all your time to corps matters."

"Doggone it, that's exactly what I planned to do—clean this place up fast, put good people in charge, grab my hat and enlist for the corps! But it's not that simple."

"Thor, no conscientious officer lets himself be relieved until his board is all green. We both knew that you had lots of lights blinking red."

"Well . . . all right, I can't make the conference. Got a few minutes?"

"Shoot," agreed "Smith."

"I think I've got a boy to hunt porcupines. Remember?"

" 'Nobody eats a porcupine.' "

"Right! Though I had to see a picture of one to understand what you meant. To put it in trader terms, the way to kill a business is to make it unprofitable. Slave-raiding is a business, the way to kill it is to put it in the red. Porcupine spines on the victims will do it."

"If we had the spines," the "X" Corps director agreed dryly. "You have an idea for a weapon?"

"Me? What do you think I am? A genius? But I think I've found one. Name is Joel de la Croix. He's supposed to be about the hottest thing M.I.T. ever turned out. I've gossiped with him about what I used to do as a firecontrolman in *Sisu*. He came up with some brilliant ideas without being prodded. Then he said, 'Thor, it's ridiculous for a ship to be put out of action by a silly little paralysis beam when it has enough power in its guts to make a small star.' "

"A *very* small star. But I agree."

"Okay. I've got him stached in our Havermeyer Labs in Toronto. As soon as your boys okay him, I want to hand him a truckload of money and give him a free hand. I'll feed him all I know about raider tactics and so forth—trance tapes, maybe, as I won't have time to work with him much. I'm being run ragged here."

"He'll need a team. This isn't a home-workshop project."

"I know. I'll funnel names to you as fast as I have them. Project Porcupine will have all the men and money it can use. But, Jake, how many of these gadgets can I sell to the Guard?"

"Eh?"

"I'm supposed to be running a business. If I run it into the ground, the courts will boost me out. I'm going to let Project Porcupine spend megabucks like water—but I've got to justify it to directors and stockholders. If we come up with something, I can sell several hundred units to Free Traders, I can sell some to ourselves—but I need to show a potential large market to justify the expenditure. How many can the Guard use?"

"Thor, you're worrying unnecessarily. Even if you don't come up with a superweapon—and your chances aren't good—*all* research pays off. Your stockholders won't lose."

"I am *not* worrying unnecessarily! I've got this job by a handful of votes; a special stockholders meeting could kick me out tomorrow. Sure research pays off, but not necessarily quickly. You can count on it that every credit I spend is reported to people who would love to see me bumped—so I've got to have reasonable justification."

"How about a research contract?"

"With a vice colonel staring down my boy's neck and telling him what to do? We want to give him a free hand."

"Mmm . . . yes. Suppose I get you a letter-of-intent? We'll make the figure as high as possible. I'll have to see the Marshal-in-Chief. He's on Luna at the moment and I can't squeeze time to go to Luna this week. You'll have to wait a few days."

"I'm not going to wait; I'm going to assume that you can do it. Jake, I'm going to get things rolling and get out of this crazy job—if you won't have me in the corps I can always be an ordnanceman."

"Come on down this evening. I'll enlist you—then I'll order you to detached duty, right where you are."

Thorby's chin dropped. "Jake! You wouldn't do that to me!"

"I would if you were silly enough to place yourself under my orders, Rudbek."

"But—" Thorby shut up. There was no use arguing; there was too much work to be done.

"Smith" added, "Anything else?"

"I guess not."

"I'll have a first check on de la Croix by tomorrow. See you."

Thorby switched off, feeling glummer than ever. It was not the Wing Marshal's half-whimsical threat, nor even his troubled conscience over spending large amounts of other people's money on a project that stood little chance of success; it was simply that he was swamped by a job more complex than he had believed possible.

He picked up the top item again, put it down, pressed the key that sealed him through to Rudbek estate. Leda was summoned to the screen. "I'll be late again. I'm sorry."

"I'll delay dinner. They're enjoying themselves and I had the kitchen make the canapés substantial."

Thorby shook his head. "Take the head of the table. I'll eat here. I may sleep here."

She sighed. "If you sleep. Look, my stupid dear, be in bed by midnight and up not before six. Promise?"

"Okay. If possible."

"It had better be possible, or you will have trouble with me. See you."

He didn't even pick up the top item this time; he simply sat in thought. Good girl, Leda . . . she had even tried to help in the business—until it had become clear that business was not her forte. But she was one bright spot in the gloom; she always bucked him up. If it wasn't patently unfair for a Guardsman to marry—But he couldn't be that unfair to Leda and he had no reason to think she would be willing anyhow. It was unfair enough for him to duck out of a big dinner party at the last minute. Other things. He would have to try to treat her better.

It had all seemed so self-evident: just take over, fumigate that sector facing the Sargony, then pick somebody else to run it. But the more he dug, the more there was to do. Taxes . . . the tax situation was incredibly snarled; it always was. That expansion program the Vegan group was pushing—how could he judge unless he went there and looked? And would he know if he did? And how could he find *time?*

Funny, but a man who owned a thousand starships automatically never had time to ride in even one of them. Maybe in a year or two—

No, those confounded wills wouldn't even be settled in that time!—two years now and the courts were still chewing it. Why couldn't death be handled decently and simply the way the People did it?

In the meantime he wasn't free to go on with Pop's work.

True, he had accomplished a little. By letting "X" Corps have access to Rudbek's files some of the picture had filled in—Jake had told him that a raid which had wiped out one slaver pesthole had resulted directly from stuff the home office knew and hadn't known that it knew.

Or *had* somebody known? Some days he thought Weemsby and Bruder had had guilty knowledge, some days not—for all that the files showed was legitimate business . . . sometimes with wrong people. But who knew that they were the wrong people?

He opened a drawer, got out a folder with no "URGENT" flag on it simply because it never left his hands. It was, he felt, the most urgent thing in Rudbek, perhaps in the Galaxy—certainly more urgent than Project Porcupine because this matter was certain to cripple, or at least hamper, the slave trade, while Porcupine was a long chance. But his progress had been slow—too much else to do.

Always too much. Grandmother used to say never to buy too many eggs for your basket. Wonder where she got that?—the People never bought eggs. He had both too many baskets and too many eggs for each. And another basket every day.

Of course, in a tough spot he could always ask himself: "What would Pop do?" Colonel Brisby had phrased that—"I just ask myself, 'What would Colonel Baslim do?' " It helped, especially when he had to remember also what the presiding judge had warned him about the day his parents' shares had been turned over to him: "No man can own a thing to himself alone, and the bigger it is, the less he owns it. You are not free to deal with this property arbitrarily nor foolishly. Your interest does not override that of other stockholders, nor of employees, nor of the public."

Thorby had talked that warning over with Pop before deciding to go ahead with Porcupine.

The judge was right. His first impulse on taking over the business had been to shut down every Rudbek activity in that infected sector, cripple the slave trade that way. But you could not do that. You *could not* injure thousands, millions, of honest men to put the squeeze on criminals. It required more judicious surgery.

Which was what he was trying to do now. He started studying the unmarked folder.

Garsch stuck his head in. "Still running under the whip? What's the rush, boy?"

"Jim, where can I find ten honest men?"

"Huh? Diogenes was satisfied to hunt for one. Gave him more than he could handle."

"You know what I mean—ten honest men each qualified to take over as a planetary manager for Rudbek." Thorby added to himself, "—and acceptable to 'X' Corps."

"Now I'll tell one."

"Know any other solution? I'll have each one relieve a manager in the smelly sector and send the man he relieves back—we can't fire them; we'll have to absorb them. Because we don't *know*. But the new men we can trust and each one will be taught how the slave trade operates and what to look for."

Garsch shrugged. "It's the best we can do. But forget the notion of doing it in one bite; we won't find that many qualified men at one time. Now look, boy, you ain't going to solve it tonight no matter how long you stare at those names. When you are as old as I am, you'll know you can't do everything at once—provided you don't kill yourself first. Either way, someday you die and somebody else has to do the work. You remind me of the man who set out to count stars. Faster he counted, the more new stars kept turning up. So he went fishing. Which you should, early and often."

"Jim, why did you agree to come here? I don't see you quitting work when the others do."

"Because I'm an old idiot. Somebody had to give you a hand. Maybe I relished a chance to take a crack at anything as dirty as the slave trade and this was my way—I'm too old and fat to do it any other way."

Thorby nodded. "I thought so. I've got another way—only, confound it, I'm so busy doing what I must do that I don't have time for what I ought to do . . . and I *never* get a chance to do what I *want* to do!"

"Son, that's universal. The way to keep that recipe from killing you is occasionally to do what you want to do anyhow. Which is right now. There's all day tomorrow ain't touched yet . . . and you are going out with me and have a sandwich and look at pretty girls."

"I'm going to have dinner sent up."

"No, you aren't. Even a steel ship has to have time for maintenance. So come along."

Thorby looked at the stack of papers. "Okay."

The old man munched his sandwich, drank his lager, and watched pretty girls, with a smile of innocent pleasure. They were indeed pretty girls; Rudbek City attracted the highest-paid talent in show business.

But Thorby did not see them. He was thinking.

A person *can't* run out on responsibility. A captain can't, a chief officer can't. But he did not see how, if he went on this way, he would ever be able to join Pop's corps. But Jim was right; here was a place where the filthy business had to be fought, too.

Even if he didn't like this way to fight it? Yes. Colonel Brisby had once said, about Pop: "It means being so devoted to freedom that you are willing to give up your own . . . be a beggar . . . or a slave . . . or die—that freedom may live."

Yes, Pop, but I don't know *how* to do this job. I'd do it . . . I'm *trying* to do it. But I'm just fumbling. I don't have any talent for it.

Pop answered, *"Nonsense! You can learn to do anything if you apply yourself. You're going to learn if I have to beat your silly head in!"*

Somewhere behind Pop Grandmother was nodding agreement and looking stern. Thorby nodded back at her. "Yes, Grandmother. Okay, Pop. I'll try."

"You'll do more than try!"

"I'll do it, Pop."

"Now eat your dinner."

Obediently Thorby reached for his spoon, then noticed that it was a sandwich instead of a bowl of stew. Garsch said, "What are you muttering about?"

"Nothing. I just made up my mind."

"Give your mind a rest and use your eyes instead. There's a time and place for everything."

"You're right, Jim."

"Goodnight, son," the old beggar whispered. *"Good dreams . . . and good luck!"*